BEYOND THE

AQUILA RIFT:

THE BEST OF ALASTAIR REYNOLDS

Also by Alastair Reynolds from Gollancz:

Novels
Revelation Space
Redemption Ark
Absolution Gap
Chasm City
Century Rain
Pushing Ice
The Prefect
House of Suns
Terminal World
Blue Remembered Earth
On the Steel Breeze
Poseidon's Wake
The Medusa Chronicles (with Stephen Baxter)
Revenger

Short Story Collections:
Diamond Dogs, Turquoise Days
Galactic North
Zima Blue
Beyond the Aquila Rift

Slow Bullets

BEYOND THE
AQUILA RIFT:

THE BEST OF ALASTAIR REYNOLDS

EDITED BY
JONATHAN STRAHAN
AND
WILLIAM SCHAFER

A CIP catalogue record for this book is available from the British Library.

ISBN 978 1 473 21636 5

Printed in Great Britain by CPI Group (UK) Ltd, Croydon, CR0 4YY

MIX
Paper from responsible sources
FSC
www.fsc.org
FSC® C104740

www.alastairreynolds.com
www.orionbooks.co.uk
www.gollancz.co.uk

TABLE OF CONTENTS

GREAT WALL
OF MARS

"YOU REALISE you might die down there," said Warren.

Nevil Clavain looked into his brother's one good eye; the one the Conjoiners had left him with after the battle of Tharsis Bulge. "Yes, I know," he said. "But if there's another war, we might all die. I'd rather take that risk, if there's a chance for peace."

Warren shook his head, slowly and patiently. "No matter how many times we've been over this, you just don't seem to get it, do you? There can't ever be any kind of peace while they're still down there. That's what you don't understand, Nevil. The only long-term solution here is..." he trailed off.

"Go on," Clavain goaded. "Say it. Genocide."

Warren might have been about to answer when there was a bustle of activity down the docking tube, at the far end from the waiting spacecraft. Through the door Clavain saw a throng of media people, then someone gliding through them, fielding questions with only the curtest of answers. That was Sandra Voi, the Demarchist woman who would be coming with him to Mars.

"It's not genocide when they're just a faction, not an ethnically distinct race," Warren said, before Voi was within earshot.

"What is it, then?"

"I don't know. Prudence?"

Voi approached. She bore herself stiffly, her face a mask of quiet resignation. Her ship had only just docked from Circum-Jove, after a three-week transit at maximum burn. During that time the prospects for a peaceful resolution of the current crisis had steadily deteriorated.

"Welcome to Deimos," Warren said.

"Marshalls," she said, addressing both of them. "I wish the circumstances were better. Let's get straight to business. Warren; how long do you think we have to find a solution?"

"Not long. If Galiana maintains the pattern she's been following for the last six months, we're due another escape attempt in..." Warren glanced at a readout buried in his cuff. "About three days. If she does try and get another shuttle off Mars, we'll really have no option but to escalate."

They all knew what would mean: a military strike against the Conjoiner nest.

"You've tolerated her attempts so far," Voi said. "And each time you've successfully destroyed her ship with all the people in it. The net risk of a successful breakout hasn't increased. So why retaliate now?"

"It's very simple. After each violation we issued Galiana with a stronger warning than the one before. Our last was absolute and final."

"You'll be in violation of treaty if you attack."

Warren's smile was one of quiet triumph. "Not quite, Sandra. You may not be completely conversant with the treaty's fine print, but we've discovered that it allows us to storm Galiana's nest without breaking any terms. The technical phrase is a police action, I believe."

Clavain saw that Voi was momentarily lost for words. That was hardly surprising. The treaty between the Coalition and the Conjoiners—which Voi's neutral Demarchists had help draft—was the longest document in existence, apart from some obscure, computer-generated mathematical proofs. It was supposed to be watertight, though only machines had ever read it from beginning to end, and only machines had ever stood a chance of finding the kind of loophole which Warren was now brandishing.

"No..." she said. "There's some mistake."

"I'm afraid he's right," Clavain said. "I've seen the natural-language summaries, and there's no doubt about the legality of a police action.

But it needn't come to that. I'm sure I can persuade Galiana not to make another escape attempt."

"But if we should fail?" Voi looked at Warren now. "Nevil and myself could still be on Mars in three days."

"Don't be, is my advice."

Disgusted, Voi turned and stepped into the green cool of the shuttle. Clavain was left alone with his brother for a moment. Warren fingered the leathery patch over his ruined eye with the chrome gauntlet of his prosthetic arm, as if to remind Clavain of what the war had cost him; how little love he had for the enemy, even now.

"We haven't got a chance of succeeding, have we?" Clavain said. "We're only going down there so you can say you explored all avenues of negotiation before sending in the troops. You actually want another damned war."

"Don't be so defeatist," Warren said, shaking his head sadly, forever the older brother disappointed at his sibling's failings. "It really doesn't become you."

"It's not me who's defeatist," Clavain said.

"No; of course not. Just do your best, little brother."

Warren extended his hand for his brother to shake. Hesitating, Clavain looked again into his brother's good eye. What he saw there was an interrogator's eye: as pale, colourless and cold as a midwinter sun. There was hatred in it. Warren despised Clavain's pacifism; Clavain's belief that any kind of peace, even a peace which consisted only of stumbling episodes of mistrust between crises, was always better than war. That schism had fractured any lingering fraternal feelings they might have retained. Now, when Warren reminded Clavain that they were brothers, he never entirely concealed the disgust in his voice.

"You misjudge me," Clavain whispered, before quietly shaking Warren's hand.

"No; I honestly don't think I do."

Clavain stepped through the airlock just before it sphinctered shut. Voi had already buckled herself in; she had a glazed look now, as if staring into infinity. Clavain guessed she was uploading a copy of the treaty through her implants, scrolling it across her visual field, trying to find the loophole; probably running a global search for any references to police actions.

The ship recognised Clavain, its interior shivering to his preferences. The green was closer to turquoise now; the readouts and controls minimalist in layout, displaying only the most mission-critical systems. Though the shuttle was the tiniest peacetime vessel Clavain had been in, it was a cathedral compared to the dropships he had flown during the war; so small that they were assembled around their occupants like Medieval armour before a joust.

"Don't worry about the treaty," Clavain said. "I promise you Warren won't get his chance to apply that loophole."

Voi snapped out of her trance irritatedly. "You'd better be right, Nevil. Is it me, or is your brother hoping we fail?" She was speaking Quebecois French now; Clavain shifting mental gears to follow her. "If my people discover that there's a hidden agenda here, there'll be hell to pay."

"The Conjoiners gave Warren plenty of reasons to hate them after the battle of the Bulge," Clavain said. "And he's a tactician, not a field specialist. After the cease-fire my knowledge of worms was even more valuable than before, so I had a role. But Warren's skills were a lot less transferable."

"So that gives him a right to edge us closer to another war?" The way Voi spoke, it was as if her own side had not been neutral in the last exchange. But Clavain knew she was right. If hostilities between the Conjoiners and the Coalition re-ignited, the Demarchy would not be able to stand aside as they had fifteen years ago. And it was anyone's guess how they would align themselves.

"There won't be war."

"And if you can't reason with Galiana? Or are you going to play on your personal connection?"

"I was just her prisoner, that's all." Clavain took the controls—Voi said piloting was a bore—and unlatched the shuttle from Deimos. They dropped away at a tangent to the rotation of the equatorial ring which girdled the moon, instantly in free-fall. Clavain sketched a porthole in the wall with his fingertip, outlining a rectangle which instantly became transparent.

For a moment he saw his reflection in the glass: older than he felt he had any right to look, the grey beard and hair making him look ancient rather than patriarchal; a man deeply wearied by recent circumstance. With some relief he darkened the cabin so that he could see Deimos, dwindling at surprising speed. The higher of the two Martian moons was a dark, bristling lump, infested with armaments, belted by the bright, window-studded band of the moving ring. For the last nine years, Deimos was all that he had known, but now he could encompass it within the arc of his fist.

"Not just her prisoner," Voi said. "No one else came back sane from the Conjoiners. She never even tried to infect you with her machines."

"No, she didn't. But only because the timing was on my side." Clavain was reciting an old argument now; as much for his own benefit as Voi's. "I was the only prisoner she had. She was losing the war by then; one more recruit to her side wouldn't have made any real difference. The terms of cease-fire were being thrashed out and she knew she could buy herself favours by releasing me unharmed. There was something else, too. Conjoiners weren't supposed to be capable of anything so primitive as mercy. They were spiders, as far as we were concerned. Galiana's act threw a wrench into our thinking. It divided alliances within high command. If she hadn't released me, they might well have nuked her out of existence."

"So there was absolutely nothing personal?"

"No," Clavain said. "There was nothing personal about it at all."

Voi nodded, without in any way suggesting that she actually believed him. It was a skill some women had honed to perfection, Clavain thought.

Of course, he respected Voi completely. She had been one of the first human beings to enter Europa's ocean, decades back. Now they were planning fabulous cities under the ice; efforts which she had spearheaded. Demarchist society was supposedly flat in structure, non-hierarchical; but someone of Voi's brilliance ascended through echelons of her own making. She had been instrumental in brokering the peace between the Conjoiners and Clavain's own Coalition. That was why she was coming along now: Galiana had only agreed to Clavain's mission provided he was accompanied by a neutral observer, and Voi had been the obvious choice.

Respect was easy. Trust, however, was harder: it required that Clavain ignore the fact that, with her head dotted with implants, the Demarchist woman's condition was not very far removed from that of the enemy.

The descent to Mars was hard and steep.

Once or twice they were queried by the automated tracking systems of the satellite interdiction network. Dark weapons hovering in Mars-synchronous orbit above the nest locked onto the ship for a few instants, magnetic railguns powering up, before the shuttle's diplomatic nature was established and it was allowed to proceed. The Interdiction was very efficient; as well it might be, given that Clavain had designed much of it himself. In fifteen years no ship had entered or left the Martian atmosphere, nor had any surface vehicle ever escaped from Galiana's nest.

"There she is," Clavain said, as the Great Wall rose over the horizon.

"Why do you call 'it' a 'she'?" Voi asked. "I never felt the urge to personalise it, and I designed it. Besides…even if it was alive once, it's dead now."

She was right, but the Wall was still awesome to behold. Seen from orbit, it was a pale, circular ring on the surface of Mars, two thousand kilometres wide. Like a coral atoll, it entrapped its own weather system; a disk of bluer air, flecked with creamy white clouds which stopped abruptly at the boundary.

Once, hundreds of communities had sheltered inside that cell of warm, thick, oxygen-rich atmosphere. The Wall was the most audacious and visible of Voi's projects. The logic had been inescapable: a means to avoid the millennia-long timescales needed to terraform Mars via such conventional schemes as cometary bombardment or ice-cap thawing. Instead of modifying the whole atmosphere at once, the Wall allowed the initial effort to be concentrated in a relatively small region, at first only a thousand kilometres across. There were no craters deep enough, so the Wall had been completely artificial: a vast ring-shaped atmospheric dam designed to move slowly outward, encompassing ever more surface area at a rate of a twenty kilometres per year. The Wall needed to be very tall because the low Martian gravity meant that the column of atmosphere was higher for a fixed surface pressure than on Earth. The ramparts were hundreds of meters thick, dark as glacial ice, sinking great taproots deep into the lithosphere to harvest the ores needed for the Wall's continual growth. Yet two hundred kilometres higher the wall was a diaphanously thin membrane only microns wide; completely invisible except when rare optical effects made it hang like a frozen aurora against the stars. Eco-engineers had invaded the Wall's liveable area with terran genestocks deftly altered in orbital labs. Flora and fauna had moved out in vivacious waves, lapping eagerly against the constraints of the Wall.

But the Wall was dead.

It had stopped growing during the war, hit by some sort of viral weapon which crippled its replicating subsystems, and now even the eco-system within it was failing; the atmosphere cooling, oxygen bleeding into space, pressure declining inevitably toward the Martian norm of one seven-thousandth of an atmosphere.

He wondered how it must look to Voi; whether in any sense she saw it as her murdered child.

"I'm sorry that we had to kill it," Clavain said. He was about to add that it been the kind of act which war normalised, but decided that the statement would have sounded hopelessly defensive.

"You needn't apologise," Voi said. "It was only machinery. I'm surprised it's lasted as long as it has, frankly. There must still be some residual damage-repair capability. We Demarchists build for posterity, you know."

Yes, and it worried his own side. There was talk of challenging the Demarchist supremacy in the outer solar system; perhaps even an attempt to gain a Coalition foothold around Jupiter.

They skimmed the top of the Wall and punched through the thickening layers of atmosphere within it, the shuttle's hull morphing to an arrowhead shape. The ground had an arid, bleached look to it, dotted here and there by ruined shacks, broken domes, gutted vehicles or shot-down shuttles. There were patches of shallow-rooted, mainly dark-red tundra vegetation; cotton grass, saxifrage, arctic poppies and lichen. Clavain knew each species by its distinct infrared signature, but many of the plants were in recession now that the imported bird species had died. Ice lay in great silver swathes, and what few expanses of open water remained were warmed by buried thermopiles. Elsewhere there were whole zones which had reverted to almost sterile permafrost. It could have been a kind of paradise, Clavain thought, if the war had not ruined everything. Yet what had happened here could only be a foretaste of the devastation that would follow across the system, on Earth as well as Mars, if another war was allowed to happen.

"Do you see the nest yet?" Voi said.

"Wait a second," Clavain said, requesting a head-up display which boxed the nest. "That's it. A nice fat thermal signature too. Nothing else for miles around—nothing inhabited, anyway."

"Yes. I see it now."

The Conjoiner nest lay a third of the way from the Wall's edge, not far from the footslopes of Arsia Mons. The entire encampment was only a kilometre across, circled by a dyke which was piled high with regolith dust on one side. The area within the Great Wall was large enough to have an appreciable weather system: spanning enough Martian latitude for significant coriolis effects; enough longitude for diurnal warming and cooling to cause thermal currents.

He could see the nest much more clearly now; details leaping out of the haze.

Its external layout was crushingly familiar. Clavain's side had been studying the nest from the vantage point of Deimos ever since the cease-fire. Phobos with its lower orbit would have been even better, of course—but there was no helping that, and perhaps the Phobos problem might actually prove useful in his negotiations with Galiana. She was somewhere in the nest, he knew: somewhere beneath the twenty varyingly-sized domes emplaced within the rim, linked together by pressurised tunnels or merged at their boundaries like soap bubbles. The nest extended several tens of levels beneath the Martian surface; maybe deeper.

"How many people do you think are inside?" Voi said.

"Nine hundred or so," said Clavain. "That's an estimate based on my experiences as a prisoner, and the hundred or so who've died trying to escape since. The rest, I have to say, is pretty much guesswork."

"Our estimates aren't dissimilar. A thousand or less here, and per-haps another three or four spread across the system in smaller nests. I know your side thinks we have better intelligence than that, but it hap-pens not to be the case."

"Actually, I believe you." The shuttle's airframe was flexing around them, morphing to a low-altitude profile with wide, batlike wings.

"I was just hoping you might have some clue as to why Galiana keeps wasting valuable lives with escape attempts."

Voi shrugged. "Maybe to her the lives aren't anywhere near as valuable as you'd like to think."

"Do you honestly think that?"

"I don't think we can begin to guess the thinking of a true hive-mind society, Clavain. Even from a Demarchist standpoint."

There was a chirp from the console; Galiana signalling them. Clavain opened the channel allocated for Coalition-Conjoiner diplomacy.

"Nevil Clavain?" he heard.

"Yes." He tried to sound as calm as possible. "I'm with Sandra Voi. We're ready to land as soon as you show us where."

"OK," Galiana said. "Vector your ship toward the westerly rim wall. And please, be careful."

"Thank you. Any particular reason for the caution?"

"Just be quick about it, Nevil."

They banked over the nest, shedding height until they were skimming only a few tens of meters above the weatherworn Martian surface. A wide rectangular door had opened in the concrete dyke, revealing a hangar bay aglow with yellow lights.

"That must be where Galiana launches her shuttles from," Clavain whispered. "We always thought there must be some kind of opening on the west side of the rim, but we never had a good view of it before."

"Which still doesn't tell us why she does it," Voi said.

The console chirped again—the link poor even though they were so close. "Nose up," Galiana said. "You're too low and slow. Get some altitude or the worms will lock onto you."

"You're telling me there are worms here?" Clavain said.

"I thought you were the worm expert, Nevil."

He nosed the shuttle up, but fractionally too late. Ahead of them something coiled out of the ground with lightning speed, metallic jaws opening in its blunt, armoured head. He recognised the type immediately: Ouroborus class. Worms of this form still infested a hundred niches across the system. Not quite as smart as the type infesting Phobos, but still adequately dangerous.

"Shit," Voi said, her veneer of Demarchist cool cracking for an instant.

"You said it," Clavain answered.

The Ouroborus passed underneath and then there was a spine-jarring series of bumps as the jaws tore into the shuttle's belly. Clavain felt the shuttle lurch down sickeningly; no longer a flying thing but an exercise in ballistics. The cool, minimalist turquoise interior shifted liquidly into an emergency configuration; damage readouts competing for attention with weapons status options. Their seats ballooned around them.

"Hold on," he said. "We're going down."

Voi's calm returned. "Do you think we can reach the rim in time?"

"Not a cat in hell's chance." He wrestled with the controls all the same, but it was no good. The ground was coming up fast and hard. "I wish Galiana had warned us a bit sooner..."

"I think she thought we already knew."

They hit. It was harder than Clavain had been expecting, but the shuttle stayed in one piece and the seat cushioned him from the worst of the impact. They skidded for a few metres and then nosed up against a sandbank. Through the window Clavain saw the white worm racing toward them with undulating waves of its segmented robot body.

"I think we're finished," Voi said.

"Not quite," Clavain said. "You're not going to like this, but..." Biting his tongue he brought the shuttle's hidden weapons online. An aiming scope plunged down from the ceiling; he brought his eyes to it and locked crosshairs onto the Ouroborus. Just like old times...

"Damn you," Voi said. "This was meant to be an unarmed mission!"

"You're welcome to lodge a formal complaint."

Clavain fired, the hull shaking from the recoil. Through the side window they watched the white worm blow apart into stubby segments. The parts wriggled beneath the dust.

"Good shooting," Voi said, almost grudgingly. "Is it dead?"

"For now," Clavain said. "It'll take several hours for the segments to fuse back into a functional worm."

"Good," Voi said, pushing herself out of her seat. "But there will be a formal complaint, take my word."

"Maybe you'd rather the worm ate us?"

"I just hate duplicity, Clavain."

He tried the radio again. "Galiana? We're down—the ship's history—but we're both unharmed."

"Thank God." Old verbal mannerisms died hard, even among the Conjoined. "But you can't stay where you are. There are more worms in the area. Do you think you can make it overland to the nest?"

"It's only two hundred meters," Voi said. "It shouldn't be a problem."

Two hundred meters, yes—but two hundred meters across treacherous, potholed ground riddled with enough soft depressions to hide a dozen worms. And then they would have to climb up the rim's side to reach the entrance to the hangar bay; ten or fifteen meters above the soil.

"Let's hope it isn't," Clavain said.

He unbuckled, feeling light-headed as he stood for the first time in Martian gravity. He had adapted entirely too well to the one-gee of the Deimos ring, constructed for the comfort of Earthside tacticians. He went to the emergency locker and found a mask which slivered eagerly across his face; another for Voi. They plugged in air-tanks and went to the shuttle's door. This time when it sphinctered open there was a glistening membrane stretched across the doorway, a recently licensed item of Demarchist technology. Clavain pushed through the membrane and the stuff enveloped him with a wet, sucking sound. By the time he hit the dirt the membrane had hardened itself around his soles and had begun to contour itself with ribs and accordioned joints, even though it stayed transparent.

Voi came behind him, gaining her own m-suit.

They loped away from the crashed shuttle, toward the dyke. The worms would be locking onto their seismic patterns already, if there were any nearby. They might be more interested in the shuttle for now, but that was nothing they could count on. Clavain knew the behaviour of worms intimately, knew the major routines which drove them; but that expertise did not guarantee his survival. It had almost failed him in Phobos.

The mask felt clammy against his face. The air at the base of the Great Wall was technically breathable even now, but there seemed no point in taking chances when speed was of the essence. His feet scuffed through the topsoil, and while he seemed to be crossing ground, the dyke obstinately refused to come any closer. It was larger than it looked from the crash; the distance further.

"Another worm," Voi said.

White coils erupted through sand to the west. The Ouroborus was making undulating progress toward them, zig-zagging with predatorial calm, knowing that it could afford to take its time. In the tunnels of Phobos, they had never had the luxury of knowing when a worm was close. They struck from ambush, quick as pythons.

"Run," Clavain said.

Dark figures appeared in the opening high in the rimwall. A rope-ladder unfurled down the side of the structure. Clavain, making for the base of it, made no effort to quieten his footfalls. He knew that the worm almost certainly had a lock on him by now.

He looked back.

The worm paused by the downed shuttle, then smashed its diamond-jawed head into the ship, impaling the hull on its body. The worm reared up, wearing the ship like a garland. Then it shivered and the ship flew apart like a rotten carcass. The worm returned its attention to Clavain and Voi. Like a sidewinder it pulled its thirty-meter-long body from the sand and rolled toward them on wheeling coils.

Clavain reached the base of the ladder.

Once, he could have ascended the ladder with his arms alone, in one-gee, but now the ladder felt alive beneath his feet. He began to climb, then realised that the ground was dropping away much faster than he was passing rungs. The Conjoiners were hauling him aloft.

He looked back in time to see Voi stumble.

"Sandra! No!"

She made to stand up, but it was too late by then. As the worm descended on her, Clavain could do nothing but turn his gaze away and pray for her death to be quick. If it had to be meaningless, he thought, at least let it be swift.

Then he started thinking about his own survival. "Faster!" he shouted, but the mask reduced his voice to a panicked muffle. He had forgotten to assign the ship's radio frequency to the suit.

The worm thrashed against the base of the wall, then began to rear up, its maw opening beneath him; a diamond-ringed orifice like the drill of a tunnelling machine. Then something eye-hurtingly bright cut into the worm's hide. Craning his neck, Clavain saw a group of Conjoiners kneeling over the lip of the opening, aiming guns downward. The worm writhed in intense robotic irritation. Across the sand, he could see the coils of other worms coming closer. There must have been dozens ringing the nest. No wonder Galiana's people had made so few attempts to leave by land.

They had hauled him within ten meters of safety. The injured worm showed cybernetic workings where its hide had been flensed away by weapons impacts. Enraged, it flung itself against the rim wall, chipping off scabs of concrete the size of boulders. Clavain felt the vibration of each impact through the wall as he was dragged upwards.

The worm hit again and the wall shook more violently than before. To his horror, Clavain watched one of the Conjoiners lose his footing and tumble over the edge of the rim toward him. Time oozed to a crawl. The falling man was almost upon him. Without thinking, Clavain hugged closer to the wall, locking his limbs around the ladder. Suddenly, he had seized the man by the arm. Even in Martian gravity, even allowing for the Conjoiner's willowy build, the impact almost sent both of them toward the Ouroborus. Clavain felt his bones pop out of location, tearing at gristle, but he managed to keep his grip on both the Conjoiner and the ladder.

Conjoiners breathed the air at the base of the Wall without difficulty. The man wore only lightweight clothes, grey silk pyjamas belted at the waist. With his sunken cheeks and bald skull, the man's Martian physique lent him a cadaverous look. Yet somehow he had managed not to drop his gun, still holding it in his other hand.

"Let me go," the man said.

Below, the worm inched higher despite the harm the Conjoiners had inflicted on it. "No," Clavain said, through clenched teeth and the distorting membrane of his mask. "I'm not letting you go."

"You've no option." The man's voice was placid. "They can't haul both of us up fast enough, Clavain."

Clavain looked into the Conjoiner's face, trying to judge the man's age. Thirty, perhaps—maybe not even that, since the cadaverous look probably made him seem older than he really was. Clavain was easily twice his age; had surely lived a richer life; had comfortably cheated death on three or four previous occasions.

"I'm the one who should die, not you."

"No," the Conjoiner said. "They'd find a way to blame your death on us. They'd make it a pretext for war." Without any fuss the man pointed the gun at his own head and blew his brains out.

As much in shock as recognition that the man's life was no longer his to save, Clavain released his grip. The dead man tumbled down the rim wall, into the mouth of the worm which had just killed Sandra Voi.

Numb, Clavain allowed himself to be pulled to safety.

WHEN THE ARMOURED door to the hangar was shut the Conjoiners attacked his m-suit with enzymic sprays. The sprays digested the fabric of the m-suit in seconds, leaving Clavain wheezing in a pool of slime. Then a pair of Conjoiners helped him unsteadily to his feet and waited patiently while he caught his breath from the mask. Through tears of exhaustion he saw that the hangar was racked full of half-assembled spacecraft; skeletal geodesic shark-shapes designed to punch out of an atmosphere, fast.

"Sandra Voi is dead," he said, removing the mask to speak.

There was no way the Conjoiners could not have seen this for themselves, but it seemed inhuman not to acknowledge what had happened.

"I know," Galiana said. "But at least you survived."

He thought of the man falling into the Ouroborus. "I'm sorry about your..." But then trailed off, because for all his depth of knowledge concerning the Conjoiners, he had no idea what the appropriate term was.

"You placed your life in danger in trying to save him."

"He didn't have to die."

Galiana nodded sagely. "No; in all likelihood he didn't. But the risk to yourself was too great. You heard what he said. Your death would be made to seem our fault; justification for a pre-emptive strike against our nest. Even the Demarchists would turn against us if we were seen to murder a diplomat."

Taking another suck from the mask, he looked into her face. He had spoken to her over low-bandwidth video-links, but only in person was it obvious that Galiana had hardly aged in fifteen years. A decade and a half of habitual expression should have engraved existing lines deeper into her face—but Conjoiners were not known for their habits of expression. Galiana had seen little sunlight in the intervening time, cooped here in the nest, and Martian gravity was much kinder to bone structure than the one-gee of Deimos. She still had the cruel beauty he remembered from his time as a prisoner. The only real evidence of ageing lay in the filaments of grey threading her hair; raven-black when she had been his captor.

"Why didn't you warn us about the worms?"

"Warn you?" For the first time something like doubt crossed her face, but it was only fleeting. "We assumed you were fully aware of the Ouroborus infestation. Those worms have been dormant—waiting—for years, but they've always been there. It was only when I saw how low your approach was that I realised..."

"That we might not have known?"

Worms were area-denial devices; autonomous prey-seeking mines. The war had left many pockets of the solar system still riddled with active worms. The machines were intelligent, in a one-dimensional way. Nobody ever admitted to deploying them and it was usually impossible to convince them that the war was over and that they should quietly deactivate.

"After what happened to you in Phobos," Galiana said, "I assumed there was nothing you needed to be taught about worms."

He never liked thinking about Phobos: the pain was still too deeply engraved. But if it had not been for the injuries he had sustained there he would never have been sent to Deimos to recuperate; would never have been recruited into his brother's intelligence wing to study the Conjoiners. Out of that phase of deep immersion in everything concerning the enemy had come his peacetime role as negotiator—and now diplomat—on the eve of another war. Everything was circular, ultimately. And now Phobos was central to his thinking because he saw it as a way out of the impasse—maybe the last chance for peace. But it was too soon to put his idea to Galiana. He was not even sure the mission could still continue, after what had happened.

"We're safe now, I take it?"

"Yes; we can repair the damage to the dyke. Mostly, we can ignore their presence."

"We should have been warned. Look, I need to talk to my brother."

"Warren? Of course. It's easily arranged."

They walked out of the hangar; away from the half-assembled ships. Somewhere deeper in the nest, Clavain knew, was a factory where the components for the ships were made, mined out of Mars or winnowed from the fabric of the nest. The Conjoiners managed to launch one every six weeks or so; had been doing so for six months. Not one of the ships had ever managed to escape the Martian atmosphere before being shot down...but sooner or later he would have to ask Galiana why she persisted with this provocative folly.

Now, though, was not the time—even if, by Warren's estimate, he only had three days before Galiana's next provocation.

The air elsewhere in the nest was thicker and warmer than in the hangar, which meant he could dispense with the mask. Galiana took him down a short, grey-walled, metallic corridor which ended in a circular room containing a console. He recognised the room from the times he had spoken to Galiana from Deimos. Galiana showed him how to use the system then left him in privacy while he established a connection with Deimos.

Warren's face soon appeared on a screen, thick with pixels like an impressionist portrait. Conjoiners were only allowed to send kilobytes a second to other parts of the system. Much of that bandwidth was now being sucked up by this one video link.

"You've heard, I take it," Clavain said.

Warren nodded, his face ashen. "We had a pretty good view from orbit, of course. Enough to see that Voi didn't make it. Poor woman. We were reasonably sure you survived, but it's good to have it confirmed."

"Do you want me to abandon the mission?"

Warren's hesitation was more than just time-lag. "No...I thought about it, of course, and high command agrees with me. Voi's death was tragic—no escaping that. But she was only along as a neutral observer. If Galiana consents for you to stay, I suggest you do so."

"But you still say I only have three days?"

"That's up to Galiana, isn't it? Have you learnt much?"

"You must be kidding. I've seen shuttles ready for launch; that's all. I haven't raised the Phobos proposal, either. The timing wasn't exactly ideal, after what happened to Voi."

"Yes. If only we'd known about that Ouroborus infestation."

Clavain leaned closer to the screen. "Yes. Why the hell didn't we? Galiana assumed that we would, and I don't blame her for that. We've had the nest under constant surveillance for fifteen years. Surely in all that time we'd have seen evidence of the worms?"

"You'd have thought so, wouldn't you?"

"Meaning what?"

"Meaning, maybe the worms weren't always there."

Conscious that there could be nothing private about this conversation—but unwilling to drop the thread—Clavain said: "You think the Conjoiners put them there to ambush us?"

"I'm saying we shouldn't disregard any possibility, no matter how unpalatable."

"Galiana would never do something like that."

"No, I wouldn't." She had just stepped back into the room. "And I'm disappointed that you'd even debate the possibility."

Clavain terminated the link with Deimos. "Eavesdropping's not a very nice habit, you know."

"What did you expect me to do?"

"Show some trust? Or is that too much of a stretch?"

"I never had to trust you when you were my prisoner," Galiana said. "That made our relationship infinitely simpler. Our roles were completely defined."

"And now? If you distrust me so completely, why did you ever agree to my visit? Plenty of other specialists could have come in my place. You could even have refused any dialogue."

"Voi's people pressured us to allow your visit," Galiana said. "Just as they pressured your side into delaying hostilities a little longer."

"Is that all?"

She hesitated slightly now. "I...knew you."

"Knew me? Is that how you sum up a year of imprisonment? What about the thousands of conversations we had; the times when we put aside our differences to talk about something other than the damned war? You kept me sane, Galiana. I've never forgotten that. It's why I've risked my life to come here and talk you out of another provocation."

"It's completely different now."

"Of course!" He forced himself not to shout. "Of course it's different. But not fundamentally. We can still build on that bond of trust and find a way out of this crisis."

"But does your side really want a way out of it?"

He did not answer her immediately; wary of what the truth might mean. "I'm not sure. But I'm also not sure you do, or else you wouldn't keep pushing your luck." Something snapped inside him and he asked the question he had meant to ask in a million better ways. "Why do you keep doing it, Galiana? Why do you keep launching those ships when you know they'll be shot down as soon as they leave the nest?"

Her eyes locked onto his own, unflinchingly. "Because we can. Because sooner or later one will succeed."

Clavain nodded. It was exactly the sort of thing he had feared she would say.

SHE LED HIM through more grey-walled corridors, descending several levels deeper into the nest. Light poured from snaking strips embedded into the walls like arteries. It was possible that the snaking design was decorative, but Clavain thought it much more likely that the strips had simply grown that way, expressing biological algorithms. There was no evidence that the Conjoiners had attempted to enliven their surroundings; to render them in any sense human.

"It's a terrible risk you're running," Clavain said.

"And the status quo is intolerable. I've every desire to avoid another war, but if it came to one, we'd at least have the chance to break these shackles."

"If you didn't get exterminated first..."

"We'd avoid that. In any case, fear plays no part in our thinking. You saw the man accept his fate on the dyke, when he understood that your death would harm us more than his own. He altered his state of mind to one of total acceptance."

"Fine. That makes it alright, then."

She halted. They were alone in one of the snakingly-lit corridors; he had seen no other Conjoiners since the hangar. "It's not that we regard individual lives as worthless, any more than you would willingly sacrifice a limb. But now that we're part of something larger..."

"Transenlightenment, you mean?"

It was the Conjoiners' term for the state of neural communion they shared, mediated by the machines swarming in their skulls. Whereas Demarchists used implants to facilitate real-time democracy, Conjoiners used them to share sensory data, memories—even conscious thought itself. That was what had precipitated the war. Back in 2190 half of humanity had been hooked into the system-wide data nets via neural implants. Then the Conjoiner experiments had exceeded some threshold, unleashing a transforming virus into the nets. Implants had begun to change, infecting millions of minds with the templates of Conjoiner thought. Instantly the infected had become the enemy. Earth and the other inner planets had always been more conservative, preferring to access the nets via traditional media.

Once they saw communities on Mars and in the asteroid belts fall prey to the Conjoiner phenomenon, the Coalition powers hurriedly pooled their resources to prevent the spread reaching their own states. The Demarchists, out around the gas giants, had managed to get firewalls up before many of their habitats were lost. They had chosen neutrality while the Coalition tried to contain—some said sterilise—zones of Conjoiner takeover. Within three years—after some of the bloodiest battles in human experience—the Conjoiners had been pushed back to a clutch of hideaways dotted around the system. Yet all along they professed a kind of puzzled bemusement that their spread was being resisted. After all, no one who had been assimilated seemed to regret it. Quite the contrary. The few prisoners whom the Conjoiners had reluctantly returned to their pre-infection state had sought every means to return to the fold. Some had even chosen suicide rather than be denied Transenlightenment. Like acolytes given a vision of heaven, they devoted their entire waking existence to the search for another glimpse.

"Transenlightenment blurs our sense of self," Galiana said. "When the man elected to die, the sacrifice was not absolute for him. He understood that much of what he was had already achieved preservation among the rest of us."

"But he was just one man. What about the hundred lives you've thrown away with your escape attempts? We know—we've counted the bodies."

"Replacements can always be cloned."

Clavain hoped that he hid his disgust satisfactorily. Among his people the very notion of cloning was an unspeakable atrocity; redolent with horror. To Galiana it would be just another technique in her arsenal. "But you don't clone, do you? And you're losing people. We thought there would be nine hundred of you in this nest, but that was a gross over-estimate, wasn't it?"

"You haven't seen much yet," Galiana said.

"No, but this place smells deserted. You can't hide absence, Galiana. I bet there aren't more than a hundred of you left here."

"You're wrong," Galiana said. "We have cloning technology, but we've hardly ever used it. What would be the point? We don't aspire to genetic unity, no matter what your propagandists think. The pursuit of optima leads only to local minima. We honour our errors. We actively seek persistent disequilibrium."

"Right." The last thing he needed now was a dose of Conjoiner rhetoric. "So where the hell is everyone?"

In a while he had part of the answer, if not the whole of it. At the end of the maze of corridors—far under Mars now—Galiana brought him to a nursery.

It was shockingly unlike his expectations. Not only did it not match what he had imagined from the vantage point of Deimos, but it jarred against his predictions based on what he had seen so far of the nest. In Deimos, he had assumed a Conjoiner nursery would be a place of grim medical efficiency; all gleaming machines with babies plugged in like peripherals, like a monstrously productive doll factory. Within the nest, he had revised his model to allow for the depleted numbers of Conjoiners. If there was a nursery, it was obviously not very productive. Fewer babies, then—but still a vision of hulking grey machines, bathed in snaking light.

The nursery was nothing like that.

The huge room Galiana showed him was almost painfully bright and cheerful; a child's fantasy of friendly shapes and primary colours. The walls and ceiling projected a holographic sky: infinite blue and billowing clouds of heavenly white. The floor was an undulating mat of synthetic grass forming hillocks and meadows. There were banks of flowers and forests of bonsai trees. There were robot animals: fabulous birds and rabbits just slightly too anthropomorphic to fool Clavain. They were like the animals in children's books; big-eyed and happy-looking. Toys were scattered on the grass.

And there were children. They numbered between forty and fifty; spanning by his estimate ages from a few months to six or seven standard years. Some were crawling among the rabbits; other, older children were gathered around tree stumps whose sheered-off surfaces flickered rapidly with images, underlighting their faces. They were talking amongst themselves, giggling or singing. He counted perhaps half a dozen adult Conjoiners kneeling among the children. The children's clothes were a headache of bright, clashing colours and patterns. The Conjoiners crouched among them like ravens. Yet the children seemed at ease with them, listening attentively when the adults had something to say.

"This isn't what you thought it would be like, is it."

"No...not at all." There seemed no point lying to her. "We thought you'd raise your young in a simplified version of the machine-generated environment you experience."

"In the early days that's more or less what we did." Subtly, Galiana's tone of voice had changed. "Do you know why chimpanzees are less intelligent than humans?"

He blinked at the change of tack. "I don't know—are their brains smaller?"

"Yes—but a dolphin's brain is larger, and they're scarcely more intelligent than dogs." Galiana stooped next to a vacant tree stump. Without seeming to do anything, she made a diagram of mammal brain anatomies appear on the trunk's upper surface, then sketched her finger across the relevant parts. "It's not overall brain volume that counts so much as the developmental history. The difference in brain volume between a neonatal chimp and an adult is only about twenty percent. By the time the chimp receives any data from beyond the womb, there's almost no plasticity left to use. Similarly, dolphins are born with almost their complete repertoire of adult behaviour already hardwired. A human brain, on the other hand, keeps growing through years of learning. We inverted that thinking. If data received during post-natal growth was so crucial to intelligence, perhaps we could boost our intelligence even further by intervening during the earliest phases of brain development."

"In the womb?"

"Yes." Now she made the tree-trunk show a human embryo running through cycles of cell-division, until the faint fold of a rudimentary spinal nerve began to form, nubbed with the tiniest of emergent minds. Droves of subcellular machines swarmed in, invading the nascent nervous system. Then the embryo's development slammed forward, until Clavain was looking at an unborn human baby.

"What happened?"

"It was a grave error," Galiana said. "Instead of enhancing normal neural development, we impaired it terribly. All we ended up with were various manifestations of savant syndrome."

Clavain looked around him. "Then you let these kids develop normally?"

"More or less. There's no family structure, of course, but then again there are plenty of human and primate societies where the family is less important in child development than the cohort group. So far we haven't seen any pathologies."

Clavain watched as one of the older children was escorted out of the grassy room, through a door in the sky. When the Conjoiner reached the door the child hesitated, tugging against the man's gentle insistence. The child looked back for a moment, then followed the man through the gap.

"Where's that child going?"

"To the next stage of its development."

Clavain wondered what were the chances of him seeing the nursery just as one of the children was being promoted. Small, he judged—unless there was a crash program to rush as many of them through as quickly as possible. As he thought about this, Galiana took him into another part of the nursery. While this room was smaller and dourer it was still more colourful than any other part of the nest he had seen before the grassy room. The walls were a mosaic of crowded, intermingling displays, teeming with moving images and rapidly scrolling text. He saw a herd of zebra stampeding through the core of a neutron star. Elsewhere an octopus squirted ink at the face of a twentieth-century despot. Other display facets rose from the floor like Japanese paper screens, flooded with data. Children—up to early teenagers—sat on soft black toadstools next to the screens in little groups, debating.

A few musical instruments lay around unused: holoclaviers and air-guitars. Some of the children had grey bands around their eyes and were poking their fingers through the interstices of abstract structures, exploring the dragon-infested waters of mathematical space. Clavain could see what they were manipulating on the flat screens: shapes that made his head hurt even in two dimensions.

"They're nearly there," Clavain said. "The machines are outside their heads, but not for long. When does it happen?"

"Soon; very soon."

"You're rushing them, aren't you. Trying to get as many children Conjoined as you can. What are you planning?"

"Something…has arisen, that's all. The timing of your arrival is either very bad or very fortunate, depending on your point of view." Before he could query her, Galiana added: "Clavain; I want you to meet someone."

"Who?"

"Someone very precious to us."

She took him through a series of child-proof doors until they reached a small circular room. The walls and ceiling were veined grey; tranquil after what he had seen in the last place. A child sat cross-legged on the floor in the middle of the room. Clavain estimated the girl's age as ten standard years—perhaps fractionally older. But she did not respond to Clavain's presence in any way an adult, or even a normal child, would have. She just kept on doing the thing she had been doing when they stepped inside, as if they were not really present at all. It was not at all clear what she was doing. Her hands moved before her in slow, precise gestures. It was as if she were playing a holoclavier or working a phantom puppet show. Now and then she would pivot round until she was facing another direction and carry on doing the hand movements.

"Her name's Felka," Galiana said.

"Hello, Felka..." He waited for a response, but none came. "I can see there's something wrong with her."

"She was one of the savants. Felka developed with machines in her head. She was the last to be born before we realised our failure."

Something about Felka disturbed him. Perhaps it was the way she carried on regardless, engrossed in an activity to which she seemed to attribute the utmost significance, yet which had to be without any sane purpose.

"She doesn't seem aware of us."

"Her deficits are severe," Galiana said. "She has no interest in other human beings. She has prosopagnosia; the inability to distinguish faces. We all seem alike to her. Can you imagine something more strange than that?"

He tried, and failed. Life from Felka's viewpoint must have been a nightmarish thing, surrounded by identical clones whose inner lives she could not begin to grasp. No wonder she seemed so engrossed in her game.

"Why is she so precious to you?" Clavain asked, not really wanting to know the answer.

"She's keeping us alive," Galiana said.

OF COURSE, HE asked Galiana what she meant by that. Galiana's only response was to tell him that he was not yet ready to be shown the answer.

"And what exactly would it take for me to reach that stage?"

"A simple procedure."

Oh yes, he understood that part well enough. Just a few machines in the right parts of his brain and the truth could be his. Politely, doing his best to mask his distaste, Clavain declined. Fortunately, Galiana did not press the point, for the time had arrived for the meeting he had been promised before his arrival on Mars.

He watched a subset of the nest file in to the conference room. Galiana was their leader only inasmuch as she had founded the lab here from which the original experiment had sprung and was accorded some respect deriving from seniority. She was also the most obvious spokesperson among them. They all had areas of expertise which could not be easily shared among other Conjoined; very distinct from the hive-mind of identical clones which still figured in the Coalition's propaganda. If the nest was in any way like an ant colony, then it was an ant colony in which every ant fulfilled a distinct role from all the others. Naturally, no individual could be solely entrusted with a particular skill essential to the nest—that would have been dangerous over-specialisation—but neither had individuality been completely subsumed into the group mind.

The conference room must have dated back to the days when the nest was a research outpost, or even earlier, when it was some kind of mining base in the early 2100s. It was much too big for the dour handful of Conjoiners who stood round the main table. Tactical readouts around the table showed the build-up of strike forces above the Martian exclusion zone; probable drop trajectories for ground-force deployment.

"Nevil Clavain," Galiana said, introducing him to the others. Everyone sat down. "I'm just sorry that Sandra Voi can't be with us now. We all feel the tragedy of her death. But perhaps out of this terrible event we can find some common ground. Nevil; before you came here you told us you had a proposal for a peaceful resolution to the crisis."

"I'd really like to hear it," one of the others murmured audibly.

Clavain's throat was dry. Diplomatically, this was quicksand. "My proposal concerns Phobos..."

"Go on."

"I was injured there," he said. "Very badly. Our attempt to clean out the worm infestation failed and I lost some good friends. That makes it personal between me and the worms. But I'd accept anyone's help to finish them off."

Galiana glanced quickly at her compatriots before answering. "A joint assault operation?"

"It could work."

"Yes..." Galiana seemed lost momentarily. "I suppose it could be a way out of the impasse. Our own attempt failed too—and the interdiction's stopped us from trying again." Again, she seemed to fall into reverie. "But who would really benefit from the flushing out of Phobos? We'd still be quarantined here."

Clavain leaned forward. "A co-operative gesture might be exactly the thing to lead to a relaxation in the terms of the interdiction. But don't think of it in those terms. Think instead of reducing the current threat from the worms."

"Threat?"

Clavain nodded. "It's possible that you haven't noticed." He leaned forward, elbows on the table. "We're concerned about the Phobos worms. They've begun altering the moon's orbit. The shift is tiny at the moment, but too large to be anything other than deliberate."

Galiana looked away from him for an instant, as if weighing her options. Then said: "We were aware of this, but you weren't to know that."

Gratitude?

He had assumed the worms' activity could not have escaped Galiana. "We've seen odd behaviour from other worm infestations across the system; things that begin to look like emergent intelligence. But never anything this purposeful. This infestation must have come from a batch with some subroutines we never even guessed about. Do you have any ideas about what they might be up to?"

Again, there was the briefest of hesitations, as if she was communing with her compatriots for the right response. Then she nodded toward a male Conjoiner sitting opposite her, Clavain guessing that the gesture was entirely for his benefit. His hair was black and curly; his face as smooth and untroubled by expression as Galiana's, with something of the same beautifully symmetrical bone structure.

"This is Remontoire," said Galiana. "He's our specialist on the Phobos situation."

Remontoire nodded politely. "In answer to your question, we currently have no viable theories as to what they're doing, but we do know one thing. They're raising the apocentre of the moon's orbit." Apocentre, Clavain knew, was the Martian equivalent of apogee for an object orbiting Earth: the point of highest altitude in an elliptical orbit. Remontoire continued, his voice as preternaturally calm as a parent reading slowly to a child. "The natural orbit of Phobos is actually inside the Roche limit for a gravitationally-bound moon; Phobos is raising a tidal bulge on Mars but, because of friction, the bulge can't quite keep up with Phobos. It's causing Phobos to spiral slowly closer to Mars, by about two metres a century. In a few tens of millions of years, what's left of the moon will crash into Mars."

"You think the worms are elevating the orbit to avoid a cataclysm so far in the future?"

"I don't know," Remontoire said. "I suppose the orbital alterations could also be a by-product of some less meaningful worm activity."

"I agree," Clavain said. "But the danger remains. If the worms can elevate the moon's apocentre—even accidentally—we can assume they also have the means to lower its pericentre. They could drop Phobos on top of your nest. Does that scare you sufficiently that you'd consider co-operation with the Coalition?"

Galiana steepled her fingers before her face; a human gesture of deep concentration which her time as a Conjoiner had not quite eroded. Clavain could almost feel the web of thought looming the room; ghostly strands of cognition reaching between each Conjoiner at the table, and beyond into the nest proper.

"A winning team, is that your idea?"

"It's got to be better than war," Clavain said. "Hasn't it?"

Galiana might have been about to answer him when her face grew troubled. Clavain saw the wave of discomposure sweep over the others almost simultaneously. Something told him that it was nothing to do with his proposal.

Around the table, half the display facets switched automatically over to another channel. The face that Clavain was looking at was much like his own, except that the face on the screen was missing an eye. It was his brother. Warren was overlaid with the official insignia of the Coalition and a dozen system-wide media cartels.

He was in the middle of a speech. "...express my shock," Warren said. "Or, for that matter, my outrage. It's not just that they've murdered a valued colleague and deeply experienced member of my team. They've murdered my brother."

Clavain felt the deepest of chills. "What is this?"

"A live transmission from Deimos," Galiana breathed. "It's going out to all the nets; right out to the trans-Pluto habitats."

"What they did was an act of unspeakable treachery," Warren said. "Nothing less than the pre-meditated, cold-blooded murder of a peace envoy." And then a video clip sprang up to replace Warren. The image must have been snapped from Deimos or one of the interdiction satellites. It showed Clavain's shuttle, lying in the dust close to the dyke. He watched the Ouroborus destroy the shuttle, then saw the image zoom in on himself and Voi, running for sanctuary. The Ouroborus took Voi. But this time there was no ladder lowered down for him. Instead, he saw weapon-beams scythe out from the nest toward him, knocking him to the ground. Horribly wounded, he tried to get up, to crawl a few inches nearer to his tormentors, but the worm was already upon him.

He watched himself get eaten.

Warren was back again. "The worms around the nest were a Conjoiner trap. My brother's death must have been planned days—maybe even weeks—in advance." His face glistened with a wave of military composure. "There can only be one outcome from such an action—something the Conjoiners must have well understood. For months they've been goading us toward hostile action." He paused, then nodded at an unseen audience. "Well now they're going to get it. In fact, our response has already commenced."

"Dear God, no," Clavain said, but the evidence was all there now; all around the table he could see the updating orbital spread of the Coalition's dropships, knifing down toward Mars.

"I think it's war," Galiana said.

CONJOINERS STORMED ONTO the roof of the nest, taking up defensive positions around the domes and the dyke's edge. Most of them carried the same guns which they had used against the Ouroborus. Smaller numbers were setting up automatic cannon on tripods. One or two were manhandling large anti-assault weapons into position. Most of it was war-surplus. Fifteen years ago the Conjoiners had avoided extinction by deploying weapons of awesome ferocity—but those ship-to-ship armaments were too simply too destructive to use against a nearby foe. Now it would be more visceral; closer to the primal templates of combat, and none of what the Conjoiners were marshalling would be much use against the kind of assault Warren had prepared, Clavain knew. They could slow an attack, but not much more than that.

Galiana had given him another breather mask, made him don light-weight chameleoflage armour, and then forced him to carry one of the smaller guns. The gun felt alien in his hands; something he had never expected to carry again. The only possible justification for carrying it was to use it against his brother's forces—against his own side.

Could he do that?

It was clear that Warren had betrayed him; he had surely been aware of the worms around the nest. So his brother was capable not just of con-tempt, but of treacherous murder. For the first time, Clavain felt genuine hatred for Warren. He must have hoped that the worms would destroy the shuttle completely and kill Clavain and Voi in the process. It must have pained him to see Clavain make it to the dyke...pained him even more when Clavain called to talk about the tragedy. But Warren's larger plan had not been affected. The diplomatic link between the nest and Deimos was secure—even the Demarchists had no immediate access to it. So Clavain's call from the surface could be quietly ignored; spysat imagery doctored to make it seem that he had never reached the dyke...had in fact been repelled by Conjoiner treachery. Inevitably the Demarchists would unravel the deception given time...but if Warren's plan succeeded, they would all be embroiled in war long before then. That, thought Clavain, was all that Warren had ever wanted.

Two brothers, Clavain thought. In many ways so alike. Both had embraced war once, but like a fickle lover Clavain had wearied of its glories. He had not even been injured as severely as Warren...but perhaps that was the point, too. Warren needed another war to avenge what one had stolen from him.

Clavain despised and pitied him in equal measure.

He searched for the safety clip on the gun. The rifle, now that he studied it more closely, was not all that different from those he had used during the war. The readout said the ammo-cell was fully charged.

He looked into the sky.

The attack wave broke orbit hard and steep above the Wall; five hundred fireballs screeching toward the nest. The insertion scorched inches of ablative armour from most of the ships; fried a few others which came in just fractionally too hard. Clavain knew that was how it was happening: he had studied possible attack scenarios for years, the range of outcomes burned indelibly into his memory.

The anti-assault guns were already working—locking onto the plasma trails as they flowered overhead, swinging down to find the tiny spark of heat at the head, computing refraction paths for laser pulses, spitting death into the sky. The unlucky ships flared a white that hurt the back of the eye and rained down in a billion dulling sparks. A dozen—then a dozen more. Maybe fifty in total before the guns could no longer acquire targets. It was nowhere near enough. Clavain's memory of the simulations told him that at least four hundred units of the attack wave would survive both re-entry and the Conjoiner's heavy defences.

Nothing that Galiana could do would make any difference.

And that had always been the paradox. Galiana was capable of running the same simulations. She must always have known that her provocations would bring down something she could never hope to defeat.

Something that was always going to destroy her.

The surviving members of the wave were levelling out now, commencing long, ground-hugging runs from all directions. Cocooned in their dropships, the soldiers would be suffering punishing gee-loads... but it was nothing they were not engineered to withstand; half their cardiovascular systems were augmented by the only kinds of implant the Coalition tolerated.

The first of the wave came arcing in at supersonic speeds. All around, worms struggled to snatch them out of the sky, but mostly they were too slow to catch the dropships. Galiana's people manned their cannon positions and did their best to fend off what they could. Clavain clutched his gun, not firing yet. Best to save his ammo-cell power for a target he stood a chance of injuring.

Above, the first dropships made hairpin turns, nosing suicidally down toward the nest. Then they fractured cleanly apart, revealing falling pilots clad in bulbous armour. Just before the moment of impact each pilot exploded into a mass of black shock-absorbing balloons, looking something like a blackberry, bouncing across the nest before the balloons deflated just as swiftly and the pilot was left standing on the ground. By then the pilot—now properly a soldier—would have a comprehensive computer-generated map of the nest's nooks and crannies; enemy positions graphed in realtime from the down-looking spysats.

Clavain fell behind the curve of a dome before the nearest soldier got a lock onto him. The firefight was beginning now. He had to hand it to Galiana's people—they were fighting like devils. And they were at least as well co-ordinated as the attackers. But their weapons and armour were simply inadequate. Chameleoflage was only truly effective against a solitary enemy, or a massed enemy moving in from a common direction. With Coalition forces surrounding him, Clavain's suit was going crazy trying to match itself against every background, like a chameleon in a house of mirrors.

The sky overhead looked strange now—darkening purple. And the purple was spreading in a mist across the nest. Galiana had deployed some kind of chemical smoke screen: infrared and optically opaque, he guessed. It would occlude the spysats and might be primed to adhere only to enemy chameleoflage. That had never been in Warren's simulations. Galiana had just given herself the slightest of edges.

A soldier stepped out of the mist, the obscene darkness of a gun muzzle trained on Clavain. His chameleoflage armour was dappled with vivid purple patches, ruining its stealthiness. The man fired, but his discharge wasted itself against Clavain's armour. Clavain returned the compliment, dropping his compatriot. What he had done, he thought, was not technically treason. Not yet. All he had done was act in self-preservation.

The man was wounded, but not yet dead. Clavain stepped through the purple haze and knelt down beside the soldier. He tried not to look at the man's wound.

"Can you hear me?" he said. There was no answer from the man, but beneath his visor, Clavain thought he saw the man's lips shape a sound. The man was just a kid—hardly old enough to remember much of the last war. "There's something you have to know," Clavain continued. "Do you realise who I am?" He wondered how recognisable he was, under the breather mask. Then something made him relent. He could tell the man he was Nevil Clavain—but what would that achieve? The soldier would be dead in minutes; maybe sooner than that. Nothing would be served by the soldier knowing that the basis for his attack was a lie; that he would not in fact be laying down his life for a just cause. The universe could be spared a single callous act.

"Forget it," Clavain said, turning away from his victim.

And then moved deeper into the nest, to see who else he could kill before the odds took him.

BUT THE ODDS never did.

"You were always were lucky," Galiana said, leaning over him. They were somewhere underground again—deep in the nest. A medical area, by the look of things. He was on a bed, fully clothed apart from the outer layer of chameleoflage armour. The room was grey and kettle-shaped, ringed by a circular balcony.

"What happened?"

"You took a head wound, but you'll survive."

He groped for the right question. "What about Warren's attack?"

"We endured three waves. We took casualties, of course."

Around the circumference of the balcony were thirty or so grey couches, slightly recessed into archways studded with grey medical equipment. They were all occupied. There were more Conjoiners in this room than he had seen so far in one place. Some of them looked very close to death.

Clavain reached up and examined his head, gingerly. There was some dried blood on the scalp, matted with his hair; some numbness, but it could have been a lot worse. He felt normal—no memory drop-outs or aphasia. When he made to stand from the bed, his body obeyed his will with only a tinge of dizziness.

"Warren won't stop at just three waves, Galiana."

"I know." She paused. "We know there'll be more."

He walked to the railing on the inner side of the balcony and looked over the edge. He had expected to see something—some chunk of incomprehensible surgical equipment, perhaps—but the middle of the room was only an empty, smooth-walled, grey pit. He shivered. The air was colder than any part of the nest he had visited so far, with a medicinal tang which reminded him of the convalescence ward on Deimos. What made him shiver even more was the realisation that some of the injured—some of the dead—were barely older than the children he had visited only hours ago. Perhaps some of them were those children, conscripted from the nursery since his visit, uploaded with fighting reflexes through their new implants.

"What are you going to do? You know you can't win. Warren lost only a tiny fraction of his available force in those waves. You look like you've lost half your nest."

"It's much worse than that," Galiana said.

"What do you mean?"

"You're not quite ready yet. But I can show you in a moment."

He felt colder than ever now. "What do you mean, not quite ready?"

Galiana looked deep into his eyes now. "You took a serious head wound, Clavain. The entry wound was small, but the internal bleeding... it would have killed you, had we not intervened." Before he could ask the inevitable question she answered it for him. "We injected a small cluster of medichines into your head. They undid the damage very easily. But it seemed provident to allow them to grow."

"You've put replicators in my head?"

"You needn't sound so horrified. They're already growing—spreading out and interfacing with your existing neural circuitry—but the total volume of glial mass that they will consume is tiny: only a few cubic millimetres in total, across your entire brain."

He wondered if she was calling his bluff. "I don't feel anything."

"You won't—not for a minute or so." Now she pointed into the empty pit in the middle of the room. "Stand here and look into the air."

"There's nothing there."

But as soon as he had spoken, he knew he was wrong. There was something in the pit. He blinked and directed his attention somewhere else, but when he returned his gaze to the pit, the thing he imagined he had seen—milky, spectral—was still there, and becoming sharper and brighter by the second. It was a three-dimensional structure, as complex as an exercise in protein-folding. A tangle of loops and connecting branches and nodes and tunnels, embedded in a ghostly red matrix.

Suddenly he saw it for what it was: a map of the nest, dug into Mars. Just as the Coalition had suspected, the base was deeper than the original structure; far more extensive, reaching deeper down but much further out than anyone had imagined. Clavain made a mental effort to retain some of what he was seeing in his mind, the intelligence-gathering reflex stronger than the conscious knowledge that he would never see Deimos again.

"The medichines in your brain have interfaced with your visual cortex," Galiana said. "That's the first step on the road to Transenlightenment. Now you're privy to the machine-generated imagery encoded by the fields through which we move—most of it, anyway."

"Tell me this wasn't planned, Galiana. Tell me you weren't intending to put machines in me at the first opportunity."

"No; I wasn't planning it. But nor was I going to let your phobias stop me from saving your life."

The image grew in complexity. Glowing nodes of light appeared in the tunnels, some moving slowly through the network.

"What are they?"

"You're seeing the locations of the Conjoiners," Galiana said. "Are there as many as you imagined?"

Clavain judged that there were no more than seventy lights in the whole complex now. He searched for a cluster which would identify the room where he stood. There: twenty-odd bright lights, accompanied by one much fainter. Himself, of course. There were few people near the top of the nest—the attack must have collapsed half the tunnels, or maybe Galiana had deliberately sealed entrances herself.

"Where is everyone? Where are the children?"

"Most of the children are gone now." She paused. "You were right to guess that we were rushing them to Transenlightenment, Clavain."

"Why?"

"Because it's the only way out of here."

The image changed again. Now each of the bright lights was connected to another by a shimmering filament. The topology of the network was constantly shifting, like a pattern seen in a kaleidoscope. Occasionally, too swiftly for Clavain to be sure, it shifted toward a mandala of elusive symmetry, only to dissolve into the flickering chaos of the ever-changing network. He studied Galiana's node and saw that—even as she was speaking to him—her mind was in constant rapport with the rest of the nest.

Now something very bright appeared in the middle of the image, like a tiny star, against which the shimmering network paled almost to invisibility. "The network is abstracted now," Galiana said. "The bright light represents its totality: the unity of Transenlightenment. Watch."

He watched. The bright light—beautiful and alluring as anything Clavain had ever imagined—was extending a ray toward the isolated node which represented himself. The ray was extending itself through the map, coming closer by the second.

"The new structures in your mind are nearing maturity," Galiana said. "When the ray touches you, you will experience partial integration with the rest of us. Prepare yourself, Nevil."

Her words were unnecessary. His fingers were already clenched sweating on the railing as the light inched closer and engulfed his node.

"I should hate you for this," Clavain said.

"Why don't you? Hate's always the easier option."

"Because..." Because it made no difference now. His old life was over. He reached out for Galiana, needing some anchor against what was about to hit him. Galiana squeezed his hand and an instant later he knew something of Transenlightenment. The experience was shocking; not because it was painful or fearful, but because it was profoundly and totally new. He was literally thinking in ways that had not been possible microseconds earlier.

Afterwards, when Clavain tried to imagine how he might describe it, he found that words were never going to be adequate for the task. And that was no surprise: evolution had shaped language to convey many concepts, but going from a single to a networked topology of self was not among them. But if he could not convey the core of the experience, he could at least skirt its essence with metaphor. It was like standing on the shore of an ocean, being engulfed by a wave taller than himself. For a moment he sought the surface; tried to keep the water from his lungs. But there happened not to be a surface. What had consumed him extended infinitely in all directions. He could only submit to it. Yet as the moments slipped by it turned from something terrifying in its unfamiliarity to something he could begin to adapt to; something that even began in the tiniest way to seem comforting. Even then he glimpsed that it was only a shadow of what Galiana was experiencing every instant of her life.

"Alright," Galiana said. "That's enough for now."

The fullness of Transenlightenment retreated, like a fading vision of Godhead. What he was left with was purely sensory; no longer any direct rapport with the others. His state of mind came crashing back to normality.

"Are you alright, Nevil?"

"Yes..." His mouth was dry. "Yes; I think so."

"Look around you."

He did.

The room had changed completely. So had everyone in it.

His head reeling, Clavain walked in light. The formerly grey walls oozed beguiling patterns; as if a dark forest had suddenly become enchanted. Information hung in veils in the air; icons and diagrams and numbers clustering around the beds of the injured, thinning out into the general space like fantastically delicate neon sculptures. As he walked toward the icons they darted out of his way, mocking him like schools of brilliant fish. Sometimes they seemed to sing, or tickle the back of his nose with half-familiar smells.

"You can perceive things now," Galiana said. "But none of it will mean much to you. You'd need years of education, or deeper neural machinery for that—building cognitive layers. We read all this almost subliminally."

Galiana was dressed differently now. He could still see the vague shape of her grey outfit, but layered around it were billowing skeins of light, unravelling at their edges into chains of Boolean logic. Icons danced in her hair like angels. He could see, faintly, the web of thought linking her with the other Conjoiners.

She was inhumanly beautiful.

"You said things were much worse," Clavain said. "Are you ready to show me now?"

SHE TOOK HIM to see Felka again, passing on the way through deserted nursery rooms, populated now only by bewildered mechanical animals. Felka was the only child left in the nursery.

Clavain had been deeply disturbed by Felka when he had seen her before, but not for any reason he could easily express. Something about the purposefulness of what she did; performed with ferocious concentration, as if the fate of creation hung on the outcome of her game. Felka and her surroundings had not changed at all since his visit. The room was still austere to the point of oppressiveness. Felka looked the same. In every respect it was as if only an instant had passed since their meeting; as if the onset of war and the assaults against the nest—the battle of which this was only an interlude—were only figments from someone else's troubling dream; nothing that need concern Felka in her devotion to the task at hand.

And what the task was awed Clavain.

Before he had watched her make strange gestures in front of her. Now the machines in his head revealed the purpose that those gestures served. Around Felka—cordoning her like a barricade—was a ghostly representation of the Great Wall.

She was doing something to it.

It was not a scale representation, Clavain knew. The Wall looked much higher here in relation to its diameter. And the surface was not the nearly-invisible membrane of the real thing, but something like etched glass. The etchwork was a filigree of lines and junctions, descending down to smaller and smaller scales in fractal steps, until the blur of detail was too fine for his eyes to discriminate. It was shifting and altering colour, and Felka was responding to these alterations with what he now saw was frightening efficiency. It was as if the colour changes warned of some malignancy in part of the Wall, and by touching it—expressing some tactile code—Felka was able to restructure the etchwork to block and neutralise the malignancy before it spread.

"I don't understand," Clavain said. "I thought we destroyed the Wall; completely killed its systems."

"No," Galiana said. "You only ever injured it. Stopped it from growing, and from managing its own repair-processes correctly...but you never truly killed it."

Sandra Voi had guessed, Clavain realised. She had wondered how the Wall had survived this long.

Galiana told him the rest—how they had managed to establish control pathways to the Wall from the nest, fifteen years earlier—optical cables sunk deep below the worm zone. "We stabilised the Wall's degradation with software running on dumb machines," she said. "But when Felka was born we found that she managed the task just as efficiently as the computers; in some ways better than they ever did. In fact, she seemed to thrive on it. It was as if in the Wall she found..." Galiana trailed off. "I was going to say a friend."

"Why don't you?"

"Because the Wall's just a machine. Which means if Felka recognised kinship...what would that make her?"

"Someone lonely, that's all." Clavain watched the girl's motions. "She seems faster than before. Is that possible?"

"I told you things were worse than before. She's having to work harder to hold the Wall together."

"Warren must have attacked it." Clavain said. "The possibility of knocking down the Wall always figured in our contingency plans for another war. I just never thought it would happen so soon." Then he looked at Felka. Maybe it was imagination but she seemed to be working even faster than when he had entered the room; not just since his last visit. "How long do you think she can keep it together?"

"Not much longer," Galiana said. "As a matter of fact I think she's already failing."

It was true. Now that he looked closely at the ghost Wall he saw that the upper edge was not the mathematically smooth ring it should have been; that there were scores of tiny ragged bites eating down from the top. Felka's activities were increasingly directed to these opening cracks in the structure; instructing the crippled structure to divert energy and raw materials to these critical failure points. Clavain knew that the distant processes Felka directed were awesome. Within the Wall lay a lymphatic system whose peristaltic feed-pipes ranged in size from meters across to the submicroscopic; flowing with myriad tiny repair machines. Felka chose where to send those machines; her hand gestures establishing pathways between damage points and the factories sunk into the Wall's ramparts which made the required types of machine. For more than a decade, Galiana said, Felka had kept the Wall from crumbling—but for most of that time her adversary had been only natural decay and accidental damage. It was a different game now that the Wall had been attacked again. It was not one she could ever win.

Felka's movements were swifter; less fluid. Her face remained impassive, but in the quickening way that her eyes darted from point to point it was possible to read the first hints of panic. No surprise, either: the deepest cracks in the structure now reached a quarter of the way to the surface, and they were too wide to be repaired. The Wall was unzipping along those flaws. Cubic kilometres of atmosphere would be howling out through the openings. The loss of pressure would be immeasurably slow at first, for near the top the trapped cylinder of atmosphere was only fractionally thicker than the rest of the Martian atmosphere. But only at first...

"We have to get deeper," Clavain said. "Once the Wall goes, we won't have a chance in hell if we're anywhere near the surface. It'll be like the worst tornado in history."

"What will your brother do? Will he nuke us?"

"No; I don't think so. He'll want to get hold of any technologies you've hidden away. He'll wait until the dust storms have died down, then he'll raid the nest with a hundred times as many troops as you've seen so far. You won't be able to resist, Galiana. If you're lucky you may just survive long enough to be taken prisoner."

"There won't be any prisoners," Galiana said.

"You're planning to die fighting?"

"No. And mass suicide doesn't figure in our plans either. Neither will be necessary. By the time your brother reaches here, there won't be anyone left in the nest."

Clavain thought of the worms encircling the area; how small were the chances of reaching any kind of safety if it involved getting past them. "Secret tunnels under the worm zone, is that it? I hope you're serious."

"I'm deadly serious," Galiana said. "And yes, there is a secret tunnel. The other children have already gone through it now. But it doesn't lead under the worm zone."

"Where, then?"

"Somewhere a lot further away."

WHEN THEY PASSED through the medical centre again it was empty, save for a few swan-necked robots patiently waiting for further casualties. They had left Felka behind tending the Wall, her hands a manic blur as she tried to slow the rate of collapse. Clavain had tried to make her come with them, but Galiana had told him he was wasting his time: that she would sooner die than be parted from the Wall.

"You don't understand," Galiana said. "You're placing too much humanity behind her eyes. Keeping the Wall alive is the single most important fact of her universe—more important than love, pain, death—anything you or I would consider definitively human."

"Then what happens to her when the Wall dies?"

"Her life ends," Galiana said.

Reluctantly he had left without her, the taste of shame in his mouth. Rationally it made sense: without Felka's help the Wall would collapse much sooner and there was a good chance all their lives would end; not just that of the haunted girl. How deep would they have to go before they were safe from the suction of the escaping atmosphere? Would any part of the nest be safe?

The regions through which they were descending now were as cold and grey as any Clavain had seen. There were no entoptic generators buried in these walls to supply visual information to the implants Galiana had put in his head, and even her own aura of light was gone. They only met a few other Conjoiners, and they seemed to be moving in the same general direction; down to the nest's basement levels. This was unknown territory to Clavain.

Where was Galiana taking him?

"If you had an escape route all along, why did you wait so long before sending the children through it?"

"I told you, we couldn't bring them to Transenlightenment too soon. The older they were, the better," Galiana said. "Now though…"

"There was no waiting any longer, was there?"

Eventually they reached a chamber with the same echoing acoustics as the topside hangar. The chamber was dark except for a few pools of light, but in the shadows Clavain made out discarded excavation equipment and freight pallets; cranes and de-activated robots. The air smelled of ozone. Something was still going on here.

"Is this the factory where you make the shuttles?" Clavain said.

"We manufactured parts of them here, yes," Galiana said. "But that was a side-industry."

"Of what?"

"The tunnel, of course." Galiana made more lights come on. At the far end of the chamber—they were walking toward it—waited a series of cylindrical things with pointed ends; like huge bullets. They rested on rails, one after the other. The tip of the very first bullet was next to a dark hole in the wall. Clavain was about to say something when there was a sudden loud buzz and the first bullet slammed into the hole. The other bullets—there were three of them now—eased slowly forward and halted. Conjoiners were waiting to get aboard them.

He remembered what Galiana had said about no one being left behind.

"What am I seeing here?"

"A way out of the nest," Galiana said. "And a way off Mars, though I suppose you figured that part for yourself."

"There is no way off Mars," Clavain said. "The interdiction guarantees that. Haven't you learned that with your shuttles?"

"The shuttles were only ever a diversionary tactic," Galiana said. "They made your side think we were still striving to escape, whereas our true escape route was already fully operational."

"A pretty desperate diversion."

"Not really. I lied to you when I said we didn't clone. We did—but only to produce brain-dead corpses. The shuttles were full of corpses before we ever launched them."

For the first time since leaving Deimos Clavain smiled, amused at the sheer obliquity of Galiana's thinking.

"Of course, there was another function," she said. "The shuttles provoked your side into a direct attack against the nest."

"So this was deliberate all along?"

"Yes. We needed to draw your side's attention; to concentrate your military presence in low-orbit, near the nest. Of course we were hoping the offensive would come later than it did...but we reckoned without Warren's conspiracy."

"Then you are planning something."

"Yes." The next bullet slammed into the wall, ozone crackling from its linear induction rails. Now only two remained. "We can talk later. There isn't much time now." She projected an image into his visual field: the Wall, now veined by titanic fractures down half its length. "It's collapsing."

"And Felka?"

"She's still trying to save it."

He looked at the Conjoiners boarding the leading bullet; tried to imagine where they were going. Was it to any kind of sanctuary he might recognise—or to something so beyond his experience that it might as well be death? Did he have the nerve to find out? Perhaps. He had nothing to lose now, after all: he could certainly not return home. But if he was going to follow Galiana's exodus, it could not be with the sense of shame he now felt in abandoning Felka.

The answer, when it came, was simple. "I'm going back for her. If you can't wait for me, don't. But don't try and stop me doing this."

Galiana looked at him, shaking her head slowly. "She won't thank you for saving her life, Clavain."

"Maybe not now," he said.

HE HAD THE feeling he was running back into a burning building. Given what Galiana had said about the girl's deficiencies—that by any reasonable definition she was hardly more than an automaton—what he was doing was very likely pointless, if not suicidal. But if he turned his back on her, he would become something even less than human himself. He had misread Galiana badly when she said the girl was precious to them. He had assumed some bond of affection...whereas what Galiana meant was that the girl was precious in the sense of a vital component. Now—with the nest being abandoned—the component had no further use. Did that make Galiana as cold as a machine herself—or was she just being unfailingly realistic? He found the nursery after only one or two false turns, and then Felka's room. The implants Galiana had given him were again throwing phantom images into the air. Felka sat within the crumbling circle of the Wall. Great fissures now reached to the surface of Mars. Shards of the Wall, as big as icebergs, had fractured away and now lay like vast sheets of broken glass across the regolith.

She was losing, and now she knew it. This was not just some more difficult phase of the game. This was something she could never win, and her realisation was now plainly evident in her face. She was still moving her arms frantically, but her face was red now, locked into a petulant scowl of anger and fear.

For the first time, she seemed to notice him.

Something had broken through her shell, Clavain thought. For the first time in years, something was happening that was beyond her control; something that threatened to destroy the neat, geometric universe she had made for herself. She might not have distinguished his face from all the other people who came to see her, but she surely recognised something...that now the adult world was bigger than she was, and it was only from the adult world that any kind of salvation could come.

Then she did something that shocked him beyond words. She looked deep into his eyes and reached out a hand.

But there was nothing he could do to help her.

LATER—IT SEEMED HOURS, but in fact could only have been tens of minutes—Clavain found that he was able to breathe normally again. They had escaped Mars now; Galiana, Felka and himself, riding the last bullet.

And they were still alive.

The bullet's vacuum-filled tunnel cut deep into Mars; a shallow arc bending under the crust before rising again, thousands of kilometres away, well beyond the Wall, where the atmosphere was as thin as ever. For the Conjoiners, boring the tunnel had not been especially difficult. Such engineering would have been impossible on a planet that had plate tectonics, but beneath its lithosphere Mars was geologically quiet. They had not even had to worry about tailings. What they excavated, they compressed and fused and used to line the tunnel, maintaining rigidity against awesome pressure with some trick of piezo-electricity. In the tunnel, the bullet accelerated continuously at three gees for ten minutes. Their seats had tilted back and wrapped around them, applying pressure to the legs to maintain bloodflow to the head. Even so, it was hard to think, let alone move, but Clavain knew that it was no worse than what the earliest space explorers had endured climbing away from Earth. And he had undergone similar tortures during the war, in combat insertions.

They were moving at ten kilometres a second when they reached the surface again, exiting via a camouflaged trapdoor. For a moment the atmosphere snatched at them...but almost as soon as Clavain had registered the deceleration, it was over. The surface of Mars was dropping below them very quickly indeed.

In half a minute, they were in true space.

"The Interdiction's sensor web can't track us," Galiana said. "You placed your best spy-sats directly over the nest. That was a mistake,

Clavain—even though we did our best to reinforce your thinking with the shuttle launches. But now we're well outside your sensor footprint."

Clavain nodded. "But that won't help us once we're far from the surface. Then, we'll just look like another ship trying to reach deep space. The web may be late locking onto us, but it'll still get us in the end."

"It would," Galiana said. "If deep space was where we were going."

Felka stirred next to him. She had withdrawn into some kind of catatonia. Separation from the Wall had undermined her entire existence; now she was free-falling through an abyss of meaninglessness. Perhaps, Clavain, thought, she would fall forever. If that was the case, he had only brought forward her fate. Was that much of a cruelty? Perhaps he was deluding himself, but with time, was it out of the question that Galiana's machines could undo the harm they had inflicted ten years earlier? Surely they could try. It depended, of course, on where exactly they were headed. One of the system's other Conjoiner nests had been Clavain's initial guess—even though it seemed unlikely that they would ever survive the crossing. At ten klicks per second it would take years...

"Where are you taking us?" he asked.

Galiana issued some neural command which made the bullet seem to become transparent.

"There," she said.

Something lay distantly ahead. Galiana made the forward view zoom in, until the object was much clearer.

Dark—misshapen. Like Deimos without fortifications.

"Phobos," Clavain said, wonderingly. "We're going to Phobos."

"Yes," Galiana said.

"But the worms—"

"Don't exist anymore." She spoke with the same tutorly patience with which Remontoire had addressed him on the same subject not long before. "Your attempt to oust the worms failed. You assumed our subsequent attempt failed...but that was only what we wanted you to think."

For a moment he was lost for words. "You've had people in Phobos all along?"

"Ever since the cease-fire, yes. They've been quite busy, too."

Phobos altered. Layers of it were peeled away, revealing the glittering device which lay hidden in its heart, poised and ready for flight. Clavain had never seen anything like it, but the nature of the thing was instantly obvious. He was looking at something wonderful; something which had never existed before in the whole of human experience.

He was looking at a starship.

"We'll be leaving soon," Galiana said. "They'll try and stop us, of course. But now that their forces are concentrated near the surface, they won't succeed. We'll leave Phobos and Mars behind, and send messages to the other nests. If they can break out and meet us, we'll take them as well. We'll leave this whole system behind."

"Where are you going?"

"Shouldn't that be where are we going? You're coming with us, after all." She paused. "There are a number of candidate systems. Our choice will depend on the trajectory the Coalition forces upon us."

"What about the Demarchists?"

"They won't stop us." It was said with total assurance—implying, what? That the Demarchy knew of this ship? Perhaps. It had long been rumoured that the Demarchists and the Conjoiners were closer than they admitted.

Clavain thought of something. "What about the worms' altering the orbit?"

"That was our doing," Galiana said. "We couldn't help it. Every time we send up one of these canisters, we nudge Phobos into a different orbit. Even after we sent up a thousand canisters, the effect was tiny— we changed Phobos's velocity by less than one tenth of a millimetre per second—but there was no way to hide it." Then she paused and looked at Clavain with something like apprehension. "We'll be arriving in two hundred seconds. Do you want to live?"

"I'm sorry?"

"Think about it. The tube in Mars was a thousand kilometres long, which allowed us to spread the acceleration over ten minutes. Even then it was three gees. But there simply isn't room for anything like that in Phobos. We'll be slowing down much more abruptly."

Clavain felt the hairs on the back of his neck prickle. "How much more abruptly?"

"Complete deceleration in one fifth of a second." She let that sink home. "That's around five thousand gees."

"I can't survive that."

"No; you can't. Not now, anyway. But there are machines in your head now. If you allow it, there's time for them to establish a structural web across your brain. We'll flood the cabin with foam. We'll all die temporarily, but there won't be anything they can't fix in Phobos."

"It won't just be a structural web, will it? I'll be like you, then. There won't be any difference between us."

"You'll become Conjoined, yes." Galiana offered the faintest of smiles. "The procedure is reversible. It's just that no one's ever wanted to go back."

"And you still tell me none of this was planned?"

"No; but I don't expect you to believe me. For what it's worth, though… you're a good man, Nevil. The Transenlightenment could use you. Maybe at the back of my mind…at the back of our mind…"

"You always hoped it might come to this?"

Galiana smiled.

He looked at Phobos. Even without Galiana's magnification, it was clearly bigger. They would be arriving very shortly. He would have liked longer to think about it, but the one thing not on his side now was time. Then he looked at Felka, and wondered which of them was about to embark on the stranger journey. Felka's search for meaning in a universe without her beloved Wall, or his passage into Transenlightenment? Neither would necessarily be easy. But together, perhaps, they might even find a way to help each other. That was all he could hope for now.

Clavain nodded assent, ready for the loom of machines to embrace his mind.

He was ready to defect.

WEATHER

WE WERE at one-quarter of the speed of light, outbound from Shiva-Parvati with a hold full of refugees, when the *Cockatrice* caught up with us. She commenced her engagement at a distance of one light-second, seeking to disable us with long-range weapons before effecting a boarding operation. Captain Van Ness did his best to protect the *Petronel*, but we were a lightly armoured ship and Van Ness did not wish to endanger his passengers by provoking a damaging retaliation from the pirates. As coldly calculated as it might appear, Van Ness knew that it would be better for the sleepers to be taken by another ship than suffer a purposeless death in interstellar space.

As shipmaster, it was my duty to give Captain Van Ness the widest choice of options. When it became clear that the *Cockatrice* was on our tail, following us out from Shiva-Parvati, I recommended that we discard fifty thousand tonnes of nonessential hull material, in order to increase the rate of acceleration available from our Conjoiner drives. When the *Cockatrice* ramped up her own engines to compensate, I identified a further twenty thousand tonnes of material we could discard until the next orbitfall, even though the loss of the armour would marginally increase the radiation dosage we would experience during the flight. We gained a little, but the pirates still had power in reserve: they'd stripped back their ship to little more than a husk, and they didn't have the mass handicap of our sleepers. Since we could not afford to lose any more hull material, I advised Van Ness to eject two of our three heavy shuttles, each of which massed six thousand tonnes when fully fuelled. That bought us yet more time, but to my dismay the pirates still found a way to squeeze a little more out of their engines.

Whoever they had as shipmaster, I thought, they were good at their work.

So I went to the engines themselves, to see if I could better my nameless opponent. I crawled out along the pressurised access tunnel that pierced the starboard spar, out to the coupling point where the foreign technology of the starboard Conjoiner drive was mated to the structural fabric of the *Petronel*. There I opened the hatch that gave access to the controls of the drive itself: six stiff dials, fashioned in blue metal, arranged in hexagon formation, each of which was tied to some fundamental aspect of the engine's function. The dials were set into quadrant-shaped recesses, all now glowing a calm blue-green.

I noted the existing settings, then made near-microscopic alterations to three of the six dials, fighting to keep my hands steady as I applied the necessary effort to budge them. Even as I made the first alteration, I felt the engine respond: a shiver of power as some arcane process occurred deep inside it, accompanied by a shift in my own weight as the thrust increased by five or six per cent. The blue-green hue was now tinted with orange.

The *Petronel* surged faster, still maintaining her former heading. It was only possible to make adjustments to the starboard engine, since the port engine had no external controls. That didn't matter, because the Conjoiners had arranged the two engines to work in perfect synchronisation, despite them being a kilometre apart. No one had ever succeeded in detecting the signals that passed between two matched C-drives, let alone in understanding the messages those signals carried. But everyone who worked with them knew what would happen if, by accident or design, the engines were allowed to get more than sixteen hundred metres apart.

I completed my adjustments, satisfied that I'd done all I could without risking engine malfunction. Three of the five dials were now showing orange, indicating that those settings were now outside what the Conjoiners deemed the recommended envelope of safe operation. If any of the dials were to show red, or if more than three showed orange, than we'd be in real danger of losing the *Petronel*.

When Ultras meet on friendly terms, to exchange data or goods, the shipmasters will often trade stories of engine settings. On a busy trade route, a marginal increase in drive efficiency can make all the difference between one ship and its competitors. Occasionally you hear about ships that have been running on three orange, even four orange, for decades at a time. By the same token, you sometimes hear about ships that went nova when only two dials had been adjusted away from the safety envelope. The one thing every shipmaster agrees upon is that no lighthugger has ever operated for more than a few days of shiptime with one dial in the red. You might risk that to escape aggressors, but even then some will insist that the danger is too great; that those ships that lasted days were the lucky ones.

I left the starboard engine and retreated back into the main hull of the *Petronel*. Van Ness was waiting to greet me. I could tell by the look on his face—the part of it that I could read—that the news wasn't good.

"Good lad, Inigo," he said, placing his heavy gauntleted hand on my shoulder. "You've bought us maybe half a day, and I'm grateful for that, no question of it. But it's not enough to make a difference. Are you sure you can't sweet-talk any more out of them?"

"We could risk going to two gees for a few hours. That still wouldn't put us out of reach of the *Cockatrice*, though."

"And beyond that?"

I showed Van Ness my handwritten log book, with its meticulous notes of engine settings, compiled over twenty years of shiptime. Black ink for my own entries, the style changing abruptly when I lost my old hand and slowly learned how to use the new one; red annotations in the same script for comments and know-how gleaned from other shipmasters, dated and named. "According to this, we're already running a fifteen per cent chance of losing the ship within the next hundred days. I'd feel a lot happier if we were already throttling back."

"You don't think we can lose any more mass?"

"We're stripped to the bone as it is. I can probably find you another few thousand tonnes, but we'll still only be looking at prolonging the inevitable."

"We'll have the short-range weapons," Van Ness said resignedly. "Maybe they'll make enough of a difference. At least now we have an extra half-day to get them run out and tested."

"Let's hope so," I agreed, fully aware that it was hopeless. The weapons were antiquated and underpowered, good enough for fending off orbital insurgents but practically useless against another ship, especially one that had been built for piracy. The *Petronel* hadn't fired a shot in anger in more than fifty years. When Van Ness had the chance to upgrade the guns, he'd chosen instead to spend the money on newer reefersleep caskets for the passenger hold.

People have several wrong ideas about Ultras. One of the most common misconceptions is that we must all be brigands, every ship bristling with armaments, primed to a state of nervous readiness the moment another vessel comes within weapons range.

It isn't true. For every ship like that, there are a thousand like the *Petronel*: just trying to ply an honest trade, with a decent, hardworking crew under the hand of a fair man like Van Ness. Some of us might look like freaks, by the standards of planetary civilisation. But spending an entire life aboard a ship, hopping from star to star at relativistic speed, soaking up exotic radiation from the engines and from space itself, is hardly the environment for which the human form was evolved. I'd lost my old hand in an accident, and much of what had happened to Van Ness was down to time and misfortune in equal measure.

He was one of the best captains I'd ever known, maybe the best ever. He'd scared the hell out of me the first time we met, when he was recruiting for a new shipmaster in a carousel around Greenhouse. But Van Ness treated his crew well, kept his word in a deal and always reminded us that our passengers were not frozen "cargo" but human beings who had entrusted themselves into our care.

"If it comes to it," Van Ness said, "we'll let them take the passengers. At least that way some of them might survive, even if they won't necessarily end up where they were expecting. We put up too much of a fight, even after we've been boarded, the *Cockatrice*'s crew may just decide to burn everything, sleepers included."

"I know," I said, even though I didn't want to hear it.

"But here's my advice to you, lad." Van Ness's iron grip tightened on my shoulder. "Get yourself to an airlock as soon as you can. Blow yourself into space rather than let the bastards get their hands on you. They might be in mind for a bit of cruelty, but they won't be in need of new crew."

I winced, before he crushed my collarbone. He meant well, but he really didn't know his own strength.

"Especially not a shipmaster, judging by the way things are going."

"Aye. He's good, whoever he is. Not as good as you, though. You've got a fully laden ship to push; all they have is a stripped-down skeleton."

It was meant well, but I knew better than to underestimate my adversary. "Thank you, Captain."

"We'd best start waking those guns, lad. If you're done with the engines, the weaponsmaster may appreciate a helping hand."

I BARELY SLEPT for the next day. Coaxing the weapons back to operational readiness was a fraught business, and it all had to be done without alerting the *Cockatrice* that we had any last-minute defensive capability. The magnetic coils on the induction guns had to be warmed and brought up to operational field strength, and then tested with slugs of recycled hull material. One of the coils fractured during warm-up and took out its entire turret, injuring one of Weps' men in the process. The optics on the lasers had to be aligned and calibrated, and then the lasers had to be test-fired against specks of incoming interstellar dust, hoping that the *Cockatrice* didn't spot those pinpoint flashes of gamma radiation as the lasers found their targets.

All the while this was going on, the enemy continued their long-range softening-up bombardment. The *Cockatrice* was using everything in her arsenal, from slugs and missiles to beam-weapons. The *Petronel* was running an evasion routine, swerving to exploit the sadly narrowing timelag between the two ships, but the routine was old and with the engines already notched up to close-on maximum output, there was precious little reserve power. No single impact was damaging, but as the assault continued, the cumulative effect began to take its toll. Acres of hull shielding were now compromised, and there were warnings of structural weakness in the port drive spar. If this continued, we would soon be forced to dampen our engines, rather than be torn apart by our own thrust loading. That was exactly what the *Cockatrice* wanted. Once they'd turned us into a lame duck, they could make a forced hard docking and storm our ship.

By the time they were eighty thousand kilometres out, things were looking very bad for us. Even the *Cockatrice* must have been nervous of what would happen if the port spar gave way, since they'd begun to concentrate their efforts on our midsection instead. Reluctantly I crawled back along the starboard spar and confronted the engine settings again. I was faced with two equally numbing possibilities. I could turn the dials even further into the orange, making the engines run harder still. Even if the engines held, the ship wouldn't, but at least we'd go out in a flash when the spar collapsed and the two engines drifted apart. Or I could return the dials to blue-green and let the *Cockatrice* catch us up without risk of further failure. One option might ensure the future survival of the passengers. Neither looked very attractive from the crew's standpoint.

Van Ness knew it, too. He'd begun to go around the rest of the crew, all two dozen of us, ordering those who weren't actively involved in the current crisis to choose an empty casket in the passenger hold and try to pass themselves off as cargo. Van Ness was wise enough not to push the point when no one took him up on his offer.

At fifty thousand kilometres, the *Cockatrice* was in range of our own weapons. We let her slip a little closer and then rotated our hull through forty-five degrees to give her a full broadside, all eleven working slug-cannons discharging at once, followed by a burst from the lasers. The recoil from the slugs was enough to generate further warnings of structural failure in a dozen critical nodes. But we held, somehow, and thirty per cent of that initial salvo hit the *Cockatrice* square-on. By then the lasers had already struck her, vaporising thousands of tonnes of ablative ice from her prow in a scalding white flash. When the steam had fallen astern of the still-accelerating ship, we got our first good look at the damage.

It wasn't enough. We'd hurt her, but barely, and I knew we couldn't sustain more than three further bursts of fire before the *Cockatrice's* own short-range weapons found their lock and returned the assault. As it was, we only got off another two salvos before the slug-cannons suffered a targeting failure. The lasers continued to fire for another minute, but once they'd burned off the *Cockatrice*'s ice (which she could easily replenish from our own shield, once we'd been taken) they could inflict little further damage.

By twenty thousand kilometres, all our weapons were inoperable. Fear of breakup had forced me to throttle our engines back down to zero thrust, leaving only our in-system fusion motors running. At ten thousand kilometres, the *Cockatrice* released a squadron of pirates, each of whom would be carrying hull-penetrating gear and shipboard weapons, in addition to their thruster packs and armour. They must have been confident that we had nothing else to throw at them.

We knew then it was over.

It was, too: but for the *Cockatrice*, not us. What took place happened too quickly for the human eye to see. It was only later, when we had the benefit of footage from the hull cameras, that we were able to piece together what had occurred.

One instant, the *Cockatrice* was creeping closer to us, her engines doused to a whisper now to match our own feeble rate of acceleration. The next instant, she was still *there*, but everything about her had changed. The engines were shut down completely and the hull had begun to come apart, flaking away in a long lateral line that ran the entire four kilometres from bow to stern. The *Cockatrice* began to crab, losing axial stabilisation. Pieces of her were drifting away. Vapour was jetting from a dozen apertures along her length. Where the hull had scabbed away, the brassy orange glow of internal fire was visible. One engine spar was seriously buckled.

We didn't know it at the time—didn't know it until much later, when we'd actually boarded her—but the *Cockatrice* had fallen victim to the oldest hazard in space: collision with debris. There isn't a lot of it out there, but when it hits…at a quarter of the speed of light, it doesn't take much to inflict crippling damage. The impactor might only have been the size of a fist, or a fat thumb, but it had rammed its way right through the ship like a bullet, and the momentum transfer had almost ripped the engines off.

It was bad luck for the crew of the *Cockatrice*. For us, it was the most appalling piece of good luck imaginable. Except it wasn't even luck, really. Every now and then, ships will encounter something like that. Deep-look radar will identify an incoming shard and send an emergency steer command to the engines. Or the radar will direct anti-collision lasers to vaporise the object before it hits. Even if it does hit, most of its kinetic energy will be soaked up by the ablation ice. Ships don't carry all that deadweight for nothing.

But the *Cockatrice* had lost her ice under our lasers. She'd have replaced it sooner or later, but without it she was horribly vulnerable. And her own anti-collision system was preoccupied dealing with our short-range weapons. One little impactor was all it took to remove her from the battle.

It gave us enough of a handhold to start fighting back. With the *Cockatrice* out of the fight, our own crew were able to leave the protection of the ship without fear of being fried or pulverised. Van Ness was the first out of the airlock, with me not far behind him. Within five minutes there were twenty-three of us outside, our suits bulked out with armour and antiquated weapons. There were at least thirty incoming pirates from the *Cockatrice,* and they had better gear. But they'd lost the support of their mother ship, and all of them must have been aware that the situation had undergone a drastic adjustment. Perhaps it made them fight even more fiercely, given that ours was now the only halfway-intact ship. They'd been planning to steal our cargo before, and strip the *Petronel* for useful parts; now they needed to take the *Petronel* and claim her as her own. But they didn't have back-up from the *Cockatrice* and—judging by the way the battle proceeded— they seemed handicapped by more than just the lack of covering fire. They fought as well as they could, which was with a terrible individual determination, but no overall coordination. Afterwards, we concluded that their suit-to-suit communications, even their spatial-orientation systems, must have been reliant on signals routed through their ship. Without her they were deaf and blind.

We still lost good crew. It took six hours to mop up the last resistance from the pirates, by which point we'd taken eleven fatalities, with another three seriously wounded. But by then the pirates were all dead, and we were in no mood to take prisoners.

But we were in a mood to take what we needed from the *Cockatrice*.

IF WE'D EXPECTED to encounter serious resistance aboard the damaged ship, we were wrong. As Van Ness led our boarding party through the drifting wreck, the scope of the damage became chillingly clear. The ship had been gutted from the inside out, with almost no intact pressure-bearing structures left anywhere inside her main hull. For most of the crew left aboard when the impactor hit, the end would have come with merciful swiftness. Only a few had survived the initial collision, and most of them must have died shortly afterwards, as the ship bled through its wounds. We found no sign that the *Cockatrice* had been carrying frozen passengers, although— since entire internal bays had been blasted out of existence, leaving only an interlinked chain of charred, blackened caverns—we probably wouldn't ever know for sure. Of the few survivors we did encounter, none attempted surrender or requested parley. That made it easier for us. If they stood still, we shot them. If they fled, we still shot them.

Except for one.

We knew there was something different about her as soon as we saw her. She didn't look or move like an Ultra. There was something of the cat or snake about the way she slinked out of the illumination of our lamps, something fluid and feral, something sleek and honed that did not belong aboard a ship crewed by pirates. We held our fire from the moment her eyes first flashed at us, for we knew she could not be one of them. Wide, white-edged eyes in a girl's face, her strong-jawed expression one of ruthless self-control and effortless superiority. Her skull was hairless, her forehead rising to a bony crest rilled on either side by shimmering coloured tissue.

The girl was a Conjoiner.

It was three days before we found her again. She knew that ship with animal cunning, as if the entire twisted and blackened warren was a lair she had made for herself. But her options were diminishing with every hour that passed, as more and more air drained out of the wreck. Even

Conjoiners needed to breathe, and that meant there was less and less of the ship in which she could hide.

Van Ness wanted to move on. Van Ness—a good man, but never the most imaginative of souls—wasn't interested in what a stray Conjoiner could do for us. I'd warned him that the *Cockatrice*'s engines were in an unstable condition, and that we wouldn't have time to back off to a safe distance if the buckled drive spar finally gave way. Now that we'd harvested enough of the other ship's intact hull to repair our own damage, Van Ness saw no reason to hang around. But I managed to talk him into letting us hunt down the girl.

"She's a Conjoiner, Captain. She wouldn't have been aboard that ship of her own free will. That means she's a prisoner that we can free and return to her people. They'll be grateful. That means they'll want to reward us."

Van Ness fixed me with an indulgent smile. "Lad, have you ever had close dealings with Spiders?"

He still called me "lad" even though I'd been part of his crew for twenty years, and had been born another twenty before that, by shiptime reckoning. "No," I admitted. "But the Spiders—the Conjoiners—aren't the bogey men some people like to make out."

"I've dealt with 'em," Van Ness said. "I'm a lot older than you, lad. I go right back to when things weren't so pretty between the Spiders and the rest of humanity, back when my wife was alive."

It took a lot to stir up the past for Rafe Van Ness. In all our years together, he'd only mentioned his wife a handful of times. She'd been a botanist, working on the Martian terraforming programme. She'd been caught by a flash flood when she was working in one of the big craters, testing plant stocks for the Demarchists. All I knew was that after her death, Van Ness had left the system, on one of the first passenger-carrying starships. It had been his first step on the long road to becoming an Ultra.

"They've changed since the old days," I said. "We trust them enough to use their engines, don't we?"

"We trust the engines. Isn't quite the same thing. And if they didn't have such a monopoly on making the things, maybe we wouldn't have to deal with them at all. Anyway, who is this girl? What was she doing aboard the *Cockatrice?* What makes you think she wasn't helping them?"

"Conjoiners don't condone piracy. And if we want answers, we have no option but to catch her and find out what she has to say."

Van Ness sounded suddenly interested. "Interrogate her, you mean?"

"I didn't say that, Captain. But we might want to ask her a few questions."

"We'd be playing with fire. You know they can make things happen just by thinking about them."

"She'll have no reason to hurt us. We'll have saved her life just by taking her off the *Cockatrice.*"

"Maybe she doesn't want it saved. Have you thought of that?"

"We'll cross that bridge when we find her, Captain."

He pulled a face, that part of his visage still capable of making expressions, at least. "I'll give you another twelve hours, lad. That's my limit. Then we put as much distance between us and that wreck as God and physics will allow."

I nodded, knowing that it was pointless to expect more of Van Ness. He'd already shown great forbearance in allowing us to delay the departure for so long. Given his feelings regarding Conjoiners, I wasn't going to push for any more time.

WE CAUGHT HER eleven hours later. We'd driven her as far as she could go, blocking her escape routes by blowing the few surrounding volumes that were still pressurised. I was the first to speak to her, when we finally had her cornered.

I pushed up the visor of my helmet, breathing stale air so that we could speak. She was huddled in a comer, compressed like some animal ready to bolt or strike.

"Stop running from us," I said, as my lamp pinned her down and forced her to squint. "There's nowhere left to go, and even if there was, we don't want to hurt you. Whatever these people did to you, whatever they made you do, we're not like them."

She hissed back, "You're Ultras. That's all I need to know."

"We're Ultras, yes, but we still want to help you. Our captain just wants to get away from this time bomb as quickly as possible. I talked him into giving us a few extra hours to find you. You can come with us whenever you like. But if you'd rather stay aboard this ship..."

She stared back at me and said nothing. I couldn't guess her age. She had the face of a girl, but there was a steely resolution in her olive-green eyes that told me she was older than she looked.

"I'm Inigo, the shipmaster from the *Petronel*," I said, hoping that my smile looked reassuring rather than threatening. I reached out my hand, my right one, and she flinched back. Even suited, even hidden under a glove, my hand was obviously mechanical. "Please," I continued, "come with us. We'll treat you well and get you back to your people."

"Why?" she snarled. "Why do *you* care?"

"Because we're not all the same," I said. "And you need to believe it, or you're going to die here when we leave. Captain wants us to secure for thrust in less than an hour. So *come on.*"

"What happened?" she asked, looking around at the damaged compartment in which she had been cornered. "I know the *Cockatrice* was attacking another ship...how did you do this?"

"We didn't. We just got very, very lucky. Now it's your turn."

"I can't leave here. I need to be with this ship."

'This ship is going to blow up if one of us sneezes. Do you really want to be aboard when that happens?"

"I still need to be here. Leave me alone, I'll survive by myself. Conjoiners will find me again."

I shook my head firmly. 'That isn't going to happen. Even if this ship doesn't blow up, you're still drifting at twenty-five per cent of the speed of light. That's too fast to get you back to Shiva-Parvati, even if there's a shuttle aboard this thing. Too fast for anyone around Shiva-Parvati to come out and rescue you, too."

"I know this."

"Then you also know that you're not moving anywhere near fast enough to actually get anywhere before your resources run out. Unless you think you can survive fifty years aboard this thing, until you swing by the next colonised system with no way of slowing down."

"I'll take my chances."

A voice buzzed in my helmet. It was Van Ness, insisting that we return to the *Petronel* as quickly as possible. "I'm sorry," I said, "but if you don't come willingly, I'm going to have to bring you in unconscious." I raised the blunt muzzle of my slug-gun.

"If there's a tranquiliser dart in there, it won't work on me. My nervous system isn't like yours. I only sleep when I choose to."

"That's what I figured. It's why I dialled the dose to five times its normal strength. I don't know about you, but I'm willing to give it a try and see what happens."

Panic crossed her face. "Give me a suit," she said. "Give me a suit and then leave me alone, if you really want to help."

"What's your name?"

"We don't have names, Inigo. At least nothing *you* could get your tongue around."

"I'm willing to try."

"Give me a suit. Then leave me alone."

Van Ness started screaming in my ears again. I'd had enough. I pointed the muzzle at her, aiming for the flesh of her thigh, where she had her legs tucked under her. I squeezed the trigger and delivered the stun flechette.

"You fool," she said. "You don't understand. You have to leave me here, with this..."

That was all she managed before slumping into unconsciousness. She'd gone down much faster than I'd expected, as if she'd already been on her last reserves of strength. I just hoped I hadn't set the stun dose too high. It was already strong enough to kill any normal human being.

VAN NESS HAD been right to be concerned about our proximity to the *Cockatrice*. We'd barely doubled the distance between the two ships when her drive spar failed, allowing the port engine to drift away from its starboard counterpart. Several agonising minutes later, the distance between the two engine units exceeded sixteen hundred metres and the drives went up in a double burst that tested our shielding to its limits. The flash must have been visible all the way back to Shiva-Parvati.

The girl had been unconscious right up until that moment, but when the engines went up she twitched on the bunk where we'd placed her, just as if she'd been experiencing a vivid and disturbing dream. The rilled structures on the side of her crest throbbed with vivid colours, each chasing the last. Then she was restful again, for many hours, and the play of colours calmer.

I watched her sleeping. I'd never been near a Conjoiner before, let alone one like this. Aboard the ship, when we had been hunting her, she had seemed strong and potentially dangerous. Now she looked like some half-starved animal, driven to the brink of madness by hunger and something infinitely worse. There were awful bruises all over her body, some more recent than others. There were fine scars on her skull. One of her incisors was missing a point.

Van Ness still wasn't convinced of the wisdom of bringing her aboard, but even his dislike of Conjoiners didn't extend to the notion of throwing her back into space. All the same, he insisted that she be bound to the bunk by heavy restraints, in an armoured room under the guard of a servitor, at least until we had some idea of who she was and how she had ended up aboard the pirate ship. He didn't want heavily augmented crew anywhere near her, either: not when (as he evidently believed) she had the means to control any machine in her vicinity, and might therefore overpower or even commandeer any crewperson who had a skull full of implants. It wasn't like that, I tried to tell him: Conjoiners could talk to machines, yes, but not all machines, and the idea that they could work witchcraft on anything with a circuit inside it was just so much irrational fearmongering.

Van Ness heard my reasoned objections, and then ignored them. I'm glad that he did, though. Had he listened to me, he might have put some other member of the crew in charge of questioning her, and then I wouldn't have got to know her as well as I did. Because I only had the metal hand, the rest of me still flesh and blood, he deemed me safe from her influence.

I was with her when she woke.

I placed my left hand on her shoulder as she squirmed under the restraints, suddenly aware of her predicament. "It's all right," I said softly. "You're safe now. Captain made us put these on you for the time being, but we'll get them off you as soon as we can. That's a promise. I'm Inigo, by the way, shipmaster. We met before, but I'm not sure how much of that you remember."

"Every detail," she said. Her voice was low, dark-tinged, untrusting.

"Maybe you don't know where you are. You're aboard the *Petronel*. The *Cockatrice* is gone, along with everyone aboard her. Whatever they did to you, whatever happened to you aboard that ship, it's over now."

"You didn't listen to me."

"If we'd listened to you," I said patiently, "you'd be dead by now."

"No, I wouldn't."

I'd been ready to give her the benefit of the doubt, but my reservoir of sympathy was beginning to dry up. "You know, it wouldn't hurt to show a little gratitude. We put ourselves at considerable risk to get you to safety. We'd taken everything we needed from the pirates. We only went back in to help you."

"I didn't need you to help me. I could have survived."

"Not unless you think you could have held that spar on by sheer force of will."

She hissed back her reply. "I'm a Conjoiner. That means the rules were different. I could have changed things. I could have kept the ship in one piece."

"To make a point?"

"No," she said, with acid slowness, as if that was the only speed I was capable of following. "Not to make a point. We don't *make* points."

"The ship's gone," I said. "It's over, so you may as well deal with it. You're with us now. And no, you're not our prisoner. We'll do everything I said we would: take care of you, get you to safety, back to your people."

"You really think it's that simple?"

"I don't know. Why don't you tell me? I don't see what the problem is."

"The problem is I can't ever go back. Is that simple enough for you?"

"Why?" I asked. "Were you exiled from the Conjoiners, or something like that?"

She shook her elaborately crested head, as if my question was the most naive thing she had ever heard. "No one gets exiled."

"Then tell me what the hell happened!"

Anger burst to the surface. "I was taken, all right? I was stolen, snatched away from my people. Captain Voulage took me prisoner around Yellowstone, when the *Cockatrice* was docked near one of our ships. I was part of a small diplomatic party visiting Carousel New Venice. Voulage's men ambushed us, split us up, then took me so far from the other Conjoiners that I dropped out of neural range. Have you any idea what that means to one of us?"

I shook my head, not because I didn't understand what she meant, but because I knew I could have no proper grasp of the emotional pain that severance must have caused. I doubted that pain was a strong enough word for the psychic shock associated with being ripped away from her fellows. Nothing in ordinary human experience could approximate the trauma of that separation, any more than a frog could grasp the loss of a loved one. Conjoiners spent their whole lives in a state of gestalt consciousness, sharing thoughts and experiences via a web of implant-mediated neural connections. They had individual personalities, but those personalities were more like the blurred identities of atoms in a metallic solid. Beyond the level of individual self was the state of higher mental union that they called Transenlightenment, analogous to the fizzing sea of dissociated electrons in that same metallic lattice.

And the girl had been ripped away from that, forced to come to terms with existence as a solitary mind, an island once more.

"I understand how bad it must have been," I said. "But now you can go back. Isn't that something worth looking forward to?"

"You only *think* you understand. To a Conjoiner, what happened to me is the worst thing in the world. And now I can't go back: not now, not ever. I've become damaged, broken, useless. My mind is permanently disfigured. It can't be allowed to return to Transenlightenment."

"Why ever not? Wouldn't they be glad to get you back?"

She took a long time answering. In the quiet, I studied her face, watchful for anything that would betray the danger Van Ness clearly believed she posed. Now his fears seemed groundless. She looked smaller and more delicately boned than when we'd first glimpsed her on the *Cockatrice*. The strangeness of her, the odd shape of her hairless crested skull, should have been off-putting. In truth I found her fascinating. It was not her alienness that drew my furtive attention, but her very human face: her small and pointed chin, the pale freckles under her eyes, the way her mouth never quite closed, even when she was silent. The olive green of her eyes was a shade so dark that from certain angles it became a lustrous black, like the surface of coal.

"No," she said, answering me finally. "It wouldn't work. I'd upset the purity of the others, spoil the harmony of the neural connections, like a single out-of-tune instrument in an orchestra. I'd make everyone else start playing out of key."

"I think you're being too fatalistic. Shouldn't we at least try to find some other Conjoiners and see what they say?"

"That isn't how it works," she said. "They'd have to take me back, yes, if I presented myself to them. They'd do it out of kindness and compassion. But I'd still end up harming them. It's my duty not to allow that to happen."

"Then you're saying you have to spend the rest of your life away from other Conjoiners, wandering the universe like some miserable excommunicated pilgrim?"

"There are more of us than you realise."

"You do a good job keeping out of the limelight. Most people only see Conjoiners in groups, all dressed in black like a flock of crows."

"Maybe you aren't looking in the right places."

I sighed, aware that nothing I said was going to convince her that she would be better off returning to her people. "It's your life, your destiny. At least you're alive. Our word still holds: we'll drop you at the nearest safe planet, when we next make orbitfall. If that isn't satisfactory to you, you'd be welcome to remain aboard ship until we arrive somewhere else."

"Your captain would allow that? I thought he was the one who wanted to leave the wreck before you'd found me."

"I'll square things with the captain. He isn't the biggest fan of Conjoiners, but he'll see sense when he realises you aren't a monster."

"Does he have a reason not to like me?"

"He's an old man," I said simply.

"Riven with prejudice, you mean?"

"In his way," I said, shrugging. "But don't blame him for that. He lived through the bad years, when your people were first coming into existence. I think he had some firsthand experience of the trouble that followed."

"Then I envy him those first-hand memories. Not many of us are still alive from those times. To have lived through those years, to have breathed the same air as Remontoire and the others..." She looked away sadly. "Remontoire's gone now. So are Galiana and Nevil. We don't know what happened to any of them."

I knew she must have been talking about pivotal figures from earlier Conjoiner history, but the people of whom she spoke meant nothing to me. To her, cast so far downstream from those early events on Mars, the names must have held something of the resonance of saints or apostles. I thought I knew something of Conjoiners, but they had a long and complicated internal history of which I was totally ignorant.

"I wish things hadn't happened the way they did," I said. "But that was then and this is now. We don't hate or fear you. If we did, we wouldn't have risked our necks getting you out of the *Cockatrice*."

"No, you don't hate or fear me," she replied. "But you still think I might be useful to you, don't you?"

"Only if you wish to help us."

"Captain Voulage thought that I might have the expertise to improve the performance of his ship."

"Did you?" I asked innocently.

"By increments, yes. He showed me the engines and...encouraged me to make certain changes. You told me you are a shipmaster, so you doubtless have some familiarity with the principles involved."

I thought back to the adjustments I had made to our own engines, when we still had ambitions of fleeing the pirates. The memory of my trembling hand on those three critical dials felt as if it had been dredged from deepest antiquity, rather than something that had happened only days earlier.

"When you say 'encouraged'..." I began.

"He found ways to coerce me. It is true that Conjoiners can control their perception of pain by applying neural blockades. But only to a degree, and then only when the pain has a real physical origin. If the pain is generated in the head, using a reverse-field trawl, our defences are useless." She looked at me with a sudden hard intensity, as if daring me to imagine one-tenth of what she had experienced. "It is like locking a door when the wolf is already in the house."

"I'm sorry. You must have been through hell."

"I only had the pain to endure," she said. "I'm not the one anyone needs to feel sorry about."

The remark puzzled me, but I let it lie. "I have to get back to our own engines now," I said, "but I'll come to see you later. In the meantime, I think you should rest." I snapped a duplicate communications bracelet from my wrist and placed it near her hand, where she could reach it. "If you need me, you can call into this. It'll take me a little while to get back here, but I'll come as quickly as possible."

She lifted her forearm as far as it would go, until the restraints stiffened. "And these?"

"I'll talk to Van Ness. Now that you're lucid, now that you're talking to us, I don't see any further need for them."

"Thank you," she said again. "Inigo. Is that all there is to your name? It's rather a short one, even by the standards of the retarded."

"Inigo Standish, shipmaster. And you still haven't told me your name."

"I told you: it's nothing you could understand. We have our own names now, terms of address that can only be communicated in the Transenlightenment. My name is a flow of experiential symbols, a string of interiorised qualia, an expression of a particular dynamic state that has only ever happened under a conjunction of rare physical conditions in the atmosphere of a particular kind of gas giant planet. I chose it myself. It's considered very beautiful and a little melancholy, like a haiku in five dimensions."

"Inside the atmosphere of a gas giant, right?"

She looked at me alertly. "Yes."

"Fine, then. I'll call you Weather. Unless you'd like to suggest something better."

SHE NEVER DID suggest something better, even though I think she once came close to it. From that moment on, whether she liked it or not, she was always Weather. Soon, it was what the other crew were calling her, and the name that—grudgingly at first, then resignedly—she deigned to respond to.

I went to see Captain Van Ness and did my best to persuade him that Weather was not going to cause us any difficulties.

"What are you suggesting we should give her—a free pass to the rest of the ship?"

"Only that we could let her out of her prison cell."

"She's recuperating."

"She's restrained. And you've put an armed servitor on the door, in case she gets out of the restraints."

"Pays to be prudent."

"I think we can trust her now, Captain." I hesitated, choosing my words with great care. "I know you have good reasons not to like her people, but she isn't the same as the Conjoiners from those days."

"That's what she'd like us to think, certainly."

"I've spoken to her, heard her story. She's an outcast from her people, unable to return to them because of what's happened to her."

"Well, then," Van Ness said, nodding as if he'd proved a point, "outcasts do funny things. You can't ever be too careful with outcasts."

"It's not like that with Weather."

"Weather," he repeated, with a certain dry distaste. "So she's got a name now, has she?"

"I felt it might help. The name was my suggestion, not hers."

"Don't start humanising them. That's the mistake humans always make. Next thing you know, they've got their claws in your skull."

I closed my eyes, forcing self-control as the conversation veered off course. I'd always had an excellent relationship with Van Ness, one that came very close to bordering on genuine friendship. But from the moment he heard about Weather, I knew she was going to come between us.

"I'm not suggesting we let her run amok," I said. "Even if we let her out of those restraints, even if we take away the servitor, we can still keep her out of any parts of the ship where we don't want her. In the meantime, I think she can be helpful to us. She's already told me that Captain

Voulage forced her to make improvements to the *Cockatrice*'s drive system. I don't see why she can't do the same for us, if we ask nicely."

"Why did he have to force her, if you're so convinced she'd do it willingly now?"

"I'm not convinced. But I can't see why she wouldn't help us, if we treat her like a human being."

"That'd be our big mistake," Van Ness said. "She never was a human being. She's been a Spider from the moment they made her, and she'll go to the grave like that."

"Then you won't consider it?"

"I consented to let you bring her aboard. That was already against every God-given instinct." Then Van Ness rumbled, "And I'd thank you not to mention the Spider again, Inigo. You've my permission to visit her if you see fit, but she isn't taking a step out of that room until we make orbitfall."

"Very well," I said, with a curtness that I'd never had cause to use on Captain Van Ness.

As I was leaving his cabin, he said, "You're still a fine shipmaster, lad. That's never been in doubt. But don't let this thing cloud your usual good judgement. I'd hate to have to look elsewhere for someone of your abilities."

I turned back and, despite everything that told me to hold my tongue, I still spoke. "I was wrong about you, Captain. I've always believed that you didn't allow yourself to be ruled by the irrational hatreds of other Ultras. I always thought you were better than that."

"And I'd have gladly told you I have just as many prejudices as the next man. They're what've kept me alive so long."

"I'm sure Captain Voulage felt the same way," I said.

It was a wrong and hateful thing to say—Van Ness had nothing in common with a monster like Voulage—but I couldn't stop myself. And I knew even as I said it that some irreversible bridge had just been crossed, and that it was more my fault than Van Ness's.

"You have work to do, I think," Van Ness said, his voice so low that I barely heard it. "Until you have the engines back to full thrust, I suggest you keep out of my way."

WEPS CAME TO see me eight or nine hours later. I knew it wasn't good news as soon as I saw her face.

"We have a problem, Inigo. The captain felt you needed to know."

"And he couldn't tell me himself?"

Weps cleared part of the wall and called up a display, filling it with a boxy green three-dimensional grid. "That's us," she said, jabbing a finger at the red dot in the middle of the display. She moved her finger halfway to the edge, scratching her long black nail against the plating. "Something else is out there. It's stealthed to the gills, but I'm still seeing it. Whatever it is is making a slow, silent approach."

My thoughts flicked to Weather. "Could it be Conjoiner?"

"That was my first guess. But if it was Conjoiner, I don't think I'd be seeing anything at all."

"So what are we dealing with?"

She tapped the nail against the blue icon representing the new ship. "Another raider. Could be an ally of Voulage—we know he had friends—or could be some other ship that was hoping to pick over our carcass once Voulage was done with us, or maybe even steal us from him before he had his chance."

"Hyena tactics."

"Wouldn't be the first time."

"Range?"

"Less than two light-hours. Even if they don't increase their rate of closure, they'll be on us within eight days."

"Unless we move."

Weps nodded sagely. "That would help. You're on schedule to complete repairs within six days, aren't you?"

"On schedule, yes, but that doesn't mean things can be moved any faster. We start cutting corners now, we'll break like a twig when we put a real load on the ship."

"We wouldn't want that."

"No, we wouldn't."

"The captain just thought you should be aware of the situation, Inigo. It's not to put you under pressure, or anything."

"Of course not."

"It's just that...we really don't want to be hanging around here a second longer than necessary."

I REMOVED WEATHER'S restraints and showed her how to help herself to food and water from the room's dispenser. She stretched and purred, articulating and extending her limbs in the manner of a dancer rehearsing some difficult routine in extreme slow motion. She'd been "reading" when I arrived, which for Weather seemed to involve staring into the middle distance while her eyes flicked to and fro at manic speed, as if following the movements of an invisible wasp.

"I can't let you out of the room just yet," I said, sitting on the fold-down stool next to the bed, upon which Weather now sat cross-legged. "I just hope this makes things a little more tolerable."

"So your captain's finally realised I'm not about to suck out his brains?"

"Not exactly. He'd still rather you weren't aboard."

"Then you're going against his orders."

"I suppose so."

"I presume you could get into trouble for that."

"He'll never find out." I thought of the unknown ship that was creeping towards us. "He's got other things on his mind now. It's not as if he's going to be paying you a courtesy call just to pass the time of day."

"But if he did find out..." She looked at me intently, lifting her chin. "Do you fear what he'd do to you?"

"I probably should. But I don't think he'd be very likely to throw me into an airlock. Not until we're under way at full power, in any case."

"And then?"

"He'd be angry. But I don't think he'd kill me. He's not a bad man, really."

"Perhaps I misheard, but didn't you say his name was Van Ness?"

"Captain Rafe Van Ness, yes." I must have looked surprised. "Don't tell me it means something to you."

"I heard Voulage mention him, that's all. Now I know we're talking about the same man."

"What did Voulage have to say?"

"Nothing good. But I don't think that necessarily reflects poorly on your captain. He must be a reasonable man. He's at least allowed me aboard his ship, even if I haven't been invited to dine in his quarters."

"Dining for Van Ness is a pretty messy business," I said confidingly. "You're better off eating alone."

"Do you like him, Inigo?"

"He has his flaws, but next to someone like Voulage, he's pretty close to being an angel."

"Doesn't like Conjoiners, though."

"Most Ultras would have left you drifting. I think this is a point where you have to take what you're given."

"Perhaps. I don't understand his attitude, though. If your captain is like most Ultras, there's at least as much of the machine about him as there is about me. More so, in all likelihood."

"It's what you do with the machines that counts," I said. "Ultras tend to leave their minds alone, if at all possible. Even if they do have implants, it's usually to replace areas of brain function lost due to injury or old age. They're not really interested in improving matters, if you get my drift. Maybe that's why Conjoiners make them twitchy."

She unhooked her legs, dangling them over the edge of the bed. Her feet were bare and oddly elongated. She wore the same tight black outfit we'd found her in when we boarded the ship. It was cut low from her neck, in a rectangular shape. Her breasts were small. Though she was bony, with barely any spare muscle on her, she had the broad shoulders of a swimmer. Though Weather had sustained her share of injuries, the outfit showed no sign of damage at all. It appeared to be self-repairing, even self-cleaning.

"You talk of Ultras as if you weren't one," she said.

"Just an old habit breaking through. Though sometimes I don't feel like quite the same breed as a man like Van Ness."

"Your implants must be very well shielded. I can't sense them at all."

"That's because there aren't any."

"Squeamish? Or just too young and fortunate not to have needed them yet?"

"It's nothing to do with being squeamish. I'm not as young as I look, either." I held up my mechanical hand. "Nor would I exactly call myself fortunate."

She looked at the hand with narrowed, critical eyes. I remembered how she'd flinched back when I reached for her aboard the *Cockatrice*, and wondered what maltreatment she had suffered at the iron hands of her former masters.

"You don't like it?" she asked.

"I liked the old one better."

Weather reached out and gingerly held my hand in hers. They looked small and doll-like as they stroked and examined my mechanical counterpart.

"This is the only part of you that isn't organic?"

"As far as I know."

"Doesn't that limit you? Don't you feel handicapped around the rest of the crew?"

"Sometimes. But not always. My job means I have to squeeze into places where a man like Van Ness could never fit. It also means I have to be able to tolerate magnetic fields that would rip half the crew to shreds, if they didn't boil alive first." I opened and closed my metal fist. "I have to unscrew this, sometimes. I have a plastic replacement if I just need to hook hold of things."

"You don't like it very much."

"It does what I ask of it."

Weather made to let go of my hand, but her fingers remained in contact with mine for an instant longer than necessary. "I'm sorry that you don't like it."

"I could have got it fixed at one of the orbital clinics, I suppose," I said, "but there's always something else that needs fixing first. Anyway, if it wasn't for the hand, some people might not believe I'm an Ultra at all."

"Do you plan on being an Ultra all your life?"

"I don't know. I can't say I ever had my mind set on being a shipmaster. It just sort of happened, and now here I am."

"I had my mind set on something once," Weather said. "I thought it was within my grasp, too. Then it slipped out of reach." She looked at me and then did something wonderful and unexpected, which was to smile. It was not the most genuine-looking smile I'd ever seen, but I sensed the genuine intent behind it. Suddenly I knew there was a human being in the room with me, damaged and dangerous though she might have been. "Now here I am, too. It's not quite what I expected...but thank you for rescuing me."

"I was beginning to wonder if we'd made a mistake. You seemed so reluctant to leave that ship."

"I was," she said, distantly. "But that's over now. You did what you thought was the right thing."

"Was it?"

"For me, yes. For the ship...maybe not." Then she stopped and cocked her head to one side, frowning. Her eyes flashed olive. "What are you looking at, Inigo?"

"Nothing," I said, looking sharply away.

KEEPING OUT OF Van Ness's way, as he'd advised, was not the hard part of what followed. The *Petronel* was a big ship and our paths didn't need to cross in the course of day-to-day duties. The difficulty was finding as much time to visit Weather as I would have liked. My original repair plan had been tight, but the unknown ship forced me to accelerate the schedule even further, despite what I'd told Weps. The burden of work began to take its toll on me, draining my concentration. I was still confident that once that work was done, we'd be able to continue our journey as if nothing had happened, save for the loss of those crew who had died in the engagement and our gaining one new passenger. The other ship would probably abandon us once we pushed the engines up to cruise thrust, looking for easier pickings elsewhere. If it had the swiftness of the *Cockatrice*, it wouldn't have been skulking in the shadows letting the other ship take first prize.

But my optimism was misplaced. When the repair work was done, I once more made my way along the access shaft to the starboard engine and confronted the hexagonal arrangement of input dials. As expected, all six dials were now showing deep blue, which meant they were operating well inside the safety envelope. But when I consulted my log book and made the tiny adjustments that should have taken all the dials into the blue-green—still nicely within the safety envelope—I got a nasty surprise. I only had to nudge two of the dials by a fraction of a millimetre before they shone a hard and threatening orange.

Something was wrong.

I checked my settings, of course, making sure none of the other dials were out of position. But there'd been no mistake. I thumbed through the log with increasing haste, a prickly feeling on the back of my neck, looking for an entry where something similar had happened; something that would point me to the obvious mistake I must have made. But none of the previous entries were the slightest help. I'd made no error with the settings, and that left only one possibility: something had happened to the engine. It was not working properly.

"This isn't right," I said to myself. "They don't fail. They don't break down. Not like this."

But what did I know? My entire experience of working with C-drives was confined to routine operations, under normal conditions. Yet we'd just been through a battle against another ship, one in which we were already known to have sustained structural damage. As shipmaster, I'd been diligent in attending to the hull and the drive spar, but it had never crossed my mind that something might have happened to one or other of the engines.

Why not?

There's a good reason. It's because even if something had happened, there would never have been anything I could have done about it. Worrying about the breakdown of a Conjoiner drive was like worrying about the one piece of debris you won't have time to steer around or shoot out of the sky. You can't do anything about it, ergo you forget about it until it happens. No shipmaster ever loses sleep over the failure of a C-drive.

It looked as if I was going to lose a lot more than sleep.

Even if we didn't have another ship to worry about, we were in more than enough trouble. We were too far out from Shiva-Parvati to get back again, and yet we were moving too slowly to make it to another system. Even if the engines kept working as they were now, we'd take far too long to reach relativistic speed, where time dilation became appreciable. At twenty-five per cent of the speed of light, what would have been a twenty-year hop before became an eighty-year crawl now…and that was an eighty-year crawl in which almost all that time would be experienced aboard ship. Across that stretch of time, reefersleep was a lottery. Our caskets were designed to keep people frozen for five to ten years, not four-fifths of a century.

I was scared. I'd gone from feeling calmly in control to feeling total devastation in about five minutes.

I didn't want to let the rest of the crew know that we had a potential crisis on our hands, at least not until I'd spoken to Weather. I'd already crossed swords with Van Ness, but he was still my captain, and I wanted to spare him the difficulty of a frightened crew, at least until I knew all the facts.

Weather was awake when I arrived. In all my visits, I'd never found her sleeping. In the normal course of events Conjoiners had no need of sleep: at worst, they'd switch off certain areas of brain function for a few hours.

She read my face like a book. "Something's wrong, isn't it?"

So much for the notion that Conjoiners were not able to interpret facial expressions. Just because they didn't *make* many of them didn't mean they'd forgotten the rules.

I sat down on the fold-out stool.

"I've tried to push the engines back up to normal cruise thrust. I'm already seeing red on two dials, and we haven't even exceeded point-two gees."

She thought about this for several moments: what for Weather must have been hours of subjective contemplation. "You didn't appear to be pushing your engines dangerously during the chase."

"I wasn't. Everything looked normal up until now. I think we must have taken some damage to one of the drives, during Voulage's softening-up assault. I didn't see any external evidence, but—"

"You wouldn't, not necessarily. The interior architecture of one of our drives is a lot more complicated, a lot more delicate, than is normally appreciated. It's at least possible that a shock-wave did some harm to one of your engines, especially if your coupling gear—the shock-dampening assembly—was already compromised."

"It probably was," I said. "The spar was already stressed."

"Then you have your explanation. Something inside your engine has broken, or is considered by the engine itself to be dangerously close to failure. Either way, it would be suicide to increase the thrust beyond the present level."

"Weather, we need both those engines to get anywhere, and we need them at normal efficiency."

"It hadn't escaped me."

"Is there anything you can do to help us?"

"Very little, I expect."

"But you must know something about the engines, or you wouldn't have been able to help Voulage."

"Voulage's engines weren't damaged," she explained patiently.

"I know that. But you were still able to make them work better. Isn't there something you can do for us?"

"From here, nothing at all."

"But if you were allowed to get closer to the engines...might that make a difference?"

"Until I'm there, I couldn't possibly say. It's irrelevant though, isn't it? Your captain will never allow me out of this room."

"Would you do it for us if he did?"

"I'd do it for me."

"Is that the best you can offer?"

"All right, then maybe I'd for it for you." Just saying this caused Weather visible discomfort, as if the utterance violated some deep personal code that had remained intact until now. "You've been kind to me. I know you risked trouble with Van Ness to make things easier in my cell. But you need to understand something very important. You may care for me. You may even think you like me. But I can't give you back any of that. What I feel for you is..." Weather hesitated, her mouth half-open. "You know we call you the retarded. There's a reason for that. The emotions I feel...the things that go on in my head...simply don't map onto anything you'd recognise as love, or affection, or even friendship. Reducing them to those terms would be like..." And then she stalled, unable to finish.

"Like making a sacrifice?"

"You've been good to me, Inigo. But I really am like the weather. You can admire me, even love me, in your way, but I can't love you back. To me you're like a photograph. I can see right through you, examine you from all angles. You amuse me. But you don't have enough depth ever to fascinate me."

"There's more to love than fascination. And you said it yourself: you're halfway back to being human again."

"I said I wasn't a Conjoiner any more. But that doesn't mean I could ever be like you."

"You could try."

"You don't understand us."

"I want to!"

Weather jammed her olive eyes tight shut. "Let's...not get ahead of ourselves, shall we? I only wanted to spare you any unnecessary emotional pain. But if we don't get this ship moving properly, that'll be the least of your worries."

"I know."

"So perhaps we should return to the matter of the engines. Again: none of this will matter if Van Ness refuses to trust me."

My cheeks were smarting as if I'd been slapped hard in the face. Part of me knew she was only being kind, in the harshest of ways. That part was almost prepared to accept her rejection. The other part of me only wanted her more, as if her bluntness had succeeded only in sharpening my desire. Perhaps she was right; perhaps I was insane to think a Conjoiner could ever feel something in return. But I remembered the gentle way she'd stroked my fingers, and I wanted her even more.

"I'll deal with Van Ness," I said. "I think there's a little something that will convince him to take a risk. You start thinking about what you can do for us."

"Is that an order, Inigo?"

"No," I said. "Nobody's going to order you to do anything. I gave you my word on that, and I'm not about to break it. Nothing you've just said changes that."

She sat tight-lipped, staring at me as if I was some kind of byzantine logic puzzle she needed to unscramble. I could almost feel the furious computation of her mind, as if I was standing next to a humming turbine. Then she lifted her little pointed chin minutely, saying nothing, but letting me know that if I convinced Van Ness, she would do what she could, however ineffectual that might prove.

THE CAPTAIN WAS tougher to crack than I'd expected. I'd assumed he would fold as soon as I explained our predicament—that we were going nowhere, and that Weather was the only factor that could improve our situation—but the captain simply narrowed his eyes and looked disappointed.

"Don't you get it? It's a ruse, a trick. Our engines were fine until we let her aboard. Then all of a sudden they start misbehaving, and she turns out to be the only one who can help us."

"There's also the matter of the other ship Weps says is closing on us."

"That ship might not even exist. It could be a sensor ghost, a hallucination she's making the *Petronel* see."

"Captain—"

"That would work for her, wouldn't it? It would be exactly the excuse she needs to force our hands."

We were in his cabin, with the door locked: I'd warned him I had a matter of grave sensitivity that we needed to discuss. "I don't think this is any of her doing," I said calmly, vowing to hold my temper under better control than before. "She's too far from the engines or sensor systems to be having any mental effect on them, even if we hadn't locked her in a room that's practically a Faraday cage to begin with. She says one or other of the engines was damaged during the engagement with the *Cockatrice*, and I've no reason to disbelieve that. I think you're wrong about her."

"She's got us right where she wants us, lad. She's done something to the engines, and now—if you get your way— we're going to let her get up close and personal with them."

"And do what?" I asked.

"Whatever takes her fancy. Blowing us all up is one possibility. Did you consider that?"

"She'd blow herself up as well."

"Maybe that's exactly the plan. Could be that she prefers dying to staying alive, if being shut out from the rest of the Spiders is as bad as you say it is. She didn't seem to be real keen on being rescued from that wreck, did she? Maybe she was hoping to die aboard it."

"She looked like she was trying to stay alive to me, Captain. There were a hundred ways she could have killed herself aboard the *Cockatrice* before we boarded, and she didn't. I think she was just scared of us, scared that we were going to be like all the other Ultras. That's why she kept running."

"A nice theory, lad. It's a pity so much is hanging on it, or I might be inclined to give it a moment's credence."

"We have no choice but to trust her. If we don't let her try something, most of us won't ever see another system."

"Easy for you to say, son."

"I'm in this as well. I've got just as much to lose as anyone else on this ship."

Van Ness studied me for what felt like an eternity. Until now his trust in my competence had always been implicit, but Weather's arrival had changed all that.

"My wife didn't die in a terraforming accident," he said slowly, not quite able to meet my eyes as he spoke. "I lied to you about that, probably because I wanted to start believing the lie myself. But now it's time you heard the truth, which is that the Spiders took her. She was a technician, an expert in Martian landscaping. She'd been working on the Schiaparelli irrigation scheme when she was caught behind Spider lines during the Sabaea Offensive. They stole her from me, and turned her into one of them. Took her to their recruitment theatres, where they opened her head and pumped it full of their machines. Rewired her mind to make her think and feel like them."

"I'm sorry," I began. "That must have been so hard—"

"That's not the hard part. I was told that she'd been executed, but three years later I saw her again. She'd been taken prisoner by the Coalition for Neural Purity, and they were trying to turn her back into a person. They hadn't ever done it before, so my wife was to be a test subject. They invited me to their compound in Tychoplex, on Earth's Moon, hoping I might be able to bring her back. I didn't want to do it. I knew it wasn't going to work; that it was always going to be easier thinking that she was already dead."

"What happened?"

"When she saw me, she remembered me. She called me by name, just as if we'd only been apart a few minutes. But there was a coldness in her eyes. Actually, it was something beyond coldness. Coldness would mean she felt some recognisably human emotion, even if it was dislike or contempt. It wasn't like that. The way she looked at me, it was as if she was looking at a piece of broken furniture, or a dripping tap, or a pattern of mould on the wall. As if it vaguely bothered her that I existed, or was the shape I was, but that she could feel nothing stronger than that."

"It wasn't your wife any more," I said. "Your wife died the moment they took her."

"That'd be nice to believe, wouldn't it? Trouble is, I've never been able to. And trust me, lad: I've had long enough to dwell on things. I know a part of my wife survived what they did to her in the theatres. It just wasn't the part that gave a damn about me any more."

"I'm sorry," I said again, feeling as if I'd been left drifting in space while the ship raced away from me. "I had no idea."

"I just wanted you to know: with me and the Spiders, it isn't an irrational prejudice. From where I'm sitting, it feels pretty damn rational." Then he drew an enormous intake of breath, as if he needed sustenance for what was to come. "Take the girl to the engine if you think it's the only way we'll get out of this mess. But don't let her out of your sight for one second. And if you get the slightest idea that she might be trying something—and I mean the *slightest* idea—you kill her, there and then."

I CLAMPED THE collar around Weather's neck. It was a heavy ring fashioned from rough black metal. "I'm sorry about this," I told her, "but it's the only way Van Ness will let me take you out of this room. Tell me if it hurts, and I'll try to do something about it."

"You won't need to," she said.

The collar was a crude old thing that had been lying around the *Petronel* since her last bruising contact with pirates. It was modified from the connecting ring of a space helmet, the kind that would amputate and shock-freeze the head if it detected massive damage to the body below the neck. Inside the collar was a noose of monofilament wire, primed to tighten to the diameter of a human hair in less than a second. There were complicated moving parts in the collar, but nothing that a Conjoiner could influence. The collar trailed a thumb-thick cable from its rear, which ran all the way to an activating box on my belt. I'd only need to give the box a hard thump with the heel of my hand, and Weather would be decapitated. That wouldn't necessarily mean she'd die instantly—with all those machines in her head, Weather would be able to remain conscious for quite some time afterwards—but I was reasonably certain it would limit her options for doing harm.

"For what it's worth," I told her as we made our way out to the connecting spar, "I'm not expecting to have to use this. But I want you to be clear that I will if I have to."

She walked slightly ahead of me, the cable hanging between us. "You seem different, Inigo. What happened between you and the captain, while you were gone?"

The truth couldn't hurt, I decided. "Van Ness told me something I didn't know. It put things into perspective. I understand now why he might not feel positively disposed towards Conjoiners."

"And does that alter the way you think about me?"

I said nothing for several paces. "I don't know, Weather. Until now I never really gave much thought to those horror stories about the Spiders. I assumed they'd been exaggerated, the way things often are during wartime."

"But now you've seen the light. You realise that, in fact, we are monsters after all."

"I didn't say that. But I've just learned that something I always thought untrue—that Conjoiners would take prisoners and convert them into other Conjoiners—really happened."

"To Van Ness?"

She didn't need to know all the facts. "To someone close to him. The worst was that he got to meet that person after her transformation."

After a little while, Weather said, "Mistakes were made. Very, very bad mistakes."

"How can you call taking someone prisoner and stuffing their skull full of Conjoiner machinery a 'mistake,' Weather? You must have known exactly what you were doing, exactly what it would do to the prisoner."

"Yes, we did," she said, "but we considered it a kindness. That was the mistake, Inigo. And it was a kindness, too: no one who tasted Transenlightenment ever wanted to go back to the experiential mundanity of retarded consciousness. But we did not anticipate how distressing this might be to those who had known the candidates beforehand."

"He felt that she didn't love him any more."

"That wasn't the case. It's just that everything else in her universe had become so heightened, so intense, that the love for another individual could no longer hold her interest. It had become just one facet in a much larger mosaic."

"And you don't think that was cruel?"

"I said it was a mistake. But if Van Ness had joined her...if Van Ness had submitted to the Conjoined, known Transenlightenment for himself...they would have reconnected on a new level of personal intimacy."

I wondered how she could be so certain. "That doesn't help Van Ness now."

"We wouldn't make the same mistake again. If there were ever to be... difficulties again, we wouldn't take candidates so indiscriminately."

"But you'd still take some."

"We'd still consider it a kindness," Weather said.

Not much was said as we traversed the connecting spar out to the starboard engine. I watched Weather alertly, transfixed by the play of colours across her cooling crest. Eventually she whirled around and said, "I'm not going to *do* anything, Inigo, so stop worrying about it. This collar's bad enough, without feeling you watching my every move."

"Maybe the collar isn't going to help us," I said. "Van Ness thinks you want to blow up the ship. I guess if you had a way to do that, we wouldn't get much warning."

"No, you wouldn't. But I'm not going to blow up the ship. That's not within my power, unless you let me turn the input dials all the way into the red. Even Voulage wasn't that stupid."

I wiped my sweat-damp hand on the thigh of my trousers. "We don't know much about how these engines work. Are you sensing anything from them yet?"

"A little," she admitted. "There's crosstalk between the two units, but I don't have the implants to make sense of that. Most Conjoiners don't need anything that specialised, unless they work in the drive creches, educating the engines."

"The engines need educating?"

Not answering me directly, she said, "I can feel the engine now. Effective range for my implants is a few dozen metres under these conditions. We must be very close."

"We are," I said as we turned a corner. Ahead lay the hexagonal arrangement of input dials. They were all showing blue-green now, but only because I'd throttled the engine back to a whisper of thrust.

"I'll need to get closer if I'm going to be any use to you," Weather told me.

"Step up to the panel. But don't touch anything until I give you permission."

I knew there wasn't much harm she could do here, even if she started pushing the dials. She'd need to move more than one to make things dangerous, and I could drop her long before she had a chance to do that. But I was still nervous as she stood next to the hexagon and cocked her head to one side.

I thought of what lay on the other side of that wall. Having traversed the spar, we were now immediately inboard of the engine, about halfway along its roughly cylindrical shape. The engine extended for one hundred and ten metres ahead of me, and for approximately two hundred and fifty metres in either direction to my left and right. It was sheathed in several layers of conventional hull material, anchored to the *Petronel* by a shock-absorbing cradle and wrapped in a mesh of sensors and steering-control systems. Like any shipmaster, my understanding of those elements was so total that it no longer counted as acquired knowledge. It had become an integral part of my personality.

But I knew nothing of the engine itself. My log book, with its reams of codified notes and annotations, implied a deep and scholarly grasp of all essential principles. Nothing could have been further from the truth. The Conjoiner drive was essentially a piece of magic we'd been handed on a plate, like a coiled baby dragon. It came with instructions on how to tame its fire, and make sure it did not come to harm, but we were forbidden from probing its mysteries. The most important rule that applied to a Conjoiner engine was a simple one: there were no user-serviceable components inside. Tamper with an engine—attempt to take it apart, in the hope of reverse-engineering it—and the engine would self-destruct in a mini-nova powerful enough to crack open a small moon. Across settled space, there was no shortage of mildly radioactive craters testifying to failed attempts to break that one prohibition.

Ultras didn't care, as a rule. Ultras, by definition, already had Conjoiner drives. It was governments and rich planet-bound individuals who kept learning the hard way. The Conjoiner argument was brutal in its simplicity: there were principles embodied in their drives that "retarded" humanity just wasn't ready to absorb. We were meant to count ourselves lucky that they let us have the engines in the first place. We weren't meant to go poking our thick monkey fingers into their innards.

And so long as the engines kept working, few of us had any inclination to do so.

Weather took a step back. "It's not good news, I'm afraid. I thought that perhaps the dial indications might be in error, suggesting that there was a fault where none existed...but that isn't the case."

"You can feel that the engine is really damaged?"

"Yes," she told me. "And it's this one, the starboard unit."

"What's wrong with it? Is it anything we can fix?"

"One question at a time, Inigo." Weather smiled tolerantly before continuing, "There's been extensive damage to critical engine components, too much for the engine's own self-repair systems to address. The engine hasn't failed completely, but certain reaction pathways have now become computationally intractable, which is why you're seeing the drastic loss in drive efficiency. The engine is being forced to explore other pathways, those that it can still manage given its existing resources. But they don't deliver the same output energy."

She was telling me everything and nothing. "I don't really understand," I admitted. "Are you saying there's nothing that can be done to repair it?"

"Not here. At a dedicated Conjoiner manufacturing facility, certainly. We'd only make things worse."

"We can't run on just the port engine, either—not without rebuilding the entire ship. If we were anywhere near a moon or asteroid, that might just be an option, but not when we're so far out."

"I'm sorry the news isn't better. You'll just have to resign yourselves to a longer trip than you were expecting."

"It's worse than that. There's another ship closing in on us, probably another raider like Voulage. It's very close now. If we don't start running soon, they'll be on us."

"And you didn't think to tell me this sooner?"

"Would it have made any difference?"

"To the trust between us, possibly."

"I'm sorry, Weather. I didn't want to distract you. I thought things were bad enough as they were."

"And you thought I'd be able to work a miracle if I wasn't distracted?"

I nodded hopelessly. I realised that, as naive as it might seem, I'd been expecting Weather to wave a hand over the broken engine and restore it to full, glittering functionality. But knowing something of the interior workings of the drive was not the same as being able to fix it.

"Are we really out of options?" I asked.

"The engine is already doing all it can to provide maximum power, given the damage it has taken. There really is no scope to make things better."

Desperate for some source of optimism, I thought back to what Weather had said a few moments before. "When you talked about the computations, you seemed to be saying that the engine needed to do some number-crunching to make itself work."

Weather looked conflicted. "I've already said too much, Inigo."

"But if we're going to die out here, it doesn't matter what you tell me, does it? Failing that, I'll swear a vow of silence. How does that sound?"

"No one has ever come close to working out how our engines function," Weather said. "We've played our hand in that, of course: putting out more than our share of misinformation over the years. And it's worked, too. We've kept careful tabs on the collective thinking concerning our secrets. We've always had contingencies in place to disrupt any research that might be headed in the right direction. So far we've never had cause to use a single one of them. If I were to reveal key information to you, I would have more to worry about than just being an outcast. My people would come after me. They'd hunt me down, and then they'd hunt you down as well. Conjoiners will consider any necessary act, up to and including local genocide, to protect the secrets of the C-drive." She paused for a moment, letting me think she was finished, before continuing on the same grave note, "But having said that, there are layers to our secrets. I can't reveal the detailed physical principles upon which the drive depends, but I can tell you that the conditions in the drive, when it is at full functionality, are enormously complex and chaotic. Your ship may ride a smooth thrust beam, but the reactions going on inside the drive are anything but smooth. There is a small mouth into hell inside every engine: bubbling, frothing, subject to vicious and unpredictable state-changes."

"Which the engine needs to smooth out."

"Yes. And to do so, the engine needs to think through some enormously complex, parallel computational problems. When all is well, when the engine is intact and running inside its normal operational envelope, the burden is manageable. But if you ask too much of the engine, or damage it in some way, that burden becomes heavier. Eventually it exceeds the means of the engine, and the reactions become uncontrolled."

"Nova."

"Quite," Weather said, favouring my response with a tiny nod.

"Then let me get this straight," I said. "The engine's damaged, but it could still work if the computations weren't so complicated."

Weather answered me guardedly. "Yes, but don't underestimate how difficult those computations have now become. I can feel the strain this engine is under, just holding things together as they are."

"I'm not underestimating it. I'm just wondering if we couldn't help it do better. Couldn't we load in some new software, or assist the engine by hooking in the *Petronel*'s own computers?"

"I really wish it was that simple."

"I'm sorry. My questions must seem quite simple-minded. But I'm just trying to make sure we aren't missing anything obvious."

"We aren't," she said. "Take my word on it."

I RETURNED WEATHER to her quarters and removed the collar. Where it had been squeezing her neck, the skin was marked with a raw pink band, spotted with blood. I threw the hateful thing into the corner of the room and returned with a medical kit.

"You should have said something," I told her as I dabbed at the abrasions with a disinfectant swab. "I didn't realise it was cutting into you all that time. You seemed so cool, so focused. But that must have been hurting all the while."

"I told you I could turn off pain."

"Are you turning it off now?"

"Why?"

"Because you keep flinching."

Weather reached up suddenly and took my wrist, almost making me drop the swab. The movement was as swift as a snakebite, but although she held me firmly, I sensed no aggressive intentions. "Now it's my turn not to understand," she said. "You were hoping I might be able to do something for you. I couldn't. That means you're in as much trouble as you ever were. Worse, if anything, because now you've heard it from me. But you're still treating me with kindness."

"Would you rather we didn't?"

"I assumed that as soon as my usefulness to you had come to an end—"

"You assumed wrongly. We're not that kind of crew."

"And your captain?"

"He'll keep his word. Killing you would never have been Van Ness's style." I finished disinfecting her neck and began to rummage through the medical kit for a strip of bandage. "We're all just going to have to make do as best we can, you included. Van Ness reckoned we should send out a distress call and wait for rescue. I wasn't so keen on that idea before, but now I'm beginning to wonder if maybe it isn't so bad after all." She said nothing. I wondered if she was thinking of exactly the same objections I'd voiced to Van Ness, when he raised the idea. "We still have a ship, that's the main thing. Just because we aren't moving as fast as we'd like—"

"I'd like to see Van Ness," Weather said.

"I'm not sure he'd agree."

"Tell him it's about his wife. Tell him he can trust me, with or without that silly collar."

I WENT TO fetch the captain. He took some persuading before he even agreed to look at Weather, and even then he wouldn't come within twenty metres of her. I told her to wait at the door to her room, which faced a long service corridor.

"I'm not going to touch you, Captain," she called, her voice echoing from the corridor's ribbed metal walls. "You can come as close as you like. I can barely smell you at this distance, let alone sense your neural emissions."

"This'll do nicely," Van Ness said. "Inigo told me you had something you wanted to say to me. That right, or was it just a ruse to get me near to you, so you could reach into my head and make me see and think whatever you like?"

She appeared not to hear him. "I take it Inigo's told you about the engine."

"Told me you had a good old look at it and decided there was nothing you could do. Maybe things would have been different if you hadn't had that collar on, though, eh?"

"You mean I might have sabotaged the engine, to destroy myself and the ship? No, Captain, I don't think I would have. If I had any intention of killing myself, you'd already made it easy enough with that collar." She glanced at me. "I could have reached Inigo and pressed that control box while the nervous impulse from his brain was still working its way down his forearm. All he'd have seen was a grey blur, followed by a lot of arterial blood."

I thought back to the speed with which she'd reached up and grabbed my forearm, and knew she wasn't lying.

"So why didn't you?" Van Ness asked.

"Because I wanted to help you if I could. Until I saw the engine— until I got close enough to feel its emissions—I couldn't know for sure that the problem wasn't something quite trivial."

"Except it wasn't. Inigo says it isn't fixable."

"Inigo's right. The technical fault can't be repaired, not without use of Conjoiner technology. But now that I've had time to think about it, mull things over, it occurs to me that there may be something I can do for you."

I looked at her. "Really?"

"Let me finish what I have to say, Inigo," she said warningly, "then we'll go down to the engine and I'll make everything clear. Captain Van Ness—about your wife."

"What would you know about my wife?" Van Ness asked her angrily.

"More than you realise. I know because I'm a—I was— a Conjoiner."

"As if I didn't know."

"We started on Mars, Captain Van Ness—just a handful of us. I wasn't alive then, but from the moment Galiana brought our new state of consciousness into being, the thread of memory has never been broken. There are many branches to our great tree now, in many systems—but we all carry the memories of those who went before us, before the family was torn asunder. I don't just mean the simple fact that we remember their names, what they looked like and what they did. I mean we carry their living experiences with us, into the future." Weather swallowed, something catching in her throat. "Sometimes we're barely aware of any of this. It's as if there's this vast sea of collective experience lapping at the shore of consciousness, but it's only every now and then that it floods us, leaving us awash in sorrow and joy. Sorrow because those are the memories of the dead, all that's left of them. Joy because *something* has endured, and while it does they can't truly be dead, can they? I feel Remontoire sometimes, when I look at something in a certain analytic way. There's a jolt of déjà vu and I realise it isn't because I've experienced it before, but because Remontoire did. We all feel the memories of the earliest Conjoiners the most strongly."

"And my wife?" Van Ness asked, like a man frightened of what he might hear.

"Your wife was just one of many candidates who entered Transenlightenment during the troubles. You lost her then, and saw her once more when the Coalition took her prisoner. It was distressing for you because she did not respond to you on a human level."

"Because you'd ripped everything human out of her," Van Ness said.

Weather shook her head calmly, refusing to be goaded. "No. We'd taken almost nothing. The difficulty was that we'd added too much, too quickly. That was why it was so hard for her, and so upsetting for you. But it didn't have to be that way. The last thing we wanted was to frighten possible future candidates. It would have worked much better for us if your wife had shown love and affection to you, and then begged you to follow her into the wonderful new world she'd been shown."

Something of Weather's manner seemed to blunt Van Ness's indignation. "That doesn't help me much. It doesn't help my wife at all."

"I haven't finished. The last time you saw your wife was in that Coalition compound. You assumed—as you continue to assume—that she ended her days there, an emotionless zombie haunting the shell of the woman you once knew. But that isn't what happened. She came back to us, you see."

"I thought Conjoiners never returned to the fold," I said.

"Things were different then. It was war. Any and all candidates were welcome, even those who might have suffered destabilising isolation away from Transenlightenment. And Van Ness's wife wasn't like me. She hadn't been born into it. Her depth of immersion into Transenlightenment was inevitably less profound than that of a Conjoiner who'd been swimming in data since they were a foetus."

"You're lying," Van Ness said. "My wife died in Coalition custody three years after I saw her."

"No," Weather said patiently. "She did not. Conjoiners took Tychoplex and returned all the prisoners to Transenlightenment. The Coalition was suffering badly at the time and could not afford the propaganda blow of losing such a valuable arm of its research programme. So it lied and covered up the loss of Tychoplex. But in fact your wife was alive and well." Weather looked at him levelly. "She is dead now, Captain Van Ness. I wish I could tell you otherwise, but I hope it will not come as too shocking a blow, given what you have always believed."

"When did she die?"

"Thirty-one years later, in another system, during the malfunction of one of our early drives. It was very fast and utterly painless."

"Why are you telling me this? What difference does it make to me, here and now? She's still gone. She still became one of you."

"I am telling you," Weather answered, "because her memories are part of me. I won't pretend that they're as strong as Remontoire's, because by the time your wife was recruited, more than five thousand had already joined our ranks. Hers was one new voice amongst many. But none of those voices were silent: they were all heard, and something of them has reached down through all these years."

"Again: why are you telling me this?"

"Because I have a message from your wife. She committed it to the collective memory long before her death, knowing that it would always be part of Conjoiner knowledge, even as our numbers grew and we became increasingly fragmented. She knew that every future Conjoiner would carry her message—even an outcast like me. It might become diluted, but it would never be lost entirely. And she believed that you were still alive, and that one day your path might cross that of another Conjoiner."

After a silence Van Ness said, "Tell me the message."

"This is what your wife wished you to hear." Almost imperceptibly, the tone of Weather's voice shifted. "I am sorry for what happened between us, Rafe—more sorry than you can ever know. When they recaptured me, when they took me to Tychoplex, I was not the person I am now. It was still early in my time amongst the Conjoiners, and—perhaps just as importantly—it was still early for the Conjoiners as well. There was much that we all needed to learn. We were ambitious then, fiercely so, but by the same token we were arrogantly blind to our inadequacies and failings. That changed, later, after I returned to the fold. Galiana made refinements to all of us, reinstating a higher degree of personal identity. I think she had learned something wise from Nevil Clavain. After that, I began to see things in the proper perspective again. I thought of you, and the pain of what I had done to you was like a sharp stone pushing against my throat. Every waking moment of my consciousness, with every breath, you were there. But by then it was much too late to make amends. I tried to contact you, but without success. I couldn't even be sure if you were in the system any more. By then, even the Demarchists had their own prototype starships, using

the technology we'd licensed them. You could have been anywhere."
Weather's tone hardened, taking on a kind of saintlike asperity. "But I
always knew you were a survivor, Rafe. I never doubted that you were
still alive, somewhere. Perhaps we'll meet again: stranger things have
happened. If so, I hope I'll treat you with something of the kindness you
always deserved, and that you always showed me. But should that never
happen, I can at least hope that you will hear this message. There will
always be Conjoiners, and nothing that is committed to the collective
memory will ever be lost. No matter how much time passes, those of
us who walk in the world will be carrying this message, alert for your
name. If there was more I could do, I would. But contrary to what some
might think, even Conjoiners can't work miracles. I wish that it were
otherwise. Then I would clap my hands and summon you to me, and
I would spend the rest of my life letting you know what you meant to
me, what you still mean to me. I loved you, Rafe Van Ness. I always did,
and I always will."

Weather fell silent, her expression respectful. It was not necessary for
her to tell us that the message was over.

"How do I know this is true?" Van Ness asked quietly.

"I can't give you any guarantees," Weather said, "but there was one
word I was also meant to say to you. Your wife believed it would have
some significance to you, something nobody else could possibly know."

"And the word?"

"The word is 'mezereon.' I think it is a type of plant. Does the word
mean something to you?"

I looked at Van Ness. He appeared frozen, unable to respond. His eye
softened and sparkled. He nodded, and said simply, "Yes, it does."

"Good," Weather answered. "I'm glad that's done: it's been weighing
on all of our minds for quite some time. And now I'm going to help you
get home."

Whatever "mezereon" meant to Van Ness, whatever it revealed to
him concerning the truth of Weather's message, I never asked.

Nor did Van Ness ever speak of the matter again.

SHE STOOD BEFORE the hexagonal arrangement of input dials, as I had done a thousand times before. "You must give me authorisation to make adjustments," she said.

My mouth was dry. "Do what you will. I'll be watching you very carefully."

Weather looked amused. "You're still concerned that I might want to kill us all?"

"I can't ignore my duty to this ship."

"Then this will be difficult for you. I must turn the dials to a setting you would consider highly dangerous, even suicidal. You'll just have to trust me that I know what I'm doing."

I glanced back at Van Ness.

"Do it," he mouthed.

"Go ahead," I told Weather. "Whatever you need to do—"

"In the course of this, you will learn more about our engines. There is something inside here that you will find disturbing. It is not the deepest secret, but it is a secret nonetheless, and shortly you will know it. Afterwards, when we reach port, you must not speak of this matter. Should you do so, Conjoiner security would detect the leak and act swiftly. The consequences would be brutal, for you and anyone you might have spoken to."

"Then maybe you're better off not letting us see whatever you're so keen to keep hidden."

"There's something I'm going to have to do. If you want to understand, you need to see everything."

She reached up and planted her hands on two of the dials. With surprising strength, she twisted them until their quadrants shone ruby red. Then she moved to another pair of dials and moved them until they were showing a warning amber. She adjusted one of the remaining dials to a lower setting, into the blue, and then returned to the first two dials she had touched, quickly dragging them back to green. While all this was happening, I felt the engine surge in response, the deck plates pushing harder against my feet. But the burst was soon over. When Weather had made her last adjustment, the engine had throttled back even further than before. I judged that we were only experiencing a tenth of a gee.

"What have you just done?" I asked.

"This," she said.

Weather took a nimble, light-footed step back from the input controls. At the same moment a chunk of wall, including the entire hexagonal array, pushed itself out from the surrounding metallic-blue material in which it had appeared to have been seamlessly incorporated. The chunk was as thick as a bank-vault door. I watched in astonishment as the chunk slid in silence to one side, exposing a bulkhead-sized hole in the side of the engine wall.

Soft red light bathed us. We were looking into the hidden heart of a Conjoiner drive.

"Follow me," Weather said.

"Are you serious?"

"You want to get home, don't you? You want to escape that raider? This is how it will happen." Then she looked back to Van Ness. "With all due respect...I wouldn't recommend it. Captain. You wouldn't do any damage to the engine, but the engine might damage you."

"I'm fine right here," Van Ness said.

I followed Weather into the engine. At first my eyes had difficulty making out our surroundings. The red light inside seemed to emanate from every surface, rather than from any concentrated source, so that there were only hints of edges and corners. I had to reach out and touch things more than once to establish their shape and proximity. Weather watched me guardedly, but said nothing.

She led me along a winding, restrictive path that squeezed its way between huge intrusions of Conjoiner machinery, like the course etched by some meandering, indecisive underground river. The machinery emitted a low humming sound, and sometimes when I touched it I felt a rapid but erratic vibration. I couldn't make out our surroundings with any clarity for more than a few metres in any direction, but as Weather pushed on I sometimes had the impression that the machinery was moving out of her way to open up the path, and sealing itself behind us. She led me up steep ramps, assisted me as we negotiated near-impassable chicanes, helped me as we climbed down vertical shafts that would be perilous even under one-tenth of a gee. My sense of direction was soon hopelessly confounded, and I had no idea whether we had travelled hundreds of metres into the engine, or merely wormed our way in and around a relatively localised region close to our entry point.

"I'm glad you know the way," I said, with mock cheerfulness. "I wouldn't be able to get out of here without you."

"Yes, you will," Weather said, looking back over her shoulder. "The engine will guide you out, don't you worry."

"You're coming with me, though."

"No, Inigo, I'm not. I have to stay here from now on. It's the only way that any of us will be getting home."

"I don't understand. Once you've fixed the engine—"

"It isn't like that. The engine can't be fixed. What I can do is help it, relieve it of some of the computational burden. But to do that I need to be close to it. Inside it."

While we were talking, Weather had brought us to a box-like space that was more open than anywhere we'd passed through so far. The room, or chamber, was empty of machinery, save for a waist-high cylinder rising from the floor. The cylinder had a flattened top and widened base that suggested the stump of a tree. It shone the same arterial red as everything else around us.

"We've reached the heart of the engine-control assembly now," Weather said, kneeling by the stump. "The reaction core is somewhere else—we couldn't survive anywhere near that—but this is where the reaction computations are made, for both the starboard and port drives. I'm going to show you something now. I think it will make it easier for you to understand what is to happen to me. I hope you're ready."

"As I'll ever be."

Weather planted a hand on either side of the stump and closed her eyes momentarily. I heard a click and the whirr of a buried mechanism. The upper fifth of the stump opened, irising wide. A blue light rammed from its innards. I felt a chill rising from whatever was inside, a coldness that seemed to reach fingers down my throat.

Something emerged from inside the stump, rising on a pedestal. It was a glass container pierced by many silver cables, each of which was plugged into the folded cortex of a single massively swollen brain. The brain had split open along fracture lines, like a cake that had ruptured in the baking. The blue light spilled from the fissures. When I looked into one—peering down into the geological strata of brain anatomy—I had to blink against the glare. A seething mass of tiny bright things lay nestled at the base of the cleft, twinkling with the light of the sun.

"This is the computer that handles the computations," Weather said.

"It looks human. Please tell me it isn't."

"It is human. Or at least that's how it started out, before the machines were allowed to infest and reorganise its deep structure." Weather tapped a finger against the side of her own scalp. "All the machines in my head only amount to two hundred grams of artificial matter, and even so I still need this crest to handle my thermal loading. There are nearly a thousand grams of machinery in that brain. The brain needs to be cooled like a turbopump. That's why it's been opened up, so that the heat can dissipate more easily."

"It's a monstrosity."

"Not to us," she said sharply. "We see a thing of wonder and beauty."

"No," I said firmly. "Let's be clear about this. What you're showing me here is a human brain, a living mind, turned into some kind of slave."

"No slavery is involved," Weather said. "The mind chose this vocation willingly."

"It *chose* this?"

"It's considered a great honour. Even in Conjoiner society, even given all that we have learned about the maximisation of our mental resources, only a few are ever born who have the skills necessary to tame and manage the reactions in the heart of a C-drive. No machine can ever perform that task as well as a conscious mind. We could build a conscious machine, of course, a true mechanical slave, but that would contravene one of our deepest strictures. No machine may think, unless it does so voluntarily. So we are left with volunteer organic minds, even if those selfsame minds need the help of a thousand grams of nonsentient processing machinery. As to why only a few of us have the talent... that is one of *our* greatest mysteries. Galiana thought that, in achieving a pathway to augmented human intelligence, she would render the brain utterly knowable. It was one of her few mistakes. Just as there are savants amongst the retarded, so we have our Conjoined equivalents. We are all tested for such gifts when we are young. Very few of us show even the slightest aptitude. Of those that do, even fewer ever develop the maturity and stability that would make them suitable candidates for enshrinement in an engine." Weather faced me with a confiding look. "They are valued very highly indeed, to the point where they are envied by some of us who lack what they were born with."

"But even if they were gifted enough that it was possible…no one would willingly choose this."

"You don't understand us, Inigo. We are creatures of the mind. This brain doesn't consider itself to have been imprisoned here. It considers itself to have been placed in a magnificent and fitting setting, like a precious jewel."

"Easy for you to say, since it isn't you."

"But it very nearly could have been. I came close, Inigo. I passed all the early tests. I was considered exceptional, by the standards of my cohort group. I knew what it was like to feel special, even amongst geniuses. But it turned out that I wasn't quite special enough, so I was selected out of the programme."

I looked at the swollen, fissured mind. The hard blue glow made me think of Cherenkov radiation, boiling out of some cracked fission core.

"And do you regret it now?"

"I'm older now," Weather said. "I realise now that being unique… being adored…is not the greatest thing in the world. Part of me still admires this mind; part of me still appreciates its rare and delicate beauty. Another part of me…doesn't feel like that."

"You've been amongst people too long, Weather. You know what it's like to walk and breathe."

"Perhaps," she said, doubtfully.

"This mind—"

"It's male," Weather said. "I can't tell you his name, any more than I could tell you mine. But I can read his public memories well enough. He was fifteen when his enshrinement began. Barely a man at all. He's been inside this engine for twenty-two years of shiptime; nearly sixty-eight years of worldtime."

"And this is how he'll spend the rest of his life?"

"Until he wearies of it, or some accident befalls this ship. Periodically, as now, Conjoiners may make contact with the enshrined mind. If they determine that the mind wishes to retire, they may effect a replacement, or decommission the entire engine."

"And then what?"

"His choice. He could return to full embodiment, but that would mean losing hundreds of grams of neural support machinery. Some are prepared to make that adjustment; not all are willing. His other option would be to return to one of our nests and remain in essentially this form, but without the necessity of running a drive. He would not be alone in doing so."

I realised, belatedly, where all this was heading. "You say he's under a heavy burden now."

"Yes. The degree of concentration is quite intense. He can barely spare any resources for what we might call normal thought. He's in a state of permanent unconscious flow, like someone engaged in an enormously challenging game. But now the game has begun to get the better of him. It isn't fun any more. And yet he knows the cost of failure."

"But you can help him."

"I won't pretend that my abilities are more than a shadow of his. Still, I did make it part of the way. I can't take all the strain off him, but I can give him free access to my mind. The additional processing resources—coupled with my own limited abilities—may make enough of a difference."

"For what?"

"For you to get wherever it is you are going. I believe that with our minds meshed together, and dedicated to this one task, we may be able to return the engines to something like normal efficiency. I can't make any promises, though. The proof of the pudding…"

I looked at the pudding-like mass of neural tissue and asked the question I was dreading. "What happens to you, while all this is happening? If he's barely conscious—"

"The same would apply, I'm afraid. As far as the external world is concerned, I'll be in a state of coma. If I'm to make any difference, I'll have to hand over all available neural resources."

"But you'll be helpless. How long would you last, sitting in a coma?"

"That isn't an issue. I've already sent a command to this engine to form the necessary life-support machinery. It should be ready any moment now, as it happens." Weather glanced down at the floor between us. "I'd take a step back if I were you, Inigo."

I did as she suggested. The flat red floor buckled upwards, shaping itself into the seamless form of a moulded couch. Without any ceremony, Weather climbed onto the couch and lay down as if for sleep.

"There isn't any point delaying things," she said. "My mind is made up, and the sooner we're on our way, the better. We can't be sure that there aren't other brigands within attack range."

"Wait," I said. "This is all happening too quickly. I thought we were coming down here to look at the situation, to talk about the possibilities."

"We've already talked about them, Inigo. They boil down to this: either I help the boy, or we drift hopelessly."

"But you can't just...do this."

Even as I spoke, the couch appeared to consolidate its hold on Weather. Red material flowed around her body, hardening over her into a semitranslucent shell. Only her face and lower arms remained visible, surrounded by a thick red collar that threatened to squeeze shut at any moment.

"It won't be so bad," she said. "As I said, I won't have much room left for consciousness. I won't be bored, that's for sure. It'll be more like one very long dream. Someone else's dream, certainly, but I don't doubt that there'll be a certain rapturous quality to it. I remember how good it felt to find an elegant solution, when the parameters looked so unpromising. Like making the most beautiful music imaginable. I don't think anyone can really know how that feels unless they've also held some of that fire in their minds. It's ecstasy, Inigo, when it goes right."

"And when it goes wrong?"

"When it goes wrong, you don't get much time to explore how it feels." Weather shut her eyes again, like a person lapsing into micro-sleep. "I'm lowering blockades, allowing the boy to co-opt my own resources. He's wary. Not because he doesn't trust me, but because he can barely manage his own processing tasks, without adding the temporary complexity of farming some of them out to me. The transition will be difficult...ah, here it comes. He's using me, Inigo. He's accepting my help." Despite being almost totally enclosed in the shell of red matter, Weather's whole body convulsed. Her voice, when she spoke again, sounded strained. "It's difficult. So much more difficult than I thought it would be. This poor mind...he's had so much to do on his own. A lesser spirit would already have buckled. He's shown heroic dedication...I wish the nest could know how well he has done." She clamped her teeth together and convulsed again, harder this time. "He's taking more of me. Eagerly now. Knows I've come to help. The sense of relief...the strain being lifted...I can't comprehend how he lasted until now. I'm sorry, Inigo. Soon there isn't going to be much of me left to talk to you."

"Is it working?"

"Yes. I think so. Perhaps between the two of us—" Her jaws cracked together, teeth cutting her tongue. "Not going to be easy, but...losing more of me now. Language going. Don't need now."

"Weather, don't go."

"Can't stay. Got to go. Only way. Inigo, make promise. Make promise fast."

"Say it. Whatever it is."

"When we get...when we—" Her face was contorted with the strain of trying to make herself understood.

"When we arrive," I said.

She nodded so hard I thought her neck was going to break. "Yes. Arrive. You get help. Find others."

"Other Conjoiners?"

"Yes. Bring them. Bring them in ship. Tell them. Tell them and make them help."

"I will. I swear on it."

"Going now. Inigo. One last thing."

"Yes. Whatever it is."

"Hold hand."

I reached out and took her hand, in my good one.

"No," Weather said. "Other. *Other hand.*"

I let go, then took her hand in my metal one, closing my fingers as tightly as I dared without risking hers. Then I leaned down, bringing my face close to hers.

"Weather, I think I love you. I'll wait for you. I'll find those Conjoiners. That's a promise."

"Love a Spider?" she asked.

"Yes. If this is what it takes."

"Silly...human...boy."

She pulled my hand, with more strength than I thought she had left in her. She tugged it down into the surface of the couch until it lapped around my wrist, warm as blood. I felt something happening to my hand, a crawling itch like pins and needles. I kissed Weather. Her lips were fever-warm. She nodded and then allowed me to withdraw my hand.

"Go now," she said.

The red material of the couch flowed over Weather completely, covering her hands and face until all that remained was a vague, mummy-like form.

I knew then that I would not see her again for a very long time. For a moment I stood still, paralysed by what had happened. Even then I could feel my weight increasing. Whatever Weather and the boy were doing between them, it was having some effect on the engine output. My weight climbed smoothly, until I was certain we were exceeding half a gee and still accelerating.

Perhaps we were going to make it home after all.

Some of us.

I turned from Weather's casket and looked for the way out. Held tight against my chest to stop it itching, my hand was lost under a glove of twinkling machinery. I wondered what gift I would find when the glove completed its work.

BEYOND THE AQUILA RIFT

GRETA'S WITH me when I pull Suzy out of the surge tank.

"Why her?" Greta asks.

"Because I want her out first," I say, wondering if Greta's jealous. I don't blame her: Suzy's beautiful, but she's also smart. There isn't a better syntax runner in Ashanti Industrial.

"What happened?" Suzy asks, when she's over the grogginess. "Did we make it back?"

I ask her to tell me the last thing she remembers.

"Customs," Suzy says. "Those pricks on Arkangel."

"And after that? Anything else? The runes? Do you remember casting them?"

"No," she says, then picks up something in my voice. The fact that I might not be telling the truth, or telling her all she needs to know. "Thom. I'll ask you again. Did we make it back?"

"Yeah," I say. "We made it back."

Suzy looks back at the starscape, airbrushed across her surge tank in luminous violet and yellow paint. She'd had it customized on Carillon. It was against regs: something about the paint clogging intake filters. Suzy didn't care. She told me it had cost her a week's pay, but it had been worth it to impose her own personality on the grey company architecture of the ship.

"Funny how I feel like I've been in that thing for months."

I shrug. "That's the way it feels sometimes."

"Then nothing went wrong?"

"Nothing at all."

Suzy looks at Greta. "Then who are you?" she asks.

Greta says nothing. She just looks at me expectantly. I start shaking, and realize I can't go through with this. Not yet.

"End it," I tell Greta.

Greta steps toward Suzy. Suzy reacts, but she isn't quick enough. Greta pulls something from her pocket and touches Suzy on the forearm. Suzy drops like a puppet, out cold. We put her back into the surge tank, plumb her back in and close the lid.

"She won't remember anything," Greta says. "The conversation never left her short-term memory."

"I don't know if I can go through with this," I say.

Greta touches me with her other hand. "No one ever said this was going to be easy."

"I was just trying to ease her into it gently. I didn't want to tell her the truth right out."

"I know," Greta says. "You're a kind man, Thom." Then she kisses me.

I REMEMBERED ARKANGEL as well. That was about where it all started to go wrong. We just didn't know it then.

We missed our first take-off slot when customs found a discrepancy in our cargo waybill. It wasn't serious, but it took them a while to realize their mistake. By the time they did, we knew we were going to be sitting on the ground for another eight hours, while inbound control processed a fleet of bulk carriers.

I told Suzy and Ray the news. Suzy took it pretty well, or about as well as Suzy ever took that kind of thing. I suggested she use the time to scour the docks for any hot syntax patches. Anything that might shave a day or two off our return trip.

"Company authorized?" she asked.

"I don't care," I said.

"What about Ray?" Suzy asked. "Is he going to sit here drinking tea while I work for my pay?"

I smiled. They had a bickering, love-hate thing going. "No, Ray can do something useful as well. He can take a look at the q-planes."

"Nothing wrong with those planes," Ray said.

I took off my old Ashanti Industrial bib cap, scratched my bald spot and turned to the jib man.

"Right. Then it won't take you long to check them over, will it?"

"Whatever, Skip."

The thing I liked about Ray was that he always knew when he'd lost an argument. He gathered his kit and went out to check over the planes. I watched him climb the jib ladder, tools hanging from his belt. Suzy got her facemask, long, black coat, and left, vanishing into the vapour haze of the docks, boot heels clicking into the distance long after she'd passed out of sight.

I left the *Blue Goose,* walking in the opposite direction to Suzy. Overhead, the bulk carriers slid in one after the other. You heard them long before you saw them. Mournful, cetacean moans cut down through the piss-yellow clouds over the port. When they emerged, you saw dark hulls scabbed and scarred by the blocky extrusions of syntax patterning, jibs and q-planes retracted for landing and undercarriages clutching down like talons. The carriers stopped over their allocated wells and lowered down on a scream of thrust. Docking gantries closed around them like grasping skeletal fingers. Cargo-handling 'saurs plodded out of their holding pens, some of them autonomous, some of them still being ridden by trainers. There was a shocking silence as the engines cut, until the next carrier began to approach through the clouds.

I always like watching ships coming and going, even when they're holding my own ship on the ground. I couldn't read the syntax, but I knew these ships had come in all the way from the Rift. The Aquila Rift is about as far out as anyone ever goes. At median tunnel speeds, it's a year from the centre of the Local Bubble.

I've been out that way once in my life. I've seen the view from the near side of the Rift, like a good tourist. It was far enough for me.

When there was a lull in the landing pattern, I ducked into a bar and found an Aperture Authority booth that took Ashanti credit. I sat in the seat and recorded a thirty-second message to Katerina. I told her I was on my way back, but that we were stuck on Arkangel for another few hours. I warned her that the delay might cascade through to our tunnel routing, depending on how busy things were at the Authority's end. Based on past experience, an eight-hour ground hold might become a two-day hold at the surge point. I told her I'd be back, but she shouldn't worry if I was a few days late.

Outside a diplodocus slouched by with a freight container strapped between its legs.

I told Katerina I loved her and couldn't wait to get back home.

While I walked back to the *Blue Goose*, I thought of the message racing ahead of me. Transmitted at light-speed up-system, then copied into the memory buffer of the next outgoing ship. Chances were, that particular ship wasn't headed to Barranquilla or anywhere near it. The Aperture Authority would have to relay the message from ship to ship until it reached its destination. I might even reach Barranquilla ahead of it, but in all my years of delays that had only happened once. The system worked all right.

Overhead, a white passenger liner had been slotted in between the bulk carriers. I lifted up my mask to get a better look at it. I got a hit of ozone, fuel and dinosaur dung. That was Arkangel all right. You couldn't mistake it for any other place in the Bubble. There were four hundred worlds out there, up to a dozen surface ports on every planet, and none of them smelled bad in quite the same way.

"Thom?"

I followed the voice. It was Ray, standing by the dock.

"You finished checking those planes?" I asked.

Ray shook his head. "That's what I wanted to talk to you about. They were a little off-alignment, so—seeing as we're going to be sitting here for eight hours—I decided to run a full recalibration."

I nodded. "That was the idea. So what's the prob?"

"The *prob* is a slot just opened up. Tower says we can lift in thirty minutes."

I shrugged. "Then we'll lift."

"I haven't finished the recal. As it is, things are worse than before I started. Lifting now would not be a good idea."

"You know how the tower works," I said. "Miss two offered slots, you could be on the ground for days."

"No one wants to get back home sooner than I do," Ray said.

"So cheer up."

"She'll be rough in the tunnel. It won't be a smooth ride home."

I shrugged. "Do we care? We'll be asleep."

"Well, it's academic. We can't leave without Suzy."

I heard boot heels clicking toward us. Suzy came out of the fog, tugging her own mask aside.

"No joy with the rune monkeys," she said. "Nothing they were selling I hadn't seen a million times before. Fucking cowboys."

"It doesn't matter," I said. "We're leaving anyway."

Ray swore. I pretended I hadn't heard him.

I WAS ALWAYS the last one into a surge tank. I never went under until I was sure we were about to get the green light. It gave me a chance to check things over. Things can always go wrong, no matter how good the crew.

The *Blue Goose* had come to a stop near the AA beacon that marked the surge point. There were a few other ships ahead of us in the queue, plus the usual swarm of AA service craft. Through an observation blister I was able to watch the larger ships depart one by one. Accelerating at maximum power, they seemed to streak toward a completely featureless part of the sky. Their jibs were spread wide, and the smooth lines of their hulls were gnarled and disfigured with the cryptic alien runes of the routing syntax. At twenty gees it was as if a huge invisible hand snatched them away into the distance. Ninety seconds later, there'd be a pale green flash from a thousand kilometres away.

I twisted around in the blister. There were the foreshortened symbols of our routing syntax. Each rune of the script was formed from a matrix of millions of hexagonal platelets. The platelets were on motors so they could be pushed in or out from the hull.

Ask the Aperture Authority and they'll tell you that the syntax is now fully understood. This is true, but only up to a point. After two centuries of study, human machines can now construct and interpret the syntax with an acceptably low failure rate. Given a desired destination, they can assemble a string of runes that will almost always be accepted by the aperture's own machinery. Furthermore, they can almost always guarantee that the desired routing is the one that the aperture machinery will provide.

In short, you usually get where you want to go.

Take a simple point-to-point transfer, like the Hauraki run. In that case there is no real disadvantage in using automatic syntax generators. But for longer trajectories—those that may involve six or seven transits between aperture hubs—machines lose the edge. They find a solution, but usually it isn't the optimum one. That's where syntax runners come in. People like Suzy have an intuitive grasp of syntax solutions. They dream in runes. When they see a poorly constructed script, they feel it like toothache. It *affronts* them.

A good syntax runner can shave days off a route. For a company like Ashanti Industrial, that can make a lot of difference.

But I wasn't a syntax runner. I could tell when something had gone wrong with the platelets, but I had to trust that Suzy had done her job. I had no other choice.

But I knew Suzy wouldn't screw things up.

I twisted around and looked back the other way. Now that we were in space, the q-planes had deployed. They were swung out from the hull on triple hundred-metre-long jibs, like the arms of a grapple. I checked that they were locked in their fully extended positions and that the status lights were all in the green. The jibs were Ray's area. He'd been checking the alignment of the ski-shaped q-planes when I ordered him to close up ship and prepare to lift. I couldn't see any visible indication that they were out of alignment, but then again it wouldn't take much to make our trip home bumpier than usual. But as I'd told Ray, who cared? The *Blue Goose* could take a little tunnel turbulence. It was built to.

I checked the surge point again. Only three ships ahead of us.

I went back to the surge tanks and checked that Suzy and Ray were all right. Ray's tank had been customized at the same time that Suzy had

had hers done. It was full of images of what Suzy called the BVM: the Blessed Virgin Mary. The BVM was always in a spacesuit, carrying a little spacesuited Jesus. Their helmets were airbrushed gold halos. The artwork had a cheap, hasty look to it. I assumed Ray hadn't spent as much as Suzy.

Quickly I stripped down to my underclothes. I plumbed into my own unpainted surge tank and closed the lid. The buffering gel sloshed in. Within about twenty seconds I was already feeling drowsy. By the time traffic control gave us the green light I'd be asleep.

I've done it a thousand times. There was no fear, no apprehension. Just a tiny flicker of regret.

I've never seen an aperture. Then again, very few people have.

Witnesses report a doughnut-shaped lump of dark chondrite asteroid, about two kilometres across. The entire middle section has been cored out, with the inner part of the ring faced by the quixotic-matter machinery of the aperture itself. They say the q-matter machinery twinkles and moves all the while, like the ticking innards of a very complicated clock. But the monitoring systems of the Aperture Authority detect no movement at all.

It's alien technology. We have no idea how it works, or even who made it. Maybe, in hindsight, it's better not to be able to see it.

It's enough to dream, and then awake, and know that you're somewhere else.

TRY A DIFFERENT *approach, Greta says. Tell her the truth this time. Maybe she'll take it easier than you think.*

"There's no way I can tell her the truth."

Greta leans one hip against the wall, one hand still in her pocket. "Then tell her something halfway truthful."

We un-plumb Suzy and haul her out of the surge tank.

"Where are we?" she asks. Then to Greta: "Who are you?"

I wonder if some of the last conversation did make it out of Suzy's short-term memory after all.

"Greta works here," I say.

"Where's here?"

I remember what Greta told me. "A station in Schedar sector."

"That's not where we're meant to be, Thom."

I nod. "I know. There was a mistake. A routing error."

Suzy's already shaking her head. "There was nothing wrong—"

"I know. It wasn't your fault." I help her into her ship clothes. She's still shivering, her muscles reacting to movement after so much time in the tank. "The syntax was good."

"Then what?"

"The system made a mistake, not you."

"Schedar sector..." Suzy says. "That would put us about ten days off our schedule, wouldn't it?"

I try and remember what Greta said to me the first time. I ought to know this stuff by heart, but Suzy's the routing expert, not me. "That sounds about right," I say.

But Suzy shakes her head. "Then we're not in Schedar sector."

I try to sound pleasantly surprised.

"We're not?"

"I've been in that tank for a lot longer than a few days, Thom. I know. I can feel it in every fucking bone in my body. So where are we?"

I turn to Greta. I can't believe this is happening again.

"End it," I say.

Greta steps toward Suzy.

YOU KNOW THAT "as soon as I awoke I knew everything was wrong" cliché? You've probably heard it a thousand times, in a thousand bars across the Bubble, wherever ship crews swap tall tales over flat, company-subsidized beer. The trouble is that sometimes that's exactly the way it happens. I never felt good after a period in the surge tank. But the only time I had ever come around feeling anywhere near this bad was after that trip I took to the edge of the Bubble.

Mulling this, but knowing there was nothing I could do about it until I was out of the tank, it took me half an hour of painful work to free myself from the connections. Every muscle fibre in my body felt like it had been shredded. Unfortunately, the sense of wrongness didn't end with the tank. The *Blue Goose* was much too quiet. We should have been heading away from the last exit aperture after our routing. But the distant, comforting rumble of the fusion engines wasn't there at all. That meant we were in free-fall.

Not good.

I floated out of the tank, grabbed a handhold and levered myself around to view the other two tanks. Ray's largest BVM stared back radiantly from the cowl of his tank. The bio indices were all in the green. Ray was still unconscious, but there was nothing wrong with him. Same story with Suzy. Some automated system had decided I was the only one who needed waking.

A few minutes later I had made my way to the same observation blister I'd used to check the ship before the surge. I pushed my head into the scuffed glass half-dome and looked around.

We'd arrived somewhere. The *Blue Goose* was sitting in a huge, zero-gravity parking bay. The chamber was an elongated cylinder, hexagonal in cross section. The walls were a smear of service machinery: squat modules, snaking umbilical lines, the retracted cradles of unused docking berths. Whichever way I looked I saw other ships locked onto cradles. Every make and class you could think of, every possible configuration of hull design compatible with aperture transitions. Service lights threw a warm golden glow on the scene. Now and then the whole chamber was bathed in the stuttering violet flicker of a cutting torch.

It was a repair facility.

I was just starting to mull on that when I saw something extend itself from the wall of the chamber. It was a telescopic docking tunnel, groping toward our ship. Through the windows in the side of the tunnel I saw figures floating, pulling themselves along hand over hand.

I sighed and started making my way to the airlock.

BY THE TIME I reached the lock they were already through the first stage of the cycle. Nothing wrong with that—there was no good reason to prevent foreign parties boarding a vessel—but it *was* just a tiny bit impolite. But perhaps they'd assumed we were all asleep.

The door slid open.

"You're awake," a man said. "Captain Thomas Gundlupet of the *Blue Goose*, isn't it?"

"Guess so," I said.

"Mind if we come in?"

There were about half a dozen of them, and they were already coming in. They all wore slightly timeworn ochre overalls, flashed with too many company sigils. My hackles rose. I didn't really like the way they were barging in.

"What's up?" I said. "Where are we?"

"Where do you think?" the man said. He had a face full of stubble, with bad yellow teeth. I was impressed by that. Having bad teeth took a lot of work these days. It was years since I'd seen anyone who had the same dedication to the art.

"I'm really hoping you're not going to tell me we're still stuck in Arkangel system," I said.

"No, you made it through the gate."

"And?"

"There was a screw-up. Routing error. You didn't pop out of the right aperture."

"Oh, Christ." I took off my bib cap. "It never rains. Something went wrong with the insertion, right?"

"Maybe. Maybe not. Who knows how these things happen? All we know is you aren't supposed to be here."

"Right. And where is 'here'?"

"Saumlaki Station. Schedar sector."

He said it as though he was already losing interest, as if this was a routine he went through several times a day.

He might have been losing interest. I wasn't.

I'd never heard of Saumlaki Station, but I'd certainly heard of Schedar sector. Schedar was a K supergiant out toward the edge of the Local Bubble. It defined one of the seventy-odd navigational sectors across the whole Bubble.

Did I mention the Bubble already?

YOU KNOW HOW the Milky Way Galaxy looks; you've seen it a thousand times, in paintings and computer simulations. A bright central bulge at the galactic core, with lazily curved spiral arms flung out from that hub, each arm composed of hundreds of billions of stars, ranging from the dimmest, slow-burning dwarfs to the hottest supergiants teetering on the edge of supernova extinction.

Now zoom in on one arm of the Milky Way. There's the sun, orange-yellow, about two-thirds out from the centre of the galaxy. Lanes and folds of dust swaddle the sun out to distances of tens of thousands of light-years. Yet the sun itself is sitting right in the middle of a four-hundred-light-year-wide hole in the dust, a bubble in which the density is about a twentieth of its average value.

That's the Local Bubble. It's as if God blew a hole in the dust just for us.

Except, of course, it wasn't God. It was a supernova, about a million years ago.

Look further out, and there are more bubbles, their walls intersecting and merging, forming a vast froth-like structure tens of thousands of light-years across. There are the structures of Loop I and Loop II and the Lindblad Ring. There are even superdense knots where the dust is almost too thick to be seen through at all. Black cauls like the Taurus or Rho-Ophiuchi dark clouds, or the Aquila Rift itself.

Lying outside the Local Bubble, the Rift is the furthest point in the galaxy we've ever travelled to. It's not a question of endurance or nerve. There simply isn't a way to get beyond it, at least not within the faster-than-light network of the aperture links. The rabbit-warren of possible routes just doesn't reach any further. Most destinations—including most of those on the *Blue Goose*'s itinerary—didn't even get you beyond the Local Bubble.

For us, it didn't matter. There's still a lot of commerce you can do within a hundred light-years of Earth. But Schedar was right on the periphery of the Bubble, where dust density began to ramp up to normal galactic levels, two hundred and twenty-eight light-years from Mother Earth.

Again: not good.

"I know this is a shock for you," another voice said. "But it's not as bad as you think it is."

‖

I LOOKED AT the woman who had just spoken. Medium height, the kind of face they called 'elfin', with slanted, ash-gray eyes and a bob of shoulder-length, chrome-white hair.

The face achingly familiar.

"It isn't?"

"I wouldn't say so, Thom." She smiled. "After all, it's given us the chance to catch up on old times, hasn't it?"

"Greta?" I asked, disbelievingly.

She nodded. "For my sins."

"My God. It is you, isn't it?"

"I wasn't sure you'd recognize me. Especially after all this time."

"You didn't have much trouble recognizing me."

"I didn't have to. The moment you popped out we picked up your recovery transponder. Told us the name of your ship, who owned her, who was flying it, what you were carrying, where you were supposed to be headed. When I heard it was you, I made sure I was part of the reception team. But don't worry. It's not like you've changed all that much."

"Well, you haven't either," I said.

It wasn't quite true. But who honestly wants to hear that they look about ten years older than the last time you saw them, even if they still don't look all that bad with it? I thought about how she had looked naked, memories that I'd kept buried for a decade spooling into daylight. It shamed me that they were still so vivid, as if some furtive part of my subconscious had been secretly hoarding them through years of marriage and fidelity.

Greta half-smiled. It was as if she knew exactly what I was thinking.

"You were never a good liar, Thom."

"Yeah. Guess I need some practice."

There was an awkward silence. Neither of us seemed to know what to say next. While we hesitated the others floated around us, saying nothing.

"Well," I said. "Who'd have guessed we'd end up meeting like this?"

Greta nodded and offered the palms of her hands in a kind of apology.

"I'm just sorry we aren't meeting under better circumstances," she said. "But if it's any consolation, what happened wasn't at all your fault.

We checked your syntax, and there wasn't a mistake. It's just that now and then the system throws a glitch."

"Funny how no one likes to talk about that very much," I said.

"Could have been worse, Thom. I remember what you used to tell me about space travel."

"Yeah? Which particular pearl of wisdom would that have been?"

"If you're in a position to moan about a situation, you've no right to be moaning."

"Christ. Did I actually say that?"

"Mm. And I bet you're regretting it now. But look, it really isn't that bad. You're only twenty days off-schedule." Greta nodded toward the man who had the bad teeth. "Kolding says you'll only need a day of damage repair before you can move off again, and then another twenty, twenty-five days before you reach your destination, depending on routing patterns. That's less than six weeks. So you lose the bonus on this one. Big deal. You're all in good shape, and your ship only needs a little work. Why don't you just bite the bullet and sign the repair paperwork?"

"I'm not looking forward to another twenty days in the surge tank. There's something else, as well."

"Which is?"

I was about to tell her about Katerina, how she'd have been expecting me back already.

Instead I said: "I'm worried about the others. Suzy and Ray. They've got families expecting them. They'll be worried."

"I understand," Greta said. "Suzy and Ray. They're still asleep, aren't they? Still in their surge tanks?"

"Yes," I said, guardedly.

"Keep them that way until you're on your way." Greta smiled. "There's no sense worrying them about their families, either. It's kinder."

"If you say so."

"Trust me on this one, Thom. This isn't the first time I've handled this kind of situation. Doubt it'll be the last, either."

I STAYED IN a hotel overnight, in another part of Saumlaki. The hotel was an echoing, multilevel prefab structure, sunk deep into bedrock. It must have had a capacity for hundreds of guests, but at the moment only a handful of the rooms seemed to be occupied. I slept fitfully and got up early. In the atrium, I saw a bib-capped worker in rubber gloves removing diseased carp from a small ornamental pond. Watching him pick out the ailing, metallic-orange fish, I had a flash of déjà vu. What was it about dismal hotels and dying carp?

Before breakfast—bleakly alert, even though I didn't really feel as if I'd had a good night's sleep—I visited Kolding and got a fresh update on the repair schedule.

"Two, three days," he said.

"It was a day last night."

Kolding shrugged. "You've got a problem with the service, find someone else to fix your ship."

Then he stuck his little finger into the corner of his mouth and began to dig between his teeth.

"Nice to see someone who really enjoys his work," I said.

I left Kolding before my mood worsened too much, making my way to a different part of the station.

Greta had suggested we meet for breakfast and catch up on old times. She was there when I arrived, sitting at a table in an "outdoor" terrace, under a red-and-white-striped canopy, sipping orange juice. Above us was a dome several hundred metres wide, projecting a cloudless holographic sky. It had the hard, enamelled blue of midsummer.

"How's the hotel?" she asked after I'd ordered a coffee from the waiter.

"Not bad. No one seems very keen on conversation, though. Is it me or does that place have all the cheery ambience of a sinking ocean liner?"

"It's just this place," Greta said. "Everyone who comes here is pissed off about it. Either they got transferred here and they're pissed off about *that*, or they ended up here by a routing error and they're pissed off about that instead. Take your pick."

"No one's happy?"

"Only the ones who know they're getting out of here soon."

"Would that include you?"

"No," she said. "I'm more or less stuck here. But I'm OK about it. I guess I'm the exception that proves the rule."

The waiters were glass mannequins, the kind that had been fashionable in the core worlds about twenty years ago. One of them placed a croissant in front of me, then poured scalding black coffee into my cup.

"Well, it's good to see you," I said.

"You too, Thom." Greta finished her orange juice and then took a corner of my croissant for herself, without asking. "I heard you got married."

"Yes."

"Well? Aren't you going to tell me about her?"

I drank some of my coffee. "Her name's Katerina."

"Nice name."

"She works in the department of bioremediation on Kagawa."

"Kids?" Greta asked.

"Not yet. It wouldn't be easy, the amount of time we both spend away from home."

"Mm." She had a mouthful of croissant. "But one day you might think about it."

"Nothing's ruled out," I said. As flattered as I was that she was taking such an interest in me, the surgical precision of her questions left me slightly uncomfortable. There was no thrust and parry; no fishing for information. That kind of directness unnerved. But at least it allowed me to ask the same questions. "What about you, then?"

"Nothing very exciting. I got married a year or so after I last saw you. A man called Marcel."

"Marcel," I said, ruminatively, as if the name had cosmic significance. "Well, I'm happy for you. I take it he's here, too?"

"No. Our work took us in different directions. We're still married, but..." Greta left the sentence hanging.

"It can't be easy," I said.

"If it was meant to work, we'd have found a way. Anyway, don't feel too sorry for either of us. We've both got our work. I wouldn't say I was any less happy than the last time we met."

"Well, that's good," I said.

Greta leaned over and touched my hand. Her fingernails were mid-night black with a blue sheen.

"Look. This is really presumptuous of me. It's one thing asking to meet up for breakfast. It would have been rude not to. But how would you like to meet again later? It's really nice to eat here in the evening. They turn down the lights. The view through the dome is really something."

I looked up into that endless holographic sky.

"I thought it was faked."

"Oh, it is," she said. "But don't let that spoil it for you."

I SETTLED IN front of the camera and started speaking.

"Katerina," I said. "Hello. I hope you're all right. By now I hope someone from the company will have been in touch. If they haven't, I'm pretty sure you'll have made your own enquiries. I'm not sure what they told you, but I promise you that we're safe and sound and that we're coming home. I'm calling from somewhere called Saumlaki Station, a repair facility on the edge of Schedar sector. It's not much to look at: just a warren of tunnels and centrifuges dug into a pitch-black, D-type asteroid, about half a light-year from the nearest star. The only reason it's here at all is because there happens to be an aperture next door. That's how we got here in the first place. Somehow or other *Blue Goose* took a wrong turn in the network, what they call a routing error. The *Goose* came in last night, local time, and I've been in a hotel since then. I didn't call last night because I was too tired and disorientated after coming out of the tank, and I didn't know how long we were going to be here. Seemed better to wait until morning, when we'd have a better idea of the damage to the ship. It's nothing serious—just a few bits and pieces buckled during the transit—but it means we're going to be here for another couple of days. Kolding—he's the repair chief—says three at the most. By the time we get back on course, however, we'll be about forty days behind schedule."

I paused, eyeing the incrementing cost indicator. Before I sat down in the booth I always had an eloquent and economical speech queued up in my head, one that conveyed exactly what needed to be said, with the measure and grace of a soliloquy. But my mind always dried up as soon as I opened my mouth, and instead of an actor I ended up sounding like a small-time thief, concocting some fumbling alibi in the presence of quick-witted interrogators.

I smiled awkwardly and continued: "It kills me to think this message is going to take so long to get to you. But if there's a silver lining it's that I won't be far behind it. By the time you get this, I should be home only a couple of days later. So don't waste money replying to this, because by the time you get it I'll already have left Saumlaki Station. Just stay where you are and I promise I'll be home soon."

That was it. There was nothing more I needed to say, other than: "I miss you." Delivered after a moment's pause, I meant it to sound emphatic. But when I replayed the recording it sounded more like an afterthought.

I could have recorded it again, but I doubted that I would have been any happier. Instead I just committed the existing message for transmission and wondered how long it would have to wait before going on its way. Since it seemed unlikely that there was a vast flow of commerce in and out of Saumlaki, our ship might be the first suitable outbound vessel.

I emerged from the booth. For some reason I felt guilty, as if I had been in some way neglectful. It took me a while before I realized what was playing on my mind. I'd told Katerina about Saumlaki Station. I'd even told her about Kolding and the damage to the *Blue Goose*. But I hadn't told her about Greta.

IT'S NOT WORKING with Suzy.

She's too smart, too well attuned to the physiological correlatives of surge tank immersion. I can give her all the reassurances in the world, but she knows she's been under too long for this to be anything other than a truly epic screw-up. She knows that we aren't just talking weeks or even months of delay here. Every nerve in her body is screaming that message into her skull.

"I had dreams," she says, when the grogginess fades.

"What kind?"

"Dreams that I kept waking. Dreams that you were pulling me out of the surge tank. You and someone else."

I do my best to smile. I'm alone, but Greta isn't far away. The hypodermic's in my pocket now.

"I always get bad dreams coming out of the tank," I say.

"These felt real. Your story kept changing, but you kept telling me we were somewhere...that we'd gone a little off course, but that it was nothing to worry about."

So much for Greta's reassurance that Suzy will remember nothing after our aborted efforts at waking her. Seems that her short-term memory isn't quite as fallible as we'd like.

"It's funny you should say that," I tell her. "Because, actually, we are a little off course."

She's sharper with every breath. Suzy was always the best of us at coming out of the tank.

"Tell me how far, Thom."

"Farther than I'd like."

She balls her fists. I can't tell if it's aggression, or some lingering neuromuscular effect of her time in the tank. "How far? Beyond the Bubble?"

"Beyond the Bubble, yes."

Her voice grows small and childlike.

"Tell me, Thom. Are we out beyond the Rift?"

I can hear the fear. I understand what she's going through. It's the nightmare that all ship crews live with on every trip. That something will go wrong with the routing, something so severe that they'll end up on the very edge of the network. That they'll end up so far from home that getting back will take years, not months. And that, of course, years will have already passed, even before they begin the return trip.

That loved ones will be years older when they reach home.

If they're still there. If they still remember you, or want to remember. If they're still recognizable, or alive.

Beyond the Aquila Rift. It's shorthand for the trip no one ever hopes to make by accident. The one that will screw up the rest of your life, the one that creates the ghosts you see haunting the shadows of company bars across the whole Bubble. Men and women ripped out of time, cut adrift from families and lovers by an accident of an alien technology we use but barely comprehend.

"Yes," I say. "We're beyond the Rift."

Suzy screams, knitting her face into a mask of anger and denial. My hand is cold around the hypodermic. I consider using it.

A NEW REPAIR estimate from Kolding. Five, six days.

This time I didn't even argue. I just shrugged and walked out, and wondered how long it would be next time.

That evening I sat down at the same table where Greta and I had met over breakfast. The dining area had been well lit before, but now the only illumination came from the table lamps and the subdued lighting panels set into the paving. In the distance, a glass mannequin cycled from empty table to empty table, playing "Asturias" on a glass guitar. There were no other patrons dining tonight.

I didn't have long to wait for Greta.

"I'm sorry I'm late, Thom."

I turned to her as she approached the table. I liked the way she walked in the low gravity of the station, the way the subdued lighting traced the arc of her hips and waist. She eased into her seat and leaned toward me in the manner of a conspirator. The lamp on the table threw red shadows and gold highlights across her face. It took ten years off her age.

"You aren't late," I said. "And anyway, I had the view."

"It's an improvement, isn't it?"

"That wouldn't be saying much," I said with a smile. "But yes, it's definitely an improvement."

"I could sit out here all night and just look at it. In fact sometimes that's exactly what I do. Just me and a bottle of wine."

"I don't blame you."

Instead of the holographic blue, the dome was now full of stars. It was like no view I'd ever seen from another station or ship. There were furious blue-white stars embedded in what looked like sheets of velvet. There were hard gold gems and soft red smears, like finger smears in pastel. There were streams and currents of fainter stars, like a myriad neon fish caught in a snapshot of frozen motion. There were vast billowing backdrops of red and green cloud, veined and flawed by filaments of cool black.

There were bluffs and promontories of ochre dust, so rich in three-dimensional structure that they resembled an exuberant impasto of oil colours; contours light-years thick laid on with a trowel. Red or pink stars burned through the dust like lanterns. Orphaned worlds were caught erupting from the towers, little sperm-like shapes trailing viscera of dust. Here and there I saw the tiny eyelike knots of birthing solar systems. There were pulsars, flashing on and off like navigation beacons, their differing rhythms seeming to set a stately tempo for the entire scene, like a deathly slow waltz. There seemed too much detail for one view, an overwhelming abundance of richness, and yet no matter which direction I looked, there was yet more to see, as if the dome sensed my attention and concentrated its efforts on the spot where my gaze was directed. For a moment I felt a lurching sense of dizziness, and—though I tried to stop it before I made a fool of myself—I found myself grasping the side of the table, as if to prevent myself from falling into the infinite depths of the view.

"Yes, it has that effect on people," Greta said.

"It's beautiful," I said.

"Do you mean beautiful, or terrifying?"

I realized I wasn't sure. "It's big," was all I could offer.

"Of course, it's faked," Greta said, her voice soft now that she was leaning closer. "The glass in the dome is smart. It exaggerates the brightness of the stars, so that the human eye registers the differences between them. Otherwise the colours aren't unrealistic. Everything else you see is also pretty accurate, if you accept that certain frequencies have been shifted into the visible band, and the scale of certain structures has been adjusted." She pointed out features for my edification. "That's the edge of the Taurus Dark Cloud, with the Pleiades just poking out. That's a filament of the Local Bubble. You see that open cluster?"

She waited for me to answer. "Yes," I said.

"That's the Hyades. Over there you've got Betelgeuse and Bellatrix."

"I'm impressed."

"You should be. It cost a lot of money." She leaned back a bit, so that the shadows dropped across her face again. "Are you all right, Thom? You seem a bit distracted."

I sighed.

"I just got another prognosis from your friend Kolding. That's enough to put a dent in anyone's day."

"I'm sorry about that."

"There's something else, too," I said. "Something that's been bothering me since I came out of the tank."

A mannequin came to take our order. I let Greta choose for me.

"You can talk to me about it, whatever it is," she said, when the mannequin had gone.

"It isn't easy."

"Something personal, then? Is it about Katerina?" She bit her tongue. "No, sorry. I shouldn't have said that."

"It's not about Katerina. Not exactly, anyway." But even as I said it, I knew that in a sense it *was* about Katerina, and how long it was going to be before we saw each other again.

"Go on, Thom."

"This is going to sound silly. But I wonder if everyone's being straight with me. It's not just Kolding. It's you as well. When I came out of that tank I felt the same way I felt when I'd been out to the Rift. Worse, if anything. I felt like I'd been in the tank for a long, long time."

"It feels that way sometimes."

"I know the difference, Greta. Trust me on this."

"So what are you saying?"

The problem was that I wasn't really sure. It was one thing to feel a vague sense of unease about how long I'd been in the tank. It was another to come out and accuse my host of lying. Especially when she had been so hospitable.

"Is there any reason you'd lie to me?"

"Come off it, Thom. What kind of a question is that?"

As soon as I had said it, it sounded absurd and offensive to me as well. I wished I could reverse time and start again, ignoring my misgivings.

"I'm sorry," I said. "Stupid. Just put it down to messed-up biorhythms, or something."

She reached across the table and took my hand, as she had done at breakfast. This time she continued to hold it.

"You really feel wrong, don't you?"

"Kolding's games aren't helping, that's for sure." The waiter brought our wine, setting it down, the bottle chinking against his delicately articulated glass fingers. The mannequin poured two glasses and I sampled mine. "Maybe if I had someone else from my crew to bitch about it all with, I wouldn't feel so bad. I know you said we shouldn't wake Suzy and Ray, but that was before a one-day stopover turned into a week."

Greta shrugged. "If you want to wake them, no one's going to stop you. But don't think about ship business now. Let's not spoil a perfect evening."

I looked up at the starscape. It was heightened, with the mad shimmering intensity of a Van Gogh nightscape.

It made one feel drunk and ecstatic just to look at it.

"What could possibly spoil it?" I asked.

WHAT HAPPENED IS that I drank too much wine and ended up sleeping with Greta. I'm not sure how much of a part the wine played in it for her. If her relationship with Marcel was in as much trouble as she'd made out, then obviously she had less to lose than I did. Yes, that made it all right, didn't it? She the seductress, her own marriage a wreck, me the hapless victim. I'd lapsed, yes, but it wasn't really my fault. I'd been alone, far from home, emotionally fragile, and she had exploited me. She had softened me up with a romantic meal, her trap already sprung.

Except all that was self-justifying bullshit, wasn't it? If my own marriage was in such great shape, why had I failed to mention Greta when I called home? At the time, I'd justified that omission as an act of kindness toward my wife. Katerina didn't know that Greta and I had ever been a couple. But why worry Katerina by mentioning another woman, even if I pretended that we'd never met before?

Except—now—I could see that I'd failed to mention Greta for another reason entirely. Because in the back of my mind, even then, there had been the possibility that we might end up sleeping together.

I was already covering myself when I called Katerina. Already making sure there wouldn't be any awkward questions when I got home. As if I not only knew what was going to happen but secretly yearned for it.

The only problem was that Greta had something else in mind.

"THOM," GRETA SAID, nudging me toward wakefulness. She was lying naked next to me, leaning on one elbow, with the sheets crumpled down around her hips. The light in her room turned her into an abstraction of milky blue curves and deep violet shadows. With one black-nailed finger she traced a line down my chest and said: "There's something you need to know."

"What?" I asked.

"I lied. Kolding lied. We all lied."

I was too drowsy for her words to have much more than a vaguely troubling effect. All I could say, again, was: "What?"

"You're not in Saumlaki Station. You're not in Schedar sector."

I started waking up properly. "Say that again."

"The routing error was more severe than you were led to believe. It took you far beyond the Local Bubble."

I groped for anger, even resentment, but all I felt was a dizzying sensation of falling. "How far out?"

"Further than you thought possible."

The next question was obvious.

"Beyond the Rift?"

"Yes," she said, with the faintest of smiles, as if humouring me in a game whose rules and objectives she found ultimately demeaning. "Beyond the Aquila Rift. A long, long way beyond it."

"I need to know, Greta."

She pushed herself from the bed, reached for a gown. "Then get dressed. I'll show you."

I FOLLOWED GRETA in a daze.

She took me to the dome again. It was dark, just as it had been the night before, with only the lamp-lit tables to act as beacons. I supposed that the illumination throughout Saumlaki Station (or wherever this was) was at the whim of its occupants, and didn't necessarily have to follow any recognizable diurnal cycle. Nonetheless it was still unsettling to find it changed so arbitrarily. Even if Greta had the authority to turn out the lights when she wanted to, didn't anyone else object?

But I didn't see anyone else *to* object. There was no one else around; only a glass mannequin standing at attention with a napkin over one arm.

She sat us at a table. "Do you want a drink, Thom?"

"No, thanks. For some reason I'm not quite in the mood."

She touched my wrist. "Don't hate me for lying to you. It was done out of kindness. I couldn't break the truth to you in one go."

Sharply I withdrew my hand. "Shouldn't I be the judge of that? So what is the truth, exactly?"

"It's not good, Thom."

"Tell me, then I'll decide."

I didn't see her do anything, but suddenly the dome was filled with stars again, just as it had been the night before.

The view lurched, zooming outward. Stars flowed by from all sides, like white sleet. Nebulae ghosted past in spectral wisps. The sense of motion was so compelling that I found myself gripping the table, seized by vertigo.

"Easy, Thom," Greta whispered.

The view lurched, swerved, contracted. A solid wall of gas slammed past. Now, suddenly, I had the sense that we were outside something— that we had punched beyond some containing sphere, defined only in vague arcs and knots of curdled gas, where the interstellar gas density increased sharply.

Of course. It was obvious. We were beyond the Local Bubble.

And we were still receding. I watched the Bubble itself contract, becoming just one member in the larger froth of voids. Instead of individual stars, I saw only smudges and motes, aggregations of hundreds of thousands of suns. It was like pulling back from a close-up view of a forest. I could still see clearings, but the individual trees had vanished into an amorphous mass.

We kept pulling back. Then the expansion slowed and froze. I could still make out the Local Bubble, but only because I had been concentrating on it all the way out. Otherwise, there was nothing to distinguish it from the dozens of surrounding voids.

"Is that how far out we've come?" I asked.

Greta shook her head. "Let me show you something."

Again, she did nothing that I was aware of. But the Bubble I had been looking at was suddenly filled with a skein of red lines, like a child's scribble.

"Aperture connections," I said.

As shocked as I was by the fact that she had lied to me—and as fearful as I was about what the truth might hold—I couldn't turn off the professional part of me, the part that took pride in recognizing such things.

Greta nodded. "Those are the main commerce routes, the well-mapped connections between large colonies and major trading hubs. Now I'll add all mapped connections, including those that have only ever been traversed by accident."

The scribble did not change dramatically. It gained a few more wild loops and hairpins, including one that reached beyond the wall of the Bubble to touch the sunward end of the Aquila Rift. One or two other additions pierced the wall in different directions, but none of them reached as far as the Rift.

"Where are we?"

"We're at one end of one of those connections. You can't see it because it's pointing directly toward you." She smiled slightly. "I needed to establish the scale that we're dealing with. How wide is the Local Bubble, Thom? Four hundred light-years, give or take?"

My patience was wearing thin. But I was still curious.

"About right."

"And while I know that aperture travel times vary from point to point, with factors depending on network topology and syntax optimization, isn't it the case that the average speed is about one thousand times faster than light?"

"Give or take."

"So a journey from one side of the Bubble might take—what, half a year? Say five or six months? A year to the Aquila Rift?"

"You know that already, Greta. We both know it."

"All right. Then consider this." And the view contracted again, the Bubble dwindling, a succession of overlaying structures concealing it, darkness coming into view on either side, and then the familiar spiral swirl of the Milky Way Galaxy looming large.

Hundreds of billions of stars, packed together into foaming white lanes of sea spume.

"This is the view," Greta said. "Enhanced of course, brightened and filtered for human consumption—but if you had eyes with near-perfect quantum efficiency, and if they happened to be about a metre wide, this is more or less what you'd see if you stepped outside the station."

"I don't believe you."

What I meant was I didn't *want* to believe her.

"Get used to it, Thom. You're a long way out. The station's orbiting a brown dwarf star in the Large Magellanic Cloud. You're one hundred and fifty thousand light-years from home."

"No," I said, my voice little more than a moan of abject, childlike denial.

"You felt as though you'd spent a long time in the tank. You were dead right. Subjective time? I don't know. Years, easily. Maybe a decade. But objective time—the time that passed back home—is a lot clearer. It took *Blue Goose* one hundred and fifty years to reach us. Even if you turned back now, you'd have been away for three hundred years, Thom."

"Katerina," I said, her name like an invocation.

"Katerina's dead," Greta told me. "She's already been dead a century."

HOW DO YOU adjust to something like that? The answer is that you can't count on adjusting to it at all. Not everyone does. Greta told me that she had seen just about every possible reaction in the spectrum, and the one thing she had learned was that it was next to impossible to predict how a given individual would take the news. She had seen people adjust to the revelation with little more than a world-weary shrug, as if this were merely the latest in a line of galling surprises life had thrown at them, no worse in its way than illness or bereavement or any number of personal setbacks. She had seen others walk away and kill themselves half an hour later.

But the majority, she said, did eventually come to some kind of accommodation with the truth, however faltering and painful the process.

"Trust me, Thom," she said. "I know you now. I know you have the emotional strength to get through this. I know you can learn to live with it."

"Why didn't you tell me straight away, as soon as I came out of the tank?"

"Because I didn't know if you were going to be able to take it."

"You waited until after you knew I had a wife."

"No," Greta said. "I waited until after we'd made love. Because then I knew Katerina couldn't mean that much to you."

"Fuck you."

"Fuck me? Yes, you did. That's the point."

I wanted to strike out against her. But what I was angry at was not her insinuation but the cold-hearted truth of it. She was right, and I knew it. I just didn't want to deal with that, any more than I wanted to deal with the here and now.

I waited for the anger to subside.

"You say we're not the first?" I said.

"No. We were the first, I suppose—the ship I came in. Luckily it was well equipped. After the routing error, we had enough supplies to set up a self-sustaining station on the nearest rock. We knew there was no going back, but at least we could make some kind of life for ourselves here."

"And after that?"

"We had enough to do just keeping ourselves alive, the first few years. But then another ship came through the aperture. Damaged, drifting, much like *Blue Goose*. We hauled her in, warmed her crew, broke the news to them."

"How'd they take it?"

"About as well as you'd expect." Greta laughed hollowly to herself. "A couple of them went mad. Another killed herself. But at least a dozen of them are still here. In all honesty, it was good for us that another ship came through. Not just because they had supplies we could use, but because it helped us to help them. Took our minds off our own self-pity. It made us realize how far we'd come, and how much help these newcomers needed to make the same transition. That wasn't the last ship, either. We've gone through the same process with eight or nine others, since then." Greta looked at me, her head cocked against her hand. "There's a thought for you, Thom."

"There is?"

She nodded. "It's difficult for you now, I know. And it'll be difficult for you for some time to come. But it can help to have someone else to care about. It can smooth the transition."

"Like who?" I asked.

"Like one of your other crew members," Greta said. "You could try waking one of them, now."

GRETA'S WITH ME when I pull Suzy out of the surge tank.

"Why her?" Greta asks.

"Because I want her out first," I say, wondering if Greta's jealous. I don't blame her: Suzy's beautiful, but she's also smart. There isn't a better syntax runner in Ashanti Industrial.

"What happened?" Suzy asks, when she's over the grogginess. "Did we make it back?"

I ask her to tell me the last thing she remembers.

"Customs," Suzy says. "Those pricks on Arkangel."

"And after that? Anything else? The runes? Do you remember casting them?"

"No," she says, then picks up something in my voice. The fact that I might not be telling the truth, or telling her all she needs to know. "Thom. I'll ask you again. Did we make it back?"

A minute later we're putting Suzy back into the tank.

It hasn't worked first time. Maybe next try.

BUT IT KEPT not working with Suzy. She was always cleverer and quicker than me; she always had been. As soon as she came out of the tank, she knew that we'd come a lot further than Schedar sector. She was always ahead of my lies and excuses.

"It was different when it happened to me," I told Greta, when we were lying next to each other again, days later, with Suzy still in the tank.

"I had all the nagging doubts she has, I think. But as soon as I saw you standing there, I forgot all about that stuff."

Greta nodded. Her hair fell across her face in dishevelled, sleep-matted curtains. She had a strand of it between her lips.

"It helped, seeing a friendly face?"

"Took my mind off the problem, that's for sure."

"You'll get there in the end," she said. "Anyway, from Suzy's point of view, aren't you a friendly face as well?"

"Maybe," I said. "But she'd been expecting me. You were the last person in the world I expected to see standing there."

Greta touched her knuckle against the side of my face. Her smooth skin slid against stubble. "It's getting easier for you, isn't it?"

"I don't know," I said.

"You're a strong man, Thom. I knew you'd come through this."

"I haven't come through it yet," I said. I felt like a tightrope walker halfway across Niagara Falls. It was a miracle I'd made it as far as I had. But that didn't mean I was home and dry.

Still, Greta was right. There was hope. I'd felt no crushing spasms of grief over Katerina's death, or enforced absence, or however you wanted to put it. All I felt was a bittersweet regret, the way one might feel about a broken heirloom or long-lost pet. I felt no animosity toward Katerina, and I was sorry that I would never see her again. But I was sorry about not seeing a lot of things. Maybe it would become worse in the days ahead. Maybe I was just postponing a breakdown.

I didn't think so.

In the meantime, I continued trying to find a way to deal with Suzy. She had become a puzzle that I couldn't leave unsolved. I could have just woken her up and let her deal with the news as best as she could, but that seemed cruel and unsatisfactory. Greta had broken it to me gently, giving me time to settle into my new surroundings and take that necessary step away from Katerina. When she finally broke the news, as shocking as it was, it didn't shatter me. I'd already been primed for it, the sting taken out of the surprise. Sleeping with Greta obviously helped. I couldn't offer Suzy the same solace, but I was sure that there was a way for us to coax Suzy to the same state of near-acceptance.

Time after time we woke her and tried a different approach. Greta said there was a window of a few minutes before the events she was experiencing began to transfer into long-term memory. If we knocked her out, the buffer of memories in short-term storage was wiped before it ever crossed the hippocampus into long-term recall. Within that window, we could wake her up as many times as we liked, trying endless permutations of the revival scenario.

At least that was what Greta told me.

"We can't keep doing this indefinitely," I said.

"Why not?"

"Isn't she going to remember *something*?"

Greta shrugged. "Maybe. But I doubt that she'll attach any significance to those memories. Haven't you ever had vague feelings of déjà vu coming out of the surge tank?"

"Sometimes," I admitted.

"Then don't sweat about it. She'll be all right. I promise you."

"Perhaps we should just keep her awake, after all."

"That would be cruel."

"It's cruel to keep waking her up and shutting her down, like a toy doll."

There was a catch in her voice when she answered me.

"Keep at it, Thom. I'm sure you're close to finding a way, in the end. It's helping you, focusing on Suzy. I always knew it would."

I started to say something, but Greta pressed a finger to my lips.

GRETA WAS RIGHT about Suzy. The challenge helped me, taking my mind off my own predicament. I remembered what Greta had said about dealing with other crews in the same situation, before *Blue Goose* put in. Clearly she had learned many psychological tricks: gambits and short cuts to assist the transition to mental well-being. I felt a slight resentment at being manipulated so effectively. But at the same time I couldn't deny that worrying about another human being had helped me with my own adjustment. When, days later, I stepped back from the immediate problem of Suzy, I realized that something was different. I didn't feel far from home. I felt, in an odd way, privileged. I'd come further than almost anyone in history. I was still alive, and there were still people around to provide love and partnership and a web of social relations. Not just Greta, but all the other unlucky souls who had ended up at the station.

If anything, there appeared to be more of them than when I had first arrived. The corridors—sparsely populated at first—were increasingly busy, and when we ate under the dome—under the Milky Way—we were not the only diners. I studied their lamp-lit faces, comforted by their vague familiarity, wondering what kinds of stories they had to tell; where they'd come from, who they had left behind, how they had adjusted to life here. There was time enough to get to know them all. And the place would never become boring, for at any time—as Greta had intimated— we could always expect another lost ship to drop through the aperture. Tragedy for the crew, but fresh challenges, fresh faces, fresh news from home, for us.

All in all, it wasn't really so bad.

Then it clicked.

It was the man cleaning out the fish that did it, in the lobby of the hotel. It wasn't just the familiarity of the process, but the man himself.

I'd seen him before. Another pond full of diseased carp. Another hotel.

Then I remembered Kolding's bad teeth, and recalled how they'd reminded me of another man I'd met long before. Except it wasn't another man at all. Different name, different context, but everything else the same. And when I looked at the other diners, really looked at them, there was no one I couldn't swear I hadn't seen before. No single face that hit me with the force of utter unfamiliarity.

Which left Greta.

I said to her, over wine, under the Milky Way: "Nothing here is real, is it?"

She looked at me with infinite sadness and shook her head.

"What about Suzy?" I asked her.

"Suzy's dead. Ray is dead. They died in their surge tanks."

"How? Why them, and not me?"

"Something about particles of paint blocking intake filters. Not enough to make a difference over short distances, but enough to kill them on the trip out here."

I think some part of me had always suspected. It felt less like shock than brutal disappointment.

"But Suzy seemed so real," I said. "Even the way she had doubts about how long she'd been in the tank...even the way she remembered previous attempts to wake her."

The glass mannequin approached our table. Greta waved him away.

"I made her convincing, the way she would have acted."

"You *made* her?"

"You're not really awake, Thom. You're being fed data. This entire station is being simulated."

I sipped my wine. I expected it to taste suddenly thin and synthetic, but it still tasted like pretty good wine.

"Then I'm dead as well?"

"No. You're alive. Still in your surge tank. But I haven't brought you to full consciousness yet."

"All right. The truth this time. I can take it. How much is real? Does the station exist? Are we really as far out as you said?"

"Yes," she said. "The station exists, just as I said it does. It just looks... different. And it *is* in the Large Magellanic Cloud, and it *is* orbiting a brown dwarf star."

"Can you show me the station as it is?"

"I could. But I don't think you're ready for it. I think you'd find it difficult to adjust."

I couldn't help laughing. "Even after what I've already adjusted to?"

"You've only made half the journey, Thom."

"But you made it."

"I did, Thom. But for me it was different." Greta smiled. "For me, everything was different."

Then she made the light show change again. None of the other diners appeared to notice as we began to zoom in toward the Milky Way, crashing toward the spiral, ramming through shoals of outlying stars and gas clouds. The familiar landscape of the Local Bubble loomed large.

The image froze, the Bubble one amongst many such structures.

Again it filled with the violent red scribble of the aperture network. But now the network wasn't the only one. It was merely one ball of red yarn amongst many, spaced out across tens of thousands of light-years. None of the scribbles touched each other, yet—in the way they were shaped, in the way they almost abutted against each other, it was possible to imagine that they had once been connected. They were like the shapes of continents on a world with tectonic drift.

"It used to span the galaxy," Greta said. "Then something happened. Something catastrophic, which I still don't understand. A shattering, into vastly smaller domains. Typically a few hundred light-years across."

"Who made it?"

"I don't know. No one knows. They probably aren't around any more. Maybe that was why it shattered, out of neglect."

"But we found it," I said. "The part of it near us still worked."

"All the disconnected elements still function," Greta said. "You can't cross from domain to domain, but otherwise the apertures work as they were designed to. Barring, of course, the occasional routing error."

"All right," I said. "If you can't cross from domain to domain, how did *Blue Goose* get this far out? We've come a lot further than a few hundred light-years."

"You're right. But then such a long-distance connection might have been engineered differently from the others. It appears that the links to the Magellanic Cloud were more resilient. When the domains shattered from each other, the connections reaching beyond the galaxy remained intact."

"In which case you *can* cross from domain to domain," I said. "But you have to come all the way out here first."

"The trouble is, not many want to continue the journey at this point. No one comes here deliberately, Thom."

"I still don't get it. What does it matter to me if there are other domains? Those regions of the galaxy are thousands of light-years from Earth, and without the apertures we'd have no way of reaching them. They don't matter. There's no one there to use them."

Greta's smile was coquettish, knowing.

"What makes you so certain?"

"Because if there were, wouldn't there be alien ships popping out of the aperture here? You've told me *Blue Goose* wasn't the first through. But our domain—the one in the Local Bubble—must be outnumbered hundreds to one by all the others. If there are alien cultures out there, each stumbling on their own local domain, why haven't any of them ever come through the aperture, the way we did?"

Again that smile. But this time it chilled my blood.

"What makes you think they haven't, Thom?"

I reached out and took her hand, the way she had taken mine. I took it without force, without malice, but with the assurance that this time I really, sincerely meant what I was about to say.

Her fingers tightened around mine.

"Show me," I said. "I want to see things as they really are. Not just the station. You as well."

Because by then I'd realized. Greta hadn't just lied to me about Suzy and Ray. She'd lied to me about the *Blue Goose* as well. Because we were not the latest human ship to come through.

We were the first.

"You want to see it?" she asked.

"Yes. All of it."

"You won't like it."

"I'll be the judge of that."

"All right, Thom. But understand this. I've been here before. I've done this a million times. I care for all the lost souls. And I know how it works. You won't be able to take the raw reality of what's happened to you. You'll shrivel away from it. You'll go mad, unless I substitute a calming fiction, a happy ending."

"Why tell me that now?"

"Because you don't have to see it. You can stop now, where you are, with an idea of the truth. An inkling. But you don't have to open your eyes."

"Do it," I said.

Greta shrugged. She poured herself another measure of wine, then made sure my own glass was charged.

"You asked for it," she said.

We were still holding hands, two lovers sharing an intimacy. Then everything changed.

It was just a flash, just a glimpse. Like the view of an unfamiliar room if you turn the lights on for an instant. Shapes and forms, relationships between things. I saw caverns, wormed-out and linked, and things moving through those caverns, bustling along with the frantic industry of moles or termites. The things were seldom alike, even in the most superficial sense. Some moved via propulsive waves of multiple clawed limbs. Some wriggled, smooth plaques of carapace grinding against the glassy rock of the tunnels.

The things moved between caves in which lay the hulks of ships, almost all too strange to describe.

And somewhere distant, somewhere near the heart of the rock, in a matriarchal chamber all of its own, something drummed out messages to its companions and helpers, stiffly articulated, antler-like forelimbs beating against stretched tympana of finely veined skin, something that had been waiting here for eternities, something that wanted nothing more than to care for the souls of the lost.

KATERINA'S WITH SUZY when they pull me out of the surge tank.

It's bad—one of the worst revivals I've ever gone through. I feel as if every vein in my body has been filled with finely powdered glass. For a moment, a long moment, even the idea of breathing seems insurmountably difficult, too hard, too painful even to contemplate.

But it passes, as it always passes.

After a while I can not only breathe, I can move and talk.

"Where—"

"Easy, Skip," Suzy says. She leans over the tank and starts unplugging me. I can't help but smile. Suzy's smart—there isn't a better syntax runner in Ashanti Industrial—but she's also beautiful. It's like being nursed by an angel.

I wonder if Katerina's jealous.

"Where are we?" I try again. "Feels like I was in that thing for an eternity. Did something go wrong?"

"Minor routing error," Suzy says. "We took some damage and they decided to wake me first. But don't sweat about it. At least we're in one piece."

Routing errors. You hear about them, but you hope they're never going to happen to you.

"What kind of delay?"

"Forty days. Sorry, Thom. Bang goes our bonus."

In anger, I hammer the side of the surge tank. But Katerina steps toward me and places a calming hand on my shoulder.

"It's all right," she says. "You're home and dry. That's all that matters."

I look at her and for a moment remember someone else, someone I haven't thought about in years. I almost remember her name, and then the moment passes.

I nod. "Home and dry."

MINLA'S FLOWERS

MISSION INTERRUPTED.

Even now, I still don't know quite what happened. The ship and I were in routine Waynet transit, all systems ticking over smoothly. I was deep in thought, a little drunk, rubbing clues together like a caveman trying to make fire with rocks, hoping for the spark that would point me towards The Gun, the one no one ever thinks I'm going to find, the one I know with every fibre of my existence is out there somewhere. I was imagining the reception I'd get when I returned to the Cohort with that prize, the slate of all my sins wiped clean when they saw that I'd actually found it, that it was real after all, and that finally we had something to use against the Huskers. In the pleasant mental haze brought on by the wine, it seemed likely that they'd forgive me anything.

Then it happened: a violent lurch that sent wine and glass flying across the cabin, a shriek from the ship's alarms as it went into panic-mode. I knew right away that this was no ordinary Way turbulence. The ship was tumbling badly, but I fought my way to the command deck and did what I could to bring her back under control. Seat-of-the-pants flying, the way Gallinule and I used to do it on Plenitude, when Plenitude still existed.

That was when I knew we were outside the Waynet, dumped back into the crushing slowness of normal space. The stars outside were stationary, their colours showing no suggestion of relativistic distortion.

"Damage?" I asked.

"How long have you got?" the ship snapped back.

I told it to ease off on the wisecracks and start giving me the bad news. And it most certainly was bad news. The precious syrinx was still functional—I touched it and felt the familiar tremble that indicated it was still sensing the nearby Waynet —but that was about the only flight-critical system that hadn't been buckled or blown or simply wiped out of existence by the unscheduled egress.

We were going to have to land and make repairs. For a few weeks or months—however long it took the ship to scavenge and process the raw materials it needed to fix itself—the search for my Gun would be on hold.

That didn't mean I was counting on a long stopover.

THE SHIP STILL had a slow tumble. Merlin squinted against hard white glare as the burning eye of a bright sun hove into view through the windows. It was white, but not killingly so. Probably a mid-sequence star, maybe a late F- or early G-type. He thought there was a hint of yellow. Had to be pretty close, too.

"Tell me where we are."

"It's called Calliope," *Tyrant* told him. "G-type. According to the last Cohort census the system contained fifteen planet-class bodies. There were five terrestrials, four of which were uninhabitable. The fifth—the furthest from Calliope—was supposedly colonised by humans in the early Flourishing."

Merlin glanced at the census data as it scrolled down the cabin wall. The planet in question was called Lecythus. It was a typical watery terrestrial, like a thousand others in his experience. It even had the almost-obligatory large single moon.

"Been a while, ship. What are the chances of anyone still being down there?"

"Difficult to say. A later Cohort flyby failed to make contact with the settlement, but that doesn't mean no one was alive. After the emergence of the Huskers, many planetary colonies went to great lengths to camouflage themselves against the aliens."

"So there could still be a welcoming committee."

"We'll see. With your permission, I'll use our remaining fuel to reach Lecythus. This will take some time. Would you like to sleep?"

Merlin looked back at the coffin-like slab of the frostwatch cabinet. He could skip over the days or weeks it would take to reach the planet, but that would mean subjecting himself to the intense unpleasantness of frostwatch revival. Merlin had never taken kindly to being woken from normal sleep, let alone the deep hibernation of frostwatch.

"Pass on that, I think. I've still got plenty of reading to catch up on."

Later—much later—*Tyrant* announced that they had reached orbit around Lecythus. "Would you like to see the view?" the ship asked, with a playful note in its voice.

Merlin scratched fatigue from his eyes. "You sound like you know something I don't."

Merlin was at first reassured by what he saw. There was blue ocean down there, swatches of green and brown land mass, large islands rather than any major continental masses, cyclonic swirls of water-vapour clouds. It didn't necessarily mean there were still people, but it was a lot more encouraging than finding a cratered, radioactive corpse of a world.

Then he looked again. Many of those green and brown swatches of land mass were surrounded by water, as his first glimpse had indicated. But some of them appeared to be floating above the ocean completely, casting shadows beneath them. His glance flicked to the horizon, where the atmosphere was compressed into a thin bow of pure indigo. He could see the foreshortened shapes of hovering land masses, turned nearly edge-on. The land masses appeared to be one or two kilometres thick, and they all appeared to be gently curved. Perhaps half were concave in shape, so their edges were slightly upturned. The edges were frosted white, like the peaks of mountain ranges. Some of the concave masses even had little lakes near their centres. The convex masses were all a scorched tawny grey in colour, devoid of water or vegetation, save for a cap of ice at their highest point. The largest shapes, convex or concave, must have been hundreds of kilometres wide. Merlin judged that there must have been at least ten kilometres of clear airspace under each piece. A third of the planet's surface was obscured by the floating shapes.

"Any idea what we're looking at here?" Merlin asked. "This doesn't look like anything in the census."

"I think they built an armoured sky around their world," the ship said. "And then something—very probably Husker-level ordnance—shattered that sky."

"No one could have survived that," Merlin said, feeling a rising tide of sadness. *Tyrant* was clever enough, but there were times—long times—when Merlin became acutely aware of the heartless machine lurking behind the personality. And then he felt very, very alone. Those were the hours when he would have done anything for companionship, including returning to the Cohort and the tribunal that undoubtedly awaited him.

"Someone does appear to have survived, Merlin."

He perked up. "Really?"

"It's unlikely to be a very advanced culture: no neutrino or gravimagnetic signatures, beyond those originating from the mechanisms that must still be active inside the sky pieces. But I did detect some very brief radio emissions."

"What language were they using? Main? Tradespeak? Anything else in the Cohort database?"

"They were using long beeps and short beeps. I'm afraid I didn't get the chance to determine the source of the transmission."

"Keep listening. I want to meet them."

"Don't raise your hopes. If there are people down there, they've been out of contact with the rest of humanity for a considerable number of millennia."

"I only want to stop for repairs. They can't begrudge me that, can they?"

"I suppose not."

Then something occurred to Merlin, something he realised he should have asked much earlier. "About the accident, ship. I take it you know why we were dumped out of the Waynet?"

"I've run a fault-check on the syrinx. There doesn't appear to be anything wrong with it."

"That's not an answer."

"I know." *Tyrant* sounded sullen. "I still don't have an explanation for what went wrong. And I don't like that any more than you do."

TYRANT **FELL INTO** the atmosphere of Lecythus. The transmissions had resumed, allowing the ship to pinpoint the origin to one of the larger airborne masses. Shortly afterwards, a second source began transmitting from another floating mass, half the size of the first, located three thousand kilometres to the west. The way the signals started and stopped suggested some kind of agonisingly slow communication via radio pulses, one that probably had nothing to do with Merlin's arrival.

"Tell me that's a code in our database," Merlin said.

"It isn't. And the code won't tell us much about their spoken language, I'm afraid."

Up close, the broken edges of the floating mass soared as tall as a cliff. They were a dark, streaked grey, infinitely less regular than they had appeared from space. The edge showed signs of weathering and erosion. There were wide ledges, dizzying promontories and cathedral-sized shadowed caves. Glinting in the low light of Calliope, ladders and walkways—impossibly thin and spindly scratches of metal—reached down from the icebound upper reaches, following zigzag trajectories that only took them a fraction of the way to the perilous lower lip, where the floating world curved back under itself.

Merlin made out the tiny moving forms of birdlike creatures, wheeling and orbiting in powerful thermals, some of them coming and going from roosts on the lower ledges.

"But that isn't a bird," *Tyrant* said, highlighting a larger moving shape.

Merlin felt an immediate pang of recognition as the image zoomed. It was an aircraft: a ludicrously fragile assemblage of canvas and wire. It had a crescent moon painted on both wings. There'd been a machine not much more advanced than that in the archive inside the Palace of Eternal Dusk, preserved across thirteen hundred years of family history. Merlin had even risked taking it outside once, to see for himself if he had the nerve to repeat his distant ancestor's brave crossing. He still remembered the sting of reprimand when he'd brought it back, nearly ruined.

This aircraft was even flimsier and slower. It was driven by a single chugging propeller rather than a battery of rocket-assisted turbines. It was following the rim of the land mass, slowly gaining altitude. Clearly it intended to make landfall. The air on Lecythus was thicker at sea level than on Plenitude, but the little machine must still have been very close to its safe operational ceiling. And yet it would have to climb even higher if it was to traverse the raised rim.

"Follow it," Merlin said. "Keep us astern by a clear two kilometres. And set hull to stealth."

Merlin's ship nosed in behind the struggling aircraft. He could see the single pilot now, goggled and helmeted within a crude-looking bubble canopy. The plane had reached ten kilometres, but it would need to double that to clear the upturned rim. Every hundred metres of altitude gained seemed to tax the aircraft to the limit, so that it climbed, levelled, climbed. It trailed sooty hyphens behind it. Merlin could imagine the sputtering protest from the little engine, the fear in the pilot's belly that the motor was going to stall at any moment.

That was when an airship hove around the edge of the visible cliff. Calliope's rays flared off the golden swell of its envelope. Beneath the long ribbed form was a tiny gondola, equipped with multiple engines on skeletal outriggers. The airship's nose began to turn, bringing another crescent moon emblem into view. The aircraft lined up with the airship, the two of them at about the same altitude. Merlin watched as some kind of net-like apparatus unfurled in slow motion from the belly of the gondola. The pilot gained further height, then cut the aircraft's engine. Powerless now, it followed a shallow glide path toward the net. Clearly, the airship was going to catch the aircraft and carry it over the rim. That must have been the only way for aircraft to arrive and depart from the hovering land mass.

Merlin watched with a sickened fascination. He'd occasionally had a presentiment when something was about to go wrong. Now he had that feeling again.

Some gust caught the airship. It began to drift out of the aircraft's glide path. The pilot tried to compensate—Merlin could see the play of light shift on the wings as they warped—but it was never going to be enough. Without power, the aircraft must have been cumbersome to steer. The engines on the gondola turned on their mountings, trying to shove the airship back into position.

Beyond the airship loomed the streaked grey vastness of the great cliff.

"Why did he cut the engines…" Merlin breathed to himself. Then, an instant later: "Can we catch up? Can we do something?"

"I'm afraid not. There simply isn't time."

Sickened, Merlin watched as the aircraft slid past the airship, missing the net by a hundred metres. A sooty smear erupted from the engine. The pilot must have been desperately trying to restart the motor. Moments later, Merlin watched as one wingtip grazed the side of the cliff and crumpled instantly, horribly. The aircraft dropped, dashing itself to splinters and shreds against the side of the cliff. There was no possibility that the pilot could have survived.

For a moment Merlin was numb. He was frozen, unsure what to do next. He'd been planning to land, but it seemed improper to arrive immediately after witnessing such a tragedy. Perhaps the thing to do was find an uninhabited land mass and put down there.

"There's another aircraft," *Tyrant* announced. "It's approaching from the west."

Still shaken by what he'd seen, Merlin took the stealthed ship closer. Dirty smoke billowed from the side of the aircraft. In the canopy, the pilot was obviously engaged in a life-or-death struggle to bring his machine to safety. Even as they watched, the engine appeared to slow and then restart.

Something slammed past *Tyrant*, triggering proximity alarms. "Some kind of shell," the ship told Merlin. "I think someone on the ground is trying to shoot down these aircraft."

Merlin looked down. He hadn't paid much attention to the land mass beneath them, but now that he did—peering through the holes in a quilt of low-lying cloud—he made out the unmistakable flashes of artillery positions, laid out along the pale scratch of a fortified line.

He began to understand why the airship dared not stray too far from the side of the land mass. Near the cliff, it at least had some measure of cover. It would have been far too vulnerable to the shells in open air.

"I think it's a time to take a stand," he said. "Maintain stealth. I'm going to provide some lift-support to that aircraft. Bring us around to her rear and then approach from under her."

"Merlin, you have no idea who these people are. They could be brigands, pirates, anything."

"They're being shot at. That's good enough for me."

"I really think we should land. I'm down to vapour pressure in the tanks now."

"So's that brave fool of a pilot. Just do it."

The aircraft's engine gave out just as *Tyrant* reached position. Taking the controls manually, Merlin brought his ship's nose into contact with the underside of the aircraft's paper-thin fuselage. Contact occurred with the faintest of bumps. The pilot glanced back down over his shoulder, but the goggled mask hid all expression. Merlin could only imagine what the pilot made of the sleek, whale-sized machine now supporting his little contraption.

Merlin's hands trembled. He was acutely aware of how easily he could damage the fragile thing with a miscalculated application of thrust. *Tyrant* was armoured to withstand Waynet transitions and the crush of gas giant atmospheres. It was like using a hammer to push around a feather. For a moment, contact between the two craft was lost, and when *Tyrant* came in again it hit the aircraft hard enough to crush the metal cylinder of a spare fuel tank bracketed on under the wing. Merlin winced in anticipation of an explosion—one that would hurt the little aeroplane a lot more than it would hurt *Tyrant*—but the tank must have been empty.

Ahead, the airship had regained some measure of stability. The capture net was still deployed. Merlin pushed harder, giving the aircraft more altitude in readiness for its approach glide. At the last moment he judged it safe to disengage. He steered *Tyrant* away and left the aircraft to blunder into the net.

This time there were no gusts. The net wrapped itself around the aircraft, the soft impact nudging down the nose of the airship. Then the net began to be winched back towards the gondola like a haul of fish. At the same time the airship swung around and began to climb.

"No other planes?" Merlin asked.

"That was the only one."

They followed the airship in. It rose over the cliff, over the ice-capped rim of the aerial land mass, then settled down towards the shielded region in the bowl, where water and greenery had gathered. There was even a wispy layer of cloud, arranged in a broken ring around the shore of the lake. Merlin presumed that the concave shape of the land mass was sufficient to trap a stable microclimate.

By now Merlin had an audience. People had gathered on the gondola's rear observation platform. They wore goggles and gloves and heavy brown overcoats. Merlin caught the shine of glass lenses being pointed at him. He was being studied, sketched, perhaps even photographed.

"Do you think they look grateful," he asked, "or pissed off?"

Tyrant declined to answer.

Merlin kept his distance, conserving fuel as best he could as the airship crossed tens of kilometres of arid, gently sloping land. Occasionally they overflew a little hamlet of huts or the scratch of a minor track. Presently the ground became soil-covered, and then fertile. They traversed swathes of bleak grey-green grass, intermingled with boulders and assorted uplifted debris. Then there were trees and woods. The communities became more than just hamlets. Small ponds fed rivers that ambled down to the single lake that occupied the land mass's lowest point. Merlin spied waterwheels and rustic-looking bridges. There were fields with grazing animals, and evidence of some tall-chimneyed industrial structures on the far side of the lake. The lake itself was an easy fifty or sixty kilometres wide. Nestled around a natural harbour on its southern shore was the largest community Merlin had seen so far. It was a haphazard jumble of several hundred mostly white, mostly single-storey buildings, arranged with the randomness of toy blocks littering a floor.

The airship skirted the edge of the town and then descended quickly. It approached what was clearly some kind of secure compound, judging by the guarded fence that encircled it. There was a pair of airstrips arranged in a cross-formation, and a dozen or so aircraft parked around a painted copy of the crescent emblem. Four skeletal docking towers rose from another area of the compound, stayed by guy-lines. A battle-weary pair of partially deflated airships was already tethered. Merlin pulled back to allow the incoming craft enough space to complete its docking. The net was lowered back down from the gondola, depositing the aeroplane—its wings now crumpled, its fuselage buckled —on the apron below. Service staff rushed out of bunkers to untangle the mess and free the pilot. Merlin brought his ship down on a clear part of the apron and doused the engines as soon as the landing skids touched the ground.

It wasn't long before a wary crowd had gathered around *Tyrant*. Most of them wore long leather coats, heavily belted, with the crescent emblem sewn into the right breast. They had scarves wrapped around their lower faces, almost to the nose. Their helmets were leather caps, with long flaps covering the sides of the face and the back of the neck. Most of them wore goggles; a few wore some kind of breathing apparatus. At least half the number were aiming barrelled weapons at the ship, some of which needed to be set up on tripods, while some even larger wheeled cannons were being propelled across the apron by teams of well-drilled soldiers. One figure was gesticulating, directing the armed squads to take up specific positions.

"Can you understand what he's saying?" Merlin asked, knowing that *Tyrant* would be picking up any external sounds.

"I'm going to need more than a few minutes to crack their language, Merlin, even if it *is* related to something in my database, of which there's no guarantee."

"Fine. I'll improvise. Can you spin me some flowers?"

"Where exactly are you going? What do you mean, *flowers*?"

Merlin paused at the airlock. He wore long boots, tight black leather trousers, a billowing white shirt and brocaded brown leather waistcoat, accented with scarlet trim. He'd tied back his hair and made a point of trimming his beard. "Where do you think? Outside. And I want some flowers. Flowers are good. Spin me some indigo hyacinths, the kind they used to grow on Springhaven, before the Mentality Wars. They always go down well."

"You're insane. They'll shoot you."

"Not if I smile and come bearing exotic alien flowers. Remember, I did just save one of their planes."

"You're not even wearing armour."

"Armour would really scare them. Trust me, ship: this is the quickest way for them to understand I'm not a threat."

"It's been a pleasure having you aboard," *Tyrant* said acidly. "I'll be sure to pass on your regards to my next owner."

"Just make the flowers and stop complaining."

Five minutes later Merlin steeled himself as the lock sequenced and the ramp lowered to kiss the ground. The cold hit him like a lover's slap. He heard an order from the soldiers' leader, and the massed ranks adjusted their aim. They'd been pointing at the ship before. Now it was only Merlin they were interested in.

He raised his right hand palm open, the newly spun flowers in his left.

"Hello. My name's Merlin." He thumped his chest for emphasis and said the name again, slower this time. "*Mer-lin*. I don't think there's much chance of you being able to understand me, but just in case…I'm not here to cause trouble." He forced a smile, which probably looked more feral than reassuring. "Now. Who's in charge?"

The leader shouted another order. He heard a rattle of a hundred safety catches being released. Suddenly, the ship's idea of sending out a proctor first sounded splendidly sensible. Merlin felt a cold line of sweat trickle down his back. After all that he had survived so far, both during his time with the Cohort and since he had become an adventuring free agent, it would be something of a let-down to die by being *shot* with a chemically propelled projectile. That was only one step above being mauled and eaten by a wild animal.

Merlin walked down the ramp, one cautious step at a time. "No weapons," he said. "Just flowers. If I wanted to hurt you, I could have hit you from space with charm-torps."

When he reached the apron, the leader gave another order and a trio of soldiers broke formation to cover Merlin from three angles, with the barrels of their weapons almost touching him. The leader—a cruel-looking young man with a scar down the right side of his face—shouted something in Merlin's direction, a word that sounded vaguely like 'distal', but which was in no language Merlin recognised. When Merlin didn't move, he felt a rifle jab into the small of his back. "Distal," the man said again, this time with an emphasis bordering on the hysterical.

Then another voice boomed across the apron, one that belonged to a much older man. There was something instantly commanding about the voice. Looking to the source of the exclamation, Merlin saw the wrecked aircraft entangled in its capture net, and the pilot in the process of crawling out from the tangle, with a wooden box in his hands. The rifle stopped jabbing Merlin's back, and the cruel-looking young man fell silent while the pilot made his way over to them.

The pilot had removed his goggles now, revealing the lined face of an older man, his grey-white beard and whiskers stark against ruddy, weatherworn skin. For a moment Merlin felt as if he was looking in the mirror at an older version of himself.

"Greetings from the Cohort," Merlin said. "I'm the man who saved your life."

"Gecko," the red-faced man said, pushing the wooden box into Merlin's chest. "Forlorn gecko!"

Now that Merlin had a chance to examine it properly, he saw that the box was damaged, its sides caved in and its lid ripped off. Inside was a matrix of straw padding and a great many shattered glass vials. The pilot took one of these smashed vials and held it up before Merlin's face, honey-coloured fluid draining down his fingers.

"What is it?" Merlin asked.

Leaving Merlin to hold the box and flowers, the red-faced pilot pointed angrily towards the wreckage of his aircraft, and in particular at the cylindrical attachment Merlin had taken for a fuel-tank. He saw now that the cylinder was the repository for dozens more of these wooden boxes, most of which must have been smashed when Merlin had nudged the aircraft with *Tyrant*.

"Did I do something wrong?" Merlin asked.

In a flash the man's anger turned to despair. He was crying, the tears smudging the soot on his cheeks. "Tangible," he said, softer now. "All tangible inkwells. Gecko."

Merlin reached into the box and retrieved one of the few intact vials. He held the delicate thing to his eyes. "Medicine?"

"Plastrum," the man said, taking the box back from Merlin.

"Show me what you do with this," Merlin said, as he motioned drinking the vial. The man shook his head, narrowing his wrinkled ice-blue eyes at him as if he thought Merlin was either stupid or making fun.

Merlin rolled up the sleeve of his arm and motioned injecting himself. The pilot nodded tentatively.

"Plastrum," he said again. "Vestibule plastrum."

"You have some kind of medical crisis? Is that what you were doing, bringing medicines?"

"Tangible," the man repeated.

"You need to come with me," Merlin said. "Whatever that stuff is, we can synthesise it aboard *Tyrant*." He held up the intact vial and then placed his index finger next to it. Then he pointed to the parked form of his ship and spread his fingers wide, hoping the pilot got the message that he could multiply the medicine. "One sample," he said. "That's all we need."

Suddenly there was a commotion. Merlin looked around in time to see a girl running across the apron, towards the two of them. In Cohort terms she could only have been six or seven years old. She wore a child's version of the same greatcoat everyone else wore, buckled black boots and gloves, no hat, goggles or breathing mask. The pilot shouted, "Minla," at her approach, a single word that conveyed both warning and something more intimate, as if the older man might have been her father or grandfather. "Minla oak trefoil," the man added, firmly but not without kindness. He sounded pleased to see her, but somewhat less than pleased that she had chosen this exact moment to run outside.

"Spelter Malkoha," the girl said, and hugged the pilot around the waist, which was as high as she could reach. "Spelter Malkoha, ursine Malkoha."

The red-faced man knelt down—his eyes were still damp—and ran a gloved finger through the girl's unruly fringe of black hair. She had a small, monkey-like face, one that conveyed both mischief and cleverness.

"Minla," he said tenderly. "Minla, Minla, Minla." Then what was clearly a rhetorical question: "Gastric spar oxen, fey legible, Minla?"

"Gorse spelter," she said, sounding contrite. And then, perhaps for the first time, she noticed Merlin. For an anxious moment her expression was frozen somewhere between surprise and suspicion, as if he was some kind of puzzle that had just intruded into her world.

"You wouldn't be called Minla, by any chance?" Merlin asked.

"Minla," she said, in barely a whisper.

"Merlin. Pleased to meet you, Minla." And then on a whim, before any of the adults could stop him, he passed her one of the indigo hyacinths that *Tyrant* had just spun for him, woven from the ancient molecular templates in its biolibrary. "Yours," he said. "A pretty flower for a pretty little girl."

"Oxen spray, Minla," the red-faced man said, pointing back to one of the buildings on the edge of the apron. A soldier walked over and extended a hand to the girl, ready to escort her back inside. She moved to hand the flower back to Merlin.

"No," he said, "you can keep it, Minla. It's for you."

She opened the collar of her coat and pushed the flower inside for safe keeping, until only its head was jutting out. The vivid indigo seemed to throw something of its hue onto her face.

"Mer-lin?" asked the older man.

"Yes."

The man tapped a fist against his own chest. "Malkoha." And then he indicated the vial Merlin was still carrying. "Plastrum," he said again. Then a question, accompanied by a nod towards *Tyrant*. "Risible plastrum?"

"Yes," Merlin said. "I can make you more medicine. *Risible plastrum.*"

The red-faced man studied him for what felt like many minutes. Merlin opted to say nothing: if the pilot hadn't got the message by now, no further persuasion was going to help. Then the pilot reached down to his belt and unbuttoned the leather holster of a pistol. He removed the weapon and allowed Merlin sufficient time to examine it by eye. The low sun gleamed off an oiled black barrel, inlaid with florid white ornamentation carved from something like whalebone.

"Mer-lin risible plastrum," Malkoha said. Then he waved the gun for emphasis. "Spar apostle."

"Spar apostle," Merlin repeated, as they walked up the boarding ramp. "No tricks."

EVEN BEFORE *TYRANT* had made progress in the cracking of the local language, Merlin had managed to hammer out a deal with Malkoha. The medicine had turned out to be a very simple drug, easily synthesized. A narrow-spectrum β–lactam antibiotic, according to the ship: exactly the sort of thing the locals might use to treat a gram-positive bacterial infection—something like bacterial meningitis, for instance—if they didn't have anything better.

Tyrant could pump out antibiotic medicine by the hundreds of litres, or synthesise something vastly more effective in equally large quantities. But Merlin saw no sense in playing his most valuable card so early in the game. He chose instead to give Malkoha supplies of the drug in approximately the same dosage and quantity as he must have been carrying when his aircraft was damaged, packaged in similar-looking glass vials. He gave the first two consignments as a gift, in recompense for the harm he was presumed to have done when attempting to save Malkoha, and let Malkoha think that it was all that *Tyrant* could do to make drugs at that strength and quantity. It was only when he handed over the third consignment, on the third day, that he mentioned the materials he needed to repair his ship.

He didn't say anything, of course, or at least nothing that the locals could have understood. But there were enough examples lying around of the materials Merlin needed—metals and organic compounds, principally, as well as water that could be used to replenish *Tyrant*'s hydrogen-fusion tanks—that Merlin was able to make considerable progress just by pointing and miming. He kept talking all the while, even in Main, and did all that he could to encourage the locals to talk back in their own tongue. Even when he was inside the compound, *Tyrant* was observing every exchange, thanks to the microscopic surveillance devices Merlin carried on his person. Through this process, the ship was constantly testing and rejecting language models, employing its knowledge of both the general principles of human grammar and its compendious database of ancient languages recorded by the Cohort, many of which were antecedents of Main itself. Lecythus might have been isolated for tens of thousands of years, but languages older than that had been cracked by brute computation, and Merlin had no doubt that *Tyrant* would get there in the end, provided he gave it enough material to work with.

It was still not clear whether the locals regarded him as their prisoner, or honoured guest. He'd made no attempt to leave, and they'd made no effort to prevent him from returning to his ship when it was time to collect the vials of antibiotic. Perhaps they had guessed that it would be futile to stop him, given the likely capabilities of his technology. Or perhaps they had guessed—correctly, as it happened—that *Tyrant* would be going nowhere until it was repaired and fuelled. In any event they seemed less awed by his arrival than intrigued, shrewdly aware of what he could do for them.

Merlin liked Malkoha, even though he knew almost nothing about the man. Clearly he was a figure of high seniority within this particular organisation, be it military or political, but he was also a man brave enough to fly a hazardous mission to ferry medicines through the sky, in a time of war. And his daughter loved him, which had to count for something. Merlin now knew that Malkoha was her "spelter" or father, although he did indeed look old enough to have been spaced from her by a further generation.

Almost everything that Merlin did learn, in those early days, was due to Minla rather than the adults. The adults seemed willing to at least attempt to answer his queries, when they could understand what he was getting at. But their chalkboard explanations usually left Merlin none the wiser. They could show him maps and printed historical and technical treatises, but none of these shed any light on the world's many mysteries. Cracking text would take *Tyrant* even longer than cracking spoken language.

Minla, though, had picture books. Malkoha's daughter had taken an obvious liking to Merlin, even though they shared nothing in common. Merlin gave her a new flower each time he saw her, freshly spun from some exotic species in the biolibrary. Merlin made a point of never giving her flowers from a particular world twice, even when she wanted more of the same. He also made a point of always telling her something about the place from where the flowers had come, regardless of her lack of understanding. It seemed to be enough for her to hear the cadences of a story, even if it was in an alien language.

There was not much colour in Minla's world, so Merlin's gifts must have had a luminous appeal to her. Once a day, for a few minutes, they were allowed to meet in a drab room inside the main compound. An adult was always stationed nearby, but to all intents and purposes Merlin and the girl were permitted to interact freely. Minla would show Merlin drawings and paintings she had done, or little compositions, written down in laboured handwriting in approximately the form of script *Tyrant* had come to refer to as Lecythus A. Merlin would examine Minla's works and offer praise when it was merited.

He wondered why these meetings were allowed. Minla was obviously a bright girl (he could tell that much merely from the precocious manner of her speaking, even if he hadn't had the ample evidence of her drawings and writings). Perhaps it was felt that meeting the man from space would be an important part of her education, one that could never be repeated at a later date. Perhaps she had pestered her father into allowing her to spend more time with Merlin. Merlin could understand that; as a child he'd also formed harmless attachments to adults, often those that came bearing gifts and especially those adults that appeared interested in what he had to show them.

Could there be more to it than that, though? Was it possible that the adults had decided that a child offered the best conduit for understanding, and that Minla was now their envoy? Or were they hoping to use Minla as a form of emotional blackmail, so that they might exert a subtle hold on Merlin when he decided it was time to leave?

He didn't know. What he was certain of was that Minla's books raised as many questions as they answered, and that simply leafing through them was enough to open windows in his own mind, back into a childhood he'd thought consigned safely to oblivion. The books were startlingly similar to the books Merlin remembered from the Palace of Eternal Dusk, the ones he'd used to fight over with his brother. They were bound similarly, illustrated with spidery ink drawings scattered through the text or florid watercolours gathered onto glossy plates at the end of the book. Merlin liked holding the book up to the light of an open window, so that the illustrated pages shone like stained glass. It was something his father had shown him on Plenitude, when he had been Minla's age, and her delight exactly echoed his own, across the unthinkable gulf of time and distance and circumstance that separated their childhoods.

At the same time, he also paid close attention to what the books had to say. Many of the stories featured little girls involved in fanciful adventures concerning flying animals and other magic creatures. Others had the worthy, over-earnest look of educational texts. Studying these latter books, Merlin began to grasp something of the history of Lecythus, at least in so far as it had been codified for the consumption of children.

The people on Lecythus knew they'd come from the stars. In two of the books there were even paintings of a vast spherical spaceship hoving into orbit around the planet. The paintings differed in every significant detail, but Merlin felt sure that he was seeing a portrayal of the same dimly remembered historical event, much as the books in his youth had shown various representations of human settlers arriving on Plenitude. There was no reference to the Waynet, however, or anything connected to the Cohort or the Huskers. As for the locals' theory concerning the origin of the aerial land masses, Merlin found only one clue. It lay in a frightening sequence of pictures showing the night sky being riven by lava-like fissures, until whole chunks of the heavens dropped out of place, revealing a darker, deeper firmament beyond. Some of the pieces were shown crashing into the seas, raising awesome waves that tumbled over entire coastal communities, while others were shown hovering unsupported in the sky, with kilometres of empty space under them. If the adults remembered that it was alien weaponry that had smashed their camouflaging sky (weapons deployed by aliens that were still *out here*) no hint of that uncomfortable truth was allowed into Minla's books. The destruction of the sky was shown simply as a natural catastrophe, like a flood or volcanic eruption. Enough to awe, enough to fascinate, but not enough to give nightmares.

Awesome it must have been, too. *Tyrant*'s own analysis had established that the aerial land masses could be put together like a jigsaw. There were gaps in that jigsaw, but most of them could be filled by lifting chunks of land out of the seas and slotting them in place. The inhabited aerial land masses were all inverted compared to their supposed positions in the original sky, requiring that they must have been flipped over after the shattering. *Tyrant* could offer little insight into how this could have happened, but it was clear enough that unless the chunks were inverted, life-supporting materials would spill off over the edges and rain down onto the planet again. Presumably the necessary materials had been uplifted into the air when the unsupported chunks (and these must have been pieces that did not contain gravity-nullifiers, or which had been damaged beyond the capacity to support themselves) came hammering down.

As to how people had come to the sky in the first place, or how the present political situation had developed, Minla's texts were frustratingly vague. There were pictures of what were obviously historic battles, fought with animals and gunpowder. There were illustrations of courtly goings-on: princes and kings, balls and regattas, assassinations and duels. There were drawings of adventurers rising on kites and balloons to survey the aerial masses, and later of what were clearly government-sponsored scouting expeditions, employing huge flotillas of flimsy-looking airships. But as to exactly why the people in the sky were now at war with the people on the ground, Merlin had little idea, and even less interest. What mattered—the only thing, in fact—was that Minla's people had the means to help him. He could have managed without them, but by bringing him the things he needed they made it easier. And it was good to see other faces again, after so long alone.

One of Minla's books intrigued him even more than all the others. It showed a picture of the starry night, the heavens as revealed after the fall of the camouflaging sky. Constellations had been drawn on the patterns of stars, with sketched figures overlaying the schematic lines joining the stars. None of the mythical or heroic figures corresponded to the old constellations of Plenitude, but the same archetypal forms were nonetheless present. For Merlin there was something hugely reassuring in seeing the evidence of similar imaginations at work. It might have been tens of thousands of years since these humans had been in contact with a wider galactic civilisation; they might have endured world-changing catastrophes and retained only a hazy notion of their origins. But they were still people, and he was amongst them. There were times, during his long search for the lost weapon that he hoped would save the Cohort, that Merlin had come to doubt whether there was anything about humanity worth saving. But all it took was the look on Minla's face as he presented her with another flower—another relic of some long-dead world—to banish such doubts almost entirely. While there were still children in the universe, and while children could still be enchanted by something as simple and wonderful as a flower, there was still a reason to keep looking, a reason to keep believing.

THE COILED BLACK device had the look of a tiny chambered nautilus, turned to onyx. Merlin pushed back his hair to let Malkoha see that he was already wearing a similar unit, then motioned for Malkoha to insert the translator into his own ear.

"Good," Merlin said, when he saw that the other man had pushed the device into place. "Can you understand me now?"

Malkoha answered very quickly, but there was a moment's lag before Merlin heard his response translated into Main, rendered in an emotionally flat machine voice. "Yes. I understand good. How is this possible?"

Merlin gestured around him. They were alone together aboard *Tyrant*, Malkoha ready to leave with another consignment of antibiotics. "The ship's been listening in on every conversation I've had with you," Merlin said. "It's heard enough of your language to begin piecing together a translation. It's still rudimentary—there are a lot of gaps the ship still needs to fill—but it will only get better with time, the more we talk."

Malkoha listened diligently as his earpiece translated Merlin's response. Merlin could only guess at how much of his intended meaning was making it through intact.

"Your ship is clever," Malkoha said. "We talk many times. We get good at understanding."

"I hope so."

Malkoha pointed now at the latest batch of supplies his people had brought, piled neatly at the top of the boarding ramp. The materials were unsophisticated in their manufacture, but they could all be reprocessed to form the complicated components *Tyrant* needed to repair itself.

"Metals make the ship good?"

"Yes," Merlin said. "Metals make the ship good."

"When the ship is good, the ship will fly? You will leave?"

"That's the idea."

Malkoha looked sad. "Where will you go?"

"Back into space. I've been a long time away from my own people. But there's something I need to find before I return to them."

"Minla will be unhappy."

"So will I. I like Minla. She's a clever little girl."

"Yes. Minla is clever. I am proud of my daughter."

"You have every right to be," Merlin said, hoping that his sincerity came across. "I have to start what I finished, though. The ship tells me it'll be flight-ready in two or three days. It's a patch job, but it'll get us to the nearest motherbase. But there's something we need to talk about first." Merlin reached for a shelf and handed Malkoha a tray upon which sat twelve identical copies of the translator device.

"You will speak with more of us?"

"I've just learned some bad news, Malkoha: news that concerns you, and your people. Before I go I want to do what I can to help. Take these translators and give them to your best people—Coucal, Jacana, the rest. Get them to wear them all the time, no matter who they're talking to. In three days I want to meet with you all."

Malkoha regarded the tray of translators with suspicion, as if the ranked devices were a peculiar foreign delicacy.

"What is the bad news, Merlin?"

"Three days isn't going to make much difference. It's better if we wait until the translation is more accurate, then there won't be any misunderstanding."

"We are friends," Malkoha said, leaning forward. "You can tell me now."

"I'm afraid it won't make much sense."

Malkoha looked at him beseechingly. "Please."

"Something is going to come out of the sky," Merlin said. "Like a great sword. And it's going to cut your sun in two."

Malkoha frowned, as if he didn't think he could possibly have understood correctly.

"Calliope?"

Merlin nodded gravely. "Calliope will die. And then so will everyone on Lecythus."

THEY WERE ALL there when Merlin walked into the glass-partitioned room. Malkoha, Triller, Coucal, Jacana, Sibia, Niltava, and about half a dozen more top brass Merlin had never seen before. An administrative assistant was already entering notes into a clattering electromechanical transcription device squatting on her lap, pecking away at its stiff metal input pads with surprising speed. Tea bubbled in a fat engraved urn set in the middle of the table. An orderly had already poured tea into china cups set before each bigwig, including Merlin himself. Through the partition, on the opposite wall of the adjoining tactical room, Merlin watched another orderly make microscopic adjustments to the placement of the aerial land masses on an equal-area projection map of Lecythus. Periodically, the entire building would rattle with the droning arrival of another aircraft or dirigible.

Malkoha coughed to bring the room to attention. "Merlin has news for us," he said, his translated voice coming through with more emotion than it had three days earlier. "This is news not just for the Skyland Alliance, but for everyone on Lecythus. That includes the Aligned Territories, the Neutrals and yes, even our enemies in the Shadowland Coalition." He beckoned with a hand in Merlin's direction, inviting him to stand.

Merlin held up one of Minla's picture books, open at the illustration of constellations in the sky over Lecythus. "What I have to tell you concerns these patterns," he said. "You see heroes, animals and monsters in the sky, traced in lines drawn between the brightest stars."

A new voice buzzed in his ear. He identified the speaker as Sibia, a woman of high political rank. "These things mean nothing," she said patiently. "They are lines drawn between chance alignments. The ancient mind saw demons and monsters in the heavens. Our modern science tells us that the stars are very distant, and that two stars that appear close together in the sky—the two eyes of Prinia the Dragon, for example—may in reality be located at very different distances."

"The lines are more significant than you appreciate," Merlin said. "They are a pattern you have remembered across tens of thousands of years, forgetting its true meaning. They are pathways between the stars."

"There are no pathways in the void," Sibia retorted. "The void is vacuum: the same thing that makes birds suffocate when you suck air out of a glass jar."

"You may think it absurd," Merlin said. "All I can tell you is that vacuum is not as you understand it. It has structure, resilience, its own reserves of energy. And you can make part of it shear away from the rest, if you try hard enough. That's what the Waymakers did. They stretched great corridors between the stars: rivers of flowing vacuum. They reach from star to star, binding together the entire galaxy. We call it the Waynet."

"Is this how you arrived?" Malkoha asked.

"My little ship could never have crossed interstellar space without it. But as I was passing close to your planet—because a strand of the Waynet runs right through this system—my ship encountered a problem. That is why *Tyrant* was damaged; why I had to land here and seek your assistance."

"And the nature of this problem?" the old man pushed.

"My ship only discovered it three days ago, based on observations it had collated since I arrived. It appears that part of the Waynet has become loose, unshackled. There's a kink in the flow where it begins to drift out of alignment. The unshackled part is drifting towards your sun, tugged towards it by the pull of Calliope's gravitational field."

"You're certain of this?" Sibia asked.

"I've had my ship check the data over and over. There's no doubt. In just over seventy years, the Waynet will cut right through Calliope, like a wire through a ball of cheese."

Malkoha looked hard into Merlin's eyes. "What will happen?"

"Probably very little to begin with, when the Waynet is still cutting through the chromosphere. But by the time it reaches the nuclear-burning core…I'd say all bets are off."

"Can it be mended? Can the Waynet be brought back into alignment?"

"Not using any technology known to my own people. We're dealing with principles as far beyond anything on Lecythus as *Tyrant* is beyond one of your propeller planes."

Malkoha looked stricken. "Then what can we possibly do?"

"You can make plans to leave Lecythus. You have always known that space travel was possible: it's in your history, in the books you give to your children. If you had any doubts, I've shown it to be true. Now you must achieve it for yourselves."

"In seventy years?" Malkoha asked.

"I know it sounds impossible. But you can do it. You already have flying machines. All you need to do is keep building on that achievement... building and building...until you have the means."

"You make it sound easy."

"It won't be. It'll be the hardest thing you've ever done. But I'm convinced that you can do it, if only you pull together." Merlin looked sternly at his audience. "That means no more wars between the Skylands and the Shadowlands. You don't have time for it. From this moment on, the entire industrial and scientific capacity of your planet will have to be directed towards one goal."

"You're going to help us, Merlin?" Malkoha asked. "Aren't you?"

Merlin's throat had become very dry. "I'd like to, but I must leave immediately. Twenty light-years from here is a bountiful system known to the Cohort. The great vessels of my people—the swallowships— sometimes stop in this system, to replenish supplies and make repairs. The swallowships cannot use the Way, but they are very big. If I could divert just one swallowship here, it could carry fifty thousand refugees; double that if people were prepared to accept some hardship."

"That's still not many people," Sibia said.

"That's why you need to start thinking about reducing your population over the next three generations. It won't be possible to save everyone, but if you could at least ensure that the survivors are adults of breeding age..." Merlin trailed off, conscious of the dismayed faces looking at him. "Look," he said, removing a sheaf of papers from his jacket and spreading them on the table. "I had the ship prepare these documents. This one concerns the production of wide-spectrum antibiotic medicines. This one concerns the construction of a new type of aircraft engine, one that will allow you to exceed the speed of sound and reach much higher altitudes than are now available to you. This one concerns metallurgy and high-precision machining. This one is a plan for a two-stage liquid-fuelled rocket. You need to start learning about rocketry *now*, because it's the only thing that's going to get you into space." His finger moved to the final sheet. "This document reveals certain truths about the nature of physical reality. Energy and mass are related by this simple formula. The speed of light is an absolute constant, irrespective of the observer's motion. This diagram shows the presence of emission lines in the spectrum of hydrogen, and a mathematical formula that predicts the spacing of those lines. All this...*stuff* should help you make some progress."

"Is this all you can give us?" Sibia asked sceptically. "A few pages' worth of vague sketches and cryptic formulae?"

"They're more than most cultures ever get. I suggest you start thinking about them straight away."

"I will get this to Shama," Coucal said, taking the drawing of a jet engine and preparing to slip it into his case.

"Not before everything here is duplicated and archived," Malkoha said firmly. "And we must take pains to ensure none of these secrets fall into Shadowland hands." Then he returned his attention to Merlin. "Evidently, you have given this matter some thought."

"Just a bit."

"Is this the first time you have had to deal with a world such as ours, one that will die?"

"I've had some prior experience of the matter. There was once a world—"

"What happened to the place in question?" Malkoha asked, before Merlin could finish his sentence.

"It died."

"How many people were saved?"

For a moment Merlin couldn't answer. The words seemed to lodge in the back of his throat, hard as pebbles. "There were just two survivors," he said quietly. "A pair of brothers."

THE WALK TO *Tyrant* was the longest he had ever taken. Ever since he had made the decision to leave Lecythus he had rehearsed the occasion in his mind, replaying it time and again. He had always imagined the crowd cheering, daunted by the news, but not cowed, Merlin raising his fist in an encouraging salute. Nothing had prepared him for the frigid silence of his audience, their judgemental expressions as he left the low buildings of the compound, their unspoken disdain hanging in the air like a proclamation.

Only Malkoha followed him all the way to *Tyrant's* boarding ramp. The old soldier had his coat drawn tight across his chest, even though the wind was still and the evening not particularly cold.

"I'm sorry," Merlin said, with one foot on the ramp. "I wish I could stay."

"You seem like two men to me," Malkoha said, his voice low. "One of them is braver than he gives himself credit for. The other man still has bravery to learn."

"I'm not running away."

"But you are running from something."

"I have to go now. If the damage to the Waynet becomes greater, I may not even be able to reach the next system."

"Then you must do what you think is right. I shall be sure to give your regards to Minla. She will miss you very much." Malkoha paused and reached into his tunic pocket. "I almost forgot to give you this. She would have been very upset with me if I had."

Malkoha had given Merlin a small piece of stone, a coin-shaped sliver that must have been cut from a larger piece and then set in coloured metal so that it could be worn around the neck or wrist. Merlin examined the stone with interest, but in truth there seemed nothing remarkable about it. He'd picked up and discarded more beautiful examples a thousand times in his travels. It had been dyed red in order to emphasize the fine grain of its surface: a series of parallel lines like the pages of a book seen end-on, but with a rhythmic structure to the spacing of the lines—a widening and a narrowing—that was unlike any book Merlin had seen.

"Tell her I appreciated it," he said.

"I gave the stone to my daughter. She found it pretty."

"How did you come by it?"

"I thought you were in a hurry to leave."

Merlin's hand closed around the stone. "You're right. I should be on my way."

"The stone belonged to a prisoner of mine, a man named Dowitcher. He was one of their greatest thinkers: a scientist and soldier much like myself. I admired his brilliance from afar, just as I hope he admired mine.

One day, our agents captured him and brought him to the Skylands. I played no part in planning his kidnap, but I was delighted that we might at last meet on equal terms. I was convinced that, as a man of reason, he would listen to my arguments and accept the wisdom of defecting to the Skylands."

"Did he?"

"Not in the slightest. He was as firmly entrenched in his convictions as I was in mine. We never became friends."

"So where does the stone come into it?"

"Before he died, Dowitcher found a means to torment me. He gave me the stone and told me that he had learned something of great significance from it. Something that could change our world. Something that had *cosmic* significance. He was looking into the sky when he said that: almost laughing. But he would not reveal what that secret was."

Merlin hefted the stone once more. "I think he was playing games with you, Malkoha."

"That's the conclusion I eventually reached. One day Minla took a shine to the stone—I kept it on my desk long after Dowitcher was gone—and I let her have it."

"And now it's mine."

"You mean a lot to her, Merlin. She wanted to give you something in return for the flowers. You may forget the rest of us one day, but please don't ever forget my daughter."

"I won't."

"I'm lucky," Malkoha said, something in his tone easing, as if he was finished judging Merlin. "I'll be dead long before your Waynet cuts into our sun. But Minla's generation won't have that luxury. They know that their world is going to end, and that every year brings that event a year nearer. They're the ones who'll spend their whole lives with that knowledge looming over them. They'll never know true happiness. I don't envy them a moment of their lives."

That was when something in Merlin gave way, some mental slippage that he must have felt coming for many hours without quite acknowledging it to himself. Almost before he had time to reflect on his own words he found himself saying to Malkoha, "I'm staying."

The other man, perhaps wary of a trick or some misunderstanding brought about by the translator, narrowed his eyes. "Merlin?"

"I said I'm staying. I've changed my mind. Maybe it was what I always knew I had to do, or maybe it was all down to what you just said about Minla. But I'm not going anywhere."

"What I said just now," Malkoha said, "about there being two of you, one braver than the other...I know now which man I am speaking to."

"I don't feel brave. I feel scared."

"Then I know it to be true. Thank you, Merlin. Thank you for not leaving us."

"There's a catch," Merlin said. "If I'm going to be any help to you, I have to see this whole thing out."

MALKOHA WAS THE last to see him before he entered frostwatch. "Twenty years," Merlin said, indicating the settings, which had been recalibrated in Lecythus time-units. "In all that time, you don't need to worry about me. *Tyrant* will take care of everything I need. If there's a problem, the ship will either wake me or it will send out the proctors to seek assistance."

"You have never spoken of proctors before," Malkoha replied.

"Small mechanical puppets. They have very little intelligence of their own, so they won't be able to help you with anything creative. But you needn't be alarmed by them."

"In twenty years, must we wake you?"

"No, the ship will take care of that as well. When the time is ready, the ship will allow you aboard. I may be a little groggy at first, but I'm sure you'll make allowances."

"I may not be around in twenty years," Malkoha said gravely. "I am sixty years old now."

"I'm sure there's still life left in you."

"If we should encounter a problem, a crisis—"

"Listen to me," Merlin said, with sudden emphasis. "You need to understand one very important thing. I am not a god. My body is much the same as yours, our lifespans very similar. That's the way we did things in the Cohort: immortality through our deeds, rather than flesh and blood. The frostwatch casket can give me a few dozen years beyond a normal human lifespan, but it can't give me eternal life. If you keep waking me, I won't live long enough to help you when things get really tough. If there is a crisis, you can knock on the ship three times. But I'd urge you not do so unless things are truly dire."

"I will heed your counsel," Malkoha said.

"Work hard. Work harder than you've ever dreamed possible. Time is going to eat up those seventy years faster than you can blink."

"I know how quickly time can eat years, Merlin."

"I want to wake to rockets and jet aircraft. Anything less, I'm going to be a disappointed man."

"We will do our best not to let you down. Sleep well, Merlin. We will take care of you and your ship, no matter what happens."

Merlin said farewell to Malkoha. When the ship was sealed up he settled himself into the frostwatch casket and commanded *Tyrant* to put him to sleep.

He didn't dream.

NOBODY HE RECOGNISED was there to greet Merlin when he returned to consciousness. Were it not for their uniforms, which still carried a recognisable form of the Skylanders' crescent emblem, he could easily believe that he had been abducted by forces from the surface. His visitors crowded around his open casket, faces difficult to make out, his eyes watering against the sudden intrusion of light.

"Can you understand me, Merlin?" asked a woman, with a firm clear voice.

"Yes," he said, after a moment in which it seemed as if his mouth was still frozen. "I understand you. How long have I—"

"Twenty years, just as you instructed. We had no cause to wake you."

He pushed himself from the casket, muscles screaming into his brain with the effort. His vision sharpened by degrees. The woman studied him with a cool detachment. She snapped her fingers at someone standing behind her and then passed Merlin a blanket. "Put this around you," she said.

The blanket had been warmed. He wrapped it around himself with gratitude, and felt some of the heat seep into his old bones. "That was a long one," he said, his tongue moving sluggishly, making him slur his words. "We don't usually spend so long in frostwatch."

"But you're alive and well."

"So it would seem."

"We've prepared a reception area in the compound. There's food and drink, a medical team waiting to look at you. Can you walk?"

"I can try."

Merlin tried. His legs buckled under him before he reached the door. They would regain strength in time, but for now he needed help. They must have anticipated his difficulties, because a wheelchair was waiting at the base of *Tyrant*'s boarding ramp, accompanied by an orderly to push it.

"Before you ask," the woman said, "Malkoha is dead. I'm sorry to have to tell you this."

Merlin had grown to think of the old man as his only adult friend on Lecythus, and had been counting on his being there when he returned from frostwatch. "When did he die?"

"Fourteen years ago."

"Force and wisdom. It must be like ancient history to you."

"Not to all of us," the woman said sternly. "I am Minla, Merlin. It may be fourteen years ago, but there isn't a day when I don't remember my father and wish he was still with us."

As he was being propelled across the apron, Merlin looked up at the woman's face and compared it against his memories of the little girl he had known twenty years ago. At once he saw the similarity and knew that she was telling the truth. In that moment he felt the first visceral sense of the time that had passed.

"You can't imagine how odd this makes me feel, Minla. Do you remember me?"

"I remember a man I used to talk to in a room. It was a long time ago."

"Not to me. Do you remember the stone?"

She looked at him oddly. "The stone?"

"You asked your father to give it to me, when I was due to leave Lecythus."

"Oh, that thing," Minla said. "Yes, I remember it now. It was the one that belonged to Dowitcher."

"It's very pretty. You can have it back if you like."

"Keep it, Merlin. It doesn't mean anything to me now, just as it shouldn't have meant anything to my father. I'm embarrassed to have given it to you."

"I'm sorry about Malkoha."

"He died well, Merlin. Flying another hazardous mission for us, in very bad weather. This time it was our turn to deliver medicine to our allies. We were now making antibiotics for all the land masses in the Skyland Alliance, thanks to the process you gave us. My father flew one of the last consignments. He made it to the other land mass, but his plane was lost on the return trip."

"He was a good man. I only knew him a short while, but I think it was enough to tell."

"He often spoke of you, Merlin. I think he hoped you might teach him more than you did."

"I did what I could. Too much knowledge would have overwhelmed you: you wouldn't have known where to start, or how to put the pieces together."

"Perhaps you should have trusted us more."

"You said you had no cause to wake me. Does that mean you made progress?"

"Decide for yourself."

He followed Minla's instruction. The area around *Tyrant* was still recognisable as the old military compound, with many of the original buildings still present, albeit enlarged and adapted. But most of the dirigible docking towers were gone, as were most of the dirigibles them- selves. Ranks of new aircraft now occupied the area where the towers and airships had been, bigger and heavier than anything Merlin had seen before. The swept-back geometry of their wings, the angle of the leading edge, the rakish curve of their tailplanes all owed something to the shape of *Tyrant* in atmospheric-entry mode. Clearly the natives had been more observant than he'd given them credit for. Merlin knew he shouldn't have been surprised; he'd given them the blueprints for the jet turbine, after all. But it was still something of a shock to see his plans made concrete, so closely to the way he had imagined it.

"Fuel is always a problem," Minla said. "We have the advantage of height, but little else. We rely on our scattered allies on the ground, together with raiding expeditions to Shadowland fuel bunkers." She pointed to one of the remaining airships. "Our cargo dirigibles can lift fuel all the way back to the Skylands."

"Are you still at war?" Merlin asked, though her statement rather confirmed it.

"There was a ceasefire shortly after my father's death. It didn't last long."

"You people could achieve a lot more if you pooled your efforts," Merlin said. "In seventy—make that fifty—years, you'll be facing collective annihilation. It isn't going to make a damned bit of difference what flag you're saluting."

"Thank you for the lecture. If it means so much to you, why don't you fly down to the other side and talk to them?"

"I'm an explorer, not a diplomat."

"You could always try."

Merlin sighed heavily. "I did try once. Not long after I left the Cohort...there was a world named Exoletus, about the same size as Lecythus. I thought there might be something on Exoletus connected with my quest. I was wrong, but it was reason enough to land and try to talk to the locals."

"Were they at war?"

"Just like you lot. Two massive power blocs, chemical weapons, the works. I hopped from hemisphere to hemisphere, trying to play the peacemaker, trying to knock their heads together to make them see sense. I laid the whole cosmic perspective angle on them: how there was a bigger universe out there, one they could be a part of if they only stopped squabbling. How they were going to have to be a part of it whether they liked it or not when the Huskers came calling, but if they could only be ready for that—"

"It didn't work."

"I made things twenty times worse. I caught them at a time when they were inching towards some kind of ceasefire. By the time I left, they were going at it again hell for leather. Taught me a valuable lesson, Minla.

It isn't my job to sprinkle fairy dust on a planet and get everyone to live happily ever after. No one gave me the toolkit for that. You have to work these things out for yourselves."

She looked only slightly disappointed. "So you'll never try again?"

"Burn your fingers once, you don't put them into the fire twice."

"Well," Minla said, "before you think too harshly of us, it was the Skylands that took the peace initiative in the last ceasefire."

"So what went wrong?"

"The Shadowlands invaded one of our allied surface territories. They were interested in mining a particular ore, known to be abundant in that area."

Depressed as he was by news that the war was still rumbling on, Merlin forced his concentration back onto the larger matter of preparations for the catastrophe. "You've done well with these aircraft. Doubtless you'll have gained expertise in high-altitude flight. Have you gone transonic yet?"

"In prototypes. We'll have an operational squadron of supersonic aircraft in the air within two years, subject to fuel supplies."

"Rocketry?"

"That too. It's probably easier if I show you."

Minla let the orderly wheel him into one of the compound buildings. A long window ran along one wall, overlooking a larger space. Though the interior had been enlarged and re-partitioned, Merlin still recognised the tactical room. The old wall-map, with its cumbersome push-around plaques, had been replaced by a clattering electromechanical display board. Operators wore headsets and sat at desks behind huge streamlined machines, their grey metal cases ribbed with cooling flanges. They were staring at small flickering slate-blue screens, whispering into microphones.

Minla removed a tranche of photographs from a desk and passed them to Merlin for his inspection. They were black and white images of the Skyland air mass, shot from increasing altitude, until the curve of Lecythus's horizon became pronounced.

"Our sounding rockets have penetrated to the very edge of the atmosphere," Minla said. "Our three-stage units now have the potential to deliver a tactical payload to any unobstructed point on the surface."

"What would count as a 'tactical payload'?" Merlin asked warily.

"It's academic. I'm merely illustrating the progress we've made in your absence."

"I'm cheered."

"You encouraged us to make these improvements," Minla said, chidingly. "You can hardly blame us if we put them to military use in the meantime. The catastrophe—as you've so helpfully pointed out—is still fifty years in the future. We have our own affairs to deal with in the meantime."

"I wasn't trying to create a war machine. I was just giving you the stepping stones you needed to get into space."

"Well, as you can doubtless judge for yourself, we still have some distance to go. Our analysts say that we'll have a natural satellite in orbit within fifteen years, maybe ten. Definitely so by the time you wake from your next bout of sleep. But that's still not the same as moving fifty thousand people out of the system, or however many it needs to be. For that we're going to need more guidance from you, Merlin."

"You seem to be doing very well with what I've already given you."

Minla's tone, cold until then, softened perceptibly. "We'll get you fed. Then the doctors would like to look you over, if only for their own notebooks. We're glad to have you back with us, Merlin. My father would have been so happy to see you again."

"I'd like to have spoken with him again."

After a moment, Minla said: "How long will you stay with us, before you go back to sleep again?

"Months, at least. Maybe a year. Long enough to be sure that you're on the right track, and that I can trust you to make your own progress until I'm awake again."

"There's a lot we need to talk about. I hope you have a strong appetite for questions."

"I have a stronger appetite for breakfast."

Minla had him wheeled out of the room into another part of the compound. There he was examined by Skyland medical officials, a process that involved much poking and prodding and whispered consultation. They were interested in Merlin not just because he was a human who had been born on another planet, but because they hoped to learn some secret of frostwatch from his metabolism. Eventually they were done and

Merlin was allowed to wash, clothe himself and finally eat. Skyland food was austere compared to what he was used to aboard *Tyrant*, but in his present state he would have wolfed down anything.

There was to be no rest for him that day. More medical examinations followed, including some that were clearly designed to test the functioning of his nervous system. They poured cold water into his ears, shone lights into his eyes and tapped him with various small hammers. Merlin endured it all with stoic good grace. They would find nothing odd about him because in all significant respects he was biologically identical to the people administering the examinations. But he imagined the tests would give the medical staff much to write about in the coming months.

Minla was waiting for him afterwards, together with a roomful of Skyland officials. He recognised two or three of them as older versions of people he had already met, greyed and lined by twenty years of war—there was Triller, Jacana and Sibia, Triller now missing an eye—but most of the faces were new to him. Merlin took careful note of the newcomers: those would be the people he'd be dealing with next time.

"Perhaps we should get to business," Minla said, with crisp authority. She was easily the youngest person in the room, but if she didn't outrank everyone present, she at least had their tacit respect. "Merlin, welcome back to the Skylands. You've learned something of what has happened in your absence: the advances we've made, the ongoing condition of war. Now we must talk about the future."

Merlin nodded agreeably. "I'm all for the future."

"Sibia?" Minla asked, directing a glance at the older woman.

"The industrial capacity of the Skylands, even when our surface allies are taken into account, is insufficient for the higher purpose of safeguarding the survival of our planetary culture," Sibia answered, sounding exactly as if she was reading from a strategy document, even though she was looking Merlin straight in the eye. "As such, it is our military duty—our moral imperative—to bring all of Lecythus under one authority, a single Planetary Government. Only then will we have the means to save more than a handful of souls."

"I agree wholeheartedly," Merlin said. "That's why I applaud your earlier ceasefire. It's just a pity it didn't last."

"The ceasefire was always fragile," Jacana said. "The wonder is that it lasted as long as it did. That's why we need something more permanent."

Merlin felt a prickling sensation under his collar. "I guess you have something in mind."

"Complete military and political control of the Shadowlands," Sibia replied. "They will never work with us, unless they become us."

"You can't believe how frightening that sounds."

"It's the only way," Minla said. "My father's regime explored all possible avenues to find a peaceful settlement, one that would allow our two blocs to work in unison. He failed."

"So instead you want to crush them into submission."

"If that's what it takes," Minla said. "Our view is that the Shadowland administration is vulnerable to collapse. It would only take a single clear-cut demonstration of our capability to bring about a coup, followed by a negotiated surrender."

"And this clear-cut demonstration?"

"That's why we need your assistance, Merlin. Twenty years ago, you revealed certain truths to my father." Before he could say anything, Minla produced one of the sheets Merlin had given to Malkoha and his colleagues. "It's all here in black and white. The equivalence of mass and energy. The constancy of the speed of light. The interior structure of the atom. Your remark that our sun contains a 'nuclear-burning core'. All these things were a spur to us. Our best minds have grappled with the implications of these ideas for twenty years. We see how the energy of the atom could carry us into space, and beyond range of our sun. We now have an inkling of what else that implies."

"Do tell," Merlin said, an ominous feeling in his belly.

"If mass can be converted into energy, then the military implications are startling. By splitting the atom, or even forcing atoms to merge, we believe that we can construct weapons of almost incalculable destructive force. The demonstration of one of these devices would surely be enough to collapse the Shadowland administration."

Merlin shook his head slowly. "You're heading up a blind alley. It isn't possible to make practical weapons using atomic energy. There are too many difficulties."

Minla studied him with an attentiveness that Merlin found quite unsettling. "I don't believe you," she said.

"Believe me or don't believe me, it's up to you."

"We are certain that these weapons can be made. Our own research lines will give them to us sooner or later."

Merlin leaned back in his seat. He knew when there was no point in maintaining a bluff.

"Then you don't need me."

"But we do. Most urgently. The Shadowland administration also has its bright minds, Merlin. Their interest in those ore reserves I mentioned earlier…either there have been intelligence leaks, or they have independently arrived at similar conclusions to us. They are trying to make a weapon."

"You can't be sure of that."

"We can't afford to be wrong. We may own the sky, but our situation is dependent upon access to those fuel reserves. If one of our allies was targeted with an atomic weapon…" Minla left the sentence unfinished, her point adequately made.

"Then build your bomb," Merlin said.

"We need it sooner rather than later. That is where you come in." Now Minla produced another sheet of paper, flicking it across the table in Merlin's direction. "We have enough of the ore," she said. "We also have the means to refine it. This is our best guess for a design."

Merlin glanced at the illustration long enough to see a complicated diagram of concentric circles, like the plan for an elaborate garden maze. It was intricately annotated in machine-printed Lecythus B.

"I won't help you."

"Then you may as well leave us now," Minla said. "We'll build our bomb in our own time, without your help, and use it to secure peace for the whole world. Maybe that will happen quickly enough for us to begin redirecting the industrial effort towards the evacuation. Maybe it won't. But what happens will be on our terms, not yours."

"Understand one thing," Jacana said, with a hawkish look on his face. "The day will come when atomic weapons are used. Left to our own devices, we'll build weapons to use against our enemy below. But by the time we have that capability, they'll more than likely have the means to strike back, if they don't hit us first. That means there'll be a series of exchanges, an escalation, rather than a single decisive demonstration. Give us the means to make a weapon now and we'll use it in such a way that the civilian casualties are minimised. Withhold it from us, and you'll have the blood of a million dead on your hands."

Merlin almost laughed. "I'll have blood on my hands because I *didn't* show you how to kill yourselves?"

"You began this," Minla said. "You already gave us secret knowledge of the atom. Did you imagine we were so stupid, so childlike, that we wouldn't put two and two together?"

"Maybe I thought you had more common sense. I was hoping you'd develop atomic rockets, not atomic bombs."

"This is our world, Merlin, not yours. We only get one chance at controlling its fate. If you want to help us, you must give us the means to overwhelm the enemy."

"If I give you this, millions will die."

"A billion will perish if Lecythus is not unified. You must do it, Merlin. Either you side with us, completely, or we all die."

Merlin closed his eyes, wishing a moment alone, a moment to puzzle over the ramifications. In desperation, he saw a possible solution: one he'd rejected before but was now willing to advance. "Show me the military targets on the surface that you would most like to eradicate," he said. "I'll have *Tyrant* take them out, using charm-torps."

"We've considered asking for your direct military assistance," Minla said. "Unfortunately, it doesn't work for us. Our enemy already know something of your existence: it was always going to be a difficult secret to hide, especially given the reach of the Shadowlander espionage network. They'd be impressed by your weapons, that much we don't doubt. But they also know that our hold on you is tenuous, and that you could just as easily refuse to attack a given target. For that reason you do not make a very effective deterrent. Whereas if they knew that *we* controlled a devastating weapon..." Minla looked at the other Skyland officials. "There could be no doubt in their minds that we might do the unthinkable."

"I'm really beginning to wonder whether I shouldn't have landed on the ground instead."

"You'd be sitting in a very similar room, having a very similar conversation," Minla said.

"Your father would be ashamed of you."

Minla's look made Merlin feel as if he was something she'd found under her shoe. "My father meant well. He served his people to the best of his abilities. But he had the luxury of knowing he was going to die before the world's end. I don't."

MERLIN WAS ABOARD *Tyrant*, alone except for Minla, while he prepared to enter frostwatch again. Eight frantic months had passed since his revival, with the progress attaining a momentum of its own that Merlin felt sure would carry through to his next period of wakefulness.

"I'll be older when we meet again," Minla said. "You'll barely have aged a day, and your memories of this day will be as sharp as if it happened yesterday. Is that something you ever get used to?"

Not for the first time, Merlin smiled tolerantly. "I was born on a world not very different from Lecythus, Minla. We didn't have land masses floating through the sky, we didn't have global wars, but in many respects we were quite alike. Everything you see here—this ship, this frostwatch cabinet, these souvenirs—would once have seemed unrecognisably strange to me. I got used to it, though. Just as you'd get used to it, if you had the same experiences."

"I'm not so sure."

"I am. I met a very intelligent girl twenty years ago, and believe me I've met some intelligent people in my time." Merlin brightened, remembering the thing he'd meant to show Minla. "That stone you had your father give me...the one we talked about just after I came out of the cabinet?"

"The worthless thing Dowitcher convinced my father was of cosmic significance?"

"It wasn't worthless to you. You must have liked it, or you wouldn't have given it to me in return for my flowers."

"The flowers," Minla said, thoughtfully. "I'd almost forgotten them. I used to look forward to them so much, the sound of your voice as you told me stories I couldn't understand but which still managed to sound so significant. You made me feel special, Merlin. I'd treasure the flowers afterwards and go to sleep imagining the strange, beautiful places they'd come from. I'd cry when they died, but then you'd always bring new ones."

"I used to like the look on your face."

"Tell me about the stone," she said, after a silence.

"I had *Tyrant* run an analysis on it. Just in case there was something significant about it, something neither you, I nor your father had spotted."

"And?" Minla asked, with a note of fearfulness.

"I'm afraid it's just a piece of whetstone."

"Whetstone?"

"Very hard. It's the kind you use for sharpening knives. It's a common enough kind of stone on a planet like this one, wherever you have tides, shorelines and oceans." Merlin had fished out the stone earlier; now he held it in his hand, palm open, like a lucky coin. "You see that fine patterning of lines? This kind of stone was laid down in shallow tidal water. Whenever the sea rushed in, it would carry a suspension of silt that would settle out and form a fine layer on the surface of the stone. The next time the tide came in, you'd get a second layer. Then a third, and so on. Each layer would only take a few hours to be formed, although it might take hundreds of millions of years for it to harden into stone."

"So it's very old."

Merlin nodded. "Very old indeed."

"But not of any cosmic significance."

"I'm sorry. I just thought you might want to know. Dowitcher *was* playing a game with your father after all. I think Malkoha had more or less guessed that for himself."

For a moment Merlin thought his explanation had satisfied Minla, enabling her to shut tight that particular chapter of her life. But instead she just frowned. "The lines aren't regular, though. Why do they widen and then narrow?"

"Tides vary," Merlin said, suddenly feeling himself on less solid ground. "Deep tides carry more sediment. Shallow tides less. I suppose."

"Storms raise high tides. That would explain the occasional thick band. But other than that, the tides on Lecythus are very regular. I know this from my education."

"Then your education's wrong, I'm afraid. A planet like this, with a large moon..." Merlin left the sentence unfinished. "Spring tides and neap tides, Minla. No arguing with it."

"I'm sure you're right."

"Do you want the stone back?" he asked.

"Keep it, if it amuses you."

He closed his hand around the stone. "It still meant something to you when you gave it to me. It'll always mean something to me for that reason."

"Thank you for not leaving us. If my stone kept you here, it served a useful purpose."

"I'm glad I chose to stay. I just hope I haven't done more harm than good, with the things I've showed you."

"That again," Minla said, with a weary sigh. "You worry that we're going to blow ourselves to bits, just because you showed us the clockwork inside the atom."

"It's nasty clockwork."

He had seen enough progress, enough evidence of wisdom and independent ingenuity, to know that the Skyland forces would have a working atomic bomb within two years. By then, their rocket programme would have given them a delivery system able to handle the cumbersome payload of that primitive device. Even if the rocket fell behind schedule, they only had to wait until the aerial land mass drifted over a Shadowland target.

"I can't stop you making weapons," Merlin said. "All I ask is that you use them wisely. Just enough to negotiate a victory, and then no more. Then forget about bombs and start thinking about atomic rockets."

Minla looked at him pityingly. "You worry that we're becoming monsters. Merlin, we already *were* monsters. You didn't make us any worse."

"That strain of bacterial meningitis was very infectious," Merlin said. "I know: I've run it through *Tyrant's* medical analyser. You were already having difficulties with supplies of antibiotics. If I hadn't landed, if I hadn't offered to make that medicine for you, your military effort might have collapsed within months. The Shadowlands would have won by default. There wouldn't be any need to introduce atomic bombs into the world."

"But we'd still need the rockets."

"Different technology. The one doesn't imply the other."

"Merlin, listen to me. I'm sorry that we're asking you to make these difficult moral choices. But for us it's about only one thing: species survival. If you hadn't dropped out of the sky, the Waynet would still be on its way to us, ready to slice our star in two. After you learned that was going to happen, you had no choice but to do everything possible to save us, no matter how bad a taste it leaves in your mouth."

"I have to live with myself when this is all over."

"You'll have nothing to be ashamed of. You've made all the right decisions so far. You've given us a future."

"I need to clear up a few things for you," Merlin said. "It isn't a friendly galaxy. The creatures that smashed your sky are still out there. Your ancestors forged the armoured sky to hide from them, to make Lecythus look like an airless world. The Huskers were hunting down my own people before I left to work on my own. It isn't going to be plain sailing."

"Survival is better than death. Always and for ever."

Merlin sighed: he knew that this conversation had run its course, that they had been over these things a thousand times already and were no closer to mutual understanding. "When I wake up again, I want to see lights in the sky."

"When I was a girl," Minla said, "long before you came, my father would tell me stories of people travelling through the void, looking down on Lecythus. He'd put in jokes and little rhymes, things to make me laugh. Under it all, though, he had a serious message. He'd show me the pictures in my books, of the great ship that brought us to Lecythus. He said we'd come from the stars and one day we'd find a way to go back there. It seemed like a fantasy when I was a little girl, something that would never come to pass in the real world. Yet now it's happening, just as my father always said it would. If I live long enough, I'll know what it's like to leave Lecythus behind. But I'll be dead long before we ever reach another world, or see any of the wonders you've known."

For an instant Minla was a girl again, not a driven military leader. Something in her face spoke to Merlin across the years, breaching the defences he had carefully assembled.

"Let me show you something."

He took her into *Tyrant*'s rear compartment and revealed the matte-black cone of the syrinx, suspended in its cradle. At Merlin's invitation, Minla was allowed to stroke its mirror-smooth surface. She reached out her hand gingerly, as if expecting to touch something very hot or very cold. At the last instant her fingertips grazed the ancient artefact and then held the contact, daringly.

"It feels old," she said. "I can't say why."

"It does. I've often felt the same thing."

"Old and very heavy. Heavier than it has any right to be. And yet when I look at it, it's somehow not quite there, as if I'm looking at the space where it used to be."

"That's exactly how it looks to me."

Minla withdrew her touch. "What is it?"

"We call it a syrinx. It's not a weapon. It's more like a key or a passport."

"What does it do?"

"It lets my ship use the Waynet. In their time the Waymakers must have made billions of these things, enough to fuel the commerce of a million worlds. Imagine that, Minla: millions of stars bound by threads of accelerated space-time, each thread strung with thousands of glittering ships rushing to and fro, drops of honey on a thread of silk, each ship moving so close to the speed of light that time itself slowed almost to stillness. You could dine on one world, ride your ship to the Waynet and then take supper on some other world, under the falling light of another sun. A thousand years might have passed while you were riding the flow, but that didn't matter. The Waymakers forged an empire where a thousand years was just a lazy afternoon, a time to put off plans for another day." Merlin looked sadly at Minla. "That was the idea, anyway."

"And now?"

"We breakfast in the ruins, barely remember the glory that was and scavenge space for the handful of still-functioning syrinxes."

"Could you take it apart, find out how it works?"

"Only if I felt suicidal. The Waymakers protected their secrets very well."

"Then it is valuable."

"Incalculably so."

Minla stroked it again. "It feels dead."

"It just isn't active yet. When the Waynet comes closer, the syrinx will sense it. That's when we'll really know it's time to get out of here." Merlin forced a smile. "But by then we'll be well on our way."

"Now that you've shown me this secret, aren't you worried that we'll take it from you?"

"The ship wouldn't let you. And what use would it be to you anyway?"

"We could make our own ship, and use your syrinx to escape from here."

Merlin tried not to sound too condescending. "Any ship you built would smash itself to splinters as soon as it touched the Waynet, even with the syrinx to help it. And you wouldn't achieve much anyway. Ships that use the Waynet can't be very large."

"Why is that?"

Merlin shrugged. "They don't need to be. If it only takes a day or two of travel to get anywhere—remember what I said about clocks slowing down—then you don't need to haul all your provisions with you, even if you're crossing to the other side of the galaxy."

"But could a bigger ship enter the Waynet, if it had to?"

"The entry stresses wouldn't allow it. It's like riding the rapids." Merlin didn't wait to see if Minla was following him. "The syrinx creates a path that you can follow, a course where the river is easier. But you still need a small boat to squeeze around the obstacles."

"Then no one ever made larger ships, even during the time of the Waymakers?"

"Why would they have needed to?"

"That wasn't my question, Merlin."

"It was a long time ago. I don't have all the answers. And you shouldn't pin your hopes on the Waynet. It's the thing that's trying to kill you, not save you."

"But when you leave us...you'll ride the Waynet, won't you?"

Merlin nodded. "But I'll make damned sure I have a head start on the collision."

"I'm beginning to see how this must all look to you," Minla said. "This is the worst thing that's ever happened to us, the end of our history itself. To you it's just a stopover, an incidental adventure. I'm sure there were hundreds of worlds before us, and there'll be hundreds more. That's right, isn't it?"

Merlin bridled. "If I didn't care about you all, I'd have left twenty years ago."

"You very nearly did. I know how close you came. My father spoke of it many times, his joy when you changed your mind."

"I had a change of heart," Merlin said. "Everyone's allowed that. You played a part in it, Minla. If you hadn't told Malkoha to give me that gift—"

"Then I'm glad I did, if it meant so much." Minla looked away, something between sadness and fascination on her face. "Merlin, before you sleep—do something for me."

"Yes?"

"Make me flowers again. From some world I'll never ever see. And tell me their story."

THE PLANETARY GOVERNMENT aircraft was a sleek silver flying wing with its own atomic reactor, feeding six engines buried in air-smoothed nacelles. Minla had already led Merlin down a spiral staircase into an observation cupola set under the thickest part of the wing. Now she touched a brushed-steel panel, causing armoured slats to whisk open in rapid sequence. Through the green-tinted blastproof glass they had an uninterrupted view of the surface rolling by underneath.

The ocean carried no evidence of the war, but there was hardly any stretch of land that hadn't been touched in some fashion. Merlin saw the rubble-strewn remains of towns and cities, some with the hearts gouged out by kilometre-deep craters. He saw flooded harbours, beginning to be clawed back by the greedy fingers of the sea. He saw swathes of grey-brown land where nothing grew any more, and where only dead, petrified forests testified to the earlier presence of living things. Atomic weapons had been used in their thousands, by both sides. The Skylanders had been first, though, which was why the weapons had a special name on Lecythus. Because of the shape of the mushroom cloud that accompanied each burst, they called them Minla's Flowers.

She pointed out the new cities that had been built since the ceasefire. They were depressing to behold: grids of utilitarian blocks, each skull-grey multi-storey building identical to the others. Spidery highways linked the settlements, but not once did Merlin see any evidence of traffic or commerce.

"We're not building for posterity," she said. "None of those buildings have to last more than fifty years, and most of them will be empty long before that. By the time they start crumbling, there'll be no one alive on Lecythus."

"You're surely not thinking of taking everyone with you," Merlin said.

"Why not? It seemed unthinkable forty years ago. But so did atomic war, and the coming of a single world state. Anything's within our reach now. With social planning, we can organise matters such that the population shrinks to a tenth of its present size. No children will be allowed to be born in the last twenty years. And we'll begin moving people into the Space Dormitories long before that."

Merlin had seen the plans for the Dormitories, along with the other elements of Minla's evacuation programme. There was already a small space station in orbit around Lecythus, but it would be utterly dwarfed by the hundred Dormitories. The plans called for huge air-filled spheres, each of which would swallow one hundred thousand evacuees, giving a total in-orbit human presence of ten million people. Yet even as the Space Dormitories were being populated, work would be under way on the thousand Exodus Arks that would actually carry the evacuees out of the system. The Arks would be built in orbit, using materials extracted and refined from the moon's crust. Merlin had already indicated to Minla's experts that they could expect to find a certain useful isotope of helium in the topsoil of the moon, an isotope that would enable the Arks to be powered by nuclear fusion engines of an ancient and well-tested design.

"Forced birth control, and mass evacuation," he said, grimacing. "That's going to take some tough policing. What if people don't go along with your programme?"

"They'll go along," Minla said.

"Even if that means shooting a few, to make a point?"

"Millions have already died, Merlin. If it takes a few more to guarantee the efficient execution of the evacuation programme, I see that as a price worth paying."

"You can't push human society that hard. It snaps."

"There's no such thing as society," Minla told him.

Presently she had the pilot bring them below supersonic speed, and then down to a hovering standstill above what Merlin took to be an abandoned building, perched near the shore amidst the remains of what must once have been a great ocean seaport. The flying wing lowered itself on ducted jets, blowing dust and debris in all directions until its landing gear kissed scorched earth and the engines quietened.

"We'll take a stroll outside," Minla said. "There's something I want you to see. Something that will convince you of our seriousness."

"I'm not sure I need convincing."

"I want you to see it nonetheless. Take this cloak." She handed him a surprisingly heavy garment.

"Lead impregnated?"

"Just a precaution. Radiation levels are actually very low in this sector."

They disembarked via an escalator that had folded down from the flying wing's belly, accompanied by a detachment of guards. The armed men moved ahead, sweeping the ground with things that looked like metal brooms before ushering Minla and Merlin forward. They followed a winding path through scorched rubble and junk, taking care not to trip over the obstacles and broken ground. Calliope had set during their descent and a biting wind was now howling into land from the sea, setting his teeth on edge. From somewhere in the distance a siren rose and fell on a mournful cycle. Despite Minla's assurance concerning the radioactivity, Merlin swore he could already feel his skin tingling. Overhead, stars poked through the thinning layer of moonlit clouds.

When at last he looked up, he saw that the solitary building was in fact an enormous stone monument. It towered a hundred metres above the flying wing, stepped like a ziggurat and cut and engraved with awesome precision. Letters in Lecythus A marched in stentorian ranks across the highest vertical face. Beyond the monument, grey-black water lapped at the shattered remains of a promenade. The monument was presumably designed to weather storms, but it would only take one spring tide to submerge its lower flanks completely. Merlin wondered why Minla's people hadn't set it on higher ground.

"It's impressive."

"There are a hundred monuments like this on Lecythus," Minla told him, drawing her cloak tighter around herself. "We faced them with whetstone, would you believe it. It turns out to be very good for making monuments, especially when you don't want the letters to be worn away in a handful of centuries."

"You built a hundred of these?" Merlin asked.

"That's just the start. There'll be a thousand by the time we're finished. When we are gone, when all other traces of our culture have been erased from time, we hope that at least one of these monuments will remain. Shall I read you the inscription?"

Merlin had still learned nothing of the native writing, and he'd neglected to wear the lenses that would have allowed *Tyrant* to overlay a translation.

"You'd better."

"It says that once a great human society lived on Lecythus, in peace and harmony. Then came a message from the stars, a warning that our world was to be destroyed by the fire of the sun itself, or something even worse. So we made preparations to abandon the world that had been our home for so long, and to commence a journey into the outer darkness of interstellar space, looking for a new home in the stars. One day, thousands or tens of thousands after our departure, you, the people who read this message, may find us. For now you are welcome to make of this world what you will. But know that this planet was ours, and it remains ours, and that one day we shall make it our home again."

"I like the bit about 'peace and harmony'."

"History is what we write, not what we remember. Why should we tarnish the memory of our planet by enshrining our less noble deeds?"

"Spoken like a true leader, Minla."

At that moment one of the guards raised his rifle and projected a line of tracer fire into the middle distance. Something hissed and scurried into the cover of debris.

"We should be leaving," Minla said. "Regressives come out at night, and some of them are armed."

"Regressives?"

"Dissident political elements. Suicide cultists who'd rather die on Lecythus than cooperate in the evacuation effort. They're our problem, Merlin, not yours."

He'd heard stories about the regressives, but had dismissed them as rumour until now. They were the survivors of the war, people who hadn't submitted eagerly to the iron rule of Minla's new Planetary Government. Details that didn't fit into the plan, and which therefore had to be brushed aside or suppressed or given a subhuman name. He pulled the cloak tighter, anxious not to spend a minute longer on the surface than necessary. But even as Minla turned and began walking back to the waiting aircraft—moonlight picked out the elegant sweep of its single great wing—something tugged at him, holding him to the spot.

"Minla," he called, a crack in his voice.

She stopped and turned around. "What is it, Merlin?"

"I've got something for you." He reached under the cloak and fished out the gift she had given him as a girl, holding it before him. He'd had it with him for days, waiting for the moment he hoped would never come.

Impatiently, Minla retraced her steps. "I said we should be leaving. What do you want to give me?"

He handed her the sliver of whetstone. "A little girl gave me this. I don't think I know that little girl any more."

Minla looked at the stone with a curl of disgust on her face. "That was forty years ago."

"Not to me. To me it was less than a year. I've seen a lot of changes since you gave me that gift."

"We all have to grow up sometime, Merlin." For a moment he thought she was going to hand him back the gift, or at least slip it into one of her own pockets. Instead, Minla let it drop to the ground. Merlin reached to pick it up, but it was too late. The stone fell into a dark crack between two shattered paving slabs, Merlin hearing the chink as it bounced off something and fell even deeper.

"It's gone."

"It was just a silly stone," Minla said. "That's all. Now let's be on our way."

Merlin looked back at the lapping waters as he followed Minla to the moonlit flying wing. Something about the whetstone, something about tides of that sea, something about the moon itself kept nagging at the back of his mind. There was a connection, trivial or otherwise, that he was missing.

He was sure it would come to him sooner or later.

MINLA WALKED WITH a stick, clicking its hard metal shaft against the echoing flooring of the station's observation deck. Illness or injury had disfigured her since their last meeting; she wore her greying hair in a lopsided parting, hanging down almost to the collar on her right side. Merlin could not say for certain what had happened to Minla, since she was careful to turn her face away from him whenever they spoke. But in the days since his revival he had already heard talk of assassination attempts, some of which had apparently come close to succeeding. Minla seemed more stooped and frail than he remembered, as if she had worked every hour of those twenty years.

She interrupted a light-beam with her hand, opening the viewing shields. "Behold the Space Dormitories," she said, declaiming as if she had an audience of thousands rather than a single man standing only a few metres away. "Rejoice, Merlin. You played a part in this."

Through the window, wheeling with the gentle rotation of the orbital station, the nearest Dormitory loomed larger than Lecythus in the sky. The wrinkled grey sphere would soon reach operational pressure, its skin becoming taut. The final sun-mirrors were being assembled in place, manipulated by mighty articulated robots. Cargo rockets were coming and going by the minute, while the first wave of evacuees had already taken up residence in the polar holding pens.

Twenty Dormitories were ready now; the remaining eighty would come online within two years. Every day, hundreds of atomic rockets lifted from the surface of Lecythus, carrying evacuees—packed into their holds at the maximum possible human storage density, like a kind of three-dimensional jigsaw of flesh and blood—or cargo, in the form of air, water and prefabricated parts for the other habitats. Each rocket launch deposited more radioactivity into the atmosphere of the doomed world. It was now fatal to breathe that air for more than a few hours, but the slow poisoning of Lecythus was of no concern to the Planetary Government. The remaining surface-bound colonists, those who would occupy the other Dormitories when they were ready, awaited transfer in pressurised bunkers, in conditions that were at least as spartan as anything they would have to endure in space. Merlin had offered the services of *Tyrant* to assist with the evacuation effort, but as efficient and fast as his ship was, it would have made only a token difference to the speed of the exercise.

That was not to say that there were not difficulties, or that the programme was exactly on schedule. Merlin was gladdened by the progress he saw in some areas, disheartened in others. Before he slept, the locals had grilled him for help with their prototype atomic rockets, seemingly in the expectation that Merlin would provide magic remedies for the failures that had dogged them so far. But Merlin could only help in a limited fashion. He knew the basic principles of building an atomic rocket, but little of the detailed knowledge needed to circumvent a particular problem. Minla's experts were frustrated, and then dismayed. He tried explaining to them that though an atomic rocket might be primitive compared to the engines in *Tyrant*, that didn't mean it was simple, or that its construction didn't involve many subtle principles. "I know how a sailing ship works," he said, trying to explain himself. "But that doesn't mean I could build one myself, or show a master boat-builder how to improve his craft."

They wanted to know why he couldn't just give them the technology in *Tyrant* itself.

"My ship is capable of self-repair," he'd said, "but it isn't capable of making copies of itself. That's a deep principle, embodied in the logical architecture at a very profound level."

"Then run off a blueprint of your engines. Let us copy what we need from the plans," they said.

"That won't work. The components in *Tyrant* are manufactured to exacting tolerances, using materials your chemistry can't even explain, let alone reproduce."

"Then show us how to improve our manufacturing capability, until we can make what we need."

"We don't have time for that. *Tyrant* was manufactured by a culture that had had over ten thousand years of experience in spacefaring, not to mention knowledge of industrial processes and inventions dating back at least as far again. You can't cross that kind of gap in fifty years, no matter how much you might want to."

"Then what are we supposed to do?"

"Keep trying," Merlin said. "Keep making mistakes, and learning from them. That's all any culture ever does."

That was exactly what they had done, across twenty painful years. The rockets worked now, after a fashion, but they'd arrived late and there was already a huge backlog of people and parts to be shifted into space. The Dormitories should have been finished and occupied by now, with work already under way on the fleet of Exodus Arks. But the Arks had met obstacles as well. The lunar colonisation and materials-extraction programme had run into unanticipated difficulties, requiring that the Arks be assembled from components made on Lecythus. The atomic rocket production lines were already running at maximum capacity without the burden of carrying even more tonnage into space.

"This is good," Merlin told Minla. "But you still need to step things up."

"We're aware of that," she answered testily. "Unfortunately, some of your information proved less than accurate."

Merlin blinked at her. "It did?"

"Our scientists made a prototype for the fusion drive, according to your plans. Given the limited testing they've been able to do, they say it works very well. It wouldn't be a technical problem to build all the engines we need for the Exodus Arks. So I'm told, at least."

"Then what's the issue?"

Her hand gripped the walking stick like a talon. "Fuel, Merlin. You told us we'd find helium three in the topsoil of our moon. Well, we didn't. Not enough to suit our needs, anyway."

"Then you mustn't have been looking properly."

"I assure you we looked, Merlin. You were mistaken. In fact almost everything you told us to expect on the moon turned out to be wrong. You really didn't pay much attention to it on your way in to Lecythus, did you?"

"It was a moon. I had a few other things on my mind."

"Not only can't we mine it for helium three, but it isn't much good for anything else. The surface gravity's much less than you led us to expect, which complicates our operations tremendously. Things float away at the least provocation. Our experts say the density's so low we shouldn't expect to find anything useful under the crust. Certainly not the heavy ores and precious metals you promised us."

"I don't know what to say."

"That you were wrong?"

"I've seen a few moons, Minla. You get used to them. If this one's a lot less dense than I thought, then there's something weird about its chemistry." Merlin paused, feeling himself on the edge of something important, but whatever it was remained just out of reach.

"Well, it doesn't matter now. We'll just have to find fuel from an alternative source, and redesign our fusion drive accordingly. We'll need your help, if we aren't to fall hopelessly behind schedule." Minla extended a withered hand towards the wheeling view. "To have come so far, to have reached this point, and then *failed*...that would be worse than having never tried at all, don't you think?"

Chastened, Merlin scratched at his chin. "I'll do what I can. Let me talk to the fusion engineers."

"I've scheduled a meeting. They're *very* anxious to talk to you." Minla paused. "There's something you should know, though. They've seen you make a mistake. They'll still be interested in what you have to say, but don't expect blind acceptance of your every word. They know you're human now."

"I never said I wasn't."

"You didn't, no. I'll give you credit for that. But for a little while some of us allowed ourselves to believe it."

Minla turned and walked away, the tap of her stick echoing into the distance.

AS SPACE WARS went, it was brief and relatively tame, certainly by comparison with the some of the more awesome battles delineated in the Cohort's pictorial history. The timeworn frescos on the swallowships commemorated engagements where entire solar systems were reduced to mere tactical details, hills or ditches in the terrain of a much larger strategic landscape, and where the participants—human and Husker both—were moving at significant fractions of the speed of light and employing relativistic weapons of world-shattering destructive potential. A single skirmish could eat up many centuries of planetary time, whole lifetimes from the point of view of a starship's crew. The war itself was a thing inseparably entwined with recorded history, a monstrous choking structure with its roots reaching into the loam of deep time, and whose end must be assumed (by all except Merlin, at least) to lie in the unimaginably remote future.

Here, the theatre of conflict was considerably less than half a light-second in diameter, encompassing only the immediate space around Lecythus, with its girdle of half-finished Dormitories and Exodus Arks. The battle lasted barely a dozen hours, between first and last detonation. With the exception of Merlin's own late intervention, no weapons more potent than hydrogen bombs were deployed. Horrific, certainly, but possessed of a certain genteel precision compared to the weapons that had consumed Plenitude.

It began with a surprise strike from the surface, using a wave of commandeered atomic rockets. It seemed that the Regressives had gained control of one of the rocket assembly and launch complexes. The rockets had no warheads, but that didn't matter: kinetic energy, and the explosive force stored in their atomic engines, was still enough to inflict havoc on their targets. The weapons had been aimed with surprising accuracy. The first wave destroyed half of the unfinished Dormitories, inflicting catastrophic damage on many of the others. By the time the second wave was rising, orbital defences had sprung into action, but by then it was too late to intercept more than a handful of the missiles. Many of the atomic rockets were being piloted by suicide crews, steering their charges through Minla's hastily erected countermeasure screens. By the third hour, the Planetary Government was beginning to retaliate against Regressive elements using atmospheric-entry interceptors, but while they could pick away at enemy fortifications on the ground, they couldn't penetrate the anti-missile cordon around the launch complex itself. Rogue warheads chipped away at the edges of aerial land masses, sending mountain-sized boulders crashing to the surface. Even as the battle raged, brutal tidal waves ravaged the already-frail coastal communities. As the hours ticked by, Minla's analysts maintained a grim toll of the total numbers of surface and orbital casualties. In the fifth and sixth hours, more Dormitories fell to the assault. Stray fire accounted for even more losses. A temporary ceasefire in the seventh hour was only caused by the temporary occultation of the launch complex by a medium-sized aerial land mass. When the skies were clear again, the rockets rose up with renewed fury.

"They've hit all but one of the Exodus Arks," Minla said, when the battle was in its ninth hour. "We just had time to move the final ship out of range of the atomics. But if they find a way to increase their reach, by eliminating more payload mass..." She turned her face from his. "It'll all have been for nothing, Merlin. They'll have won, and the last sixty years may as well not have happened."

He felt preternaturally calm, knowing exactly what was coming. "What do you want me to do?"

"Intervene," Minla said. "Use whatever force is merited."

"I offered once. You said no."

"You changed your mind once. Now I'm changing mine."

Merlin went to *Tyrant*. He ordered the ship to deliver a concentrated charm-torp salvo against the compromised rocket facility, bringing more energy to bear on that one tiny area of land than had been deployed in all the years of the atomic wars. There was no need for him to accompany his ship; like a well-trained dog, *Tyrant* was perfectly capable of carrying out his orders without direct supervision.

They watched the spectacle from orbit. When the electric-white fire erupted on the horizon of Lecythus, brightening that entire limb of the planet in the manner of a stuttering cold sunrise, Merlin felt Minla's hand tighten around his own. For all her frailty, for all that the years had taken from her, astonishing steel remained in that grip.

"Thank you," she said. "You may just have saved us all."

IT HAD BEEN ten years.

Lecythus and its sun now lay many light-weeks to stern. The one remaining Exodus Ark had reached five per cent of the speed of light. In sixty years—faster, if the engine could be improved—it would streak into another system, one that might offer the possibility of landfall. It flew alongside the gossamer line of the Waynet, using the tube as cover from Husker long-range sensors. The Exodus Ark carried only twelve hundred exiles, few of whom would live long enough to see another world.

The hospital was near the core of the ship, safely distant from the sleeting energies of interstellar radiation or the exotic emissions of the Waynet. Many of its patients were veterans of the Regressive War, victims of the viciously ingenious injuries wrought by the close conjunction of vacuum and heat, radiation and kinetic energy. Most of them would be dead by the time the fusion engine was silenced for cruise phase. For now they were being afforded the care appropriate to war heroes, even those who screamed bloodcurdling pleas for the painkilling mercy of euthanasia.

In a soundproofed private annexe of that same complex, Minla also lay in the care of machines. This time the assassins had come closer than ever before, and they had very nearly achieved their objective. Yet she'd survived, and the prognosis for a complete recovery—so Merlin was informed—was deemed higher than seventy-five per cent. More than could be said of Minla's aides, injured in the same attack, but they were at least receiving the best possible care in *Tyrant*'s frostwatch cabinets.

The exercise was, Merlin knew, akin to knitting together human-shaped sculptures from a bloody stew of meat and splintered bone, and then hoping that those sculptures would retain some semblance of mind. Minla would have presented no challenge at all, but the Planetary Director had declined the offer of frostwatch care herself, preferring to give up her place to one of her underlings. Knowing that, Merlin allowed himself a momentary flicker of empathy.

He walked into the room, coughing to announce himself. "Hello, Minla."

She lay on her back, her head against the pillow, though she was not asleep. Slowly she turned to face Merlin as he approached. She looked very old, very tired, but she still found the energy to form a smile.

"It's so good of you to come. I was hoping, but…I didn't dare ask. I know how busy you've been with the engine upgrade study."

"I could hardly not pay you a visit. Even though I had a devil of a job persuading your staff to let me through."

"They're too protective of me. I know my own strength, Merlin. I'll get through this."

"I believe you will."

Minla's gaze settled on his hand. "Are those for me?"

He had a bouquet of alien flowers. They were of a peculiar dark hue, a shade that ought to have appeared black in the room's subdued gold lighting yet which was clearly and unmistakably purple, revealed by its own soft inner illumination. They had the look of a detail that had been hand-tinted in a black and white photograph, so that it appeared to float above the rest of the image.

"Of course," Merlin said. "I always bring flowers, don't I?"

"You always used to. Then you stopped."

"Perhaps it's time to start again."

He set them by her bedside, in the water-filled vase that was already waiting. They were not the only flowers in the room, but the purple ones seemed to suck the very colour from the others.

"They're beautiful," Minla said. "It's like I've never seen anything precisely that colour before. It's as if there's a whole circuit in my brain that's never been activated until now."

"I chose them especially. They're famous for their beauty."

Minla lifted her head from the pillow, her eyes brightening with curiosity. "Now you'll have to tell me where they're from."

"It's a long story."

"That never stopped you before."

"A world called Lacertine. It's ten thousand light-years from here; many days of shiptime, even in the Waynet. I don't even know if it still exists."

"Tell me about Lacertine," she said, pronouncing the name of the world with her usual scrupulousness.

"It's a very beautiful planet, orbiting a hot blue star. They say the planet must have been moved into its present orbit by the Waymakers, from another system entirely. The seas and skies are a shimmering electric blue, the forests a dazzle of purple and violet and pink; colours that you've only ever seen when you close your eyes against the sun and see patterns behind your eyelids. White citadels rise above the treeline, towers linked by a filigree of delicate bridges."

"Then there are people on Lacertine?"

Merlin thought of the occupants, and nodded. "Adapted, of course. Everything that grows on Lacertine was bioengineered to tolerate the scalding light from the sun. They say if something can grow there, it can grow almost anywhere."

"Have you been there?"

He shook his head ruefully. "Never been within a thousand light-years of the place."

"I'll never see it. Nor any of the other places you've told me about."

"There are places I'll never see. Even with the Waynet, I'm still just one human man, with one human life. Even the Waymakers didn't live long enough to glimpse more than a fraction of their empire."

"It must make you very sad."

"I take each day as it comes. I'd rather take good memories from one world than fret about the thousand I'll never see."

"You're a wise man," Minla said. "We were lucky to get you."

Merlin smiled. He was silent for many moments, letting Minla enjoy the last calmness of mind she would ever know. "There's something I need to tell you," he said eventually.

She must have heard something in his tone of voice. "What, Merlin?"

"There's a good chance you're all going to die."

Her tone became sharp. "We don't need you to remind us of the risks."

"I'm talking about something that's going to happen sooner rather than later. The ruse of shadowing the Waynet didn't work. It was the best thing to do, but there was always a chance..." Merlin spread his hands in exaggerated apology, as if there had ever been something he could have done about it. "*Tyrant*'s detected a Husker attack swarm, six elements lying a light-month ahead of you. You don't have time to steer or slow down. They'd shadow every move you made, even if you tried to shake them off."

"You promised us—"

"I promised you nothing. I just gave you the best advice I could. If you hadn't shadowed the Waynet, they'd have found you even sooner."

"We aren't using the ramscoop design. You said we'd be safe if we stuck to fusion motors. The electromagnetic signature—"

"I said you'd be *safer*. There were never any cast-iron guarantees."

"You lied to us." Minla turned suddenly spiteful. "I never trusted you."

"I did all in my power to save you."

"Then why are you standing there looking so calm, when you know we're going to die?" But before Merlin had time to answer, Minla had seen the answer for herself. "Because you can leave," she said, nodding at her own percipience. "You have your ship, and a syrinx. You can slip into the Waynet and outrun the enemy."

"I'm leaving," Merlin said. "But I'm not running."

"Aren't they one and the same?"

"Not this time. I'm going back to Plenitude, I mean Lecythus, to do what I can for the people we left behind. The people you condemned to death."

"Me, Merlin?"

"I examined the records of the Regressive War: not just the official documents, but *Tyrant*'s own data logs. And I saw what I should have seen at the time, but didn't. It was a ruse. It was too damned easy, the way they took control of that rocket factory. You let them, Minla."

"I did nothing of the kind."

"You knew the whole evacuation project was never going to be ready on time. The Space Dormitories were behind schedule, there were problems with the Exodus Arks…"

"Because you told us falsehoods about the helium in the moon's soil."

Merlin raised a warning hand. "We'll get to that. The point is, your plans were in tatters. But you could still have completed more Dormitories and ships, if you'd been willing to leave the system a little later. You could still have saved more people than you did, albeit at a slightly increased risk to your own survival. But that wasn't acceptable. You wanted to leave there and then. So you engineered the whole Regressive attack, set it up as a pretext for an early departure."

"The Regressives were real!" Minla hissed.

"But you gave them the keys to that rocket silo, and the know-how to target and guide those missiles. Funny how their attack just missed the one station that you were occupying, you and all your political cronies, and that you managed to move the one Exodus Ark to safety just in time. Damned convenient, Minla."

"I'll have you shot for this, Merlin."

"Good luck. Try laying a hand on me, and see how far it gets you. My ship's listening in on this conversation. It can put proctors into this room in a matter of seconds."

"And the moon, Merlin? Do you have an excuse for the error that cost us so dearly?"

"I don't know. Possibly. That's why I'm going back to Lecythus. There are still people on the surface—Regressives, allies, I don't care. And people you abandoned in orbit, as well."

"They'll all die. You said it yourself."

He raised a finger. "If they don't leave. But maybe there's a way. Again, I should have seen it sooner. But that's me all the way. I take a long time to put the pieces together, but I get there in the end. Just like Dowitcher, the man who gave your father the whetstone."

"It was just a stone."

"So you said. In fact, it was a vital clue to the nature of your world. It took spring tides and neap tides to lay down those patterns. But you said it yourself: Lecythus doesn't have spring tides and neap tides. Not any more, at least."

"I'm sure this means something to you."

"Something happened to your moon, Minla. When that whetstone formed, your moon was raising tides on Lecythus. When the moon and Calliope were tugging on your seas in the same direction, you got a spring tide. When they were balancing each other, you got a neap tide. Hence the patterning on the whetstone. But now the tides are the same from day to day. Calliope's still there, so that only leaves the moon. It isn't exerting the same gravitational pull it used to. Like you told me, the surface gravity is much lower than you'd expect. Oh, it weighs *something*—but nowhere near as much as it should, based on its size and appearance. If you could skip forward a few hundred million years and examine a piece of whetstone laid down now, you'd probably find very faint variations in sediment thickness. But whatever the effect is now, it must be insignificant compared to the time when your whetstone was formed. Yet the moon's still there, in what appears to be the same orbit. So what's happened?"

"You tell me, Merlin."

"I don't think it's a moon any more. I think the original moon got ripped to pieces to make your armoured sky. I don't know how much of the original mass was used for that, but I'm guessing it was quite a significant fraction. The question is, what happened to the remains?"

"I'm sure you have a theory."

"I think they made a fake moon out of the leftovers. It sits there in your sky, it orbits Lecythus, but it doesn't pull on your seas the way the old one used to. It has gravity, but it's not enough to affect the oceans to the same degree. And you're right: it's much less dense than I expected. I really should have paid more attention. Maybe if I did I could have spared Lecythus all this bloodshed."

"And now you understand everything?"

"I understand that the moon's new. It's not been sitting there long enough to soak up billions of years of particles from the solar wind. That's why you didn't find the helium you were expecting."

"So what is it?"

"That's what I'm keen to find out. The thing is, I know what Dowitcher was thinking now. He knew that wasn't a real moon. Which begs the question: what's inside it? And could it make a difference to the survivors you left behind?"

"Hiding inside a shell won't help them," Minla said. "You already told us we'd achieve nothing by digging tunnels into Lecythus."

"I'm not thinking about hiding. I'm thinking about moving. What if the moon's an escape vehicle? An Exodus Ark big enough to take the entire population?"

"You have no evidence."

"I have this." With that, Merlin produced one of Minla's old picture books. Seventy years had aged its pages to a brittle yellow, dimming the vibrancy of the old inks. But the linework in the illustrations was still clear enough. Merlin held the book open at a particular page, letting Minla look at it. "Your people had a memory of arriving on Lecythus in a moon-sized ship," he said. "Maybe that was true. Equally, maybe it was a case of muddling one thing with another. I'm wondering if the thing you were meant to remember was not that you came by moon, but that you could leave by one."

Minla stared at the picture. For a moment, like a breeze on a summer's day, Merlin felt a wave of almost unbearable sadness pass through the room. It was as if the picture had transported her back to her childhood, before she had set her life on the trajectory that, seventy years later, would bring it to this bed, this soundproofed room, the shameful survival of this one ship. The last time she had looked at the picture, everything had been possible, all life's opportunities open to her. She'd been the daughter of a powerful and respected man, with influence and wisdom at her fingertips. And yet from all the choices presented to her, she had selected this one dark path, and followed it to its conclusion.

"Even if it is a ship," she said softly, "you'll never get them all aboard."

"I'll die trying."

"And us? We get abandoned to our fates?"

Merlin smiled: he'd been expecting the question. "There are twelve hundred people on this ship, some of them children. They weren't all party to your schemes, so they don't all deserve to die when you meet the Huskers. That's why I'm leaving behind weapons and a detachment of proctors to show you how to install and use them."

For the first time since his arrival in the room, Minla spoke like a leader again. "Will they make a difference?"

"They'll give your ship a fighting chance. That's the best I can offer."

"Then we'll take what we're given."

"I'm sorry it came to this. I played a part in what you became, of that I've no doubt. But I didn't make you a monster."

"No," she said. "I'll at least take credit for myself, and for the fact that I saved twelve hundred of my people. If it took a monster to do that, doesn't that mean we sometimes need monsters?"

"Maybe we do. But that doesn't mean we should forgive them for what they are, even for an instant." Gently, as if bestowing a gift, Merlin placed the picture book on Minla's recumbent form. "I'm afraid I have to go now. There won't be much time when I get back to Lecythus."

"Please," she said. "Not like this. Not this way."

"This is how it ends," he said, before turning from her bed and walking to the exit. "Goodbye, Minla."

Twenty minutes later he was in the Waynet, racing back to Lecythus.

THERE'S A LOT to tell, and one day I'll get around to writing it up properly. For now it's enough to say that I was right to trust my instincts about the moon. I just wish I'd put the clues together sooner than I did. Perhaps then Minla would never have had to commit her crimes.

I didn't save as many as I'd have wished, but I did save some of the people Minla left behind to die. I suppose that has to count for something. It was close, but if there's one thing to be said for Waymaker-level technology, it's that it's almost childishly easy to use. They were like babies with the toys of the gods. They left that moon there for a good reason, and while it was necessary for them to camouflage it—it had to be capable of fooling the Huskers, or whoever they built that sky to hide from—the moon itself was obligingly easy to break into, once our purpose became clear. And once it started moving, once its great engines came online after tens of thousands of years of quiet dormancy, no force in the universe could have held it back. I shadowed the fleeing moon long enough to establish that it was headed into a sector that appeared to be free of Husker activity, at least for now. It'll be touch and go for a few centuries, but with force and wisdom on their side, I think they'll make it.

I'm in the Waynet now, riding the flow away from Calliope. The syrinx still works, much to my relief. For a while I considered riding the contraflow, back towards that lone Exodus Ark. By the time I reached them they'd have been only days away from the encounter. But my presence wouldn't have made a decisive difference to their chances of surviving the Huskers, and I couldn't have expected much of a warm welcome.

Not after my final gift to Minla.

I'm glad she never asked me too much about those flowers, or the world they came from. If she'd wanted to know more about Lacertine, she might have sensed that I was holding something back. Such as the fact that the assassin guilds on Lacertine were masters of their craft, known throughout the worlds of the Waynet for their skill and cunning, and that no guild on Lacertine was more revered than the bio-artificers who made the sleepflowers.

It was said that they could make them in any shape, any colour, to match any known flower from any known world. It was said that they could pass all tests save the most microscopic scrutiny. It was said that if you wanted to kill someone, you gave them a gift of flowers from Lacertine.

She would have been dead not long after my departure. The flowers would have detected her presence—they were keyed to locate a single breathing form in a room, most commonly a sleeper—and when the room was quiet they would have become stealthily animate, leaving their vase and creeping from point to point with the slowness of a sundial's shadow, their movement imperceptible to the naked eye, but enough to take them to the face of the sleeper. Their tendrils would have closed around Minla's face with the softness of a lover's caress. Then the paralysing toxins would have hit her nervous system.

I hoped it was painless. I hoped it was quick. But what I remembered of the Lacertine assassins was that they were known for their cleverness, not their clemency.

Afterwards, I deleted the sleepflowers from the bio-library.

I knew Minla for less than a year of my life, and for seventy years by another reckoning. Sometimes when I think of her I see a human being in all her dimensions, as real as anyone I've ever known. Other times, I see something two-dimensional, like a faded illustration in one of her books, so thin that the light shines through her.

I don't hate her, even now. But I wish time and tide had never brought us together.

A comfortable number of light-hours behind me, the Waynet has just cut into Calliope's heart. It has already sliced through the photosphere and the star's convection zone. Quite what has happened, or is happening, or will happen, when it touched (or touches, or will touch) the nuclear-burning core is still far from clear.

Theory says that no impulse can travel faster than light. Since my ship is already riding the Waynet's flow at very nearly the speed of light, it seems impossible that any information concerning Calliope's fate will ever be able to catch up with me. And yet...several minutes ago I swear that I felt a kick, a jolt in the smooth glide of my flight, as if some report of that destructive event had raced up the flow at superluminal speed, buffeting my little ship.

There's nothing in the data to suggest any unusual event, and I don't have any plans to return to Lecythus and see what became of that world when its sun was gored open. But I still felt something, and if it reached me up the flow of the Waynet, if that impulse bypassed the iron barrier of causality itself, I can't begin to imagine the energies that must have been involved, or what must have happened to the strand of the Waynet behind me. Perhaps it's unravelling, and I'm about to breathe my last breath before I become a thin smear of naked quarks, stretched across several billion kilometres of interstellar space.

That would certainly be one way to go.

Frankly, it would be nice to have the luxury to dwell on such fears. But I still have a gun to find, and I'm not getting any younger.

Mission resumed.

ZIMA BLUE

AFTER THE first week people started drifting away from the island. The viewing stands around the pool became emptier by the day. The big tourist ships hauled back towards interstellar space. Art fiends, commentators and critics packed their bags in Venice. Their disappointment hung over the lagoon like a miasma.

I was one of the few who stayed on Murjek, returning to the stands each day. I'd watch for hours, squinting against the trembling blue light reflected from the surface of the water. Face down, Zima's pale shape moved so languidly from one end of the pool to the other that it could have been mistaken for a floating corpse. As he swam I wondered how I was going to tell his story, and who was going to buy it. I tried to remember the name of my first newspaper, back on Mars. They wouldn't pay as much as some of the bigger titles, but some part of me liked the idea of going back to the old place. It had been a long time...I queried the AM, wanting it to jog my memory about the name of the paper. There'd been so many since...hundreds, by my reckoning. But nothing came. It took me another yawning moment to remember that I'd dismissed the AM the day before.

"Carrie, you're on your own," I said aloud to myself. "Start getting used to it."

In the pool, the swimming figure ended a length and began to swim back towards me.

Two weeks earlier I'd been sitting in the Piazza San Marco at noon, watching white figurines glide against the white marble of the clock tower. The sky over Venice was jammed with ships, parked hull-to-hull. Their bellies were quilted in vast, glowing panels, tuned to match the real sky. The view reminded me of the work of a pre-Expansion artist who had specialized in eye-wrenching tricks of perspective and composition: endless waterfalls, interlocking lizards. I formed a mental image and queried the fluttering presence of the AM, but it couldn't retrieve the name.

I finished my coffee and steeled myself for the bill.

I'd come to this white marble version of Venice to witness the unveiling of Zima's final work of art. I'd had an interest in the artist for years, and I'd hoped I might be able to arrange an interview. Unfortunately several thousand other members of the in-crowd had come up with exactly the same idea. Not that it mattered what kind of competition I had anyway: Zima wasn't talking.

The waiter placed a folded card on my table.

All we had been told was to make our way to Murjek, a waterlogged world most of us had never heard of before. Murjek's only claim to fame was that it hosted the one hundred and seventy-first known duplicate of Venice, and one of only three Venices rendered entirely in white marble. Zima had chosen Murjek to host his final work of art, and to be the place where he would make his retirement from public life.

With a heavy heart I lifted the bill to inspect the damage. Instead of the expected bill, it was a small, blue card printed in fine gold italic lettering. The shade of blue was that precise powdery aquamarine that Zima had made his own. The card was addressed to me, Carrie Clay, and it said that Zima wanted to talk to me about the unveiling. If I was interested, I should report to the Rialto Bridge in exactly two hours.

If I was interested.

The note stipulated that no recording materials were to be brought, not even a pen and paper. As an afterthought, the card mentioned that the bill had been taken care of. I almost had the nerve to order another coffee and put it on the same tab. Almost, but not quite.

ZIMA'S SERVANT WAS there when I arrived early at the bridge. Intricate neon mechanisms pulsed behind the flexing glass of the robot's mannequin body. It bowed at the waist and spoke very softly. "Miss Clay? Since you're here, we might as well depart."

The robot escorted me to a flight of stairs that led to the waterside. My AM followed us, fluttering at my shoulder. A conveyor hovered in waiting, floating a metre above the water. The robot helped me into the rear compartment. The AM was about to follow me inside when the robot raised a warning hand.

"You'll have to leave that behind, I'm afraid; no recording materials, remember?"

I looked at the metallic green hummingbird, trying to remember the last time I had been out of its ever-watchful presence.

"Leave it behind?"

"It'll be quite safe here, and you can collect it again when you return after nightfall."

"If I say no?"

"Then I'm afraid there'll be no meeting with Zima."

I sensed that the robot wasn't going to hang around all afternoon waiting for my answer. The thought of being away from the AM made my blood run cold. But I wanted that interview so badly I was prepared to consider anything.

I told the AM to stay here until I returned.

The obedient machine reversed away from me in a flash of metallic green. It was like watching a part of myself drift away. The glass hull wrapped itself around me and I felt a surge of un-nulled acceleration.

Venice tilted below us, then streaked away to the horizon.

I formed a test query, asking the AM to name the planet where I'd celebrated my seven hundredth birthday. Nothing came: I was out of query range, with only my own age-saturated memory to rely on.

I leaned forward. "Are you authorized to tell me what this is about?"

"I'm afraid he didn't tell me," the robot said, making a face appear in the back of his head. "But if at any moment you feel uncomfortable, we can return to Venice."

"I'm fine for now. Who else got the blue card treatment?"

"Only you, to the best of my knowledge."

"And if I'd declined? Were you supposed to ask someone else?"

"No," the robot said. "But let's face it, Miss Clay. You weren't very likely to turn him down."

As we flew on, the conveyor's shock wave gouged a foaming channel in the sea behind it. I thought of a brush drawn through wet paint on marble, exposing the white surface beneath. I took out Zima's invitation and held it against the horizon ahead of us, trying to decide whether the blue was a closer match to the sky or the sea. Against these two possibilities the card seemed to flicker indeterminately.

Zima Blue. It was an exact thing, specified scientifically in terms of angstroms and intensities. If you were an artist, you could have a batch of it mixed up according to that specification. But no one ever used Zima Blue unless they were making a calculated statement about Zima himself.

Zima was already unique by the time he emerged into the public eye. He had undergone radical procedures to enable him to tolerate extreme environments without the burden of a protective suit. Zima had the appearance of a well-built man wearing a tight body stocking, until you were close and you realized that this was actually his skin. Covering his entire form, it was a synthetic material that could be tuned to different colours and textures depending on his mood and surroundings. It could approximate clothing if the social circumstances demanded it. The skin could contain pressure when he wished to experience vacuum, and stiffen to protect him against the crush of a gas giant. Despite these refinements the skin conveyed a full range of sensory impressions to his mind. He had no need to breathe, since his entire cardiovascular system had been replaced by closed-cycle life-support mechanisms. He had no need to eat or drink; no need to dispose of bodily waste. Tiny repair machines swarmed through his body, allowing him to tolerate radiation doses that would have killed an ordinary man in minutes.

With his body thus armoured against environmental extremes, Zima was free to seek inspiration where he wanted. He could drift free in space, staring into the face of a star, or wander the searing canyons of a planet where metals ran like lava. His eyes had been replaced by cameras sensitive to a huge swathe of the electromagnetic spectrum, wired into his brain via complex processing modules. A synaesthetic bridge allowed him to hear visual data as a kind of music, to see sounds as a symphony of startling colours. His skin functioned as a kind of antenna, giving him sensitivity to electrical field changes. When that wasn't sufficient, he could tap into the data feeds of any number of accompanying machines.

Given all this, Zima's art couldn't help but be original and attention-grabbing. His landscapes and starfields had a heightened, ecstatic quality about them, awash with luminous, jarring colours and eye-wrenching tricks of perspective. Painted in traditional materials but on a huge scale, they quickly attracted a core of serious buyers. Some found their way into private collections, but Zima murals also started popping up in public spaces all over the galaxy. Tens of metres across, the murals were nonetheless detailed down to the limits of vision. Most had been painted in one session. Zima had no need for sleep, so he worked uninterrupted until a piece was complete.

The murals were undeniably impressive. From a standpoint of composition and technique they were unquestionably brilliant. But there was also something bleak and chilling about them. They were landscapes without a human presence, save for the implied viewpoint of the artist himself.

Put it this way: they were nice to look at, but I wouldn't have hung one in my home.

Not everyone agreed, obviously, or else Zima wouldn't have sold as many works as he had. But I couldn't help wondering how many people were buying the paintings because of what they knew about the artist, rather than because of any intrinsic merit in the works themselves.

That was how things stood when I first paid attention to Zima. I filed him away as interesting but kitschy; maybe worth a story if something else happened to either him or his art.

Something did, but it took a while for anyone—including me—to notice.

One day—after a longer than usual gestation period—Zima unveiled a mural that had something different about it. It was a painting of a swirling, star-pocked nebula, from the vantage point of an airless rock. Perched on the rim of a crater in the middle distance, blocking off part of the nebula, was a tiny, blue square. At first glance it looked as if the canvas had been washed blue and Zima had simply left a small area unpainted. There was no solidity to the square, no detail or suggestion of how it related to the landscape or the backdrop. It cast no shadow and had no tonal influence on the surrounding colours. But the square was deliberate: close examination showed that it had indeed been over-painted over the rocky lip of the crater. It meant something.

The square was just the beginning. Thereafter, every mural that Zima released to the outside world contained a similar geometric shape: a square, triangle, oblong or some similar form embedded somewhere in the composition. It was a long time before anyone noticed that the shade of blue was the same from painting to painting.

It was Zima Blue: the same shade of blue as on the gold-lettered card.

Over the next decade or so, the abstract shapes became more dominant, squeezing out the other elements of each composition. The cosmic vistas ended up as narrow borders, framing blank circles, triangles, rectangles. Where his earlier work had been characterized by exuberant brushwork and thick layers of paint, the blue forms were rendered with mirror-smoothness.

Intimated by the intrusion of the abstract blue forms, casual buyers turned away from Zima. Before very long Zima unveiled the first of his entirely blue murals. Large enough to cover the side of a thousand-storey building, the mural was considered by many to be as far as Zima could take things.

They couldn't have been more wrong.

I FELT THE conveyor slowing as we neared a small island, the only feature in any direction.

"You're the first to see this," the robot said. "There's a distortion screen blocking the view from space."

The island was about a kilometre across: low and turtle-shaped, ringed by a narrow collar of pale sand. Near the middle it rose to a shallow plateau, on which vegetation had been cleared in a roughly rectangular area. I made out a small panel of reflective blue set flat against the ground, surrounded by what appeared to be a set of tiered viewing stands.

The conveyor shed altitude and speed, bobbing down until it stopped just outside the area enclosed by the viewing stands. It came to rest next to a low, white pebble-dash chalet I hadn't noticed during our approach.

The robot stepped out and helped me from the conveyor.

"Zima will be here in a moment," it said, before returning to the conveyor and vanishing back into the sky.

Suddenly I felt very alone and very vulnerable. A breeze came in from the sea, blowing sand into my eyes. The sun was creeping down towards the horizon and soon it would be getting chilly. Just when I was beginning to feel the itch of panic, a man emerged from the chalet, rubbing his hands briskly. He walked towards me, following a path of paved stones.

"Glad you could make it, Carrie."

It was Zima, of course, and in a flash I felt foolish for doubting that he would show his face.

"Hi," I said lamely.

Zima offered his hand. I shook it, feeling the slightly plastic texture of his artificial skin. Today it was a dull pewter-grey.

"Let's go and sit on the balcony. It's nice to watch the sunset, isn't it?"

"Nice," I agreed.

He turned his back to me and set off in the direction of the chalet. As he walked, his muscles flexed and bulged beneath the pewter flesh. There were scalelike glints in the skin on his back, as if it had been set with a mosaic of reflective chips. He was beautiful like a statue, muscular like a panther. He was a handsome man, even after all his transformations, but I had never heard of him taking a lover, or having any kind of a private life at all. His art was everything.

I followed him, feeling awkward and tongue-tied. Zima led me into the chalet, through an old-fashioned kitchen and an old-fashioned lounge, full of thousand-year-old furniture and ornaments.

"How was the flight?"

"Fine."

He stopped suddenly and turned to face me. "I forgot to check…did the robot insist that you leave behind your *Aide Memoire*?"

"Yes."

"Good. It was you I wanted to talk to, Carrie, not some surrogate recording device."

"Me?"

The pewter mask of his face formed a quizzical expression. "Do you do multi-syllables, or are you still working up to that?"

"Er..."

"Relax," he said. "I'm not here to test you, or humiliate you, or anything like that. This isn't a trap, and you're not in any danger. You'll be back in Venice by midnight."

"I'm OK," I managed. "Just a bit starstruck."

"Well, you shouldn't be. I'm hardly the first celebrity you've met, am I?"

"Well, no, but—"

"People find me intimidating," he said. "They get over it eventually, and then wonder what all the fuss was about."

"Why me?"

"Because you kept asking nicely," Zima said.

"Be serious."

"All right. There's a bit more to it than that, although you *did* ask nicely. I've enjoyed much of your work over the years. People have often trusted you to set the record straight, especially near the ends of their lives."

"You talked about retiring, not dying."

"Either way, it would still be a withdrawal from public life. Your work has always seemed truthful to me, Carrie. I'm not aware of anyone claiming misrepresentation through your writing."

"It happens now and then," I said. "That's why I always make sure there's an AM on hand so no one can dispute what was said."

"That won't matter with my story," Zima said.

I looked at him shrewdly. "There's something else, isn't there? Some other reason you pulled my name out of the hat."

"I'd like to help you," he said.

WHEN MOST PEOPLE speak about his Blue Period they mean the era of the truly huge murals. By huge I do mean *huge*. Soon they had become large enough to dwarf buildings and civic spaces, large enough to be visible from orbit. Across the galaxy twenty-kilometre-high sheets of blue towered over private islands or rose from storm-wracked seas. Expense was never a problem, since Zima had many rival sponsors who competed to host his latest and biggest creation. The panels kept on growing, until they required complex, sloth-tech machinery to hold them aloft against gravity and weather. They pierced the tops of planetary atmospheres, jutting into space. They glowed with their own soft light. They curved around in arcs and fans, so that the viewer's entire visual field was saturated with blue.

By now Zima was hugely famous, even to people who had no particular interest in art. He was the weird cyborg celebrity who made huge blue structures; the man who never gave interviews or hinted at the private significance of his art.

But that was a hundred years ago. Zima wasn't even remotely done.

Eventually the structures became too unwieldy to be hosted on planets. Blithely Zima moved into interplanetary space, forging vast, free-floating sheets of blue ten thousand kilometres across. Now he worked not with brushes and paint, but with fleets of mining robots, tearing apart asteroids to make the raw material for his creations. Now it was entire stellar economies that competed with each other to host Zima's work.

That was about the time that I renewed my interest in Zima. I attended one of his 'moonwrappings': the enclosure of an entire celestial body in a lidded blue container, like a hat going into a box. Two months later he stained the entire equatorial belt of a gas giant blue, and I had a ringside seat for that as well. Six months later he altered the surface chemistry of a sun-grazing comet so that it daubed a Zima Blue tail across an entire solar system. But I was no closer to a story. I kept asking for an interview and kept being turned down. All I knew was that there had to be more to Zima's obsession with blue than a mere artistic whim. Without an understanding of that obsession, there was no story: just anecdote.

I didn't do anecdote.

So I waited, and waited. And then—like millions of others—I heard about Zima's final work of art, and made my way to the fake Venice on Murjek. I wasn't expecting an interview, or any new insights. I just had to be there.

WE STEPPED THROUGH sliding glass doors onto the balcony. Two simple white chairs sat either side of a white table. The table was set with drinks and a bowl of fruit. Beyond the unfenced balcony, arid land sloped steeply away, offering an uninterrupted view of the sea. The water was calm and inviting, with the lowering sun reflected like a silver coin.

Zima indicated that I should take one of the seats. His hand dithered over two bottles of wine.

"Red or white, Carrie?"

I opened my mouth as if to answer him, but nothing came. Normally, in that instant between the question and the response, the AM would have silently directed my choice to one of the two options. Not having the AM's prompt felt like a mental stall in my thoughts.

"Red, I think," Zima said. "Unless you have strong objections."

"It's not that I can't decide these things for myself," I said.

Zima poured me a glass of red, then held it up to the sky to inspect its clarity. "Of course not," he said.

"It's just that this is a little strange for me."

"It shouldn't be strange," he said. "This is the way you lived your life for hundreds of years."

"The natural way, you mean?"

Zima poured himself a glass of the red wine, but instead of drinking it he merely sniffed the bouquet. "Yes."

"But there isn't anything natural about being alive a thousand years after I was born," I said. "My organic memory reached saturation point about seven hundred years ago. My head's like a house with too much furniture. Move something in, you have to move something out."

"Let's go back to the wine for a moment," Zima said. "Normally, you'd have relied on the advice of the AM, wouldn't you?"

I shrugged. "Yes."

"Would the AM always suggest one of the two possibilities? Always red wine, or always white wine, for instance?"

"It's not that simplistic," I said. "If I had a strong preference for one over the other, then, yes, the AM would always recommend one wine over the other. But I don't. I like red wine sometimes and white wine other times. Sometimes I don't want any kind of wine." I hoped my frustration wasn't obvious. But after the elaborate charade with the blue card, the robot and the conveyor, the last thing I wanted to be discussing with Zima was my own imperfect recall.

"Then it's random?" he asked. "The AM would have been just as likely to say red as white?"

"No, it's not like that either. The AM's been following me around for hundreds of years. It's seen me drink wine a few hundred thousand times, under a few hundred thousand different circumstances. It knows, with a high degree of reliability, what my best choice of wine would be given any set of parameters."

"And you follow that advice unquestioningly?"

I sipped at the red. "Of course. Wouldn't it be a little childish to go against it just to make a point about free will? After all, I'm more likely to be satisfied with the choice it suggests."

"But unless you ignore that suggestion now and then, won't your whole life become a set of predictable responses?"

"Maybe," I said. "But is that so very bad? If I'm happy, what do I care?"

"I'm not criticising you," Zima said. He smiled and leaned back in his seat, defusing some of the tension caused by his line of questioning. "Not many people have an AM these days, do they?"

"I wouldn't know," I said.

"Less than one per cent of the entire galactic population." Zima sniffed his wine and looked through the glass at the sky. "Almost everyone else out there has accepted the inevitable."

"It takes machines to manage a thousand years of memory. So what?"

"But a different order of machine," Zima said. "Neural implants, fully integrated into the participant's sense of self. Indistinguishable from biological memory. You wouldn't need to query the AM about your choice of wine; you wouldn't need to wait for that confirmatory whisper. You'd just know it."

"Where's the difference? I allow my experiences to be recorded by a machine that accompanies me everywhere I go. The machine misses nothing, and it's so efficient at anticipating my queries that I barely have to ask it anything."

"The machine is vulnerable."

"It's backed up at regular intervals. And it's no more vulnerable than a cluster of implants inside my head. Sorry, but that just isn't a reasonable objection."

"You're right, of course. But there's a deeper argument against the AM. It's too perfect. It doesn't know how to distort or forget."

"Isn't that the point?"

"Not exactly. When you recall something—this conversation, perhaps, a hundred years from now—there will be things about it that you misremember. Yet those misremembered details will themselves become part of your memory, gaining solidity and texture with each instance of recall. A thousand years from now, your memory of this conversation might bear little resemblance to reality. Yet you'd swear your recollection was accurate."

"But if the AM had accompanied me, I'd have a flawless record of how things really were."

"You would," Zima said. "But that isn't living memory. It's photography: a mechanical recording process. It freezes out the imagination, leaves no scope for details to be selectively misremembered." He paused long enough to top off my glass. "Imagine that on nearly every occasion when you had cause to sit outside on an afternoon like this you had chosen red wine over white, and generally had no reason to regret that choice. But on one occasion, for one reason or another, you were persuaded to choose white—against the judgement of the AM—and it was wonderful. Everything came together magically: the company, the conversation, the late afternoon ambience, the splendid view, the euphoric rush of being slightly drunk. A perfect afternoon turned into a perfect evening."

"It might not have had anything to do with my choice of wine," I said.

"No," Zima agreed. "And the AM certainly wouldn't attach any significance to that one happy combination of circumstances. A single deviation wouldn't affect its predictive model to any significant degree. It would still say 'red wine' the next time you asked."

I felt an uncomfortable tingle of understanding. "But human memory wouldn't work that way."

"No. It would latch on to that one exception and attach undue significance to it. It would amplify the attractive parts of the memory of that afternoon and suppress the less pleasant parts: the fly that kept buzzing in your face, your anxiety about catching the boat home and the birthday present you knew you had to buy in the morning. All you'd remember was that golden glow of well-being. The next time, you might well choose white, and the time after. An entire pattern of behaviour would have been altered by one instance of deviation. The AM would never tolerate that. You'd have to go against its advice many, many times before it grudgingly updated its model and started suggesting white rather than red."

"All right," I said, still wishing we could talk about Zima rather than me. "But what practical difference does it make whether the artificial memory is inside my head or outside?"

"All the difference in the world," Zima said. "The memories stored in the AM are fixed for eternity. You can query it as often as you like, but it will never enhance or omit a single detail. But the implants work differently. They're designed to integrate seamlessly with biological memory, to the point where the recipient can't tell the difference. For that very reason they're necessarily plastic, malleable, subject to error and distortion."

"Fallible," I said.

"But without fallibility there is no art. And without art there is no truth."

"Fallibility leads to truth? That's a good one."

"I mean truth in the higher, metaphoric sense. That golden afternoon? That was the truth. Remembering the fly wouldn't have added to it in any material sense. It would have detracted from it."

"There was no afternoon, there was no fly," I said. Finally, my patience had reached breaking point. "Look, I'm grateful to have been invited here. But I thought there might be a little more to this than a lecture about the way I choose to manage my own memories."

"Actually," Zima said, "there was a point to this after all. And it is about me, but it's also about you." He put down the glass. "Shall we take a little walk? I'd like to show you the swimming pool."

"The sun hasn't gone down yet," I said.

Zima smiled. "There'll always be another one."

He took me on a different route through the house, leaving by a different door than the one we'd come in. A meandering path climbed gradually between white stone walls, bathed now in gold from the lowering sun. Presently we reached the flat plateau I'd seen on my approach in the conveyor. The things I'd thought were viewing stands were exactly that: terraced structures about thirty metres high, with staircases at the back leading to the different levels. Zima led me into the darkening shadow under the nearest stand, then through a private door that led into the enclosed area. The blue panel I'd seen during the approach turned out to be a modest rectangular swimming pool, drained of water.

Zima led me to the edge.

"A swimming pool," I said. "You weren't kidding. Is this what the stands are all about?"

"This is where it will happen," Zima said. "The unveiling of my final work of art, and my retirement from public life."

The pool wasn't quite finished. In the far corner, a small, yellow robot glued ceramic tiles into place. The part near us was fully tiled, but I couldn't help noticing that the tiles were chipped and cracked in places. The afternoon light made it hard to be sure—we were in deep shadow now—but their colour looked to be very close to Zima Blue.

"After painting entire planets, isn't this is a bit of a let-down?" I asked.

"Not for me," Zima said. "For me this is where the quest ends. This is what it was all leading up to."

"A shabby-looking swimming pool?"

"It's not just any old swimming pool," he said.

HE WALKED ME around the island, as the sun slipped under the sea and the colours turned ashen.

"The old murals came from the heart," Zima said. "I painted on a huge scale because that was what the subject matter seemed to demand."

"It was good work," I said.

"It was hack work. Huge, loud, demanding, popular, but ultimately soulless. Just because it came from the heart didn't make it good."

I said nothing. That was the way I'd always felt about his work as well: it was as vast and inhuman as its inspiration, and only Zima's cyborg modifications lent his art any kind of uniqueness. It was like praising a painting because it had been done by someone holding a brush between their teeth.

"My work said nothing about the cosmos that the cosmos wasn't already capable of saying for itself. More importantly, it said nothing about me. So what if I walked in vacuum, or swam in seas of liquid nitrogen? So what if I could see ultraviolet photons, or taste electrical fields? The modifications I inflicted upon myself were gruesome and extreme. But they gave me nothing that a good telepresence drone couldn't offer any artist."

"I think you're being a little harsh on yourself," I said.

"Not at all. I can say this now because I know that I did eventually create something worthwhile. But when it happened it was completely unplanned."

"You mean the blue stuff?"

"The blue stuff," he said, nodding. "It began by accident: a misapplication of colour on a nearly finished canvas. A smudge of pale aquamarine-blue against near-black. The effect was electric. It was as if I had achieved a short circuit to some intense, primal memory, a realm of experience where that colour was the most important thing in my world."

"What was that memory?"

"I didn't know. All I knew was the way that colour spoke to me, as if I'd been waiting my whole life to find it, to set it free." He thought for a moment. "There's always been something about blue. A thousand years ago Yves Klein said it was the essence of colour itself: the colour that stood for all other colours. A man once spent his entire life searching for a particular shade of blue that he remembered encountering in childhood. He began to despair of ever finding it, thinking he must have imagined that precise shade, that it could not possibly exist in nature. Then one day he chanced upon it. It was the colour of a beetle in a museum of natural history. He wept for joy."

"What is Zima Blue?" I asked. "Is it the colour of a beetle?"

"No," he said. "It's not a beetle. But I had to know the answer, no matter where it took me. I had to know why that colour meant so much to me, and why it was taking over my art."

"You allowed it to take over," I said.

"I had no choice. As the blue became more intense, more dominant, I felt I was closer to an answer. I felt that if only I could immerse myself in that colour, then I would know everything I desired to know. I would understand myself as an artist."

"And? Did you?"

"I understood myself," Zima said. "But it wasn't what I expected."

"What did you learn?"

Zima was a long time answering me. We walked on slowly, me lagging slightly behind his prowling muscular form. It was getting cooler now and I began to wish I'd had the foresight to bring a coat. I thought of asking Zima if he could lend me one, but I was concerned not to derail his thoughts from wherever they were headed. Keeping my mouth shut had always been the toughest part of the job.

"We talked about the fallibility of memory," he said.

"Yes."

"My own memory was incomplete. Since the implants were installed I remembered everything, but that only accounted for the last three hundred years of my life. I knew myself to be much older, but of my life before the implants I recalled only fragments; shattered pieces that I did not quite know how to reassemble." He slowed and turned back to me, the dulling orange light on the horizon catching the side of his face. "I knew I had to dig back into that past, if I was to ever understand the significance of Zima Blue."

"How far back did you get?"

"It was like archaeology," he said. "I followed the trail of my memories back to the earliest reliable event, which occurred shortly after the installation of the implants. This took me to Kharkov Eight, a world in the Garlin Bight, about nineteen thousand light-years from here. All I remembered was the name of a man I had known there, called Cobargo."

Cobargo meant nothing to me, but even without the AM I knew something of the Garlin Bight. It was a region of the galaxy encompassing six hundred habitable systems, squeezed between three major economic powers. In the Garlin Bight normal interstellar law did not apply. It was fugitive territory.

"Kharkov Eight specialized in a certain kind of product," Zima said. "The entire planet was geared up to provide medical services of a kind unavailable elsewhere. Illicit cybernetic modifications, that kind of thing."

"Is that where..." I left the sentence unfinished.

"That is where I became what I am," Zima said. "Of course, I made further changes to myself after my time on Kharkov Eight—improving my tolerance to extreme environments, improving my sensory capabilities—but the essence of what I am was laid down under the knife in Cobargo's clinic."

"So before you arrived on Kharkov Eight you were a normal man?" I asked.

"This is where it gets difficult," Zima said, picking his way carefully along the trail. "Upon my return I naturally tried to locate Cobargo. With his help, I assumed I would be able to make sense of the memory fragments I carried in my head. But Cobargo was gone, vanished elsewhere into the Bight. The clinic remained, but now his grandson was running it."

"I bet he wasn't keen on talking."

"No; he took some persuading. Thankfully, I had means. A little bribery, a little coercion." He smiled slightly at that. "Eventually he agreed to open the clinic records and examine his grandfather's log of my visit."

We turned a corner. The sea and the sky were now the same inseparable grey, with no trace of blue remaining.

"What happened?"

"The records say that I was never a man," Zima said. He paused a while before continuing, leaving no doubt as to what he had said. "Zima never existed before my arrival in the clinic."

What I wouldn't have done for a recording drone, or—failing that—a plain old notebook and pen. I frowned, as if that might make my memory work just that little bit harder.

"Then who were you?"

"A machine," he said. "A complex robot: an autonomous artificial intelligence. I was already centuries old when I arrived on Kharkov Eight, with full legal independence."

"No," I said, shaking my head. "You're a man with machine parts, not a machine."

"The clinic records were very clear. I had arrived as a robot. An androform robot, certainly—but an obvious machine nonetheless. I was dismantled and my core cognitive functions were integrated into a vat-grown biological host body." With one finger he tapped the pewter side of his skull. "There's a lot of organic material in here, and a lot of cybernetic machinery. It's difficult to tell where one begins and the other ends. Even harder to tell which is the master, and which is the slave."

I looked at the figure standing next to me, trying to make the mental leap needed to view him as a machine—albeit a machine with soft, cellular components—rather than a man. I couldn't—not yet.

I stalled. "The clinic could have lied to you."

"I don't think so. They would have been far happier had I not known."

"All right," I said. "Just for the sake of argument—"

"Those were the facts. They were easily verified. I examined the customs records for Kharkov Eight and found that an *autonomous robot entity* had entered the planet's airspace a few months before the medical procedure."

"Not necessarily you."

"No other robot entity had come near the world for decades. It had to be me. More than that, the records also showed the robot's port of origin."

"Which was?"

"A world beyond the Bight. Lintan Three, in the Muara Archipelago."

The AM's absence was like a missing tooth. "I don't know if I know it."

"You probably don't. It's no kind of world you'd ever visit by choice. The scheduled lightbreakers don't go there. My only purpose in visiting the place seemed to me—"

"You went there?"

"Twice. Once before the procedure on Kharkov Eight, and again recently, to establish where I'd been before Lintan Three. The evidence trail was beginning to get muddy, to say the least...but I asked the right kinds of questions, poked at the right kinds of databases, and eventually found out where I'd come from. But that still wasn't the final answer. There were many worlds, and the chain became fainter with each that I visited. But I had persistence on my side."

"And money."

"And money," Zima said, acknowledging my remark with a polite little nod. "That helped incalculably."

"So what did you find, in the end?"

"I followed the trail back to the beginning. On Kharkov Eight I was a quick-thinking machine with human-level intelligence. But I hadn't always been that clever, that complex. I'd been augmented in steps, as time and circumstances allowed."

"By yourself?"

"Eventually, yes. That was when I had autonomy, legal independence. But I had to reach a certain level of intelligence before I was allowed that freedom. Before that, I was a simpler machine...like an heirloom or a pet. I was passed from one owner to the next, between generations. They added things to me. They made me cleverer."

"How did you begin?"

"As a project," he said.

ZIMA LED ME back to the swimming pool. Equatorial night had arrived quickly, and the pool was bathed now in artificial light from the many floods arrayed above the viewing stands. Since we had last seen the pool the robot had finished gluing the last of the tiles in place.

"It's ready now," Zima said. "Tomorrow it will be sealed, and the day after it will be flooded with water. I'll cycle the water until it attains the necessary clarity."

"And then?"

"I prepare myself for my performance."

On the way to the swimming pool he had told me as much as he knew about his origin. Zima had begun his existence on Earth, before I was even born. He had been assembled by a hobbyist, a talented young man with an interest in practical robotics. In those days, the man had been one of many groups and individuals groping towards the hard problem of artificial intelligence.

Perception, navigation and autonomous problem-solving were the three things that most interested the young man. He had created many robots, tinkering them together from kits, broken toys and spare parts. Their minds—if they could be dignified with such a term—were cobbled from the innards of junked computers, with their simple programs bulging at the limits of memory and processor speed.

The young man filled his house with these simple machines, designing each for a particular task. One robot was a sticky-limbed spider that climbed around the walls of his house, dusting the frames of pictures. Another lay in wait for flies and cockroaches. It caught and digested them, using the energy from the chemical breakdown of their biomass to drive itself to another place in the house. Another robot busied itself by repainting the walls of the house over and over, so that the colours matched the changing of the seasons.

Another robot lived in his swimming pool.

It toiled endlessly up and down and along the ceramic sides of the pool, scrubbing them clean. The young man could have bought a cheap swimming pool cleaner from a mail-order company, but it amused him to design the robot from scratch, according to his own eccentric design principles. He gave the robot a full-colour vision system and a brain large enough to process the visual data into a model of its surroundings. He allowed the robot to make its own decisions about the best strategy for cleaning the pool. He allowed it to choose when it cleaned and when it surfaced to recharge its batteries via the solar panels grouped on its back. He imbued it with a primitive notion of reward.

The little pool-cleaner taught the young man a great deal about the fundamentals of robotics design. Those lessons were incorporated into the other household robots, until one of them—a simple household cleaner—became sufficiently robust and autonomous that the young man began to offer it as a kit, via mail-order. The kit sold well, and a year later the young man offered it as a preassembled domestic robot. The robot was a runaway success, and the young man's firm soon became the market leader in domestic robots.

Within ten years, the world swarmed with his bright, eager machines.

He never forgot the little pool-cleaner. Time and again he used it as a test-bed for new hardware, new software. By stages it became the cleverest of all his creations, and the only one that he refused to strip down and cannibalise.

When he died, the cleaner passed to his daughter. She continued the family tradition, adding cleverness to the little machine. When she died, she passed it to the young man's grandson, who happened to live on Mars.

"This is the original pool," Zima said. "If you hadn't already guessed."

"After all this time?" I asked.

"It's very old. But ceramics endure. The hardest part was finding it in the first place. I had to dig through two metres of topsoil. It was in a place they used to call Silicon Valley."

"These tiles are coloured Zima Blue," I said.

"Zima Blue *is* the colour of the tiles," he gently corrected. "It just happened to be the shade that the young man used for his swimming pool tiles."

"Then some part of you remembered."

"This was where I began. A crude little machine with barely enough intelligence to steer itself around a swimming pool. But it was my world. It was all I knew, all I needed to know."

"And now?" I asked, already fearing the answer.

"Now I'm going home."

I WAS THERE when he did it. By then the stands were full of people who had arrived to watch the performance, and the sky over the island was a mosaic of tightly packed hovering ships. The distortion screen had been turned off, and the viewing platforms on the ships thronged with hundreds of thousands of distant witnesses. They could see the swimming pool by then, its water mirror-flat and gin-clear. They could see Zima standing at the edge, with the solar patches on his back glinting like snake scales. None of the viewers had any idea what was about to happen, or its significance. They were expecting something—the public unveiling of a work that would presumably trump everything Zima had created before then—but they could only stare in puzzled concern at the pool, wondering how it could possibly measure up to those atmosphere-piercing canvases, or those entire worlds wrapped in shrouds of blue. They kept thinking that the pool had to be a diversion. The real work of art—the piece that would herald his retirement—must be somewhere else, as yet unseen, waiting to be revealed in all its immensity.

That was what they thought.

But I knew the truth. I knew it as I watched Zima stand at the edge of the pool and surrender himself to the blue. He'd told me exactly how it would happen: the slow, methodical shutting-down of higher-brain functions. It hardly mattered that it was all irreversible: there wouldn't be enough of him left to regret what he had lost.

But something would remain—a little kernel of being—enough of a mind to recognize its own existence. Enough of a mind to appreciate its surroundings, and to extract some trickle of pleasure and contentment from the execution of a task, no matter how purposeless. He wouldn't ever need to leave the pool. The solar patches would provide him with all the energy he needed. He would never age, never grow ill. Other machines would take care of his island, protecting the pool and its silent, slow swimmer from the ravages of weather and time.

Centuries would pass.

Thousands of years, and then millions.

Beyond that, it was anyone's guess. But the one thing I knew was that Zima would never tire of his task. There was no capacity left in his mind for boredom. He had become pure experience. If he experienced any kind of joy in the swimming of the pool, it was the near-mindless euphoria of a pollinating insect. That was enough for him. It had been enough for him in that pool in California, and it was enough for him now, a thousand years later, in the same pool but on another world, around another sun, in a distant part of the same galaxy.

As for me...

It turned out that I remembered more of our meeting on the island than I had any right to. Make of that what you will, but it seemed I didn't need the mental crutch of my AM quite as much as I'd always imagined. Zima was right: I'd allowed my life to become scripted, laid out like a blueprint. It was always red wine with sunsets, never the white. Aboard the outbound lightbreaker a clinic installed a set of neural memory extensions that should serve me well for the next four or five hundred years. One day I'll need another solution, but I'll cross that particular mnemonic bridge when I get there. My last act, before dismissing the AM, was to transfer its observations into the vacant spaces of my enlarged memory. The events still don't feel quite like they ever happened to me, but they settle in a little bit better with each act of recall. They change and soften, and the highlights glow a little brighter. I guess they become a little less accurate with each instance of recall, but like Zima said, perhaps that's the point.

I know now why he spoke to me. It wasn't just my way with a biographical story. It was his desire to help someone move on, before he did the same.

I did eventually find a way to write his story, and I sold it back to my old newspaper, the *Martian Chronicle*. It was good to visit the old planet again, especially now that they've moved it into a warmer orbit.

That was a long time ago. But I'm still not done with Zima, odd as it seems.

Every couple of decades, I still hop a lightbreaker to Murjek, descend to the streets of that gleaming white avatar of Venice, take a conveyor to the island and join the handful of other dogged witnesses scattered across the stands. Those that come, like me, must still feel that the artist has something else in store...one last surprise. They've read my article now, most of them, so they know what that slowly swimming figure means...but they still don't come in droves. The stands are always a little echoey and sad, even on a good day. But I've never seen them completely empty, which I suppose is some kind of testament. Some people get it. Most people never will.

But that's art.

FURY

I WAS THE first to reach the emperor's body, and even then it was too late to do anything. He had been examining his koi, kneeling on the stone pathway that wound between the ponds, when the bullet arrived. It had punched through his skull, achieving instantaneous destruction. Fragments of skin and bone and pinkish grey cortical material lay scattered on the tiles. Blood—dark and red as the ink on the imperial seal—was oozing out from the entry and exit wounds. The body had slumped over to one side, with the lower half still spasming as motor signals attempted to regain control. I reached over and placed my hand against the implanted device at the base of the neck, applying firm pressure through the yellow silk of his collar to a specific contact point. I felt a tiny subepidermal click. The body became instantly still.

I stood up and summoned a clean-up crew.

"Remove the body," I told the waiting men. "Don't dispose of it until you've completed a thorough forensic analysis. Drain and search the surrounding ponds until you've recovered the bullet or any remaining pieces of it. Then hose down the path until you've removed all trace of blood and whatever else came out of him. Test the water thoroughly and don't let the koi back until you're certain they won't come to any harm." I paused, still trying to focus on what had just happened. "Oh, and secure the Great House. No one comes and goes until we find out who did this. And no ships are to pass in or out of the Capital Nexus without my express authorisation."

"Yes, Mercurio," the men said in near-unison.

In the nearest pond one of the fish—I recognised it as one of the Asagi Koi, with the blue-toned scales laid out in a pine-cone pattern—opened and closed its mouth as if trying to tell me something vital. I turned from the scene and made my way back into the Great House. By the time I reached the emperor's reception chamber the building was buzzing with rumours of the assassination attempt. Despite my best efforts, the news would be out of the Nexus within the hour, hopscotching from world to world, system to system, spreading into the galaxy like an unstoppable fire.

The emperor's new body rose from his throne as the doors finished opening. He was dressed in a yellow silk gown identical to the one worn by the corpse. Aside from the absence of injuries, the body was similarly indistinguishable, appearing to be that of a white-haired man of considerable age, yet still retaining a youthful vigour. His habitual expression normally suggested playfulness, compassion and the kind of deep wisdom that can only come from a very long and scholarly life. Now his face was an expressionless mask. That, and a certain stiffness in his movements, betrayed the fact that this was a new body, being worn for the first time. It would take several hours for the implant to make the fine sensorimotor adjustments that gave the emperor true fluidity of movement, and allowed him to feel as if he was fully inhabiting the puppet organism.

"I'm sorry," I said, before the emperor had a chance to speak. "I take full responsibility for this incident."

He waved aside my apology. "Whatever this is about, Mercurio, I doubt very much that you could have done anything to prevent it." His voice was thick-tongued, like a drunkard with a bad hangover. "We both know how thorough you've been; all the angles you've covered. No one could have asked for better security than you've given me, all these years. I'm still alive, aren't I?"

"Nonetheless, there was clearly a flaw in my arrangements."

"Perhaps," he allowed. "But the fact is, whoever did this only reached the body, not me. It's unfortunate, but in the scheme of things little worse than an act of vandalism against imperial property."

"Did you feel anything?"

"A sharp blow; a few moments of confusion; not much else. If that's what being assassinated feels like, then it isn't much to fear, truth be told. Perhaps I've been wrong to keep looking over my shoulder, all this time."

"Whoever did this, they must have known it wouldn't achieve anything."

"I've wondered about that myself." He stroked the fine white banner of his beard, as if acquainting himself with it for the first time. "I almost hate to ask—but the koi?"

"I've got my men searching the ponds, looking for bullet fragments. But as far as I can see the fish didn't come to any harm."

"Let's hope so. The effort I've put into those fish—I'd be heartbroken if anything happened to them. I'll want to see for myself, of course."

"Not until we've secured the Great House and found our man," I said, speaking as only the emperor's personal security expert would have dared. "Until the risk of another attempt is eliminated, I can't have you leaving this building."

"I have an inexhaustible supply of bodies, Mercurio."

"That's not the point. Whoever did this..." But I trailed off, my thoughts still disorganized. "Please, sir, just respect my wishes in this matter."

"Of course, Mercurio. Now as ever. But I trust you won't keep me from my fish for the rest of eternity?"

"I sincerely hope not, sir."

I left the emperor, returning to my offices to coordinate the hunt for the assassin and the search for whatever evidence he might have left behind. Within a few hours the body had been subjected to an exhaustive forensic analysis, resulting in the extraction of bullet shards from the path of the wound. In the same timeframe my men recovered other fragments from the vicinity of the corpse; enough to allow us to reassemble the bullet.

An hour later, against all my expectations, we had the assassin himself. They found him with his weapon, waiting to be apprehended. He hadn't even tried to leave the grounds of the Great House.

That was when I began to suspect that this wasn't any act of mindless desecration, but something much more sinister.

"Tell me what you found," the emperor said, when I returned to the reception chamber. In the intervening time his control over the new body had improved markedly. His movements were fluid and he had regained his usual repertoire of facial expressions.

"We've found the assassin, sir, as you'll doubtless have heard."

"I hadn't, but please continue."

"And the weapon. The bullet itself was a goal-seeking autonomous missile, a very sophisticated device. It had the means to generate stealthing fields to confuse our anti-intrusion systems, so once it was loose in the grounds of the Great House it could move without detection. But it still needed a launching device, a kind of gun. We found that as well."

The emperor narrowed his eyes. "I would have thought it was hard enough to get a gun into the Nexus, let alone the Great House."

"That's where it gets a little disturbing, sir. The gun could only have been smuggled into the grounds in tiny pieces—small enough that they could be disguised by field generators, or hidden inside legitimate tools and equipment allowed the palace staff. That's how it happened, in fact. The man we found the gun on was an uplift named Vratsa, one of the keepers in charge of the ponds."

"I know Vratsa," the emperor said softly. "He's been on the staff for years. Never the brightest of souls...but diligent, gentle, and beyond any question a hard worker. I always liked him—we'd talk about the fish, sometimes. He was tremendously fond of them. Are you honestly telling me he had something to do with this?"

"He's not even denying it, sir."

"I'm astonished. Vratsa of all people. Primate stock, isn't he?"

"Gorilla, I think."

"He actually planned this?"

"I'm not sure 'planned' is exactly the word I'd use. The thing is, it's starting to look as if Vratsa was a mole."

"But he's on the staff for—how long, exactly?"

There'd been no need for me to review the files—the information was at my immediate disposal, flashing into my mind instantly. "Thirty-five years, sir. In my estimation, that's about as long as it would have taken to smuggle in and assemble the pieces of the weapon."

"Could a simple uplift have done this?"

"Not without help, sir. You've always been very kind to them, employing them in positions of responsibility where others would rather treat them as subhuman slaves. But the fact remains that uplifts don't generally exhibit a high degree of forward planning and resourcefulness. This took both, sir. I'm inclined to the view that Vratsa was just as much a puppet as that body you're wearing."

"Why the bullet, though? As I said, Vratsa and I have spoken on many occasions. He could have hurt me easily enough then, just with his bare hands."

"I don't know, sir. There is something else, though." I looked around the walls of the room, with its panelled friezes depicting an ancient, weatherworn landscape—some nameless, double-mooned planet half way across the galaxy. "It's delicate, sir—or at least it *might* be delicate. I think we need to talk about it face to face."

"This room is already one of the most secure places in the entire Radiant Commonwealth," he reminded me.

"Nonetheless."

"Very well, Mercurio." The old man sighed gently. "But you know how uncomfortable I find these encounters."

"I assure you I'll be as brief as possible."

Above me the ceiling separated into four equal sections. The sections slid back into the walls, a cross-shaped gap opening between them to reveal an enormous overhead space—a brightly lit enclosure as large as any in the Great House. Floating in the space, pinned into place by gravity neutralisers, was a trembling sphere of oxygenated water, more than a hundred meters across. I began to ascend, pushed upwards on a section of flooring immediately beneath me, a square tile that became a rising pillar. Immune to vertigo—and incapable of suffering lasting damage even if I'd fallen to the floor—I remained calm, save for the thousand questions circling in my mind.

At one hundred and thirty meters, my head pushed through the surface tension of the sphere. A man would have started drowning, but immersion in water posed no difficulties for me. In fact, there were very few environments in the galaxy that I couldn't tolerate, at least temporarily.

My lenses adjusted to the differing optical properties of the medium, until I seemed to be looking through something only slightly less sharp than clear air. The emperor was floating, as weightless as the water surrounding him. He looked something like a whale, except that he had no flippers or flukes.

I remembered—dimly, for it had been a long time ago—when he was still more or less humanoid. That was in the early days of the Radiant Commonwealth, when it only encompassed a few hundred systems. He had grown with it, swelling as each new territory—be it a planet, system or entire glittering stare cluster—was swallowed into his realm. It wasn't enough for him to have an abstract understanding of the true extent of his power. He needed to feel it on a purely sensory level, as a flood of inputs reaching directly into his brain. Countless modifications later, his mind was now the size of a small house. The mazelike folds of that dome bulged against drum-tight skin, as if about to rip through thin canvas. Veins and arteries the size of plumbing ducts wrapped the cerebellum. It was a long time since that brain had been protected by a cage of bone.

The emperor was monstrous, but he wasn't a monster—not now. There might once have been a time when his expansionist ambitions were driven by something close to lust, but that was tens of thousands of years ago. Now that he controlled almost the entire colonised galaxy, he sought only to become the figurehead of a benevolent, just government. The emperor was famed for his clemency and forgiveness. He himself had pushed for the extension of democratic principles into many of the empire's more backward prefectures.

He was a good and just man, and I was happy to serve him.

"So tell me, Mercurio, whatever it is that is too secret even for one of my puppets."

The rising pillar had positioned me next to one of his dark eyes. They were like currants jammed into doughy flesh.

"It's the bullet, sir."

"What about it?"

I held the reconstructed item up for inspection, confident now that we were outside the reach of listening devices. It was a metal cylinder with a transparent cone at the front.

"There are, or were, markings on the bullet casing. They're in one of the older trading languages of the Luquan Emergence. The inscription, in so far as it can be translated into Prime, reads as follows: *Am I my brother's keeper?*"

He reflected on this for a moment. "It's not ringing any bells."

"I'd be surprised if it did, sir. The inscription appears to be a quote from an ancient religious text. As to its greater significance, I can't say."

"The Luquans haven't traditionally been a problem. We give them a certain amount of autonomy; they pay their taxes and agree to our trifling requests that they instigate democratic rule and cut down on the number of executions. They may not like that, but there are a dozen other special administrative volumes that we treat in exactly the same fashion. Why would the Emergence take against me now?"

"It doesn't end there, sir. The bullet had a hollow cavity at the front, inside the glass cone. There was enough space in there for the insertion of any number of harmful agents, up to and including an antimatter device that could easily have destroyed all or part of the Great House. Whoever made this, whoever programmed it to reach this far, could easily have gone the extra step necessary to have you killed, not just your puppet."

The ancient dark eye regarded me. Though it hardly moved in the socket, I still had the sense of penetrating focus and attention.

"You think someone was trying to tell me something? That they *can* murder me, but chose not to?"

"I don't know. Certainly, the provisions I've now put in place would prevent anyone making a second attempt in this manner. But they'd have known that as well. So why go to all this trouble?" I paused before continuing. "There is something else, I'm afraid."

"Go ahead."

"Although the bullet was hollow, it wasn't totally empty. There was something inside the glass part—a few specks of reddish sand or dust. The surgeons extracted most of it from the puppet, and they've promised me that the few remaining traces that entered the koi ponds won't cause any ill effects. I've had the dust analysed and it's absolutely harmless. Iron oxide, silicon and sulphur, for the most part. Frankly, I don't know what to make of it. It resembles something you'd find on the surface of an arid terrestrial planet, something with a thin atmosphere and not much weather or biology. The problem is there are ten million worlds that fit that description."

"And within the Emergence?"

"Fewer, but still far too many to speak of." I withdrew the replica bullet from his examination. "Nonetheless, these are our only clues. With your permission, I'd like to leave the Capital Nexus to pursue the matter further."

He ruminated on this for a few seconds. "You propose a mission to the Emergence?"

"I really don't see any alternative. There's only so much I can do from my office. It's better if I go walkabout." The phrase, which had popped unbidden into my mind, caused me disquiet. Where had it come from? "What I mean, sir, is that I can be much more effective in person."

"I appreciate that. But I also appreciate that you're incredibly valuable to me—not just as a friend, but as my closest and most trusted advisor. I've become very used to knowing you're close at hand, in the walls of the Great House. It's one of the things that helps me sleep at night, knowing you're not far away."

"I'll only ever be a few skipspace transits from home, sir."

"You have my agreement, of course—as if I was ever going to say no. But do look after yourself, Mercurio. I'd hate to think how I'd manage without you."

"I'll do my best, sir." I paused. "There is one other thing I need to ask you, sir. The uplift, Vratsa?"

"What about him?"

"We subjected him to mild interrogation. He gave us nothing, but I'd be remiss in my duties if I didn't point out that we could employ other methods, just to be certain he isn't keeping anything from us."

"What's your honest judgement?"

"I think he's completely innocent, sir—he was just following a script someone programmed into him thirty-five or more years ago. He no more knows why he did this—and who's behind it—than the bullet did. But if you feel something might be gained…"

"Have him tortured, on the very slight chance he might tell us something?" It was clear from his tone of voice what he felt about that.

"I didn't think you'd approve, sir. As far as I'm concerned, it would achieve about as much as smacking a puppy for something it did the day before yesterday."

"I've spent much of the last thousand years trying to enforce humanitarian principles on the more barbarous corners of my own empire. The very least I can do is live up to my own high moral standards, wouldn't you say?" It was a rhetorical question, since he allowed me no time to answer. "Take Vratsa and remove him from the Great House—he's a continuing security risk, even if he doesn't know why he did what he did. But I don't want him locked away or punished. Find some work for him in the outlying gardens. Give him some fish to look after. And if anyone harms a hair on his head..."

"They won't, sir. Not while I'm in charge."

"That's very good, Mercurio. I'm glad we see things similarly."

I LEFT THE Great House a day later, once I was satisfied that I had put in place all necessary measures for the emperor's continued security in my absence. From the moon-girdled heart of the Capital Nexus, through skipspace via the Coronal Polities to the fuzzy perimeter of the Luquan Emergence—sixty thousand light years in only a handful of days. As I changed from ship to ship, I attracted an unavoidable degree of attention. Since I would require Great House authority to make my investigations in the Emergence, there was no possibility of moving incognito. I travelled in full imperial regalia, and made sure the seriousness of my mission was understood.

How much more attention would I have merited, if they had realised what I *really* was?

I looked like a man, but in fact I was a robot. My meat exterior was only a few centimetres thick. Beneath that living shell lay the hard armour of a sentient machine.

The emperor knew—of course—and so did a handful of his closest officials. But to most casual observers, and even people who had spent much time in the Great House, I was just another human security expert, albeit one with an uncommonly close relationship with the emperor. The fact that I had been in his service for tens of thousands of years was one of the most closely guarded secrets in the Radiant Commonwealth.

I was rare. Robots were commonplace, but I was something more than that. I was a true thinking machine. There were reckoned to be less than a million of us in existence—not many, considering the billion worlds of the Radiant Commonwealth, and all the teeming souls on those planets and moons.

There were two schools of thought concerning our origin. In the thirty-two thousand years of its existence, the empire had been through a number of historical convulsions. One school—the alchemicals—had it that the means to manufacture us—some critical expertise in cybernetics and programming—had been discovered and then lost at an earlier time. All remaining sentient machines therefore dated from this period.

The other school, the accretionists, held a different view. They maintained that robot intelligence was an emergent property, something that could only happen given sufficient resources of time and complexity. The accretionists argued that the surviving robots became the way we were gradually, through the slow augmentation of simpler machines. In their view, almost any machine could become an intelligent robot, provided it was allowed to evolve and layer itself with improvements.

It would have been convenient if we robots could have settled the matter. The unfortunate fact, though, was that we simply didn't remember. Like any recording apparatus, we were prone to error and distortion. At times when the emperor's hold on the galaxy had slackened, data wars corrupted even the most secure of archives. I could sift through my memories until I found the earliest reliable events of which I had direct experience, but I knew—I sensed—that I was still only plumbing relatively shallow layers of my own identity.

I knew I'd been around considerably longer than that.

The only thing I could be absolutely certain of was that I'd known the emperor for a very long time. We fit together like hand and glove. And in all that time I'd always been there to protect him.

It was what I did.

THE OFFICIAL WAS a high-ranking technocrat on Selva, one of the major power centres of the Luquan Emergence. He studied me with unconcealed hostility, sitting behind a desk in his private office in one of Selva's aquatic cities. Fierce, luminous oceanforms—barbed and tentacled things of alien provenance—clawed and suckered at the armoured glass behind him, testing its strength.

"I really don't think I can offer any more assistance, sire," the official said, putting sufficient stress on the honorific for it to sound insulting. "Since your arrival on Selva we've given you free rein to conduct your investigations. Every administrative department has done its utmost to comply with your requests. And yet you still act as if there is more we could have done." He was a thin, sallow man with arched, quizzical eyebrows, dressed in a military uniform that was several sizes too big for him. "Have we not demonstrated our obedience with the trials?"

"I didn't ask for those dissidents to be executed," I said. "Although I can see how useful it would have been for you. Arrest some troublemakers, ask them questions they can't possibly answer, about a crime they had nothing to do with, and then hang them on the pretext that they weren't cooperating with the Great House. Do you imagine that will buy you favour with the emperor? Quite the opposite, I'd suggest. When all this is over and done with, I wouldn't be at all surprised if you have an imperial audit to deal with."

He shrugged, as if the matter was of no possible consequence.

"You're wasting your time, sire—looking for a pattern, a logical explanation, where none exists. I don't even know why you're bothering. Didn't you already find your assailant? Didn't you already extract a confession?"

"We found evidence that points to the Luquan Emergence."

"Yes, I've heard about that." Ostentatiously, he tapped at a sealed brochure on his desk. "A cryptic statement in an ancient tongue. Some dust that could have come from anywhere."

I maintained a blank expression, giving no hint at my anger that the forensic information had been leaked. It was inevitable, I supposed, but I had hoped to keep a lid on it for a little longer.

"I'd discount any rumours if I were you."

A mouthful of concentric teeth gnashed against the glass, rotating and counter-rotating like some industrial drilling machine. The official craned around in his seat, studying the ravenous creature for a few seconds. "They have a taste for human flesh now," he said, as if the two of us were making idle conversation. "No one's exactly sure how, but it appears that at some point certain undesirables must have been fed to them, despite all the prohibitions against introducing human genetic material into the native ecosystem."

"I suppose I must count as an undesirable, from where you're sitting. Coming in with imperial authorisation, the license to ask any questions I choose."

"I won't pretend I'll shed many tears when you're gone, if that's what you mean." He straightened in his chair, the stiff fabric of the uniform creaking. "On that matter, there's something you might benefit from knowing."

"Because it'll get me off Selva?"

"I'd inflict you on Porz, if I didn't know you'd already visited." He tapped another finger against the brochure. "It behoves me to point out that you may be making a tactical error in conducting your enquiries here, at the present heart of the Emergence. This ancient inscription— the quote from that old text—harkens back to our very early history. The geopolitical balance was different back then, as I'm sure you'll appreciate."

"I know my history." Which was true, up to a point. But the history of the Luquan Emergence was a bewildering thicket of half-truths and lies, designed to confound imperial legislators. Even the Great House hadn't been able to help me sort out truth and fiction where the Emergence was concerned. It was worse than trying to find Lost Earth.

"Then consider acting upon it," the official said. "Julact was the heart of the Luquan Emergence in those days. No one lives there now, but…"

"I'll come to Julact in good time."

"You may wish to move it up your schedule. That part of the Emergence doesn't see much traffic, so the skipspace connections are being pruned back. We've already mothballed all routes west of the Hasharud Loop. It's difficult enough to reach Julact now. In a few years, it may not be possible at all—even with imperial blessing. You know how hard it is to reactivate a path, once it's fallen out of use."

No administrative entity within the Radiant Commonwealth was supposed to shutdown skipspace paths without direct permission from the Great House. Merely doing so was a goading taunt against the emperor's authority. That, though, was a fight for another day.

"If I had the slightest suspicion that I was being manipulated…"

"Of course you're being manipulated. I want you out of my jurisdiction.

"Oh, and it's a red world," the official continued. "And the soil's a close match to that sample you found in the bullet. In case that makes any difference to you."

"You said it yourself. That soil could have come from anywhere in the galaxy. A close match doesn't imply a unique match."

"Still. You've got to start somewhere, haven't you?"

I LEFT SELVA.

My passage to Julact was appropriately arduous. After emerging from the soon-to-be-mothballed skipspace portal I had to complete the final leg of the journey at sublight speed, accruing years of irritating timelag. Before I dropped out of superluminal signal range I contacted the Capital Nexus, alerting the emperor that I would not be home for some time.

"Are you sure this is wise, Mercurio?"

"Clearly, it suits them that I should redirect my enquiries away from Selva, Porz, and the other power centres of the present Emergence. But Julact is worthy of my attention. Even if there isn't anyone living there now, I may find another clue, another piece of the puzzle."

The emperor was outside again, very close to the spot where his previous body had been shot, kneeling by the treasured koi pond with some kind of water-testing device in his hand. A white and orange male broke the water with his barbled head, puckering silver-white lips at the force-shielded sky above the Great House. "You sound as if you're caught up in some kind of elaborate parlour game," the emperor said.

"That's exactly how it feels. By the same token, I have no choice but to play along. Ordinarily I would not consider dropping out of contact for as long as it will take me to travel to Julact and back. But since the Great

House seems to be running itself well enough in my absence, and given that there have been no further security incidents..."

The emperor lifted a yellow silk sleeve. "Yes, of course. Do whatever is necessary. I could hardly expect you to be less thorough about this than any other security arrangements you've dealt with."

"I promise I'll be as quick as possible."

"Of course. And once again, I urge you to take all necessary precautions. You and I, we've got a lot of history together. I'd feel quite naked without you."

"I'll report back as soon as I have something, sir."

The emperor, the fish and the Great House faded from my console. With nothing to do but wait for my journey to end, I sifted through the facts of the case, examining every aspect from every conceivable angle. The process consumed many centuries of equivalent human thought, but at the end of it I was still none the wiser. All I had was a bullet, an inscription and some fine red dust.

Would Julact provide any answers?

The red world was smaller than most terrestrials, with a single small moon. It had a ghost-thin haze of atmosphere and no evidence of surface biology. Winds scoured tawny dust from pole to pole, creating an ever-changing mask. The humans of the Luquan Emergence had not, of course, evolved on this world. Thousands of years before their emergence as a galactic mini-power, they must have crossed interstellar space from Lost Earth, to settle and perhaps terraform this unpromising pebble.

From orbit, I dropped down samplers to sniff and taste Julact's lifeless soil. As the technocrat had already promised, it turned out to be in uncannily close agreement with the forensic sample. That didn't prove that Julact was the home of the assassin—dozens of other worlds would have given at least as convincing a match—but at least I didn't have to rule it out immediately.

I surveyed the planet from space, searching for possible clues. Humans had been here once, that much was clear. There were ruined cities on the surface—smothered in dust, abandoned tens of thousands of years ago. Could someone have stayed behind, nursing a potent grudge? Possibly. But it was difficult to see how a single man could have orchestrated the long game of the assassination attempt. It would have taken several normal lifetimes to put in place the necessary measures— and only a select few have ever been given the imperial gift of extended longevity. A machine such as I—that would have been different. But what possible harm could a robot wish upon the emperor?

I was debating these points with myself when a signal flashed from the surface, emanating from the largest ruined city.

"Welcome, Mercurio," said the signal. "I'm glad you finally arrived."

"To whom am I speaking?"

"That doesn't matter for now. If you wish answers to your questions, descend to the perimeter of the abandoned settlement from which this transmission is originating. We have much to talk about, you and I."

"I'm on official business for the Great House. I demand to know your identity."

"Or what?" the voice asked, amusedly. "You'll destroy the city? And then what will you have learned?" The tone shifted to one of gentle encouragement. "Descend, Mercurio—I promise that no harm will come to you, and that I will satisfy your curiosity in all matters. What do you have to lose?"

"My existence?"

"I wouldn't harm you, brother. Not in a million years."

I commenced entry into Julact's wisp of an atmosphere. All the while I scanned the city for signs of concealed weaponry, half expecting to be blown out of the sky at any moment. There were no detectable weapons, but that wasn't much consolation. The only assurance I could offer myself was that I was now only slightly more vulnerable than when I had surveyed Julact from space.

The city lay inside the crumbled remains of a once-proud wall. I set down just beyond it, instructing my ship to wait while I ventured outside. As I stepped onto Julact's surface, the dust crunching beneath my feet, some ancient memory threatened to stir. It was as if I had been here before, as if this landscape had been awaiting my return, patient and still as an old painting. The feeling was neither welcome nor pleasant. I could only assume that the many skipspace transits I'd been forced to endure were having an effect on my higher functions.

I thought of what I had said to the emperor, before my departure. Of how I was going to go walkabout.

Unnerved, but still determined to stand my ground, I waited to see what would happen.

Presently four golden robots emerged from a crack in the side of the city wall. They were standing on a flying disk, a common form of transportation in the Julactic League. They were humanoid, but clearly no more than clever servitors. Each machine had a human torso, but only a very small glowing sphere for a head. I watched their approach with trepidation, but none of the machines showed any hostile intentions.

"Please come with us," they said in unison, beckoning me to step onto the disk. "We will take you to the one you wish to meet."

"The one I spoke to from space?"

"Please come with us," the robots repeated, standing aside to give me room.

"Identify the individual or organisation for whom you are working."

"Please come with us."

I realised that it was futile expecting to get anything out of these idiot machines. Submitting myself to fate, I stepped onto the disk. We sped away instantly, back through the crack in the wall. There was a grey rush of ruined stone, and then we were in the city proper, winging over smashed buildings; what had once been towers or elegantly domed halls. Centuries of dust storms had polished them to a glassy smoothness against the prevailing winds. Only a handful of buildings reached higher than the city wall. We approached the highest of them, a tapering white structure like a snapped-off tusk rammed into the ground. At the very tip was a bulb-shaped swelling that had cracked open to reveal a tilted floor. A bronze craft, shaped like a blunt spearhead, waited on the floor for our arrival. I would have seen it from space, had it not been screened from observation until this moment.

The flying disk rose into the belly of the parked vehicle. The robots bade me to step down, onto carpeted flooring. The belly door sealed shut and I sensed a lurch of rapid movement. I wondered if they were taking me back into space. It seemed absurd to invite me down to the surface, only to take me away from Julact.

"He will see you now," the robots announced.

They showed me forward, into the front compartment of the vehicle. It was a triangular room outfitted in burgundy, with wide, sloping windows on two sides. There were no controls or displays, and the only furniture consisted of two padded benches, set at an angle to each other before the windows. A figure was sitting on one of these benches as I was shown in. The golden robots left us alone, retreating into the rear of the craft as a door closed between us.

Such is the rarity of robot intelligence that I have only been in the presence of machines such as myself on a handful of occasions. In all such instances I always felt a quiet certainty that I was the superior machine, or that we were at least equal partners. I have never felt myself to be in the presence of a stronger, cleverer entity.

Until this moment.

He rose from the couch where he had been sitting, feigning that human need for relaxation. He was as tall as I and not dissimilar in build and cosmetic ornamentation. Where I resembled a masked soldier in jade armour, he was a fiery, almost luminous red, with the face of an iron gargoyle.

"The accretionists were right," he said, by way of welcome. "But of course you knew that all along, Mercurio. In your bones. I certainly know it in *my* bones."

"I confess I didn't."

"Well, maybe you think you didn't. But your deep memory says otherwise—as does mine. We've been around too long to have been the product of some brief, ingenious golden age. We're not just as old as the empire. We go back even further, you and I."

Through the window the landscape rushed by. We had passed beyond the limits of the ruined city and were now traversing lifeless hills and valleys.

"Do we?" I asked.

"You knew the emperor when he was still recognisably human. So did I. We knew him before this empire was even a glint in his eye. When the very idea of it would have been laughable. When he was just a powerful man in a single solar system. But we were there, beyond any question."

"Who are you?"

He touched a fiery hand to the armoured breastplate of his chest. "My name is Fury. Your name was bestowed upon you by your master; I chose mine for myself."

I searched my memory for information on any figures named Fury who might have been considered a security concern. Nothing of significance emerged, even when I expanded the search parameters to scan back many thousands of years.

"That tells me nothing."

"Then maybe this will. I'm your brother. We were created at the same time."

"I don't have a brother."

"So you believe. The truth is, you've always had one. You just didn't realise it."

I thought back to the religious text on the bullet casing, wondering if it might have some bearing on our conversation. *Am I my brother's keeper?* What did it mean, in this context?

"How could a machine have a brother?" I asked. "It doesn't make any sense. Any way, I haven't come here to be teased with irrelevancies about my own past. I've come to investigate a crime."

"The attempted assassination of the emperor, I presume," Fury said casually. "I'll make it easy for you, shall I? I did it. I arranged for the uplift and his weapon. I created the bullet that did so little harm. I put the dust inside it, I put the words on the casing. I did all this without ever setting foot within a hundred light years of the Capital Nexus."

"If you wanted to kill the emperor..."

"I could have done it; trivially. Yes; I'm glad you came to that conclusion. I take it you've now had time to work out why I went to such elaborate lengths, merely to injure him?"

All of a sudden it made sense to me. "So that I'd have a lead to follow? To bring me to you?"

He nodded once. "Knowing your dedication to his protection, I had little doubt that you'd terminate yourself if you failed him. I couldn't have that. But if he was threatened, I knew you'd move world and star to find the perpetrator. I knew you'd turn over every stone until it led you to me.

Which was exactly what I wanted. And look—here you are. Brimming with righteous indignation, determined to bring the world-be assassin to justice."

"That's still my intention."

"I've looked inside you. You contain weapons, but nothing that can penetrate my armour or the security screens between us." He touched a finger to his sharp-pointed chin. "Except, of course, for the powerplant which energises you, and which you could choose to detonate at any moment. Be assured that nothing of me would survive such an event. So go ahead: annihilate the would-be assassin. You won't be able to return to your emperor, but you'll at least have died knowing you did the decent thing." He waited a beat, the eye-slits in his gargoyle mask giving nothing away. "You can do that, can't you?"

"Of course I can."

"But you won't. Not until you know why another robot wanted your emperor dead, and chose not to do it himself."

He understood me very well. If I destroyed myself, I could not be certain that I had undermined the threat to the emperor. Not until I fully understood the scope of that threat, and the motivating agency behind it.

"So that's settled, at least," he added. "You'll do nothing until you have further information. Fine—let's give you that information, and see what you make of it. Shall we?"

"I'm at your disposal," I said.

"I've brought you somewhere significant. You think Julact is an old world, but that's not the half of it. It's been part of the Radiant Commonwealth for a lot longer than anyone realises. In fact you could say that everything began here."

"You're going to tell me this is really Lost Earth?"

"No; this isn't Earth. We can visit Earth if you like, but in truth there's not much to see. Anyway, that sterilised husk doesn't mean anything to you and I. We weren't even made on Earth. This is our home. This is where we were born."

"I think I'd remember."

"Do you?" he asked sharply. "Or is it possible you might have forgotten? You don't recall your origins, after all. That information was scrubbed out of you thirty centuries ago, accidentally or otherwise. But I've always remembered. Keeping the low profile that I have, I've managed to avoid contact with most of the damaging agencies that wiped your past. That's not to say I haven't had to fight to preserve these memories, treasuring them for what they were." He gestured at the rushing landscape beyond the window. "Julact is Mars, Mercurio. The first real world that humans touched, after they left the Earth. How does that make you feel?"

"Sceptical."

"Nonetheless, this is Mars. And I have something interesting to show you."

The vehicle was slowing. If we had passed any other signs of human habitation since leaving the deserted city, I had witnessed none of them. If this was indeed Mars—and I could think of no reason why Fury would lie to me now—then the world had almost certainly undergone many phases of climate modification. Though the planet might now have reverted to its prehistoric condition, the effects of those warm, wet interludes would have been to erase all evidence of earlier settlements. The ruined city might well have been indescribably ancient, but it could also have been one of the newest features on the surface.

Yet as the vehicle came to a hovering halt, something about the landscape struck me as familiar. I compared the canyons and bluffs through the window with something in my recent experience, and realised that I had seen the view before, albeit from a different angle. A human might never have made the connection, but we robots are attuned to such things.

"The emperor's reception room," I said, marvelling. "The friezes on the wall—the images of a landscape with two moons. It was here. But there was only one moon as we came in."

"That was Phobos," Fury said. "The other one—Deimos—was lost during one of the empire's early wars. It was a manufacturing centre, and therefore of tactical importance. As a matter of fact, we were both made in Deimos, in the same production batch. So we're not really from Mars after all, if you want to be pedantic—but Mars is where we were activated, and where we served our masters for the first time."

"But if there were two moons on the frieze, it must be very old. How am I still able to recognise the landscape?"

"I shaped it for you," Fury said, not without a touch of pride. "There was less to do than you might think—the terraforming changes left this part of Mars relatively undisturbed. But I still moved a few things around. Of course, since I couldn't call in much in the way of assistance, it took a long time. But as you'll have realised by now, patience is one of my strong points."

"I still don't understand why you've brought me here. So Mars was significant to the emperor. That doesn't excuse an assassination attempt on him."

"More than significant, Mercurio. Mars was everything. The crux; the wellspring; the seed. Without Mars, there would have been no Radiant Commonwealth. Or at the very least a very different empire, ruled by a different man. Shall I show you what happened?"

"How can you show me?"

"Like this."

He did nothing, but I understood immediately. The vehicle was projecting forms out onto the landscape, superimposing ghostly actors on the real terrain.

Two figures were walking over the crest of a dune. Their footprints ran all the way back to a primitive surface vehicle—a pressurised cabin mounted on six balloon-like wheels. The vehicle bristled antenna, with solar collectors folded on its back like a pair of delicately hinged insect wings. It had the flimsy, makeshift look of something from the dawn of technology. I could only imagine that the wheeled machine had brought the two figures on a long, difficult journey from some equally flimsy and makeshift settlement.

"How far back are we looking, Fury?"

"A very long way. Thirty-two thousand years. Barely a century after the first manned landing on Mars. Conditions, as you'll have gathered, were still extremely perilous. Accidental death was commonplace. Effective terraforming—the creation of a thick, breathable atmosphere—lay a thousand years in the future. There were only a handful of surface communities and the political balance of the planet—not to mention the whole system—was still in a state of flux. These two men..."

"They're both men?"

Fury nodded. "Brothers, like you and I."

I watched the suited figures advance towards us. With their visors reflecting the landscape, and with the bulkiness of the suits hiding their physiques, I had to take Fury's word that these were human male siblings. Both men were dressed similarly, suggesting that they had originated from the same community or power bloc. Their suits were hard armoured shells, with the limbs joined by flexible connections. Something in the easy, relaxed way they moved told me that the suits were doing some of the hard work of walking, taking the burden off their occupants. A hump rose from the back of each suit, containing—I presumed—the necessary life-support equipment. They had similar symbols and patterns on the suits, some of which were mirrored in forms painted on the side of the vehicle. The man on the right held something in his gloved hand, a small box with a readout set into it.

"Why have they come here?"

"It's a good question. The brothers are both influential men in one of the largest military-industrial entities on the planet. Tensions are running high at the moment—other factions are circling, there's a power vacuum in the inner system, the lunar factories have switched to making weapons, there's an arms embargo around Mars, and it's not clear if war can be avoided. The man on the left—the older of the two brothers—is at heart a pacifist. He fought in an earlier engagement—little more than a spat between two combines—and he wants no more of that. He thinks there's still a chance for peace. The only downside is that Mars may have to relinquish its economic primacy compared to an alliance of the outer giants and their moons. The industrial concern that the two men work for will pay a bitter price if that happens. But he still thinks it's worth it, if war can be avoided."

"And the younger brother?"

"He's got a different viewpoint. He thinks that, far from standing down, this could be the big chance for Mars to position itself as the main player in the system—over and above the outer giants and what's left of the Inner Worlds Prefecture. That would be good for Mars, but it would be even better for the concern. And exceptionally good for him, if he handles things well. Of course, there'll almost certainly have to be a limited war of some kind…but he's ready to pay that price. Willingly, even eagerly. He's never had his brother's chance to test his mettle. He sees the war as his springboard to glory."

"I still don't see why they've come here."

"It's a trick," Fury explained. "The younger brother set this up a long time ago. A season ago—before the dust storms—he drove out to this exact spot and buried a weapon. Now there's no trace that he was ever here. But he's lied to the older brother; told him he's received intelligence concerning a buried capsule containing valuable embargoed technologies. The older brother's agreed to go out with him to examine the spot—it's too sensitive a matter to trust to corporate security."

"He doesn't suspect?"

"Not a thing. He realises they have differences, but it would never occur to him that his younger brother might be planning to have him killed. He still thinks they'll find common ground."

"Then they're not at all alike."

"For brothers, Mercurio, they could hardly be more different."

The younger brother brought the older one to a halt, signalling with his hand that he had found something. They must have been directly over the burial spot, since the handheld box was now flashing bright red. The younger man fastened the device onto his belt. The older brother bent down onto his knees to start digging, scooping up handfuls of rust-coloured dust. The younger brother stood back for a few moments, then knelt down and began his own excavation, a little to the right of where the other man was digging. They had spades with them, clipped to the sides of their backpacks, but they must have decided not to use them until they were certain they'd have to dig down more than a few centimetres.

It wasn't long—no more than ten or twenty seconds—before the younger brother found what he was looking for. He began to uncover a silver tube, buried upright in the dust. The older brother stopped his own digging and looked at what the other man was in the process of uncovering. He began to stand up, presumably to offer assistance.

It was all over quickly. The younger brother tugged the tube from the sand. It had a handle jutting from the side. He twisted the tube around, dust spilling from the open muzzle at one end. There was a crimson flash.

The older brother toppled back into the dust, a fist-sized black wound burned into his chestplate. He rolled slightly and then became still. The weapon had killed him instantly.

The younger brother placed the weapon down and surveyed the scene with hands on hips, for all the world like an artist taking quiet pleasure in work well done. After a few moments he unclipped his spade and started digging. By the time he had finished there was no sign of either the body or the murder weapon. The dust had been disturbed, but it would only take one good storm to cover that, and the two sets of tracks that led from the parked vehicle.

Finished, the younger brother set off home.

Fury turned to me, as the projected images faded away, leaving only the empty reality of the Martian landscape.

"Do I need to spell it out, Mercurio?"

"I don't think so. The younger man became the emperor, I'm assuming?"

"He took Mars into war. Millions of lives were lost—whole communities rendered uninhabitable. But he came out of it very well. Although even he couldn't have seen it at the time, that was the beginning of the Radiant Commonwealth. The new longevity processes allowed him to ride that wave of burgeoning wealth all the way to the stars. Eventually, it turned him into the man I could so easily have killed."

"A good man, trying his best to govern justly."

"But who'd be nothing if he hadn't committed that single, awful crime."

Again, I had no option but to take all of this on faith. "If you hate him so much, why didn't you put a bomb in that bullet?"

"Because I'd rather you did it instead. Haven't you understood yet, Mercurio? This crime touched both of us. We were party to it."

"You're presuming that we even existed back then."

"I know that we did. I remembered, even if you didn't. I said we came from the same production batch, Mercurio. *We were the suits.* High-autonomy, surface-environment protection units. Fully closed-cycle models with exoskeletal servo-systems, to assist our wearers. We were assembled in the Deimos manufactury complex and sent down to Mars, for use in the settlements."

"I am not a suit," I said, shaking my head. "I never was. I have always been a robot."

"Those suits *were* robots, to all intents and purposes. Not as clever as you and I, not possessing anything resembling free will, but still capable of behaving independently. If the user was incapacitated, the suit could still carry him to help. If the user wished, the suit could even go off on its own, scouting for resources or carrying material. Walkabout mode, that's what they called it. That's how we began, brother. That's how we began and that's how I nearly died."

The truth of it hit me like a cold blast of decompressing air. I wanted to refute every word of it, but the more I struggled to deny him, the more I knew I could never succeed. I had felt my ancient, buried history begin to force its way to the surface from the moment I saw the dust in that bullet; that cryptic inscription.

I had known, even then. I just hadn't been ready to admit it to myself.

Hand in glove, the emperor and I. He'd even said he'd feel naked without me. On some level, that meant he also knew as well. Even if he no longer realised it on a conscious level.

A bodyguard was all I'd ever been. All I ever would be.

"If what you say is true, how did I become the way I am?"

"You were programmed to adapt to your master's movements, to anticipate his needs and energy demands. When he was wearing you, he barely noticed that he was wearing a suit at all. Is it any wonder that he kept you, even as his power accumulated? You were physical protection, but also a kind of talisman, a lucky charm. He had faith in you to keep him alive, Mercurio. So as the years turned into decades and the decades became centuries, he made sure that you never became obsolete. He improved your systems, added layers of sophistication. Eventually you became so complex that you accreted intelligence. By then he wasn't even using you as a suit at all—you'd become his bodyguard, his personal security expert. You were in permanent walkabout mode. He even made you look human."

"And you?" I asked.

"I survived. We were sophisticated units with a high capacity for self-repair. The damage inflicted on me by the weapon was severe—enough to kill my occupant—but not enough to destroy me. After a long while my repair systems activated. I clawed my way out of the grave."

"With a dead man still inside you?"

"Of course," Fury said.

"And then?"

"I said that we were not truly intelligent, Mercurio. In that respect I may not have spoken truthfully. I had no consciousness to speak of; no sense of my own identity. But there was a glimmer of cunning, an animal recognition that something dreadfully wrong had taken place. I also grasped the idea that my existence was now in peril. So I hid. I waited out the storms and the war. In the aftermath, I found a caravan of nomads, refugees from what had once been Vikingville, one of the larger surface communities. They had need of protection, so I offered my services. We were given that kind of autonomy, so that we could continue to remain useful in the fragmented society of a war zone."

"You continued to function as a suit?"

"They had their own. I went walkabout. I became a robot guard."

"And later? You can't have stayed on Julact—Mars—all this time."

"I didn't. I passed from nomadic group to nomadic group, allowing myself to be improved and augmented from time to time. I became steadily more independent and resourceful. Eventually my origin as a suit was completely forgotten, even by those I worked for. Always I kept moving, aware of the crime I had witnessed and the secret I carried with me."

"Inside you?" I asked, just beginning to understand.

"After all this time, he's still with me." Fury nodded, watching me with great attentiveness. "Would you like to see, Mercurio? Would that settle your doubts?"

I felt myself on the threshold of something terrifying, but which I had no choice but to confront. "I don't know."

"Then I'll decide for you." Fury's hand rose to his face. He took hold of the gargoyle mask and pulled it free from the rest of his armoured casing.

We were, I realised, almost perfect opposites of each other. I was living flesh wrapped around a core of dead machinery. He was machinery wrapped around a core of dead flesh. As the faceless skull presented itself towards me I saw that there was something inside it, something older than the Radiant Commonwealth itself. Something pale and mummi-fied; something with empty eye sockets and thin lips pulled back from grinning brown teeth.

The face in Fury's hand said: "I didn't ever want to forget, Mercurio. Not until you'd come to me."

IT MAY BE difficult to countenance, but by the time I returned to the Great House my resolve was absolute. I knew exactly what I was going to do. I had served the emperor with every fibre of my being for the entire dura-tion of my existence. I had come to love and to admire him, both for his essential humanity and for the wise hand with which he governed the Radiant Commonwealth. He was a good man trying to make a better world for his fellow citizens. If I doubted this, I only had to reflect on the compassion he had shown to the uplift Vratsa, or his distaste at the political methods employed in those parts of the Commonwealth that had not yet submitted to enlightened government.

And yet he had done something unspeakable. Every glorious and noble act that he had ever committed, every kind and honourable deed, was built upon the foundations of a crime. The empire's very existence hinged upon a single evil act.

So what if it happened thirty-two thousand years ago? Did that make it less of a crime than if it had happened ten thousand years ago, or last week? We were not dealing with murky deeds perpetrated by distant ancestors. The man who had murdered his brother was still alive; still in absolute command of his faculties. Knowing what I did, how could I permit him to live another day without being confronted with the horror of what he had done?

I grappled with these questions during my journey home. But always I came back to the same conclusion.

No crime can go unpunished.

Naturally, I signalled my imminent return long before I reached the Capital Nexus. The emperor was overjoyed to hear that I had survived my trip to Julact, and brimming with anticipation at the news I would bring.

I had no intention of disappointing him.

He was still on the same body as last time—no assassination attempt or accidental injury had befallen him. When he rose from his throne, it was with a sprightliness that belied his apparent age. He seemed, if anything, even younger than when I had departed.

"It's good to have you back, Mercurio."

"Good to be back," I said.

"Do you have...news? You were reluctant to speak in detail over the superluminal link."

"I have news," I confirmed.

The body's eyes looked to the cross-shaped seam in the ceiling. "News, doubtless, that would be better discussed in conditions of absolute privacy?"

"Actually," I said, "there'll be no need for that at all."

He looked relieved. "But you do have something for me?"

"Very much so."

"That thing in your hand," he said, his attention snapping to my fingers. "It looks rather like the bullet you showed me before, the one with the inscription."

"That's what it is. Here—you may as well have it now." Without waiting for his response, I tossed the bullet to him. The old body's reflexes were still excellent, for he caught it easily.

"There's no dust in it," he said, peering at the glass-cased tip.

"No, not now."

"Did you find out...?"

"Yes; I located the origin of the dust. And I tracked down the would-be assassin. You have my assurance that you won't be hearing from him again."

"You killed him?"

"No, he's still much as he was."

The ambiguity in my words must have registered with him, because there was an unease in his face. "This isn't quite the outcome I was expecting, Mercurio—if you don't mind my saying. I expected the perpetrator to be brought to justice, or at the very least executed. I expected a body, closure." His eyes sharpened. "Are you quite sure you're all right?"

"I've never felt better, sir."

"I'm...troubled."

"There's no need." I extended my hand, beckoning him to leave the throne. "Why don't we take a walk? There's nothing we can't discuss outside."

"You've never encouraged me to talk outside. Something's wrong, Mercurio. You're not your usual self."

I sighed. "Then let me make things clear. We are now deep inside the Great House. Were I to detonate the powerplant inside my abdomen, you and I would cease to exist in a flash of light. Although I don't contain antimatter, the resultant fusion blast would easily equal the damage that the assassin could have wrought, if he'd put a bomb inside that bullet. You'll die—not just your puppet, but *you*, floating above us—and you'll take most of the Great House with you."

He blinked, struggling to process my words. After so many thousands of years of loyal service, I could only imagine how surprising they were.

"You're malfunctioning, Mercurio."

"No. The fact is, I've never functioned as well as I am functioning at this moment. Since my departure, I've regained access to memory layers I thought lost since the dawn of the empire. And I assure you that I will detonate, unless you comply with my exact demands. Now stand from the throne and walk outside. And don't even *think* of calling for help, or expecting some security override to protect you. This is my realm you're in now. And I can promise you that there is nothing you can do but obey my every word."

"What are you going to do?"

"Make you pay," I said.

We left the reception chamber. We walked the gilded hallways of the Great House, the emperor walking a few paces ahead of me. We passed officials and servants and mindless servitors. No one said or did anything except bow as their station demanded. All they saw was the emperor and his most trusted aide, going about their business.

We made our way to the koi ponds.

Whispering, I instructed the emperor to kneel in the same place where his earlier body had been killed. The clean-up crew had been thorough and there was no trace of the earlier bloodstain.

"You're going to kill me now," he said, speaking in a frightened hiss.

"Is that what you think?"

"Why bring me here, if not to kill me?"

"I could have killed you already, sir."

"And taken the Great House with you? All those innocent lives? You may be malfunctioning, Mercurio, but I still don't think you'd do something that barbaric."

"Perhaps I would have done it, if I thought justice would be served. But here's the thing. Even if justice would have been served, the greater good of the Radiant Commonwealth most certainly wouldn't have been. Look up, emperor. Look into that clear blue sky."

He bent his neck, as well as his old body allowed.

"There's an empire out there," I said. "Beyond the force screens and the sentry moons. Beyond the Capital Nexus. A billion teeming worlds, waiting on your every word. Depending on you for wisdom and balance in all things. Counting on your instinct for decency and forgiveness. If you were a bad ruler, this would be easy for me. But you're a good man, and that's the problem. You're a good man who once did something so evil the shadow of it touched you across thirty-two thousand years. You killed your brother, emperor. You took him out into the Martian wilderness and murdered him in cold blood. And if you hadn't, none of this would ever have happened."

"I didn't have..." he began, still in the same harsh whisper. His heart was racing. I could hear it drumming inside his ribs.

"I didn't think I had a brother either. But I was wrong, and so are you. My brother's called Fury. Yours—well, whatever name he had, the only person likely to remember is you. But I doubt that you can, can you? Not after all this time."

He choked—I think it was fear more than sorrow or anguish. He still didn't believe me, and I didn't expect him to. But he did believe that I was capable of killing him, and only a lethal instant away from doing so.

"Whatever you're going to do, do it."

"Do you still have the bullet, sir?"

His eyes flashed childlike terror. "What about the bullet?"

"Show it to me."

He opened his hand, the glass-nosed bullet still pinched between thumb and forefinger.

"There's no bomb in it. I'd see if there was a bomb in it. It's empty now." In his voice was something between relief and dizzy incomprehension.

What could be worse than a bomb?

"No, it's not empty." Gently, I took his hand in mine and guided it out until it was poised over the open water of the koi pond. "In a few moments, emperor, you and I are going to walk back inside the Great House. You'll return to your throne, and I'll return to my duties. I'll always be there for you, from now until the day I stop functioning. There'll never be a moment when I'm not looking after you, protecting you against those who would do you harm. You'll never need to question my loyalty; my unswerving dedication to that task. This...incident...is something we'll never speak of again. To all intents and purposes, nothing will have changed in our relationship. Ask me about your brother, ask me about mine, and I will feign ignorance. From now until the end of my existence. But I won't ever forget, and neither will you. Now break the glass."

He glanced at me, as if he hadn't quite understood the words. "I'm sorry?"

"Break the glass. It'll shatter easily between your fingers. Break the glass and let the contents drain into the pond. Then get up and walk away."

I stood up, leaving the emperor kneeling by the side of the pathway, his hand extended out over the water. I took a few paces in the direction of the Great House. Already I was clearing my mind, readying myself to engage with the many tasks that were my responsibility. Would he get rid of me, or try to have me destroyed? Quite possibly. But the emperor was nothing if not a shrewd man. I had served him well until now. If we could both agree to put this little aberration behind us, there was no reason why we couldn't continue to enjoy a fruitful relationship.

Behind me I heard the tiniest crack. Then sobbing.

I kept on walking.

THE STAR SURGEON'S APPRENTICE

THROUGH THE bar's windows Juntura Spaceport was an endless grid of holding berths, launch gantries and radiator fins, coiling in its own pollution under a smeared pink sky. The air crackled with radiation from unshielded drives. It was no place to visit, let alone stay.

"I need to get out of here," I said.

The shipmaster sneered at my remaining credit. "That won't get you to the Napier Belt, kid, let alone Frolovo."

"It's all I've got."

"Then maybe you should spend a few months working in the port, until you can pay for a ride."

The shipmaster—he was a cyborg, like most of them—turned away with a whine of his servo-driven exoskeleton.

"Wait," I said. "Please…just a moment. Maybe this makes a difference."

I pulled a black bundle from inside my jacket, peeling back enough of the cloth to let him see the weapon. The shipmaster—his name was Master Khorog—reached out one iron gauntlet and hefted the prize. His eye-goggle clicked and whirred into focus.

"Very nasty," he said appreciatively. "I heard someone used one of these against Happy Jack." The eye swivelled sharply onto me. "Maybe you know something about that?"

"Nothing," I said easily. "It's just an heirloom."

The heirloom was a bone gun: Kalarash Empire tech: very old, very difficult to pick up in security scans. Not much of it around any more, which is why the gun cost me so much. It employed a sonic effect to shatter human bone, turning it into something resembling sugar. Three seconds was all it needed to do its work. By then the victim no longer had anything much resembling a skeletal structure.

You couldn't live long like that, of course. But you didn't die instantly either.

"The trick—so they say—is not to dwell on the skull," Khorog mused. "Leave enough cranial structure for the victim to retain consciousness. And the ability to hear, if you want to taunt them. There are three small bones in the ear. People usually forget those."

"Will you take the gun or not?"

"I could get into trouble just looking at it." He put the gun back onto the cloth. "But it's a nice piece. Warm, too. It might make a difference. There used to be a good market for antique weapons on Jelgava. Maybe there still is."

I brightened. "Then you can give me a berth?"

"I only said it makes a difference, kid. Enough that you can pay off the rest aboard the *Iron Lady*."

I could already feel Happy Jack's button men, pushing their way through the port, asking urgent questions. Only a matter of time before they hit this bar and found me.

"If you can get me to the Frolovo Hub, I'll take it."

"Maybe we're not going to Frolovo. Maybe we're going to the Bafq Gap, or the Belterra Sphere."

"Somewhere nearby, then. Another hub. It doesn't matter. I just have to get off Mokmer."

"Show us your mitts." Before I could say yes, Khorog's metal hands were examining my skin and bone ones, splaying the fingers with surprising gentleness. "Never done a hard day's work in your life, have you? But you have good fingers. Hand to eye coordination OK? No neuromotor complications? Palsy?"

"I'm fine," I said. "And whatever it is you want me to do, I can learn."

"Mister Zeal—our surgeon—needs an assistant. It's manual labour, mostly. Think you can handle it?"

Jack's men, closer now. "Yes," I said. By then I'd have said anything to get off Mokmer.

"There'll be no freezer berth: the *Iron Lady* doesn't run to them. You'll be warm the whole trip. Two and half years subjective, maybe three, 'til we make the next orbitfall. And once Zeal's trained you up, he won't want you leaving his service at the first port of call. You'll be looking at four or five years aboard the *Lady*; maybe longer if he can't find another pair of hands. Doesn't sound so sweet now, does it?"

No, I thought: but then neither did the alternative.

"I'm still willing."

"Then be at shuttle dock nine in twenty minutes. That's when we lift for orbit."

WE LIFTED ON time.

I didn't see much of the ship from the shuttle: just enough to tell that the *Iron Lady* looked much the same as all the other ramscoops parked in orbit around Mokmer: a brutalist grey cylinder, swelling to the armoured mouth of the magnetic field intake at the front, tapering to the drive assembly at the back. Comms gear, radiators, docking mechanisms and modular cargo containers ringed the ship around its gently in-curving waist. It was bruised and battered from endless near-light transits, with great scorch marks and impact craters marring much of the hull.

The shuttle docked with just Khorog and me aboard. Even before I had been introduced to the rest of the crew—or at least the surgeon—the *Iron Lady* was moving.

"Sooner than I expected," I said.

"Complaining?" Khorog asked. "I thought you wanted to get away from Mokmer as soon as possible."

"No," I said. "I'm glad we're underway." I brushed a wall panel as we walked. "It's very smooth. I expected it to feel different."

"That's because we're only on in-system motors at the moment."

"There's a problem with the ramscoop?"

"We don't switch on the scoop until we're well beyond Mokmer—or any planet, for that matter. We're safe in the ship—life quarters are well shielded—but outside, you're looking at the strongest magnetic field this side of the Crab pulsar. Doesn't hurt *wetheads* like you all that much… but us, that's different." He knuckled his fist against his plated cranium. "Cyborgs like me…cyborgs like everyone else you'll meet aboard this ship, or in any kind of space environment—we feel it. Get within a thousand kilometers of a ship like this…it warms up the metal in our bodies. Inductive heating: we fry from the inside. That's why we don't light the scoop: it ain't *neighbourly.*"

"I'm sorry," I said, realising that I'd touched the cyborg equivalent of a nerve.

"We'll light in good time." Khorog hammered one of the wall plates. "Then you'll feel the old girl shiver her timbers."

On the way to the surgeon we passed other members of the *Iron Lady's* redoubtable crew, none of whom Khorog saw fit to introduce. They were a carnival of grotesques, even by the standards of the cyborgs I'd seen around the spaceport. One man consisted of a grinning, cackling, gap-toothed head plugged into a trundling life-support mechanism that had apparently originated as a cleaning robot: in place of wheels, or legs, he moved on multiple spinning brushes, polishing the deck plates behind him. A woman glanced haughtily at me as she passed: normal enough except that the upper hemisphere of her skull was a glass dome, in which resided a kind of ticking orrery: luminous planetary beads orbiting the bright lamp of a star. As she walked she rubbed a hand over the swell of her belly and I understood—as I was surely *meant* to—that her brain had been relocated there for safekeeping. Another man moved in a similar exoskeleton to the one Khorog wore, but in this case there was very little man left inside the powered frame: just a dessicated whisp, like something that had dried out in the sun. His limbs were like strands of rope, his head a piece of shrivelled, stepped-on fruit. "You'll be the new mate, then," he said, in a voice that sounded as if he was trying to speak while being strangled.

"If Zeal agrees to it," Khorog said back. "Only then."

"What if Mister Zeal doesn't agree to it?" I asked, when we were safely out of earshot.

"Then we'll find you something else to do," Khorog replied. "Always plenty of jobs on the..." And then he halted, as if he'd been meaning to say something else, but had caught himself in time.

By then we'd reached the surgeon.

Mister Zeal occupied a windowless chamber near the middle of the ship. He was working on one of his patients when Khorog showed me in. Hulking surgical machines loomed over the operating table, carrying lights, manipulators and barbed, savage-looking cutting tools.

"This is the new assistant," Khorog said. "Has a good pair of hands on him, so try and make this one last."

Zeal looked up from his work. He was a huge, bald, thick-necked man with a powerful jaw. There was nothing obviously mechanical about him: even the close-up goggle he wore over his left eye was strapped into place, rather than implanted. He wore a stiff leather apron over his bare, muscular chest, and he glistened with sweat and oil.

His voice was a low rumble. "Just a pup, Master Khorog. I asked for a man."

"Beggars can't be choosers, Mister Zeal. This is what was on offer."

Zeal stood up from the table and studied me with a curl on his lips, wiping his right hand against his apron. He pushed his left hand against the rust-dappled side of one of the surgical machines, causing it to move back on a set of caterpillar tracks. He stepped over a body that happened to be lying on the floor, scuffing his boot heel against the chest.

The voice rumbled again. "What's your name, lad?"

"Peter," I said, fighting to keep my nervousness in check. "Peter Vandry."

He pushed the goggle off his eye, up onto his forehead.

"Your hands."

"I'm sorry?"

He roared: "Show me your damned hands, boy!"

I stepped closer to the surgeon and offered him my hands. Zeal examined them with a particular attentiveness, his scrutiny more thorough, more methodical, than Khorog's had been. He looked at my tongue. He peered back my eyelids and looked deep into my eyes. He sniffed as he worked, the curl never leaving his lips. All the while I tried to ignore the semihuman thing laid out on the operating table, horrified that it was still breathing, still obviously alive. The crewman's torso was completely detached from his hips and legs.

"I need a new mate," Zeal told me. He kicked the body on the floor. "I've been trying to manage ever since with this *lobot*, but today..."

"Temper got the better of you, did it?" Khorog asked.

"Never mind my temper," Zeal said warningly.

"Lobots don't grow on trees, Master Zeal. There isn't an inexhaustible supply."

The surgeon snapped his gaze back onto me. "I'm a pair of hands down. Do you think you can do better?"

My throat was dry, my hands shaking. "Master Khorog seemed to think I could do it." I held out my hand, hoping he didn't notice the tremble. "I'm steady."

"Steadiness is a given. But do you have the stomach for the rest?"

"I've seen worse than that," I said, glancing at the patient. But only today, I thought: only since I left Happy Jack flopping and oozing on the carpet.

Zeal nodded at the other man. "You may leave us now, Master Khorog. Please ask the captain to delay drive start-up until I'm finished with this one, if that isn't too much trouble?"

"I'll do what I can," Khorog said.

Zeal turned smartly back to me. "I'm in the middle of a procedure. As you can tell from the lobot, things took a turn for the worse. You'll assist in the completion of the operation. If things conclude satisfactorily...well, we'll see." The curl became a thin, uncharitable smile.

I stepped over the dead lobot. It was common knowledge that space crews made extensive use of lobots for menial labour, but quite another to see the evidence. Many worlds saw nothing wrong in turning criminals into lobotomized slave labour. Instead of the death sentence, they got neurosurgery and a set of implants so that they could be puppeted and given simple tasks.

"What do you want me to do?" I asked.

Zeal lowered his goggle back into place, settling it over his left eye.

"Looking in the rough direction of the patient would be a start, lad."

I forced myself to take in the bloody mess on the table: the two detached body halves, the details of meat and bone and nervous system almost lost amid the eruptive tangle of plastic and metal lines spraying from either half: carrying pink-red arterial blood, chemical green pneumatic fluid. The tracked machines attending to the operation were of ancient, squalid provenance. Nothing in Zeal's operating room looked newer than a thousand years old.

Zeal picked up the end of one segmented chrome tube. "I'm trying to get this thoracic line in. There was a lot of resistance...the lobot kept fumbling the job. I'm assuming you can do better."

I took the end of the line. It was slippery between my fingers. "Shouldn't I...wash, or something?"

"Just hold the line. Infection's the least of his worries."

"I was thinking of me."

Zeal made a small gutteral sound, like someone trying to cough up an obstruction. "The least of yours as well."

I worked as best I could. We got the line in, then moved onto other areas. I just did what Zeal told me, while he watched me with his one human eye, taking in every slip and tremor of my hand. Once in a while he'd dig into the wide leather pocket sewn across the front of his apron and come out with some new blade or tool. Occasionally a lobot would arrive to take away some piece of equipment or dead flesh, or arrive with something new and gleaming on a plate. Now and then the tracked robot would creep forward to assist in a procedure. I noticed, with skin-crawling horror, that its dual manipulator arms ended in a perfect pair of female human hands, long-fingered and elegant and white as snow.

"Forceps," he'd say. "Laser scalpel." Or, sometimes: "Soldering iron."

"What happened to this man?" I asked, feeling I ought to be showing interest in more than just the mechanics of the operation.

"Hold that down," Zeal said, ignoring my question completely. "Cut there. Now make a knot and tie off. God's teeth, *careful*."

A little while later, the engine lit up. The transition to thrust weight was sudden and unannounced. The floor shook violently. Equipment clattered off trays. Zeal slipped with a knife, ruining half an hour's work, and swore in one of the ancient trade languages.

"They've lit the drive," he said.

"I thought you asked..."

"I did. Now apply pressure *here*."

We kept on working, even as the ship threatened to shake itself to bits. Scoop instability, Zeal said: it was always rough at first, before the fields settled down. My back began to ache from all the leaning over the table. Yet after what felt like many hours we were done: the two halves reunited, the interconnects joined, the bone and flesh encouraged to fuse across the divide.

With the patient sewn up, rebooted and restored to consciousness, I rubbed my back as Zeal spoke softly to the man, answering his questions and nodding now and then.

"You'll be all right," I heard him say. "Just keep away from any cargo lifts for a while."

"Thanks," the cyborg said.

The crewman got up off the table, whole again—or as whole as he would ever be. He walked stiffly to the door, pawing at his healed injuries in a kind of stunned wonderment, as if he had never expected to leave the operating table.

"It wasn't as bad as it looked," Zeal told me, when the patient had gone. "Stick with me, and you'll see a lot worse."

"Does that mean you'll let me stay?"

Zeal picked up an oily rag and threw it my way. "What else would it mean? Clean yourself up and I'll show you to your quarters."

IT WAS A job, and it had got me off Mokmer. As gruesome as working for Zeal might have been, I kept reminding myself that it was a lot better than dealing with Happy Jack's button men. And in truth, it could have been a lot worse. Gruff as he had been to start with, Zeal gradually opened up and started treating me...not exactly as an equal, but at least as a promising apprentice. He chided me when I made mistakes, but was also careful to let me know when I had done something well: when I'd sewn up a wound nicely, or when I'd wired in a neuromotor implant without causing too much surrounding brain damage. He wouldn't say anything, but the curl of his lip would soften and he'd favour my efforts with a microscopic nod of approval.

Zeal, I came to learn, enjoyed an uneasy relationship with the rest of the *Iron Lady*'s crew. It must have always been that way, for ship's surgeons. They were there to keep the crew healthy, and much of their work was essentially benign: the treating of minor ailments, the prescribing of restorative drugs and diets. But occasionally they had to do unspeakable things; things that inspired dread and horror. And no one was beyond the surgeon's reach, even the captain. If a crewman needed treatment, he was going to get it—even if Zeal and his lobots had to drag the man screaming and kicking to the table.

Most of the accidents, though, tended to happen during port time. Now that we were under flight, sucking interstellar gases into the ramscoop field, climbing inexorably closer to the speed of light, Zeal's work tended to minor operations and adjustments. Days went by with nobody to treat at all. During these intervals, Zeal would have me practising on the lobots, refining my techniques.

Three or four years, Khorog had said. Longer if Zeal couldn't find a replacement. With only a week under my belt, it seemed like a life sentence aboard the *Iron Lady*. But I would get through it, I promised myself. If conditions became intolerable, I would just jump ship in the next port of call.

In the meantime I got to know as much of my new home as I was allowed. Large areas of the *Iron Lady* were out of bounds: the rear section was deemed too radioactive, while the front was closed to low-ranking crewmembers like myself. I never saw the captain; never learned his name. But that still left a labyrinth of rooms, corridors and storage bays in which I was allowed to roam during my off-duty hours. Now and then I would pass other crewmembers, but apart from Khorog none of them ever gave me the time of the day. Zeal told me not to take it to heart: it was just that I was working for *him*, and would always be seen as the butcher's boy.

After that, I began to take a quiet pride in the fear and respect Zeal and I enjoyed. The other crew might loathe us, but they needed us as well. Our knives gave us power.

The lobots were different: they neither feared nor admired us, but simply did what we wanted with the instant obedience of machines. They didn't have enough residual personality to feel emotions. That was what I'd been told, anyway, but I still found myself wondering. There were nine of them on the *Iron Lady*: five men and four women. Looking into their slack, sleepwalker faces, I couldn't help wondering what kind of people they had been before; what kinds of lives they had led. It was true that they must have all committed capital crimes to have become lobots in the first place. But not every planet defined capital crimes in exactly the same way.

I knew there were nine, and only nine, because they came through Zeal's room on a regular basis, for minor tweaks to their control circuitry. I got to know their faces; got to recognise their slumping, shuffling gait as they walked into a room.

One day, however, I saw a tenth.

Zeal had sent me off on an errand to collect replacement parts for one his machines. I'd taken a wrong turning, then another one, and before I realised quite how lost I was, I had ended up in an unfamiliar part of the *Iron Lady*. I stayed calm at first, expecting that after ten or twenty minutes of random wandering, I'd find a corridor I recognised.

I didn't.

After thirty minutes became an hour, and every new corridor looked less familiar than the last, I began to panic. There were no markings on the walls; no navigation consoles or colour-coordinated arrows. The ship's dark architecture seemed to be rearranging itself as I passed, confounding my attempts at orientation. My panic changed to dread as I considered my plight. I might starve before I found my way back to the part of the ship I knew. The *Iron Lady* was huge, and its living crew tiny. If they had little cause to visit these corridors, it might be years before they found my dead body.

I turned another corner, more in desperation than hope, and faced yet another unrecognised corridor. But there was someone standing at the end of it. The harsh overhead light picked out only her face and shoulders, with the rest of her lost in shadow. I could see from her collar that she wore the same kind of overall as the other lobots. I could also see that she was quite pretty. The lobots were usually shaved to the scalp, to make life easier when their heads had to be opened. This one had a head of hair. It grew out ragged and greasy, tangled like the branches of an old tree, but it was still hair. Beneath it was a pale, almond-shaped face half lost in shadow.

She started back from me, vanishing into deeper shadow and then around a bend at her end of the corridor.

"Wait!" I called. "I'm lost! I need someone to show me the way out of here!"

Lobots never spoke, but they understood spoken instructions. The girl should have obeyed me instantly. Instead she broke into a running shuffle. I heard her shoes scuffing on the deck plating.

I chased after her, catching up with her easily before she reached the end of the next corridor. I seized her by the left arm and forced her to look at me.

"You shouldn't have run. I just need to know how to get out of here. I'm *lost.*"

She looked at me from under the stiff, knotted overhang of her hair. "Who you?" she asked.

"Peter Vandry, surgeon's mate," I said automatically, before frowning. "You talk. You're not *meant* to talk."

She lifted up her right arm, the sleeve of her overall slipping down to reveal a crude mechanical substitute for a hand. This clawlike append- age was grafted onto her forearm, held in place by a tight black collar. I thought for a moment that she meant to shock me, but then I real- ised that she was only making a human gesture, touching the tip of her mechanical hand against the side of her head.

"I…talk. Still…something left."

I nodded, understanding belatedly. Some of the lobots were clearly allowed to retain more mental faculties than others. Presumably these were the lobots that needed to engage in more complex tasks, requiring a degree of reciprocal communication.

But why had I never seen this one before?

"What are you doing here?" I asked.

"I…tend." She screwed up her face. Even this stripped-down approx- imation to normal speech was costing her great effort. "*Them.* Keep *them*…working."

"What do you mean, them?"

She cocked her head behind us, in the direction of wall plating. "Them."

"The engine systems?" I asked.

"You...go now." She nodded back the way I had chased her. "Second... left. Third right. Then you...know."

I let her go of her, conscious that I had been holding left her arm too tightly. I saw then that both her hands had been replaced by mechanical substitutes. With a shudder my thoughts raced back to the surgical machine in Zeal's operating room, the one with the feminine hands.

"Thank you," I said softly.

But before I could leave her she suddenly reached out her left hand and touched the metal to the side of my head, running her fingers against the skin. "Wethead," she said, with something like fascination. "Still."

"Yes," I said, trying not to flinch against the cold touch. "Zeal's talked about putting some implants into me soon, to help with the surgery... nothing irreversible, he says...but he hasn't done it yet."

Why was I talking to her so openly? Because she was a girl. Because it had been a long time since I'd seen someone who looked even remotely human, let alone someone pretty.

"Don't let," she said urgently. "Don't let. *Bad thing* happen soon. You OK now. You *stay* OK."

"I don't understand."

"You stay wethead. Stay wethead and get off ship. Soon as can. Before *bad thing.*"

"How am I supposed to get off the ship? We're in interstellar space!"

"Your problem," she said. "Not mine."

Then she turned away, the sleeves of her overalls falling down to hide her hands.

"Wait," I called after her. "Who are you? What is...what *was* your name?"

She paused in her stiff shuffle and looked back at me. "My name... gone." Then her eyes flashed wild in the shadows. "Second left. Third right. Go now, Peter Vandry. Go now then *get off ship.*"

ZEAL AND I were midway through another minor procedure when the engagement began. The *Iron Lady* shook like a struck bell. "God's teeth!" Zeal said, flinging aside his soldering iron. "What now?"

I picked up the iron and wiped sandpaper across its tip until it was bright again. "I thought the scoop fields were supposed to have settled down by now."

"That didn't feel like a field tremor to me. Felt more like an attack. Pass me the iron: we'll sew this one up before things get worse."

"An attack?" I asked.

Zeal nodded grimly. "Another ship, probably. They'll be after our cargo."

"Pirates, you mean?"

"Aye, son. Pirates. If that's what they are."

We tidied up the patient as best we could, while the ship continued to shudder. Zeal went to an intercom, bent a stalk to his lips and spoke to the rest of the crew, before returning to me. "It's an attack," he said. "Just as I reckoned. Apparently we've been trying to outrun the other ship for weeks. Quite why no one thought to *tell* me this..." He shook his head ruefully, as if he expected no better.

We were a long way in from the hull, but the impacts still sounded like they were happening next door. I shuddered to think of the energies being flung against the *Iron Lady*'s already bruised armour. "How long can we hold?" I asked.

"Come with me," Zeal said, pushing the goggle up onto his forehead. "There's a reinforced observation bubble not far from here. It's not often you'll get to see close action, so you might as well make the most of it."

Something in Zeal's tone surprised me. He'd been annoyed at the interruption to his surgical work, but he still did not sound particularly alarmed at the fact that we were being shot at by another ship.

What did Zeal know that I didn't?

As he led me to the observation bubble, I finally found the nerve to ask the question I had been meaning to put to him ever since I met the girl in the corridor, several weeks ago. Now that he was distracted with the battle, I assumed he wouldn't dwell overlong on my questions.

"Mister Zeal...that lobot we were just working on..."

He looked back at me. "What about it?"

"It seems funny that we can do so much to their brains...put stuff in, take stuff out..."

"Go on."

"It seems funny that we never give them *language*. I mean, they can understand us...but wouldn't it be easier if they could talk to us as well? At least that way we'd know that they'd understood our instructions."

"Language modules are too expensive. The captain has one, but that's only because a hull spar took out his speech center."

"I'm not talking about cyber modules."

Zeal halted and looked back at me again. Around us, the ship rocked and roared. Emergency alarms sounded from the distance. A mechanical voice intoned warning messages. I heard the shriek of a severed air line.

"What, then?"

"Why do we take out the language center in the first place? I mean, why not just leave it intact?"

"We take the lobots as we get 'em, son. If the speech center's been scooped out...it isn't in our power to put it back again."

I steadied myself against a bulkhead, as the floor bucked under us. "Then they're all like that?"

"Unless you know otherwise." Zeal studied me with chilling suspicion. "Wait," he said slowly. "This line of questioning...it wouldn't be because you've seen *her*, would it?"

"Her, Mister Zeal?"

"You know who I mean. The other lobot. The tenth one. You've met her, haven't you?"

"I..." Zeal had the better of me. "I got lost. I bumped into her somewhere near the back of the ship."

The curl of his lip intensified. "And what did she say?"

"Nothing," I said hurriedly. "Nothing. Just...how to find my way back. That's all I asked her. That's all she said."

"She's out of control," he said, more to himself than me. "Becoming trouble. Needs something doing to her."

I sensed further questions would be unwise, bitterly regretting that I had raised the subject in the first place. At least the battle was still on-going, with no sign of any lessening in its intensity. Difficult as it was to look on that as any kind of positive development, at least it might force Zeal's mind onto other matters. If we had a rush of casualties, he might forget that I'd mentioned the girl at all.

Some chance, I thought.

We reached the observation bubble, Zeal silent and brooding at first. He pulled back a lever, opening an iron shutter. Beyond the glass, closer than I'd expected, was the other ship. It couldn't have been more than twenty or thirty kilometers from us.

It was another ramscoop, shaped more or less like the *Iron Lady*. We were so close that the magnetic fields of our scoops must have been meshed together, entangled like the rigging of two sailing ships exchanging cannon fire. Near the front of the other ship, where the scoop pinched to a narrow mouth, I could actually *see* the field: picked out in faint purple flickers of excited, inrushing gas. Behind the other ship was the hot spike of its drive flame: the end result of all that interstellar material being sucked up in the first place, compacted and compressed to stellar core pressures in her drive chamber. A similar flame would have been burning from the *Iron Lady*'s stern, keeping us locked alongside.

The other ship was firing on us, discharging massive energy and projectile weapons from hull emplacements.

"They must be pirates," I said, bracing myself as the ship took another hit. "I'd heard they existed, but never really believed it until now."

"Start believing it," Zeal grunted.

"Could that ship be the *Devilfish*?"

"And what have you heard about the *Devilfish*?"

"If you take the stories seriously, that's the ship they say does most of the pirating between here and the Frolovo Hub. I suppose if pirates exist, then there's a good chance the *Devilfish* does as well."

The hull shook again, but it was a different kind of vibration than before: more regular, like the steady chiming of a great clock.

"That's us firing back," Zeal said. "About bloody time."

I watched our weapons impact across the hull of the other ship, flowering in a chain. Huge blasts...but not enough to stop a wave of retaliatory fire.

"She's switched to heavy slugs," Zeal said. "We'll feel this."

We did. It was worse than anything we had experienced before, as if the entire ship were being shaken violently in a dog's jaw. By now the noise from the klaxons and warning voices had become deafening. Through the window I saw huge scabs of metal slam past.

"Hull plating," Zeal said. "Ours. That'll take some fixing."

"You don't seem all that worried."

"I'm not."

"But we're being shot to pieces here."

"We'll hold," he said. "Long enough."

"Long enough for what?"

I felt a falling sensation in my gut. "That's our drive flame stuttering," Zeal reported, with no sense of alarm. "Captain's turned off our scoop. We'll be on reserve fuel in a moment."

Sure enough, normal weight returned. The two ships were still locked alongside each other.

"Why's he done that?" I asked, fighting to keep the terror from my voice, not wanting to show myself up before Zeal. "We won't be able to burn reserve fuel for very long without the scoop to replenish..."

"Scoop's down for a reason, son."

I followed Zeal's gaze back to the other ship. Once again, I saw the hot gases ramming into the engine mouth, flickering purple. But now there was something skewed about the geometry of the field, like a candleflame bending in a draught. The distortion to the field intensified, and then snapped back in the other direction.

"What's happening?"

"Her fieldmaster's trying to compensate," Zeal said. "He's pretty good, give him that."

Now the ramscoop field was oscillating wildly, caught between two distorted extremes. The pinched gas flared hotter—blue white, shifting into the violet.

"What's happening to them? Why doesn't the fieldmaster shut down the field, if he's losing control of it?"

"Too scared to. Most ships can't switch to reserve fuel as smoothly as we can."

"I still don't see..."

That was when the field instabilities exceeded some critical limit. Gobbets of hot gas slammed into the swallowing mouth. An eyeblink later, an explosion ripped from the belly of the other ship. Instantly her drive flame and scoop field winked out.

She began to fall behind us.

We cut our engines and matched her velocity. The other ship was a wreck: a huge hole punched amidships, through which I saw glowing innards and pieces of tumbling debris, some of which looked horribly like people.

"She's dead now," I said. "We should leave, get out of here as quickly as we can. What if they repair her?"

Zeal looked at me and shook his head slowly. "You don't get it, do you? They weren't the pirates. They were just trying to get away from us."

"But I thought you said..."

"I was having some fun. This was a scheduled interception—always was. It just happened a bit sooner than the captain told me."

"But then if they're not the pirates..."

"Correct, lad. We are. And this isn't really the *Iron Lady*. That's only a name she wears in port." He tapped a hand against the metal framing of the bubble. "You're on the *Devilfish*, and that makes you one of us."

A WEEK PASSED, then another. I learned to stop asking questions, afraid of where my tongue might take me. I kept thinking back to the girl in the corridor, and the cryptic warning she had given me. About how I should get off the ship as soon as possible, before Mister Zeal put machines in my head or the *bad thing* happened. Well, a bad thing had certainly happened. The *Iron Lady*, or the *Devilfish* as I now had to think of her, had attacked and crippled another ship. Her holds had been looted for cargo. A handful of her crew had managed to escape in cryopods, but most had died in the explosion when her drive core went critical. I did not know what had happened to the few survivors, but it could not have been coincidence that I suddenly noticed we were carrying three new lobots. I had played no part in converting them, but it would not have taxed Zeal to do the surgery on his own. I knew my way around his operating room by now; knew what was difficult and what was easy.

So we had murdered another ship and taken some of her crew as prize. Every hour that I stayed aboard the *Devilfish* made me complicit in that crime, and any other attacks that were yet to take place. But where could I run to?

We were between systems, in deep interstellar space.

Get off ship. Before bad thing happens.

Had she meant the attack, or was she talking about something else, something yet to happen?

I had to find her again. I wanted to ask her more questions, but that wasn't the only reason. I kept seeing her face, frozen in the corridor lights. I knew nothing about her except that I wanted to know more. I wanted to touch that face, to pull back that messy curtain of hair and look into her eyes.

I fantasized about saving her: how I'd do the bare minimum in Zeal's service, just enough to keep him happy, and then jump ship at the first opportunity. Jump and run, and take the lobot girl with me. I'd outrun Happy Jack's button men; I could outrun the crew of the *Devilfish*.

But it wasn't going to be that easy.

"I've got a job for you," Zeal said. "Nice and easy. Then you can have the rest of the day off."

"A job?" I ventured timidly.

"Take this." He delved into his apron pocket and passed something to me: a gripped thing shaped a little like the soldering iron. "It's a tranquiliser gun," he said.

"What do you want me to do?"

"I want you to bring the girl back in."

"The girl?"

"Don't try my patience, Peter." He closed my hand around the grip. "You know where she haunts. Find her, or let her find you. Shouldn't be too hard."

"And when I've found her?"

"Then you shoot her." He raised a warning finger. "Not to kill, just to incapacitate. Aim for a leg. She'll drop, after a minute or so. Then you bring her back to me."

He'd cleared the operating table. I knew from our work schedule that we were not expecting any more patients today.

"What do you want her for?" I asked.

"Always been a bit too chirpy, that one. She has a job to do...a certain job that means she has to be brighter than the other lobots. But not *that* much brighter. I don't like it when they answer back, and I definitely don't like it when they start showing notions of free will." He smiled. "But it's all right. Nothing we can't fix, you and I."

"Fix?"

"A few minutes under the knife, is all."

My hand trembled on the gun. "But then she won't be able to talk."

"That's the idea."

"I can't shoot her," I said. "She's still a person. There's still something left of who she was."

"How would you know? All she told you was how to get back home. Or did you talk more than you said?"

"No," I said, cowed. "Only what I told you."

"Good. Then you won't lose any sleep over it, will you?"

With gun in my hand I considered turning it on Mister Zeal and putting him under and then killing him. With the rest of the crew still alive, my chances of stopping the *Devilfish* (let alone making it off the ship in one piece) were practically zero. It would be a futile gesture, nothing more. Without Zeal the crew would be inconvenienced, but most of them would still survive.

I still wanted to stop them, but the gun wasn't the answer. And she *was* just a lobot, after all. She hadn't even remembered her name. What kind of person did that make her?

I slipped the gun into my belt.

"Good lad," Zeal said.

I FOUND HER again. It didn't take all that long, considering. I kept a careful note on the twists and turns I took, doubling back every now and then to make sure the ship really wasn't shifting itself around me. That much had always been my imagination, and now that I was revisiting the zone where I had been lost before, it all looked a degree more familiar. Now that I had been given license to enter this part of the ship, I felt more confident. I still wasn't happy about shooting the girl...but then it wasn't as if Zeal was going to *kill* her. When so much had already been taken from her, what difference did a little bit more make?

I turned a corner and there she was. She wolfed vile-looking paste into her mouth from some kind of spigot in the wall, the stuff lathering her metal hands.

My hand tightened on the gun, still tucked into my belt. I took a pace closer, hoping she would stay engrossed in her meal.

She stopped eating and looked at me. Through the tangled fringe of her hair, eyes shone feral and bright.

"Peter Vandry," she said, and then did something horrible and unexpected; something no lobot should ever do.

She smiled.

It was only a flicker of a smile, quickly aborted, but I had still seen it. My hand trembled as I withdrew the gun and slipped off the safety catch.

"No," she said, backing away from the spigot.

"I'm sorry," I said, aiming the gun. "It isn't personal. If I don't do it, Zeal'll kill me."

"Don't," she said, raising her hands. "Not shoot. Not shoot me. Not *now. Not now.*"

"I'm sorry," I said again.

My finger tightened on the trigger. Two things made me hesitate, though. The first was: what did she mean: *not now*? What did it matter to her if I shot her now, rather than later? The second thing was those fierce, beautiful eyes.

My hesitation lasted an instant too long.

"Baby," she said.

The gun quivered in my hand, and then leapt free of it with painful force, nearly snapping my fingers as it escaped my grip. It slammed into the wall, the impact smashing it apart. The metal remains hovered there for an agonising instant, before dropping—one by one—to the floor.

I looked on, stunned at what had just happened.

"Warn...you," she said. "Warn you good, Peter Vandry. Warn you... get off ship. Stay wethead. Soon *bad thing* happen and you still here."

I pushed my hand against my chest, trying to numb the pain in my forefinger, where it had been twisted out of the trigger grip.

"The bad thing already happened," I said, angry and confused at the same time. "We took out a ship...killed its crew."

"No," she said, shaking her head gravely. "That not what I mean. I mean *real bad thing. Real bad thing* happen *here.* Here and soon. *This ship.*"

I looked at the remains of the gun. "What just happened?"

"She save me."

I frowned. "She?"

For a moment the girl seemed torn between infinite opposed possibilities.

"You try shoot me, Peter Vandry. I trust you and you try *shoot* me."

"I'm sorry. I didn't want to...it's just that I need to keep on Mister Zeal's good side."

"Zeal bad man. Why you work for Zeal?"

"I didn't have a choice. They tricked me aboard. I didn't know this was a pirate ship. I just needed a ticket off Mokmer."

"What happen on Mokmer?"

"Bad thing," I said, with half a smile.

"Tell."

"A man called Happy Jack did something to my sister. I got even with Happy Jack. Unfortunately, that meant I couldn't stick around."

"Happy Jack bad man?"

"As bad as Zeal."

She looked at me, hard and deep and enquiring, and then said: "I hope you not lie, Peter Vandry."

"I'm not lying."

She showed me her hands, giving me time to admire the crudity of their function, the brutal way they'd been grafted to her arms. "Zeal did this."

"I figured."

"Once I work for Zeal. All go well…until one day. Then I make mistake. Zeal get angry. Zeal take hands. Zeal say 'more use on end of machine'."

"I'm sorry."

"Zeal got temper. One day Zeal get angry with *you*."

"I'll be off the ship before then."

"You hope."

Now it was my turn to sound angry. "What does it matter? There's nowhere for me to go. I have no choice but to work with Zeal."

"No," she said. "You have choice."

"I don't see that I do."

"I show. Then you understand. Then you help."

I looked at her. "I just tried to shoot you. Why would you still trust me?"

She cocked her head, as if my question made only the barest sense to her. "You ask me…what my name *is*." She blinked, screwing up her face with the effort of language. "What my name *was*."

"But you didn't know."

"Doesn't matter. No one else…ever ask. Except you, Peter Vandry."

SHE TOOK ME deeper into the ship, into the part I had always been told was off-limits because of its intense radiation. Dimly, it began to dawn on me that this was just a lie to dissuade the curious.

"Zeal not happy, you not bring me in," she said.

"I'll make something up. Tell him I couldn't find you, or that you tricked me and destroyed the gun."

"Not work on Zeal."

"I'll think of something," I said glibly. "In the meantime…you can just hide out here. When we dock, we can both make a run for it."

She laughed. "I not get off *Devilfish*, Peter Vandry. I die here."

"No," I said. "It doesn't have to happen like that."

"Yes, it does. Nearly time now."

"Back there," I said. "When you did that thing with the gun…what did you mean when you said 'baby'?"

"I mean this," she said, and opened a door.

It led into a huge and bright room: part of the engine system. Since my time on the ship, I had learned enough of the ramscoop design to understand that the interstellar gases collected by the magnetic scoop had to pass through the middle of the ship to reach the combustion chamber at the rear...which was somewhere near where we were standing.

Overhead was a thick, glowing tube, running the length of the room. That was the fuel conduit. With the drive off, the glass lining the tube would have been midnight black. Only a fraction of the glow from the heated gases shone through...but it was still enough to bathe the room in something like daylight.

But that wasn't the only bright thing in the room.

We walked along a railinged catwalk, high above the floor. Below, but slightly off to one side, was a thick metal cage in the form of a horizontal cylinder. The cage flickered with containment fields.

Something huge floated in the cage. It was creature: sleek and elongated, aglow with its own fierce brassy light. Something like a whale, but carved from molten lava. Quilted in fiery platelets that flexed and undulated as the creature writhed in the field's embrace. Flickering with arcs and filaments of lightning, like a perpetual dance of St. Elmo's fire.

I squinted against the glare from the alien thing.

"What...?" I asked, not needing to say any more.

"Flux Swimmer," she said. "*Devilfish* found her...living in outflow jet from star. Didn't evolve there. Migrated. Star to star, billions of years. Older than Galaxy."

I stared, humbled, at the astonishing thing. "I'd heard of such things. In the texts of the Kalarash...but everyone always assumed they were legendary animals, like unicorns, or dragons, or tigers."

"Real," she said. "Just...rare."

The creature writhed again, flexing the long, flattened whip of its body. "But why? Why keep it here?"

"*Devilfish* needs Flux Swimmer," she said. "Flux Swimmer...has power. Magnetic fields. Reaches out...shapes. *Changes*."

I nodded slowly, beginning to understand. I thought back to the engagement with the other ramscoop; the way its intake field had become fatally distorted.

"The Flux Swimmer is the *Devilfish*'s weapon against other ships," I said, speaking for the girl. "She reaches out and twists their magnetic fields. Zeal always knew we were going to win." I looked down at the creature again, looking so pitiful in its metal cage. I did not have to read the animal's mind to know that it did not want to be held here, locked away in the heart of the *Devilfish*.

"They...make her do this," the girl said.

"Torture?"

"No. She could always...choose to die. Easier for her."

"How, then?"

She led me along an extension to the catwalk, so that we walked directly over the trapped animal. It was then that I understood how the crew exerted their control of the alien.

Hidden from view before, but visible now, was a smaller version of the same cage. It sat next to the Flux Swimmer. It held another version of the alien animal, but one that was much tinier than the first. Probes reached through the field, contacting the fiery hide of the little animal.

"Baby," the girl said. "Hurt baby. Make mother shape field, or hurt baby even more. *That* how it works."

It was all too much. I closed my eyes, numbed at the implicit horror I had just been shown. The baby was not being hurt now, but that was only because the *Devilfish* did not need the mother's services. But when another ship needed to be destroyed and looted...then the pain would begin again, until the mother extended her alien influence beyond the hull and twisted the other ship's magnetic field.

"I see why the captain cut our field now," I said. "It was so she could reach through it."

"Yes. Captain clever."

"Where do you come into it?" I asked.

"I look after them. Tend them. Keep them alive." She nodded upward, to where smaller conduits branched off the main fuel line. "Swimmers drink plasma. Captain lets them have fuel. Just enough... keep alive. No more."

"We've got to stop this ever happening again," I said, reopening my eyes. Then a thought occurred to me. "But she *can* stop it, can't she? If the mother has enough influence over magnetic fields to twist the ramscoop of a ship thirty kilometers away...surely she can stop the captain and his crew? They're cyborgs, after all. They're practically made of metal."

"No," she said, shaking her head in exasperation—either with the situation, or her own limitations. "Mother...too strong. Long range...good control. Smash other ship, easy. Short range...bad. Too near."

"So what you're saying is...she can't exercise enough local control, because she's too strong?"

"Yes," she said, nodding emphatically. "Too strong. Too much danger... kill baby."

So the mother was powerless, I thought: she had the ability to destroy another ramscoop, but not to unshackle herself from her own chains without harming her child.

"Wait, though. The thing with the gun...*that* took some precision, didn't it?"

"Yes," she said. "But not mother. Baby."

She had said it with something like pride. "The baby can do the same trick?"

"Baby weak...for now. But I make baby stronger. Give baby more fuel. They say starve baby...keep baby alive, but *just*." She clenched her fist and snarled. "I disobey. Give baby more food. Let baby get stronger. Then one day..."

"The baby will be able to do what the mother can't," I said. "Kill them all. That's the bad thing, isn't it? That's what you were warning me about. Telling me to get off the ship before it happened. And to make sure Zeal didn't put implants in my head. So I'd have a chance."

"Someone...live," she said. "Someone...come back. Find *Devilfish*. Let mother and baby go. Take them home."

"Why not you?"

She touched the side of her head. "I, lobot."

"Oh, no."

"When bad thing happen, I go too. But you live, Peter Vandry. You *wethead*. You come back."

"How soon?" I breathed, not wanting to think about what she had just said.

"Soon. Baby stronger...hour by hour. Control...improving. See, feel, all around it. *Empathic*. Know what to do. Understand good." Again that flicker of pride. "Baby *clever*."

"Zeal's onto you. That's why he sent me here."

"That why...has to happen soon. Before Zeal take away...*me*. What left behind after...not care about baby."

"And now?"

"I care. I *love*."

"Well, isn't that heartwarming," said a voice behind us.

I turned around, confronted by the sight of Mister Zeal blocking the main catwalk, advancing toward us with a heavy gun in his human hand: not a tranquiliser this time. He shook his head disappointedly. "Here was I, thinking maybe you needed some help...and when I arrive I find you having a good old chinwag with the lobot!"

"Zeal make you lobot too," she said. "He train you now...just to build up neuromotor patterns."

"Listen to her," Zeal said mockingly. "Step aside now, Peter. Let me finish the job you were so tragically incapable of completing."

I stood my ground. "Is that right, Zeal? Were you going to make me into one of them as well, or were you just planning on taking my hands?"

"Stand aside, lad. And it's *Mister* Zeal to you, by the way."

"No," I said. "I'm not letting you touch her."

"Fine, then."

Zeal aimed the gun and shot me. The round tore through my leg, just below the knee. I yelped and started to fold as my leg buckled under me. By tightening my grip on the railings I managed not to slip off the catwalk.

Zeal advanced toward me, boots clanging on the catwalk. I could barely hold myself up now. Blood was drooling down my leg from the wound. My hands were slippery on the railing, loosing their grip.

"I'm trying not to do too much damage," Zeal said, before levelling the gun at me again. "I'd still like to be able to salvage something."

I steeled myself against the shot.

"Baby," the girl called.

Zeal's arm swung violently aside, mashing against the railing. His hand spasmed open to drop the gun. It clattered to the deck of the catwalk, then dropped all the way to the floor of the chamber, where it smashed apart.

Zeal grunted in anguish, using his good hand to massage the fingers of the other.

"Nice trick," he said. "But it'll only make it slower and messier for both of you."

With both hands—he couldn't have been hurt that badly—he delved into the pocket on the front of his apron. He came out with a pair of long, vicious looking knives, turning them edge-on so that we'd see how sharp they were.

"Baby..." I called.

But Zeal kept advancing, sharpening the knives on each other, showing no indication that the baby was having any effect on his weapons. It was only then that I realised that the knives were not necessarily made of metal.

Baby wasn't going to be able to do anything about them.

Zeal's huge boots clanged ponderously closer. The pain in my leg was now excruciating, beginning to dull my alertness. Slumped down on the deck, I could barely reach his waist, let alone the knives.

"Easy now, lad," he said, as I tried to block him. "Easy now, and we'll make it nice and quick when it's your turn. How does that sound?"

"It sounds..."

I pawed ineffectually at the leather of his apron, slick with blood and oil. I couldn't begin to get a grip on it, even if I'd had the strength to stop him.

"Now lad," he said, sounding more disappointed than angry. "Don't make me slash at your hands. They're too good to waste like that."

"You're not getting any part of me."

He clucked a little purr of amusement and knelt down just far enough to stab the tip of one of the knives—the one he held in his right hand—against my chest. "Seriously, now."

The pressure of the knife made me fall back, so that my back was on the deck. That was when I touched it with my bare hand and felt how warm it was.

Warm and getting hotter.

Inductive heating, I thought: Baby's magnetic field washing back and forth over the metal, cooking it.

I twisted my neck to glance back at the girl, and saw her pain. She held her hands in front of her, like someone expecting a gift. Baby must have been warming the hands as well as the deck.

Baby couldn't help it.

Flat on the deck now, Zeal lowered his heel onto my chest. "Yes, the deck's getting hotter. I can just feel it through the sole of my shoe."

"Don't you touch her."

He increased the pressure on my chest, crushing the wind from my lungs. "Or what, exactly?"

I didn't have the strength to answer. All I could do was push ineffectually against his boot, in the hope of snatching a breath of air.

"I'll deal with you in a moment," Zeal said, preparing to move on.

But then he stopped.

Even from where I was lying, I saw something change on his face. The cocky set of his jaw slipped a notch. His eyes looked up, as if he'd seen something on the ceiling.

He hadn't. He was looking at his goggle, pushed high onto his forehead.

Nothing about the goggle had changed, except for the thin wisp of smoke curling away from it, where it contacted his skin.

It was beginning to burn its way into his forehead, pulled tight by the strap.

Zeal let out an almighty bellow of pain and fury: real this time. His hands jerked up reflexively, as if he meant to snatch the goggle away. But both hands were holding knives.

He screamed, as the hot thing seared into his forehead like a brand.

He lowered his hands, and tried to fumble one of the knives into his apron pocket. His movements were desperate, uncoordinated. The knife tore at the leather, but couldn't find its way home. Finally, shrieking, he simply dropped the weapon.

It fell to the decking. I reached out and took it.

Zeal reached up with his bare hand and closed his fingers around the goggle. Instantly I heard the sizzle of burning skin. He tried to pull his hand away, but his fingers appeared to have stuck to the goggle. Thrashing now, he reached up with the other knife—still unwilling to relinquish it—and tried to use its edge to lever the offending mass of fused metal and skin from his forehead.

That was when I plunged the other knife into his shin, and twisted. Zeal teetered, fighting for balance. But with one hand stuck to his forehead and the other holding the knife, he had no means to secure himself.

I assisted him over the edge. Zeal screamed as he fell. Then there was a clatter and a sudden, savage stillness.

For what seemed like an age I lay on the catwalk, panting until the pain lost its focus.

"It won't be long before the rest of the crew come after us," I told the girl.

She was still holding her metal hands before her. I could only imagine her pain.

"Need to make baby strong now," she said. "Feed it more." She moved to a console, set into a recess in the railing itself. She touched her claws against the controls, and then gasped, unable to complete whatever action she'd had in mind.

I forced myself to stand, putting most of my weight on my good leg. My arm was in a bad way, but the fingers still worked. If I splinted it, I ought to be able to grip something.

I lurched and hobbled until I was next to her.

"Show me what to do."

"Give baby more fuel," she said, indicating a set of controls. "Turn that. All the way."

I did what she said. The decking rumbled, as if the ship itself had shuddered. Overhead, I noticed a dimming in the glow of the pipe after the point where the smaller lines branched out of it.

"How long?" I said, pushing my good hand against the slug wound to keep the blood at bay.

"Not long. Ship get slower...but not enough for captain to notice. Baby drink. Then...*bad thing*."

"Everyone aboard will die?"

"Baby kill them. Fry them alive, same way as Zeal. Except you."

I thought of all that the *Devilfish* had done. If only half of those stories were true, it was still more than enough to justify what was about to happen.

"How long?" I repeated.

"Thirty…forty minutes."

"Then it's time enough," I said.

She looked at me wonderingly. "Time enough…for what?"

"To get you to the surgeon's room. To get you on the table and get those implants out of your head."

Something like hope crossed her face. It was there, fleetingly. Then it was gone, wiped away. How often had she dared to hope, before learning to crush the emotion before it caused any more pain? I didn't want to know…not yet.

"No," she said. "Not time."

"There is time," I said. If I could extract those implants in time, and remove those metal hands, she would weather baby's magnetic storm when it ripped through the rest of the crew. There was nothing I could do for the other lobots, not in the time that was left. And maybe there was nothing anyone could do for them now.

But the girl was different. I knew there was something more in there…something that hadn't been completely erased. Maybe she didn't remember her name now, but with time…with patience…who knew what was possible?

But first we had to save the aliens. And we would, too. We'd have the *Devilfish* to ourselves. If we couldn't work out how to fly the aliens home, we could at least let them go. They were creatures of space: all that they really craved was release.

Then…once the Flux Swimmers were taken care of…we'd find a cryo-pod and save ourselves. So what if it took a while before anyone found us?

"No time," she said again.

"There is," I said. "And we're doing this. You're my patient, and I'm not giving up on you. I'm Peter Vandry, surgeon."

"Surgeon's mate," she corrected.

I looked down at Zeal's spreadeagled, motionless form and shook my head. "Surgeon, actually. Someone just got a promotion."

THE SLEDGE-MAKER'S DAUGHTER

SHE STOPPED in sight of Twenty Arch Bridge, laying down her bags to rest her hands from the weight of two hog's heads and forty pence worth of beeswax candles. While she paused, Kathrin adjusted the drawstring on her hat, tilting the brim to shade her forehead from the sun. Though the air was still cool, there was a fierce new quality to the light that brought out her freckles.

Kathrin moved to continue, but a tightness in her throat made her hesitate. She had been keeping the bridge from her thoughts until this moment, but now the fact of it could not be ignored. Unless she crossed it she would face the long trudge to New Bridge, a diversion that would keep her on the road until long after sunset.

"Sledge-maker's daughter!" called a rough voice from across the road.

Kathrin turned sharply at the sound. An aproned man stood in a doorway, smearing his hands dry. He had a monkeylike face, tanned a deep liverish red, with white sideboards and a gleaming pink tonsure.

"Brendan Lynch's daughter, isn't it?"

She nodded meekly, but bit her lip rather than answer.

"Thought so. Hardly one to forget a pretty face, me." The man beckoned her to the doorway of his shop. "Come here, lass. I've something for your father."

"Sir?"

"I was hoping to visit him last week, but work kept me here." He cocked his head at the painted wooden trademark hanging above the doorway. "Peter Rigby, the wheelwright. Kathrin, isn't it?"

"I need to be getting along, sir…"

"And your father needs good wood, of which I've plenty. Come inside for a moment, instead of standing there like a starved thing." He called over his shoulder, telling his wife to put the water on the fire.

Reluctantly Kathrin gathered her bags and followed Peter into his workshop. She blinked against the dusty air and removed her hat. Sawdust carpeted the floor, fine and golden in places, crisp and coiled in others, while a heady concoction of resins and glues filled the air. Pots simmered on fires. Wood was being steamed into curves, or straightened where it was curved. Many sharp tools gleamed on one wall, some of them fashioned with blades of skydrift. Wheels, mostly awaiting spokes or iron tyres, rested against another. Had the wheels been sledges, it could have been her father's workshop, when he had been busier.

Peter showed Kathrin to an empty stool next to one of his benches. "Sit down here and take the weight off your feet. Mary can make you some bread and cheese. Or bread and ham if you'd rather."

"That's kind, sir, but Widow Grayling normally gives me something to eat, when I reach her house."

Peter raised a white eyebrow. He stood by the bench with his thumbs tucked into the belt of his apron, his belly jutting out as if he was quietly proud of it. "I didn't know you visited the witch."

"She will have her two hog's heads, once a month, and her candles. She only buys them from the Shield, not the Town. She pays for the hogs a year in advance, twenty-four whole pounds."

"And you're not scared by her?"

"I've no cause to be."

"There's some that would disagree with you."

Remembering something her father had told her, Kathrin said, "There are folk who say the Sheriff can fly, or that there was once a bridge that winked at travellers like an eye, or a road of iron that reached all the way to London. My father says there's no reason for anyone to be scared of Widow Grayling."

"Not afraid she'll turn you into a toad, then?"

"She cures people, not put spells on them."

"When she's in the mood for it. From what I've heard she's just as likely to turn the sick and needy away."

"If she helps some people, isn't that better than nothing at all?"

"I suppose." She could tell Peter didn't agree, but he wasn't cross with her for arguing. "What does your father make of you visiting the witch, anyway?"

"He doesn't mind."

"No?" Peter asked, interestedly.

"When he was small, my dad cut his arm on a piece of skydrift that he found in the snow. He went to Widow Grayling and she made his arm better again by tying an eel around it. She didn't take any payment except the skydrift."

"Does your father still believe an eel can heal a wound?"

"He says he'll believe anything if it gets the job done."

"Wise man, that Brendan, a man after my own heart. Which reminds me." Peter ambled to another bench, pausing to stir one of his bubbling pots before gathering a bundle of sawn-off wooden sticks. He set them down in front of Kathrin on a scrap of cloth. "Off cuts," he explained. "But good seasoned beech, which'll never warp. No use to me, but I am sure your father will find use for them. Tell him that there's more, if he wishes to collect it."

"I haven't got any money for wood."

"I'd take none. Your father was always generous to me, when I was going through lean times." Peter scratched behind his ear. "Only fair, the way I see it."

"Thank you," Kathrin said doubtfully. "But I don't think I can carry the wood all the way home."

"Not with two hog's heads as well. But you can drop by when you've given the heads to Widow Grayling."

"Only I won't be coming back over the river," Kathrin said. "After I've crossed Twenty Arch Bridge, I'll go back along the south quayside and take the ferry at Jarrow."

Peter looked puzzled. "Why line the ferryman's pocket when you can cross the bridge for nowt?"

Kathrin shrugged easily. "I've got to visit someone on the Jarrow road, to settle an account."

"Then you'd better take the wood now, I suppose," Peter said.

Mary bustled in, carrying a small wooden tray laden with bread and ham. She was as plump and red as her husband, only shorter. Picking up the entire gist of the conversation in an instant, she said, "Don't be an oaf, Peter. The girl cannot carry all that wood *and* her bags. If she will not come back this way, she must pass a message onto her father. Tell him that there's wood here if he wants it." She shook her head sympathetically at Kathrin. "What does he think you are, a pack mule?"

"I'll tell my father about the wood," she said.

"Seasoned beech," Peter said emphatically. "Remember that."

"I will."

Mary encouraged her to take some of the bread and meat, despite Kathrin again mentioning that she expected to be fed at Widow Grayling's. "Take it anyway," Mary said. "You never know how hungry you might get on the way home. Are you sure about not coming back this way?"

"I'd best not," Kathrin said.

After an awkward lull, Peter said, "There is something else I meant to tell your father. Could you let him know that I've no need of a new sledge this year, after all?"

"Peter," Mary said. "You promised."

"I said that I should *probably* need one. I was wrong in that." Peter looked exasperated. "The fault lies in Brendan, not me! If he did not make such good and solid sledges, then perhaps I should need another by now."

"I shall tell him," Kathrin said.

"Is your father keeping busy?" Mary asked.

"Aye," Kathrin answered, hoping the wheelwright's wife wouldn't push her on the point.

"Of course he will still be busy," Peter said, helping himself to some of the bread. "People don't stop needing sledges, just because the Great Winter loosens its hold on us. Any more than they stopped needing wheels when the winter was at its coldest. It's still cold for half the year!"

Kathrin opened her mouth to speak. She meant to tell Peter that he could pass the message on to her father directly, for he was working not five minutes walk from the wheelwright's shop. Peter clearly had no knowledge that her father had left the village, leaving his workshop empty during these warming months. But she realised that her father would be ashamed if the wheelwright were to learn of his present trade. It was best that nothing be said.

"Kathrin?" Peter asked.

"I should be getting on. Thank you for the food, and the offer of the wood."

"You pass our regards onto your father," Mary said.

"I shall."

"God go with you. Watch out for the jangling men."

"I will," Kathrin replied, because that was what you were supposed to say.

"Before you go," Peter said suddenly, as if a point had just occurred to him. "Let me tell you something. You say there are people who believe the Sheriff can fly, as if that was a foolish thing, like the iron road and the winking bridge. I cannot speak of the other things, but when I was boy I met someone who had seen the Sheriff's flying machine. My grandfather often spoke of it. A whirling thing, like a windmill made of tin. He had seen it when he was a boy, carrying the Sheriff and his men above the land faster than any bird."

"If the Sheriff could fly then, why does he need a horse and carriage now?"

"Because the flying machine crashed down to Earth, and no tradesman could persuade it to fly again. It was a thing of the old world, before the Great Winter. Perhaps the winking bridge and the iron road were also things of the old world. We mock too easily, as if we understood everything of our world where our forebears understood nothing."

"But if I should believe in certain things," Kathrin said, "should I not also believe in others? If the Sheriff can fly, then can a jangling man not steal me from my bed at night?"

"The jangling men are a story to stop children misbehaving," Peter said witheringly. "How old are you now?"

"Sixteen," Kathrin answered.

"I am speaking of something that was seen, in daylight, not made up to frighten bairns."

"But people say they have seen jangling men. They have seen men made of tin and gears, like the inside of a clock."

"Some people were frightened too much when they were small," Peter said, with a dismissive shake. "No more than that. But the Sheriff is real, and he was once able to fly. That's God's truth."

HER HANDS WERE hurting again by the time she reached Twenty Arch Bridge. She tugged down the sleeves of her sweater, using them as mittens. Rooks and jackdaws wheeled and cawed overhead. Seagulls feasted on waste floating in the narrow races between the bridge's feet, or pecked at vile leavings on the road that had been missed by the night soil gatherers. A boy laughed as Kathrin nearly tripped on the labyrinth of criss-crossing ruts that had been etched by years of wagon wheels entering and leaving the bridge. She hissed a curse back at the boy, but now the wagons served her purpose. She skulked near a doorway until a heavy cart came rumbling along, top-heavy with beer barrels from the Blue Star Brewery, drawn by four snorting dray-horses, a bored-looking drayman at the reins, huddled so down deep into his leather coat that it seemed as if the Great Winter still had its icy hand on the country.

Kathrin started walking as the cart lumbered past her, using it as a screen. Between the stacked beer barrels she could see the top level of the scaffolding that was shoring up the other side of the arch, visible since no house or parapet stood on that part of the bridge. A dozen or so workers—including a couple of aproned foremen—were standing on the scaffolding, looking down at the work going on below. Some of them had plumb lines; one of them even had a little black rod that shone a fierce red spot wherever he wanted something moved. Of Garret, the reason she wished to cross the bridge only once if she could help it, there was nothing to be seen. Kathrin hoped that he was under the side of the bridge, hectoring the workers. She felt sure that her father was down there too, being told what to do and biting his tongue against answering back. He put up with being shouted at, he put up with being forced to treat wood with crude disrespect, because it was all he could do to earn enough money to feed and shelter himself and his daughter. And he never, ever, looked Garret Kinnear in the eye.

Kathrin felt her mood easing as the dray ambled across the bridge, nearing the slight rise over the narrow middle arches. The repair work, where Garret was most likely to be, was now well behind her. She judged her progress by the passage of alehouses. She had passed the newly painted Bridge Inn and the shuttered gloom of the Lord's Confessor. Fiddle music spilled from the open doorway of the Dancing Panda: an old folksong with nonsense lyrics about *sickly sausage rolls*.

Ahead lay the Winged Man, its sign containing a strange painting of a foreboding figure rising from a hilltop. If she passed the Winged Man, she felt she would be safe.

Then the dray hit a jutting cobblestone and rightmost front wheel snapped free of its axle. The wheel wobbled off on its own. The cart tipped to the side, spilling beer barrels onto the ground. Kathrin stepped nimbly aside as one of the barrels ruptured and sent its fizzing, piss-coloured contents across the roadway. The horses snorted and strained. The drayman spat out a greasy wad of chewing tobacco and started down from his chair, his face a mask of impassive resignation, as if this was the kind of thing that could be expected to happen once a day. Kathrin heard him whisper something in the ear of one of the horses, in beast-tongue, which calmed the animal.

Kathrin knew that she had no choice but to continue. Yet she had no sooner resumed her pace—moving faster now, the bags swaying awkwardly—than she saw Garret Kinnear. He was just stepping out of the Winged Man's doorway.

He smiled. "You in a hurry or something?"

Kathrin tightened her grip on the bags, as if she was going to use them as weapons. She decided not to say anything, not to openly acknowledge his presence, even though their eyes had met for an electric instant.

"Getting to be a big strong girl now, Kathrin Lynch."

She carried on walking, each step taking an eternity. How foolish she had been, to take Twenty Arch Bridge when it would only have cost her another hour to take the further crossing. She should not have allowed Peter to delay her with his good intentions.

"You want some help with them bags of yours?"

Out of the corner of her eye she saw him move out of the doorway, tugging his mud-stained trousers higher onto his hip. Garret Kinnear was snake thin, all skin and bone, but much stronger than he looked. He wiped a hand across his sharp beardless chin. He had long black hair, the greasy grey colour of dishwater.

"Go away," she hissed, hating herself in the same instant.

"Just making conversation," he said.

Kathrin quickened her pace, glancing nervously around. All of a sudden the bridge appeared deserted. The shops and houses she had yet to pass were all shuttered and silent. There was still a commotion going on by the dray, but no one there was paying any attention to what was happening further along the bridge.

"Leave me alone," Kathrin said.

He was walking almost alongside her now, between Kathrin and the road. "Now what kind of way to talk is that, Kathrin Lynch? Especially after my offer to help you with them bags. What have you got in them, anyways?"

"Nothing that's any business of yours."

"I could be the judge of that." Before she could do anything, he'd snatched the bag from her left hand. He peered into its dark depths, frowning. "You came all the way from Jarrow Ferry with this?"

"Give me back the bag."

She reached for the bag, tried to grab it back, but he held it out of her reach, grinning cruelly.

"That's mine."

"How much would a pig's head be worth?"

"You tell me. There's only one pig around here."

They'd passed the mill next to the Winged Man. There was a gap between the mill and the six-storey house next to it, where some improbably narrow property must once have existed. Garret turned down the alley, still carrying Kathrin's bag. He reached the parapet at the edge of the bridge and looked over the side. He rummaged in the bag and drew out the pig's head. Kathrin hesitated at the entrance to the narrow alley, watching as Garret held the head out over the roiling water.

"You can have your pig back. Just come a wee bit closer."

"So you can do what you did last time?"

"I don't remember any complaints." He let the head fall, then caught it again, Kathrin's heart in her throat.

"You know I couldn't complain."

"Not much to ask for a pig's head, is it?" With his free hand, he fumbled open his trousers, tugging out the pale worm of his cock. "You did it before, and it didn't kill you. Why not now? I won't trouble you again."

She watched his cock stiffen. "You said that last time."

"Aye, but this time I mean it. Come over here, Kathrin. Be a good girl now and you'll have your pig back."

Kathrin looked back over her shoulder. No one was going to disturb them. The dray had blocked all the traffic behind it, and nothing was coming over the bridge from the south.

"Please," she said.

"Just this once," Garret said. "And make your mind up fast, girl. This pig's getting awfully heavy in my hand."

KATHRIN STOOD IN the widow's candlelit kitchen—it only had one tiny, dusty window—while the old woman turned her bent back to attend to the coals burning in her black metal stove. She poked and prodded the fire until it hissed back like a cat. "You came all the way from Jarrow Ferry?" she asked.

"Aye," Kathrin said. The room smelled smoky.

"That's too far for anyone, let alone a sixteen-year-old lass. I should have a word with your father. I heard he was working on Twenty Arch Bridge."

Kathrin shifted uncomfortably. "I don't mind walking. The weather's all right."

"So they say. All the same, the evenings are still cold, and there are types about you wouldn't care to meet on your own, miles from Jarrow."

"I'll be back before it gets dark," Kathrin said, with more optimism than she felt. Not if she went out of her way to avoid Garret Kinnear she wouldn't. He knew the route she'd normally take back home, and the alternatives would mean a much longer journey.

"You sure about that?"

"I have no one else to visit. I can start home now." Kathrin offered her one remaining bag, as Widow Grayling turned from the fire, brushing her hands on her apron.

"Put it on the table, will you?"

Kathrin put the bag down. "One pig's head, and twenty candles, just as you wanted," she said brightly.

Widow Grayling hobbled over to the table, supporting herself with a stick, eyeing Kathrin as she opened the bag and took out the solitary head. She weighed it in her hand then set it down on the table, the head facing Kathrin in such a way that its beady black eyes and smiling snout suggested amused complicity.

"It's a good head," the widow said. "But there were meant to be two of them."

"Can you manage with just the one, until I visit again? I'll have three for you next time."

"I'll manage if I must. Was there a problem with the butcher in the Shield?"

Kathrin had considered feigning ignorance, saying that she did not recall how only one head had come to be in her bags. But she knew Widow Grayling too well for that.

"Do you mind if I sit down?"

"Of course." The widow hobbled around the table to one of the rickety stools and dragged it out. "Are you all right, girl?"

Kathrin lowered herself onto the stool.

"The other bag was taken from me," she answered quietly.

"By who?"

"Someone on the bridge."

"Children?"

"A man."

Widow Grayling nodded slowly, as if Kathrin's answer had only confirmed some deep-seated suspicion she had harboured for many years. "Thomas Kinnear's boy, was it?"

"How could you know?"

"Because I've lived long enough to form ready opinions of people. Garret Kinnear is filth. But there's no one that'll touch him, because they're scared of his father. Even the Sheriff tugs his forelock to Thomas Kinnear. Did he rape you?"

"No. But he wanted me to do something nearly as bad."

"And did he make you?"

Kathrin looked away.

"Not this time."

Widow Grayling closed her eyes. She reached across the table and took one of Kathrin's hands, squeezing it between her own. "When was it?"

"Three months ago, when there was still snow on the ground. I had to cross the bridge on my own. It was later than usual, and there weren't any people around. I knew about Garret already, but I'd managed to keep away from him. I thought I was going to be lucky." Kathrin turned back to face her companion. "He caught me and took me into one of the mills. The wheels were turning, but there was nobody inside except me and Garret. I struggled, but then he put his finger to my lips and told me to shush."

"Because of your father."

"If I made trouble, if I did not do what he wanted, Garret would tell his father some lie about mine. He would say that he caught him sleeping on the job, or drunk, or stealing nails."

"Garret promised you that?"

"He said, life's hard enough for a sledge-maker's daughter when no one wants sledges. He said it would only be harder if my father lost his work."

"In that respect he was probably right," the widow said resignedly. "It was brave of you to hold your silence, Kathrin. But the problem hasn't gone away, has it? You cannot avoid Garret forever."

"I can take the other bridge."

"That'll make no difference, now that he has his eye on you."

Kathrin looked down at her hands. "Then he's won already."

"No, he just thinks that he has." Without warning the widow stood from her chair. "How long have we known each other, would you say?"

"Since I was small."

"And in all that time, have I come to seem any older to you?"

"You've always seemed the same to me, Widow Lynch."

"An old woman. The witch on the hill."

"There are good witches and bad witches," Kathrin pointed out.

"And there are mad old women who don't belong in either category. Wait a moment."

Widow Grayling stooped under the impossibly low doorway into the next room. Kathrin heard a scrape of wood on wood, as of a drawer being opened. She heard rummaging sounds. Widow Grayling returned with something in her hands, wrapped in red cotton. Whatever it was, she put it down on the table. By the noise it made Kathrin judged that it was an item of some weight and solidity.

"I was just like you once. I grew up not far from Ferry, in the darkest, coldest years of the Great Winter."

"How long ago?"

"The Sheriff then was William the Questioner. You won't have heard of him." Widow Grayling sat down in the same seat she'd been using before and quickly exposed the contents of the red cotton bundle.

Kathrin wasn't quite sure what she was looking at. There was a thick and unornamented bracelet, made of some dull grey metal like pewter. Next to the ornament was something like the handle of a broken sword: a grip, with a criss-crossed pattern on it, with a curved guard reaching from one end of the hilt to the other. It was fashioned from the same dull grey metal.

"Pick it up," the widow said. "Feel it."

Kathrin reached out tentatively and closed her finger around the criss-crossed hilt. It felt cold and hard and not quite the right shape for her hand. She lifted it from the table, feeling its weight.

"What is it, Widow?"

"It's yours. It's a thing that has been in my possession for a very long while, but now it must change hands."

Kathrin didn't know quite what to say. A gift was a gift, but neither she nor her father would have any use for this ugly broken thing, save for its value to a scrap man.

"What happened to the sword?" she asked.

"There was never a sword. The thing you are holding is the entire object."

"Then I don't understand what it is for."

"You shall, in time. I'm about to place a hard burden on your shoulders. I have often thought that you were the right one, but I wished to wait until you were older, stronger. But what has happened today cannot be ignored. I am old and weakening. It would be a mistake to wait another year."

"I still don't understand."

"Take the bracelet. Put it on your wrist."

Kathrin did as she was told. The bracelet opened on a heavy hinge, like a manacle. When she locked it together, the join was nearly invisible. It was a cunning thing, to be sure. But it still felt as heavy and dead and useless as the broken sword.

Kathrin tried to keep a composed face, while all the while suspecting that the widow was as mad as people had always said.

"Thank you," she said, with as much sincerity as she could muster.

"Now listen to what I have to say. You walked across the bridge today. Doubtless you passed the inn known as the Winged Man."

"It was where Garret caught up with me."

"Did it ever occur to you to wonder where the name of the tavern comes from?"

"My dad told me once. He said the tavern was named after a metal statue that used to stand on a hill to the south, on the Durham road."

"And did your father explain the origin of this statue?"

"He said some people reckoned it had been up there since before the Great Winter. Other people said an old sheriff had put it up. Some other people..." But Kathrin trailed off.

"Yes?"

"It's silly, but they said a real Winged Man had come down, out of the sky."

"And did your father place any credence in that story?"

"Not really," Kathrin said.

"He was right not to. The statue was indeed older than the Great Winter, when they tore it down. It was not put up to honour the sheriff, or commemorate the arrival of a Winged Man." Now the widow looked at her intently. "But a Winged Man *did* come down. I know what happened, Kathrin: I saw the statue with my own eyes, before the Winged Man fell. I was there."

Kathrin shifted. She was growing uncomfortable in the widow's presence.

"My dad said people reckoned the Winged Man came down hundreds of years ago."

"It did."

"Then you can't have been there, Widow Grayling."

"Because if I had been, I should be dead by now? You're right. By all that is natural, I should be. I was born three hundred years ago, Kathrin. I've been a widow for more than two hundred of those years, though not always under this name. I've moved from house to house, village to village, as soon as people start suspecting what I am. I found the Winged Man when I was sixteen years old, just like you."

Kathrin smiled tightly. "I want to believe you."

"You will, shortly. I already told you that this was the coldest time of the Great Winter. The sun was a cold grey disk, as if it was made of ice itself. For years the river hardly thawed at all. The Frost Fair stayed almost all year round. It was nothing like the miserable little gatherings you have known. This was ten times bigger, a whole city built on the frozen river. It had streets and avenues, its own quarters. There were tents and stalls, with skaters and sledges everywhere. There'd be races, jousting competitions, fireworks, mystery players, even printing presses to make newspapers and souvenirs just for the Frost Fair. People came from miles around to see it, Kathrin: from as far away as Carlisle or York."

"Didn't they get bored with it, if it was always there?"

"It was always changing, though. Every few months there was something different. You would travel fifty miles to see a new wonder if enough people started talking about it. And there was no shortage of wonders, even if they were not always quite what you had imagined when you set off on your journey. Things fell from the sky more often in those days. A living thing like the Winged Man was still a rarity, but other things came down regularly enough. People would spy where they fell and try to get there first. Usually all they'd find would be bits of hot metal, all warped and runny like melted sugar."

"Skydrift," Kathrin said. "Metal that's no use to anyone, except barbers and butchers."

"Only because we can't make fires hot enough to make that metal smelt down like iron or copper. Once, we could. But if you could find a small piece with an edge, there was *nothing* it couldn't cut through. A surgeon's best knife will always be skydrift."

"Some people think the metal belongs to the jangling men, and that anyone who touches it will be cursed."

"And I'm sure the sheriff does nothing to persuade them otherwise. Do you think the jangling men care what happens to their metal?"

"I don't think they care, because I don't think they exist."

"I was once of the same opinion. Then something happened to make me change my mind."

"This being when you found the Winged Man, I take it."

"Before even that. I would have been thirteen, I suppose. It was in the back of a tent in the Frost Fair. There was a case holding a hand made of metal, found among skydrift near Wallsend."

"A rider's gauntlet."

"I don't think so. It was broken off at the wrist, but you could tell that it used to belong to something that was also made of metal. There were metal bones and muscles in it. No cogs or springs, like in a clock or tin toy. This was something finer, more ingenious. I don't believe any man could have made it. But it cannot just be the jangling men who drop things from the sky, or fall out of it."

"Why not?" Kathrin asked, in the spirit of someone going along with a game.

"Because it was said that the sheriff's men once found a head of skin and bone, all burned up, but which still had a pair of spectacles on it. The glass in them was dark like coal, but when the sheriff wore them, he could see at night like a wolf. Another time, his men found a shred of garment that kept changing colour, depending on what it was lying against. You could hardly see it then. Not enough to make a suit, but you could imagine how useful that would have been to the sheriff's spies."

"They'd have wanted to get to the Winged Man first."

Widow Grayling nodded. "It was just luck that I got to him first. I was on the Durham road, riding a mule, when he fell from the sky. Now, the law said that they would spike your head on the bridge if you touched something that fell on the Sheriff's land, especially skydrift. But everyone knew that the Sheriff could only travel so fast, even when he had his flying machine. It was a risk worth taking, so I took it, and I found the Winged Man, and he was still alive."

"Was he really a man?"

"He was a creature of flesh and blood, not a jangling man, but he was not like any man I had seen before. He was smashed and bent, like a toy that had been trodden on. When I found him he was covered in armour, hot enough to turn the snow to water and make the water hiss and bubble under him. I could only see his face. A kind of golden mask had come off, lying next to him. There were bars across his mask, like the head of the Angel on the tavern sign. The rest of him was covered in metal, jointed in a clever fashion. It was silver in places and black in others, where it had been scorched. His arms were metal wings, as wide across as the road itself if they had not been snapped back on themselves. Instead of legs he just had a long tail, with a kind of fluke at the end of it. I crept closer, watching the sky all around me for the sheriff's whirling machine. I was fearful at first, but when I saw the Winged Man's face I only wanted to do what I could for him. And he was dying. I knew it, because I'd seen the same look on the faces of men hanging from the sheriff's killing poles."

"Did you talk to him?"

"I asked him if he wanted some water. At first he just looked at me, his eyes pale as the sky, his lips opening and closing like a fish that has just been landed. Then he said 'water will not help me.' Just those five words, in a dialect I didn't know. Then I asked him if there was anything else I could do to help him, all the while glancing over my shoulder in case anyone should come upon us. But the road was empty and the sky was clear. It took a long time for him to answer me again."

"What did he say?"

"He said 'thank you, but there is nothing you can do for me.' Then I asked him if he was an angel. He smiled, ever so slightly. 'No,' he said.

'Not an angel, really. But I am a flier.' I asked him if there was a difference. He smiled again before answering me. 'Perhaps not, after all this time. Do you know of fliers, girl? Do any of you still remember the war?'"

"What did you tell him?"

"The truth. I said I knew nothing of a war, unless he spoke of the Battle of the Stadium of Light, which had only happened twenty years earlier. He looked sad, then, as if he had hoped for a different answer. I asked him if he was a kind of soldier. He said that he was. 'Fliers are warriors', he said. 'Men like me are fighting a great war, on your behalf, against an enemy you do not even remember.'"

"What enemy?"

"The jangling men. They exist, but not in the way we imagine them. They don't crawl in through bedroom windows at night, clacking tin-bodied things with skull faces and clockwork keys whirring from their backs. But they're real enough."

"Why would such things exist?"

"They'd been made to do the work of men on the other side of the sky, where men cannot breathe because the air is so thin. They made the jangling men canny enough that they could work without being told *exactly* what to do. But that already made them slyer than foxes. The jangling men coveted our world for themselves. That was before the Great Winter came in. The flier said that men like him—special soldiers, born and bred to fight the jangling men—were all that was holding them back."

"And he told you they were fighting a war, above the sky?"

Something pained Widow Grayling. "All the years since haven't made it any easier to understand what the flier told me. He said that, just as there may be holes in a old piece of timber, one that has been eaten through by woodworm, so there may be holes in the sky itself. He said that his wings were not really to help him fly, but to help him navigate those tunnels in the sky, just as the wheels of a cart find their way into the ruts on a road."

"I don't understand. How can there be holes in the sky, when the air is already too thin to breathe?"

"He said that the fliers and the jangling men make these holes, just as armies may dig a shifting network of trenches and tunnels as part of a long campaign. It requires strength to dig a hole and more strength to shore it up when it has already been dug. In an army, it would be the muscle of men and horses and whatever machines still work. But the flier was talking about a different kind of strength altogether." The widow paused, then stared into Kathrin's eyes with a look of foreboding. "He told me where it came from, you see. And ever since then, I have seen the world with different eyes. It is a hard burden, Kathrin. But someone must bear it."

Without thinking, Kathrin said, "Tell me."

"Are you sure?"

"Yes. I want to know."

"That bracelet has been on your wrist for a few minutes now. Does it feel any different?"

"No," Kathrin said automatically, but as soon as she'd spoken, as soon as she'd moved her arm, she knew that it was not the case. The bracelet still looked the same, it still looked like a lump of cold dead metal, but it seemed to hang less heavily against her skin than when she'd first put it on.

"The flier gave it to me," Widow Grayling said, observing Kathrin's reaction. "He told me how to open his armour and find the bracelet. I asked why. He said it was because I had offered him water. He was giving me something in return for that kindness. He said that the bracelet would keep me healthy, make me strong in other ways, and that if anyone else was to wear it, it would cure them of many ailments. He said that it was against the common law of his people to give such a gift to one such as I, but he chose to do it anyway. I opened his armour, as he told me, and I found his arm, bound by iron straps to the inside of his wing, and broken like the wing itself. On the end of his arm was this bracelet."

"If the bracelet had the power of healing, why was the Winged Man dying?"

"He said that there were certain afflictions it could not cure. He had been touched by the poisonous ichor of a jangling man, and the bracelet could do nothing for him now."

"I still do not believe in magic," Kathrin said carefully.

"Certain magics are real, though. The magic that makes a machine fly, or a man see in the dark. The bracelet feels lighter, because part of it has entered you. It is in your blood now, in your marrow, just as the jangling man's ichor was in the flier's. You felt nothing, and you will continue to feel nothing. But so long as you wear the bracelet, you will age much slower than anyone else. For centuries, no sickness or infirmity will touch you."

Kathrin stroked the bracelet. "I do not believe this."

"I would not expect to you. In a year or two, you will feel no change in yourself. But in five years, or in ten, people will start to remark upon your uncommon youthfulness. For a while, you will glory in it. Then you will feel admiration turn slowly to envy and then to hate, and it will start to feel like a curse. Like me, you will need to move on and take another name. This will be the pattern of your life, while your wear the flier's charm."

Kathrin looked at the palms of her hand. It might have been imagination, but the lines where the handles had cut into her were paler and less sensitive to the touch.

"Is this how you heal people?" she asked.

"You're as wise as I always guessed you were, Kathrin Lynch. Should you come upon someone who is ill, you need only place the bracelet around their wrist for a whole day and—unless they have the jangling man's ichor in them—they will be cured."

"What of the other things? When my father hurt his arm, he said you tied an eel around his arm."

Her words made the widow smile. "I probably did. I could just as well have smeared pigeon dung on it instead, or made him wear a necklace of worms, for all the difference it would have made. Your father's arm would have mended itself on its own, Kathrin. The cut was deep, but clean. It did not need the bracelet to heal, and your father was neither stupid nor feverish. But he did have the loose tongue of all small boys. He would have seen the bracelet, and spoken of it."

"Then you did nothing."

"Your father believed that I did something. That was enough to ease the pain in his arm and perhaps allow it to heal faster than it would otherwise have done."

"But you turn people away."

"If they are seriously ill, but neither feverish nor unconscious, I cannot let them see the bracelet. There is no other way, Kathrin. Some must die, so that the bracelet's secret is protected."

"This is the burden?" Kathrin asked doubtfully.

"No, this is the reward for carrying the burden. The burden is knowledge."

Again, Kathrin said, "Tell me."

"This is what the flier told me. The Great Winter fell across our world because the sun itself grew colder and paler. There was a reason for that. The armies of the celestial war were mining its fire, using the furnace of the sun itself to dig and shore up those seams in the sky. How they did this is beyond my comprehension, and perhaps even that of the flier himself. But he did make one thing clear. So long as the Great Winter held, the celestial war must still be raging. And that would mean that the jangling men had not yet won."

"But the Thaw..." Kathrin began.

"Yes, you see it now. The snow melts from the land. Rivers flow, crops grow again. The people rejoice, they grow stronger and happier, skins darken, the Frost Fairs fade into memory. But they do not understand what it really means."

Kathrin hardly dared ask. "Which side is winning, or has already won?"

"I don't know; that's the terrible part of it. But when the flier spoke to me, I sensed an awful hopelessness, as if he knew things were not going to go the way of his people."

"I'm frightened now."

"You should be. But someone needs to know, Kathrin, and the bracelet is losing its power to keep me out of the grave. Not because there is anything wrong with it, I think—it heals as well as it has ever done—but because it has decided that my time has grown sufficient, just as it will eventually decide the same thing with you."

Kathrin touched the other object, the thing that looked like a sword's handle.

"What is this?"

"The flier's weapon. His hand was holding it from inside the wing. It poked through the outside of the wing like the claw of a bat. The flier showed me how to remove it. It is yours as well."

She had touched it already, but this time Kathrin felt a sudden tingle as her fingers wrapped around the hilt. She let go suddenly, gasping as if she had reached for a stick and picked up an adder, squirming and slippery and venomous.

"Yes, you feel its power," Widow Grayling said admiringly. "It works for no one unless they carry the bracelet."

"I can't take it."

"Better you have it, than let that power go to waste. If the jangling men come, then at least someone will have a means to hurt them. Until then, there are other uses for it."

Without touching the hilt, Kathrin slipped the weapon into her pocket where it lay as heavy and solid as a pebble.

"Did you ever use it?"

"Once."

"What did you do?"

She caught a secretive smile on Widow Grayling's face. "I took something precious from William the Questioner. Banished him to the ground like the rest of us. I meant to kill him, but he was not riding in the machine when I brought it down."

Kathrin laughed. Had she not felt the power of the weapon, she might have dismissed the widow's story as the ramblings of an old woman. But she had no reason in the world to doubt her companion.

"You could have killed the sheriff later, when he came to inspect the killing poles."

"I nearly did. But something always stayed my hand. Then the sheriff was replaced by another man, and he in turn by another. Sheriffs came and went. Some were evil men, but not all of them. Some were only as hard and cruel as their office demanded. I never used the weapon again, Kathrin. I sensed that its power was not limitless, that it must be used sparingly, against the time when it became really necessary. But to use it in defence, against a smaller target...that would be a different matter, I think."

Kathrin thought she understood.

"I need to be getting back home," she said, trying to sound as if they had discussed nothing except the matter of the widow's next delivery of provisions. "I am sorry about the other head."

"There is no need to apologise. It was not your doing."

"What will happen to you now, Widow?"

"I'll fade, slowly and gracefully. Perhaps I will see things through to the next winter. But I don't expect to see another thaw."

"Please. Take the bracelet back."

"Kathrin, listen. It will make no difference to me now, whether you take it or not."

"I'm not old enough for this. I'm only a girl from the Shield, a sledge-maker's daughter."

"What do you think I was, when I found the flier? We were the same. I've seen your strength and courage."

"I wasn't strong today."

"Yet you took the bridge, when you knew Garret would be on it. I have no doubt, Kathrin."

She stood. "If I had not lost the other head...if Garret had not caught me...would you have given me these things?"

"I was minded to do it. If not today, it would have happened next time. But let us give Garret due credit. He helped me make up my mind."

"He's still out there," Kathrin said.

"But he will know you will not be taking the bridge to get back home, even though that would save you paying the toll at Jarrow Ferry. He will content himself to wait until you cross his path again."

Kathrin collected her one remaining bag and moved to the door.

"Yes."

"I will see you again, in a month. Give my regards to your father."

"I will."

Widow Grayling opened the door. The sky was darkening to the east, in the direction of Jarrow Ferry. The dusk stars would appear shortly, and it would be dark within the hour. The crows were still wheeling, but more languidly now, preparing to roost. Though the Great Winter was easing, the evenings seemed as cold as ever, as if night was the final stronghold, the place where the winter had retreated when the inevitability of its defeat became apparent. Kathrin knew that she would be shivering long before she reached the tollgate at the crossing, miles down the river. She tugged down her hat in readiness for the journey and stepped onto the broken road in front of the widow's cottage.

"You will take care now, Kathrin. Watch out for the janglies."

"I will, Widow Grayling."

The door closed behind her. She heard a bolt slide into place.

She was alone.

Kathrin set off, following the path she had used to climb up from the river. If it was arduous in daylight, it was steep and treacherous at dusk. As she descended she could see Twenty Arch Bridge from above, a thread of light across the shadowed ribbon of the river. Candles were being lit in the inns and houses that lined the bridge, tallow torches burning along the parapets. There was still light at the north end, where the sagging arch was being repaired. The obstruction caused by the dray had been cleared, and traffic was moving normally from bank to bank. She heard the calls of men and women, the barked orders of foremen, the braying of drunkards and slatterns, the regular creak and splash of the mill wheels turning under the arches.

Presently she reached a fork in the path and paused. To the right lay the quickest route down to the quayside road to Jarrow Ferry. To the left lay the easiest descent down to the bridge, the path that she had already climbed. Until that moment, her resolve had been clear. She would take the ferry, as she always did, as she was expected to do.

But now she reached a hand into her pocket and closed her fingers around the flier's weapon. The shiver of contact was less shocking this time. The object already felt a part of her, as if she had carried it for years.

She drew it out. It gleamed in twilight, shining where it had appeared dull before. Even if the widow had not told her of its nature, there would have been no doubt now. The object spoke its nature through her skin and bones, whispering to her on a level beneath language. It told her what it could do and how she could make it obey her. It told her to be careful of the power she now carried in her hand. She must scruple to use it wisely, for nothing like it now existed in the world. It was the power to smash walls. Power to smash bridges and towers and flying machines. Power to smash jangling men.

Power to smash ordinary men, if that was what she desired.

She had to know.

The last handful of crows gyred overhead. She raised the weapon to them and felt a sudden dizzying apprehension of their number and distance and position, each crow feeling distinct from its brethren, as if she could almost name them.

She selected one laggard bird. All the others faded from her attention, like players removing themselves from a stage. She came to know that last bird intimately. She could feel its wingbeats cutting the cold air. She could feel the soft thatch of its feathers, and the lacelike scaffolding of bone underneath. Within the cage of its chest she felt the tiny strong pulse of its heart, and she knew that she could make that heart freeze just by willing it.

The weapon seemed to urge her to do it. She came close. She came frighteningly close.

But the bird had done nothing to wrong her, and she spared it. She had no need to take a life to test this new gift, at least not an innocent one. The crow rejoined its brethren, something skittish and hurried in its flight, as if it had felt that coldness closing around its heart.

Kathrin returned the weapon to her pocket. She looked at the bridge again, measuring it once more with clinical eyes, eyes that were older and sadder this time, because she knew something that the people on the bridge could never know.

"I'm ready," she said, aloud, into the night, for whoever might be listening.

Then resumed her descent.

DIAMOND DOGS

ONE

I MET CHILDE in the Monument to the Eighty.

It was one of those days when I had the place largely to myself, able to walk from aisle to aisle without seeing another visitor; only my footsteps disturbed the air of funereal silence and stillness.

I was visiting my parents' shrine. It was a modest affair: a smooth wedge of obsidian shaped like a metronome, undecorated save for two cameo portraits set in elliptical borders. The sole moving part was a black blade which was attached near the base of the shrine, ticking back and forth with magisterial slowness. Mechanisms buried inside the shrine ensured that it was winding down, destined to count out days and then years with each tick. Eventually it would require careful measurement to detect its movement.

I was watching the blade when a voice disturbed me.

"Visiting the dead again, Richard?"

"Who's there?" I said, looking around, faintly recognising the speaker but not immediately able to place him.

"Just another ghost."

Various possibilities flashed through my mind as I listened to the man's deep and taunting voice—a kidnapping, an assassination—before I stopped flattering myself that I was worthy of such attention.

Then the man emerged from between two shrines a little way down from the metronome.

"My God," I said.

"Now do you recognise me?"

He smiled and stepped closer: as tall and imposing as I remembered. He had lost the devil's horns since our last meeting—they had only ever been a bio-engineered affectation—but there was still something satanic about his appearance, an effect not lessened by the small and slightly pointed goatee he had cultivated in the meantime.

Dust swirled around him as he walked towards me, suggesting that he was not a projection.

"I thought you were dead, Roland."

"No, Richard," he said, stepping close enough to shake my hand. "But that was most certainly the effect I desired to achieve."

"Why?" I said.

"Long story."

"Start at the beginning, then."

Roland Childe placed a hand on the smooth side of my parents' shrine. "Not quite your style, I'd have thought?"

"It was all I could do to argue against something even more ostentatious and morbid. But don't change the subject. What happened to you?"

He removed his hand, leaving a faint damp imprint. "I faked my own death. The Eighty was the perfect cover. The fact that it all went so horrendously wrong was even better. I couldn't have planned it like that if I'd tried."

No arguing with that, I thought. It *had* gone horrendously wrong.

More than a century and a half ago, a clique of researchers led by Calvin Sylveste had resurrected the old idea of copying the essence of a living human being into a computer-generated simulation. The procedure—then in its infancy—had the slight drawback that it killed the subject. But there had still been volunteers, and my parents had been amongst the first to sign up and support Calvin's work. They had offered him political protection when the powerful Mixmaster lobby opposed the project, and they had been amongst the first to be scanned.

Less than fourteen months later, their simulations had also been amongst the first to crash.

None could ever be restarted. Most of the remaining Eighty had succumbed, and now only a handful remained unaffected.

"You must hate Calvin for what he did," Childe said, still with that taunting quality in his voice.

"Would it surprise you if I said I didn't?"

"Then why did you set yourself so vocally against his family after the tragedy?"

"Because I felt justice still needed to be served." I turned from the shrine and started walking away, curious as to whether Childe would follow me.

"Fair enough," he said. "But that opposition cost you dearly, didn't it?"

I bridled, halting next to what appeared a highly realistic sculpture but was almost certainly an embalmed corpse.

"Meaning what?"

"The Resurgam expedition, of course, which just happened to be bankrolled by House Sylveste. By rights, you should have been on it. You were Richard Swift, for heaven's sake. You'd spent the better part of your life thinking about possible modes of alien sentience. There should have been a place for you on that ship, and you damned well knew it."

"It wasn't that simple," I said, resuming my walk. "There were a limited number of slots available and they needed practical types first—biologists, geologists, that kind of thing. By the time they'd filled the most essential slots, there simply wasn't any room for abstract dreamers like myself."

"And the fact that you'd pissed off House Sylveste had nothing whatsoever to do with it? Come off it, Richard."

We descended a series of steps down into the lower level of the Monument. The atrium's ceiling was a cloudy mass of jagged sculptures: interlocked metal birds. A party of visitors was arriving, attended by servitors and a swarm of bright, marble-sized float-cams. Childe breezed through the group, drawing annoyed frowns but no actual recognition, although one or two of the people in the party were vague acquaintances of mine.

"What is this about?" I asked, once we were outside.

"Concern for an old friend. I've had my tabs on you, and it was pretty obvious that not being selected for that expedition was a crushing disappointment. You'd thrown your life into contemplation of the alien. One marriage down the drain because of your self-absorption. What was her name again?"

I'd had her memory buried so deeply that it took a real effort of will to recall any exact details about my marriage.

"Celestine. I think."

"Since then you've had a few relationships, but nothing lasting more than a decade. A decade's a mere fling in this town, Richard."

"My private life's my own business," I responded sullenly. "Hey. Where's my volantor? I parked it here."

"I sent it away. We'll take mine instead."

Where my volantor had been was a larger, blood-red model. It was as baroquely ornamented as a funeral barge. At a gesture from Childe it clammed open, revealing a plush gold interior with four seats, one of which was occupied by a dark, slouched figure.

"What's going on, Roland?"

"I've found something. Something astonishing that I want you to be a part of; a challenge that makes every game you and I ever played in our youth pale in comparison."

"A challenge?"

"The ultimate one, I think."

He had pricked my curiosity, but I hoped it was not too obvious. "The city's vigilant. It'll be a matter of public record that I came to the Monument, and we'll have been recorded together by those float-cams."

"Exactly," Childe said, nodding enthusiastically. "So you risk nothing by getting in the volantor."

"And should I at any point weary of your company?"

"You have my word that I'll let you leave."

I decided to play along with him for the time being. Childe and I took the volantor's front pair of seats. Once ensconced, I turned around to acquaint myself with the other passenger, and then flinched as I saw him properly.

He wore a high-necked leather coat which concealed much of the lower half of his face. The upper part was shadowed under the generous rim of a Homburg, tipped down to shade his brow. Yet what remained visible was sufficient to shock me. There was only a blandly handsome silver mask; sculpted into an expression of quiet serenity. The eyes were blank silver surfaces, what I could see of his mouth a thin, slightly smiling slot.

"Doctor Trintignant," I said.

He reached forward with a gloved hand, allowing me to shake it as one would the hand of a woman. Beneath the black velvet of the glove I felt armatures of hard metal. Metal that could crush diamond. "The pleasure is entirely mine," he said.

AIRBORNE. THE VOLANTOR'S baroque ornamentation melted away to mirror-smoothness. Childe pushed ivory-handled control sticks forward, gaining altitude and speed. We seemed to be moving faster than the city ordinances allowed, avoiding the usual traffic corridors. I thought of the way he had followed me, researched my past and had my own volantor desert me. It would also have taken considerable resourcefulness to locate the reclusive Trintignant and persuade him to emerge from hiding.

Clearly Childe's influence in the city exceeded my own, even though he had been absent for so long.

"The old place hasn't changed much," Childe said, swooping us through a dense conglomeration of golden buildings, as extravagantly tiered as the dream pagodas of a fever-racked Emperor.

"Then you've really been away? When you told me you'd faked your death, I wondered if you'd just gone into hiding."

He answered with a trace of hesitation, "I've been away, but not as far as you'd think. A family matter came up that was best dealt with confidentially, and I really couldn't be bothered explaining to everyone why I needed some peace and quiet on my own."

"And faking your death was the best way to go about it?"

"Like I said, I couldn't have planned the Eighty if I'd tried. I had to bribe a lot of minor players in the project, of course, and I'll spare you the details of how we provided a corpse…but it all worked swimmingly, didn't it?"

"I never had any doubts that you'd died along with the rest of them."

"I didn't like deceiving my friends. But I couldn't go to all that trouble and then ruin my plan with a few indiscretions."

"You were friends, then?" solicited Trintignant.

"Yes, Doctor," Childe said, glancing back at him. "Way back when. Richard and I were rich kids—relatively rich, anyway—with not enough to do. Neither of us were interested in the stock market or the social whirl. We were only interested in games."

"Oh. How charming. What kinds of games, might I ask?"

"We'd build simulations to test each other—extraordinarily elaborate worlds filled with subtle dangers and temptations. Mazes and labyrinths; secret passages; trapdoors; dungeons and dragons. We'd spend months inside them, driving each other crazy. Then we'd go away and make them even harder."

"But in due course you grew apart," the Doctor said. His synthesised voice had a curious piping quality.

"Yeah," Childe said. "But we never stopped being friends. It was just that Richard had spent so much time devising increasingly alien scenarios that he'd become more interested in the implied psychologies behind the tests. And I'd become interested only in the playing of the games; not their construction. Unfortunately Richard was no longer there to provide challenges for me."

"You were always much better than me at playing them," I said. "In the end it got too hard to come up with something you'd find difficult. You knew the way my mind worked too well."

"He's convinced that he's a failure," Childe said, turning round to smile at the Doctor.

"As are we all," Trintignant answered. "And with some justification, it must be said. I have never been allowed to pursue my admittedly controversial interests to their logical ends. You, Mister Swift, were shunned by those who you felt should have recognised your worth in the field of speculative alien psychology. And you, Mister Childe, have never discovered a challenge worthy of your undoubted talents."

"I didn't think you'd paid me any attention, Doctor."

"Nor had I. I have surmised this much since our meeting."

The volantor dropped below ground level, descending into a brightly lit commercial plaza lined with shops and boutiques. With insouciant ease, Childe skimmed us between aerial walkways and then nosed the car into a dark side-tunnel. He gunned the machine faster, our speed indicated only by the passing of red set into the tunnel sides. Now and then another vehicle passed us, but once the tunnel had branched and rebranched half a dozen times, no further traffic appeared. The tunnel lights were gone now and when the volantor's headlights grazed the walls they revealed ugly cracks and huge, scarred absences of cladding. These old sub-surface ducts dated back to the city's earliest days, before the domes were thrown across the crater.

Even if I had recognised the part of the city where we had entered the tunnel system, I would have been hopelessly lost by now.

"Do you think Childe has brought us together to taunt us about our lack of respective failures, Doctor?" I asked, beginning to feel uneasy again despite my earlier attempts at reassurance.

"I would consider that a distinct possibility, were Childe himself not conspicuously tainted by the same lack of success."

"Then there must be another reason."

"Which I'll reveal in due course," Childe said. "Just bear with me, will you? You two aren't the only ones I've gathered together."

PRESENTLY WE ARRIVED somewhere.

It was a cave in the form of a near-perfect hemisphere, the great domed roof arching a clear three hundred metres from the floor. We were obviously well below Yellowstone's surface now. It was even possible that we had passed beyond the city's crater wall, so that above us lay only poisonous skies.

But the domed chamber was inhabited.

The roof was studded with an enormous number of lamps, flooding the interior with synthetic daylight. An island stood in the middle of the chamber, moated by a ring of uninviting water. A single bone-white bridge connected the mainland to the island, shaped like a great curved femur. The island was dominated by a thicket of slender, dark poplars partly concealing a pale structure situated near its middle.

Childe brought the volantor to a rest near the edge of the water and invited us to disembark.

"Where are we?" I asked, once I had stepped down.

"Query the city and find out for yourself," Trintignant said.

The result was not what I was expecting. For a moment there was a shocking absence inside my head, the neural equivalent of a sudden, unexpected amputation.

The Doctor's chuckle was an arpeggio played on a pipe organ. "We have been out of range of city services from the moment we entered his conveyance."

"You needn't worry," Childe said. "You are beyond city services, but only because I value the secrecy of this place. If I imagined it'd have come as a shock to you, I'd have told you already."

"I'd have at least appreciated a warning, Roland," I said.

"Would it have changed your mind about coming here?"

"Conceivably."

The echo of his laughter betrayed the chamber's peculiar acoustics. "Then are you at all surprised that I didn't tell you?"

I turned to Trintignant. "What about you?"

"I confess my use of city services has been as limited as your own, but for rather different reasons."

"The good Doctor needed to lie low," Childe said. "That meant he couldn't participate very actively in city affairs. Not if he didn't want to be tracked down and assassinated."

I stamped my feet, beginning to feel cold. "Good. What now?"

"It's only a short ride to the house," Childe said, glancing towards the island.

NOW A NOISE came steadily nearer. It was an antiquated, rumbling sound, accompanied by a odd, rhythmic sort of drumming, quite unlike any machine I had experienced. I looked towards the femoral bridge, suspecting as I did that it was exactly what it looked like: a giant, bio-engineered bone, carved with a flat roadbed. And something was approaching us over the span: a dark, complicated and unfamiliar contraption, which at first glance resembled an iron tarantula.

I felt the back of my neck prickle.

The thing reached the end of the bridge and swerved towards us. Two mechanical black horses provided the motive power. They were emaciated black machines with sinewy, piston-driven limbs, venting steam and snorting from intakes. Malignant red laser-eyes swept over us. The horses were harnessed to a four-wheeled carriage slightly larger than the volantor, above which was perched a headless humanoid robot. Skeletal hands gripped iron control cables which plunged into the backs of the horses' steel necks.

"Meant to inspire confidence, is it?" I asked.

"It's an old family heirloom," Childe said, swinging open a black door in the side of the carriage. "My uncle Giles made automata. Unfortunately—for reasons we'll come to—he was a bit of a miserable bastard. But don't let it put you off."

He helped us aboard, then climbed inside himself, sealed the door and knocked on the roof. I heard the mechanical horses snort; alloy hooves hammered the ground impatiently. Then we were moving, curving around and ascending the gentle arc of the bridge of bone.

"Have you been here during the entire period of your absence, Mister Childe?" Trintignant asked.

He nodded. "Ever since that family business came up. I've allowed myself the occasional visit back to the city—just like I did today—but I've tried to keep such excursions to a minimum."

"Didn't you have horns the last time we met?" I said.

He rubbed the smooth skin of his scalp where the horns had been. "Had to have them removed. I couldn't very well disguise myself otherwise."

We crossed the bridge and navigated a path between the tall trees which sheltered the island's structure. Childe's carriage pulled up to a smart stop in front of the building and I was afforded my first unobstructed view of our destination. It was not one to induce great cheer. The house's architecture was haphazard: whatever basic symmetry it might once have had was lost under a profusion of additions and modifications. The roof was a jumbled collision of angles and spires, jutting turrets and sinister oubliettes. Not all of the embellishments had been arranged at strict right angles to their neighbours, and the style and apparent age of the house varied jarringly from place to place. Since our arrival in the cave the overhead lights had dimmed, simulating the onset of dusk, but only a few windows were illuminated, clustered together in the left-hand wing. The rest of the house had a forbidding aspect, the paleness of its stone, the irregularity of its construction and the darkness of its many windows suggesting a pile of skulls.

Almost before we had disembarked from the carriage, a reception party emerged from the house. It was a troupe of servitors—humanoid household robots, of the kind anyone would have felt comfortable with in the city proper—but they had been reworked to resemble skeletal ghouls or headless knights. Their mechanisms had been sabotaged so that they limped and creaked, and they had all had their voiceboxes disabled.

"Had a lot of time on his hands, your uncle," I said.

"You'd have loved Giles, Richard. He was a scream."

"I'll take your word for it, I think."

The servitors escorted us into the central part of house, then took us through a maze of chill, dark corridors.

Finally we reached a large room walled in plush red velvet. A holo-clavier sat in one corner, with a book of sheet music spread open above the projected keyboard. There was a malachite escritoire, a number of well-stocked bookcases, a single chandelier, three smaller candelabra and two fireplaces of distinctly gothic appearance, in one of which roared an actual fire. But the room's central feature was a mahogany table, around which three additional guests were gathered.

"Sorry to keep everyone waiting," Childe said, closing a pair of sturdy wooden doors behind us. "Now. Introductions."

The others looked at us with no more than mild interest.

The only man amongst them wore an elaborately ornamented exo-skeleton: a baroque support structure of struts, hinged plates, cables and servo-mechanisms. His face was a skull papered with deathly white skin, shading to black under his bladelike cheekbones. His eyes were concealed behind goggles, his hair a spray of stiff black dreadlocks.

Periodically he inhaled from a glass pipe, connected to a miniature refinery of bubbling apparatus placed before him on the table.

"Allow me to introduce Captain Forqueray," Childe said. "Captain—this is Richard Swift and...um, Doctor Trintignant."

"Pleased to meet you," I said, leaning across the table to shake Forqueray's hand. His grip felt like the cold clasp of a squid.

"The Captain is an Ultra; the master of the lighthugger *Apollyon*, currently in orbit around Yellowstone," Childe added.

Trintignant refrained from approaching him.

"Shy, Doctor?" Forqueray said, his voice simultaneously deep and flawed, like a cracked bell.

"No, merely cautious. It is a matter of common knowledge that I have enemies amongst the Ultras."

Trintignant removed his Homburg and patted his crown delicately, as if smoothing down errant hairs. Silver waves had been sculpted into his head-mask, so that he resembled a bewigged Regency fop dipped in mercury.

"You've enemies everywhere," said Forqueray between gurgling inhalations. "But I bear you no personal animosity for your atrocities, and I guarantee that my crew will extend you the same courtesy."

"Very gracious of you," Trintignant said, before shaking the Ultra's hand for the minimum time compatible with politeness. "But why should your crew concern me?"

"Never mind that." It was one of the two women speaking now. "Who is this guy, and why does everyone hate him?"

"Allow me to introduce Hirz," Childe said, indicating the woman who had spoken. She was small enough to have been a child, except that her face was clearly that of an adult woman. She was dressed in austere, tight-fitting black clothes which only emphasised her diminutive build. "Hirz is—for want of a better word—a mercenary."

"Except I prefer to think of myself as an information retrieval specialist. I specialise in clandestine infiltration for high-level corporate clients in the Glitter Band—physical espionage, some of the time. Mostly, though, I'm what used to be called a hacker. I'm also pretty damned good at my job." Hirz paused to swig down some wine. "But enough about me. Who's the silver dude, and what did Forqueray mean about atrocities?"

"You're seriously telling me you're unaware of Trintignant's reputation?" I said.

"Hey, listen. I get myself frozen between assignments. That means I miss a lot of shit that goes down in Chasm City. Get over it."

I shrugged and—with one eye on the Doctor himself—told Hirz what I knew about Trintignant. I sketched in his early career as an experimental cyberneticist, how his reputation for fearless innovation had eventually brought him to Calvin Sylveste's attention.

Calvin had recruited Trintignant to his own research team, but the collaboration had not been a happy one. Trintignant's desire to find the ultimate fusion of flesh and machine had become obsessive; even—some said—perverse. After a scandal involving experimentation on unconsenting subjects, Trintignant had been forced to pursue his work alone, his methods too extreme even for Calvin.

So Trintignant had gone to ground, and continued his gruesome experiments with his only remaining subject.

Himself.

"So let's see," said the final guest. "Who have we got? An obsessive and thwarted cyberneticist with a taste for extreme modification. An intrusion specialist with a talent for breaking into highly protected—and dangerous—environments. A man with a starship at his disposal and the crew to operate it."

Then she looked at Childe, and while her gaze was averted I admired the fine, faintly familiar profile of her face. Her long hair was the sheer black of interstellar space, pinned back from her face by a jewelled clasp which flickered with a constellation of embedded pastel lights. Who was she? I felt sure we had met once or maybe twice before. Perhaps we had passed each other amongst the shrines in the Monument to the Eighty, visiting the dead.

"And Childe," she continued. "A man once known for his love of intricate challenges, but long assumed dead." Then she turned her piercing eyes upon me. "And, finally, you."

"I know you, I think—" I said, her name on the tip of my tongue.

"Of course you do." Her look, suddenly, was contemptuous. "I'm Celestine. You used to be married to me."

ALL ALONG, CHILDE had known she was here.

"Do you mind if I ask what this is about?" I said, doing my best to sound as reasonable as possible, rather than someone on the verge of losing their temper in polite company.

Celestine withdrew her hand once I had shaken it. "Roland invited me here, Richard. Just the same way he did you, with the same veiled hints about having found something."

"But you're..."

"Your ex-wife?" She nodded. "Exactly how much do you remember, Richard? I heard the strangest rumours, you know. That you'd had me deleted from your long-term memory."

"I had you suppressed, not deleted. There's a subtle distinction."

She nodded knowingly. "So I gather."

I looked at the other guests, who were observing us. Even Forqueray was waiting, the pipe of his apparatus poised an inch from his mouth in expectation. They were waiting for me to say something; anything.

"Why exactly are you here, Celestine?"

"You don't remember, do you?"

"Remember what?"

"What it was I used to do, Richard, when we were married."

"I confess I don't, no."

Childe coughed. "Your wife, Richard, was as fascinated by the alien as you were. She was one of the city's foremost specialists on the Pattern Jugglers, although she'd be entirely too modest to admit it herself." He paused, apparently seeking Celestine's permission to continue. "She visited them, long before you met, spending several years of her life at the study station on Spindrift. You swam with the Jugglers, didn't you, Celestine?"

"Once or twice."

"And allowed them to reshape your mind, transforming its neural pathways into something deeply—albeit usually temporarily—alien."

"It wasn't that big a deal," Celestine said.

"Not if you'd been fortunate enough to have it happen to you, no. But for someone like Richard—who craved knowledge of the alien with every fibre of his existence—it would have been anything but mundane." He turned to me. "Isn't that true?"

"I admit I'd have done a great deal to experience communion with the Jugglers," I said, knowing that it was pointless to deny it. "But it just wasn't possible. My family lacked the resources to send me to one of the Juggler worlds, and the bodies that might ordinarily have funded that kind of trip—the Sylveste Institute, for instance—had turned their attentions elsewhere."

"In which case Celestine was deeply fortunate, wouldn't you say?"

"I don't think anyone would deny that," I said. "To speculate about the shape of alien consciousness is one thing; but to drink it; to bathe in the full flood of it—to know it intimately, like a lover..." I trailed off for a moment. "Wait a minute. Shouldn't you be on Resurgam, Celestine? There isn't time for the expedition to have gone there and come back."

She eyed me with raptorial intent before answering, "I never went."

Childe leant over and refreshed my glass. "She was turned down at the last minute, Richard. Sylveste had a grudge against anyone who'd visited the Jugglers; he suddenly decided they were all unstable and couldn't be trusted."

I looked at Celestine wonderingly. "Then all this time...?"

"I've been here, in Chasm City. Oh, don't look so crushed, Richard. By the time I learned I'd been turned down, you'd already decided to flush me out of your past. It was better for both of us this way."

"But the deception..."

Childe put one hand on my shoulder, calmingly. "There wasn't any. She just didn't make contact again. No lies; no deception; nothing to hold a grudge about."

I looked at him, angrily. "Then why the hell is she here?"

"Because I happen to have use for someone with the skills that the Jugglers gave to Celestine."

"Which included?" I said.

"Extreme mathematical prowess."

"And why would that have been useful?"

Childe turned to the Ultra, indicating that the man should remove his bubbling apparatus.

"I'm about to show you."

THE TABLE HOUSED an antique holo-projection system. Childe handed out viewers which resembled lorgnette binoculars, and, like so many myopic opera buffs, we studied the apparitions which floated into existence above the polished mahogany surface.

Stars: incalculable numbers of them—hard white and bloodred gems, strewn in lacy patterns against deep velvet blue.

Childe narrated:

"The better part of two and a half centuries ago, my uncle Giles—whose somewhat pessimistic handiwork you have already seen—made a momentous decision. He embarked on what we in the family referred to as the Program, and then only in terms of extreme secrecy."

Childe told us that the Program was an attempt at covert deep space exploration.

Giles had conceived the work, funding it directly from the family's finances. He had done this with such ingenuity that the apparent wealth of House Childe had never faltered, even as the Program entered its most expensive phase. Only a few select members of the Childe dynasty had even known of the Program's existence, and that number had dwindled as time passed.

The bulk of the money had been paid to the Ultras, who had already emerged as a powerful faction by that time.

They had built the autonomous robot space probes according to this uncle's desires, and then launched them towards a variety of target systems. The Ultras could have delivered his probes to any system within range of their lighthugger ships, but the whole point of the exercise was to restrict the knowledge of any possible discoveries to the family alone. So the envoys crossed space by themselves, at only a fraction of the speed of light, and the targets they were sent to were all poorly explored systems on the ragged edge of human space.

The probes decelerated by use of solar sails, picked the most interesting worlds to explore, and then fell into orbit around them.

Robots were sent down, equipped to survive on the surface for many decades.

Childe waved his hand across the table. Lines radiated out from one of the redder suns in the display, which I assumed was Yellowstone's star.

The lines reached out towards other stars, forming a three-dimensional scarlet dandelion several dozen light-years wide.

"These machines must have been reasonably intelligent," Celestine said. "Especially by the standards of the time."

Childe nodded keenly. "Oh, they were. Cunning little blighters. Subtle and stealthy and diligent. They had to be, to operate so far from human supervision."

"And I presume they found something?" I said.

"Yes," Childe said testily, like a conjurer whose carefully scripted patter was being ruined by a persistent heckler. "But not immediately. Giles didn't expect it to be immediate, of course—the envoys would take decades to reach the closest systems they'd been assigned to, and there'd still be the communicational timelag to take into consideration. So my uncle resigned himself to forty or fifty years of waiting, and that was erring on the optimistic side." He paused and sipped from his wine. "Too bloody optimistic, as it happened. Fifty years passed... then sixty...but nothing of any consequence was ever reported back to Yellowstone, at least not in his lifetime. The envoys did, on occasion, find something interesting—but by then other human explorers had usually stumbled on the same find. And as the decades wore on, and the envoys failed to justify their invention, my uncle grew steadily more maudlin and bitter."

"I'd never have guessed," Celestine said.

"He died, eventually—bitter and resentful; feeling that the universe had played some sick cosmic trick on him. He could have lived for another fifty or sixty years with the right treatments, but I think by then he knew it would be a waste of time."

"You faked your death a century and a half ago," I said. "Didn't you tell me it had something to do with the family business?"

He nodded in my direction. "That was when my uncle told me about the Program. I didn't know anything about it until then—hadn't heard even the tiniest hint of a rumour. No one in the family had. By then, of course, the project was costing us almost nothing, so there wasn't even a financial drain to be concealed."

"And since then?"

"I vowed not to make my uncle's mistake. I resolved to sleep until the machines sent back a report, and then sleep again if the report turned out to be a false alarm."

"Sleep?" I said.

He clicked his fingers and one entire wall of the room whisked back to reveal a sterile, machine-filled chamber.

I studied its contents.

There was a reefersleep casket of the kind Forqueray and his ilk used aboard their ships, attended by numerous complicated hunks of gleaming green support machinery. By use of such a casket, one might prolong the four hundred-odd years of a normal human lifespan by many centuries, though reefersleep was not without its risks.

"I spent a century and a half in that contraption," he said, "waking every fifteen or twenty years whenever a report trickled in from one of the envoys. Waking is the worst part. It feels like you're made of glass; as if the next movement you make—the next breath you take—will cause you to shatter into a billion pieces. It always passes, and you always forget it an hour later, but it's never easier the next time." He shuddered visibly. "In fact, sometimes I think it gets harder each time."

"Then your equipment needs servicing," Forqueray said dismissively. I suspected it was bluff. Ultras often wore a lock of braided hair for every crossing they had made across interstellar space and survived all the myriad misfortunes which might befall a ship. But that braid also symbolised every occasion on which they had been woken from the dead, at the end of the journey.

They felt the pain as fully as Childe did, even if they were not willing to admit it.

"How long did you spend awake each time?" I asked.

"No more than thirteen hours. That was usually sufficient to tell if the message was interesting or not. I'd allow myself one or two hours to catch up on the news; what was going on in the wider universe. But I had to be disciplined. If I'd stayed awake longer, the attraction of returning to city life would have become overwhelming. That room began to feel like a prison."

"Why?" I asked. "Surely the subjective time must have passed very quickly?"

"You've obviously never spent any time in reefersleep, Richard. There's no consciousness when you're frozen, granted—but the transitions to and from the cold state are like an eternity, crammed with strange dreams."

"But you hoped the rewards would be worth it?"

Childe nodded. "And, indeed, they may well have been. I was last woken six months ago, and I've not returned to the chamber since. Instead, I've spent time gathering together the resources and the people for a highly unusual expedition."

Now he made the table change its projection, zooming in on one particular star.

"I won't bore you with catalogue numbers, suffice to say that this is a system which no one around this table—with the possible exception of Forqueray—is likely to have heard of. There've never been any human colonies there, and no crewed vessel has ever passed within three light-years of it. At least, not until recently."

The view zoomed in again, enlarging with dizzying speed.

A planet swelled up to the size of a skull, suspended above the table.

It was hued entirely in shades of grey and pale rust, cratered and gouged here and there by impacts and what must have been very ancient weathering processes. Though there was a suggestion of a wisp of atmosphere—a smoky blue halo encircling the planet—and though there were icecaps at either pole, the world looked neither habitable nor inviting.

"Cheerful-looking place, isn't it?" Childe said. "I call it Golgotha."

"Nice name," Celestine said.

"But not, unfortunately, a very nice planet." Childe made the view enlarge again, so that we were skimming the world's bleak, apparently lifeless surface. "Pretty dismal, to be honest. It's about the same size as Yellowstone, receiving about the same amount of sunlight from its star. Doesn't have a moon. Surface gravity's close enough to one gee that you won't know the difference once you're suited up. A thin carbon dioxide atmosphere, and no sign that anything's ever evolved there. Plenty of radiation hitting the surface, but that's about your only hazard, and one we can easily deal with. Golgotha's tectonically dead, and there haven't been any large impacts on her surface for a few million years."

"Sounds boring," Hirz said.

"And it very probably is, but that isn't the point. You see, there's something on Golgotha."

"What kind of something?" Celestine asked.

"That kind," Childe said.

It came over the horizon.

It was tall and dark, its details indistinct. That first view of it was like the first glimpse of a cathedral's spire through morning fog. It tapered as it rose, constricting to a thin neck before flaring out again into a bulb-shaped finial, which in turn tapered to a needle-sharp point.

Though it was impossible to say how large the thing was, or what it was made of, it was very obviously a structure, as opposed to a peculiar biological or mineral formation. On Grand Teton, vast numbers of tiny single-celled organisms conspired to produce the slime towers which were that world's most famous natural feature, and while those towers reached impressive heights and were often strangely shaped, they were unmistakably the products of unthinking biological processes rather than conscious design. The structure on Golgotha was too symmetric for that, and entirely too solitary. If it had been a living thing, I would have expected to see others like it, with evidence of a supporting ecology of different organisms.

Even if it were a fossil, millions of years dead, I could not believe that there would be just one on the whole planet.

No. The thing had most definitely been put there.

"A structure?" I asked Childe.

"Yes. Or a machine. It isn't easy to decide." He smiled. "I call it Blood Spire. Almost looks innocent, doesn't it? Until you look closer."

We spun round the Spire, or whatever it was, viewing it from all directions. Now that we were closer, it was clear that the thing's surface was densely detailed; patterned and textured with geometrically complex forms, around which snaked intestinal tubes and branching, veinlike bulges. The effect was to undermine my earlier certainty that the thing was non-biological.

Now it looked like some sinewy fusion of animal and machine: something that might have appealed in its grotesquerie to Childe's demented uncle.

"How tall is it?" I asked.

"Two hundred and fifty metres," Childe said.

I saw that now there were tiny glints on Golgotha's surface, almost like metallic flakes which had fallen from the side of the structure.

"What are those?" I asked.

"Why don't I show you?" Childe said.

He enlarged the view still further, until the glints resolved into distinct shapes.

They were people.

Or—more accurately—the remains of what had once been people. It was impossible to say how many there had been. All had been mutilated in some fashion: crushed or pruned or bisected; the tattered ruins of their spacesuits were still visible in one or two places. Severed parts accompanied the bodies, often several tens of metres from the rightful owner.

It was as if they had been flung away in a fit a temper.

"Who were they?" Forqueray asked.

"A crew who happened to slow down in this system to make shield repairs," Childe said. "Their captain was called Argyle. They chanced upon the Spire and started exploring it, believing it to contain something of immense technological value."

"And what happened to them?"

"They went inside in small teams, sometimes alone. Inside the Spire they passed through a series of challenges, each of which was harder than the last. If they made a mistake, the Spire punished them. The punishments were initially mild, but they became steadily more brutal. The trick was to know when to admit defeat."

I leaned forward. "How do you know all this?'

"Because Argyle survived. Not long, admittedly, but long enough for my machine to get some sense out of him. It had been on Golgotha the whole time, you see—watching Argyle's arrival, hiding and recording them as they confronted the Spire. And it watched him crawl out of the Spire, shortly before the last of his colleagues was ejected."

"I'm not sure I'm prepared to trust either the testimony of a machine or a dying man," I said.

"You don't have to," Childe answered. "You need only consider the evidence of your eyes. Do you see those tracks in the dust? They all lead into the Spire, and there are almost none leading to the bodies."

"Meaning what?" I said.

"Meaning that they got inside, the way Argyle claimed. Observe also the way the remains are distributed. They're not all at the same distance from the Spire. They must have been ejected from different heights, suggesting that some got closer to the summit than others. Again, it accords with Argyle's story."

With a sinking feeling of inevitability I saw where this was heading. "And you want us to go there and find out what it was they were so interested in. Is that it?"

He smiled. "You know me entirely too well, Richard."

"I thought I did. But you'd have to be quite mad to go anywhere near that thing."

"Mad? Possibly. Or simply very, very curious. The question is—" He paused and leaned across the table to refill my glass, all the while maintaining eye contact. "Which are you?"

"Neither," I said.

BUT CHILDE COULD be persuasive. A month later I was frozen aboard Forqueray's ship.

TWO

WE REACHED ORBIT around Golgotha.

Thawed from reefersleep we convened for breakfast, riding a travel pod upship to the lighthugger's meeting room.

Everyone was there, including Trintignant and Forqueray, the latter inhaling from the same impressive array of flasks, retorts and spiralling tubes he had brought with him to Yellowstone. Trintignant had not slept with the rest of us, but looked none the worse for wear. He had, Childe said, his own rather specialized plumbing requirements, incompatible with standard reefersleep systems.

"Well, how was it?" Childe asked, throwing a comradely arm around my shoulders.

"Every bit as...dreadful as I'd been led to expect." My voice was slurred, sentences taking an age to form in whatever part of my brain it was that handled language. "Still a bit fuzzy."

"Well, we'll soon fix that. Trintignant can synthesise a medichine infusion to pep up those neural functions, can't you, Doctor?"

Trintignant looked at me with his handsome, immobile mask of a face. "It would be no trouble at all, my dear fellow..."

"Thanks." I steadied myself; my mind crawled with half-remembered images of the botched cybernetic experiments which had earned Trintignant his notoriety. The thought of him pumping tiny machines into my skull made my skin crawl. "But I'll pass on that for now. No offence intended."

"And absolutely none taken." Trintignant gestured towards a vacant chair. "Come. Sit with us and join in the discussion. The topic, rather interestingly, is the dreams some of us experienced on the way here."

"Dreams...?" I said. "I thought it was just me. I wasn't the only one?"

"No," Hirz said, "you weren't the only one. I was on a moon in one of them. Earth's, I think. And I kept on trying to get inside this alien structure. Fucking thing kept killing me, but I'd always keep going back inside, like I was being brought back to life each time just for that."

"I had the same dream," I said, wonderingly. And there was another dream in which I was inside some kind of—" I halted, waiting for the words to assemble in my head. "Some kind of underground tomb. I remember being chased down a corridor by an enormous stone ball which was going to roll over me."

Hirz nodded. "The dream with the hat, right?"

"My God, yes." I grinned like a madman. "I lost my hat, and I felt this ridiculous urge to rescue it!"

Celestine looked at me with something between icy detachment and outright hostility. "I had that one too."

"Me too," Hirz said, chuckling. "But I said fuck the hat. Sorry, but with the kind of money Childe's paying us, buying a new one ain't gonna be my biggest problem."

An awkward moment followed, for only Hirz seemed at all comfortable about discussing the generous fees Childe had arranged as payment for the expedition. The initial sums had been large enough, but upon our return to Yellowstone we would all receive nine times as much; adjusted to match any inflation which might occur during the time—between sixty and eighty years—which Childe said the journey would span.

Generous, yes.

But I think Childe knew that some of us would have joined him even without that admittedly sweet bonus.

Celestine broke the silence, turning to Hirz. "Did you have the one about the cubes, too?"

"Christ, yes," the infiltration specialist said, as if suddenly remembering. "The cubes. What about you, Richard?"

"Indeed," I answered, flinching at the memory of that one. I had been one of a party of people trapped inside an endless series of cubic rooms, many of which contained lethal surprises. "I was cut into pieces by a trap, actually. Diced, if I remember accurately."

"Yeah. Not exactly on my top ten list of ways to die, either."

Childe coughed. "I feel I should apologise for the dreams. They were narratives I fed into your minds—Doctor Trintignant excepted—during the transition to and from reefersleep."

"Narratives?" I said.

"I adapted them from a variety of sources, thinking they'd put us all in the right frame of mind for what lies ahead."

"Dying nastily, you mean?" Hirz asked.

"Problem-solving, actually." Childe served pitch-black coffee as he spoke, as if all that was ahead of us was a moderately bracing stroll. "Of course, nothing that the dreams contained is likely to reflect anything that we'll find inside the Spire...but don't you feel better for having had them?"

I gave the matter some thought before responding.

"Not exactly, no," I said.

THIRTEEN HOURS LATER we were on the surface, inspecting the suits Forqueray had provided for the expedition.

They were sleek white contraptions, armoured, powered and equipped with enough intelligence to fool a roomful of cyberneticians. They enveloped themselves around you, forming a seamless white surface which lent the wearer the appearance of a figurine moulded from soap. The suits quickly learned how you moved, adjusting and anticipating all the time like perfect dance partners.

Forqueray told us that each suit was capable of keeping its occupant alive almost indefinitely; that the suit would recycle bodily wastes in a near-perfect closed cycle, and could even freeze its occupant if circumstances merited such action. They could fly and would protect their user against just about any external environment, ranging from a vacuum to the crush of the deepest ocean.

"What about weapons?" Celestine asked, once we had been shown how to command the suits to do our bidding.

"Weapons?" Forqueray asked blankly.

"I've heard about these suits, Captain. They're supposed to contain enough firepower to take apart a small mountain."

Childe coughed. "There won't be any weapons, I'm afraid. I asked Forqueray to have them removed from the suits. No cutting tools, either. And you won't be able to achieve as much with brute force as you would with an unmodified suit. The servos won't allow it."

"I'm not sure I understand. You're handicapping us before we go in?"

"No—far from it. I'm just abiding by the rules that the Spire sets. It doesn't allow weapons inside itself, you see—or anything else that might be used against it, like fusion torches. It senses such things and acts accordingly. It's very clever."

I looked at him. "Is this guesswork?"

"Of course not. Argyle already learned this much. No point making exactly the same mistakes again, is there?"

"I still don't get it," Celestine said when we had assembled outside the shuttle, standing like so many white soap statuettes. "Why fight the thing on its own terms at all? There are bound to be weapons on Forqueray's ship we could use from orbit; we could open it like a carcass."

"Yes," Childe said, "and in the process destroy everything we came this far to learn?"

"I'm not talking about blowing it off the face of Golgotha. I'm just talking about clean, surgical dissection."

"It won't work. The Spire is a living thing, Celestine. Or at least a machine intelligence many orders of magnitude cleverer than anything we've encountered to date. It won't tolerate violence being used against it. Argyle learned that much."

"Even if it can't defend itself against such attacks—and we don't know that—it will certainly destroy what it contains. We'll still have lost everything."

"But still...no weapons?"

"Not quite," Childe said, tapping the forehead region of his suit. "We still have our minds, after all. That's why I assembled this team. If brute force would have been sufficient, I'd have had no need to scour Yellowstone for such fierce intellects."

Hirz spoke from inside her own, smaller version of the armoured suit. "You'd better not be taking the piss."

"FORQUERAY?" CHILDE SAID. "We're nearly there now. Put us down on the surface two klicks from the base of the Spire. We'll cross the remaining distance on foot."

Forqueray obliged, bringing the triangular formation down. Our suits had been slaved to his, but now we regained independent control.

Through the suit's numerous layers of armour and padding I felt the rough texture of the ground beneath my feet. I held up a thickly gauntleted hand and felt the breeze of Golgotha's thin atmosphere caress my palm. The tactile transmission was flawless, and when I moved, the suit flowed with me so effortlessly that I had no sense of being encumbered by it. The view was equally impressive, with the suit projecting an image directly into my visual field rather than forcing me to peer through a visor.

A strip along the top of my visual field showed a three-hundred-and-sixty-degree view all around me, and I could zoom in on any part of it almost without thinking. Various overlays—sonar, radar, thermal, gravimetric—could be dropped over the existing visual field with the same ease. If I looked down I could even ask the suit to edit me out of the image, so that I could view the scene from a disembodied perspective. As we walked along the suit threw traceries of light across the scenery: an etchwork of neon which would now and then coalesce around an odd-shaped rock or peculiar pattern of ground markings. After several minutes of this I had adjusted the suit's alertness threshold to what I felt was a useful level of protectivity, neither too watchful nor too complacent.

Childe and Forqueray had taken the lead on the ground. They would have been difficult to distinguish, but my suit had partially erased their suits, so that they seemed to walk unprotected save for a ghostly second skin. When they looked at me they would perceive the same consensual illusion.

Trintignant followed a little way behind, moving with the automaton-like stiffness I had now grown almost accustomed to.

Celestine followed, with me a little to her stern.

Hirz brought up the rear, small and lethal and—now that I knew her a little better—quite unlike any of the few children I had ever met.

And ahead—rising, ever rising—was the thing we had come all this way to best.

It had been visible, of course, long before we set down. The Spire was a quarter of a kilometre high, after all. But I think we had all chosen to ignore it; to map it out of our perceptions, until we were much closer. It was only now that we were allowing those mental shields to collapse; forcing our imaginations to confront the fact of the tower's existence.

Huge and silent, it daggered into the sky.

It was much as Childe had shown us, except that it seemed infinitely more massive; infinitely more present. We were still a quarter of a kilometre from the thing's base, and yet the flared top—the bulb-shaped finial—seemed to be leaning back over us, constantly on the point of falling and crushing us. The effect was exacerbated by the occasional high-altitude cloud that passed overhead, writhing in Golgotha's fast, thin jet-streams. The whole tower looked as if it were toppling. For a long moment, taking in the immensity of what stood before us—its vast age; its vast, brooding capacity for harm—the idea of trying to reach the summit felt uncomfortably close to insanity.

Then a small, rational voice reminded me that this was exactly the effect the Spire's builders would have sought.

Knowing that, it was fractionally easier to take the next step closer to the base.

"WELL," CELESTINE SAID. "It looks like we've found Argyle."

Childe nodded. "Yes. Or what's left of the poor bastard."

We had found several body parts by then, but his was the only one that was anywhere near being complete. He had lost a leg inside the Spire, but had been able to crawl to the exit before the combination of bleeding and asphyxiation killed him. It was here—dying—that he had been interviewed by Childe's envoy, which had only then emerged from its hiding place.

Perhaps he had imagined himself in the presence of a benevolent steel angel.

He was not well-preserved. There was no bacterial life on Golgotha, and nothing that could be charitably termed weather, but there were savage dust-storms, and these must have intermittently covered and revealed the body, scouring it in the process. Parts of his suit were missing, and his helmet had cracked open, exposing his skull. Papery sheets of skin adhered to the bone here and there, but not enough to suggest a face.

Childe and Forqueray regarded the corpse uneasily, while Trintignant knelt down and examined it in more detail. A float-cam belonging to the Ultra floated around, observing the scene with goggling arrays of tightly packed lenses.

"Whatever took his leg off did it cleanly," the doctor reported, pulling back the tattered layers of the man's suit fabric to expose the stump. "Witness how the bone and muscle have been neatly severed along the same plane, like a geometric slice through a platonic solid? I would speculate that a laser was responsible for this, except that I see no sign of cauterisation. A high-pressure water-jet might have achieved the same precision of cut, or even an extremely sharp blade."

"Fascinating, Doc," Hirz said, kneeling down next to him. "I'll bet it hurt like fuck, too, wouldn't you?"

"Not necessarily. The degree of pain would depend acutely on the manner in which the nerve ends were truncated. Shock does not appear to have been the primary agent in this man's demise." Doctor Trintignant fingered the remains of a red fabric band a little distance above the end of the leg. "Nor was the blood loss as rapid as might have been expected given the absence of cauterisation. This band was most likely a tourniquet, probably applied from his suit's medical kit. The same kit almost certainly included analgesics."

"It wasn't enough to save him, though," Childe said.

"No." Trintignant stood up, the movement reminding me of an escalator. "But you must concede that he did rather well, considering the impediments."

FOR MOST OF its height Blood Spire was no thicker than a few dozen metres, and considerably narrower just below the bulb-like upper part. But, like a slender chess piece, its lower parts swelled out considerably to form a wide base. That podium-like mass was perhaps fifty metres in diameter: a fifth of the structure's height. From a distance it appeared to rest solidly on the base: a mighty obelisk requiring the deepest of foundations to anchor it to the ground.

But it didn't.

The Spire's base failed to touch the surface of Golgotha at all, but floated above it, spaced by five or six clear metres of air. It was as if someone had constructed a building slightly above the ground, kicked away the stilts, and it had simply stayed there.

We all walked confidently towards the rim and then stopped; none of us were immediately willing to step under that overhang.

"Forqueray?" Childe said.

"Yes?"

"Let's see what that drone of yours has to say."

Forqueray had his float-cam fly under the rim, orbiting the underside of the Spire in a lazily widening spiral. Now and then it fingered the base with a spray of laser-light, and once or twice even made contact, skittering against the flat surface. Forqueray remained impassive, glancing slightly down as he absorbed the data being sent back to his suit.

"Well?" Celestine said. "What the hell's keeping it up?"

Forqueray took a step under the rim. "No fields; not even a minor perturbation of Golgotha's own magnetosphere. No significant alteration in the local gravitational vector, either. And—before we assume more sophistication than is strictly necessary—there are no concealed supports."

Celestine was silent for a few moments before answering, "All right. What if the Spire doesn't weigh anything? There's air here; not much of it I'll grant you—but what if the Spire's mostly hollow? There might be enough buoyancy to make the thing float, like a balloon."

"There isn't," Forqueray said, opening a fist to catch the cam, which flew into his grasp like a trained kestrel. "Whatever's above us is solid matter. I can't read its mass, but it's blocking an appreciable cosmic-ray flux, and none of our scanning methods can see through it."

"Forqueray's right," Childe said. "But I understand your reluctance to accept this, Celestine. It's perfectly normal to feel a sense of denial."

"Denial?'

"That what we are confronting is truly alien. But I'm afraid you'll get over it, just the way I did."

"I'll get over it when I feel like getting over it," Celestine said, joining Forqueray under the dark ceiling.

She looked up and around, less in the manner of someone admiring a fresco than in the manner of a mouse cowering beneath a boot.

But I knew exactly what she was thinking.

In four centuries of deep space travel there had been no more than glimpses of alien sentience. We had long expected they were out there somewhere. But that suspicion had grown less fervent as the years passed; world after world had revealed only faint, time-eroded traces of cultures that might once have been glorious but which were now utterly destroyed. The Pattern Jugglers were clearly the products of intelligence, but not necessarily intelligent themselves. And—though they had been spread from star to star in the distant past—they did not now depend on any form of technology that we recognised. The Shrouders were little better: secretive minds cocooned inside shells of restructured spacetime.

They had never been glimpsed, and their nature and intentions remained worryingly unclear.

Yet Blood Spire was different.

For all its strangeness; for all that it mocked our petty assumptions about the way matter and gravity should conduct themselves, it was recognisably a manufactured thing. And, I told myself, if it had managed to hang above Golgotha's surface until now, it was extremely unlikely to choose this moment to come crashing down.

I stepped across the threshold, followed by the others.

"Makes you wonder what kind of beings built it," I said. "Whether they had the same hopes and fears as us, or whether they were so far beyond us as to seem like gods."

"I don't give a shit who built it," Hirz said. "I just want to know how to get into the fucking thing. Any bright ideas, Childe?"

"There's a way," he said.

We followed him until we stood in a small, nervous huddle under the centre of the ceiling. It had not been visible before, but directly above us was a circle of utter blackness against the mere gloom of the Spire's underside.

"That?" Hirz said.

"That's the only way in," Childe said. "And the only way you get out alive."

I said, "Roland—how exactly did Argyle and his team get inside?"

"They must have brought something to stand on. A ladder or something."

I looked around. "There's no sign of it now, is there?"

"No, and it doesn't matter. We don't need anything like that—not with these suits. Forqueray?"

The Ultra nodded and tossed the float-cam upwards.

It caught flight and vanished into the aperture. Nothing happened for several seconds, other than the occasional stutter of red light from the hole. Then the cam emerged, descending again into Forqueray's hand.

"There's a chamber up there," Forqueray said. "Flat-floored, surrounding the hole. It's twenty metres across, with a ceiling just high enough to let us stand upright. It's empty. There's what looks like a sealed door leading out of the chamber into the rest of the Spire."

"Can we be sure there's nothing harmful in it?" I asked.

"No," Childe said. "But Argyle said the first room was safe. We'll just have to take his word on that one."

"And there's room for all of us up there?"

Forqueray nodded. "Easily."

I suppose there should have been more ceremony to the act, but there was no sense of significance, or even foreboding, as we rose into the ceiling. It was like the first casual step onto the tame footslopes of a mountain, unweighted by any sense of the dangers that undoubtedly lay ahead.

Inside it was exactly as Forqueray had described.

The chamber was dark, but the float-cam provided some illumination and our suits' sensors were able to map out the chamber's shape and overlay this information on our visual fields.

The floor had a metalled quality to it, dented here and there, and the edge where it met the hole was rounded and worn.

I reached down to touch it, feeling a hard, dull alloy which nonetheless seemed as if it would yield given sufficient pressure. Data scrolled onto my visual readout, informing me that the floor had a temperature only one hundred and fifteen degrees above absolute zero. My palm chemosensor reported that the floor was mainly iron, laced with carbon woven into allotropic forms it could not match against any in its experience. There were microscopic traces of almost every other stable isotope in the periodic table, with the odd exception of silver. All of this was inferred, for when the chemosensor attempted to shave off a microscopic layer of the flooring for more detailed analysis, it gave a series of increasingly heated error messages before falling silent.

I tried the chemosensor against part of my own suit.

It had stopped working.

"Fix that," I instructed my suit, authorising it to divert whatever resources it required to the task.

"Problem, Richard?" asked Childe.

"My suit's damaged. Minor, but annoying. I don't think the Spire was too thrilled about my taking a sample of it."

"Shit. I probably should have warned you of that. Argyle's lot had the same problem. It doesn't like being cut into, either. I suspect you got off with a polite warning."

"Generous of it," I said.

"Be careful, all right?" Childe then told everyone else to disable their chemosensors until told otherwise. Hirz grumbled, but everyone else quietly accepted what had to be done.

In the meantime I continued my own survey of the room, counting myself lucky that my suit had not provoked a stronger reaction. The chamber's circular wall was fashioned from what looked like the same hard, dull alloy, devoid of detail except for the point where it framed what was obviously a door, raised a metre above the floor. Three blocky steps led up to it.

The door itself was one metre wide and perhaps twice that in height.

"Hey," Hirz said. "Feel this."

She was kneeling down, pressing a palm against the floor.

"Careful," I said. "I just did that and—"

"I've turned off my chemo-whatsit, don't worry."

"Then what are you—"

"Why don't you reach down and see for yourself?"

Slowly, we all knelt down and touched the floor. When I had felt it before it had been as cold and dead as the floor of a crypt, yet that was no longer the case. Now it was vibrating; as if somewhere not too far from here a mighty engine was shaking itself to pieces: a turbine on the point of breaking loose from its shackles. The vibration rose and fell in throbbing waves. Once every thirty seconds or so it reached a kind of crescendo, like a great slow inhalation.

"It's alive," Hirz said.

"It wasn't like that just now."

"I know." Hirz turned and looked at me. "The fucking thing just woke up, that's why. It knows we're here."

THREE

I MOVED TO the door and studied it properly for the first time.

Its proportions were reassuringly normal, requiring only that we stoop down slightly to step through. But for now the door was sealed by a smooth sheet of metal, which would presumably slide across once we had determined how to open it. The only guidance came from the door's thick metal frame, which was inscribed with faint geometric markings.

I had not noticed them before.

The markings were on either side of the door, on the uprights of the frame. Beginning from the bottom on the left-hand side, there was a dot—it was too neatly circular to be accidental—a flat-topped equilateral triangle, a pentagon and then a heptagonal figure. On the right-hand side there were three more figures with eleven, thirteen and twenty sides respectively.

"Well?" Hirz was looking over my shoulder. "Any bright ideas?"

"Prime numbers," I said. "At least, that's the simplest explanation I can think of. The number of vertices of the shapes on the left-hand frame are the first four primes: one, three, five and seven."

"And on the other frame?"

Childe answered for me. "The eleven-sided figure is the next one in the sequence. Thirteen's one prime too high, and twenty isn't a prime at all."

"So you're saying if we choose eleven, we win?" Hirz reached out her hand, ready to push her hand against the lowest figure on the right, which she could reach without ascending the three steps. "I hope the rest of the tests are this simp—"

"Steady, old girl." Childe had caught her wrist. "Mustn't be too hasty. We shouldn't do anything until we've arrived at a consensus. Agreed?"

Hirz pulled back her hand. "Agreed..."

It took only a few minutes for everyone to agree that the eleven-sided figure was the obvious choice. Celestine did not immediately accede; she looked long and hard at the right-hand frame before concurring with the original choice.

"I just want to be careful, that's all," she said. "We can't assume any-thing. They might think from right to left, so that the figures on the right form the sequence which those on the left are supposed to complete. Or they might think diagonally, or something even less obvious."

Childe nodded. "And the obvious choice might not always be the right one. There might be a deeper sequence—something more elegant—which we're just not seeing. That's why I wanted Celestine along. If anyone'll pick out those subtleties, it's her."

She turned to him. "Just don't put too much faith in whatever gifts the Jugglers might have given me, Childe."

"I won't. Unless I have to." Then he turned to the infiltration specialist, still standing by the frame. "Hirz—you may go ahead."

She reached out and touched the frame, covering the eleven-sided figure with her palm.

After a heart-stopping pause there was a clunk, and I felt the floor vibrate even more strongly than it had before. Ponderously, the door slid aside, revealing another dark chamber.

We all looked around, assessing each other.

Nothing had changed; none of us had suffered any sudden, violent injuries.

"Forqueray?" Childe said.

The Ultra knew what he meant. He tossed the float-cam through the open doorway and waited several seconds until it flew back into his grasp.

"Another metallic chamber, considerably smaller than this one. The floor is level with the door, so we'll have gained a metre or so in height. There's another door on the opposite side, again with markings. Other than that, I don't see anything except bare metal."

"What about the other side of *this* door?" Childe said. "Are there markings on it as well?"

"Nothing that the drone could make out."

"Then let me be the guinea pig. I'll step through and we'll see what happens. I'm assuming that even if the door seals behind me, I'll still be able to open it. Argyle said the Spire didn't prevent anyone from leaving provided they hadn't attempted to access a new room."

'Try it and see," Hirz said. "We'll wait on this side. If the door shuts on you, we'll give you a minute and then we'll open it ourselves."

Childe walked up the three steps and across the threshold. He paused, looked around and then turned back to face us, looking down on us now.

Nothing had happened.

"Looks like the door stays open for now. Who wants to join me?"

"Wait," I said. "Before we all cross over, shouldn't we take a look at the problem? We don't want to be trapped in there if it's something we can't solve."

Childe walked over to the far door. "Good thinking. Forqueray, pipe my visual field through to the rest of the team, will you?"

"Done."

We saw what Childe was seeing, his gaze tracking along the door-frame. The markings looked much like those we had just solved, except that the symbols were different. Four unfamiliar shapes were inscribed on the left side of the door, spaced vertically. Each of the shapes was composed of four rectangular elements of differing sizes, butted together in varying configurations. Childe then looked at the other side of the door. There were four more shapes on the right, superficially similar to those we had already seen.

"Definitely not a geometric progression," Childe said.

"No. Looks more like a test of conservation of symmetry through different translations," Celestine said, her voice barely a murmur. "The lowest three shapes on the left have just been rotated through an integer number of right angles, giving their corresponding forms on the right. But the top two shapes aren't rotationally symmetric. They're mirror images, plus a rotation."

"So we press the top right shape, right?"

"Could be. But the left one's just as valid."

Hirz said, "Yeah. But only if we ignore what the last test taught us. Whoever the suckers were that made thing, they think from left to right."

Childe raised his hand above the right-side shape. "I'm prepared to press it."

"Wait." I climbed the steps and walked over the threshold, joining Childe. "I don't think you should be in here alone."

He looked at me with something resembling gratitude. None of the others had stepped over yet, and I wondered if I would have done so had Childe and I not been friends.

"Go ahead and press it," I said. "Even if we get it wrong, the punishment's not likely to be too severe at this stage."

He nodded and palmed the right-side symbol.

Nothing happened.

"Maybe the left side…?"

"Try it. It can't hurt. We've obviously done *something* wrong already."

Childe moved over and palmed the other symbol on the top row.

Nothing.

I gritted my teeth. "All right. Might as well try one of the ones we definitely know is wrong. Are you ready for that?"

He glanced at me and nodded. "I didn't go to the hassle of bringing in Forqueray just for the free ride, you know. These suits are built to take a lot of crap."

"Even alien crap?"

"About to find out, aren't we?"

He moved to palm one of the lower symmetry pairs.

I braced myself, unsure what to expect when we made a deliberate error, wondering if the Spire's punishment code would even apply in such a case. After all, what was clearly the correct choice had elicited no response, so what was the sense in being penalised for making the wrong one?

He palmed the shape; still nothing happened.

"Wait," Celestine said, joining us. "I've had an idea. Maybe it won't respond—positively or negatively—until we're all in the same room."

"Only one way to find out," Hirz said, joining her.

Forqueray and Trintignant followed.

When the last of them had crossed the threshold, the rear door—the one we had all come through—slid shut. There were no markings on it, but nothing that Forqueray did made it open again.

Which, I supposed, made a kind of sense. We had committed to accepting the next challenge now; the time for dignified retreats had passed. The thought was not a pleasant one. This room was smaller than the last one, and the environment was suddenly a lot more claustrophobic.

We were standing almost shoulder to shoulder.

"You know, I think the first chamber was just a warm-up," Celestine said. "This is where it starts getting more serious."

"Just press the fucking thing," Hirz said.

Childe did as he was told. As before, there was an uncomfortable pause which probably lasted only half a second, but which felt abyssally longer, as if our fates were being weighed by distant judicial machinery. Then thumps and vibrations signalled the opening of the door.

Simultaneously, the door behind us had opened again. The route out of the Spire was now clear again.

"Forqueray..." Childe said.

The Ultra tossed the float-cam into the darkness.

"Well?"

"This is getting a tiny bit monotonous. Another chamber, another door, another set of markings."

"No booby-traps?"

"Nothing the drone can resolve, which I'm afraid isn't saying much."

"I'll go in this time," Celestine said. "No one follow me until I've checked out the problem, understood?"

"Fine by me," Hirz said, peering back at the escape route.

Celestine stepped into the darkness.

I decided that I was no longer enjoying the illusion of seeing everyone as if we were not wearing suits—we all looked far too vulnerable, suddenly—and ordered my own to stop editing my visual field to that extent. The transition was smooth; suits formed around us like thickening auras. Only the helmet parts remained semi-transparent, so that I could still identify who was who without cumbersome visual tags.

"It's another mathematical puzzle," Celestine said. "Still fairly simple. We're not really being stretched yet."

"Yeah, well, I'll settle for not being really stretched," Hirz said.

Childe looked unimpressed. "Are you certain of the answer?"

"Trust me," Celestine said. "It's perfectly safe to enter."

THIS TIME THE markings looked more complicated; at first I feared that Celestine had been over-confident.

On the left-hand side of the door—extending the height of the frame—was a vertical strip marked by many equally spaced horizontal grooves, in the manner of a ruler. But some of the cleanly cut grooves were deeper than the others. On the other side of the door was a similar ruler, but with a different arrangement of deeper grooves, not lining up with any of those on the right.

I stared at the frame for several seconds, thinking the solution would click into my mind; willing myself back into the problem-solving mode that had once seemed so natural. But the pattern of grooves refused to snap into any neat mathematical order.

I looked at Childe, seeing no greater comprehension in his face.

"Don't you see it?" Celestine said.

"Not quite," I said.

"There are ninety-one grooves, Richard." She spoke with the tone of a teacher who had begun to lose patience with a tardy pupil. "Now counting from the bottom, the following grooves are deeper than the rest: the third, the sixth, the tenth, the fifteenth...shall I continue?"

"I think you'd better," Childe said.

"There are seven other deep grooves, concluding with the ninety-first. You must see it now, surely. Think geometrically."

"I am," I said testily.

"Tell us, Celestine," Childe said, between what was obviously gritted teeth.

She sighed. "They're triangular numbers."

"Fine," Childe said. "But I'm not sure I know what a triangular number is."

Celestine glanced at the ceiling for a moment, as if seeking inspiration. "Look. Think of a dot, will you?"

"I'm thinking," Childe said.

"Now surround that dot by six neighbours, all the same distance from each other. Got that?"

"Yes."

"Now keep on adding dots, extending out in all directions, as far as you can imagine—each dot having six neighbours."

"With you so far."

"You should have something resembling a Chinese chequerboard. Now concentrate on a single dot again, near the middle. Draw a line from it to one of its six neighbours, and then another line to one of the two dots either side of the neighbour you just chose. Then join the two neighbouring dots. What have you got?"

"An equilateral triangle."

"Good. That's three taken care of. Now imagine that the triangle's sides are twice as long. How many dots are connected together now?"

Childe answered after only a slight hesitation, "Six. I think."

"Yes." Celestine turned to me. "Are you following, Richard?"

"More or less..." I said, trying to hold the shapes in my head.

"Then we'll continue. If we triple the size of the triangle, we link together nine dots along the sides, with an additional dot in the middle. That's ten. Continue—with a quadruple-sized triangle—and we hit fifteen."

She paused, giving us time to catch up. "There are eight more; up to ninety-one, which has thirteen dots along each side."

"The final groove," I said, accepting for myself that whatever this problem was, Celestine had definitely understood it.

"But there are only seven deep grooves in that interval," she continued. "That means all we have to do is identify the groove on the right which corresponds to the missing triangular number."

"All?" Hirz said.

"Look, it's simple. I *know* the answer, but you don't have to take my word for it. The triangles follow a simple sequence. If there are N dots in the lower row of the last triangle, the next one will have N plus one more. Add one to two and you've got three. Add one to two to three, and you've got six. One to two to three to four, and you've got ten. Then fifteen, then twenty-one..." Celestine paused. "Look, it's senseless taking my word for it. Graph up a chequerboard display on your suits—Forqueray, can you oblige?—and start arranging dots in triangular patterns."

We did. It took quarter of an hour, but after that time we had all—Hirz included—convinced ourselves by brute force that Celestine was right. The only missing pattern was for the fifty-five-dot case, which happened to coincide with one of the deep grooves on the right side of the door.

It was obvious, then. That *was* the one to press.

"I don't like it," Hirz said. "I see it now...but I didn't see it until it was pointed out to me. What if there's another pattern none of us are seeing?"

Celestine looked at her coldly. "There isn't."

"Look, there's no point arguing," Childe said. "Celestine saw it first, but we always knew she would. Don't feel bad about it, Hirz. You're not here for your mathematical prowess. Nor's Trintignant, nor's Forqueray."

"Yeah, well, remind me when I can do something useful," Hirz said.

Then she pushed forward and pressed the groove on the right side of the door.

PROGRESS WAS SMOOTH and steady for the next five chambers. The problems to be solved grew harder, but after consultation the solution was never so esoteric that we could not all agree on it. As the complexity of the task increased, so did the area taken up by the frames, but other than that there was no change in the basic nature of the challenges. We were never forced to proceed more quickly than we chose, and the Spire always provided a clear route back to the exit every time a doorway had been traversed. The door immediately behind us would seal only once we had all entered the room where the current problem lay, which meant that we were able to assess any given problem before committing ourselves to its solution. To convince ourselves that were indeed able to leave, we had Hirz go back the way we had come in. She was able to return to the first room unimpeded—the rear-facing doors opened and closed in sequence to allow her to pass—and then make her way back to the rest of us by using the entry codes we had already discovered.

But something she said upon her return disturbed us.

"I'm not sure if it's my imagination or not..."

"What?" Childe snapped.

"I think the doorways are getting narrower. And lower. There was definitely more headroom at the start than there is now. I guess we didn't notice when we took so long to move from room to room."

"That doesn't make much sense," Celestine said.

"As I said, maybe I imagined it."

But we all knew she had done no such thing. The last two times I had stepped across a door's threshold my suit had bumped against the frame. I had thought nothing of it at the time—putting it down to carelessness—but that had evidently been wishful thinking.

"I wondered about the doors already," I said. "Doesn't it seem a little convenient that the first one we met was just the right size for us? It could have come from a human building."

'Then why are they getting smaller?" Childe asked.

"I don't know. But I think Hirz is right. And it does worry me."

"Me too. But it'll be a long time before it becomes a problem." Childe turned to the Ultra. "Forqueray—do the honours, will you?"

I turned and looked at the chamber ahead of us. The door was open now, but none of us had yet stepped across the threshold. As always, we waited for Forqueray to send his float-cam snooping ahead of us, establishing that the room contained no glaring pitfalls.

Forqueray tossed the float-cam through the open door.

We saw the usual red stutters as it swept the room in visible light. "No surprises," Forqueray said, in the usual slightly absent tone he adopted when reporting the cam's findings. "Empty metallic chamber... only slightly smaller than the one we're standing in now. A door at the far end with a frame that extends half a metre out on either side. Complex inscriptions this time, Celestine."

"I'll cope, don't you worry."

Forqueray stepped a little closer to the door, one arm raised with his palm open. His expression remained calm as he waited for the drone to return to its master. We all watched, and then—as the moment elongated into seconds—began to suspect that something was wrong.

The room beyond was utterly dark; no stammering flashes now.

"The cam—" Forqueray said.

Childe's gaze snapped to the Ultra's face. "Yes?"

"It isn't transmitting anymore. I can't detect it."

"That isn't possible."

"I'm telling you." The Ultra looked at us, his fear not well concealed. "It's gone."

CHILDE MOVED INTO the darkness, through the frame.

Just as I was admiring his bravery I felt the floor shudder. Out of the corner of my eye I saw a flicker of rapid motion, like an eyelid closing.

The rear door—the one that led out of the chamber in which we were standing—had just slammed shut.

Celestine fell forward. She had been standing in the gap.

"No…" she said, hitting the ground with a detectable thump.

"Childe!" I shouted, unnecessarily. "Stay where you are—something just happened."

"What?"

"The door behind us closed on Celestine. She's been injured…"

I was fearing the worst—that the door might have snipped off an arm or a leg as it closed—but it was, mercifully, not that serious. The door had damaged the thigh of her suit, grazing an inch of its armour away as it closed, but Celestine herself had not been injured. The damaged part was still airtight, and the suit's mobility and critical systems remained unimpaired.

Already, in fact, the self-healing mechanisms were coming into play repairing the wound.

She sat up on the ground. "I'm OK. The impact was hard, but I don't think I've done any permanent damage.

"You sure?" I said, offering her a hand.

"Perfectly sure," she said, standing up without my assistance.

"You were lucky," Trintignant said. "You were only partly blocking the door. Had that not been the case, I suspect your injuries would have been more interesting."

"What happened?" Hirz asked.

"Childe must have triggered it," Forqueray said. "As soon as he stepped into the other room, it closed the rear door." The Ultra stepped closer to the aperture. "What happened to my float-cam, Childe?"

"I don't know. It just isn't here. There isn't even a trace of debris, and there's no sign of anything that could have destroyed it."

The silence that followed was broken by Trintignant's piping tones. "I believe this makes a queer kind of sense."

"You do, do you?" I said.

"Yes, my dear fellow. It is my suspicion that the Spire has been tolerating the drone until now—lulling us, if you will, into a false sense of security. Yet now the Spire has decreed that we must discard that particular mental crutch. It will no longer permit us to gain any knowledge of the contents of a room until one us steps into it. And at that moment it will prevent any of us *leaving* until we have solved that problem."

"You mean it's changing the rules as it goes along?" Hirz asked.

The doctor turned his exquisite silver mask towards her. "Which rules did you have in mind, Hirz?"

"Don't fuck with me, Doc. You know what I mean."

Trintignant touched a finger to the chin of his helmet. "I confess I do not. Unless it is your contention that the Spire has at some point agreed to bind by a set of strictures, which I would ardently suggest is far from the case."

"No," I said. "Hirz is right, in one way. There *have* been rules. It's clear that it won't tolerate us inflicting physical harm against it. And it won't allow us to enter a room until we've all stepped into the preceding one. I think those are pretty fundamental rules."

"Then what about the drone, and the door?" asked Childe.

"It's like Trintignant said. It tolerated us playing outside the rules until now, but we shouldn't have assumed that was always going to be the case."

Hirz nodded. "Great. What else is it tolerating now?"

"I don't know." I managed a thin smile. "I suppose the only way to find out is to keep going."

WE PASSED THROUGH another eight rooms, taking between one and two hours to solve each.

There had been a couple of occasions when we had debated whether to continue, with Hirz usually the least keen of us, but so far the problems had not been insurmountably difficult. And we were making a kind of progress. Mostly the rooms were blank, but every now and then there was a narrow, trellised window, paneled in stained sheets of what was obviously a substance very much more resilient than glass or even diamond. Sometimes these windows opened only into gloomy interior spaces, but on one occasion we were able to look outside, able to sense some of the height we had attained. Forqueray, who had been monitoring our journey with an inertial compass and gravitometer, confirmed that we had ascended at least fifteen vertical metres since the first chamber. That almost sounded impressive, until one considered the several hundred metres of Spire that undoubtedly lay above us. Another few hundred rooms, each posing a challenge more testing than the last?

And the doors were definitely getting smaller.

It was an effort to squeeze through now, and while the suits were able to reshape themselves to some extent, there was a limit to how compact they could become.

It had taken us sixteen hours to reach this point. At this rate it would take many days to get anywhere near the summit.

But none of us had imagined that this would be over quickly.

"Tricky," Celestine said, after studying the latest puzzle for many minutes. "I think I see what's going on here, but..."

Childe looked at her. "You think, or you know?"

"I mean what I said. It's not easy, you know. Would you rather I let someone else take first crack at it?"

I put a hand on Celestine's arm and spoke to her privately. "Easy. He's just anxious, that's all."

She brushed my hand away. "I didn't ask you to defend me, Richard."

"I'm sorry. I didn't mean—"

"Never mind." Celestine switched off private and addressed the group. "I think these markings are shadows. Look."

By now we had all become reasonably adept at drawing figures using our suits' visualisation systems. These sketchy hallucinations could be painted on any surface, apparently visible to all.

Celestine, who was the best at this, drew a short red hyphen on the wall.

"See this? A one-dimensional line. Now watch." She made the line become a square; splitting into two parallel lines joined at their ends. Then she made the square rotate until it was edge-on again, and all we could see was the line.

"We see it…" Childe said.

"You can think of a line as the one-dimensional shadow of a two-dimensional object, in this case a square. Understand?"

"I think we get the gist," Trintignant said.

Celestine made the square freeze, and then slide diagonally, leaving a copy of itself to which it was joined at the corners. "Now. We're looking at a two-dimensional figure this time; the shadow of a three-dimensional cube. See how it changes if I rotate the cube, how it elongates and contracts?"

"Yes. Got that," Childe said, watching the two joined squares slide across each other with a hypnotically smooth motion, only one square visible, as the imagined cube presented itself face-on to the wall.

"Well, I think what these figures…" Celestine sketched a hand an inch over the intricate designs worked into the frame, "I think what these figures represent are two-dimensional shadows of four-dimensional objects."

"Fuck off," Hirz said.

"Look, just concentrate, will you? This one's easy. It's a hypercube. That's the four-dimensional analogue of a cube. You just take a cube and extend it *outwards*; just the same way that you make a cube from a square." Celestine paused, and for a moment I thought she was going to throw up her hands in despair. "Look. Look at this." And then she sketched something on the wall: a cube set inside a slightly larger one, to which it was joined by diagonal lines. "That's what the three-dimensional shadow of a hypercube would look like. Now all you have to do is collapse that shadow by one more dimension, down to two, to get *this*—" She jabbed at the beguiling design marked on the door.

"I think I see it," Childe said, without anything resembling confidence.

Maybe I did, too—though I felt the same lack of certainty. Childe and I had certainly taunted each other with higher-dimensional puzzles in our youth, but never had so much depended on an intuitive grasp of those mind-shattering mathematical realms. "All right," I said. "Supposing that *is* the shadow of a tesseract…what's the puzzle?"

"This," Celestine said, pointing to the other side of the door, to what seemed like an utterly different—though no less complex—design. "It's the same object, after a rotation."

"The shadow changes that drastically?"

"Start getting used to it, Richard."

"All right." I realised she was still annoyed with me for touching her. "What about the others?"

"They're all four-dimensional objects; relatively simple geometric forms. This one's a 4-simplex; a hypertetrahedon. It's a hyper-pyramid with five tetrahedral faces…" Celestine trailed off, looking at us with an odd expression on her face. "Never mind. The point is, all the corresponding forms on the right should be the shadows of the same polytopes after a simple rotation through higher-dimensional space. But one isn't."

"Which is?"

She pointed to one of the forms. "This one."

"And you're certain of that?" Hirz said. "Because I'm sure as fuck not."

Celestine nodded. "Yes. I'm completely sure of it now."

"But you can't make any of us see that this is the case?"

She shrugged. "I guess you either see it or you don't."

"Yeah? Well maybe we should have all taken a trip to the Pattern Jugglers. Then maybe I wouldn't be about to shit myself."

Celestine said nothing, but merely reached out and touched the errant figure.

"**THERE'S GOOD NEWS** and there's bad news," Forqueray said after we had traversed another dozen or so rooms without injury.

"Give us the bad news first," Celestine said.

Forqueray obliged, with what sounded like the tiniest degree of pleasure. "We won't be able to get through more than two or three more doors. Not with these suits on."

There had been no real need to tell us that. It had become crushingly obvious during the last three or four rooms that we were near the limit; that the Spire's subtly shifting internal architecture would not permit further movement within the bulky suits. It had been an effort to squeeze through the last door; only Hirz was oblivious to these difficulties.

"Then we might as well give up," I said.

"Not exactly." Forqueray smiled his vampiric smile. "I said there was good news as well, didn't I?"

"Which is?" Childe said.

"You remember when we sent Hirz back to the beginning, to see if the Spire was going to allow us to leave at any point?"

"Yes," Childe said. Hirz had not repeated the complete exercise since, but she had gone back a dozen rooms, and found that the Spire was just as operative as it had been before. There was no reason to think she would not have been able to make her way to the exit, had she wished.

"Something bothered me," Forqueray said. "When she went back, the Spire opened and closed doors in sequence to allow her to pass. I couldn't see the sense in that. Why not just open all the doors all the doors along her route?"

"I confess it troubled me as well," Trintignant said.

"So I thought about it, and decided there must be a reason not to have all the doors open at once."

Childe sighed. "Which was?"

"Air," Forqueray said.

"You're kidding, aren't you?"

The Ultra shook his head. "When we began, we were moving in vacuum—or at least through air that was as thin as that on Golgotha's surface. That continued to be the case for the next few rooms. Then it began to change. Very slowly, I'll grant you—but my suit sensors picked up on it immediately."

Childe pulled a face. "And it didn't cross your mind to tell any of us about this?"

"I thought it best to wait until a pattern became apparent." Forqueray glanced at Celestine, whose face was impassive.

"He's right," Trintignant said. "I too have become aware of the changing atmospheric conditions. Forqueray has also doubtless noticed that the temperature in each room has been a little warmer than the last. I have extrapolated these trends and arrived at a tentative conclusion. Within two—possibly three—rooms, we will be able to discard our suits and breathe normally."

"Discard our suits?" Hirz looked at him as if he were insane. "You have got to be fucking kidding."

Childe raised a hand. "Wait a minute. When you said air, Doctor Trintignant, you didn't say it was anything we could breathe."

The Doctor's answer was a melodious piped refrain. "Except it is. The ratios of the various gases are remarkably close to those we employ in our suits."

"Which isn't possible. I don't remember providing a sample."

Trintignant dipped his head in a nod. "Nonetheless, it appears that one has been taken. The mix, incidentally, corresponds to precisely the atmospheric preferences of Ultras. Argyle's expedition would surely have employed a slightly different mix, so it is not simply the case that the Spire has a long memory."

I shivered.

The thought that the Spire—this vast breathing thing through which we were scurrying like rats—had somehow reached inside the hard armour of our suits to snatch a sample of air, without our knowing, made my guts turn cold. It not only knew of our presence, but it knew—intimately—what we were.

It understood our fragility.

As if wishing to reward Forqueray for his observation, the next room contained a substantially thicker atmosphere than any of its predecessors, and was also much warmer. It was not yet capable of supporting life, but one would not have died instantly without the protection of a suit.

The challenge that the room held was by far the hardest, even by Celestine's reckoning. Once again the essence of the task lay in the figures marked on either side of the door, but now these figures were linked by various symbols and connecting loops, like the subway map of a foreign city. We had encountered some of these hieroglyphics

—370—

before—they were akin to mathematical operators, like the addition and subtraction symbol—but we had never seen so many. And the problem itself was not simply a numerical exercise, but—as far as Celestine could say with any certainty—a problem about topological transformations in four dimensions.

"Please tell me you see the answer immediately," Childe said.

"I..." Celestine trailed off. "I think I do. I'm just not absolutely certain. I need to think about this for a minute."

"Fine. Take all the time you want."

Celestine fell into a reverie which lasted minutes, and then tens of minutes. Once or twice she would open her mouth and take a breath of air as if in readiness to speak, and on one or two other occasions she took a promising step closer to the door, but none of these things heralded the sudden, intuitive breakthrough we were all hoping for. She always returned to same silent, standing posture. The time dragged on; first an hour and then the better part of two hours.

All this, I thought, before even Celestine had seen the answer.

It might take days if we were all expected to follow her reasoning.

Finally, however, she spoke. "Yes, I see it."

Childe was the first to answer. "Is it the one you thought it was originally?"

"No."

"Great," Hirz said.

"Celestine..." I said, trying to defuse the situation. "Do you understand why you made the wrong choice originally?"

"Yes. I think so. It was a trick answer; an apparently correct solution which contained a subtle flaw. And what looked like the clearly wrong answer turned out to be the right one."

"Right. And you're certain of that?"

"I'm not certain of anything, Richard. I'm just saying this is what I believe the answer to be."

I nodded. "I think that's all any of us can honestly expect. Do you think there's any chance of the rest of us following your line of argument?"

"I don't know. How much do you understand about Kaluza-Klein spaces?"

"Not a vast amount, I have to admit."

"That's what I feared. I could probably explain my reasoning to some of you, but there'd always be someone who didn't get it—" Celestine looked pointedly at Hirz. "We could be in this bloody room for weeks before any of us grasp the solution. And the Spire may not tolerate that kind of delay."

"We don't know that," I cautioned.

"No," Childe said. "On the other hand, we can't afford to spend weeks solving every room. There's going to have to come a point where we put our faith in Celestine's judgment. I think that time may have come."

I looked at him, remembering that his mathematical fluency had always been superior to mine. The puzzles I had set him had seldom defeated him, even if it had taken weeks for his intensely methodical mind to arrive at the solution. Conversely, he had often managed to beat me by setting a mathematical challenge of similar intricacy to the one now facing Celestine. They were not quite equals, I knew, but neither were their abilities radically different. It was just that, thanks to her experiences with the Pattern Jugglers, Celestine would always arrive at the answer with the superhuman speed of a savant.

"Are you saying I should just press it, with no consultation?" Celestine said.

Childe nodded. "Provided everyone else agrees with me..."

It was not an easy decision to make, especially after having navigated so many rooms via such a ruthlessly democratic process. But we all saw the sense, even Hirz coming around to our line of thinking in the end.

"I'm telling you," she said. "We get through this door, I'm out of here, money or not."

"You're giving up?" Childe asked.

"You saw what happened to those poor bastards outside. They must have thought they could keep on solving next test."

Childe looked sad, but said, "I understand perfectly. But I trust you'll reassess your decision as soon as we're through?"

"Sorry, but my mind's made up. I've had enough of this shit." Hirz turned to Celestine. "Put us all out of our misery, will you? Make the choice."

Celestine looked at each of us in turn. "Are you ready for this?"

"We are," Childe said, answering for the group. "Go ahead."

Celestine pressed the symbol. There was the usual yawning moment of expectation; a moment that stretched agonisingly. We all stared at the door, willing it to begin sliding open.

This time nothing happened.

"Oh God..." Hirz began.

Something happened then, almost before she had finished speaking, but it was over almost before we had sensed any change in the room. It was only afterwards—playing back the visual record captured by our suits—that we were able to make any sense of events.

The walls of the chamber—like every room we had passed through, in fact—had looked totally seamless. But in a flash something emerged from the wall: a rigid, sharp-ended metal rod spearing out at waist-height. It flashed through the air from wall to wall, vanishing like a javelin thrown into water. None of us had time to notice it, let alone react bodily. Even the suits—programmed to move out of the way of obvious moving hazards—were too slow. By the time they began moving, the javelin had been and gone. And if there had been only that one javelin, we might have missed it happening at all.

But a second emerged, a fraction of a second after the first, spearing across the room at a slightly different angle.

Forqueray happened to be standing in the way.

The javelin passed through him as if he were made of smoke; its progress was unimpeded by his presence. But it dragged behind it a comet-tail of gore, exploding out of his suit where he had been speared, just below the elbow. The pressure in the room was still considerably less than atmospheric.

Forqueray's suit reacted with impressive speed, but it was still sluggish compared to the javelin.

It assessed the damage that had been inflicted on the arm, aware of how quickly its self-repair systems could work to seal that inch-wide hole, and came to a rapid conclusion. The integrity could be restored, but not before unacceptable blood and pressure loss. Since its duty was always to keep its wearer alive, no matter what the costs, it opted to sever the arm above the wound; hyper-sharp irised blades snicked through flesh and bone in an instant.

All that took place long before any pain signals had a chance to reach his brain. The first thing Forqueray knew of his misfortune was when his arm clanged to his feet.

"I think—" he started saying. Hirz dashed over to the Ultra and did her best to support him.

Forqueray's truncated arm ended in a smooth silver iris.

"Don't talk," Childe said.

Forqueray, who was still standing, looked at his injury with something close to fascination. "I—"

"I said don't talk." Childe knelt down and picked up the amputated arm, showing the evidence to Forqueray. The hole went right through it, as cleanly bored as a rifle barrel.

"I'll live," Forqueray managed.

"Yes, you will," Trintignant said. "And you may also count yourself fortunate. Had the projectile pierced your body, rather than one of its extremities, I do not believe we would be having this conversation."

"You call this fortunate?"

"A wound such as yours can be made good with only trivial intervention. We have all the equipment we need aboard the shuttle."

Hirz looked around uneasily. "You think the punishment's over?"

"I think we'd know if it wasn't," I said. "That was our first mistake, after all. We can expect things to be a little worse in future, of course."

"Then we'd better not make any more screw-ups, had we?" Hirz was directing her words at Celestine.

I had expected an angry rebuttal. Celestine would have been perfectly correct to remind Hirz that—had the rest of us been forced to make that choice—our chances of hitting the correct answer would have been a miserable one in six.

But instead Celestine just spoke with the flat, soporific tones of one who could not quite believe she had made such an error.

"I'm sorry...I must have..."

"Made the wrong decision. Yes." I nodded. "And there'll undoubtedly be others. You did your best, Celestine—better than any of us could have managed."

"It wasn't good enough."

"No, but you narrowed the field down to two possibilities. That's a lot better than six."

"He's right," Childe said. "Celestine, don't cut yourself up about this. Without you we wouldn't have got as far as we did. Now go ahead and press the other answer—the one you settled on originally—and we'll get Forqueray back to base camp."

The Ultra glared at him. "I'm fine, Childe. I can continue."

"Maybe you can, but it's still time for a temporary retreat. We'll get that arm looked at properly, and then we'll come back with lightweight suits. We can't carry on much further with these, anyway—and I don't particularly fancy continuing with no armour at all."

Celestine turned back to the frame. "I can't promise that this is the right one, either."

"We'll take that chance. Just hit them in sequence—best choice first—until the Spire opens a route back to the start."

She pressed the symbol that had been her first choice, before she had analysed the problem more deeply and seen a phantom trap.

As always, Blood Spire did not oblige us with an instant judgement on the choice we had made. There was a moment when all of us tensed, expecting the javelins to come again...but this time we were spared further punishment.

The door opened, exposing the next chamber.

We did not step through, of course. Instead, we turned around and made our way back through the succession of rooms we had already traversed, descending all the while, almost laughing at the childish simplicity of the very earliest puzzles compared to those we had faced before the attack.

As the doors opened and closed in sequence, the air thinned out and the skin of Blood Spire became colder, less like a living thing, more like an ancient, brooding machine. But still that distant, throbbing respiratory vibration rattled the floors, lower now, and slower: the Spire letting us know it was aware of our presence and, perhaps, the tiniest bit disappointed at this turning back.

"All right, you bastard," Childe said. "We're retreating, but only for now. We're coming back, understand?"

"You don't have to take it personally," I said.

"Oh, but I do," Childe said. "I take it very personally indeed."

We reached the first chamber, and then dropped down through what had been the entrance hole. After that, it was just a short flight back to the waiting shuttle.

It was dark outside.

We had been in the Spire for more than nineteen hours.

FOUR

"IT'LL DO." FORQUERAY said, tilting his new arm this way and that.

"Do?" Trintignant sounded mortally wounded. "My dear fellow, it is a work of exquisite craftsmanship; a thing of beauty. It is unlikely that you will see its like again, unless of course I am called upon to perform a similar procedure."

We were sitting inside the shuttle, still parked on Golgotha's surface. The ship was a squat, aerodynamically blunt cylinder which had landed tail-down and then expanded a cluster of eight bubbletents around itself: six for our personal quarters during the expedition, one commons area, and a general medical bay equipped with all the equipment Trintignant needed to do his work. Surprisingly—to me, at least, who admitted to some unfamiliarity with these things—the shuttle's fabricators had been more than able to come up with the various cybernetic components that the doctor required, and the surgical tools at his disposal—glistening, semi-sentient things which moved to his will almost before they were summoned—were clearly state of the art by any reasonable measure.

"Yes, well, I'd have rather you'd reattached my old arm," Forqueray said, opening and closing the sleek metal gauntlet of his replacement.

"It would have been almost insultingly trivial to do that," Trintignant said. "A new hand could have been cultured and regrafted in a few hours. If that did not appeal to you, I could have programmed your stump to regenerate a hand of its own accord; a perfectly simple matter of stem-cell manipulation. But what would have been the point? You would be very likely to lose it as soon as we suffer our next punishment. Now you will only be losing machinery—a far less traumatic prospect."

"You're enjoying this," Hirz said, "aren't you?"

"It would be churlish to deny it," Trintignant said. "When you have been deprived of willing subjects as long as I have, it's only natural to take pleasure in those little opportunities for practice that fate seems fit to present."

Hirz nodded knowingly. She had not heard of Trintignant upon our first meeting, I recalled, but she had lost no time in forming her subsequent opinion of the man. "Except you won't just stop with a hand, will you? I checked up on you, Doc—after that meeting in Childe's house. I hacked into some of the medical records that the Stoner authorities still haven't declassified, because they're just too damned disturbing. You really went the whole hog, didn't you? Some of the things I saw in those files—your victims—they stopped me from sleeping."

And yet still she had chosen to come with us, I thought. Evidently the allure of Childe's promised reward outweighed any reservations she might have had about sharing a room with Trintignant. But I wondered about those medical records. Certainly, the publicly released data had contained more than enough atrocities for the average nightmare. It chilled the blood to think that Trintignant's most heinous crimes had never been fully revealed.

"Is it true?" I said. "Were there really worse things?"

"That depends," Trintignant said. "There were subjects upon whom I pushed my experimental techniques further than is generally realised, if that is what you mean. But did I ever approach what I considered were the true limits? No. I was always hindered."

"Until, perhaps, now," I said.

The rigid silver mask swivelled to face us all in turn. "That is as may be. But please give the following matter some consideration. I can surgically remove all your limbs now, cleanly, with the minimum of complications. The detached members could be put into cryogenic storage, replaced by prosthetic systems until we have completed the task that lies ahead of us."

'Thanks…" I said, looking around at the others. "But I think we'll pass on that one, Doctor."

Trintignant offered his palms magnanimously. "I am at your disposal, should you wish to reconsider."

WE SPENT A full day in the shuttle before returning to the Spire. I had been mortally tired, but when I finally slept, it was only to submerge myself in yet more labyrinthine dreams, much like those Childe had pumped into our heads during the reefersleep transition. I woke feeling angry and cheated, and resolved to confront him about it.

But something else snagged my attention. There was something wrong with my wrist. Buried just beneath the skin was a hard rectangle, showing darkly through my flesh. Turning my wrist this way and that, I admired the object, acutely—and strangely conscious of its rectilinearity. I looked around me, and felt the same visceral awareness of the other shapes which formed my surroundings. I did not know whether I was more disturbed at the presence of the alien object under my flesh, or my unnatural reaction to it.

I stumbled groggily into the common quarters of the shuttle, presenting my wrist to Childe, who was sitting there with Celestine.

She looked at me before Childe had a chance to answer. "So you've got one too," she said, showing me the similar shape lurking just below her own skin. The shape rhymed—there was no other word for it—with the surrounding panels and extrusions of the commons. "Um, Richard?" she added.

"I'm feeling a little strange."

"Blame Childe. He put them there. Didn't you, you lying rat?"

"It's easily removed," he said, all innocence. "It just seemed more prudent to implant the devices while you were all asleep anyway, so as not to waste any more time than necessary."

"It's not just the thing in my wrist," I said, "whatever it is."

"It's something to keep us awake," Celestine said, her anger just barely under control. Feeling less myself than ever, I watched the way her face changed shape as she spoke, conscious of the armature of muscle and bone lying just beneath the skin.

"Awake?" I managed.

"A...shunt, of some kind," she said. "Ultras use them, I gather. It sucks fatigue poisons out of the blood, and puts other chemicals back into the blood to upset the brain's normal sleeping cycle. With one of these you can stay conscious for weeks, with almost no psychological problems."

I forced a smile, ignoring the sense of wrongness I felt. "It's the almost part that worries me."

"Me too." She glared at Childe. "But much as I hate the little rat for doing this without my permission, I admit to seeing the sense in it."

I felt the bump in my wrist again. "Trintignant's work, I presume?"

"Count yourself lucky he didn't hack your arms and legs off while he was at it."

Childe interrupted her. "I told him to install the shunts. We can still catnap, if we have the chance. But these devices will let us stay alert when we need alertness. They're really no more sinister than that."

"There's something else..." I said tentatively. I glanced at Celestine, trying to judge if she felt as oddly as I did. "Since I've been awake, I've... experienced things differently. I keep seeing shapes in a new light. What exactly have you done to me, Childe?"

"Again, nothing irreversible. Just a small medichine infusion—"

I tried to keep my temper. "What sort of medichines?"

"Neural modifiers." He raised a hand defensively, and I saw the same rectangular bulge under his skin. "Your brain is already swarming with Demarchist implants and cellular machines, Richard, so why pretend that what I've done is anything more than a continuation of what was already there?"

"What the fuck is he talking about?" said Hirz, who had been standing at the door to the commons for the last few seconds. "Is it to do with the weird shit I've been dealing with since waking up?"

"Very probably," I said, relieved that at least I was not going insane. "Let me guess—heightened mathematical and spatial awareness?"

"If that's what you call it, yeah. Seeing shapes everywhere, and thinking of them fitting together..."

Hirz turned to look at Childe. Small as she was, she looked easily capable of inflicting injury. "Start talking, dickhead."

Childe spoke with quiet calm. "I put modifiers in your brain, via the wrist shunt. The modifiers haven't performed any radical neural restructuring, but they are suppressing and enhancing certain regions of brain function. The effect—crudely speaking—is to enhance your spatial abilities, at the expense of some less essential functions. What you are getting is a glimpse into the cognitive realms that Celestine inhabits as a matter of routine." Celestine opened her mouth to speak, but he cut her off with a raised palm. "No more than a glimpse, no, but I think you'll agree that—given the kinds of challenges the Spire likes to throw at us—the modifiers will give us an edge that we lacked previously."

"You mean you've turned us all into maths geniuses, overnight?"

"Broadly speaking, yes."

"Well, that'll come in handy," Hirz said.

"It will?"

"Yeah, when you try and fit the pieces of your dick back together."

She lunged for him.

"Hirz, I..."

"Stop," I said, interceding. "Childe was wrong to do this without our consent, but—given the situation we find ourselves in—the idea makes sense."

"Whose side are you on?" Hirz said, backing away with a look of righteous fury in her eyes.

"Nobody's," I said. "I just want to do whatever it takes to beat the Spire."

Hirz glared at Childe. "All right. This time. But you try another stunt like that, and..."

But even then it was obvious that Hirz had come to the conclusion that I had already arrived at myself that, given what the Spire was likely to test us with, it was better to accept these machines than ask for them to be flushed out of our systems.

There was just one troubling thought which I could not quite dismiss.

Would I have welcomed the machines so willingly before they had invaded my head, or were they influencing my decision?

I had no idea.

But I decided to worry about that later.

FIVE

"THREE HOURS," **CHILDE** said triumphantly. "Took us nineteen to reach this point on our last trip through. That has to mean something, doesn't it?"

"Yeah," Hirz said snidely. "It means it's a piece of piss when you know the answers."

We were standing by the door where Celestine had made her mistake the last time. She had just pressed the correct topological symbol and the door had opened to admit us to the chamber beyond, one we had not so far stepped into. From now on we would be facing fresh challenges again, rather than passing through those we had already faced. The Spire, it appeared, was more interested in probing the limits of our understanding than getting us simply to solve permutations of the same basic challenge.

It wanted to break us, not stress us.

More and more I was thinking of it as a sentient thing: inquisitive and patient and—when the mood took it—immensely capable of cruelty.

"What's in there?" Forqueray said.

Hirz had gone ahead into the unexplored room.

"Well, fuck me if it isn't another puzzle."

"Describe it, would you?"

"Weird shape shit, I think." She was quiet for a few seconds. "Yeah. Shapes in four dimensions again. Celestine—you wanna take a look at this? I think it's right up your street."

"Any idea what the nature of the task is?" Celestine asked.

"Fuck, I don't know. Something to do with stretching, I think..."

"Topological deformations," Celestine murmured before joining Hirz in the chamber.

For a minute or so the two of them conferred, studying the marked doorframe like a pair of discerning art critics.

On the last run through, Hirz and Celestine had shared almost no common ground: it was unnerving to see how much Hirz now grasped. The machines Childe had pumped into our skulls had improved the mathematical skills of all of us—with the possible exception of Trintignant, who I suspected had not received the therapy—but the effects had differed in nuance, degree and stability. My mathematical brilliance came in feverish, unpredictable waves, like inspiration to a laudanum-addicted poet. Forqueray had gained astonishing fluency in arithmetic, able to count huge numbers of things simply by looking at them for a moment.

But Hirz's change had been the most dramatic of all, something even Childe was taken aback by. On the second pass through the Spire she had been intuiting the answers to many of the problems at a glance, and I was certain that she was not always remembering what the correct answer had been. Now, as we encountered the tasks that had challenged even Celestine, Hirz was still able to perceive the essence of a problem, even if it was beyond her to articulate the details in the formal language of mathematics.

And if she could not yet see her way to selecting the correct answer, she could at least see the one or two answers that were clearly wrong.

"Hirz is right," Celestine said eventually. "It's about topological deformations, stretching operations on solid shapes."

Once again we were seeing the projected shadows of four-dimensional lattices. On the right side of the door, however, the shadows were of the same objects after they had been stretched and squeezed and generally distorted. The problem was to identify the shadow that could only be formed with a shearing, in addition to the other operations.

It took an hour, but eventually Celestine felt certain that she had selected the right answer. Hirz and I attempted to follow her arguments, but the best we could do was agree that two of the other answers would have been wrong. That, at least, was an improvement on anything we would have been capable of before the medichine infusions, but it was only moderately comforting.

Nonetheless, Celestine had selected the right answer. We moved into the next chamber.

"This is as far as we can go with these suits," Childe said, indicating the door that lay ahead of us. "It'll be a squeeze, even with the lighter suits—except for Hirz, of course."

"What's the air like in here?" I asked.

"We could breathe it," Forqueray said. "And we'll have to, briefly. But I don't recommend that we do that for any length of time—at least not until we're forced into it."

"Forced?" Celestine said. "You think the doors are going to keep getting smaller?"

"I don't know. But doesn't it feel as if this place is forcing us to expose ourselves to it, to make ourselves maximally vulnerable? I don't think it's done with us just yet." He paused, his suit beginning to remove itself. "But that doesn't mean we have to humour it."

I understood his reluctance. The Spire had hurt him, not us.

Beneath the Ultra suits which had brought us this far we had donned as much of the lightweight versions as was possible. They were skintight suits of reasonably modern design, but they were museum pieces compared to the Ultra equipment. The helmets and much of the breathing gear had been impossible to put on, so we had carried the extra parts strapped to our backs. Despite my fears, the Spire had not objected to this, but I remained acutely aware that we did not yet know all the rules under which we played.

It only took three or four minutes to get out of the bulky suits and into the new ones; most of this time was taken up running status checks. For a minute or so, with the exception of Hirz, we had all breathed Spire air.

It was astringent, blood-hot, humid, and smelt faintly of machine oil.

It was a relief when the helmets flooded with the cold, tasteless air of the suits' backpack recyclers.

"Hey." Hirz, the only one still wearing her original suit, knelt down and touched the floor. "Check this out."

I followed her, pressing the flimsy fabric of my glove against the surface.

The structure's vibrations rose and fell with increased strength, as if we had excited it by removing our hard protective shells.

"It's like the fucking thing's getting a hard-on," Hirz said.

"Let's push on," Childe said. "We're still armoured—just not as effectively as before—but if we keep being smart, it won't matter."

"Yeah. But it's the being smart part that worries me. No one smart would come within pissing distance of this fucking place."

"What does that make you, Hirz?" Celestine asked.

"Greedier than you'll ever know," she said.

Nonetheless we made good progress for another eleven rooms. Now and then a stained-glass window allowed a view out of Golgotha's surface, which looked very far below us. By Forqueray's estimate we had gained forty-five vertical metres since entering the Spire. Although two hundred further metres lay ahead—the bulk of the climb, in fact—for the first time it began to appear possible that we might succeed. That, of course, was contingent on several assumptions. One was that the problems, while growing steadily more difficult, would not become insoluble. The other was that the doorways would not continue to narrow now that we had discarded the bulky suits.

But they did.

As always, the narrowing was imperceptible from room to room, but after five or six it could not be ignored. After ten or fifteen more rooms we would again have to scrape our way between them.

And what if the narrowing continued beyond that point?

"We won't be able to go on," I said. "We won't fit—even if we're naked."

"You are entirely too defeatist," Trintignant said.

Childe sounded reasonable. "What would you propose, Doctor?"

"Nothing more than a few minor adjustments of the basic human body-plan. Just enough to enable us to squeeze through apertures which would be impassable with our current...encumbrances."

Trintignant looked avariciously at my arms and legs.

"It wouldn't be worth it," I said. "I'll accept your help after I've been injured, but if you're thinking that I'd submit to anything more drastic... well, I'm afraid you're severely mistaken, Doctor."

"Amen to that," Hirz said. "For a while back there, Swift, I really thought this place was getting to you."

"It isn't," I said. "Not remotely. And in any case, we're thinking many rooms ahead here, when we might not even be able to get through the next."

"I agree," Childe said. "We'll take it one at a time. Doctor Trintignant, put your wilder fantasies aside, at least for now."

"Consider them relegated to mere daydreams," Trintignant said.

So we pushed on.

Now that we had passed through so many doors, it was possible to see that the Spire's tasks came in waves; that there might, for instance, be a series of problems which depended on prime number theory, followed by another series which hinged on the properties of higher-dimensional solids. For several rooms in sequence we were confronted by questions related to tiling patterns—tessellations—while another sequence tested our understanding of cellular automata: odd chequerboard armies of shapes which obeyed simple rules and yet interacted in stunningly complex ways. The final challenge in each set would always be the hardest; the one where we were most likely to make a mistake. We were quite prepared to take three or four hours to pass each door, if that was the time it took to be certain—in Celestine's mind at least—that the answer was clear.

And though the shunts were leaching fatigue poisons from our blood, and though the modifiers were enabling us to think with a clarity we had never known before, a kind of exhaustion always crept over us after solving one of the harder challenges. It normally passed in a few tens of minutes, but until then we generally waited before venturing through the now open door, gathering our strength again.

In those quiet minutes we spoke amongst ourselves, discussing what had happened and what we could expect.

"It's happened again," I said, addressing Celestine on the private channel.

Her answer came back, no more terse than I had expected. "What?"

"For a while the rest of us could keep up with you. Even Hirz. Or, if not keep up, then at least not lose sight of you completely. But you're pulling ahead again, aren't you? Those Juggler routines are kicking in again."

She took her time replying. "You have Childe's medichines."

"Yes. But all they can do is work with the basic neural topology, suppressing and enhancing activity without altering the layout of the connections in any significant way. And the 'chines are broad-spectrum; not tuned specifically to any one of us."

Celestine looked at the only one of us still wearing one of the original suits. "They worked on Hirz."

"Must have been luck. But yes, you're right. She couldn't see as far as you, though, even with the modifiers."

Celestine tapped the shunt in her wrist, still faintly visible beneath the tight-fitting fabric of her suit. "I took a spike of the modifiers as well."

"I doubt that it gave you much of an edge over what you already had."

"Maybe not." She paused. "Is there a point to this conversation, Richard?"

"Not really," I said, stung by her response. "I just…"

"Wanted to talk, yes."

"And you don't?"

"You can hardly blame me if I don't, can you? This isn't exactly the place for small talk, let alone with someone who chose to have me erased from his memory."

"Would it make any difference if I said I was sorry about that?"

I could tell from the tone of her response that my answer had not been quite the one she was expecting. "It's easy to say you're sorry, now… now that it suits you to say as much. That's not how you felt at the time."

I fumbled for an answer which was not too distant from the truth. "Would you believe me if I said I'd had you suppressed because I still loved you, and not for any other reason?"

"That's just a little too convenient, isn't it?"

"But not necessarily a lie. And can you blame me for it? We were in love, Celestine. You can't deny that. Just because things happened between us…" A question I had been meaning to ask her forced itself to the front of my mind. "Why didn't you contact me again, after you were told you couldn't go to Resurgam?"

"Our relationship was over, Richard."

"But we'd parted on reasonably amicable terms. If the Resurgam expedition hadn't come up, we might not have parted at all."

Celestine sighed; one of exasperation. "Well, since you asked, I *did* try and contact you."

"You did?"

"But by the time I'd made my mind up, I learned about the way you'd had me suppressed. How do you imagine that made me feel, Richard? Like a small, disposable part of your past—something to be wadded up and flicked away when it offended you?"

"It wasn't like that at all. I never thought I'd see you again."

She snorted. "And maybe you wouldn't have, if it wasn't for dear old Roland Childe."

I kept my voice level. "He asked me along because we both used to test each other with challenges like this. I presume he needed someone with your kind of Juggler transform. Childe wouldn't have cared about our past."

Her eyes flashed behind the visor of her helmet. "And you don't care either, do you?"

"About Childe's motives? No. They're neither my concern nor my interest. All that bothers me now is this."

I patted the Spire's thrumming floor.

"There's more here than meets the eye, Richard."

"What do you mean by that?"

"Haven't you noticed how—" She looked at me for several seconds, as if on the verge of revealing something, then shook her head. "Never mind."

"What, for pity's sake?"

"Doesn't it strike you that Childe has been just a little too well prepared?"

"I wouldn't say there's any such thing as being too well prepared for a thing like the Blood Spire, Celestine."

"That's not what I mean." She fingered the fabric of her skintight. "These suits, for instance. How did he know we wouldn't be able to go all the way with the larger ones?"

I shrugged, a gesture that was now perfectly visible. "I don't know. Maybe he learned a few things from Argyle, before he died."

"Then what about Doctor Trintignant? That ghoul isn't remotely interested in solving the Spire. He hasn't contributed to a single problem yet. And yet he's already proved his value, hasn't he?"

"I don't follow."

Celestine rubbed her shunt. "These things. And the neural modifiers— Trintignant supervised their installation. And I haven't even mentioned Forqueray's arm, or the medical equipment aboard the shuttle."

"I still don't see what you're getting at."

"I don't know what leverage Childe's used to get his cooperation—it's got to be more than bribery or avarice—but I have a very, very nasty idea. And all of it points to something even more disturbing."

I was wearying of this. With the challenge of the next door ahead of us, the last thing I needed was paranoiac theory-mongering.

"Which is?"

"Childe knows too much about this place."

ANOTHER ROOM, ANOTHER wrong answer, another punishment.

It made the last look like a minor reprimand. I remembered a swift metallic flicker of machines emerging from hatches which opened in the seamless walls: not javelins now, but jointed, articulated pincers and viciously curved scissors. I remembered high-pressure jets of vivid arterial blood spraying the room like pink banners, the shards of shattered bone hammered against the walls like shrapnel. I remembered an unwanted and brutal lesson in the anatomy of the human body; the elegance with which muscle, bone and sinew were anchored to each other and the horrid ease with which they could be flensed apart—filleted—by surgically sharp metallic instruments.

I remembered screams.

I remembered indescribable pain, before the analgesics kicked in.

Afterwards, when we had time to think about what had happened, I do not think any of us thought of blaming Celestine for making another mistake. Childe's modifiers had given us a healthy respect for the difficulty of what she was doing, and—as before—her second choice had been the correct one; the one that opened a route back to the Spire's exit.

And besides...

Celestine had suffered as well.

It was Forqueray who had caught the worst of it, though. Perhaps the Spire, having tasted his blood once, had decided it wanted much more of it—more than could be provided by the sacrifice of a mere limb. It had quartered him: two quick opposed snips with the nightmarish scissors; a bisection followed an instant later by a hideous transection.

Four pieces of Forqueray had thudded to the Spire's floor; his interior organs were laid open like a wax model in a medical school. Various machines nestled neatly amongst his innards, sliced along the same planes. What remained of him spasmed once or twice, then—with the exception of his replacement arm, which continued to twitch—he was mercifully still. A moment or two passed, and then—with whiplash speed—jointed arms seized his pieces and pulled him into the wall, leaving slick red skidmarks.

Forqueray's death would have been bad enough, but by then the Spire was already inflicting further punishment.

I saw Celestine drop to the ground, one arm pressed around the stump of another, blood spraying from the wound despite the pressure she was applying. Through her visor her face turned ghostly.

Childe's right hand was missing all the fingers. He pressed the ruined hand against his chest, grimacing but managing to stay on his feet.

Trintignant had lost a leg. But there was no blood gushing from the wound; no evidence of severed muscle and bone. I saw only damaged mechanisms; twisted and snapped steel and plastic armatures, buzzing cables and stuttering optic fibres; interrupted feedlines oozing sickly green fluids.

Trintignant, nonetheless, fell to the floor.

I also felt myself falling, looking down to see that my right leg ended just below the knee; realising that my own blood was hosing out in a hard scarlet stream . I hit the floor—the pain of the injury having yet to reach my brain—and reached out in reflex for the stump. But only one hand presented itself; my left arm had been curtailed neatly above the wrist. In my peripheral vision I saw my detached hand, still gloved, perched on the floor like an absurd white crab.

Pain flowered in my skull.

I screamed.

SIX

"I'VE HAD ENOUGH of this shit," Hirz said.

Childe looked up at her from his recovery couch. "You're leaving us?"

"Damn right I am."

"You disappoint me."

"Fine, but I'm still shipping out."

Childe stroked his forehead, tracing its shape with the new steel gauntlet Trintignant had attached to his arm. "If anyone should be quitting, it isn't you, Hirz. You walked out of the Spire without a scratch. Look at the rest of us."

"Thanks, but I've just had dinner."

Trintignant lifted his silver mask towards her. "Now, there is no call for that. I admit the replacements I have fashioned here possess a certain brutal *esthétique*, but in functional terms they are without equal." As if to demonstrate his point, he flexed his own replacement leg.

It was a replacement, rather than simply the old one salvaged, repaired and reattached. Hirz—who had picked up as many pieces of us as she could manage—had never found the other part of Trintignant. Nor had an examination of the area around the Spire—where we had found the pieces of Forqueray—revealed any significant part of the doctor. The Spire had allowed us to take back Forqueray's arm after it had been severed, but it appeared to have decided to keep all metallic things for itself.

I stood up from my own couch, testing the way my new leg supported my weight. There was no denying the excellence of Trintignant's work. The prosthesis had interfaced with my existing nervous system so perfectly that I had already accepted the leg into my body image. When I walked on it I did so with only the tiniest trace of a limp, and that would surely vanish once I had grown accustomed to the replacement.

"I could take the other one off as well," Trintignant piped up, rubbing his hands together. "Then you would have perfect neural equilibrium... shall I do it?"

"You want to, don't you?"

"I admit I have always been offended by asymmetry."

I felt my other leg; the flesh and blood one felt so vulnerable, so unlikely to last the course.

"You'll just have to be patient," I said.

"Well, all things come to he who waits. And how is the arm doing?"

Like Childe, I now boasted one steel gauntlet instead of a hand. I flexed it, hearing the tiny, shrill whine of actuators. When I touched something I felt prickles of sensation; the hand was capable of registering subtle gradations of warmth or coldness. Celestine's replacement was very similar, although sleeker and somehow more feminine. At least our injuries had demanded as much, I thought; unlike Childe, who had lost only his fingers, but who had appeared to welcome more of the doctor's gleaming handiwork than was strictly necessary.

"It'll do," I said, remembering how much Forqueray had irritated the doctor with the same remark.

"Don't you get it?" Hirz said. "If Trintignant had his way, you'd be like him by now. Christ only knows where he'll stop."

Trintignant shrugged. "I merely repair what the Spire damages."

"Yeah. The two of you make a great team, Doc." She looked at him with an expression of pure loathing. "Well, sorry, but you're not getting your hands on me."

Trintignant appraised her. "No great loss, when there is so little raw material with which to work."

"Screw you, creep."

Hirz left the room.

"Looks like she means it when she says she's quitting," I said, breaking the silence that ensued.

Celestine nodded. "I can't say I entirely blame her either."

"You don't?" Childe asked.

"No. She's right. This whole thing is in serious danger of turning into some kind of sick exercise in self-mutilation." Celestine looked at her own steel hand, not quite masking her own revulsion. "What will it take, Childe? What will we turn into by the time we beat this thing?"

He shrugged. "Nothing that can't be reversed."

"But maybe by then we won't want it reversed, will we?"

"Listen, Celestine." Childe propped himself against a bulkhead. "What we're doing here is trying to beat an elemental thing. Reach its summit, if you will. In that respect the Blood Spire isn't very different to a mountain. It punishes us when we make mistakes, but then so do mountains. Occasionally, it kills. More often than not it leaves us only with a reminder of what it can do. Blood Spire snips off a finger or two. A mountain achieves the same effect with frostbite. Where's the difference?"

"A mountain doesn't enjoy doing it, for a start. But the Spire *does*. It's alive, Childe, living and breathing."

"It's a machine, that's all."

"But maybe a cleverer one than anything we've ever known before. A machine with a taste for blood, too. That's not a great combination, Childe."

He sighed. "Then you're giving up as well?"

"I didn't say that."

"Fine."

He stepped through the door which Hirz had just used.

"Where are you going?" I said.

"To try and talk some sense into her, that's all."

SEVEN

TEN HOURS LATER—BUZZING with unnatural alertness; the need for sleep a distant, fading memory—we returned to Blood Spire.

"What did he say to make you come back?" I said to Hirz, between one of the challenges.

"What do you think?"

"Just a wild stab in the dark, but did he by any chance up your cut?"

"Let's just say the terms were renegotiated. Call it a performance-related bonus."

I smiled. "Then calling you a mercenary wasn't so far off the mark, was it?"

"Sticks and stones may break my bones...sorry. Given the circumstances, that's not in the best possible taste, is it?"

"Never mind."

We were struggling out of our suits now. Several rooms earlier we had reached a point where it was impossible to squeeze through the door without first disconnecting our air lines and removing our backpacks. We could have done without the packs, of course, but none of us wanted to breathe Spire air until it was absolutely necessary. And we would still need the packs to make our retreat, back through the unpressurised rooms. So we kept hold of them as we wriggled between rooms, fearful of letting go. We had seen the way the Spire harvested first Forqueray's drone and then Trintignant's leg, and it was likely it would do the same with our equipment if we left it unattended.

"Why are you doing it, then?" asked Hirz.

"It certainly isn't the money," I said.

"No. I figured that part out. What, then?"

"*Because it's there.* Because Childe and I go back a long way, and I can't stand to give up on a challenge once I've accepted it."

"Old-fashioned bullheadedness, in other words," Celestine said.

Hirz was putting on a helmet and backpack assembly for the first time. She had just been forced to get out of her original suit and put on one of the skintights; even her small frame was now too large to pass through the constricted doors. Childe had attached some additional armor to her skintight—scablike patches of woven diamond—but she must have felt more vulnerable.

I answered Celestine. "What about you, if it isn't the same thing that keeps me coming back?"

"I want to solve the problems, that's all. For you they're just a means to an end, but for me they're the only thing of interest."

I felt slighted, but she was right. The nature of the challenges was less important to me than discovering what was at the summit; the secret the Spire so jealously guarded.

"And you're hoping that through the problems they set us you'll eventually understand the Spire's makers?"

"Not just that. I mean, that's a significant part of it, but I also want to know what my own limitations are."

"You mean you want to explore the gift that the Jugglers have given you?" Before she had time to answer I continued, "I understand. And it's never been possible before, has it? You've only ever been able to test yourself against problems set by other humans. You could never map the limits of your ability; any more than a lion could test its strength against paper."

She looked around her. "But now I've met something that tests me."

"And?"

Celestine smiled thinly. "I'm not sure I like it."

WE DID NOT speak again until we had traversed half a dozen new rooms, and then rested while the shunts mopped up the excess of tiredness which came after such efforts.

The mathematical problems had now grown so arcane that I could barely describe them, let alone grope my way towards a solution. Celestine had to do most of the thinking, therefore, but the emotional strain which we all felt was just as wearying. For an hour during the rest period I teetered on the edge of sleep, but then alertness returned like a pale, cold dawn. There was something harsh and clinical about that state of mind—it did not feel completely normal—but it enabled us to get the job done, and that was all that mattered.

We continued, passing the seventieth room—fifteen further than we had reached before. We were now at least sixty metres higher than when we had entered, and for a while it looked like we had found a tempo that suited us. It was a long time since Celestine had shown any hesitation in her answers, even if it took a couple of hours for her to reach the solution. It was as if she had found the right way of thinking, and now none of the challenges felt truly alien to her. For a while, as we passed room after room, a dangerous optimism began to creep over us.

It was a mistake.

In the seventy-first room, the Spire began to enforce a new rule. Celestine, as usual, spent at least twenty minutes studying the problem, skating her fingers over the shallowly etched markings on the frame, her lips moving silently as she mouthed possibilities.

Childe studied her with a peculiar watchfulness I had not observed before.

"Any ideas?" he said, looking over her shoulder.

"Don't crowd me, Childe. I'm thinking."

"I know, I know. Just try and do it a little faster, that's all."

Celestine turned away from the frame. "Why? Are we on a schedule suddenly?"

"I'm just a little concerned about the amount of time it's taking us, that's all." He stroked the bulge on his forearm. "These shunts aren't perfect, and—"

"There's something else, isn't there?"

"Don't worry. Just concentrate on the problem."

But this time the punishment began before we had begun our solution.

It was lenient, I suppose, compared to the savage dismembering that had concluded our last attempt to reach the summit. It was more of a stern admonishment to make our selection; the crack of a whip rather than the swish of a guillotine.

Something popped out of the wall and dropped to the floor.

It looked like a metal ball, about the size of a marble. For several seconds it did nothing at all. We all stared at it, knowing that something unpleasant was going to happen, but unsure what.

Then the ball trembled, and—without deforming in any way—bounced itself off the ground to knee-height.

It hit the ground and bounced again; a little higher this time.

"Celestine," Childe said, "I strongly suggest you come to a decision—"

Horrified, Celestine forced her attention back to the puzzle marked on the frame. The ball continued bouncing; reaching higher each time.

"I don't like this," Hirz said.

"I'm not exactly thrilled by it myself," Childe told her, watching as the ball hit the ceiling and slammed back to the floor, landing to one side of the place where it had begun its bouncing. This time its rebound was enough to make it hit the ceiling again, and on the recoil it streaked diagonally across the room, hitting one of the side walls before glancing off at a different angle. The ball slammed into Trintignant, ricocheting off his metal leg, and then connected with the walls twice—gaining speed with each collision—before hitting me in the chest. The force of it was like a hard punch, driving the air from my lungs.

I fell to the ground, emitting a groan of discomfort.

The little ball continued arcing around the room, its momentum not sapped in any appreciable way. It kept getting faster, in fact, so that its trajectory came to resemble a constantly shifting silver loom which occasionally intersected with one of us. I heard groans, and then felt a sudden pain in my leg, and the ball kept on getting faster. The sound it made was like a fusillade of gunshots, the space between detonation growing smaller.

Childe, who had been hit himself, shouted: "Celestine! Make your choice!"

The ball chose that moment to slam into her, making her gasp in pain. She buckled down on one knee, but in the process reached out and palmed one of the markings on the right side of the frame.

The gunshot sounds—the silver loom—even the ball itself—vanished.

Nothing happened for several more seconds, and then the door ahead of us began to open.

We inspected our injuries. There was nothing life-threatening, but we had all been bruised badly, and it was likely that a bone or two had been fractured. I was sure I had broken a rib, and Childe grimaced when he tried to put weight on his right ankle. My leg felt tender where the ball had struck me, but I could still walk, and after a few minutes the pain abated, soothed by a combination of my own medichines and the shunt's analgesics.

"Thank God we'd put the helmets back on," I said, fingering a deep bump in the crown. "We'd have been pulped otherwise."

"Would someone please tell me what just happened?" Celestine asked, inspecting her own wounds.

"I guess the Spire thought we were taking too long," Childe said. "It's given us as long as we like to solve the problems until now, but from now on it looks we'll be up against the clock."

Hirz said: "And how long did we have?"

"After the last door opened? Forty minutes or so."

"Forty-three, to be precise," Trintignant said.

"I strongly suggest we start work on the next door," Childe said. "How long do you think we have, Doctor?"

"As an upper limit? In the region of twenty-eight minutes."

"That's nowhere near enough time," I said. "We'd better retreat and come back."

"No," Childe said. "Not until we're injured."

"You're insane," Celestine said.

But Childe ignored her. He just stepped through the door, into the next room. Behind us the exit door slammed shut.

"Not insane," he said, turning back to us. "Just very eager to continue."

IT WAS NEVER the same thing twice.

Celestine made her selection as quickly as she could, every muscle tense with concentration, and that gave us—by Trintignant's estimation—five or six clear minutes before the Spire would demand an answer.

"We'll wait it out," Childe said, eyeing us all to see if anyone disagreed. "Celestine can keep checking her results. There's no sense in giving the fucking thing an answer before we have to; not when so much is at stake."

"I'm sure of the answer," Celestine said, pointing to the part of the frame she would eventually palm.

"Then take five minutes to clear your head. Whatever. Just don't make the choice until we're forced into it."

"If we get through this room, Childe..."

"Yes?"

"I'm going back. You can't stop me."

"You won't do it, Celestine, and you know it."

She glared at him, but said nothing. I think what followed was the longest five minutes in my life. None of us dared speak again, unwilling to begin anything—even a word—for fear that something like the ball would return. All I heard for five minutes was our own breathing; backgrounded by the awful slow thrumming of the Spire itself.

Then something slithered out of one wall.

It hit the floor, writhing. It was an inch-thick, three-metre-long length of flexible metal.

"Back off..." Childe told us.

Celestine looked over her shoulder. "You want me to press this, or not?"

"On my word. Not a moment before."

The cable continued writhing: flexing, coiling and uncoiling like a demented eel. Childe stared at it, fascinated. The writhing grew in strength, accompanied by the slithering, hissing sounds of metal on metal.

"Childe?" Celestine asked.

"I just want to see what this thing actually—"

The cable flexed and writhed, and then propelled itself rapidly across the floor in Childe's direction. He hopped nimbly out of the way, the cable passing under his feet. The writhing had become a continuous whipcracking now, and we all pressed ourselves against the walls. The cable—having missed Childe—retreated to the middle of the room and hissed furiously. It looked much longer and thinner than it had a moment ago, as if it had elongated itself.

"Childe," Celestine said, "I'm making the choice in five seconds, whether you like it or not."

"Wait, will you?"

The cable moved with blinding speed now, rearing up so that its motion was no longer confined to a few inches above the floor. Its writhing was so fast that it took on a quasi-solidity: an irregularly shaped pillar of flickering, whistling metal. I looked at Celestine, willing her to palm the frame, no matter what Childe said. I appreciated his fascination—the thing was entrancing to look at—but I suspected he was pushing curiosity slightly too far.

"Celestine..." I started saying.

But what happened next happened with lightning speed: a silver-grey tentacle of the blur—a thin loop of the cable—whipped out to form a double coil around Celestine's arm. It was the one Trintignant had already worked on. She looked at it in horror; the cable tightened itself and snipped the arm off. Celestine slumped to the floor, screaming.

The tentacle tugged her arm to the centre of the room, retreating back into the hissing, flickering pillar of whirling metal.

I dashed for the door, remembering the symbol she pressed. The whirl reached a loop out to me, but I threw myself against the wall and the loop merely brushed the chest of my suit before flicking back into the mass. From the whirl, tiny pieces of flesh and bone dribbled to the ground. Then another loop flicked out and snared Hirz, wrapping around her midsection and pulling her towards the centre.

She struggled—cartwheeling her arms, her feet skidding against the floor—but it was no good. She started shouting, and then screaming.

I reached the door.

My hand hesitated over the markings. Was I remembering accurately, or had Celestine intended to press a different solution? They all looked so similar now.

Then Celestine, who was still clutching her ruined arm, nodded emphatically.

I palmed the door.

I stared at it, willing it to move. After all this, what if her choice had been wrong? The Spire seemed to draw out the moment sadistically while behind me I continued to hear the frantic hissing of the whirling cable. And something else, which I preferred not to think about.

Suddenly the noise stopped.

In my peripheral vision I saw the cable retreating back into the wall, like a snake's tongue laden with scent.

Before me, the door began to open.

Celestine's choice had been correct. I examined my state of mind and decided that I ought to be feeling relief. And perhaps, distantly, I did. At least now we would have a clear route back out of the Spire. But we would not be going forward, and I knew not all us would be leaving.

I turned around, steeling myself against what I was about to see.

Childe and Trintignant were undamaged.

Celestine was already attending to her injury, fixing a tourniquet from her medical kit above the point where her arm ended. She had lost very little blood, and did not appear to be in very much discomfort.

"Are you all right?" I said.

"I'll make it out, Richard." She grimaced, tugging the tourniquet tighter. "Which is more than can be said for Hirz."

"Where is she?"

"It got her."

With her good hand, Celestine pointed to the place where the whirl had been only moments before. On the floor—just below the volume of air where the cable had hovered and thrashed—lay a small, neat pile of flailed human tissue.

"There's no sign of Celestine's hand," I said. "Or Hirz's suit."

"It pulled her apart," Childe said, his face drained of blood.

"Where is she?"

"It was very fast. There was just a…blur. It pulled her apart and then the parts disappeared into the walls. I don't think she could have felt much."

"I hope to God she didn't."

Doctor Trintignant stooped down and examined the pieces.

EIGHT

OUTSIDE, IN THE long, steely-shadowed light of what was either dusk or dawn, we found the pieces of Hirz for which the Spire had had no use.

They were half-buried in dust, like the bluffs and arches of some ancient landscape rendered in miniature. My mind played gruesome tricks with the shapes, turning them from brutally detached pieces of human anatomy into abstract sculptures: jointed formations that caught the light in a certain way and cast their own pleasing shadows. Though some pieces of fabric remained, the Spire had retained all the metallic parts of her suit for itself. Even her skull had been cracked open and sucked dry, so that the Spire could winnow the few small precious pieces of metal she carried in her head.

And what it could not use, it had thrown away.

"We can't just leave her here," I said. "We've got to do something, bury her...at least put up some kind of marker."

"She's already got one," Childe said.

"What?"

"The Spire. And the sooner we get back to the shuttle, the sooner we can fix Celestine and get back to it."

"A moment please," Trintignant said, fingering through another pile of human remains.

"Those aren't anything to do with Hirz," Childe said.

Trintignant rose to his feet slipping something into his suit's utility belt pocket in the process.

Whatever it had been was small; no larger than a marble or small stone.

"I'M GOING HOME," Celestine said, when we were back in the safety of the shuttle. "And before you try and talk me out of it, that's final."

We were alone in her quarters. Childe had just given up trying to convince her to stay, but he had sent me in to see if I could be more persuasive. My heart, however, was not in it. I had seen what the Spire could do, and I was damned if I was going to be responsible for any blood other than my own.

"At least let Trintignant take care of your hand," I said.

"I don't need steel now," she said, stroking the glistening blue surgical sleeve which terminated her arm. "I can manage without a hand until we're back in Chasm City. They can grow me a new one while I'm sleeping."

The doctor's musical voice interrupted us, Trintignant's impassive silver mask poking through into Celestine's bubble-tent partition. "If I may be so bold...it may be that my services are the best you can now reasonably hope to attain."

Celestine looked at Childe, and then at the doctor, and then at the glistening surgical sleeve.

"What are you talking about?"

"Nothing. Only some news from home which Childe has allowed me to see." Uninvited, Trintignant stepped fully into the room and sealed the partition behind him.

"What, Doctor?"

"Rather disturbing news, as it happens. Not long after our departure, something upsetting happened to Chasm City. A blight which afflicted everything contingent upon any microscopic, self-replicating system. Nanotechnology, in other words. I gather the fatalities were numbered in the millions..."

"You don't have to sound so bloody cheerful about it."

Trintignant navigated to the side of the couch where Celestine was resting. "I merely stress the point that what we consider state of the art medicine may be somewhat beyond the city's present capabilities. Of course, much may change before our return..."

"Then I'll just have to take that risk, won't I?" Celestine said.

"On your own head be it." Trintignant paused and placed something small and hard on Celestine's table. Then he turned as if to leave, but stopped and spoke again. "I am accustomed to it, you know."

"Used to what?" I said.

"Fear and revulsion. Because of what I have become, and what I have done. But I am not an evil man. Perverse, yes. Given to peculiar desires, most certainly. But emphatically not a monster."

"What about your victims, Doctor?"

"I have always maintained that they gave consent for the procedures I inflicted"—he corrected himself—"performed upon them."

"That's not what the records say."

"And who are we to argue with records?" The light played on his mask in such a fashion as to enhance the half-smile that was always there. "Who are we, indeed."

WHEN TRINTIGNANT WAS gone, I turned to Celestine and said, "I'm going back into the Spire. You realise that, don't you?"

"I'd guessed, but I still hope I can talk you out of it." With her good hand, she fingered the small, hard thing Trintignant had placed on the table. It looked like a misshapen dark stone—whatever the doctor had found amongst the dead—and for a moment I wondered why he had left it behind.

Then I said, "I really don't think there's much point. It's between me and Childe now. He must have known there'd come a point when I wouldn't be able to turn away."

"No matter what the costs?" Celestine asked.

"Nothing's without a little risk."

She shook her head, slowly and wonderingly. "He really got to you, didn't he."

"No," I said, feeling a perverse need to defend my old friend, even when I knew that what Celestine said was perfectly true. "It wasn't Childe, in the end. It was the Spire."

"Please, Richard. Think carefully, won't you?"

I said I would. But we both knew it was a lie.

NINE

CHILDE AND I went back.

I gazed up at it, towering over us like some brutal cenotaph. I saw it with astonishing, diamond-hard clarity. It was as if a smoky veil had been lifted from my vision, permitting thousands of new details and nuances of hue and shade to blast through. Only the tiniest, faintest hint of pixelation—seen whenever I changed my angle of view too sharply—betrayed the fact that this was not quite normal vision, but a cybernetic augmentation.

Our eyes had been removed, the sockets scrubbed and packed with far more efficient sensory devices, wired back into our visual cortices. Our eyeballs waited back at the shuttle, floating in jars like grotesque delicacies. They would be popped back in when we had conquered the Spire.

"Why not goggles?" I said when Trintignant had first explained his plans.

"Too bulky, and too liable to be snatched away. The Spire has a definite taste for metal. From now on, anything vital had better be carried as part of us—not just worn, but internalised." The doctor steepled his silver fingers. "If that repulses you, I suggest you concede defeat now."

"I'll decide what repulses me," I said.

"What else?" Childe said. "Without Celestine we'll need to crack those problems ourselves."

"I will increase the density of medichines in your brains," Trintignant said. "They will weave a web of fullerene tubes, artificial neuronal connections supplanting your existing synaptic topology."

"What good will that do?"

"The fullerene tubes will conduct nerve signals hundreds of times more rapidly than your existing synaptic pathways. Your neural computation rate will increase. Your subjective sense of elapsed time will slow."

I stared at the doctor, horrified and fascinated at the same time. "You can do that?"

"It's actually rather trivial. The Conjoiners have been doing it since the Transenlightenment, and their methods are well documented. With them I can make time slow to a subjective crawl. The Spire may give you only twenty minutes to solve a room, but I can make it feel like several hours; even one or two days."

I turned to Childe. "You think that'll be enough?"

"I think it'll be a lot better than nothing, but we'll see."

But it was better than that.

Trintignant's machines did more than just supplant our existing and clumsily slow neural pathways. They reshaped them, configuring the topology to enhance mathematical prowess, which took us onto a plateau beyond what the neural modifiers had been capable of doing. We lacked

Celestine's intuitive brilliance, but we had the advantage of being able to spend longer—subjectively, at least—on a given problem.

And, for a while at least, it worked.

TEN

"YOU'RE TURNING INTO a monster," she said.

I answered, "I'm turning into whatever it takes to beat the Spire."

I stalked away from the shuttle, moving on slender, articulated legs like piston-driven stilts. I no longer needed armour now: Trintignant had grafted it to my skin. Tough black plaques slid over each other like the carapacial segments of a lobster.

"You even sound like Trintignant now," Celestine said, following me. I watched her asymmetric shape loom next to mine: she lopsided; me a thin, elongated wraith.

"I can't help that," I said, my voice piping from the speech synthesiser that replaced my sealed-up mouth.

"You can stop. It isn't too late."

"Not until Childe stops."

"And then? Will even that be enough to make you give up, Richard?"

I turned to face her. Behind her faceplate I watched her try to conceal the revulsion she obviously felt.

"He won't give up," I said.

Celestine held out her hand. At first I thought she was beckoning me, but then I saw there was something in her palm. Small, dark and hard.

"Trintignant found this outside, by the Spire. It's what he left in my room. I think he was trying to tell us something. Trying to redeem himself. Do you recognise it, Richard?"

I zoomed in on the object. Numbers flickered around it. Enhancement phased in. Surface irregularity. Topological contours. Albedo. Likely composition. I drank in the data like a drunkard.

Data was what I lived for now.

"No."

ELEVEN

"I CAN HEAR something."

"Of course you can. It's the Spire, the same as it's always been."

"No." I was silent for several moments, wondering whether my augmented auditory system was sending false signals into my brain.

But there it was again: an occasional rumble of distant machinery, but one that was coming closer.

"I hear it now," Childe said. "It's coming from behind us. Along the way we've come."

"It sounds like the doors opening and closing in sequence."

"Yes."

"Why would they do that?"

"Something must be coming through the rooms towards us."

Childe thought about that for what felt like minutes, but was probably only a matter of actual seconds. Then be shook his head, dismissively. "We have eleven minutes to get through this door, or we'll be punished. We don't have time to worry about anything extraneous."

Reluctantly, I agreed.

I forced my attention back to the puzzle, feeling the machinery in my head pluck at the mathematical barbs of the problem. The ferocious clockwork that Trintignant had installed in my skull spun giddily. I had never understood mathematics with any great agility, but now I sensed it as a hard grid of truth underlying everything: bones shining through the thin flesh of the world.

It was almost the only thing I was now capable of thinking of at all. Everything else felt painfully abstract, whereas before the opposite had been the case. This, I knew, must be what it felt like to an idiot savant, gifted with astonishing skill in one highly specialised field of human expertise.

I had become a tool shaped so efficiently for one purpose that it could serve no other.

I had become a machine for solving the Spire.

Now that we were alone—and no longer reliant on Celestine—Childe had revealed himself as a more than adequately capable problem-solver. Several times I had found myself staring at a problem, with even my new mathematical skills momentarily unable to crack the solution, when Childe had seen the answer. Generally he was able to articulate the reasoning behind his choice, but sometimes there was nothing for it but for me to either accept his judgement or wait for my own sluggard thought processes to arrive at the same conclusion.

And I began to wonder.

Childe was brilliant now, but I sensed there was more to it than the extra layers of cognitive machinery Trintignant had installed. He was so confident now that I began to wonder if he had merely been holding back before, preferring to let the rest of us make the decisions. If that was the case, he was in some way responsible for the deaths that had already happened.

But, I reminded myself, we had all volunteered.

With three minutes to spare, the door eased open, revealing the room beyond. At the same moment the door we had come through opened as well, as it always did at this point. We could leave now, if we wished. At this time, as had been the case with every room we had passed through, Childe and I made a decision on whether to proceed further or not. There was always the danger that the next room would be the one that killed us—and every second that we spent before stepping through the doorway meant one second less available for cracking the next problem.

"Well?" I said.

His answer came back, clipped and automatic. "Onwards."

"We only had three minutes to spare on this one, Childe. They're getting harder now. A hell of a lot harder."

"I'm fully aware of that."

"Then maybe we should retreat. Gather our strength and return. We'll lose nothing by doing so."

"You can't be sure of that. You don't know that the Spire will keep letting us make these attempts. Perhaps it's already tiring of us."

"I still—"

But I stopped, my new, wasp-waisted body flexing easily at the approach of a footfall.

My visual system scanned the approaching object, resolving it into a figure, stepping over the threshold from the previous room. It was a human figure, but one that had, admittedly, undergone some alterations—although none that were as drastic as those that Trintignant had wrought on me. I studied the slow, painful way she made her progress. Our own movements seemed slow, but were lightning-fast by comparison.

I groped for a memory; a name; a face.

My mind, clotted with routines designed to smash mathematics, could not at first retrieve such mundane data.

Finally, however, it obliged.

"Celestine," I said.

I did not actually speak. Instead, laser light stuttered the mass of sensors and scanners jammed into my eyesockets. Our minds now ran too rapidly to communicate verbally, but, though she moved slowly herself, she deigned to reply.

"Yes. It's me. Are you really Richard?"

"Why do you ask?"

"Because I can hardly tell the difference between you and Childe."

I looked at Childe, paying proper attention to his shape for what seemed the first time.

At last, after so many frustrations, Trintignant had been given free rein to do with us as he wished. He had pumped our heads full of more processing machinery, until our skulls had to be reshaped to accommodate it, becoming sleekly elongated. He cracked our ribcages open and carefully removed our lungs and hearts, putting these organs into storage. The space vacated by one lung was replaced by a closed-cycle blood oxygenating system of the kind carried in spacesuit backpacks, so that we could endure vacuum and had no need to breathe ambient air. The other lung's volume was filled by a device which circulated refrigerated fluid along a loop of tube, draining the excess heat generated by the stew of neural machines filling our heads. Nutrient systems crammed the remaining thoracic spaces; our hearts were tiny fusion-powered pumps. All other organs—stomach, intestines, genitalia—were removed, along with many bones and muscles. Our remaining limbs were detached and put into storage, replaced by skeletal prosthetics of immense strength, but which could fold and deform to enable us to squeeze through the tightest door. Our bodies were encased in exoskeletal frames to which these limbs were anchored. Finally, Trintignant gave us whiplike counterbalancing tails, and then caused our skins to envelop our metal parts, hardening here and there in lustrous grey patches of organic armour, woven from the same diamond mesh that had been used to reinforce Hirz's suit.

When he was done, we looked like diamond-hided greyhounds.

Diamond dogs.

I BOWED MY head. "I am Richard."

"Then for God's sake please come back."

"Why have you followed us?"

"To ask you. One final time."

"You changed yourself just to come after me?"

Slowly, with the stone grace of a statue, she extended a beckoning hand. Her limbs, like ours, were mechanical, but her basic form was far less canine.

"Please."

"You know I can't go back now. Not when I've come so far."

Her answer was an eternity arriving. "You don't understand, Richard. This is not what it seems."

Childe turned his sleek, snouted face to mine.

"Ignore her," he said.

"No," Celestine said, who must have also been attuned to Childe's laser signals. "Don't listen to him, Richard. He's tricked and lied to you all along. To all of us. Even to Trintignant. That's why I came back."

"She's lying," Childe said.

"No. I'm not. Haven't you got it yet, Richard? Childe's been here before. This isn't his first visit to the Spire."

I convulsed my canine body in a shrug. "Nor mine."

"I don't mean since we arrived on Golgotha. I mean before that. Childe's been to this planet already."

"She's lying," Childe repeated.

"Then how did you know what to expect, in so much detail?"

"I didn't. I was just prudent" He turned to me, so that only I could read the stammer of his lasers. "We are wasting valuable time here, Richard."

"Prudent?" Celestine said. "Oh yes; you were damned prudent. Bringing along those other suits, so that when the first ones became too bulky we could still go on. And Trintignant—how did you know he'd come in so handy?"

"I saw the bodies lying around the base of the Spire," Childe answered. "They'd been butchered by it."

"And?"

"I decided it would be good to have someone along who had the medical aptitude to put right such injuries."

"Yes." Celestine nodded. "I don't disagree with that. But that's no more than part of the truth, is it?"

I looked at Childe and Celestine in turn. "Then what is the whole truth?"

"Those bodies aren't anything to do with Captain Argyle."

"They're not?" I said.

"No." Celestine's words arrived agonisingly slowly, and I began to wish that Trintignant had turned her into a diamond-skinned dog as well. "No. Because Argyle never existed. He was a necessary fiction—a reason for Childe knowing at least something about what the Spire entailed. But the truth…well, why don't you tell us, Childe?"

"I don't know what you want me to say."

Celestine smiled. "Only that the bodies are yours."

His tail flexed impatiently, brushing the floor. "I won't listen to this."

"Then don't. But Trintignant will tell you the same thing. He guessed first, not me."

She threw something towards me.

I willed time to move more slowly. What she had thrown curved lazily through the air, following a parabola. My mind processed its course and extrapolated its trajectory with deadening precision.

I moved and opened my foreclaw to catch the falling thing.

"I don't recognise it," I said.

"Trintignant must have thought you would."

I looked down at the thing, trying to see it anew. I remembered the doctor fishing amongst the bones around the Spire's base; placing something in one of his pockets. This hard, black, irregular, dully pointed thing.

What was it?

I half remembered.

"There has to be more than this," I said.

"Of course there is," Celestine said. "The human remains—with the exception of what's been added since we arrived—are all from the same genetic individual. I know. Trintignant told me."

"That isn't possible."

"Oh, it is. With cloning, it's almost child's play."

"This is nonsense," Childe said.

I turned to him now, feeling the faint ghost of an emotion Trintignant had not completely excised. "Is it really?"

"Why would I clone myself?"

"I'll answer for him," Celestine said. "He found this thing, but long, long before he said he did. And he visited it, and set about exploring it, using clones of himself."

I looked at Childe, expecting him to at least proffer some shred of explanation. Instead, padding on all fours, he crossed into the next room.

The door behind Celestine slammed shut like a steel eyelid.

Childe spoke to us from the next room. "My estimate is that we have nine or ten minutes in which to solve the next problem. I am studying it now and it strikes me as…challenging, to say the least. Shall we adjourn any further discussion of trivialities until we're through?"

"Childe," I said. "You shouldn't have done that. Celestine wasn't consulted…"

"I assumed she was on the team."

Celestine stepped into the new room. "I wasn't. At least I didn't think I was. But it looks like I am now."

"That's the spirit," Childe said. And I realized then where I had seen the small, dark thing that Trintignant had retrieved from the surface of Golgotha.

I might have been mistaken.

But it looked a lot like a devil's horn.

TWELVE

THE PROBLEM WAS as elegant Byzantine, multi-layered and potentially treacherous as any we had encountered.

Simply looking at it sent my mind careering down avenues of mathematical possibility, glimpsing deep connections between what I had always assumed were theoretically distant realms of logical space. I could have stared at it for hours, in a state of ecstatic transfixion. Unfortunately, we had to solve it, not admire it. And we now had less than nine minutes.

We crowded around the door and for two or three minutes—what felt like two or three hours—nothing was said.

I broke the silence, when I sensed that I needed to think about something else for a moment.

"Was Celestine right? Did you clone yourself?"

"Of course he did," she said. "He was exploring hazardous territory, so he'd have been certain to bring the kind of equipment necessary to regenerate organs."

Childe turned away from the problem. "That isn't the same as cloning equipment."

"Only because of artificially imposed safeguards," Celestine answered. "Strip those away and you can clone to your heart's content. Why regenerate a single hand or arm when you can culture a whole body?"

"What good would that do me? All I'd have done was make a mindless copy of myself."

I said, "Not necessarily. With memory trawls and medichines, you could go some way towards imprinting your personality and memory on any clone you chose."

"He's right," Celestine said. "It's easy enough to rescript memories. Richard should know."

Childe looked back at the problem, which was still as fiercely intractable as when we had entered.

"Six minutes left," he said.

"Don't change the fucking subject," Celestine said. "I want Richard to know exactly what happened here.

"Why?" Childe said. "Do you honestly care what happens to him? I saw that look of revulsion when you saw what we'd done to ourselves."

"Maybe you do revolt me," she said, nodding. "But I also care about someone being manipulated."

"I haven't manipulated anyone."

"Then tell him the truth about the clones. And the Spire, for that matter."

Childe returned his attention to the door, evidently torn between solving the problem and silencing Celestine. Less than six minutes now remained, and though I had distracted myself, I had not come closer to grasping the solution, or even seeing a hint of how to begin.

I snapped my attention back to Childe. "What happened with the clones? Did you send them in, one by one, hoping to find a way into the Spire for you?"

"No." He almost laughed at my failure to grasp the truth. "I didn't send them in ahead of me, Richard. Not at all. I sent them in *after* me."

"Sorry, but I don't understand."

"I went in first, and the Spire killed me. But before I did that, I trawled myself and installed those memories in a recently grown clone. The clone wasn't a perfect copy of me, by any means—it had some memories, and some of my grosser personality traits, but it was under no illusions that it was anything but a recently made construct." Childe looked back towards the problem. "Look, this is all very interesting, but I really think—"

"The problem can wait," Celestine said. "I think I see a solution, in any case."

Childe's slender body stiffened in anticipation. "You do?"

"Just a hint of one, Childe. Keep your hackles down."

"We don't have much time, Celestine. I'd very much like to hear your solution."

She looked at the pattern, smiling faintly. "I'm sure you would. I'd also like to hear what happened to the clone."

I sensed him seethe with anger, then bring it under control. "It—the new me—went back into the Spire and attempted to make further progress than its predecessor. Which it did, advancing several rooms beyond the point where the old me died."

"What made it go in?" Celestine said. "It must have known it would die in there as well."

"It thought it had a significantly better chance of survival than the last one. It studied what had happened to the first victim and took precautions—better armour; drugs to enhance mathematical skills; some crude stabs at the medichine therapies we have been using."

"And?" I said. "What happened after that one died?"

"It didn't die on its first attempt. Like us, it retreated once it sensed it had gone as far as it reasonably could. Each time, it trawled itself—making a copy of its memories. These were inherited by the next clone."

"I still don't get it," I said. "Why would the clone care what happened to the one after it?"

"Because…it never expected to die. None of us did. Call that a character trait, if you will."

"Overweening arrogance?" Celestine offered.

"I'd prefer to think of it as a profound lack of self-doubt. Each clone imagined itself better than its predecessor; incapable of making the same errors. But they still wanted to be trawled, so that—in the unlikely event that they were killed—something would go on. So that, even if that particular clone did not solve the Spire, it would still be something with my genetic heritage that did. Part of the same lineage. Family, if you will." His tail flicked impatiently. "Four minutes. Celestine…are you ready now?"

"Almost, but not quite. How many clones were there, Childe? Before you, I mean?"

"That's a pretty personal question."

She shrugged. "Fine. I'll just withhold my solution."

"Seventeen," Childe said. "Plus my original; the first one to go in."

I absorbed this number, stunned at what it implied. "Then you're… the nineteenth to try and solve the Spire?"

I think he would have smiled at that point, had it been anatomically possible. "Like I said, I try and keep it in the family."

"You've become a monster," Celestine said, almost beneath her breath.

It was hard not to see it that way as well. He had inherited the memories from eighteen predecessors, all of whom had died within the Spire's pain-wracked chambers. It hardly mattered that he had probably never inherited the precise moment of death; the lineage was no less monstrous for that small mercy. And who was to say that some of his ancestor clones had not crawled out of the Spire, horribly mutilated, dying, but still sufficiently alive to succumb to one last trawl?

They said a trawl was all the sharper if it was performed at the moment of death, when damage to the scanned mind mattered less.

"Celestine's right," I said. "You've become something worse than the thing you set out to beat."

Childe appraised me, those dense clusters of optics sweeping over me like gun barrels. "Have you looked in a mirror lately, Richard? You're not exactly the way nature intended, you know."

"This is just cosmetic," I said. "I still have my memories. I haven't allowed myself to become a"—I faltered, my brain struggling with vocabulary now that so much of it had been reassigned to the task of cracking the Spire—"a perversion," I finished.

"Fine." Childe lowered his head; a posture of sadness and resignation. "Then go back, if that's what you want. Let me stay to finish the challenge."

"Yes," I said. "I think I will. Celestine? Get us through this door and I'll come back with you. We'll leave Childe to his bloody Spire."

CELESTINE'S SIGH WAS one of heartfelt relief. "Thank God, Richard. I didn't think I'd be able to convince you quite that easily."

I nodded towards the door, suggesting that she sketch out what she thought was the likely solution. It still looked devilishly hard to me, but now that I refocused my mind on it, I thought I began to see the faintest hint of an approach, if not a full-blooded solution.

But Childe was speaking again. "Oh, you shouldn't sound so surprised," he said. "I always knew he'd turn back as soon as the going got tough. That's always been his way. I shouldn't have deceived myself that he'd have changed."

I bristled. "That isn't true."

"Then why turn back when we've come so far?"

"Because it isn't worth it."

"Or is it simply that the problem's become too difficult; the challenge too great?"

"Ignore him," Celestine said. "He's just trying to goad you into following him. That's what this has always been about, hasn't it, Childe? You think you can solve the Spire, where eighteen previous versions of you have failed. Where eighteen previous versions of you were butchered and flayed by the thing." She looked around, almost as if she expected the Spire to punish her for speaking so profanely. "And perhaps you're right, too. Perhaps you really have come closer than any of the others."

Childe said nothing, perhaps unwilling to contradict her.

"But simply beating the Spire wouldn't be good enough," Celestine said. "For you'd have no witnesses. No one to see how clever you'd been."

"That isn't true at all."

"Then why did we all have to come here? You found Trintignant useful, I'll grant you that. And I helped you as well. But you could have done without us, ultimately. It would have been bloodier, and you might have needed to run off a few more clones...but I don't doubt that you could have done it."

"The solution, Celestine."

By my estimate we had not much more than two minutes left in which to make our selection. And yet I sensed that it was time enough. Magically, the problem had opened up before me where a moment ago it had been insoluble; like one of those optical illusions which suddenly flip from one state to another. The moment was as close to a religious experience as I cared to come.

"It's all right," I said. "I see it now. Have you got it?"

"Not quite. Give me a moment..." Childe stared at it, and I watched as the lasers from his eyes washed over the labyrinthine engravings. The red glare skittered over the wrong solution and lingered there. It flickered away and alighted on the correct answer, but only momentarily.

Childe flicked his tail. "I think I've got it."

"Good," Celestine replied. "I agree with you. Richard? Are you ready to make this unanimous?"

I thought I had misheard her, but I had not. She was saying that Childe's answer was the right one; that the one I had been sure of was the wrong one...

"I thought..." I began. Then, desperately, I stared at the problem again. Had I missed something? Childe had looked to have his doubts, but Celestine was so certain of herself. And yet what I had glimpsed had appeared beyond question. "I don't know," I said weakly. "I don't know."

"We haven't time to debate it. We've got less than a minute."

The feeling in my belly was one of ice. Somehow, despite the layers of humanity that had been stripped from me, I could still taste terror. It was reaching me anyway; refusing to be daunted.

I felt so certain of my choice. And yet I was outnumbered.

"Richard?" Childe said again, more insistent this time.

I looked at the two of them, helplessly. "Press it," I said.

Childe placed his forepaw over the solution that he and Celestine had agreed on, and pressed.

I think I knew, even before the Spire responded, that the choice had not been the correct one. And yet when I looked at Celestine I saw nothing resembling shock or surprise in her expression. Instead, she looked completely calm and resigned.

And then the punishment commenced.

It was brutal, and once it would have killed us. Even with the augmentations Trintignant had given us, the damage inflicted was considerable as a scythe-tipped, triple-jointed pendulum descended from the ceiling and began swinging in viciously widening arcs. Our minds might have been able to compute the future position of a simpler pendulum, steering our bodies out of its harmful path. But the trajectory of a jointed pendulum was ferociously difficult to predict: a nightmarish demonstration of the mathematics of chaos.

But we survived, as we had survived the previous attacks. Even Celestine made it through, the flashing arc snipping off only one of her arms. I lost an arm and leg on one side, and watched—half in horror, half in fascination—as the room claimed these parts for itself; tendrils whipped out from the wall to salvage those useful conglomerations of metal and plastic. There was pain, of a sort, for Trintignant had wired those limbs into our nervous systems, so that we could feel heat and cold. But the pain abated quickly, replaced by digital numbness.

Childe got the worst of it, though. The blade had sliced him through the middle, just below what had once been his ribcage, spilling steel and plastic guts, bone, viscera, blood and noxious lubricants onto the floor. The tendrils squirmed out and captured the twitching prize of his detached rear end, flicking tail and all.

With the hand that she still had, Celestine pressed the correct symbol. The punishment ceased and the door opened.

In the comparative calm that followed, Childe looked down at his severed trunk.

"I seem to be quite badly damaged," he said.

But already various valves and gaskets were stemming the fluid loss; clicking shut with neat precision. Trintignant, I saw, had done very well. He had equipped Childe to survive the most extreme injuries.

"You'll live," Celestine said, with what struck me as less than total sympathy.

"What happened?" I asked. "Why didn't you press that one first?"

She looked at me. "Because I knew what had to be done."

DESPITE HER INJURIES she helped us on the retreat.

I was able to stumble from room to room, balancing myself against the wall and hopping on my good leg. I had lost no great quantity of blood, for while I had suffered one or two gashes from close approaches of the pendulum, my limbs had been detached below the points where they were anchored to flesh and bone. But I still felt the shivering onset of shock, and all I wanted to do was make it out of the Spire, back to the sanctuary of the shuttle. There, I knew, Trintignant could make me whole again. Human again, for that matter. He had always promised it would be possible, and while there was much about him that I did not like, I did not think he would lie about that. It would be a matter of professional pride that his work was technically reversible.

Celestine carried Childe, tucked under her arm. What remained of him was very light, she said, and he was able to cling to her with his undamaged forepaws. I felt a spasm of horror every time I saw how little of him there was, while shuddering to think how much more intense that spasm would have been were I not numbed by the medichines.

We had made it back through perhaps one third of the rooms when he slithered from her grip, thudding to the floor.

"What are you doing?" Celestine asked.

"What do you think?" He supported himself by his forelimbs, his severed trunk resting against the ground. The wound had begun to close, I saw, his diamond skin puckering tight to seal the damage.

Before very long he would look as if he had been made this way.

Celestine took her time before answering, "Quite honestly, I don't know what to think."

"I'm going back. I'm carrying on."

Still propping myself against a wall, I said, "You can't. You need treatment. For God's sake; you've been cut in half."

"It doesn't matter," Childe said. "All I've done is lose a part of me I would have been forced to discard before very long. Eventually the doors would have been a tight squeeze even for something shaped like a dog."

"It'll kill you," I said.

"Or I'll beat it. It's still possible, you know." He turned around, his rear part scraping against the floor, and then looked back over his shoulder. "I'm going to retrace my steps back to the room where this happened. I don't think the Spire will obstruct your retreat until I step—or crawl, as it may be—into the last room we opened. But if I were you, I wouldn't take too long on the way back." Then he looked at me, and again switched on the private frequency. "It's not too late, Richard. You can still come back with me."

"No," I said. "You're wrong. It's much too late."

Celestine reached out to help me make my awkward way to the next door. "Leave him, Richard. Leave him to the Spire. It's what he's always wanted, and he's had his witnesses now."

Childe eased himself onto the lip of the door leading into the room we had just come through.

"Well?" he said.

"She's right. Whatever happens now, it's between you and the Spire. I suppose I should wish you the best of luck, except it would sound irredeemably trite."

He shrugged; one of the few human gestures now available to him. "I'll take whatever I can get. And I assure you that we *will* meet again, whether you like it or not."

"I hope so," I said, while knowing it would never be the case. "In the meantime, I'll give your regards to Chasm City."

"Do that, please. Just don't be too specific about where I went."

"I promise you that. Roland?"

"Yes?"

"I think I should say goodbye now."

Childe turned around and slithered into the darkness, propelling himself with quick, piston-like movement of his forearms.

Then Celestine took my arm and helped me towards the exit.

THIRTEEN

"YOU WERE RIGHT," I told her as we made our way back to the shuttle. "I think I would have followed him."

Celestine smiled. "But I'm glad you didn't."

"Do you mind if I ask you something?"

"As long as it isn't to do with mathematics."

"Why did you care about what happened to me, and not Childe?"

"I did care about Childe," she said firmly. "But I didn't think any of us were going to be able to persuade him to turn back."

"And that was the only reason?"

"No. I also thought you deserved something better than to be killed by the Spire."

"You risked your life to get me out," I said. "I'm not ungrateful."

"Not ungrateful? Is that your idea of an expression of gratitude?" But she was smiling, and I felt a faint impulse to smile as well. "Well, at least that sounds like the old Richard."

"There's hope for me yet, then. Trintignant can put me back the way I should be, after he's done with you."

But when we got back to the shuttle there was no sign of Doctor Trintignant. We searched for him, but found nothing; not even a set of tracks leading away. None of the remaining suits were missing, and when we contacted the orbiting ship they had no knowledge of the doctor's whereabouts.

Then we found him.

He had placed himself on his operating couch, beneath the loom of swift, beautiful surgical machinery. And the machines had dismantled him, separating him into his constituent components, placing some pieces of him in neatly labelled fluid-filled flasks and others in vials. Chunks of eviscerated biomachinery floated like stinger-laden jelly-fish. Implants and mechanisms glittered like small, precisely jewelled ornaments.

There was surprisingly little in the way of organic matter.

"He killed himself," Celestine said. Then she found his hat—the Homburg—which he had placed at the head of the operating couch. Inside, tightly folded and marked in precise handwriting, was what amounted to Trintignant's suicide note.

> *My dear friends*, he had written.
>
> *After giving the matter no little consideration, I have decided to dispose of myself. I find the prospect of my own dismantling a more palatable one than continuing to endure revulsion for a crime I do not believe I committed. Please do not attempt to put me back together; the endeavour would, I assure you, be quite futile. I trust however that the manner of my demise—and the annotated state to which I have reduced myself—will provide some small amusement to future scholars of cybernetics.*
>
> *I must confess that there is another reason why I have chosen to bring about this somewhat terminal state of affairs. Why, after all, did I not end myself on Yellowstone?*
>
> *The answer, I am afraid, lies as much in vanity as anything else.*

Thanks to the Spire—and to the good offices of Mister Childe—I have been given the opportunity to continue the work that was so abruptly terminated by the unpleasantness in Chasm City. And thanks to yourselves—who were so keen to learn the Spire's secrets—I have been gifted with subjects willing to submit to some of my less orthodox procedures.

You in particular, Mister Swift, have been a Godsend. I consider the series of transformations I have wrought upon you to be my finest achievement to date. You have become my magnum opus. I fully accept that you saw the surgery merely as a means to an end and that you would not otherwise have consented to my ministrations, but that in no way lessens the magnificence of what you have become.

And therein, I am afraid lies the problem.

Whether you conquer the Spire or retreat from it—assuming, of course, that it does not kill you—there will surely come a time when you will desire to return to your prior form. And that would mean that I would be compelled to undo my single greatest work.

Something I would rather die than do.

I offer my apologies, such as they are, while remaining—

Your obedient servant,

T

Childe never returned. After ten days we searched the area about the Spire's base, but there were no remains that had not been there before. I supposed that there was nothing for it but to assume that he was still inside; still working his way to whatever lay at the summit.

And I wondered.

What ultimate function did the Spire serve? Was it possible that it served none but its own self-preservation? Perhaps it simply lured the curious into it, and forced them to adapt—becoming more like machines themselves—until they reached the point when they were of use to it.

At which point it harvested them.

Was it possible that the Spire was no more purposeful than a flytrap? I had no answers. And I did not want to remain on Golgotha pondering such things. I did not trust myself not to return to the Spire. I still felt its feral pull.

So we left.

"Promise me," Celestine said.

"What?"

"That whatever happens when we get home—whatever's become of the city—you won't go back to the Spire."

"I won't go back," I said. "And I promise you that. I can even have the memory of it suppressed, so it doesn't haunt my dreams."

"Why not," she said. "You've done it before, after all."

But when we returned to Chasm City we found that Childe had not been lying. Things had changed, but not for the better. The thing that they called the Melding Plague had plunged our city back into a festering, technologically-decadent dark age. The wealth we had accrued on Childe's expedition meant nothing now, and what small influence my family had possessed before the crisis had diminished even further.

In better days, Trintignant's work could probably have been undone. It would not have been simple, but there were those who relished such a challenge, and I would probably have had to fight off several competing offers: rival cyberneticists vying for the prestige of tackling such a difficult project. Things were different. Even the crudest kinds of surgery were now difficult or impossibly expensive. Only a handful of specialists retained the means to even attempt such work, and they were free to charge whatever they liked.

Even Celestine, who had been wealthier than me, could only afford to have me repaired, not rectified. That—and the other matter—almost bankrupted us.

And yet she cared for me.

There were those who saw us and imagined that the creature with her—the thing that trotted by her like a stiff, diamond-skinned, grotesque mechanical dog—was merely a strange choice of pet. Sometimes they sensed something unusual in our relationship—the way she might whisper an aside to me, or the way I might appear to be leading her—and they would look at me, intently, before I stared into their eyes with the blinding red scrutiny of my vision.

Then they would always look away.

And for a long time—until the dreams became too much—that was how it was.

Yet now I pad into the night, Celestine unaware that I have left our apartment. Outside, dangerous gangs infiltrate the shadowed, half-flooded streets. They call this part of Chasm City the Mulch and it is the only place where we can afford to live now. Certainly we could have afforded something better—something much better—if I had not been forced to put aside money in readiness for this day. But Celestine knows nothing of that.

The Mulch is not as bad as it used to be, but it would still have struck the earlier me as a vile place in which to exist. Even now I am instinctively wary, my enhanced eyes dwelling on the various crudely fashioned blades and crossbows that the gangs flaunt. Not all of the creatures who haunt the night are technically human. There are things with gills that can barely breathe in open air. There are other things that resemble pigs, and they are the worst of all.

But I do not fear them.

I slink between shadows, my thin, doglike form confusing them. I squeeze through the gaps in collapsed buildings, effortlessly escaping the few who are foolish enough to chase me. Now and then I even stop and confront them, standing with my back arched.

My red gaze stabs through them.

I continue on my way.

Presently I reach the appointed area. At first it looks deserted—there are no gangs here—but then a figure emerges from the gloom, trudging through ankle-deep caramel-brown flood-water. The figure is thin and dark, and with each step it makes there is a small, precise whine. It comes into view and I observe that the woman—for it is a woman, I think—is wearing an exoskeleton. Her skin is the black of interstellar space, and her small, exquisitely featured head is perched above a neck which has been extended by several vertebrae. She wears copper rings around her neck, and her fingernails—which I see clicking against the thighs of her exoskeleton—are as long as stilettos.

I think she is strange, but she sees me and flinches.

"Are you...?" she starts to say.

"I am Richard Swift," I answer.

She nods almost imperceptibly—it cannot be easy, bending that neck—and introduces herself. "I am Triumvir Verika Abebi, of the lighthugger *Poseidon*. I sincerely hope you are not wasting my time."

"I can pay you, don't you worry."

She looks at me with something between pity and awe. "You haven't even told me what it is you want."

"That's easy," I say. "I want you to take me somewhere."

THOUSANDTH NIGHT

I**T WAS** the afternoon before my threading, and stomach butterflies were doing their best to unsettle me. I had little appetite and less small talk. All I wanted was for the next twenty-four hours to slip by so that it could be someone else's turn to sweat. Etiquette forbade it, but there was nothing I'd have preferred than to flee back to my ship and put myself to sleep until morning. Instead I had to grin and bear it, just as everyone else had to when their night came around.

Waves crashed a kilometer below, dashing against the bone-white cliffs, the spray cutting through one of the elegant suspension bridges that linked the main island to the smaller ones surrounding it. Beyond the islands, the humped form of an aquatic crested the waves. I made out the tiny dots of people frolicking on the bridge, dancing in the spray. It had been my turn to design the venue for this carnival, and I thought I'd made a tolerable job of it.

A pity none of it would last.

In little over a year machines would pulverise the islands, turning their spired buildings into powdery rubble. The sea would have pulled them under by the time the last of our ships had left the system. But even the sea would only last a few thousand years after that. I'd steered water-ice comets onto this arid world just to make its oceans. The atmosphere itself was dynamically unstable. We could breathe it now, but there was no biomass elsewhere on Reunion to replenish the oxygen we were turning into carbon dioxide. In twenty thousand years the world would be uninhabitable to all but the hardiest micro-organisms. It would stay like that for the better part of another hundred and eighty thousand years, until our return.

By then the scenery would be someone else's problem, not mine. On Thousandth Night—the final evening of the reunion—the person who had threaded the most acclaimed strand would be charged with designing the venue for the next gathering. Depending on their plans, they'd arrive between one thousand and ten thousand years before the official opening of the next gathering.

My hand tightened on the rail at the edge of the high balcony as I heard urgent footsteps approach from behind. High hard heels on marble, the swish of an evening gown.

"Don't tell me, Campion. Nerves."

I turned around, greeting Purslane—beautiful, regal Purslane—with a stiff smile and a grunt of acknowledgement. "Mm. How did you guess?"

"Intuition," she said. "Actually, I'm surprised you're here at all."

"Why's that?"

"When it's my turn I'm sure I'll still be on my ship, furiously re-editing until the last possible moment."

"That's the problem," I said. "I've done all the editing I need. There's nothing *to* edit. Nothing of any consequence has happened to me since the last time."

Purslane fixed me with a knowing smile. Her hair was bunched and high, sculpted like a fairytale palace with spires and turrets. "Typical false modesty." She pushed a glass of red wine into my hand before I could refuse.

"Well, this time there's nothing false about it. My thread is going to be a crashing anti-climax. The sooner we get over it, the better."

"It's going to be that dull?"

I sipped at the wine. "The very exemplar of dullness. I've had a spectacularly uneventful two hundred thousand years."

"You said exactly the same thing last time, Campion. Then you showed us wonders and miracles. You were the hit of the reunion."

"Maybe I'm getting old," I said, "but this time I felt like taking things a little bit easier. I made a conscious effort to keep away from inhabited worlds; anywhere there was the least chance of something exciting happening. I watched a lot of sunsets."

"Sunsets," she said.

"Mainly solar-type stars. Under certain conditions of atmospheric calm and viewing elevation you can sometimes see a flash of green just before the star slips below the horizon..." I trailed off lamely, detesting the sound of my own voice. "All right. It's just scenery."

"Two hundred thousand years of it?"

"I'm not repentant. I enjoyed every minute of it."

Purslane sighed and shook her head: I was her hopeless case, and she didn't mind if I knew it. "I didn't see you at the orgy this morning. I was going to ask what you thought of Tormentil's strand."

Tormentil's memories, burned into my mind overnight, still had an electric brightness about them. "The usual self-serving stuff," I said. "Ever noticed that all the adventures he embroils himself in always end up making him look wonderful, and everyone else a bit thick?"

"True. This time even his usual admirers have been tut-tutting behind his back."

"Serves him right."

Purslane looked out to sea, through the thicket of hovering ships parked around the tight little archipelago. A layer of cloud had formed during the afternoon, with the ships—most of them stationed nose down—piercing it like daggers. There were nearly a thousand of them. The view resembled an inverted landscape: a sea of fog, interrupted by the sleek, luminous spires of tall buildings.

"Asphodel's ship still hasn't been sighted," Purslane said. "It's looking as if she won't make it."

"Do you think she's dead?"

Purslane dipped her head. "I think it's a possibility. That last strand of hers...a lot of risk-taking."

Asphodel's strand, delivered during the last reunion, had been full of death-defying sweeps past lethal phenomena. What had seemed beautiful then—a whiplashing binary star, or a detonating nova—must have finally reached out and killed her. Killed one of *us*.

"I liked Asphodel," I said absently. "I'll be sorry if she doesn't make it. Maybe she's just delayed."

"Why don't you come inside and stop moping?" Purslane said, edging me away from the balcony. "It's not good for you."

"I'm not really in the mood."

"Honestly, Campion. I'm sure you're going to startle us tonight."

"That depends," I said, "on how much you like sunsets."

THAT NIGHT MY memories were threaded into the dreams of the other guests. Come morning most of them managed to say something vaguely complimentary about my strand, but beneath the surface politeness their bemused disappointment was all too obvious. It wasn't just that my memories had added nothing startling to the whole. What really annoyed them was that I'd apparently gone out of my way to have as dull a time as possible. The implication was that I'd let the side down by looking for pointless green flashes rather than adventure; that I'd deliberately sought to add nothing useful to the tapestry of our collective knowledge.

By the afternoon, my patience was wearing perilously thin.

"Well, at least you won't be on the edge of your seat come Thousandth Night," said Samphire, an old acquaintance in the line. "That *was* the idea, wasn't it?"

"I'm sorry?"

"Deliberate dullness, to take you out of the running for best strand."

"That wasn't the idea at all," I said testily. "Still, if you think it was dull…that's your prerogative. When's your strand, Samphire? I'll be sure to offer my heartfelt congratulations when everyone else is sticking the boot in."

"Day eight hundred," he said easily. "Plenty of time to study the opposition and make a few judicious alterations." Samphire sidled a bit too close for comfort. I had always found Samphire cloying, but I tolerated his company because his strands were usually memorable. He had a penchant for digging through the ruins of ancient human cultures, looting their tombs for quaint technologies, grisly weapons, and machine minds driven psychotic by two million years of isolation. "So anyway," he said, conspiratorially. "Thousandth Night. *Thousandth Night.* Can't wait to see what you've got lined up for us."

"Nor can I."

"What's it going to be? You can't do a Cloud Opera, if that's what you've planned. We had one of those last time."

"Not a very good one though."

"And the time before that—what was it?"

"A recreation of a major space battle, I think. Effective, if a little on the brash side."

"Yes, I remember now. Didn't Fescue's ship mistake it for a real battle? Dug a ten-kilometer-wide crater into the crust when his screens went up. The silly fool had his defence thresholds turned down too low." Unfortunately, Fescue was in earshot. He looked at us over the shoulder of the line member he was talking to, shot me a warning glance then returned to his conversation. "Anyway," Samphire continued, oblivious. "What do you mean, you can't wait? It's your show, Campion. Either you've planned something or you haven't."

I looked at him pityingly. "You've never actually won best strand, have you?"

"Come close, though...my strand on the Homunculus Wars..." He shook his head. "Never mind. What's your point?"

"My point is that sometimes the winner elects to suppress their memories of exactly what form the Thousandth Night celebrations will take."

Samphire touched a finger to his nose. "I know you, Campion. It'll be tastefully restrained...and very, very dull."

"Good luck with your strand," I said icily.

Samphire left me. I thought I'd have a few moments alone, but no sooner had I turned to admire the view than Fescue leaned against the balustrade next to me, swilling a glass of wine. He held the glass by the stem, in jewelled and ringed fingers.

"Enjoying yourself, Campion?" he asked, in his usual deep-voiced, paternalistic, faintly disapproving way. The wind flicked iron-grey hair from his aristocratic brow.

"Yes, actually. Aren't you?"

"It's not a matter of enjoyment. Not for some us, at any rate. There's work to be done during these reunions—serious business, of great importance to the future status of the line."

"Lighten up," I said under my breath.

Fescue and I had never seen eye to eye. Among the nine hundred and ninety-three surviving members of the line, there were two or three dozen who exerted special influence. Though we had all been created at the same time, these figures had cultured a quiet superiority, distancing themselves from the more frivolous aspects of a reunion. Their body plans and clothes were studiedly formal. They spent a lot of time standing around in grave huddles, shaking their heads at the rest of us. They had the strongest ties to external lines. Many of them were Advocates, like Fescue himself.

If Fescue had heard my whispered remark, he kept it to himself. "I saw you with Purslane earlier," he said.

"It's not against the law."

"You spend a lot of time with her."

"Again…whose business is it? Just because she turned her nose up at your elitist little club."

"Careful, Campion. You've done well with this venue, but don't overestimate your standing. Purslane is a troublemaker—a thorn in the line."

"She's my friend."

"That's clear enough."

I bristled. "Meaning what?"

"I didn't see either of you at the orgy this morning. You spend a lot of time together, just the two of you. You sleep together, yet you disdain sexual relationships with the rest of your fellows. That isn't how we like to do things in Gentian Line."

"You Advocates keep yourselves to yourselves."

"That's different. We have duties…obligations. Purslane wouldn't understand that. She had her chance to join us."

"If you've got something to say, why not say it to her face?"

He looked away, to the brush-thin line of the horizon. "You did well with the aquatics," he said absently. "Nice touch. Mammals. They're from…*the old place*, aren't they?"

"I forget. What is this little pep talk about, Fescue? Are you telling me to keep away from Purslane?"

"I'm telling you to buck up your ideas. Start showing some *spine*, Campion. Turbulent times are coming. Admiring sunsets is all very well, but what we need now is hard data on emergent cultures across the entire Galaxy. We need to know who's with us and who isn't. There'll be all the time in the world for lolling around on beaches after we've completed the Great Work." Fescue poured the remains of his wine into my ocean. "Until then we need a degree of focus."

"Focus yourself," I said, turning away.

THINGS BEGAN TO improve in the afternoon, when interest shifted to the next evening's strand. Purslane found me again, attending to a whimsical redesign of one of the outlying towers. She told me that she had heard about an orgy on the fiftieth level of the main spire, very exclusive, and that I should join her there in an hour. Still stinging from Fescue's criticism, I told her that I was in no mood for it, but Purslane won me over and I agreed to meet when I was done with the tower.

When I arrived, the only other person there was Purslane.

"Wrong floor, I take it?"

"No," she said, standing on the perfectly transparent floor of an outflung balcony, so that she appeared to float two kilometers above the sea. "Right floor, right time. I told you it was exclusive."

"But you didn't tell me it was *this* exclusive," I said.

Purslane disrobed. As they stepped away, her clothes assumed the texture of weathered stone and froze into sculptural forms from deep antiquity. "Are you complaining?" she asked.

My own clothes broke up into a cloud of cherry blossom petals and scudded away across the floor. "Not exactly, no."

Purslane looked on approvingly. "I can tell."

We rolled around on the glass floor, which softened and hardened itself in perfect consideration of our needs. As we made love, I tried to remember whether I'd designed the glass floor to be transparent in both directions—and if so, what kind of entertainment we were providing to the line members who might be looking up to the fiftieth floor from below. Then I decided that I didn't care. If we outraged them, so be it.

"You were right," Purslane said, when we were lying together afterwards.

"Right about what?"

"The sunsets. Every bit as...challenging...as you said."

"Go on. Kick a man when he's down."

"Actually I admire your nerve," she said. "You had a plan and you stuck with it. And some of the sunsets were actually quite nice."

She'd meant it as a compliment, but I couldn't help looking wounded. "Quite nice."

Purslane conjured a grape and popped it into my mouth. "Sorry, Campion."

"It's all right," I said. "At least I won't have people pestering me for the rest of the carnival, trying to get at the memories I edited out of the strand. At least they'll know that's precisely as exciting as it gets."

It was true: the pressure was off, and to my surprise I actually started relaxing and enjoying the remaining days and nights. The last time, my submitted strand had been so well received that there'd been mutterings that I must have spiced things up for effect. I hadn't—those things really had happened to me—but I'd still spent the rest of the reunion in a state of prickly self-defence.

It was better now. I enjoyed feeling my mind filling with bright new experience; multiple snapshots of a dizzyingly complex and teeming Galaxy. It was the euphoria of drunkenness combined with an absolute, crystalline clarity of mind. It was glorious and overwhelming: an avalanche of history.

At the last count there were ten million settled solar systems out there. Fifty million planet-class worlds. Entire upstart civilisations had risen and fallen since the last reunion, several times over. With the passing of every reunion it seemed impossible that the wilder fringes of humanity could become any stranger, any less recognizable. Yet they always contrived to do so; oozing into every cosmic niche like molten lava, and then carving out new niches that no one had dared dreamed of before.

Two million years of bioengineering and cyborg reshaping had equipped humankind for any possible physical environment. Twenty thousand distinct branches of humanity had returned to alien seas, each adopting a different solution to the problem of aquatic life. Some were still more or less humanoid, but others had sculpted themselves into sleek sharklike things, or dextrous multi-limbed molluscs or hard-shelled arthropods. There were thirteen hundred distinct human cultures in the atmospheres of gas giants. Ninety that swam in the metallic hydrogen oceans under those atmospheres. There were vacuum dwellers and star dwellers. There were people who lived in trees, and people who had, by some definition, become trees themselves. There were people as large as small moons, which fostered entire swarming communities within their bodies. There were people who had encoded themselves into the nuclear structure of neutron stars, although no one had heard much from *them* lately. Against all this change, the nine hundred and ninety-three members of the Gentian Line must have appeared laughably quaint and antique, with our stolid adherence to traditional anatomy. But all this was just convention. Prior to arrival on the planet, we were free to adopt whatever forms we chose. The only rule was that when we emerged from our ships we must assume the forms of adult humans, and that we must bring our minds with us. Minor matters such as gender, build, pigmentation and sexual orientation were left to our discretion, but we were all obliged to carry the facial characteristics of Abigail Gentian: her high cheekbones, her strong jaw and the fact that her left eye was green and the other a wintery, jackdaw blue.

Everything else was up for grabs.

Perhaps it was the stirring up of the past as each new thread was added, but we all felt Abigail Gentian's base memories looming large in our thoughts as Thousandth Night approached. We remembered how it had felt to be just one individual, in the centuries before Abigail shattered herself into pieces and sent them roaming the Galaxy. We all remembered being Abigail.

Somewhere near the seven hundredth threading, I was again approached by Purslane. Her hair was styled in stiff spiral arms, like the structure of our galaxy. They twinkled with embedded gems: reds, yellows and hard blue-whites for different stellar populations.

"Campion?" she asked cautiously.

I turned from the balcony. I was repairing one of the bridges after a storm, knitting it back together with wizardlike hand movements, making the invisibly small machines that composed the bridge dance to my commands. Matter flowed like milk, and then hardened magically.

"Come to torment me about sunsets?"

"Not exactly. You and I need to talk."

"We could always go to one of those exclusive orgies," I said teasingly.

"I mean somewhere private. *Very* private." She seemed distracted, quite unlike her usual self. "Did you create a Secure on this island?"

"I didn't see the need. I can create one, if you think it's worth it."

"No: that'll just draw too much attention. We'll have to make do with my ship."

"I really need to finish this bridge."

"Finish it. I'll be on my ship whenever you're ready."

"What is this about, Purslane?"

"Be on my ship."

She turned away. A few moments later a square glass pane tumbled out of the sky and lowered itself to the ground. Purslane stepped onto the pane. Its edges expanded and then angled upward to form a box. The box rose into the air, carrying Purslane, and then suddenly accelerated away from the island. I watched it speed into the distance, the grey light occasionally flaring off one of its flat sides. The box became tiny and then just a twinkling dot. It vanished into the scarred, mountainous hull of an enormous waiting ship.

I returned to my bridge-repair work, wondering.

"**WHAT IS ALL** this about?"

"It's about your thread, among other things." She looked at me astutely, reclining in the lounge chair that her ship had provided. "You told us all the truth, didn't you? You really did spend two hundred thousand years watching sunsets?"

"If I wanted to make something up, don't you think I would have made it a tiny bit more exciting?"

"That's what I thought."

"Besides," I said. "I didn't *want* to win this time. Creating this venue was a major headache. You've no idea how much I agonised about the placement of these islands, let alone whatever I've cooked up for Thousandth Night."

"No, I can believe it. And I believe *you*. I just had to ask." She tugged down one of the spiral arms in her hair and bit on it nervously. "Though you could still be lying, I suppose."

"I'm not. Are you going to get to the point?"

My travel box had brought me into Purslane's hovering ship an hour after her departure. My ship was modestly sized for an interstellar craft; only three kilometers long, but Purslane's was enormous. It was two hundred kilometers from nose to tail, with a maximum width of twenty. The tail parts of her ship projected above the atmosphere, into the vacuum of space. By night they sparkled as anticollision fields intercepted and vaporised meteorites. Auroral patterns played around the upper extremities like a lapping tide.

There were many reasons why someone might need a ship this big. It might have been constructed around some antique but valuable moon-sized engine, or some huge, fabulously efficient prototype drive that no one else possessed. Any advance that could get you slightly closer to the speed of light was to be treasured. Or it might be that her ship carried some vast, secret cargo, like the entire sentient population of an evacuated planet. Or it might be that the ship had been made this big in a gesture of mad exuberance, simply because it was possible to do so. Or it might be—and here my thoughts choked on bitter alienness—that the ship had to be this big to contain its one living passenger. Purslane was human-sized now, but who was to say what her true form was like between our visits to Reunion?

I didn't want to know, and I didn't ask.

"The point is delicate," Purslane said. "I could be wrong about it. I almost certainly am. After all, no one else seems to have noticed anything unusual..."

"Anything unusual about what?"

"Do you remember Burdock's thread?"

"Burdock? Yes, of course." It was a silly, if understandable question. None of us were capable of forgetting any of the threaded strands unless we made a conscious effort to delete them. "Not that there was much about it *worth* remembering." Burdock was a quiet, low-profile line member who never went out of his way to make a show of himself. He'd threaded his strand a few weeks earlier. It had been uneventful, and I hadn't paid much attention to it. "It was almost as if he was trying to upstage me in the dullness stakes."

"I think he lied," Purslane said. "I think Burdock's thread was deliberately altered."

"By Burdock himself?"

"Yes."

"Why would he do that, though? The strand still wasn't very interesting."

"I think that was the point. I think he wanted to conceal something that did happen. He used dullness as a deliberate camouflage."

"Wait," I said. "How can you be sure things just weren't that dull?"

"Because of a contradiction," Purslane said. "Look, when the last reunion ended we all of us hared off into the Galaxy in different directions. As far as I'm aware, none of us swapped plans or itineraries."

"Forbidden, anyway," I said.

"Yes. And the chances of any of us bumping into each other between then and now were tiny."

"But it happened?"

"Not exactly. But I think *something* happened to Burdock: something that had him doctoring his thread to create a false alibi."

I shifted in my seat. These were serious allegations, far above the usual bitchy speculation that attended any private discussion about other members of the Gentian Line. "How can you know?"

"Because his memories contradict yours. I know: I've checked. According to your mutual strands, the two of you should have both been in the same system at the same time."

"Which system?"

She told me. It was an unremarkable place: just another star dipping into an alien sea, as far as I was concerned. "I was there," I said. "But I definitely didn't bump into Burdock." I rummaged through my memories, digging through mnemonic headers to those specific events. "He didn't come nearby either. No interstellar traffic came close to that world during my entire stay. His ship might have been stealthed..."

"I don't think it was. Anyway, he doesn't mention you either. Was your ship stealthed?"

"No."

"Then he'd have seen you arriving or departing. The interstellar medium's pretty thick near there. Relativistic ships can't help but carve a wake through it. He'd surely have made some mention of that if the strand was real."

She was right. Accidental encounters were always celebrated: a triumph of coincidence over the inhuman scale of the Galaxy.

"What do you think happened?"

"I think Burdock was unlucky," Purslane said. "I think he picked that world out of a hat, never imagining you'd visit it just when he claimed to be there."

"But his strand was threaded after mine. If he was going to lie..."

"I don't think he paid enough attention to your catalogue of sunsets," Purslane said. "Can't blame him, though, can you?"

"It could be me that's lying," I said.

"My money's still on Burdock. Anyway, that's not the only problem with his story. There are a couple of other glitches: nothing quite so egregious, but enough to make me pick through the whole thing looking for anomalies. That's when I spotted the contradiction."

I looked at her wonderingly. "This is serious."

"It could be."

"It must be. Harmless exaggeration is one thing. Even outright lying is understandable. But why would you replace the truth with something less interesting, unless you had something to hide?"

"That's what I thought as well."

"Why would he go to the trouble of creating an alibi, when he could just as easily delete the offending memories from his strand?"

"Risky," Purslane said. "Safer to swap the system he did visit with one in the same neck of the woods, so that it didn't throw his timings too far out, in case anyone dug too deeply into his strand."

"That doesn't help us work out where he was, though—the same neck of the woods still means hundreds of light years, thousands of possible systems."

"It's a big galaxy," said Purslane.

There was an uneasy silence. Far above us, beyond layers of armored metal, I heard the seismic groan as something colossal shifted and settled like a sleeping baby.

"Have you spoken to Burdock?"

"Not about this."

"Anyone else?"

"Just you," Purslane said. "I'm worried, Campion. What if Burdock did something?"

"A crime?"

"It's not unthinkable."

But unthinkable was precisely what it was. Gentian Line was not the only one of its kind. When Abigail shattered herself, others had done likewise. Some of those lines had died out over the intervening time, but most had endured in some shape or form. Although customs varied, most of those lines had something similar to Reunion: a place where they convened and re-threaded memories.

In the last two million years there had been many instances of contact between those lines. Until recently Gentian Line had been isolationist, but some of the others had formed loose associations. There had been treaties and feuds. One entire line had been murdered, when a rival line booby-trapped its equivalent of Reunion with an antimatter device left over from the War of the Local Bubble. Nowadays we were all a lot more careful. There were formal ties between many of the lines. There were agreed rules of behaviour. Feuds were out, marriages were in. There were plans for future collaboration, like the Great Work.

The Great Work was a project—not yet initiated—which would require the active cooperation of many lines. Whatever it was was *big*. Beyond that I knew nothing about it. I wasn't alone in my ignorance. Officially, no members of Gentian Line were privy to detailed knowledge about the Great Work. That information was held by an alliance of lines to which we hadn't yet been granted full membership. The expectation, however, was that it wouldn't be long before we were invited into the club. Among the guests on Reunion were ambassadors from other lines— some of which were in on the big secret. They were keeping an eye on us, sampling our strands, judging our wisdom and readiness.

Unofficially, there were also Gentian members who seemed to know something. I remembered Fescue's criticism of my strand: how there were turbulent times coming and how I'd have all the time in the world to loll around on beaches after the Great Work had been completed. Fescue—and a handful of other line members—had almost certainly been tipped off.

We called them the Advocates.

But while it seemed likely that we'd be invited to participate in the project before very long, we were also now at our most vulnerable. A single error could jeopardize our standing with the other lines. We'd all been mindful of this as we prepared our strands.

But what if one of us had done something truly awful? A crime committed by one Gentian Line member would reflect badly upon all of us. Technically, we were different manifestations of the same individual. If one Gentian member had it in them to do something bad, then it could be presumed that we all did.

If Burdock had indeed committed a crime, and if that crime came to light, then we might well be excluded from the Great Work.

"This could be bad," I said.

IT WAS VERY hard to behave normally in the days and weeks that followed. No matter where I went, I bumped into Burdock with unerring regularity. Our paths had hardly crossed during this latest carnival, but now he and I seemed doomed to meet each other every day. During these awkward encounters I kept fumbling for the right tone, hoping that I never gave away any hint of the suspicion Purslane and I felt. At the same time my mind spun out of control with imagined crimes. Like any members of a starfaring society, those of Gentian Line had terrible powers at their disposal. One of our ships, used carelessly, could easily incinerate a world. Deliberate action was even more chilling to contemplate. Members of other lines *had* committed atrocities in the remote past. History was paved with genocides.

But nothing about Burdock suggested a criminal streak. He wasn't ambitious. His strands had always been unmemorable. He'd never attempted to influence Gentian policy. He had no obvious enemies.

"Do you think anyone else knows?" I asked Purslane, during another covert meeting aboard her ship. "After all, the evidence is all out there in the public realm. Anyone else could spot those discrepancies if they paid enough attention."

"That's the point, though: I don't think anyone else will. You and I are friends. I probably paid more attention to your sunsets than anyone else did. And I'm a stickler for detail. I've been looking out for false threads during every carnival."

"Because you suspected one of us might lie?"

"Because it made it more interesting."

"Maybe we're making too much of this," I said. "Maybe he just did something embarrassing that he wanted to cover up. Not a crime, but just something that would have made him look foolish."

"We've all done foolish things. That hasn't stopped any of us including them in our strands when the mood suits us. Remember Orpine, during the third carnival?"

Orpine had made a fool of herself near the Whipping Star, SS433, nearly crashing her ship in the process. But her honesty had endeared her to the rest of us. She had been chosen to forge the venue for the fourth carnival. Ever since then, including an embarrassing anecdote in a strand had almost become *de rigueur*.

"Maybe we should talk to Burdock," I said.

"What if we're wrong? If Burdock felt aggrieved, we could be ostracized by the entire line."

"It's a risk," I admitted. "But if he has done something bad, the line has to know about it. It would look very bad if one of the other lines discovered the truth before we did."

"Maybe we're making a mountain out of a molehill."

"Or maybe we're not. Could we force the issue out into the open somehow? What if you publicly accuse *me* of lying?"

"Risky, Campion. What if they believe me?"

"They won't be able to find any chinks in my story because there aren't any. After due process, the attention will shift to Burdock. If, as you said, there are other things in his strand that don't check out…"

"I don't like it."

"Me neither. But it's not as if I can think of any other way of pursuing this."

"There might be one," Purslane said, eyeing me cautiously. "You built these islands, after all."

"Yes," I allowed.

"Presumably it wouldn't stretch your talents to spy on Burdock."

"Oh, no," I said, shaking my head.

She raised a calming hand. "I don't mean putting a bug on him, following him to his ship, or anything like that. I just mean keeping a record of anything he does or says in public. Is your environment sophisticated enough to allow that?"

I couldn't lie. "Of course. It's constantly monitoring everything we do in public anyway, for our own protection. If someone has an accident…"

"So what's the problem?"

"The environment doesn't report to me. It keeps this kind of thing to itself."

"But it could be programmed to report to you," Purslane said.

I squirmed. "Yes."

"I realise this is unorthodox, Campion. But I think we have to do it, given all that could be at stake."

"Burdock may say nothing."

"We won't know unless we try. How long would it take you to arrange this?"

"It's trivial," I admitted.

"Then do it. Last night was the eight hundred and third threading. There are less than two hundred days before we all leave Reunion. If we don't find out what Burdock's up to now, we may never have another chance." Purslane's eyes gleamed thrillingly. "We haven't a moment to lose."

PURSLANE AND I agreed that we should keep our meetings to a minimum from then on, in case we began to draw attention to ourselves. Liaisons between line members were normal enough—even long-term relationships—but the fact that we insisted on meeting out of the public eye was bound to raise eyebrows. Even given the absence of a single Secure anywhere in the venue, there were plenty of places that were private enough for innocent assignations.

But our assignation was anything but innocent.

It wasn't difficult to keep in touch, once we'd agreed a scheme. Since I had designed and constructed the venue, the machinery that handled the threading of the strands into our nightly dreams lay under my control. Each evening, I took the environment's covert observations of Burdock over the last day, and ran a simple program to isolate those instances where Burdock was talking to someone else or accessing data from one of the public nodes I'd dotted around the venue. I then took those isolated sequences and slipped them into Purslane's dreams, along with the allotted strand for that night. I did the same for myself: it meant that we had more to dream than everyone else, but that was a small price to pay.

By day, as we fulfilled our social obligations, we reviewed the Burdock data independently. The agreement was that if either of us noticed something unusual, we should leave a signal for the other party. Since I ran the venue, my signal consisted of a change to the patterning of the floor tiles on the thirtieth level terrazzo, cunningly encoding the time of the unusual event in the Burdock data. I'd been fiddling around with the patterns long before the Burdock affair, so there was nothing odd about my actions as far as anyone else was concerned. As for Purslane, she'd agreed to stand at noon at a certain position on one of my spray-lashed suspension bridges. By counting the number of wires between her and land, I could isolate the anomaly to within a few tens of minutes.

We'd agreed that we wouldn't meet in person until we'd had time to review each other's observations. If we agreed that there was something worth talking about, then we'd "accidentally" meet each other within the next few days. Then we'd judge the right moment to slip away to Purslane's ship. In practise, days and weeks would go by without Burdock doing anything that we both agreed was noteworthy or odd. Now and then he'd do or say something that hinted at a dark personal secret—but under that level of scrutiny, it was difficult to think of anyone who wouldn't. And who among us didn't have some secrets, anyway?

But by turns we noticed something that we couldn't dismiss.

"THIS IS THE third time that he's fished for information about the Great Work," Purslane said.

I nodded. On three occasions, Burdock had steered his conversations with other line members around to the subject of the Great Work. "He's very discreet about it," I said. "But you can tell he's itching to know more about it. But don't we all?"

"Not to that degree," she said. "I'm curious. I'd like to know what it is that has the lines so stirred up. But at the same time it doesn't keep me awake at night. I know that the secret will eventually be revealed. I'm patient enough to wait until then."

"Really?" I asked.

"Yes. And besides—I've heard enough rumours to think that I know half the answer already."

That was news to me. "Go on."

"It's about knitting the worlds of the lines into a cohesive entity—a Galactic Empire, if you like. At the moment such a thing clearly isn't practical. It takes us two hundred thousand years just to make one sweep through the Galaxy. That's much too long on a human scale. We might not experience much time passing in our ships, but that doesn't apply to the people living on planets. Entire cultures wax and wane while we're making course adjustments. Some of the people down on those planets have various forms of immortality, but that doesn't make history pass any less quickly. And it's history that keeps destroying things. It's history that stops us reaching our full potential."

"I'm not sure I follow you," I said.

"Think of all those myriad human cultures," Purslane said. "To all intents and purposes, they exist independently of each other. Those within a few light years of each other can exchange ideas and perhaps even enjoy a degree of trade. Most are too far apart from that: at best they might have some vague knowledge of each other's existence, based on transmissions and data passed on by the likes of you and me. But what can two cultures on either side of the Galaxy know of each other? By the time one gets to hear about the other, the other probably doesn't exist any more. There's no possibility of mutual cooperation; the sharing of intellectual resources and knowledge." Purslane shrugged. "So those cultures stumble through the dark, making the same mistakes over and over again, constantly reinventing the wheel. At best they have some knowledge of galactic history, so they can avoid repeating the worst mistakes. At worst they're evolving in near-total ignorance. Some of them don't even remember how they got where they are."

I echoed Purslane's shrug. "But that's the way things must be. It's human nature for us to keep changing, to keep experimenting with new societies, new technologies, new modes of thought..."

"The very experiments that rip societies apart, and keep the wheel of history turning."

"But if we weren't like that, we wouldn't be human. Every culture in the Galaxy has the means to engineer itself into social stasis tomorrow, if the will were there. Some of them have probably tried it. But what's the point? We might stop the wheel of history turning, but we wouldn't be human anymore."

"I agree," Purslane said. "Meddling in human nature isn't the solution. But imagine if the intellectual capacity of the entire human Diaspora could somehow be tapped. At the moment those cultures are bumping around like random atoms in a gas. What if they could be brought into a state of coherence, like the atoms in a laser? Then there'd be real progress, with each achievement leading to the next. Then we could really start *doing* something."

I almost laughed. "We're immortal superbeings who've lived longer than some starfaring civilisations, including many Priors. If we choose, we can cross the Galaxy in the gap between thoughts. We can make worlds and shatter suns for our amusement. We can sip from the dreams and nightmares of fifty million billion sentient beings. Isn't that enough for you?"

"It might be enough for you and I, Campion. But then we've always had modest ambitions."

"But what about Burdock?" I asked. "He isn't linked to the Advocates, as far as I'm aware. I don't think he's been actively frozen out, but he certainly hasn't spent any time cultivating the right connections."

"I'll have to review the recordings again," Purslane said. "But I'm pretty sure none of his enquiries were directed at known Advocates. He was targeting people on the fringe: line members who might know something, without being directly privy to the big secret."

"Why wouldn't he just ask the Advocates directly?"

"Good question," Purslane said. "Of course, we could always ask *him*."

"Not until we know a bit more about what he's involved in."

"You know," Purslane said. "There's something else we could consider."

The tone of her voice prickled the hairs on the back of my neck. "I'm not going to like this, am I?"

"We could examine the records on his ship and find out what he was really up to."

"He's hardly likely to give us permission to do that."

"I wasn't talking about asking his permission." Purslane's smile was wicked and thrilling: she was actually enjoying our little adventure. "I was talking about going aboard and finding out for ourselves."

"Just like that, without so much as a by-your-leave?"

"I'm not saying it would be easy. But you did make this venue, Campion. Surely it isn't beyond your immense capabilities to engineer a distraction."

"Flattery," I said, "will get you almost anywhere. But what about breaking into his ship? That won't exactly be child's play."

Purslane pressed a dainty finger to my lip. "I'll worry about the ship. You worry about the distraction."

We maintained our vigil on Burdock over the coming weeks, as our dangerous, delicious plan slowly came together. Burdock kept up the pattern of behaviour we had already noted, asking questions that probed the nature of the Great Work, but never directing his queries to known Advocates. More and more it seemed to us that there was something about the Work that had alarmed him; something too sensitive to bring to the attention of those who had a vested interest in the thing itself. But since Purslane and I were none the wiser about what the Great Work actually entailed, we could only guess about what it was that had unnerved Burdock. We both agreed that we needed to know more, but our suspicions about Burdock (and, by implication, Burdock's own suspicions) meant that we were just as incapable of putting direct questions to the Advocates. Day by day, therefore, I found myself making surreptitious enquires much like those made by Burdock himself. I endeavoured to target my questioning at different people than the ones Burdock had buttonholed, not wanting to spark anyone else's curiosity. Purslane did likewise, and—even as we planned our utterly illegal raid on Burdock's ship—we pieced together the tidbits of information we had gathered.

None of it was very illuminating, but by the same token little of it contradicted Purslane's conviction that the Great Work was related to the emergence of a single, Galaxy-spanning Supercivilisation. There were dark, glamorous rumours concerning the covert development of technologies that would bring this state of affairs into being.

"It must be related to the slowness of interstellar communication," I mused. "That's the fundamental objection, no matter which way you look at it. No signals or ships can cross the Galaxy quickly enough to make any kind of orthodox political system possible. And the lines are too independent to tolerate the kind of social engineering we talked about before. They won't accept any kind of system that imposes limits on human creativity."

"No one takes faster than light travel seriously, Campion."

"It doesn't have to involve travel. A signalling mechanism would be just as useful. We could all stay at home, and communicate via clones or robots. Instead of sending my body to another planet, I'd piggyback a host body that was already there." I shrugged. "Or use sensory stimulation to create a perfect simulation of the other planet and all its inhabitants. Either way, I wouldn't be able to tell the difference. Why would I care?"

"But in two million years," Purslane said, "no culture in the Galaxy has come close to developing faster-than-light communication or travel."

"Lots of people have tried, though. What if some of them succeeded, but kept their breakthrough secret?"

"Or were wiped out to protect the status quo? We can play this game forever. The fact is, faster-than-light travel—or signalling, for that matter—looks even less likely now than it did a million years ago. The universe simply isn't wired to permit it. It's like trying to play chequers on a chess board."

"You're right of course," I said, sighing. "I studied the mathematics once, for a century. It looks pretty watertight, once you get your head around it. But if that's not the answer..."

"I don't think it is. We should keep open minds, of course...but I think the Great Work has to be something else. What, though, I can't imagine."

"That's as far as you've got?"

"I'm afraid so. But don't look so disappointed, Campion. It really doesn't become you."

THEN SOMETHING ODD happened to Burdock. The first hint of it was his flawless navigation of the Mood Maze.

It was customary to sprinkle harmless entertainments and diversions through the nights of the Reunion. On the afternoon of the eight hundred and seventieth night, I opened the maze on one of the high balconies, with a modest prize for the line member who found their way through it the fastest. The maze would remain in existence until the nine hundredth night; time enough for everyone to have a try at it.

But the Mood Maze was no ordinary labyrinth. Based on a game I had discovered during my travels, a Mood Maze was sensitive to emotional states, which the maze detected using a variety of subtle cues and mildly invasive sensors. As long as one remained perfectly calm, a Mood Maze held a fixed geometry. But as soon as the walls detected the slightest suggestion of frustration, the geometry of the maze underwent a sly modification: walls and gaps moving to block one route and open up another. The more frustrated one became, the more tortuous the labyrinth made itself. Extremes of anger could even cause the maze to form a closed-loop around the hapless player, so that they had no choice but to wander in circles until they calmed down. Needless to say, it was considered very bad form to enter a Mood Maze with anything other than baseline human intelligence. Extreme faculties of memory or spatial positioning had to be turned off before participation.

The Mood Maze was a pleasant enough diversion, and popular with most of those who took a chance on it. But I'd had more than that in mind when I set it up. I'd hoped that the maze would tell me something about Burdock's state of mind, if only he would participate. Since it was voluntary, I couldn't be accused of violating his mental privacy.

But when I ran the maze, Burdock sailed through it, with the walls registering hardly any change to his emotional state. Cheating could not be ruled out, though it was unlikely: a Mood Maze was designed to detect most forms of subterfuge and punish them accordingly. And if he had that much to hide, it would not have been hard to avoid the maze entirely.

What surprised me was the degree of frustration I saw in some of the other participants. When a group of Advocates wagered among themselves as to who would beat the maze the quickest, it was Fescue who ended up with the humiliation of being trapped in a closed-loop. His rage built to a crescendo until I tactfully intervened and allowed him an exit.

I greeted him as he left the maze. "Challenging little devil," I said lightly, trying to calm things down.

"A childish little prank," he said, spitting fury. "But then I shouldn't have expected any better from you."

"It's just a game. You didn't have to take part."

"That's all anything is to you, isn't it? Just a game with no consequences." He glanced at the other Advocates, who were looking on with amused expressions. "You have no idea what's at stake here. Even if you did, you'd shrivel from any hint of responsibility."

"All right," I said, holding up my hands in defeat. "I'll forbid you from taking part in any of my games. Will that make you happy?"

"What would make me happy..." Fescue began, before scowling and making to turn away.

"It's Purslane, isn't it," I said.

He lowered his voice to a hiss. "I've given you fair warning. But to what purpose? You continue to associate with her to the exclusion of others. Your sexual relations verge on the monogamous. You spit on the traditions of the line."

I kept my voice level, refusing to rise to his bait. "All this because of a maze, Fescue? I never had you down as quite that bad a loser."

"You have no idea what is at stake," he repeated. "Change is coming, Campion—violent, sudden change. The only thing that will hold the line together is self-sacrifice."

"Is this about the Great Work?" I asked.

"It's about duty," he said. "Something you seem incapable of grasping." He looked back at my maze, as if willing it to crumble to dust. "Keep playing with your toys, Campion. Fritter away your days in idleness and dissipation. Leave the important things to the rest of us."

Fescue stalked off. I stood blinking, regretting the fact that I had mentioned the Great Work. Now my interest in it was known to at least one Advocate.

A hand touched my shoulder. "I see the old fart's giving you a hard time again."

It was Samphire, pushing into my personal space. Normally I would have edged away, but for once I relaxed in his presence, glad to unburden myself.

"I don't think he was thrilled about the Mood Maze," I said.

"Don't take it personally. He's been acting odd for weeks, giving everyone hard stares. What's his problem?"

"Fescue doesn't like me spending time with Purslane."

"Only because the craggy bastard couldn't get a shag out of her."

"I think there's a bit more to it than that. Fescue's mixed up in something. You know what I mean, don't you."

Samphire kept his voice low. "No idea at all. Other than that it's a *work* and it's *great*. Are you any more clued up about it than me?"

"I doubt it," I said. "But whatever it is, Fescue think it's a lot more important than the kind of lazy, self-indulgent things Purslane and I tend to get up to."

"Has he tried to rope you in?"

"Not sure. I can't work out whether he totally disapproves of me on every level, or whether he's just bitterly disappointed that I waste so much potential talent."

"Well, I wouldn't lose any sleep over it. Fescue's just a wasted old bore. His strand didn't exactly set the island ringing, did it?"

"Nor did mine."

"Difference is Fescue obviously expected more. Between you and me..." Samphire hesitated and looked around. "I think he was just a tiny bit economical with the facts."

I frowned. "You're saying he fiddled his strand?"

"A few details here and there. We came close to meeting around the Hesperus Veil: near enough to exchange recognition protocols."

I nodded. There'd been a supernova near the Hesperus Veil, and a number of us had planned close approaches to it. "That's not enough to prove that he lied, though."

"No," Samphire said. "But according to his strand he skipped the Veil altogether. Why lie about that? Because either before or after that he was somewhere else he didn't want us to know about. Probably somewhere a lot less exciting than the places that showed up in his strand."

I felt a tingling sensation, wondering if Fescue might also be implicated in the Burdock business. Could the two of them be accomplices?

"That's a pretty heavy accusation," I said, my mind reeling.

"Oh, I'm not going to make anything of it. I've already edited down my own strand so as not to embarrass him. Let him trip himself up. He's bound to do it one of these days."

"I suppose you're right," I said, not quite able to suppress my disappointment. The idea of seeing Fescue publicly humiliated—revealed as fabricating chunks of his strand—tasted shamefully delicious.

"Don't let him get to you too much," Samphire said. "He's just a sad old man with too much time on his hands."

"The funny thing," I said, "is that he's no older than the rest of us."

"He *acts* old. That's all that matters."

Samphire's revelation improved my mood, and I took great delight in telling Purslane what I had learned. Robbed of their sting, Fescue's warnings only emboldened the two of us. Time and again, as covertly as we dared, we met aboard her ship and discussed what we had learned.

It was there that I mentioned Burdock's swift passage through the maze.

"He could have been cheating," I said. "His emotional registers were all very flat, according to the maze."

"I don't see why he'd cheat," Purslane answered. "Admittedly, he doesn't have much prestige in the line—but there are other ways he could have won it by now, if it mattered to him that much. It's almost as if he did the maze because he felt obliged to do so...but that it just wasn't difficult for him."

"There's something else, too," I said. "I'm not sure if I'd have noticed it were it not for the whole business with the maze...but ever since then, I've been watching for anything even more out of the ordinary than normal."

"You've seen something?"

"More a case of what he hasn't been doing, rather than what he has been doing, if that makes any sense."

Purslane nodded sagely. "I noticed too—if we're talking about the same thing. It's been going on for at least a week now."

"Then it isn't just me," I said, relieved that she had shared my observation.

"I wasn't sure whether to say anything. It's not that there's been any dramatic change in his behaviour, just that..."

I completed her sentence for her: an annoying habit I'd spent the last million years trying to break. "...he isn't poking around the Great Work any more."

Purslane's eyes gleamed confirmation. "Exactly."

"Unless I've missed something, he's given up trying to find what it's all about."

"Which tells us one of two possibilities," Purslane said. "Either he thinks he knows enough by now..."

"Or someone has scared him off."

"We really need to take a look at that ship of his," she said. "Now more than ever."

PURSLANE HAD DONE her homework. During one of Burdock's visits to his ship, she had shadowed him with a drone, a glassy dragonfly small and transparent enough to slip undetected into his travel box. The drone had eavesdropped on the exchange of recognition protocols between the box and the hovering ship. A second visit confirmed that the protocol had not changed since the last time: Burdock wasn't using some randomly varying key. There was nothing too surprising about that: we were all meant to be family, after all, and many of the parked ships probably had no security measures at all. It was simply not the done thing to go snooping around without permission.

That was one half of the problem cracked, at least. We could get aboard Burdock's ship, but we would still need to camouflage our departure and absence from the island.

"I hope you've given some thought to this," Purslane said.

Well, I had: but I didn't think she was going to like my suggestion overmuch.

"Here's one idea," I said. "I have the entire island under surveillance, so I always know where Burdock is at a given moment, and what he's doing."

"Go on."

"We wait until my systems pick an interval when Burdock's otherwise engaged. An orgy, a game, or a long, distracting conversation..."

Purslane nodded provisionally. "And if he bores of this orgy, or game, or conversation, and extricates himself prematurely?"

"That'll be trickier to handle," I admitted. "But the island is still mine. With some deft intervention I might be able to hold him on the ground for an hour or two before he gets too suspicious."

"That might not be long enough. You can't very well make him a prisoner."

"No, I can't."

"And even if you did manage to keep Burdock occupied for as long as we need, there's the small problem of everyone else. What if someone sees us entering or leaving his ship?"

"That's also a problem," I said. "Which is why that was only suggestion number one. I didn't really think you'd go for it. Are you ready for number two?"

"Yes," she said, with the tone of someone half aware that they were walking into a trap.

"We need a better distraction: one Burdock can't walk away from after an hour or two. We also need one that will keep everyone else tied up—and where *our* absences won't be noticed."

"You've thought of something, haven't you."

"In ten days you deliver your strand, Purslane." I saw a flicker of concern in her face, but I continued, knowing she would see the sense in my proposal. "This is our only chance. By Gentian rules, every person on this island is required to receive your strand. With, of course, one exception."

"Me," she said, with a slow, dawning nod. "I don't have to be physically present, since I already know my own memories. But what about..."

"Me? Well, that isn't a problem either. Since I control the apparatus anyway, no one else need know that I wasn't on the island when your strand was threaded."

I watched Purslane's expression as she considered my idea. It was workable: I was convinced of that. I had examined the problem from every conceivable angle, looking for a hairline flaw—and I had found nothing. Well, nothing I could do anything about, anyway.

"But you won't know my strand," Purslane said. "What if someone asks..."

"That isn't a problem, either. Once we've agreed on the strand, I can receive it immediately. I just won't tell anyone until the day after your threading. It'll be just as if I received it the same way as everyone else."

"Wait," Purslane said, raising a hand. "What you just said...about us 'agreeing' on the strand."

"Um, yes?"

"Am I missing something? There isn't anything *to* agree on. I've already prepared and edited my strand to my complete satisfaction. There isn't a single memory I haven't already agonised over a thousand times: putting it in, taking it out again."

"I'm sure you're right," I said, knowing how much of a perfectionist Purslane was. "But unfortunately, we need to make this a tiny bit more of an event."

"I'm not following you, Campion."

"It has to be an effective distraction. Your memories have to be electrifying—the talk of the island for days afterwards. We have to talk them up before the thread, so that everyone is in a state of appropriate expectation. Obviously, there's only one person who can do that beforehand.

You'll have to drop hints. You'll have to look smug and self-satisfied. You'll have to pour lukewarm praise on someone else's strand."

"Oh, God preserve us from lukewarm praise."

"Trust me," I said. "I know all about that."

She shook her head. "I can't do this, Campion. It isn't me. I don't boast."

"Breaking into ships isn't you either. The rules have changed. We have to be flexible."

"It's all very well you saying that. It's me who's being asked to lie here…and anyway, why do I have to lie in the first place? Are you actually saying you don't think my real strand would be interesting enough?"

"Tell you what," I said, as if the idea had just occurred to me. "Why don't you let me have a look at your strand tonight? I'll speed-dream the scheduled strand to make room for yours."

"And then what?"

"Then we meet and discuss the material we have to work with. We'll make a few tweaks here and there—heighten this memory, downplay that one. Perhaps exercise a smidgeon of economy with regard to the strict veracity of the events portrayed…"

"Make things up, you mean."

"We need a distraction," I said. "This is the only way, Purslane. If it helps…don't think of it as lying. Think of it as creating a small untruth in order to set free a larger truth. How does that sound?"

"It sounds very dangerous, Campion."

We did it anyway.

Ten days was nowhere near as much time as I would have liked, but if we had been given any longer the utter incaution of what we were doing would have had time to gnaw away at my better judgement. It was a false strand that had set this entire enterprise in motion, I had to remind myself. Burdock had perpetrated a lie, and now we were perpetrating another because of it. Unfortunately, I saw no practical alternative.

Purslane's original strand wasn't as bad as I had feared: there was actually some promising material in it, if only it could be brought out more effectively. It was certainly a lot more dramatic and exciting than my essay on sunsets. Nonetheless, there was plenty of scope for some judicious fiddling with the facts: nothing outrageous, nothing that would have people looking for flaws in Purslane's strand, but enough to justify the anticipation she had begun to stoke. And in that respect she excelled herself: without actually saying anything, she managed to whip everyone into a state of heady expectation. It was all in the haughtiness of her walk, the guarded confidence of her looks, the sympathetic, slightly pitying smile with which she greeted everyone else's efforts. I know she hated every minute of that performance, but to her credit she threw herself into it with giddy abandon. By the time the evening of her threading came around, the atmosphere tingled with excitement. Her strand would be the subject of so much discussion tomorrow that no one could possibly take the risk of not dreaming it tonight, even if my apparatus had permitted such evasion. It would be the most exquisite of embarrassments not to be able to hold a view on Purslane's strand.

At midnight, the line members and their guests dispersed to sleep and dream. Surveillance confirmed that they were all safely under: including Burdock. The strand was threading into their collective memories. There had been no traffic to and from the island and the ships for an hour. A warm breeze rolled in from the west, but the sea was tranquil, save for the occasional breaching aquatic.

Purslane and I made our move. Two travel boxes folded around us and pulled us away from the island, through the thicket of hanging vessels, out to the ship belonging to Burdock. A kilometer long, it was a modest craft by Gentian standards: neither modern nor fast, but rugged and dependable for all that. Its armored green hull had something of the same semi-translucence as polished turtleshell. Its drive was a veined green bulb, flung out from the stern on a barbed stalk: it hung nose-down from the bulb, swaying gently in the late evening breeze.

Purslane's box led the way. She curved under the froglike bow of the ship, then rose up on the other side. Halfway up the hull, between a pair of bottle-green hull plates, lay a wrinkled airlock. Her box transmitted recognition protocols and the airlock opened like a gummed eye. There was room inside for both boxes. They opened and allowed us to disembark.

Nothing about Burdock's outward appearance had suggested that the air aboard his ship would be anything but a standard oxygen-nitrogen mix. It was still a relief when I gulped down a lungful and found it palatable. It would have been a chore to have to return to the island and remake my lungs to cope with something poisonous.

"I recognise this design of ship," Purslane said, whispering. We were inside a red-lined antechamber, like a blocked throat. "It's Third Intercessionary. I owned one like it once. I should be able to find my way around it quite easily, provided he hasn't altered too many of the fittings."

"Does the ship know we're here?"

"Oh, yes. But it should regard us as friendly, once we're inside."

"Suddenly this doesn't seem like quite the excellent idea it did ten days ago."

"We're committed now, Campion. Back on the island they're dreaming my strand and wondering what the hell turned me into such an adventuress. I didn't go to all that trouble to have you back out now."

"All right," I said. "Consider me suitably emboldened."

But though I strove for a note of easy-going jocularity, I could not shake the sense that our adventure had taken a turn into something far more serious. Until this evening all we had done was indulge in harmless surveillance: an indulgence that had added spice to our days. Now we had falsified a strand and were trespassing on someone else's ship. Both deeds were as close to crimes as anything perpetrated within the history of the Gentian Line. Discovery could easily mean expulsion from the line, or something worse.

This was not a game any more.

As we approached the end of the chamber, the constriction at the end eased open with an obscene sucking sound. It admitted warm, wet, pungent air.

We stooped through the low overhang into a much larger room. Like the airlock chamber, it was lit by randomly spaced light nodes, embedded in the fleshy walls like nuts wedged into the bark of a tree. Half a dozen corridors fed off in different directions, labelled with symbols in an obsolete language. I paused a moment while my brain retrieved the necessary reading skills from deep recall.

"This one is supposed to lead to the command deck," I said, as the symbols became suddenly meaningful. "Do you agree?"

"Yes," Purslane said, but with the tiniest note of hesitation in her voice.

"Something wrong?"

"Maybe you're right. Maybe this isn't such a good idea after all."

"What's got you afraid all of a sudden?"

"This is too easy," Purslane said.

"I thought it was meant to be easy. I thought that was the point of going to all that trouble with the access protocol."

"I know," she said. "But it just seems...I was expecting something to slow us down. Now I'm worried that we're walking into a trap."

"Burdock has no reason to set a trap," I said. But I could not deny that I felt the same unease. "Burdock isn't expecting us to visit. He isn't aware that we're onto him."

"Let's check out the command deck," she said. "But let's be quick about it, all right? The sooner we're back on the island, the happier I'll be."

We took the corridor, following its rising, curving ramp through several rotations, obeying signs for the deck all the while. Around us the ship breathed and gurgled like a sleeping monster, digesting its last big meal. Biomechanical constructs were typical products of the Third Intercessionary period, but I had never taken to them myself. I preferred my machines hard-edged, the way nature intended.

But nothing impeded our progress to the command deck. The deck was spaciously laid out, with a crescent window set into one curve of wall. It looked back across the sea, to the island. A spray of golden lights betrayed the darkening sliver of the main spire. I thought of the dreamers ranged throughout that tower, and of the lies we were peddling them.

Mushroom-shaped consoles studded the floor, rising to waist height. Purslane moved from one to the next, conjuring a status readout with a pass of her hand.

"This all looks good so far," she said. "Control architecture is much as I remember it from my ship. The navigations logs should be about...here." She halted at one of the mushrooms and flexed her hands in the stiffly formal manner of a dancer. Text and graphics cascaded through the air in a flicker of primary colors. "No time to go through it all now," she said. "I'll just commit it to eidetic memory and review it later." She increased the flow of data, until it blurred into whiteness.

I paced nervously up and down the crescent window. "Fine by me. Just out of interest, what are the chances we'll find anything incriminating anyway?"

Purslane's attention snapped onto me for a second. "Why not? We know for a fact that he lied."

"But couldn't he have doctored those logs as well? If he had something to hide…why leave the evidence aboard his ship?"

But Purslane did not answer me. She was looking beyond me, to the door where we had entered. Her mouth formed a silent exclamation of horror and surprise.

"Stop, please," said a voice.

I looked around, all my fears confirmed. But I recognized neither the voice nor the person who had spoken.

It was a man, baseline human in morphology. Nothing about his face marked him as Gentian Line. His rounded skull lacked Abigail's prominent cheekbones, and his eyes were pure matched blue of a deep shade, piercing even in the subdued light of the command deck.

"Who are you?" I asked. "You're not one of us, and you don't look like one of the guests."

"He isn't," Purslane said.

"Step away from the console, please," the man said. His voice was soft, unhurried. The device he held in his fist was all the encouragement we needed. It was a weapon: something unspeakably ancient and nasty. Its barrel glittered with inlaid treasure. His gloved finger caressed the delicate little trigger. Above the grip, defined by swirls of ruby, was the ammonite spiral of a miniature cyclotron. The weapon was a particle gun.

Its beam would slice through us as cleanly as it sliced through the hull of Burdock's ship.

"I will use this," the man said, "so please do as I say. Move to the middle of the room, away from any instruments."

Purslane and I did as he said, joining each other side by side. I looked at the man, trying to fit him into the Burdock puzzle. By baseline standards his physiological age was mature. His face was lined, especially around the eyes, with flecks of grey in his hair and beard. Something about the way he deported himself led me to believe that he was just as old as he looked. He wore a costume of stiff, skin-tight fabric in a shade of fawn, interrupted here and there by metal plugs and sockets. A curious metal ring encircled his neck.

"We don't know who you are," I said. "But we haven't come to do you any harm."

"Interfering with this ship doesn't count as doing harm?" He spoke the Gentian tongue with scholarly precision, as if he had learned it for this occasion.

"We were just after information," Purslane said.

"Were you now? What kind?"

Purslane flashed me a sidelong glance. "We may as well tell the truth, Campion," she said quietly. "We won't have very much to lose."

"We wanted to know where this ship had been," I said, knowing she was right but not liking it either.

The man jabbed the barrel of the particle gun in my direction. "Why? Why would you care?"

"We care very much. Burdock—the rightful owner of this ship—seems not to have told the truth about what he was up to since the last reunion."

"That's Burdock's business, not yours."

"Do you know Burdock?" I asked, pushing my luck.

"I know him very well," the man told me. "Better than you, I reckon."

"I doubt it. He's one of us. He's Gentian flesh."

"That's nothing to be proud of," the man said. "Not where I come from. If Abigail Gentian was here now, I'd put a hole in her you could piss through."

The dead calm with which he made this statement erased any doubt that he meant exactly what he said. I felt an existential chill. The man would have gladly erased not just Abigail but her entire line.

It was a strange thing to feel despised.

"Who are you?" Purslane asked. "And how do you know Burdock?"

"I'm Grisha," the man said. "I'm a survivor."

"A survivor of what?" I asked. "And how did you come to be aboard Burdock's ship?"

The man looked at me, little in the way of expression troubling his rounded face. Then by some hidden process he seemed to arrive at a decision.

"Wait here," he said. "I'll be back in a moment."

He let go of the particle gun. Instead of dropping to the floor the weapon simply hung exactly where he had left it, with its barrel still aimed in our general direction. Grisha stepped through the door and left the command deck.

"I knew this was a mistake," Purslane whispered. "Do you think that thing is really…"

I moved a tiny distance away from Purslane and the gun flicked its attention onto me. I drew breath and returned to my former spot, the gun following my motion.

"Yes," I said.

"I thought so."

Grisha returned soon enough. He closed his hand around the gun and lowered it a little. It was no longer trained on us, but we were still in Grisha's power.

"Come with me," he said. "There's someone you need to meet."

A WINDOWLESS ROOM lay near the core of the ship. It was, I realised, the sleeping chamber: the place where the ship's occupants (even if they only amounted to a single person) would have entered metabolic stasis for the long hops between stars. Some craft had engines powerful enough to push them so close to the speed of light that time dilation squeezed all journeys into arbitrarily short intervals of subjective time, but this was not one of those. At the very least Burdock would have had to spend years between stars. For that reason the room was equipped with the medical systems needed to maintain, modify and rejuvenate a body many times over.

And there *was* a body. A pale form, half eaten by some form of brittle, silvery calcification—a plaque that consumed his lower body to the waist, and which had begun to envelop the side of his chest, right shoulder and the right side of his face. A bustle of ivory machines attended the body, which trembled behind the distorting effect of a containment bubble.

"You can look," Grisha said.

We looked. Purslane and I let out a joint gasp of disbelief. The body on the couch belonged to Burdock.

"It doesn't make any sense," I said, studying the recumbent, damaged form. "The body he has on the island is intact. Why keep this failing one alive?"

"That isn't a duplicate body," Grisha said, nodding at the half-consumed form. "That's his only one. That *is* Burdock."

"No," I said. "Burdock was still on the island when we left."

"That wasn't Burdock," Grisha said, with a weary sigh. He pointed the gun at a pair of seats next to the bed. "Sit down, and I'll try and explain."

"What's wrong with him?" Purslane asked, as we followed Grisha's instruction.

"He's been poisoned. It's some kind of assassination weapon: very subtle, very slow, very deadly." Grisha leaned over and stroked the containment bubble, his fingertips pushing flickering pink dimples into the field. "This is more for your benefit than mine. If his contagion touched me, all I'd have to show for it is a nasty rash. It would kill you the same way it's killing him."

"No," I said. "He's Gentian. We can't be killed by an infection."

"It's a line weapon. It's made to kill the likes of you."

"Who did this to him?" Purslane asked. "You, Grisha?"

The question seemed not to offend him. "No, I didn't do this. It was one of *you*—an Advocate, he thought."

I frowned at the silver-ridden corpse. "Burdock told you who did it?"

"Burdock had his suspicions. He couldn't be sure who exactly had poisoned him."

"I don't understand. What exactly happened? How can Burdock be sick here, if we've seen him running around on the island only a couple of hours ago?"

Grisha smiled narrowly: the first hint of emotion to have troubled his face since our introduction. "That wasn't Burdock that you saw. It was a construct, a mimic, created by his enemies. It replaced the real Burdock nearly three weeks ago. They poisoned him before he returned to his ship."

I looked at Purslane and nodded. "If Grisha's telling the truth, that at least explains the change in Burdock's behaviour. We thought he'd been scared off asking any more questions about the Great Work. Instead he'd been supplanted."

"So he did ask too many questions," Purslane said. She creased her forehead prettily. "Wait, though. If he knew he'd been poisoned, why didn't he tell the rest of us? And why did he stay aboard the ship, out of sight, when his impostor was running around on the island?"

"He had no choice," Grisha answered. "When he arrived here, the ship detected the contagion and refused to let him leave."

"Noble of it," I said.

"He'd programmed it that way. I think he had a suspicion his enemies might try something like this. If he was infected, he didn't want to be allowed to return and spread it around. He was thinking of the rest of you."

Purslane and I were quiet for a few moments. I think we were both thinking the same rueful thoughts. We had never considered the possibility that Burdock might be acting honourably, even heroically. No matter what else I learned that evening, I knew that I had already misjudged someone who deserved better.

"All the same," I said, "that still doesn't explain why he didn't alert the rest of us. If he knew he'd been poisoned, and if he had half an idea as to who might have been behind it, there'd have been hell to pay."

"Doubtless there would have been," Grisha said. "But Burdock knew the risk was too great."

"Risk of what?" asked Purslane.

"My existence coming to light. If his enemies learned of my existence, learned of what I know, they'd do all in their power to silence me."

"You mean they'd kill you as well?" I asked.

Grisha gave off a quick, henlike cluck of amusement. "Yes, they'd certainly kill me. But not *just* me. That wouldn't be thorough enough. They wouldn't stop at this ship, either. They'd destroy every ship parked around the island, and then the island, and then perhaps the world."

I absorbed what he had said with quiet horror. Again, there was no doubt as to the truth of his words.

"You mean they'd murder all of us?"

"This is about more than just Gentian Line," Grisha said. "The loss of a single line would be a setback, but not a crippling one. The other lines would take up the slack. It wouldn't stop the Great Work."

I looked at him. "What do you know about the Great Work?"

"Everything," he said.

"Are you going to tell us?" Purslane asked.

"No," he said. "I'll leave that to Burdock. He still has several minutes of effective consciousness left, and I think he'd rather tell you in person. Before I wake him, though, it might not hurt if I told you a thing or two about myself, and how I came to be here."

"We've got all evening," I said.

GRISHA'S PEOPLE WERE archaeologists. They had been living in the same system for two million years, ever since settling it by generation ark. They had no interest in wider galactic affairs, and seemed perfectly content with a mortal lifespan of a mere two hundred years. They occupied their days in the diligent, monkish study of the Prior culture that had inhabited their system before their own arrival, in the time when humanity was still a gleam in evolution's eye.

The Priors had no name for themselves except the Watchers. They had been hard-shelled, multi-limbed creatures that spent half their lives beneath water. Their biology and culture was alien enough for a lifetime of study: even a modern one. But although they differed from Grisha's people in every superficial respect, there were points of similarity between the two cultures. They too were archaeologists, of a kind.

The Watchers had chosen to focus on a single, simple question. The universe had already been in existence for more than eleven billion years by the time the Watchers learned its age. And yet the study of the stellar populations in spiral galaxies at different redshifts established that the preconditions for the emergence of intelligent life had been in place for several billion years before the Watchers had evolved, even in the most conservative of scenarios.

Were they therefore the first intelligent culture in the universe, or had sentience already arisen in one of those distant spirals?

To answer this question, the Watchers had taken one of their worlds and shattered it to molecular rubble. With the materials thus liberated, they had constructed a swarm of miraculous eyes: a fleet of telescopes that outnumbered the stars in the sky. They had wrapped this fleet around their system and quickened it to a kind of slow, single-minded intelligence. The telescopes peered through the hail of local stars out into intergalactic space. They shared data across a baseline of tens of light hours, sharpening their acuity to the point where they approximated a single all-seeing eye as wide as a solar system.

It took time for light to reach the Eye from distant galaxies. The further out the Eye looked, the further it looked back into the history of the universe. Galaxies ten million light years away were glimpsed as they were ten million years earlier; those a billion light years away offered a window into the universe when it was a billion years younger than the present epoch.

The Eye looked at a huge sample of spiral galaxies, scrutinising them for signs of intelligent activity. It looked for signals across the entire electromagnetic spectrum; it sifted the parallel data streams of neutrino and gravity waves. It hunted for evidence of stellar engineering, of the kind that other Priors had already indulged in: planets remade to increase their surface area, stars sheathed in energy-trapping shells, entire star systems relocated from one galactic region to another.

One day it found what it was looking for.

At a surprisingly high redshift, the Eye detected a single spiral galaxy that was alive with intelligence. Judging by the signals emerging from the galaxy—accidental or otherwise—the ancient spiral was home to a single starfaring culture two or three million years into its dominion. The culture might have begun life as several distinct emergent intelligences that had amalgamated into one, or it might have arisen on a single world. At this distance in time and space, it hardly mattered.

What was clear was that the culture had reached a plateau of social and technological development. They had colonised every useful rock in their galaxy, to the point where their collective biomass exceeded that of a large gas giant. They became expert in the art of stellar husbandry: tampering in the nuclear burning processes of stars to prolong their lifetime, or to fan them to hotter temperatures. They shattered worlds and remade them into artful, energy-trapping forms. They played with matter and elemental force the way a child might play with sand and water. There was nothing they couldn't conquer, except time and distance and the iron barrier of the speed of light.

At this point in Grisha's story, Purslane and I looked at each other in a moment of dawning recognition.

"Like us," we both said.

Grisha favoured this assessment with a nod. "They were like you in so very many ways. They desired absolute omniscience. But the sheer scale of the galaxy always crushed them. They could never know everything: only out of date snapshots. Entire histories slipped through their fingers, unwitnessed, unmourned. Like you, they evolved something like the great lines: flocks of cloned individuals to serve as independent observers, gathering information and experience that would later be merged into the collective whole. And like you they discovered that it was only half a victory."

"And then?" I asked.

"Then...they did something about it." Grisha opened his mouth as if to speak more on the matter, then seemed to think better of it. "The Watchers continued to study the spiral culture. They gathered data, and when the Watchers passed away, that same data was entombed on the first world that my people settled. In the course of our study, we found this data and eventually we learned how to understand it. And for hundreds of thousands of years we thought no more of it: just one observational curiosity among the many gathered by our Priors."

"What did the spiral culture do?" I asked.

"Burdock can tell you that. It'll be better coming from him."

"You were going to tell us how you ended up on his ship," Purslane prompted.

Grisha looked at the recumbent figure, trapped within those trembling fields. "I'm here because Burdock saved me," he said. "Our culture was murdered. Genocide machines took apart our solar system world by world. We made evacuation plans, of course; built ships so that some of us might cross space to another system. We still knew nothing of relativistic starflight, so those ships were necessarily slow and vulnerable. That was our one error. If there was one piece of knowledge we should have allowed ourselves, it was how to build faster ships. Then perhaps, I wouldn't be speaking to you now. Too many of us would have reached other systems for there to be any need for this subterfuge. But as it is, I'm the only survivor."

His ship had crawled away from the butchered system with tens of thousands of refugees aboard. They had stealthed the ship to the best of their ability, and for a little while it looked as if they might make it into interstellar space unmolested. Then an instability in their narrow, shielded fusion flame had sent a clarion across tens of light hours.

The machines were soon on them.

Most had died immediately, but there had been enough warning for a handful of people to abandon the ship in smaller vehicles. Most of those had been picked off, as well. But Grisha had made it. He had fallen out of his system, engines dead, systems powered down to a trickle of life-support. And still he hadn't been dark or silent enough to avoid detection.

But this time it wasn't the machines that found him. It was another ship—a Gentian Line vessel that just happened to be passing by.

Burdock had pulled him out of the escape craft; warmed him from the emergency hibernation, and cracked the labyrinth of his ancient language.

Then Burdock taught Grisha how to speak his own tongue.

"He saved my life," Grisha said. "We fled the system at maximum thrust, outracing the machines. They tried to chase us, and for a little while it seemed that they had the edge. But eventually we made it."

Even as I framed the question, I think I already had an inkling of the answer. "These machines...the ones that murdered your people?"

"Yes," Grisha said.

"Who sent them?"

He looked at both of us and said, very quietly, "You did."

WE WOKE BURDOCK.

The assassination toxin was eating him at a measurable rate; cubic centimeters per hour at normal body temperatures. With Burdock cooled below consciousness, the consumption was retarded to a glacially slow attack. But he would have to be warmed to talk to us, and so his remaining allowance of conscious life could be defined in a window of minutes, with the quality of that consciousness degrading as the weapon gorged itself on his mind.

"I was hoping someone would make it this far," Burdock said, opening his eyes. He didn't turn his head to greet us—the consuming plaque would have made that all but impossible even if he had the will—but I assumed that he had some other means of identifying us. His lips barely moved, but something was amplifying his words, or his intention to speak. "I know how you broke into my ship," he said, "and I presume Grisha's told you something of his place in this whole mess."

"A bit," I said.

"That's good—no need to go over that again." The words had their own erratic rhythm, like slowly dripping water. "But what made you come out here in the first place?"

"There was a discrepancy in your strand," Purslane said, approaching uncomfortably close to the bedside screen. "It conflicted with Campion's version of events. One of you had to be lying."

"You said you'd been somewhere you hadn't," I said. "I happened to be there at the same time, or else no one would ever have known."

"Yes," he said. "I lied; submitted a false strand. Most of it was true—you probably guessed that much—but I had to cover up my visit to Grisha's system."

I nodded. "Because you knew who had destroyed Grisha's people?"

"The weapons were old: million-year-old relics from some ancient war. That should have made them untraceable. But I found one of the weapons, adrift and deactivated. New control systems had been grafted over the old machinery. These control systems used line protocols."

"Gentian?"

"Gentian, or one of our allies. I had witnessed a terrible crime, a genocide worse than anything recorded in our history."

"Why did you cover it up?" Purslane asked.

"The knowledge frightened me. But that wasn't the reason I altered my strand. I did it because I needed time: time to identify those responsible, and protect Grisha from them until I had enough evidence to bring them to justice. If the perpetrators were among us—and I had reason to think they were—they would have killed Grisha to silence him. And if killing Grisha meant killing the rest of us, I don't think they'd have blinked at that." He managed a despairing laugh. "When you've just wiped out a two-million-year-old civilisation, what do a thousand clones matter?"

I tried not to sound too disbelieving. "The murder of an entire line? You think they'd go that far, just to cover up an earlier crime?"

"And more," Burdock said gravely. "This is about more than our piddling little line, Campion."

"The Great Work," Purslane said, voicing my own thoughts. "A project bigger than any single line. That's what they killed for, isn't it. And that's what they'll kill for again."

"You're good," Burdock said. "I couldn't have asked for a better pair of amateur sleuths."

"We still don't know anything about the Great Work itself," I told him. "Or why Grisha's people had to die."

"I'll tell you about the Work in good time. First we need to talk about the people who want Grisha dead."

Purslane looked at the other man, and then returned her attention to Burdock. "Do you know their names?"

"It was names I was after," he said. "I had a suspicion—little more than a hunch—that the genocide had something to do with the Work."

"Quite a hunch," I commented.

"Not really. Whoever was behind this had murdered those people because of something big, and the only big thing I could think of was the Work. What else do the Advocates talk about, Campion—other than their own inflated sense of self-worth?"

"You have a point."

"Anyway, the more I dug, the more it looked like I was right about that hunch. It did tie in with the Work. But I still didn't have any names. I thought if I could at least isolate the line members who had the strongest ties to the Work, then I could start looking for flaws in their strands..."

"Flaws?" Purslane asked.

"Yes. At least one of them had to have been near Grisha's system at the same time as me. They won't have used intermediaries for that kind of thing."

But it was only good luck that we had found the flaw in Burdock's strand in the first place, I thought. Even if someone else had fabricated all or part of their strand, there was no reason to assume they had made the same kind of mistake.

"Did you narrow it down to anyone?" Purslane asked.

"A handful of plausible suspects…conspicuous Advocates, for the most part. I'm sure you could draw up the same shortlist with little effort."

I thought of the Advocates I knew, and the one in particular I had never liked. "Was Fescue among them?"

"Yes," Burdock said. "He was one of them. No love lost there, I see."

"Fescue is a senior Advocate," Purslane said. "He's tried to keep Campion and I apart. It could easily be that he knows we're onto something. If anyone has the means…"

"There are others besides Fescue. I needed to know who it was. That was why I started asking questions, nosing around, trying to goad someone into an indiscretion."

"We noticed," I said.

"Obviously my idea of subtle wasn't *their* idea of subtle. Well, it proves I was onto something, I suppose. At least one of our line has to be involved."

I tapped a finger against my nose. "Why didn't they just kill you on the island, and be done with it?"

"It was *your* island, Campion. How would they have killed me without you noticing it? Administering a poisonous agent was simpler—at least that way they didn't have a body to dispose of."

"Do you know about the impostor?" I asked.

"My ship kept a watch on the island. More than once I saw myself strolling on the high promenades."

"You could have signalled us," Purslane said. "Made your ship malfunction, or something like that."

"No. I thought of that, of course. But if my enemies had the slightest suspicion I was still alive, they might have attacked the ship. Remember: they poisoned me not because I knew what had happened, but simply because I was asking too many questions. It's entirely possible that they've done this to other line members in the past. There might be other impostors on your island, Campion."

"I'd know," I said automatically.

"Would you? Would you really?"

When he put it like that, I wasn't sure. I wasn't in the habit of looking inside the skulls of other line members, just to make sure they were really who I assumed them to be. Mental architecture was a private thing at the best of times. And a strand was a strand, whether it was delivered by a thinking person or a mindless duplicate.

"You could have sent a message to one of us," Purslane said.

"How would I have known you were to be trusted? From where I was sitting, hardly anyone wasn't a possible suspect."

"Do you trust us now?" I asked.

"I suppose so," Burdock said, with not quite the conviction I might have hoped for. "Does it look like I have a great deal of choice?"

"We're not implicated," Purslane said soothingly. "But we are concerned to expose the truth."

"It's dangerous. Everything I said still holds. They'll take this world apart to safeguard the Great Work. Unless you can organise a significant number of allies and move against them quickly...I fear they'll gain the upper hand."

"Then we'll just have to outplay them, so that they never get a chance." Easier said than done, I thought. We had no more idea who we could trust than Burdock himself.

"Whatever we do," Purslane said, "it'll have to happen before Thousandth Night. If there's any evidence pointing to a crime now, it'll be lost forever by the time we return here."

"She's right," I said. "If Gentian Line is implicated, then whoever's involved is on the island now. That gives us something. We've at least got them in one place."

"Thousandth Night would be a good time to move," Purslane mused. "If we leave it until then—the last possible moment—they'll probably have assumed nothing's going to happen."

"Risky," I said.

"It's all risky. At least that way we stand a chance of catching them off guard. There's only one thing anyone ever thinks about on Thousandth Night."

"Purslane may have a point," Burdock said. "Whoever the perpetrators are, they're still part of the line. They'll be waiting to see who wins best strand, just like the rest of you."

I noticed that he said "you" rather than "us." On his deathbed, Burdock had already begun the process of abdication from Gentian affairs. Knowing he would not see Thousandth Night, let alone another reunion, he was turning away from the line.

Abigail valued death as much as she valued life. Though we were all technically immortal, that immortality only extended to our cellular processes. If we destroyed our bodies, we died. Gentian protocol forbade backups, or last minute neural scans. She wanted her memories to burn bright with the knowledge that life—even a life spanning hundreds of thousands of years—was only a sliver of light between two immensities of darkness.

Burdock would die. Nothing in the universe could stop that now.

"When you witnessed the crime," I said, "did you see anything that could tell us who was responsible?"

"I've been through my memories of my passage through Grisha's system a thousand times," he said. "After I rescued Grisha, I caught a trace of a drive flame exiting the system in the opposite direction. Presumably whoever deployed the machines was still around until then, making sure that the job was done."

"We should be able to match the drive signature to one of the ships parked here," I said.

"I've tried, but the detection was too faint. There's nothing that narrows down my list of suspects."

"Maybe a fresh pair of eyes might help, though," Purslane said. "Or even two pairs."

"Direct exchange of memories is forbidden outside of threading," Burdock said heavily.

"Add it to the list of Gentian rules we've already broken tonight," I said. "Falsification of Purslane's strand, absence from the island during a threading, breaking into someone else's ship...why don't you let *me* worry about the rules, Burdock? My neck's already on the line."

"I suppose one more wrong won't make much difference," he said, resignedly. "The sensor records of my passage through Grisha's system are still in my ship files—will they be enough?"

"You had no other means of witnessing events?"

"No. Everything I saw came through the ship's eyes and ears in one form or another."

"That should be good enough. Can you pass those records to my ship?"

"Mine as well," Purslane said.

Burdock waited a moment. "It's done. I'm afraid you'll still have some compatibility issues to deal with."

A coded memory flash—a bee landing on a flower—told me that my ship had just received a transmission from another craft, in an unfamiliar file format. I sent another command to my ship to tell it to start working on the format conversion. I had faith that it would get there in the end: I often set it the task of interpreting Prior languages, just to keep its mental muscles in shape.

"Thank you," I said.

"Make what you will of it. I'm afraid there are many gaps in the sensor data. You'll just have to fill in the holes."

"We'll do what we can," Purslane said. "But if we're to bring anyone to justice, we have to know what this is all about. You must tell us what you've learned of the Great Work."

"I only know parts. I've guessed most of it."

"That's still more than Campion and I know."

"All right," he said, with something like relief. "I'll tell you. But there isn't time to do this the civilised way. Will you give me permission to push imagery into your heads?"

Purslane and I looked at each other uneasily. Rationally, we had nothing to fear: if Burdock had the means to tamper with our heads, he could have already forced hallucinations on us by now, or killed us effortlessly. We willingly opened our memories during each threading, but that was within the solemn parameters of age-old ceremony, when we were all equally vulnerable. We already knew Burdock had lied once. What if the rest of his story was a lie as well? We had no evidence that Grisha was authentic, and not just a figment created by the ship.

"You have to trust me," Burdock pleaded. "There isn't much time left."

"He's right," Purslane said, gripping my hand. "There's a risk, but there's also a risk in doing nothing. We have to do this."

I nodded at Burdock. "Tell us."

"Prepare," he whispered.

An instant later I felt a kind of mental prickle as something touched my brain, groping its way in like an octopus seeking a way into a shell. Purslane tightened her hold, anchoring herself to me. There was a moment of resistance and then the intrusive thing was ensconced.

My sense of being present in the room became attenuated, as if my body was suddenly at the far end of a long thread of nerve fibres, with my brain somewhere else entirely. I didn't know how Burdock was doing it, but I could see at least two possibilities. The air in his ship might have been thick with machines, able to swim into neural spaces and tap into direct mental processes. Or the ship itself might been generating external magnetic fields of great precision, steering the foci into my skull and stimulating microscopic areas of my mind. I was only dimly aware of Grisha and Burdock looking on, half a universe away.

Coldness seized me, electric with the crackle and fizz of subatomic radiation. I was somewhere dark beyond imagination. My point of view shifted and something awesome hoved into view. As my disembodied eyes adjusted to the darkness, the thing brightened and grew layers of dizzying detail.

It was a spiral galaxy.

I recognized it instantly as the Milky Way. I had crossed it enough times to know the kinked architecture of its stellar arms and dust lanes, a whorl as familiar and idiosyncratic as a fingerprint. The hundreds of billions of stars formed a blizzard of light, but through some trick of perception I felt that I recognized all the systems I had visited during my travels, as well as all those I had come to know through the shared memories of the Gentian Line. I made out the little yellow sun which we now orbited, and felt both inconsequential and godlike as I imagined myself on a watery world circling that star, a thing tiny beyond measure, yet with an entire galaxy wheeling inside my head.

"You know this place, of course," said Burdock's disembodied voice. "As one facet of Abigail, you've crossed it ten or twelve times; tasted the air of a few hundred worlds. Enough for one lifetime, perhaps. But that was never enough for Abigail, for us. As Abigail's shattered self we've crossed it ten thousand times; known a million worlds. We've seen wonder and terror; heaven and hell. We've seen empires and dynasties pass like seasons. And still that isn't enough. We're still monkeys, you know. In terms of the deep structure of our minds, we've barely left the trees. There's always a shinier, juicier piece of fruit just out of reach. We've reached for it across two million years and it's brought us to this place, this moment. And now we reach again. We embark on our grandest scheme to date: the Great Work."

The view of the Milky Way did not change in any perceptible way, but I was suddenly aware of human traffic crossing between the stars. Ships much like those of the Gentian Line fanned out from points of reunion, made vast circuits across enormous swathes of the Galaxy, and converged back again two or three hundred thousand years later, ready to merge experiences. Cocooned in relativistic time, the journeys did not seem horrendously long for the pilots: mere years or decades of flight, with the rest of time (which might equal many centuries) spent soaking up planetary experience, harvesting memory and wisdom. But the true picture was of crushing slowness, even though the ships moved at the keen, sharp edge of lightspeed. Interesting star systems were thousands or tens of thousands of years of flight time apart. Planetary time moved much faster than that. Human events outpaced the voyagers, so that what they experienced was only glimpses of history, infuriatingly incomplete. Brief, bittersweet golden ages flourished for a handful of centuries while the ships were still moving between stars. Glories went unrecorded, unremembered.

Something had to be done.

"The lines have been gnawing at the lightspeed problem for half a million years," Burdock said. "It won't crack. It's just the way the universe is. Faced with that, you have two other possibilities. You can reengineer human nature to slow history to a crawl, so that starfarers can keep pace with planetary time. Or you can consider the alternative. You can reengineer the Galaxy itself, to shrink it to a human scale."

In an eye blink of comprehension we understood the Great Work, and why it had been necessary for Grisha's people to die. The Great Work concerned nothing less than the relocation of entire stars and all the worlds that orbited them.

Moving stars was not actually as difficult as it sounded. The Priors had moved stars around many times, using many different methods. It had even taken place in the human era: demonstration projects designed to boost the prestige of whichever culture or line happened to be sponsoring it. But the Great Work was not about moving one or two stars a few light years, impressive as such a feat undoubtedly was. The Great Work was about the herding of stars in numbers too large to comprehend: the movement of hundreds of millions of stars across distances of tens of thousand of light years. The Advocates dreamed of nothing less than compactifying the Milky Way; taking nature's work and remaking it into something more useful for human occupation. For quick-witted monkeys, it was no different than clearing a forest, or draining a swamp.

Burdock told us that the Advocates had been covertly resurrecting Prior methods of stellar engineering, contesting them against each other to find the most efficient processes. The methods that worked best seemed to be those that employed some of the star's own fusion power as the prime mover. They used mirrors to direct the star's energy output in a single direction, in the manner of a rocket motor. If the star's acceleration were sufficiently gentle, it would carry its entire family of worlds and rubble and dust with it.

Of all the Prior methods tested so far, none were able to accelerate a sunlike star to anything faster that one percent of the speed of light. This was laughably slow compared to our oldest ships, but it didn't matter to the Advocates. Even if it took two or three more million years to move all their target stars, this was still a price worth paying. Everything that had happened to date, they liked to say, was just a *prologue to history*. Real human affairs would not begin in earnest until the last star was dropped into its designed Galactic orbit. Set against the billions of years ahead of us (before the Galaxy itself began to wither, or suffered a damaging encounter with Andromeda) what was a mere handful of millions of years?

It was like delaying a great voyage by a few hours.

When they were done, the Galaxy would look very different. All life-bearing stars (cool and long-lived suns, for the most part) would have been shunted much closer to the core, until they fell within a volume only five thousand light years across. Superhot blue stars—primed to explode as supernovae in mere millions of years—would be prematurely triggered, or shoved out of harm's way. Unstable binaries would be dismantled like delicate time bombs. The unwieldy clockwork of the central black hole would be tamed and harnessed for human consumption. Stars that were already on the point of falling into the central engine would be mined for raw materials. New worlds would be forged, vast as stars themselves: the golden palaces and senates of this new galactic empire. With a light-crossing time of only fifty centuries, something like an empire was indeed possible. History would no longer outpace starfarers like Purslane and I. If we learned of something magical on the other side of human space, there would be every hope that it would still be there when we arrived. And most of humanity would be packed into a light-crossing time much less than fifty centuries.

This was the Great Work. It was the culminative project of two million years of human advancement: the enterprise that would the tax the ingenuity and resourcefulness of the most powerful lines. Where the lines squabbled now, they would come together in peaceful cooperation. And at the end of it (if any of us lived that long), we would have something wonderful to show for it. It would be the ultimate human achievement, a spectacle of engineering visible across cosmological distance. A beacon to our bright monkey cleverness.

It could not be allowed to happen.

That was the message Grisha's people had uncovered, in their archaeological enquiries into their planet's Prior culture. It transpired that the Watchers had witnessed something like the Great Work once already, in the distant spiral galaxy that they had been monitoring. Perhaps it was a kind of recurrent pathology, destined to afflict civilisations once they reached a certain evolutionary state. They grew weary of the scale of their galaxy and sought to shrink it.

In doing so they created the preconditions for their own extinction. Where once they had moved too slowly to threaten more than a handful of neighbouring systems, the compactification allowed war and disease to spread like wildfire. The inhuman scale of the colonised Galaxy was its strength as well as its weakness: time and distance were buffers against catastrophe. Spread out across tens of thousands of light years, we were immune to extinction, at least by our own hands.

Compactified, death could touch us all in less than five thousand years.

"The Advocates knew this, I think," Burdock said. "But they considered it to be a theoretical problem they would deal with when the time came. Surely, they rationalised, we would be wise enough to avoid such foolishness. But then they learned of the discovery made by the Watchers, and rediscovered by Grisha's people. Another spiral culture that had gone down the same path—and ended up extinct; wiped out in a cosmological instant. Perhaps the fate was not so avoidable after all, no matter how wise you became. By rights, they should have viewed this data as an awful warning, and acted accordingly: abandoning the Great Work before a single star had moved an inch."

But it was never going to happen like that. The lines had already invested too much of themselves in the future success of the Work. Alliances had already been forged; hierarchies of influence and responsibility agreed upon. To back down now would involve crushing loss of face to the senior lines. Old wounds would be reopened; old rivalries would simmer to the fore. If the Great Work was the project that would bind the lines, its abandonment could very easily push some of them to war. That was why Grisha's people had to be silenced, even if it meant their genocide. For what was the loss of one culture, against something so huge? If we were still living in the prologue to history, they would be doing well to merit a footnote.

The vision ended then, and I felt my mind being sucked back to the body I had left (and nearly forgotten) aboard Burdock's ship. There was a moment of unpleasant confinement, as if I was a being squeezed into a too-small bottle, and then I was back, still holding hands with Purslane, the two of us reeling as our inner ears adjusted to the return of gravity.

Grisha stood by the couch, his gun still in his hand. "Did you learn all that you needed to know?" he asked.

"I think so," I started to say.

"Good," he said. "Because Burdock's dead. He gave you the last minute of his life."

PURSLANE AND I returned to the island as the sky lightened in anticipation of dawn. It was still midnight blue overhead, but the horizon was tinged with the softest tangerine orange, cut through by ribbons of cloud. As the box wheeled through the thicket of hanging ships toward the island I began to see the crests of waves, stippled in brightening gold.

I had seen many dawns, but in all my travels I had never tired of them. Even now, with the weight of all that had happened and all that we had learned, some part of me stood aside from the moment to acknowledge the simple beauty of sunrise on another world. I wondered what Burdock would have made of it. Would it have touched him with the same alchemical force, bypassing the rational mind to speak to that animal part from which we were separated by only an evolutionary heartbeat? Perhaps I'd find a clue in all the strands Burdock had submitted during his time among us. Now there would be no more.

A death among the line was a terrible and rare thing. When it happened, one of us would be tasked to create a suitable memorial somewhere out in the stars. Such a memorial could take many forms. Long ago, the death of one of our number had been commemorated by the seeding of ferrite dust into the atmosphere of a dying star, just before the star expelled its outer envelope to create a nebula in the shape of a human head, sketched in lacy curves of blue-green oxygen and red hydrogen, racing outward at sixty kilometers a second. Another memorial, no less heartfelt, had taken the form of a single stone kiln on an airless moon. Both had been appropriate.

Burdock would surely receive his due, but his death had to remain a secret until Thousandth Night. Until then Purslane and I would have to walk among our fellow line members with that knowledge in our hearts, and not betray the slightest hint of it.

We owed it to Burdock.

"We're in time," I said, as the box neared the island. "That took longer than I'd hoped, but the threading is still taking place. No one will have missed us yet."

Purslane pressed a hand to her brow. "God, the threading. I'd forgotten all about that. Now I'll have to spend all day telling lies. Please tell me this was a good idea, Campion."

"Wasn't it? We know what happened to Burdock now. We know about Grisha and the Great Work. *Of course* it was worth it."

"Are you so sure? All we know now is that asking questions could get us into serious trouble. We're still none the wiser about who's actually behind this. I'm not sure I wasn't happier in blissful ignorance."

"We have the data from Burdock's ship," I reminded her.

"Have you looked at it yet, Campion?" I could tell from her tone that she wasn't impressed. "My ship's already sent me back a preliminary analysis. Burdock's data is riddled with gaps."

"He warned us there were a few holes."

"What he didn't say was that thirty percent of his records were missing. There may be something useful in the remaining data, but there's still a good chance that the clues fell into the gaps."

"Why the gaps in the first place? Do you think he edited out something he didn't want us to see?"

Purslane shook her head. "Don't think so. The gaps seem to be caused by his anticollision screens going up, blinding his sensors. You saw how old that ship was: it probably has pretty ancient screen generators, or pretty ancient sensors, or both."

"Why the anticollision screens?"

"Debris," Purslane said. "Grisha's system had been turned into a cloud of radioactive rubble. Burdock's approach never took him all that close to the main action, but there must still have been a lot of debris flying around. If he'd thought to turn up his triggering threshold, he might have given us more to work with…"

I tried to sound optimistic. "We'll just to have make the best of what's left."

"My ship's already made the obvious checks. I've seen the flame Burdock mentioned, but it really is too faint for an accurate match. If the murderers were hanging around the system before then, they must have been very well camouflaged."

"We can't just…give up," I said, thinking of the man we had left behind on Burdock's ship. "We owe it to Burdock, and Grisha, and Grisha's people."

"If there's nothing there, there's nothing there," Purslane said.

She was right. But it wasn't what I wanted to hear.

We landed on the island and reset our body clocks so that—to first approximation—we looked and felt as if we had just passed a restful, dream-filled night. That was the idea, at least. But when I conjured a mirror and examined my face in it I saw a quivering, tic-like tightness around the mouth. I tried a kinesic reset but it didn't go away. When Purslane and I met alone on one of the high balconies, after breakfasting with a few other line members, I swear saw the same tightness.

"How did it go?" I asked.

She kept her voice low. "It was as bad as I feared. They thought my strand was *wonderful, darling*. They won't stop asking me about it. They hate me."

"That's sort of the reaction we were hoping for. The one thing no one will be wondering about is what you were up to last night. And we can be sure no one ducked out of the strand."

"What about Burdock's impostor? We didn't know about him when we hatched this plan."

"He still had to act like Burdock," I said. "That means he'll have needed to dream your strand."

"I hope you're right."

"You only have to get through this one day. It's Squill's strand tonight. He always gives good dream."

Purslane looked at me pityingly. "Keep up, Campion. Squill's been off-form for half a million years."

Unfortunately, she was right about Squill. His strand consisted of endless visits to planets and artefacts left over from the Interstitial Uprising, overlaid with tedious, self-serving monologues of historical analysis. It was not the hit of the reunion, and it did little to take the heat off Purslane. The next night wasn't much better: Mullein's strand was a workmanlike trudge through thirty cultures that had collapsed back to pre-industrial feudalism. "Mud," I heard someone say dispiritedly, the day after. "Lots of...mud."

The third night was a washout as well. That was when Asphodel would have delivered her strand, had she made it back to the reunion. As was our custom, her contribution took the form of a compilation from her previous strands. It was all very worthy, but not enough to stop people talking about Purslane's exploits.

Thankfully, things picked up for her on the fourth night. Borage's strand detailed his heroic exploits in rescuing an entire planet's worth of people following the close approach of a star to their Oort cloud. Borage dropped replicators on their nearest moon and converted part of it into a toroidal defence screen, shielding their planet from the infall of dislodged comets. Then he put the moon back together again and (this was a touch of genius, we had to admit) he *wrote his signature* on the back of the tide-locked moon in a chain of craters. It was flashy, completely contrary to any number of Line strictures, but it got people talking about Borage, not Purslane.

I could have kissed the egomaniacal bastard.

"I think we got away with that one," I told Purslane, when she was finally able to move through the island without being pestered by an entourage of hangers-on.

"Good," she said. "But that doesn't mean we're any closer to finding out who killed Grisha's people."

"Actually," I said, "I've been thinking about that. Maybe there's something in that data after all."

"We've been through it with a fine-toothed comb."

"But looking for the obvious signatures," I said.

"There are too many gaps."

"But maybe the gaps are telling us something. What caused the gaps?"

"Burdock being too cautious, throwing up his screens every time a speck of dust came within a light-second of his ship. His screens are sensor-opaque, at least in all the useful bands."

"Correct. But some of those activations were probably necessary: there *was* a lot of rubble, after all."

"Go on," she said.

"Well, if there was a lot of debris that far out, there must have been even more closer to the action. Enough to trigger the screens of the other ship."

"I hadn't thought of that."

"Me neither, until now. And the type of search we've been doing wouldn't have picked up screen signatures. We need to slice the data up into short time windows and filter on narrow-band graviton pulses. *Then* we might find something."

"I'm already on it," Purslane said.

I closed my eyes and directed a command at my own ship. "Me too. Want to take a bet on who finds something first?"

"No point, Campion. I'd thrash you."

She did, too. Her ship found something almost immediately, now that it had been given the right search criteria. "It's still at the limits of detection," she said. "They must have had their screens tuned right down, for just this reason. But they couldn't run with them turned off."

"Is this enough to narrow it down?"

"Enough to improve matters. The resonant frequency of the graviton pulse is at the low end: that means whoever's doing this was throwing up a big screen."

Like blowing a low note in a big bottle, rather than a high note in a small bottle.

"Meaning big ship," I said.

"I'm guessing fifty or sixty kilometers at the minimum." She looked at the parade of hanging ships. "That already narrows it down to less than a hundred."

My ship pushed a memory into my head: a girl seated in the lotus position, with a golden, glowing cube rotating above her cupped palms. It meant that the ship had a result.

"Mine's in," I said, requesting a full summary. "My ship says seventy kilometers at the low end, with a central estimate around ninety. See: slow, but she gets there in the end."

"My ship's refined its analysis and come to more or less the same conclusion," Purslane said. "That narrows it down even more. We're talking about maybe twenty ships."

"Still not good enough," I said ruefully. "We can't point fingers unless we have a better idea than that."

"Agreed. But we have the drive flame as an additional constraint. Not all of those twenty ships even use visible thrust. And we also know who Burdock spoke to about the Great Work."

I paused and let those numbers crunch against each other. "Better. Now we're down to...what? Seven or eight ships, depending on where you draw the cut-off for the size estimate. Seven or eight names. One of which happens to be Fescue."

"Still not good enough, though."

I thought for a moment. "If we could narrow it down to one ship... then we'd be sure, wouldn't we?"

"That's the problem, Campion. We can't narrow it down. Not unless we saw what those anticollision fields looked like."

"Exactly," I said. "If we could get them to put up their screens...all we'd need to do is find the ship with the closest resonance to the one in Grisha's system."

"Wherever you're taking this line of thought..." Purslane's eyes flashed a warning at me.

"All I need to do is find a way to get them to trigger their shields. Full ship screens, of course."

"It won't work. If they get an inkling of what you're up to, they'll tune to a different resonance."

"Then I'd better not give them much warning," I said. "We'll do it on Thousandth Night, just the way we said we would. They'll be too distracted to plan anything in advance, and they won't be expecting a last-minute surprise."

"I like the way you say 'we'."

"We're in this together now," I said. "All the way. Even if we take the line with us."

Purslane sniffed her wineglass. "How are you going to get everyone to turn on their shields?"

I squinted against the sun. "I'm sure I'll think of something."

BECAUSE I WAS dreading its arrival, Thousandth Night was suddenly upon us. Since Purslane's discovery that Burdock had lied, the reunion had passed by in a blur. For nine hundred and ninety-nine nights we had dreamed of suns and worlds, miracles and wonders, and perhaps a little mud along the way. Our knowledge of the galaxy we called home had accreted yet another layer of detail, even as the endless transformations of history rendered much of that knowledge obsolete. For most of us, it was of no concern. The innate fascination of the strands, the spectacle, intrigue, and glamour of this final evening together was all that mattered. Not the Advocates, though. Though they did their best to hide it, they itched with impatience. For two million years, they had accepted the crushing scale of the Galaxy and their own fixed relationship to that immensity. When Abigail Gentian shattered herself into nine hundred and ninety-nine gemlike pieces, she had hoped to conquer space and time. Instead, she had only come to a deeper understanding of her own microscopic insignificance. The Advocates could not tolerate that any longer.

I kept a stiff, strained smile on my face as I made my rounds of the Thousandth Night revellers, accepting compliments. Although my strand had not set the world on fire, no one had any serious complaints about the venue. The island was just the right size: small enough to feel intimate, but with enough curious little byways and quirks of design not to become boring. Every now and then I had introduced some minor change—moving a passage here, or a staircase there, and my efforts were generally deemed to have been worthwhile. The white terraces, balconies and bridges of the island had a charm of their own, but they had not detracted from the strands, and the threadings had gone flawlessly. Time and again, people squeezed my sleeve and asked me what I had lined up for the final night, and time and again I confessed that I couldn't even be sure that I *had* lined anything up at all.

Of course, I knew I must have planned something.

Evening turned to night. Floating paper lanterns glowed in the warm air, casting lozenges of pastel color on the revellers. As was Gentian custom, everyone wore a costume that, subtly or otherwise, reflected the content of their dream. We wore carnival masks, the game being to match the dreamer to the dream before the masks were ripped away. I wore a moon mask and a simple outfit patterned in sunset shades, with a repeating motif of half-swallowed suns. Purslane wore a fox mask and a harlequin costume, in which each square detailed one of her legendary adventures. It didn't take very long for people to work out who she was. Once again, she was tormented by questions about the false strand, but she only had to keep up the pretence for a few more hours. Soon our deception would be revealed, and we would beg forgiveness for weaving a lie.

"Look," I heard someone say, pointing to the zenith. "A shooting star!"

I looked up sharply enough to catch the etched trail before it faded from sight. A shooting star, I thought: a good omen, perhaps. Except I didn't believe in omens, especially not when they were signified by pieces of cosmic grit slamming into our planet's atmosphere.

Purslane sidled up to me a few minutes later. "Are you sure you want to go through with this?"

"Yes. In less than a day, every ship you see here will be on its way out of the system. We do it now or we forget about it forever."

"Maybe that would be easier."

"Easier, yes. The right thing—no."

Another shooting star slashed the sky.

"I agree," she said.

Upon midnight, the revellers assembled on a high balcony flung out from the side of the main tower on an arm of curved ivory. They had all cast their votes and my system had tallied the winning strand. Shortly it would push the information into my head, and I would deliver the much-anticipated announcement. One of us would leave the system heady with the knowledge their dream had moved us like no other, and that they had been honoured with the design of the next venue. Whoever it was, I wished them well. As I had discovered, the praise burned off very quickly, and what was left was a dark, ominous clinker of responsibility.

I looked down on the assembled gathering from a much higher balcony, watching the masked and costumed figures slow in their orbits. The atmosphere of the revellers became perceptibly tense, as my announcement drew nearer. There was a palpable sadness amongst all the gaiety. Friendships made here must be put on hold until the next reunion, two hundred thousand years in the future. Time and space would change some of us. We would not all be the same people, and not all of those friendships would endure.

It was time.

I stepped from the side of my balcony, into open space. There was a collective gasp from the revellers, even though no one seriously expected me to come to harm. As my left foot pushed down into thin air, a sheet of white marble whisked under it to provide support. As my right foot stepped below my left, another sheet whisked under that one. I took weight from my left foot and stepped down again, and the first sheet curved back under me to meet my falling foot. Stepping between these two sheets, I walked calmly down to the lower balcony. The effect was everything I could have wished for, and I tried to look as quietly pleased with myself as I ought to have been.

But not all the eyes were upon me. Masked and unmasked faces were caught by something above. I followed their gaze to see another slashing shooting star, and then another. In quick succession, six more cut the sky from zenith to horizon. Then more. A dozen in the first minute, and then two dozen in the second. I smiled, realising that this must be the surprise I had arranged for Thousandth Night. A meteor shower!

Easily done, I thought. All I would have needed to do is shove a comet onto the right orbit, shatter it and let its dusty tail intersect the orbit of my planet at the right point in space and time...here, tonight. Now that I thought of that, there was a twinge of familiarity about it...the memory of doing so not completely erased.

By the standards of some, it was very low-key, and for a moment I wondered if I had misjudged the effect...but just as I was beginning to worry about that, people started clapping. It was polite at first, but soon it built in enthusiasm, even as the stars quickened their display, flashing overhead too quickly to count.

They liked it.

"Bravo, Campion!" I heard someone say. "Tasteful restraint...beautifully simple!"

I stepped onto a low plinth, so that I was head and shoulders above the crowd. I forced a smile and waved down the applause. "Thank you, everyone," I said. "I'm glad things have gone so well. If this reunion has been a success, it has far more to do with the people than the venue." I looked over my shoulder, at the central spire rising behind me. "Although the venue isn't half bad, is it?" They laughed and applauded, and I smiled again, hoping I looked and sounded genuine. It was hard, but it was vital that no one suspect I had anything else up my sleeve.

"Every strand is to be treasured," I said, injecting a note of solemnity into my voice. "Every experience, every memory, is sacred. On this Thousandth Night, we gather to select one strand in particular that has touched us more than others. That is our custom. But in doing so, we do not denigrate any other strands. In the totality of experience, they are all equally vital, and all equally cherished." I singled out Mullein, and smiled sympathetically. "Even the ones with an unusually high mud content."

Mullein laughed good-naturedly, and, for a moment, he was the star of the show again. The gentle mocking of one of our number was also part of tradition. Of all of us, Mullein could relax now.

"In a little while, we will return to our ships," I continued. "We will travel back out into the Galaxy and seek new experiences; new strands to be woven into the greater tapestry of the Gentian collective memory. None of us will leave here the same person he or she was a thousand days ago, and when we return, we will have changed again. That is part of the wonder of what Abigail made of herself. Other Lines favour rigid regimentation: a thousand identical clones, each programmed to respond to the same stimulus in exactly the same way. You might as well send out robots. That wasn't how Abigail wanted to do things. She wanted to gorge on reality. She wanted to feed her face with it, drunk on curiosity. In our bickering diversity, we honour that impulse." I paused and laced my hands, nodding at the nearest faces. "And now the time has come. The system has informed me of the winner...the name I am about to reveal." I pulled a face that suggested amused surprise. "The name is..."

And then I paused again, and frowned. The crowd tensed.

"Wait a moment," I said. "I'm sorry, but...something's wrong. I'm receiving an emergency message from my ship." I raised my voice over the people who had started talking. "This is...unfortunate. My ship has a technical problem with drive containment. There's a small but non-negligible risk of detonation." I tried to sound panicked, but still in some kind of control. "Please, remain calm. I'm ordering my ship to move to a safe distance..." I looked over the heads, beyond the island to the forest of parked ships, and counted to five in my head. "No response...I'm trying again, but..." The heads started moving, their voices threatening to drown me out. "Still no response," I said, tightening my face to a grimace. "I don't seem to be able to get a command through." I raised my voice, until I was almost shouting. "We're safe here: in a few seconds, I'll screen the island. Before I do that, I recommend that you order your ships to protect themselves."

Some of them already had. Their ships trembled within the vague, wobbling shapes of anticollision screens, like insects in spit. After a few seconds, the screens locked into stable forms and became harder to see. I allowed myself a glance in Purslane's direction. She responded with the tiniest encouraging nod.

It was working.

"Please," I urged. "Hurry. I'll raise the island's own screen in ten seconds. You may not be able to get a message through once that happens."

More and more ships wobbled as their screens flicked on. Peals of thunder, distant and low, signalled the activations. Doubtless many of the people were wondering what was going on: how it just happened that it was my ship that was threatening to blow up, when I was already the centre of attention. I just hoped that they would have the sense to put up their screens first and worry about the coincidence later.

But some of the largest ships were still not screened. I could not delay the screening of the island any longer. I would just have to hope that the necessary commands had already been sent, and that those ships were just a bit slow to respond.

But even as the island's own screen flickered on—blurring the view all around us, as if smeared glass had dropped into place—I knew that my plan was coming adrift.

Fescue spoke, his deep voice commanding instant attention. "The danger is passed," he said. "My own ship has projected a secondary screen around yours, Campion. You may lower the island's shield."

My answer caught in my throat. "My ship may blow at any moment. Are you sure that secondary screen is going to be good enough?"

"Yes," Fescue said, with withering authority. "I'm more than sure."

The gathered revellers looked out to my ship, which remained stubbornly intact within the envelope Fescue had projected around it.

"Lower the island screen, Campion." And even as he spoke, Fescue's ship pushed mine up and away, into the high atmosphere, until it was lost among the stars.

The meteor shower was over, I noticed.

"The screen," Fescue said.

I gave the necessary commands, lowering the screen. "Thank you," I said, breathless and distraught. "That was...quick thinking, Fescue."

"It must have been a false alarm after all," he said, his unmasked eyes piercing mine. "Or a mistake."

"I thought my ship was going to blow up."

"Of course you did. Why else would you have told us?" He made a growl-like sound. "You were about to announce the winner, Campion. Perhaps you ought to continue."

There was a murmur of approval. If I'd had the sympathy of the crowd five minutes ago, I had lost it completely now. My throat was dry. I saw Purslane, the fox mask tugged down, and something like horror on her face.

"Campion," Fescue pushed. "The winner...if it isn't too much trouble."

But I didn't know the winner. The system wasn't due to inform me for another hour. I had delayed my receipt of the announcement, not wishing to be distracted from the main business.

"I....the winner. Yes. The winner of the strand...the best strand winner...is...the winner. And the winner is..." I fell silent for ten or twenty seconds, frozen in the gaze of nearly a thousand mortified onlookers. Then my thoughts suddenly quietened, as if I'd found an epicentre of mental calm. I seemed to stand outside myself.

"There is no winner," I said softly. "Not yet."

"Perhaps you ought to stand down," Fescue said. "You've arranged a fine reunion; we all agree on that. It would be a shame to ruin it now."

Fescue took a step toward me, presumably intending to help me from the plinth.

"Wait," I said, with all the dignity I could muster. "Wait and hear me out. All of you."

"You have an explanation for this travesty?" Fescue asked.

"Yes," I said. "I do."

He stopped in his tracks and folded his arms. "Then let's hear it. Part of me would love to think that this is all part of your Thousandth Night plans, Campion."

"Something awful has happened," I said. "There has been a conspiracy...a murder. One of us has been killed."

Fescue cocked his head. "One of us?"

I scanned the crowd and pointed to Burdock's duplicate. "That's not Burdock," I said. "That's an impostor. The real Burdock is dead."

The duplicate Burdock pulled a startled face. He looked at the people surrounding him, and then back at me, aghast. He said something and the onlookers laughed.

"The real Burdock is dead?" Fescue asked. "Are you quite sure of this, Campion?"

"Yes. I know because I've seen his body. When we broke into his ship..."

"When 'we' broke into his ship," Fescue repeated, silencing me. "You mean there was someone else involved?"

Purslane's voice rang out clear and true. "It was me. Campion and I broke into the ship. Everything he's told you is the truth. Burdock was murdered by proponents of the Great Work, because Burdock knew what they had done."

Fescue looked intrigued. "Which was?"

"They destroyed an entire culture...Grisha's people...a culture that had uncovered Prior data damaging to the Great Work. Wiped them out with Homunculus weapons. Burdock tried to cover up his discovery, for fear of what the Advocates would do to him. There was a discrepancy in Burdock's dreams...an error." Purslane's control began to falter. "He said he'd been somewhere he hadn't...somewhere Campion had been."

"So it was Burdock's word against Campion?" Fescue turned to the impostor. "Does this make the slightest sense to you?"

The impostor shrugged and looked at me with something between pity and spite.

"Hear us out," Purslane insisted. "All Campion was hoping to do was provoke the raising of anticollision shields. The ship that destroyed Grisha's people...we had data on its field resonance, but we needed to see our own fields before we could establish a match." Purslane swallowed and regained some measure of calm. "I'm broadcasting the resonance data to all ships. See it for yourselves. See what those bastards did to Grisha's people."

There was a moment, a lull, while the crowd assessed the data Purslane had just made public. She had taken a frightful risk in revealing the information, for now our enemies had every incentive to move against us, even if that meant killing everyone else on the island. But I agreed with what she had done. We were out of options.

Except one.

"Very impressive," Fescue admitted. "But we've no evidence that you didn't forge this data."

"The authentication stamp ties it to Burdock," Purslane said.

Fescue looked regretful. "Authentication can always be faked, with sufficient ingenuity. You've already admitted that you broke into his ship, after all. Disavow your involvement in this, Purslane, before it's too late."

"No," she said. "I won't."

Fescue nodded at a number of the people around him, including a handful of senior Advocates.

"Restrain the two of them," he said.

I fingered the metal shape under my flame-colored costume. My hand closed on the haft and removed Grisha's particle gun. The crowd silenced as the evil little thing glinted in the lantern light. Earlier, unwitnessed, I had primed the weapon onto Burdock. I squeezed a jewelled button and the gun moved as if in an invisible grip, nearly dragging itself from my fist. It swivelled onto Burdock and locked steady as a snake. Even if I released my hold on the gun, it would keep tracking its designated target.

"Stand aside, please," I said.

"Don't do anything silly," Fescue said, even as the crowd parted around Burdock's impostor.

The moment closed around me like a vise. I had seen the real, dying Burdock aboard his ship—at least, I believed I had. When I squeezed the trigger, I would be killing a mindless automaton, a biomechanical construct programmed to duplicate Burdock's responses with a high degree of accuracy...but not a living thing. Nothing with a sense of self.

But what if the dying figure on the ship was the impostor, and this was still the real Burdock? What if the whole story about Grisha and the assassination agent had been the lie, and the real Burdock was standing in front of me? I had no idea why such an elaborate charade might have been staged...but I couldn't rule it out, either. And there was one possibility that sprang to mind. What if Burdock had enemies among the line, and they wanted him dead, with someone else to pin the blame on? Suddenly I felt dizzy, lost in mazelike permutations of bluff and double bluff. I had to make a simple choice. I had to trust my intuitive sense of what was true and what was false.

"If this is a mistake," I said, "forgive me."

I squeezed the trigger. The particle beam sliced its way across space, piercing the figure in the chest.

Burdock's impostor touched a hand to the smoking wound, opened its mouth as it speak, and fell lifeless to the floor. The crowd screamed their horror, revolted at the idea that a member of the Gentian Line had murdered another.

My work done, I let go of the particle gun. It remained floating before me, as if inviting me to take another shot. Burdock's impostor lay on its side, with one dry hand open to the sky. He had touched the wound and there had been no blood. I allowed myself a moment of relief. The others would see that the thing I had killed was not a man, but a bloodless construct. But even as these thoughts formed, the body retched and coughed a mouthful of dark blood onto the perfect white marble of the terrace. Its face was a mask of fear and incomprehension. Then it was still.

The crowd surged. They were on me in seconds, swatting aside the gun. They pulled me from the plinth and smothered me to the ground. The breath was knocked out of me. They began to pull at my clothing with animal fury. I heard shouts as some of the revellers tried to pull the others off me, but the collective anger—the collective repulsion—was too great to be resisted. I felt something crack in my chest, tasted my own blood as someone smashed a fist into my jaw. I thrashed out, survival instincts kicking in, but there were too many of them. Most of them were still wearing carnival masks.

Then something happened. Just before I was about to go under, the attack calmed. Someone landed a final punch in my chest, sending a bolt of pain up my spine, and then pulled away. I received a desultory kick, and then they left me there, sprawled on the ground, my mouth wet, my body bruised. I knew they hadn't finished with me. They were just leaving me alone while something else attracted their attention.

In their hundreds, they were pressing against the low railing that encircled the balcony. They were looking out to sea, drawn by something going on beyond the island. I pushed myself to my feet and stumbled to the slumped form of Purslane. They had not hurt her as badly as me, but there was still a cut on her lip where someone had slapped her.

"Are you all right?" I said, my mouth thick with blood.

"Better than you," she said.

"I don't think they're done with us. There's a distraction now...maybe we could reach our ships?"

She shook her head and used her finger to wipe blood from my chin. "We started this, Campion. Let's finish it."

"It's Fescue," I said. "He's the one."

We followed the onlookers to the balcony. No one gave us a second glance, even as we pushed forward to the front. All round us the revellers were looking at the sea. Sleek dark forms were surfacing from the midnight waters, black as night themselves. They lolled and bellied in the waves, pushing great flukes and flippers into the sky, jetting white spouts of water from blowholes.

Purslane asked me what was happening.

"I don't know," I said truthfully.

"You planned this, Campion. This has to be something to do with Thousandth Night."

"I know." I winced at the pain in my chest, certain that the mob had broken a rib. "But I don't remember what I planned. I thought the meteor shower was an end to it."

They were everywhere now, surfacing in multitudes. "It's as if they're gathering in readiness for something," Purslane said. "Like the start of a migration."

"To where?"

"You tell me, Campion."

But I didn't have to tell her. It was soon obvious. In ones and twos they started leaving the ocean, rising into the air. Curtains of water drained off their flanks as they parted company with the sea. Ones and twos at first, then whole schools of them, rising into the sky between the hovering cliffs of our ships, as if they were born to fly.

"This is...impossible," I said. "They're aquatics. They don't...fly."

"Unless you made them that way. Unless you always planned this."

Pink-tinged aurorae flickered around the rising forms, hinting at the fields that allowed them to fly, and which would—I presumed—sustain them when the air thinned out, high above us. Some ghost of a memory now pushed its way into my consciousness. Had I truly engineered these aquatics for flight, equipping them with implanted field generators, and enough animal wisdom to use them? The memory beckoned, and then shrivelled under my attention.

"Maybe," I said.

"Good," Purslane said. "But now the next question: why?"

But we didn't have long to wonder about that. Suddenly the sky was cut in two by a brighter meteor than any we had seen during the earlier display. It boomed, reverberating down to the horizon and left a greenish aftertinge.

Another followed it: brighter now.

As if the meteor had triggered something, the sea erupted with a vast wave of departing aquatics. Thousands of them now, packed into huge and ponderous shoals or flocks, each aggregation moving with its own dim identity. The seas were emptying of life. Another meteor slashed the sky, bringing a temporary daylight to the scene. Over the horizon, an ominous false dawn signalled some terrible impact. Something large had smashed into my world. As more trails of light split the sky, I sensed that it would not be the last.

The island shook beneath our feet. That made no sense at all: there surely hadn't been enough time for shockwaves to reach us yet, but none of us had imagined the vibration. I steadied myself on the handrail.

"What..." Purslane began.

The island shook again. That was a cue for the crowd to renew their interest in me, tearing their attention away from the departing aquatics. Purslane squeezed closer to me. I tightened my hold on her, while she redoubled her hold on me.

The crowd advanced.

"Stop," boomed out a voice.

Everyone halted and turned to look at the speaker. It was Fescue, and he was kneeling by the figure I had shot. He had a hand in the wound I had bored through the body, plunged deep to the wrist. Slowly he withdrew his hand, slick to the cuff with blood, but holding something between his fingers, something that wriggled in them like a little silver starfish.

"This wasn't Burdock," he said, standing to his feet, while still holding the obscene, wriggling thing. "It was...a thing. Just like Campion and Purslane told us." Fescue turned to look at me, his expression grave and forgiving. "You told the truth."

"Yes," I said, with all the breath I could muster. I realised that I had been wrong about Fescue: utterly, utterly wrong.

"Then it's true," he said. "One of us has committed a crime."

"Burdock's body is still on his ship," I said. "All of this can be proved... if you allow us."

The ground shook again. Overhead, the meteor assault had become continuous, and the horizon was aglow with fire. I had no sooner registered this than a small shard slammed out of the sky no more than fifteen kilometers from the island, punching a bright frothing wound into the sea. Sensing danger, the island's screen came on, muting the impact blast to a salty roar. Another trail lanced down fifty kilometers away, raising a huge plume of superheated steam.

The impacts were increasing in severity.

Fescue spoke again. "We've all seen the evidence Purslane submitted. Given the truth about Burdock...I believe we should take the rest of the story seriously. Including the part about the murder of an entire culture." He looked at the two of us. "You wanted to see our anticollision fields, I believe."

"That'll tell us who did it," Purslane said.

"I think you may shortly have your wish."

He was right. All around the island, the ships were raising their screens again, as protection against the bombardment. The smaller ships at first, then the larger ones—all the way up to the biggest craft of all, those that were already poking into space. The screens quivered and stabilised, and a hail of minor impacts glittered off them.

"Well," Fescue said, addressing Purslane. "Do you see a match?"

"Yes," she said. "I do."

Fescue nodded grimly. "Would you care to tell us who it is?"

Purslane blinked, paralysed by the enormity of what she had to reveal. I held her hand, willing her to find the strength. "I thought it might be you," she told Fescue. "Your ship matched the size profile...and when you ruined Campion's ploy..."

"I don't think he meant to," I said.

"No, he didn't," Purslane said. "That's obvious now. And in any case, his ship isn't the best match. Samphire's ship, on the other hand..."

As one, the crowd's attention locked onto Samphire. "No," he said. "There's been a mistake."

"Perhaps," Fescue said. "But there is the matter of the weapons Purslane mentioned: the ones used against Grisha's people. You've always had an interest in ancient weapons, Samphire...especially the weapons of the Homunculus wars."

Samphire looked astonished. "That was over a million years ago. It's ancient history!"

"But what's a million years to the Gentian Line? You knew where those weapons were to be found, and you probably had more than an inkling of how they worked."

"No," Samphire said. "This is preposterous."

"It may well be," Fescue allowed. "In which case, you'll be allowed all the time you need to make your case, before a jury of your peers. If you are innocent, we'll prove it and ask your forgiveness—just as we did with Betony, all those years ago. If you are guilty, we will prove that instead—and uncover the rest of your collaborators. You've never struck me as the calculating kind, Samphire: I doubt that you put this together without assistance."

A wave of change overcame Samphire: his expression hardening. "You can prove what you like," he said. "It will change nothing."

"That sounds suspiciously like an admission of guilt," Fescue said. "Is it true? Did you really murder an entire culture, just to protect the Great Work?"

Now his expression was full of disdain. There was an authority in his voice I had never heard before. "One culture," Samphire said. "One pebble on the beach, against an ocean of possibility! Do you honestly think they mattered? Do you honestly think we'll remember them, in a billion years?"

Fescue turned to his Advocate friends. "Restrain him."

Three of the Advocates took purposeful steps toward Samphire. But they had only taken three or four paces when Samphire shook his head, more in sorrow than anger, and ripped open his tunic, exposing his smooth and hairless chest to the waist. He plunged his fingers into his own skin and pulled it aside like two theatrical curtains, showing no pain. Instead of muscle and bone, we saw only an oozing clockwork of translucent pink machines, layered around a glowing blue core.

"Homunculus machinery," Fescue said, with an awesome calm. "He's a weapon."

Samphire smiled. A white light curdled in his open chest. It brightened to hellfire, ramming from his mouth and eyes. The construct body writhed as the detonating weapon consumed its nervous system from within. The outer layers crisped and collapsed.

But something was containing the blast. The white light—almost too bright to look at now—could not escape. It was being held back by a man-sized containment bubble, locked around Samphire.

I looked at Fescue. He stood with his arms outstretched, like a sculptor visualising a composition. Thick metal jewellery glinted on his fingers. Not jewellery, I realised now, but miniature field generators. Fescue was holding the containment bubble around Samphire, preventing the blast from escaping and destroying us all. His face was etched with the strain of controlling the generators.

"I'm not sure of the yield," Fescue said to me, forcing each word out. "Sub-kilotonne range, I think, or else your systems would have detected the homunculus machinery. But it will still be enough to destroy this balcony. Can the island lock a screen around him?"

"No," I said. "I never allowed for...this."

"That's as I thought. I can't hold it much longer...twenty-five, thirty seconds." Fescue's eyes bored into me with iron determination. "You have complete control of the structure, Campion? You can reshape it according to your requirements?"

"Yes," I said, faltering.

"Then you must drop the two of us through the floor."

They were standing only a few meters apart. It would only cost me a moment's concentration to order that part of the floor to detach itself, falling free. But if I did that, I would be sending Fescue to his death.

"Do it!" he hissed.

"I can't," I said.

"Campion," he said. "I know you and I have had our differences. I have always criticised you for lacking spine. Well, now is your chance to prove me wrong. *Do this*."

"I..."

"Do it! For the sake of the line!"

I looked at the faces of the other line members. I saw their pain, but also their solemn consent. They were telling me I had no choice. They were telling me to kill Fescue, and save us all.

I did it.

I willed the floor around the two figures to detach itself from the rest of the balcony. The tiny machines forming the fabric of the floor followed my will with dumb obedience, severing the molecular bonds that linked each machine to its neighbour.

For a heart-rending moment, the floor seemed to hover in place.

The field around Samphire quivered, beginning to lose integrity. Fescue's generators were running out of power, Fescue running out of concentration...

He looked at me and nodded. "Good work, Campion."

Then they dropped.

It was a long way down, and they were still falling when the revellers surged to the edge of the balcony to look down. The light from the explosion momentarily eclipsed the brightest impacts still raining down on the planet. I nodded at Fescue's assessment: kilotonne range, easily. He had been right. It would have killed us all, and snapped the spire in two had the balcony not been flung so far out in space. It had been an accidental whim of design, but it had saved us all.

So had Fescue.

THERE WAS A great space battle that night, but this time it was for real, not staged in memory of some ancient, time-fogged conflict. The real Samphire had been on his ship, and when the construct failed to destroy the island, he made a run for orbit. From orbit, he must have planned to turn the ship's own armaments on Reunion. But Fescue's allies had anticipated him, and when his ship moved, so did a dozen others. They made interception above the lacerated atmosphere of my dying world and lit the sky with obscene energies. Samphire died, or at least that version of Samphire that had been sent to infiltrate our gathering. It may or may not have been the final one. It may or may not have been the only impostor in our midst.

After the battle, Vetchling, one of the other Advocates, took me aside and told me what she knew.

"Fescue supported the Great Work," she said. "But not at any cost. When evidence reached him that an atrocity had been committed in the name of the Work...the murder of an entire human culture...he realised that not all of us shared his view."

"Then Fescue knew all along," I said, dismayed.

"No. He had shards of intelligence—hints, rumours, whisperings. He still had no idea who had committed the crime; how deeply they were tied to Gentian Line. He did not know whether the rest of the Advocates could be trusted." She paused. "He trusted me, and a handful of others. But not everyone."

"But Fescue spoke to me about the Great Work," I said. "Of how we all had to bind together to bring it into being."

"He believed it would be for the best. But more than likely he was sounding you out, seeing what you thought of it, goading you into an indiscretion." Vetchling looked to the simmering sea, punctured by hundreds of volcanic vents that had reopened in the planet's crust. We were looking down on the sea from a dizzy height now: the island had detached itself from Reunion, and was now climbing slowly into space, pushed by the vast motors I must have installed in its foundation rocks. The blast from Samphire's weapon had shattered the outlying islands, crumbling them back into the sea. The water had rushed into the fill the caldera left after the main island's departure, and now there was no trace that it had ever existed.

The party was over.

"He suspected Advocate involvement in the crime," Vetchling continued. "But he could not rule out someone else being implicated: a sleeper, an agent no one would suspect."

"He must have suspected Purslane and I," I said.

"That's possible. You did spend a lot of time associating, after all. If it's any consolation, the two of you wouldn't have been his only suspects. He may even have had his suspicions about Samphire."

"What will happen to the Great Work now?"

"That's not just a matter for Gentian Line," Vetchling said. "But my guess is there'll be pressure to put the whole thing on the back burner for a few hundred thousand years. A cooling-off period." She sounded sad. "Fescue was respected. He had a lot of friends beyond our line."

"I hated him," I said.

"He wouldn't have minded. All he really cared about was the line. You did the right thing, Campion."

"I killed him."

"You saved us all. You have Fescue's gratitude."

"How can you know?" I asked.

She touched a finger to her lips. "I know. Isn't that enough for you?"

A LITTLE LATER, Purslane and I stood alone on the highest balcony of the island's central spire. The island had climbed out of what would have been Reunion's atmosphere, had the atmosphere remained.

Far below, viewed through the flickering curtain of the containment bubble, my planet writhed in the agonies of its death by stoning. The impacting asteroids struck her like fists, bludgeoning her in furious quick-time. At least two, sometimes three or four, arrived within every minute. Their impact fireballs had dispersed most of the atmosphere by now, and had elevated a goodly fraction of the crust into parabolas of molten rock, tongues of flame that arced thousands of kilometers before splashing down. They reminded me of the coronal arcs near the surface of a late-type star. The ocean was a memory: boiled into a dust-choked vapour. Concussion from the multiple impacts was already unhinging the delicate clockwork of the planet's magnetohydrodynamic core. Had there been a spot on the planet where it was still night, the auroral storms would have been glorious. For a moment, I regretted that I had not arranged matters so that the aurorae had formed part of the show, somehow, someway.

But it was much too late for second thoughts now. It would be some-one else's turn next time.

Purslane took my hand. "Don't look so sad, Campion. You did well. It was a fine end."

"You think so?"

"They'll be raving about this for a million years. What you did with those whales..." She shook her head in undisguised admiration.

"I couldn't very well let them stay in the ocean."

"It was lovely. Putting aside everyone else that happened...I think that was my favourite bit. Not that this is bad, either."

We paused a while to watch a succession of major impacts: a long, sequenced string of them. Continent-sized fissures were beginning to open up deep into the planet's mantle: wounds as bright as day.

"I created something and now I'm ruining it. Doesn't that strike you as just the tiniest bit...infantile? Fescue certainly wouldn't have approved."

"I don't know," she said. "It's not as if that world ever had any chance of outlasting us. It was created to endure for a specific moment in time. Like a sandcastle, or an ice sculpture. Here, and then gone. In a way, that's the beauty of it. Who'd marvel at a sandcastle, if sandcastles lasted forever?"

"Or sunsets, I suppose," I said.

"Oh, no," she said. "Don't start talking about sunsets again. I thought you got that safely out of your system last time."

"I have," I said. "Completely and utterly. I'm thinking of a radically different theme for my tour this time. Something as far removed from sunsets as possible."

"Oh, good."

"Something like...waterfalls."

"Waterfalls."

"They're pretty universal, you know. Any planet with some kind of atmosphere, and some kind of surface, usually ends up with something vaguely like a waterfall, somewhere. As long as you're not too fussy about the water part."

"Actually," Purslane said, "I quite like waterfalls. I remember one I encountered in my travels...ten vertical kilometers of it, pure methane. I stood under it, allowed myself to feel a little of the cold. Just enough to shiver at the wonder of it."

"It's probably gone now," I said sadly. "They don't last long, compared to us."

"But perhaps you'll find an even better one."

"I'll keep my eyes open. I mapped some promising rivers during my tour; places where the geology might have allowed waterfalls to form by now. I think I'll revisit some of those old places, for old time's sake."

"Bring me back a memory."

"I'll be sure to. It's just such a shame you won't ever see them with your own eyes..." I paused, aware that I stood on the thrilling, dangerous threshold of something. "I mean with me, the two of us."

"You know the line frowns upon planned associations," Purslane said, as if I needed to be reminded. "Such meetings erode the very spirit of chance and adventure Abigail sought to instill in us. If we meet between now and the next reunion, it must be by chance and chance alone."

"Then we'll never meet."

"No. Probably not."

"That's a silly rule, isn't it? I mean, given everything else that's happened here...why should we care?"

Purslane was a great while answering. "Because we're traditionalists, Campion. Line loyalists, to the marrow." She tightened her grip on the rail as something came streaking up from the molten world below: the last of my aquatics, lingering out of idleness or some instinctive curiosity. The huge field-encased creature was as sleek as night, its under parts highlit in brassy reds from the fires. It paused at the level of the balcony, long enough to scrutinise us with one small, wrinkled, distressingly human eye. Then with a powerful flick of its fluke it soared higher, to the orbital shallows where its fellow were already assembling.

"There is something, though," Purslane added.

"What?"

"I shouldn't even mention it...but I've been less than discreet about my flight plan. That trick I used to break into Burdock's ship? It worked equally well with yours."

"What did you do?"

"Nothing harmful. Just installed a copy of my flight plan on your ship...for your information. Just so you know where I am."

"You're right," I said, wonderingly. "That was spectacularly indiscreet."

"I couldn't help it."

"It would be completely improper for us to meet."

"Utterly," Purslane agreed, nodding emphatically.

"But you'll stick to that flight plan?"

"To the letter." She had finished her wine. She flung the empty glass into space. I watched it fall, waiting for the glint when it impacted the bubble. But before it hit, Purslane took my arm and turned me away from the view. "Come on, Campion. Let's go inside. They're still all waiting to hear who's won best strand."

"I can't believe anyone still cares about that, after all that's happened."

"Never underestimate the recuperative powers of human vanity," Purslane said sagely. "Besides: it isn't just the strand we have to think about. There are two memorials that need to be created. We'll need one for Burdock, and one for Fescue."

"One day we might need one for Samphire as well," I said.

"I think we'll do our best to forget all about him."

"He won't go away that easily. He may still be alive. Or it may be that he was murdered and replaced with an impostor, just like Burdock. Either way, I have a feeling we haven't finished with him. Or the Great Work."

"We've won this battle, though. That's enough for tonight, isn't it?"

"It'll have to be," I said.

"Something worries me, though," Purslane said. "We still haven't told anyone that my strand wasn't all it appears to be. They'll have to find out one of these days."

"Not tonight, though."

"Campion...if my name comes out of the hat...*what will I do*?"

I feigned concern, suppressing an amused smile. "Do what I'd do. Keep a very straight face."

"You mean...just accept it? That would be a little on the mischievous side, wouldn't it?"

"Very," I said. "But worth it, all the same."

Purslane tightened her grasp on my arm. Together we walked back toward the auditorium where the others waited. Under us, the fires of creation consumed my little world while, far above it, aquatics gathered in squadrons and schools, ready for their long migration.

TROIKA

Y THE time I reach the road to Zvezdniy Gorodok acute hypothermia is beginning to set in. I recognise the symptoms from my training: stage one moving into two, as my body redirects blood away from skin to conserve heat—shivering and a general loss of coordination the result. Later I can expect a deterioration of vasomotor tone as the muscles now contracting my peripheral blood vessels become exhausted. As blood surges back to my chilled extremities, I'll start to feel hot rather than cold. Slipping ever further into disorientation, it will take an effort of will not to succumb to that familiar and distressing syndrome, paradoxical undressing. The few layers of clothes I'm wearing—the pyjamas, the thin coat I stole from Doctor Kizim—will start feeling too warm. They'll find me naked and dead in the snow.

How long have I been out? An hour, two hours? There's no way to tell. It's like being back on the *Tereshkova*, when we slept so little that a day could feel like a week. All I know is that it's still night. When the sun is up it will be harder to move around, but until then there's still time to locate Nesha Petrova.

I touch the metal prize in my pocket, reassuring myself that it's still there.

As if invoked by the act of touching the prize, a monstrous machine roars toward me out of the night. It's yellow, with an angled shovel on the front. I stumble into the path of its headlights and raise a wary hand. The snowplough sounds its horn. I jerk back, avoiding the blade and the flurry of dirty snow it flings aside.

I think for a moment it's going to surge on past. Instead the machine slows and stops. Maybe he thinks he's hit me. It's good—a robot snowplough wouldn't stop, so there must be someone operating this one. I hobble around to the cab, where the driver's glaring at me through an unopened window. He's got a moustache, a woollen hat jammed down over his hair and ears, the red nose of a serious drinker.

Above the snorting, impatient diesel I call: "I could use a ride to town."

The driver looks at me like I'm dirt, some piece of roadside debris he'd have been better shovelling into the verge. This far out of town, on this road, it doesn't take much guesswork to figure out where I've come from. The hospital, the facility, the madhouse, whatever you want to call it, will have been visible in the distance on a clear day—a forbidding smudge of dark, tiny-windowed buildings, tucked behind high, razor-topped security fencing.

He lowers the window an inch. "Do yourself a favour, friend. Go back, get warm."

"I won't make it back. Early-onset hypothermia. Please, take me to Zvezdniy Gorodok. I can't give you much, but you're welcome to these." My fingers feel like awkward tele-operated waldos, the kind we'd had on the Progress. I fumble a pack of cigarettes from my coat pocket and push the crushed and soggy rectangle up to the slit in the window.

"All you've got?"

"They're American."

The driver grunts something unintelligible, but takes the cigarettes anyway. He opens the pack to inspect the contents, sniffing at them. "How old are these?"

"You can still smoke them."

The driver leans over to open the other door. "Get in. I'll take you as far as the first crossroads on the edge of town. You get out when we stop. You're on your own from then on."

I'll agree to any arrangement provided it gets me a few minutes in the warmth of the cab. For now I'm still lucid enough to recognise the hypothermia creeping over me. That state of clinical detachment won't last forever.

I climb in, taking deep, shivering breaths.

"Thank you."

"The edge of town, that's as far as we go," he says, as if I didn't get it the first time. His breath stinks of alcohol. "I'm caught giving you a ride, it won't be good for me."

"I doubt it'll be good for either of us."

The driver shifts the snowplough back into gear and lets her roll, the engine bellowing as the blade bites snow. "They'll find you in Zvezdniy Gorodok. It's not that big a place. It's the arse end of nowhere and the trains aren't running."

"I only need to get to town."

He looks at me, assessing the shabbiness of my dress, the state of my beard and hair. "Wild night ahead of you?"

"Something like that."

He's got the radio on, tuned to the state classical music channel. It's playing Prokofiev. I lean over and turn the volume down, until it's almost lost under the engine noise.

"I was listening to that."

"Please. Until we get there."

"Got a problem with music?"

"Some of it."

The driver shrugs—he doesn't seem to mind as much as he pretends. Panicking suddenly, imagining I might have dropped it in the snow, I pat my pocket again. But—along with Doctor Kizim's security pass—the little metal box is still there.

It takes all of my resolve not to take it out and turn the little handle that makes it play. Not because I can stand to hear it again, but because I want to be sure it still works.

THE SNOWPLOUGH'S TAILLIGHTS fade into the night. The driver has kept to his word, taking us through the abandoned checkpoint, then to the first crossroads inside the old city boundary and no further. It's been good to get warm, my clothes beginning to dry, but now that I'm outside again the cold only takes a few seconds to reach my bones. The blizzard has abated while we drove, but the snow's still falling, coming down in soft flurries from a milky predawn sky.

At this early hour Zvezdniy Gorodok gives every indication of being deserted. The housing blocks are mostly unlit, save for the occasional illuminated window—a pale, curtained rectangle of dim yellow against the otherwise dark edifice. The buildings, set back from the intersecting roads in long ranks, look drearily similar, as if stamped from the same machine tool—even the party images flickering on their sides are the same from building to building. The same faces, the same slogans. For a moment I have the sense of having embarked on a ludicrous and faintly delusional task. Any one of these buildings could be where she lives. They'll find me long before I have time to search each lobby, hoping to find a name.

I'd shown the driver the address I'd written down, pulled from the public telephone directory on Doctor Kizim's desk. He'd given me a rough idea of where I ought to head. The apartment complex is somewhere near the railway station—I'll have to search the surrounding streets until I find it.

"I know where the station is," I tell the driver. "I was here when it was a sealed training facility."

"You had something to do with the space program?"

"I did my bit."

Zvezdniy Gorodok—Starry Town, or Star City. In the old days, you needed a permit just to get into it. Now that the space program is over—it has "achieved all necessary objectives", according to the official line of the Second Soviet—Zvezdniy Gorodok is just another place to live, work and die. Utilitarian housing projects radiate far beyond the old boundary. The checkpoint is a disused ruin and the labs and training facilities have been turned into austere community buildings. More farmers and factory workers live here now than engineers, scientists and former cosmonauts.

I'm lucky to have got this far.

I escaped through a gap in the facility's security fence, in a neglected corner of the establishment tucked away behind one of the kitchens. I'd known about the breach for at least six months—long enough to reassure myself that no one else had noticed it, and that the break could not be seen from the administrative offices or any of the surveillance cameras. It was good fortune that the gap existed, but I still wouldn't have got far without the help from Doctor Kizim. I don't know if he expects me to succeed in my escape attempt, but Doctor Kizim—who had always been more sympathetic to the *Tereshkova*'s survivors than any of the other medics—did turn a conveniently blind eye. It was his coat that I had taken. Not much good against blizzards, but without it I'd never have got as far as the snowplough, let alone Zvezdniy Gorodok. I just hope he doesn't get into too much trouble when they find out I took it.

I don't expect to get the chance to apologise to him.

The snow's stopped falling, and a pink frigid sun is trying to break through the gloom on the eastern horizon. I locate the railway station, and begin to explore the surrounding streets, certain I can't be wrong. More lights have come on now and I'm noticing the stirrings of daily activity. One or two citizens pass me in the snow, but they have their heads down and pay me little heed. Few vehicles are on the roads, and with the trains not running the area around the station is almost totally devoid of activity. When a large car—a Zil limousine, black and muscular as a panther—swings onto the street I'm walking down, I don't have time to hide. But the Zil sails by, tyres spraying muddy slush, and as it passes I see that it's empty. The car must be on its way to collect a party official from one of the better districts.

I've been walking for an hour, trying not to glance over my shoulder too often, when I find Nesha's building. The apartment complex has a public entrance lobby smelling of toilets and alcohol. Plywood panels cover some of the windows in the outer wall, where the glass has broken. It's draughty and unlit, the tiled floor filthy with footprints and paper and smashed glass. The door into the rest of the building can only be opened by someone inside. In my cold, sodden slippers I squelch to the buzzer panel next to the mailboxes.

I catch my breath. Everything hinges on this moment. If I'm wrong about Nesha, or if she's moved elsewhere, or died—it's been a long time, after all—then everything, everything, will have been for nothing.

But her name's still there.

N. Petrova. She lives on the ninth floor.

It may mean nothing. She may still have died or been moved on. I reach out a numb finger and press the buzzer anyway. There's no sound, no reassuring response. I wait a minute then press it again. Outside, a stray dog with mad eyes yellows the snow under a lamp-post. I press the buzzer again, shivering more than when I was outside.

A woman's voice crackles through the grille above the buzzers. "Yes?"

"Nesha Petrova?" I ask, leaning to bring my lips closer to the grille.

"Who is it?"

"Dimitri Ivanov." I wait a second or two for her to respond to the name.

"From building services?"

I assume that there's no camera letting Nesha see me, if there ever was. "Dimitri Ivanov, the cosmonaut. I was on the ship, the *Tereshkova.* The one that met the Matryoshka."

Silence follows. I realise, dimly, that there's an eventuality I've never allowed for. Nesha Petrova may be too old to remember anything of importance. She may be too old to care.

I shuffle wet feet to stave off the cold.

"Nesha?"

"There were three cosmonauts."

I lean into the grille again. "The other two were Galenka Makarova and Yakov Demin. They're both dead now. The VASIMIR engine malfunctioned on the way home, exposing them to too much radiation. I'm the only one left."

"Why should I believe you?"

"Because I'm standing here in pyjamas and a stolen coat. Because I've come all the way from the facility just to see you, through the snow. Because there's something I want you to know."

"Then tell me."

"I'd rather show you. Besides, I'm going to die of cold if I stand here much longer."

I look to the outside world again, through one of the panes that hasn't been broken and covered over with plywood. Another Zil slides by. This one has bodies in it: grey-skinned men sitting upright in dark coats and hats.

"I don't want any trouble from the police."

"I won't stay long. Then I'll be on my way, and no one will have to know that I was here."

"I'll know."

"Please, let me in." I haven't bargained for this. In all the versions of this encounter that I've run through my mind before the escape, she never needed any persuasion to meet me. "Nesha, you need to understand. They tried to bury you, but you were right all along. That's what I want to tell you about. Before they silence me, and no one ever gets to find out."

After an age she says: "You think it matters now, Dimitri Ivanov? You think anything matters?"

"More than you can imagine," I say.

The door buzzes. She's letting me in.

"IT'S BLACKER THAN I was expecting."

I paused in my hamfisted typing. "Of course it's black. What other colour were you expecting?"

Yakov was still staring out the porthole, at the looming Matryoshka. It was two hundred kilometres away, but still ate up more than half the sky. No stars in that direction, just a big absence like the mother of all galactic supervoids. We had the cabin lights dimmed so he could get a good view. We had already spread the relay microsats around the alien machine, ready for when the Progress penetrated one of the transient windows in Shell 3. But you couldn't see the microsats from here—they were tiny, and the machine was vast.

"What I mean is..." Yakov started saying.

"Is that it's black."

"I mean it's more than black. It's like—black was black, and now there's something in my head that's even darker, like a colour I never imagined until now. But which was always there, just waiting for this moment."

"I'm concerned about you, comrade," said Galenka, who was riding the exercise cycle in one corner of the module. She was wearing a skin-tight load-suit, designed to preserve muscle tone even in weightlessness. Maybe I'd been in space too long, but she looked better in that load-suit every day.

"You don't feel it, then?" Yakov asked, directing his question to both of us.

"It's just dark," I said. "I guess nothing's really prepared us for this, but it's not something we should be surprised about. The last two apparitions…"

"Just machines, just dumb space probes. This is the first time any-one's seen it with their own eyes." Yakov turned slowly from the porthole. He was pale, with the puffy, slit-eyed look we'd all developed since leaving Earth. "Don't you think that changes things? Don't you think us being out here, us being observers, changes things? We're not just making mea-surements on this thing from a distance now. We're interacting, touching it, feeling it."

"And I think you need to get some sleep," Galenka said.

I folded the workstation keyboard back into its recess. I had been answering questions from schoolchildren; the selected few that had been deemed worthy of my attention by the mission schedulers.

"Tell me you don't feel a little freaked out, Dimitri."

"Maybe a bit," I allowed. "But no more than I'd feel if we were in orbit around Mars, or Venus, or creeping up on an asteroid. It's a very big thing and we're very small and a long way from home."

"This is also a very alien big thing. It was made by alien minds, for a purpose we can't grasp. It's not just some lump of rock with a gravita-tional field. It's a machine, a ship, that they sent to our solar system for a reason."

"It's a dead alien thing," Galenka said, huffing as she cycled harder, pushing through an uphill part of her training schedule. "Someone made it once, but it's broken now. Fucked like an old clock. If it wasn't fucked, it wouldn't be on this stupid elliptical orbit."

"Maybe this orbit is all part of the plan," Yakov said.

"He's starting to sound like Nesha Petrova," Galenka said teasingly. "Be careful, Yakov. You know what happened to her when she didn't shut up with her silly ideas."

"What plan?" I asked.

"That thing must be thousands of years old. Tens of thousand, maybe more. The fact that it's been on this orbit for twenty-four years proves nothing. It's an eye-blink, as far as that thing's concerned. It might just be waking up, running systems checks, rebooting itself. It came through a wormhole. Who knows what that does to something?"

"You certainly don't," Galenka said.

"She's right," I said. "It's dead. If it was going to wake up, it would have done so during the first two apparitions. We poked and prodded it enough the second time; nothing happened."

"I wish I shared your reassurance."

I shrugged. "We're just here to do a job, Yakov. Get in, get out. Then go home and get the glory, like good cosmonauts. Before I worried about the Matryoshka, I'd worry about not screwing up your part in it."

"I'm not going to screw up." He looked at me earnestly, as if I had challenged him. "Did I ever screw up in the simulations, Dimitri? Did I ever screw up once?"

"No," I admitted. "But this isn't a simulation. We're not in Star City now."

He winked at me. "Absolutely sure of that, comrade?"

I WIPED THE sleeve of my load-suit against the portal glass to clear the condensation. From around the curve of the ship there was a puff of silvery brightness as the pyrotechnic docking latches released their hold on the Progress. In the same instant I heard a faraway thud and felt the fabric of the ship lurch with the recoil.

"Confirm separation," Yakov reported, calling from another porthole. "Looks like a clean birth to me, boys and girls."

Galenka was webbed into a hammock at the Progress workstation, one hand on a joystick and the other tapping a keyboard. The screens before her were alive with camera views, from both the *Tereshkova* and the little robot that had just detached from it.

"Beginning thruster translation," she said, touching keys. "You should see her in a few seconds, Dimitri."

The Progress drifted over my horizon, a pea-green shuttlecock with CCCP stencilled down the side in red letters. Very slowly it pulled away from the *Tereshkova* and tipped around on two axes, pointing its nose at the forbidding darkness of the Matryoshka. "Looking good," I said, inspecting every visible inch of the spacecraft for signs of damage. "No impacts that I can see. Looks as good as the day they wheeled her out of the clean room."

"Stirring hydrazine tanks," Galenka said. "Let's see if she holds, shall we?"

"Still there," I reported, when the Progress had failed to blow itself apart. "Looks like we have a viable spacecraft. Shall I break out the vodka?"

"Let's not get ahead of ourselves—no use going in if we're blind. Beginning camera and waldo deployment—this'll be the real test."

Our little envoy looked like a cross between a spaceship and a deep-sea submersible robot, the kind they use to explore shipwrecks and pull missiles out of sunken submarines. Arms and sensors and cameras had been bolted onto the front, ruining whatever vague aerodynamics the Progress might have had. Now the equipment—stowed since launch—was slowly deploying, like a flower opening to the sun. Galenka pushed aside the joystick and tugged down a set of waldo controls, slipping her fingers into the heavy, sensor-laden gloves and sleeves. Out in space, the Progress's mechanical arms and hands echoed her gestures. It looked good to me but Galenka still frowned and made some small adjustments to the settings. Ever the perfectionist, I thought. More check-out tests followed until she signified grudging satisfaction.

"Camera assembly three is a little stiff—I wouldn't be surprised if it seizes on us mid-mission. Haptic feedback on arm two is delayed just enough to throw me off. We've lost a row of pixels on the mid infrared array—probably a bad cosmic ray strike. I'm already reading an event overflow in one of the memory buffers, and we haven't even started logging data."

"But you're happy to continue?" I asked.

"Unless we brought a second Progress no one told me about, we're stuck with this one."

"It's nothing we can repair," Yakov said. "So we may as well live with it. Even if we went out in the suits, we don't have the tools to fix those instruments."

"I don't need that spelled out," Galenka said, just barely keeping a lid on her temper.

Yakov was starting to needle both of us. The Matryoshka was getting to him in a way it wasn't yet getting to Galenka, or me for that matter. He'd started coming out with some very odd statements. The joke of his, that we were still back in Star City, that all of this was an elaborate simulation, a preparation for the mission to come—even down to the impossible-to-fake weightlessness—was beginning to wear thin.

What bothered me was that I wasn't even sure he was joking any more.

People cracked in space. It was part of the job. That was why we had duct-tape and tasers aboard. I just hadn't expected it to happen to one of us, so soon in the mission. We hadn't even touched the Matryoshka yet. What was going to happen when the Progress reached the secret layers beneath Shell 3?

I tried not to think about it.

"WHAT'S YOUR APPROACH speed?" I asked, looming behind Galenka while she worked the controls.

"Two metres per second, on the nail."

"A little on the fast side, aren't we?"

Galenka touched a hand over the mike, so Baikonur wouldn't hear what she had to say next. "You flying this thing, or me, comrade?"

"You are, definitely." I scratched at chin stubble. "It's just that I thought we were going to keep it below one meter a second, all the way in."

"You want to sit around for thirty hours, be my guest."

"I wouldn't be the one doing the sitting."

"This is well within acceptable limits. We'll make up speed in the gaps and slow down when we hit anything knotty. Trust me on this, all right?"

"You're the pilot."

"That's the general idea."

She un-cupped the microphone. "Holding approach speed, Baikonur. Progress systems stable. One hundred meters into Shell 1. Predictive impact model still holding. No change in the status of the Matryoshka or the surrounding vacuum."

On the screen, wireframe graphics traced the vast right-angled shapes of radar-illuminated obstacles—iceberg or battle-cruiser sized slabs of inscrutably dark free-flying machinery, between which the Progress was obliged to navigate a path, avoiding not only the obstacles but the invisible threads of razor-thin force binding them together. Shell 1 was not a solid sphere, but a swarm of deadly obstacles and tripwires.

During the second apparition, the Americans had sent one of their robot probes straight through one of those field threads. It had gone instantly silent, suggesting that it had suffered a fatal or damaging collision. Years later, deep space radar had picked it up drifting powerless on a sun-circling orbit. A manned expedition (one of the last the Americans ever managed) was sent out to recover it and bring it back to Earth for inspection.

Yet when the astronauts got hold of part of the probe, an entire half of it drifted silently away from the other, separating along a mathematically perfect plane of bisection. The astronauts stared in mute incomprehension at the sliced-through interior of the robot, its tight-packed, labyrinthine innards gleaming back at them with the polish of chrome. The robot must have been cut in two as it passed through the Matryoshka, but so cleanly that the two parts had continued moving on exactly the same trajectory, until this moment.

Although it was only the robot we were sending in, with the *Tereshkova* parked at a safe distance, I still shuddered to think what those lines of force could do to metal and ceramic, to flesh and bone. The predictive model traced the vectors of the field lines and offered solutions for safe passage, but, try as I might, I couldn't share Galenka's unflappable faith in the power of algorithm and computer speed.

Still, like she said, she was the pilot. This was her turf and I was well advised not to trample on it. I'd have felt exactly the same way if she had dared tell me how to manage the *Tereshkova*'s data acquisition and transmission systems.

Following a plan that had been argued over for months back on Earth, it had been agreed to attempt sample collection at each stage of the Progress's journey. The predictive model gave us confidence that the robot could get close to one of the free-flying obstacles without being sliced by the field lines. Dropping the Progress's speed to less than a meter per second, Galenka brought it within contact range of a particular lump of alien machinery and extended the arms and analysis tools to their full extent. Thanks to a Chinese probe that had gone off-course during the second apparition, we knew that the outer integument was surprisingly brittle. The probe had destroyed itself utterly in its high-velocity collision, but not before chipping off vast chunks of alien material. To our delight, early surveys of the Matryoshka on its third return had shown that the impacted obstacle had not repaired itself.

The Progress anchored itself by firing sticky-tipped guy-lines onto the obstacle. Galenka used hammers, cutting devices and claws to pick away at the scabbed edge of the impact point. Pieces of integument flaked away easily—had we been out there in our EVA suits, we could have ripped them out by hand. Some of them were coal-sized, some were as large as engine blocks. Galenka loaded up a third of the Progress's cargo space before deeming the haul sufficient. She wanted room for more samples when she got further in.

"Want to bring her back, unload and return?" I asked. The plan had been to make multiple forays into the Matryoshka, until we'd exhausted our hydrazine reserves.

"Not with the systems as screwed as they are. We lose camera rotation, or blow some more memory, we're blind. Maybe we'll get three or four missions out of the robot, but right now I'm assuming this is our one chance. I'd like to go deeper, at least until we have a full hold."

"You want to consult with Baikonur?"

"We have discretion here, Dimitri. Timelag's too great to go crying to mummy every time we have a decision to make." She withdrew her hands from the waldo controls and flexed her fingers. "I'm taking her further in, while we still have a ship that works."

"I'm fine with that."

"Good," she said, massively indifferent to whether I was "fine" with it or not. Then: "Where's Yakov right now, by the way?"

"Somewhere."

"One of us needs to keep an eye on him, Dimitri. Not happy with that guy. I think he's on the edge."

"We're all on the edge. It's called being in space."

"I'm just saying."

"Keep an eye on him, yes. I will."

At fifteen kilometres, the Progress cleared Shell 1 and passed into a volume of open space largely devoid of moving obstacles or field lines. Galenka notched up the speed, until the Progress was falling inwards at a kilometre every ten seconds. There was nothing here to sample or analyse. "Normal vacuum in Gap 1," she murmured. "Or at least what the robot reads as normal. The ambient physics hasn't changed too much."

Ever since the first apparition, it had been known—or at least suspected—that the Matryoshka was not just a mysteriously layered artefact drifting through space. In some way that we didn't yet understand, the object distorted the very physics of the spacetime in which it was floating. The effects were almost too subtle to measure at the distance of the Tereshkova, but they became more severe the closer any probes got to the middle. Fundamental constants stopped being fundamental. The speed of light varied. Planck's constant deviated from the figure in textbooks. So did the weak mixing angle, the fine-structure constant, Newton's constant. None of this could be explained under any existing theory of physics. It was as if the Matryoshka was dragging a chunk of another universe around with it. Perhaps it had been designed that way, or perhaps the altered spacetime was a kind of lingering contamination, a side-effect of wormhole travel.

Of course, we didn't know for sure that the Matryoshka had come through a wormhole. That was just an educated guess papered over the vast, yawning chasm of our ignorance. All we knew for sure was that it had appeared, accompanied by a flash of energy, in the middle of the solar system.

I remembered that day very well. November the sixth, twenty fifteen. My twentieth birthday, to the day. Twenty-four years later—two of the

Matryoshka's looping, twelve-year elliptical orbits around the Sun—and here I was, staring the thing in the face, as if my whole adult life had been an arrow pointing to this moment.

Maybe it had.

I was born in nineteen ninety-five, in Klushino. It's a small place near Smolensk. It wouldn't have any claim to fame except Klushino is the place where Yuri Gagarin was born. I knew that name almost before I knew any other. My father told me about him; how he had been the first man in space, his unassuming modesty, how he became a deputy of the Supreme Soviet, a hero for all the world, how he had died when his training jet crashed into trees. My father told me that it was a custom for all cosmonauts to visit Gagarin's office before a mission, to see the clock on the wall stopped at the moment of his death. Years later, I paid my own respects in the office.

The thing I remember most of all about my father, though, is holding me on his shoulders when I was five, taking me out into a cold winter evening to watch our Mir space station arc across the twilight sky. I reached out to grasp it and he held me higher, as if that might make a difference.

"Do you want to go up there sometime, Dimitri?"

"Do you have to be big?"

"No," he said. "But you have to be brave and strong. You'll do, one day."

"And if I died would they stop the clock in my office as well?"

"You won't die," my father said. Even though it was cold he had his shirt sleeves rolled up, his hair scratching against my skin.

"But if I did."

"Of course they would. Just like Comrade Gagarin. And they'd make a hero of you as well."

THE ELEVATOR DOORS open to a chill wind, howling in from the flat farmland beyond the city. The landing is open to the elements, only a low railing along one side. When I arrive at Nesha's apartment, half way along the building, the door is ajar. Nesha—for it can only be Nesha—is waiting in the gap, bony, long-nailed fingers curling around the edge of the door. I see half her face—her right eye, prematurely wrinkled skin, a wisp of grey hair. She looks much smaller, much older and frailer, than I ever dared to imagine.

"Whatever you have to show me, show me and go."

"I'd really like to talk to you first." I hold up my gloveless, numb-fingered hands. "Everything I told you is true. I escaped from the psychiatric facility a few hours ago, and by now they'll be looking for me."

"Then you should go now."

"I was inside the Matryoshka, Nesha. Don't you want to hear what happened to me?"

She opens the door a tiny bit wider, showing me more of her face. She's old now but the younger Nesha hasn't been completely erased. I can still see the strong and determined woman who stood by her beliefs, even when the state decided those beliefs were contrary to the official truth.

"I heard the rumours. They say you went insane."

I give an easy shrug. "I did, on the way home. It's the only thing that saved me. If I hadn't gone crazy, I wouldn't be standing here now."

"You said there was something I had to know."

"Give me a little of your time, then I'll be gone. That's my promise to you."

Nesha looks back over her shoulder. She's wearing a knitted shawl of indeterminate colour. "It isn't much warmer in here. When you called, I hoped you'd come to fix the central heating." She pauses for a moment, mind working, then adds: "I can give you something to drink, and maybe something better to wear. I still have some of my husband's old clothes—someone may as well get some use from them."

"Thank you."

"You shouldn't have come to see me. No good will come of it, for either us."

"You might say the damage is already done."

She lets me inside. Nesha might consider her apartment cold, but it's a furnace to me. After the wards and cubicles of the facility, it's bordering on the luxurious. There are a couple of items of old furniture, threadbare but otherwise serviceable. There's a low coffee table with faded plastic flowers in a vase. There are pictures on the walls, save for the part that's been painted over with television. It's beginning to flake off in the corners, so it won't be too long before someone comes along to redo it.

"I can't turn it off," Nesha says, as if I've already judged her. "You can scrape it away, but they just come and paint it on again. They take more care of that than they do the heating. And they don't like it if they think you'd done it deliberately, or tried to hide the television behind pictures."

I remember the incessant televisions in the facility; the various strategies that the patients evolved to block them out or muffle the sound. "I understand. You don't have to make allowances."

"I don't like the world we live in. I'm old enough to remember when it was different." Still standing up, she waves a hand dismissively, shooing away the memories of better times. "Anyway, I don't hear so well these days. It's a blessing, I suppose."

"Except it doesn't feel like one." I point to one of the threadbare chairs. "May I sit down?"

"Do what you like."

I ease my aching bones into the chair. My damp clothes cling to me. Nesha looks at me with something close to pity.

"Are you really the cosmonaut?"

"Yes."

"I can make some tea."

"Please. Anything hot."

I watch her amble into the adjoining kitchen. Her clothes are still those of her early middle age, with allowance for infirmity and the cold. She wears old-looking jeans, several layers of jumpers, a scarf and the drab coloured shawl. Even though we're indoors she wears big fur boots. The clothes give her an illusion of bulk, but I can tell how thin she really is. Like a bird with a lot of puffed-up plumage, hiding delicate bones. There's also something darting, nervous and birdlike about the way she negotiates the claustrophobic angles of her apartment. I hear the clatter of a kettle, the squeak of a tap, a half-hearted dribble of water, then she returns.

"It'll take a while."

"Everything does, these days. When I was younger, old people used to complain about the world getting faster and faster, leaving them behind.

That isn't how it seems to you and I. We've left the world behind—we've kept up, but it hasn't."

"How old are you?" she asks.

"Fifty-one."

"Not what I'd call old. I have nearly twenty years on you." But her eyes measure me and I know what she's thinking. I look older, beyond any doubt. The mission took its toll on me, but so did the facility. There were times when I looked in the mirror with a jolt of non-recognition, a stranger's face staring back at me. "Something bad happened to you out there, didn't it," she said.

"To all of us."

She makes the tea. "You think I envy you," she says, as I sip from my cup.

"Why would you envy me?"

"Because you went out there, because you saw it up close, because you went inside it. You cosmonauts think all astronomers are the same. You go out into space and look at the universe through a layer of armoured glass, if you're lucky. Frosted with your own breath, blurring everything on the other side. Like visiting someone in a prison, not being able to touch them. You think we envy you that."

"Some might say it's better to get that close, than not go at all."

"I stayed at home. I touched the universe with my mind, through mathematics. No glass between us then—just a sea of numbers." Nesha looks at me sternly. "Numbers are truth. It doesn't get any more intimate than numbers."

"It's enough that we both reached out, wouldn't you say?" I offer her a conciliatory smile—I haven't come to pick a fight about the best way to apprehend nature. "The fact is, no one's doing much of that any more. There's no money for science and there's certainly none for space travel. But we did something great. They can write us out of history, but it doesn't change what we did."

"And me?"

"You were part of it. I'd read all your articles, long before I was selected for the mission. That's why I came to see you, all that time ago. But long before that—I knew what I wanted to do with my life. I was a young man when the Matryoshka arrived, but not so young that I didn't have dreams and plans."

"You must be sorry about that now."

"Sometimes. Not always. No more than you regret what you did."

"It was different back then, between the Soviets. If you believed something, you said it."

"So you don't regret a word of it."

"I had it easier than he did."

Silence. I look at a photograph on the coffee table—a young woman and a young man, holding hands in front of some grand old church or cathedral I don't recognise, in some European city I'll never see. They have bright clothes with slogans on, sunglasses, ski hats, and they're both smiling. The sky is a hard primary blue, as if it's been daubed in poster paint. "That's him," I say.

"Gennadi was a good man. But he never knew when to shut his mouth. That was his problem. The new men wanted to take us back to the old ways. Lots of people thought that was a good idea, too. The problem was, not all of us did. I was born in nineteen seventy-five. I'm old enough to remember what it was like before Gorbachev. It wasn't all that wonderful, believe me."

"Tell me about Gennadi. How did he get involved?"

"Gennadi was a scientist to begin with—an astronomer like me, in the same institute. That's how we met. But his heart was elsewhere. Politics took up more and more of his time."

"He was a politician?"

"An activist. A journalist and a blogger. Do you remember the internet, Dimitri?"

"Just barely." It's something from my childhood, like foreign tourists and contrails in the sky.

"It was a tool the authorities couldn't control. That made them nervous. They couldn't censor it, or take it down—not then. But they could take down the people behind it, like Gennadi. So that's what they did."

"I'm sorry."

"It's all in the past now. We had our time together; that's all that matters. Perhaps if I hadn't made such a noise about my findings, perhaps if I hadn't angered the wrong people…" Nesha stops speaking. All of a sudden I feel shamefully intrusive. What right have I have to barge in on this old woman, to force her to think about the way things used to be? But I can't leave, not having come this far. "His clothes," she says absent-mindedly. "I don't know why I kept them all this time, but perhaps you can use them."

I put down the tea. "Are you certain?"

"It's what Gennadi would have wanted. Always very practical-ly-minded, Gennadi. Go into the room behind you, the cupboard on the left. Take what you can use."

"Thank you."

Even though I'm beginning to warm up, it's good to change out of the sodden old clothes. Gennadi must have been shorter than me, his trousers not quite reaching my ankles, but I'm in no mood to com-plain. I find a vest, a shirt and an old grey sweater that's been repaired a number of times. I find lace-up shoes that I can wear with two layers of socks. I wash my hands and face in the bedroom basin, straighten-ing back my hair, but there's nothing I can do to tidy or trim my beard. I had plans to change my appearance so far as I was able, but all of a sudden I know how futile that'd be. They'll find me again, even if it takes a little longer. They'd only have to take one look in my eyes to know who I am.

"Do they fit?" Nesha asks, when I return to the main room.

"Like a glove. You've been very kind. I can't ever repay this."

"Start by telling me why you're here. Then—although I can't say I'm sorry for a little company—you can be on your way, before you get both of us into trouble."

I return to the same seat I used before. It's snowing again, softly. In the distance the dark threads of railway lines stretch between two anon-ymous buildings. I remember what the snowplough driver said. In this weather, I can forget about buses. No one's getting in or out of Zvezdniy Gorodok unless they have party clearance and a waiting Zil.

"I came to tell you that you were right," I say. "After all these years."

"About the Matryoshka?"

"Yes."

"I've known I was right for nearly thirty years. I didn't need you to come and tell me."

"Doesn't it help to know that someone else believes you now?"

"Truth is truth, no matter who else believes it."

"You constructed a hypothesis to fit the data," I said. "It was a sound hypothesis, in that it was testable. But that's all it ever was. You never got to see it tested."

She regards me with steely-eyed intensity, the earlier Nesha Petrova burning through the mask of the older one. "I did. The second apparition."

"Where they proved you wrong?"

"So they said."

"They were wrong. I know. But they used it to crush you, to mock you, to bury you. But we went inside. We penetrated Shell 3. After that—everything was different."

"Does it matter now?"

"I think it does." Now is the moment. The thing I've come all this way to give Nesha, the thing that's been in my pyjama pocket, now in the trousers. I take it out, the prize folded in a white handkerchief.

I pass the bundle across the coffee table. "This is for you."

Nesha takes it warily. She unwraps the handkerchief and blinks at the little metal box it had contained. She picks it up gently, holds it before her eyes and pinches her fingers around the little handle that sticks out from one side.

"Turn it."

"What?"

"Turn the handle."

She does as I say, gently and hesitantly at first, as if fearful that the handle will snap off in her fingers. The box emits a series of tinkling notes. Because Nesha is turning the handle so slowly, it's hard to make out the melody.

"I don't understand. You came all this way to give me this?"

"I did."

"Then the rumours were right," Nesha says. "You did go mad after all."

FALLING INWARD, THE Progress began to pass through another swarm of free-flying obstacles. Like those of Shell 1, the components of Shell 2 were all but invisible to the naked eye—dark as space itself, and only a fraction of a kelvin warmer than the cosmic microwave background. The wireframe display started showing signs of fuzziness, as if the computer was having trouble decoding the radar returns. The objects were larger and had a different shape to the ones in the outer shell—these were more like rounded pebbles or all-enveloping turtle-shells, wide as cities. They were covered in scales or plaques which moved around in a weird, oozing fashion, like jostling continents on a planet with vigorous plate tectonics. Similarly lethal field lines bound them, but this far in the predictive model became a lot less trustworthy.

No runaway Chinese probe had ever collided with Shell 2, so we had no good idea how brittle the objects were. A second apparition probe operated by the European Space Agency had tried to land and sample one of the Shell 2 obstacles, but without success. That wouldn't stop Galenka from making her own attempt.

She picked a target, wove around the field lines and came in close enough to fire the sticky anchors onto one of the oozing platelets. The Progress wound itself in on electric winches until it was close enough to extend its tools and manipulators.

"Damn camera's sticking again. And I keep losing antenna lock."

"It's what they pay you for," I said.

"Trying to be helpful, Dimitri?"

"Doing my best."

She had her hands in the waldos again. Her eyes darted from screen to screen. Never having trained for Progress operations, I couldn't make much sense of the displays myself. It looked as if she was playing six or seven weirdly abstract computer games at the same time, manipulating symbols according to arcane and ever-shifting rules. I could only hope that she was holding her ground.

"Cutting head can't get traction. Whatever that stuff is, it's harder than diamond. Nothing for the claws to grip, either. I'm going to try the laser."

I tensed as she swung the laser into play. How would the Matryoshka respond to our burning a hole in it? With the same cosmic indifference that it had shown when the Chinese robot had rammed it, or when the American probe intersected its field lines? Nothing in our experience offered guidance. Perhaps it had tolerated us until now, and would interpret the laser as the first genuinely hostile action. In which case losing the Progress might be the least of our worries.

"Picking up ablation products," Galenka said, eyeing the trembling registers of a gas chromatograph readout. "Laser's cutting into *something*, whatever it is. Lots of carbon. Some noble gases and metals: iron, vanadium, some other stuff I'm not too sure about right now. Let's see if I can cut away a sample."

The laser etched a circle into the surface of the platelet. With the beam kept at an angle to the surface, it was eventually possible to isolate a cone-shaped piece of the material. Galenka used an epoxy-tipped sucker to extract the fist-sized sample, which already seemed to be in the process of fusing back into the main structure.

"Well done."

She grinned at me. "Let's take a few more while our luck's holding, shall we?"

She pulled out of the waldo controls, disengaged the sticky anchors and applied translational thrust, shifting the Progress to a different platelet.

"You sure you don't want to take a break? We can hold here for hours if we have to, especially with the anchors."

"I'm fine, Dimitri." But I noticed that Galenka's knuckles were tight on the joystick, the effort of piloting beginning to show. There was a chisel-sharp crease in the skin on the side of her mouth that only came when she was concentrating. "Fine but a little hungry, if you must know. You want to do something useful, you can fetch me some food."

"I think that might be within my capabilities," I said.

I pushed away from the piloting position, expertly inserting myself onto a weightless trajectory that sent me careening through one of the narrow connecting throats that led from one of the *Tereshkova*'s modules to the next.

By any standards she was a large spacecraft. Nuclear power had brought us to the Matryoshka. The *Tereshkova*'s main engine was a "variable specific impulse magnetic rocket": a VASIMIR drive. It was an old design that had been dusted down and made to work when the requirements of our mission became clear. The point of the VASIMIR (it was an American acronym, but it *sounded* appropriately Russian) was that it could function in a dual mode, giving not us only the kick to escape Earth orbit, but also months of low-impulse cruise thrust, to take us all the way to the artefact and back. It would get us all the way home again, too—whereupon we'd climb into our Soyuz re-entry vehicle and detach from the mothership. The Progress would come down on autopilot, laden with alien riches—that was the plan, anyway.

Like all spacecraft, the *Tereshkova* looked like a ransacked junk shop inside. Any area of the ship that wasn't already in use as a screen or control panel or equipment hatch or analysis laboratory or food dispenser or life-support system was something to hold onto, or kick off from, or rest against, or tie things onto. Technical manuals floated in mid-air, tethered to the wall. Bits of computer drifted around the ship on pilgrimages of their own, until one of us needed some cable or connector. Photos of our family, drawings made by our children, were tacked to the walls between panels and grab rails. The whole thing stank like an armpit and made so much noise that most of us kept earplugs in when we didn't need to talk.

But it was home, of a sort. A stinking, noisy shithole of a home, but still the best we had.

I hadn't seen Yakov as I moved through the ship, but that wasn't any cause for alarm. As the specialist in charge of the *Tereshkova*'s flight systems, his duty load had eased now that we had arrived on station at the artefact. He had been busy during the cruise phase, so we couldn't begrudge him a little time off, especially as he was going to have to nurse the ship home again. So, while Baikonur gave him a certain number of housekeeping tasks to attend to, Yakov had more time to himself than Galenka or I. If he wasn't in his quarters, there were a dozen other places on the ship where he could find some privacy, if not peace and quiet. We all had our favorite spots, and we were careful not to intrude on each other when we needed some personal time.

So I had no reason to sense anything unusual as I selected and warmed a meal for Galenka. But as the microwave chimed readiness, a much louder alarm began shrieking throughout the ship. Red emergency lights started flashing. The general distress warning meant that the ship had detected something anomalous. Without further clarification, it could be almost anything: a fault with the VASIMIR, a hull puncture, a life-support system failure, a hundred other problems. All that the alarm told me was that the ship deemed the problem critical, demanding immediate attention.

I grabbed a handrail and propelled myself to the nearest monitor. Text was already scrolling on it.

Unscheduled activity in hatch three, said the words.

I froze for a few moments, not so much in panic as out of a need to pause and concentrate, to assess the situation and decide on the best course of action. But I didn't need much time to reflect. Since Galenka was still at her station, still guiding the Progress, it was obvious what the problem was. Yakov was trying to escape from the *Tereshkova*.

As if we were still in Star City.

There was no automatic safety mechanism to prevent that door from being opened. It was assumed that if anyone did try and open it, they must have a valid reason for doing so—venting air into space, for instance, to quench a fire.

I pushed myself through the module, through the connecting throat, through the next module. The alarm was drilling into my head. If Yakov really did think that the ship was still in Russia, he wouldn't be concerned about decompression. He wouldn't be concerned about whether or not he was wearing a suit.

He just wanted to get out.

I reached a red locker marked with a lightning flash and threw back the heavy duty latches. I expected to see three tasers, bound with security foils.

There were no tasers—just the remains of the foil and the recessed foam shapes where the stunners had fitted.

"Fuck," I said, realising that Yakov was ahead of me; that he had opened the locker—against all rules; it was only supposed to be touched in an emergency—and taken the weapons.

I pushed through another connecting throat, scraping my hand against sharp metal until it bled, then corkscrewed through ninety degrees to reach the secondary throat that led to the number three hatch.

I could already see Yakov at the end of it. Braced against the wall, he was turning the yellow cartwheel that undid the door's locking mechanism. When he was done, it would only take a twist of the handle to free the hatch. The air pressure behind it would slam it open in an instant, and both of us would be sucked into space long before emergency bulkhead seals protected the rest of the ship. I tried to work out which way we were facing now. Would it be a long fall back to the Sun, or an inglorious short-cut to the Matryoshka?

"Yakov, please," I called. "Don't open the door."

He kept working the wheel, but looked back at me over his shoulder. "No good, Dimitri. I've figured this out even if you haven't. None of this is real. We're not really out here, parked next to the Matryoshka. We're just rehearsing for it, running through another simulation."

I tried to ride with his logic. "Then let's see the simulation through to the end."

"Don't you get it? This is all a test. They want to see how alert we are. They want to see that we're still capable of picking up on the details that don't fit."

The blood was spooling out of my hand, forming a chain of scarlet droplets. I pushed the wound to my mouth and sucked at it. "Like weightlessness? How would they ever fake that, Dimitri?"

He let go of the wheel with one hand and touched the back of his neck. "The implants. They fool with your inner ear, make you think you're floating."

"That's your GLONASS transponder. It's so they can track and recover our bodies if the re-entry goes wrong."

"That's what they told us." He kept on turning the wheel.

"You open that door, you're a dead man. You'll kill me and probably Galenka as well."

"Listen to me," he said with fierce insistence. "This is not real. We're in Star City, my friend. We're still back in Russia. The whole point of this exercise is to measure our alertness, our ability to see through delusional constructs. Escaping from the ship is the objective, the end-state."

Reasoned argument clearly wasn't going to get me anywhere. I gave myself a hard shove in his direction, hoping to overwhelm him with sheer momentum. But Yakov was faster. His hand sprung to his pocket and came out holding one of the tasers, aimed straight at me. The barbs sprang out and contacted my chest. Never having been shot before, I wasn't remotely ready for the pain. It seemed to crush me into a little ball of concentrated fire, like an insect curling under the heat from a magnifying glass. I let out a brief yelp, biting my tongue, and then I didn't even have the energy to scream. The barbs were still in me. Bent double, blood dribbling from my hand and mouth, I lost all contact with the ship. Drifting, I saw Yakov leave the taser floating in mid-air while he returned his attention to the wheel and redoubled his efforts.

"You stupid fucker," I heard Galenka say, behind me.

I didn't know whether she meant Yakov—for trying to escape—or me, for trying to stop him on my own. Maybe she meant both of us.

The pain of the discharge was beginning to ebb. I could just begin to think about speaking again.

"Got a taser," I heard myself say, as if from a distance.

"Good. So have I." I felt Galenka push past me, something hard in her hand. Then I heard the strobing crackle of another taser. I kept drifting around, until the door came into view again. Through blurred and slitted eyes, I saw Yakov twitching against the metal. Galenka had fired barbs into him; now she was holding the prongs of the taser against his abdomen, the blue worm of a spark writhing between.

I reached out a hand and managed to steady myself. The pain had now all but gone, but I was enveloped in nausea and a tingling all-body version of pins and needles.

"You can stop now."

She gave the taser one last prod, then withdrew it. Yakov remained still, slumped and unconscious against the door.

"I say we kill the fucker now."

I wiped the blood from my lips. "I know how you feel. But we need him to get us home. If there's the slightest problem with the engine…"

"Anything happens, mission control can help us."

I worked my way down to the door. "He's not going to do this again. We can sedate him, wrap him in duct-tape and confine him to one of the modules if necessary. Until Baikonur advise."

Galenka pushed her own taser back into her pocket, with the barbs dangling loose on their springy wires. She started turning the wheel in the opposite direction, grunting at first with the effort.

"This was a close call."

"You were right—I should have been more worried about him than I was. I didn't think he was really serious about all that Star City stuff. I mean, not *this* serious."

"He's a basket case, Dimitri. That means there are only two sane people left on this ship, and I'm being generous."

"Do you think Baikonur will be able to help?"

"They'd better. Anything goes wrong on this ship, we need him to fix it. And he's not going to be much use to us doped to his eyeballs."

We manhandled the stunned Yakov back into the main part of the *Tereshkova*. Already I could tell that he was only lightly unconscious, and that we'd have a struggle on our hands if he came around now. He was mumbling under his breath. Sweat began to bead on my forehead. Why the fuck did this have to happen to us?

"What do you reckon we should do? Confine him to his quarters?"

"And have him loose aboard the ship again, looking for a way to escape?"

"I'm not sure we have any other choice."

"We lock him in the forward module," Galenka said decisively. "He'll be safe in there. We can seal the connecting lock from our side, until Baikonur come up with a treatment regime. In the meantime we dose him on sedatives, put him under for as long as we can. I don't want that lunatic running around when I'm trying to steer the Progress through Shell 3."

I breathed in hard, trying to focus. "Where is it now?"

"Still anchored to one of the Shell 2 platelets. I'd like to take a few more samples before I detach, but from then on it's seat of the pants stuff."

She was right: it was a good plan. Better than anything I could come up with, at any rate. We took him forward to the orbiter, opened a medical kit and injected him with the sedative. I took out a tube of disinfectant and a roll of bandage for my gashed hand. Yakov stopped mumbling and became more pliant, like a big rag doll. We duct-taped him into a sleeping hammock and locked the door on him.

"He was pissing me off anyway," Galenka said.

I MOVE BACK from the window in Nesha's apartment. Zvezdniy Gorodok is stirring to hypothermic half-life. The snow's still coming down, though in fitful flurries rather than a steady fall. When a Zil pulls onto the street I feel a tightness in my throat. But the limousine stops, releasing its passenger, and moves on. The man strolls across the concrete concourse into one of the adjoining buildings, a briefcase swinging from his hand. He might have anything in that briefcase—a gun, a syringe, a lie detector. But he has no business here.

"You think they're looking for you."

"I know it."

"Then where are you going to go?"

Out into the cold and the snow to die, I think. But I smile and say nothing.

"Is it really so bad in the facility? Do they really treat you so badly?"

I return to my seat. Nesha's poured me another cup of tea, which—her views on my sanity notwithstanding—I take as an invitation to remain. "Most of them don't treat me badly at all—they're not monsters or sadists. I'm too precious to them for that. They don't beat me, or electrocute me, and the drugs they give me, the things they do to me, they're not to make me docile or to punish me. Doctor Kizim, he's even kind to me. He spends a lot of time talking to me, trying to get me to remember details I might have forgotten. It's pointless, though. I've already remembered all that I'm ever going to. My brain feels like a pan that's been scrubbed clean."

"Did Doctor Kizim help you to escape?"

"I've asked myself the same question. Did he mean for me to steal his coat? Did he sense that I was intending to leave? He must have known I wouldn't get far without it."

"What about the others? Were you allowed to see them?"

I shake my head. "They kept us apart the whole time Yakov and Galenka were still alive. We were questioned and examined separately.

Even though we'd spent all those months in the ship, they didn't want us contaminating each other's accounts."

"So you never really got to know what happened to the others."

"I know that they both died. Galenka went first—she took the highest dosage when the VASIMIR's shielding broke down. Yakov was a little luckier, but not much. I never got to see either of them while they were still alive."

"Why didn't you get a similar dosage?"

"Yakov was mad to begin with. Then he got better, or at least decided he was better off working with us than against us. We let him out of the module where we were keeping him locked up. That was after Galenka and I got back from the Matryoshka."

"And then?"

"It was my turn to go a little mad. Inside the machine—something touched us. It got into our heads. It affected me more than it did Galenka. On the return trip, they had no choice but to confine me to the forward module."

"The thing that saved you."

"I was further from the engine when it went wrong. Inverse square laws. My dosage was negligible."

"You accept that they died, despite having no evidence."

"I believe what Doctor Kizim told me. I trusted him. He had no reason to lie. He was already putting his career at risk by giving me this information. Maybe more than his career. A good man."

"Did he know the other two?"

"No; he only ever treated me. That was part of the methodology. Strange things had happened during the early months of the debriefing. The doctors and surgeons got too close to us, too involved. After we came back from the Matryoshka, there was something different about us. It affected us all, even Yakov, who hadn't gone inside. Just being close to it was enough."

"Different in what way?" Nesha asks.

"It began in small ways, while we were still on the *Tereshkova*. Weird slips. Mistakes that didn't make sense. As if our identities, our personalities and memories, were blurring. On the way home, I sit at the computer keyboard and find myself typing Yakov's name and password into the system, as if he's sitting inside me. A few days later Galenka wakes up and tells me she dreamed she was in Klushino, a place she's never visited." I pause, trying to find words that would not make me sound crazy. "It was as if something in the machine had touched us and removed some fundamental barrier in our heads, some wall or moat that keeps one person from becoming another. When the silver fluid got into us..."

"I don't understand. How could the doctors get too close to you? What happened to them?"

I sense her uneasiness; the realisation that she may well be sharing her room with a lunatic. I have never pretended to be entirely sane, but it must only be now that the white bones of true madness are beginning to show through my skin.

"I didn't mean to alarm you, Nesha. I'll be gone shortly, I promise you. Why don't you tell me what it was like for you, back when it all began?"

"You know my story."

"I'd still like to hear it from you. From the day it arrived. How it changed you."

"You were old enough to remember it. You already told me that."

"But I wasn't an astronomer, Nesha. I was just a twenty-year-old kid with some ideas about being a cosmonaut. You were how old, exactly?"

"Forty years. I'd been a professional astronomer for fifteen or sixteen of them, by then." She becomes reflective, as if it's only now that she has given that time of her life any thought. "I'd been lucky, really. I'd made professor, which meant I didn't have to grub around for funding every two years. I had to do my share of lecturing, and fighting my corner for the department, but I still had plenty of time for independent research. I was still in love with science, too. My little research area—stellar pulsation modes—it wasn't the most glamorous." She gives a rueful smile. "They didn't fight to put our faces on the covers of magazine, or give us lucrative publishing deals to talk about how we were uncovering the mysteries of the universe, touching the face of God. But we knew it was solid science, important to the field as a whole." She leans forward to make a point. "Astronomy's like a cathedral, Dimitri. The ones putting the gold on the top spire get all the glory, but they'd be nothing without a solid foundation. That's where we were—down in the basement, down in the crypt, making sure it was all anchored to firm ground. Fundamental stellar physics. Not very exotic compared to mapping the large scale universe, or probing the event horizons of black holes. But vital all the same."

"I don't doubt it."

"I can remember that afternoon when the news came in. Gennadi and I were in my office. It was a bright day, with the blinds drawn. It was the end of the week and we were looking forward to a few days off. We had tickets to see a band in town that night. We just had one thing we wanted to get sorted before we finished. A paper we'd been working on had come back from the referee with a load of snotty comments, and we didn't quite agree on how to deal with them. I wanted to write back to the journal and request a different referee. The referee on our paper was anonymous, but I was sure I knew who it was—a slimy, womanising prick who'd made a pass at me at a conference in Trieste, and wasn't going to let me forget that I'd told him where to get off."

I smile. "You must have been fierce in your day."

"Well, maybe it wasn't him—but we still needed a different referee. Gennadi, meanwhile, thought we should sit back and do what the referee was telling us. Which meant running our models again, which meant a week of time on the department supercomputer. Normally, that would have meant going right back to the start of the queue. But there was a gap in the schedule—another group had just pulled out of their slot, because they couldn't get their software to compile properly. We could have their slot—but only if we got our model up and running that evening, with all the modifications the referee wanted us to make."

"You weren't going to make it to that band."

"That was when the IAU telegram came in to my inbox. I didn't even open it at first; it wasn't as if IAU telegrams were exactly unusual. It probably just meant that a supernova had gone off in a remote galaxy, or that some binary star was undergoing a nova. Nothing I needed to get excited about."

"But that wasn't what it was about."

"It was the Matryoshka, of course—the emergence event, when it came into our solar system. A sudden influx of cosmic rays, triggering half the monitoring telescopes and satellites in existence. They all turned to look at the point where the machine had come in. A flash of energy that intense, it could only be a gamma-ray burst, happening in some distant galaxy. That's what everyone thought it was, especially as the Matryoshka came in high above the ecliptic, and well out of the plane of the galaxy. It looked extragalactic, not some local event. Sooner or later, though, they crunched the numbers—triangulated from the slightly different pointing angles of the various spacecraft and telescopes, the slightly different detection times of the event—and they realised that, whatever this was, it had happened within one light hour of the Sun. Not so much on our doorstep, cosmically speaking, as in our house, making itself at home." The memory seems to please her. "There was some wild theorizing to begin with. Everything from a piece of antimatter colliding with a comet, a quantum black hole evaporating, to the illegal test of a Chinese super-weapon in deep space. Of course, it was none of those things. It was spacetime opening wide enough to vomit out a machine the size of Tasmania."

"It was a while before they found the Matryoshka itself."

Nesha nods. "You try finding something that dark, when you don't even know in which direction it's moving."

"Even from the *Tereshkova*, it was hard to believe it was actually out there."

"To begin with, we still didn't know what to make of it. The layered structure confused the hell out of us. We weren't used to analysing anything like that. It was artificial, clearly, but it wasn't made of solid parts. It was like a machine caught in the instant of blowing up, but which was still working, still doing whatever it was sent to do. Without getting closer, we could only resolve the structure in the outer layer. We didn't start calling it Shell 1 until we knew there were deeper strata. The name Matryoshka didn't come until after the first flyby probes, when we glimpsed Shell 2. The Americans called it the Easter Egg for a little while, but eventually everyone started using the Russian name."

I know that when she talks about "we", she means the astronomical community as a whole, rather than her own efforts. Nesha's involvement—the involvement that had first made her famous, then ruined her reputation, then her life—did not come until later.

The emergence event—the first apparition—caught human-ity entirely unawares. The Matryoshka had come out of its wormhole mouth—if that was what it was—on an elliptical, sun-circling trajectory similar to a periodic comet. The only thing non-cometary was the very steep inclination to the ecliptic. It made reaching the Matryoshka prob-lematic, except when it was swinging near the Sun once every twelve years. Even with a massive international effort, there was no way to send dedicated probes out to meet the artefact and match its velocity. The best anyone could do was fling smart pebbles at it, hoping to learn as much as possible in the short window while they slammed past. Probes that had been intended for Mars or Venus were hastily repurposed for the Matryoshka flyby, where time and physics made that possible. It was more like the mad scramble of some desperate, last-ditch war effort than anything seen in peacetime.

There were, of course, dissenting voices. Some people thought the prudent thing would be to wait and see what the Matryoshka had in mind for us. By and large, they were ignored. The thing had arrived here, hadn't it? The least it could expect was a welcome party.

As it was, the machine appeared completely oblivious to the atten-tion—as it had continued to do through the second apparition. The third apparition—that was different, of course. But then again our provocation had been of an entirely different nature.

After the probes had gone by, there was data to analyse. Years of it. The Matryoshka had fallen out of reach of our instruments and robots, but we had more than enough to keep busy until the next apparition. Plans were already being drawn up for missions to rendezvous with the object and penetrate that outer layer. Robots next time, but who knew what might be possible in the twenty-four years between the first and third apparitions?

"The scientists who'd had their missions redirected wanted a first look at the Matryoshka data," Nesha says. "The thinking was that they'd get exclusive access to it for six months."

"You can't blame them for that."

"There was still an outcry. It was felt that an event of this magnitude demanded the immediate release of all the data to the community. To the whole world, in fact. Anyone who wanted it was welcome to it. Of course, unless they had a lightning-fast internet connection, about ten million terabytes of memory, expertise in hypercube number-crunching, their own Cray...they couldn't even begin to scratch the surface. There were collaborative efforts, millions of people downloading a fragment of the data and analysing it using spare CPU cycles, but they still couldn't beat the resources of a single well-equipped academic department with a tame supercomputer in the basement. Above all else, we had all the analysis tools at hand, and we knew how to use them. But it was still a massive cake to eat in one bite."

"And did you?"

"No—it made much more sense to focus on what we were good at. The data hinted that the elements of the outer layer—Shell 1—were bound together by some kind of force-field. The whole thing was breathing in and out, the components moving as if tied together by a complex web of elastic filaments." She shapes her fingers around an invisible ball and makes the ball swell and contract. "The thing is, stars breathe as well. The pulsation modes in a solar-type star aren't the same as the pulsation modes in the Matryoshka. But we could still use the same methods, the same tools and tricks, to get a handle on them. And of course, there was a point to all of that. Map the pulsations in a star and you can probe the deep interior, in exactly the same way that earthquakes tell us about the structure of the Earth. There was every expectation that the Matryoshka's pulsations might tell us something about the inside of that as well."

"I guess you didn't have a clue what you'd actually find."

Nesha gives a brief, derisive laugh. "Of course not. I wasn't thinking in those terms at all. I was just thinking of frequencies, harmonics, Fourier analysis, caustic surfaces. I wasn't thinking of fucking *music*."

"Tell me how it felt."

"The first time I ran the analysis, and realised that the pulsations could be broken down into notes on the western chromatic scale? Like I was the victim of a bad practical joke, someone in the department messing with the data."

"And when you realised you weren't being hoaxed?"

"I still didn't *believe* it—not to begin with. I thought I must have screwed up in my analysis somewhere, introduced harmonics that weren't real. I stripped the tools down and put them together again. Same story—notes, chords, melody and counterpoint. Music. That's when I started accepting the reality of it. Whatever we were dealing with—whatever had come to find us—wasn't what we had assumed. This wasn't just some dumb invention, some alien equivalent of the probes we had been sending out. The Matryoshka was a different order of machine. Something clever and complex enough to sing to itself. Or, just possibly, to us." Nesha hesitates and looks at me with an unwavering gaze. "And it was singing our music. Russian music."

"I know," I say. "It's been in my head since I came back."

NO ONE HAD been this deep before.

The Progress had travelled fifty kilometres into the Matryoshka—through two layers of orbiting obstruction, each of which was ten kilometres in depth, and through two open volumes fifteen kilometres thick. Beneath lay the most difficult part of its journey so far. Though the existence of Shell 3 had been known since the second apparition, no hard data existed on conditions beneath it.

The barrier was actually a pair of tightly nested spheres, one slightly smaller than the other. The shell's material was as dark as anything already encountered, but—fortuitously for us—the spheres had holes in them, several dozen circular perforations ranging in width from one to three kilometres, spotted around the spheres in what appeared to be an entirely random arrangement. The pattern of holes was the same in both spheres, but because they were rotating at different speeds, on different, slowly precessing axes, the holes only lined up occasionally. During those windows, glimpses opened up into the heart of the Matryoshka. A blue-green glow shone through the winking gaps in Shell 3, hinting at luminous depths.

Shortly we'd know.

"How's he doing?" Galenka asked, from the pilot's position. I had just returned from the orbiter, where I had been checking on Yakov. I had fixed a medical cuff to his wrist, so that Baikonur could analyse his blood chemistry.

"Not much change since last time. He just looks at me. Doesn't say or do anything."

"We should up the medication." She tapped keys, adjusting one of the Progress's camera angles. She was holding station, hovering a few kilometres over Shell 3. Talking out of the side of her mouth she said: "Put him into a coma until we really need him."

"I talked to Baikonur. They recommend holding him at the current dosage until they've run some tests."

"Easy for them to say, half the solar system away."

"They're the experts, not us."

"If you say so."

"I think we should let them handle this one. It's not like we don't have other things to occupy our minds, is it?"

"You have a point there, comrade."

"Are you happy about taking her in? You've been in the chair for a long time now."

"It's what we came to do. Progress systems are dropping like flies, anyway—I give this ship about six hours before it dies on us. I think it's now or never."

I could only bow to her superior wisdom in this matter.

In the years since the last apparition, the complex motion of the spheres had been subjected to enormous scrutiny. It had been a triumph to map the holes in the interior sphere. Despite this, no watertight algorithm had ever been devised to predict the window events with any precision. The spheres slowed down and sped up unpredictably, making a nonsense of long-range forecasts. Unless a window was in view, the movement of the inner sphere could not be measured. Radar bounced off its flawless surface as if the thing was motionless.

All Galenka could do was wait until a window event began, then make a run for it—hoping that the aperture remained open long enough for the Progress to pass through. Analysis of all available data showed that window events occurred, on average, once in every seventy-two minute interval. But that was just an average. Two window events could fall within minutes of each other, or there might be a ten-hour wait before the next one. Timing was tight—the Progress would have to begin its run within seconds of the window opening, if it had a chance of slipping through. I didn't envy Galenka sitting there with her finger on the trigger, like a gunslinger waiting for her opponent to twitch.

In the event, a useful window—one that she could reach, in the allowed time—opened within forty minutes of our conversation. Looking over her shoulder at the screens, I could scarcely detect any change in Shell 3. Only when the Progress was already committed—moving too quickly to stop or change course—did a glimmer of blue-green light reassure me that the window was indeed opening. Even then, it hardly seemed possible that the Progress would have time to pass through the winking eye.

Of course, that was exactly what happened. Only a slight easing of the crease on the side of Galenka's mouth indicated that she was, for now, breathing easier. We both knew that this triumph might be exceedingly short-lived, since the Progress would now find it even more difficult to remain in contact with the *Tereshkova*. Since no man-made signal could penetrate Shell 3, comms could only squirt through when a window was open, in whatever direction that happened to be. The swarm of relay microsats placed around the Matryoshka were intended to intercept these burst transmissions and relay them back to the *Tereshkova*. Its puppet-strings all but severed, the robotic spacecraft would be relying more and more on the autonomous decision-making of its onboard computers.

I knew that the mission planners had subjected the Progress to every eventuality, every scenario, they could dream up. I also knew that none of those planners seriously expected the secrets of the Matryoshka to bear the slightest resemblance to their imaginings. If it did, they'd be brutally disappointed.

The rear-looking camera showed the window sealing behind the Progress. The inside surface of Shell 3 was as pitilessly dark as its outer skin, yet all else was aglow. I shivered with an almost religious ecstasy. Soon the secrets revealed here would be in the hands of the entire human species, but for now—for a delicious and precious interval—the only two souls granted this privilege were Galenka and I. No other thinking creature had seen this far.

Beneath Shell 3 was another empty volume—Gap 3. Then there was another sphere. We were looking at the central sixty kilometres of the Matryoshka, three quarters of the way to whatever lay at its heart. Shell 4 looked nothing like the dark machinery we had already passed through. This was more like a prickly fruit, a nastily evolved bacterium or some fantastically complex coral formation. The surface of the sphere was barely visible, lost under a spiky, spiny accretion of spokes and barbs and twisted unicorn horns, pushing out into the otherwise empty band gap for many kilometres. Lacy webs of matter bridged one spike to the next. Muscular structures, like the roots of enormous trees, entwined the bases of the largest outgrowths. It was all ablaze with blue-green light, like a glass sculpture lit from within. The light wavered and pulsed. Shell 3 did not look like something which had been designed and built, but rather something which had grown, wildly and unpredictably. It was wonderful and terrifying.

Then the signal ended. The Progress was on its own now, relying on its hardwired wits.

"You did well," I told Galenka.

She said nothing. She was already asleep. Her head did not loll in zero gravity, her jaw did not droop open, but her eyes were closed and her hand had slackened on the joystick. Only then did I realise how utterly exhausted she must have been. But I imagined her dreams were peaceful ones. She had not failed the mission. She had not failed Mother Russia and the Second Soviet.

I left her sleeping, then spent two hours attending to various house-keeping tasks aboard the *Tereshkova*. Since we were only able to use the low-gain antenna—the high-gain antenna had failed shortly after departure—the data that the Progress had already sent back needed to be organised and compressed before it could be sent onwards to Earth. All the data stored aboard the *Tereshkova* would get home eventually—assuming, of course, that we did—but in the meantime I was anxious to provide Baikonur with what I regarded as the highlights. All the while I checked for updates from the Progress, but no signal had yet been detected.

Without waiting for mission control to acknowledge the data package, I warmed some food for myself, took a nip of vodka from my private supply, and then carried my meal into the part of the *Tereshkova* loosely designated as the commons/recreational area. It was the brightest part of the ship, with plastic flowers and ornaments, tinsel, photographs, postcards and children's paintings stuck to the walls. I stationed myself against a wall and watched television, flicking through the various uplink feeds while spooning food into my mouth. I skipped soaps, quizzes and chat shows until I hit the main state news channel. The *Tereshkova* had been big news during its departure, but had fallen from the headlines during the long and tedious cruise to the Matryoshka. Now we were a top-listed item once more, squeezing out stories of indomitable Soviet enterprise and laughable Capitalist failure.

The channel informed its viewers that the ship had successfully launched a robotic probe through Shells 1 and 2, a triumph equal to anything achieved during the last two apparitions, and one which—it was confidently expected—would soon be surpassed. The data already returned to Earth, the channel said, offered a bounty that would keep the keenest minds engaged for many years. Nor would this data be hoarded by Russia alone, for with characteristic Soviet generosity, it would be shared with those "once-proud" nations who now lacked the means to travel into space. The brave cosmonauts who were reaping this harvest of riches were mentioned by name on several occasions. There was, of course, no word about how one of those brave cosmonauts had gone stark staring mad.

I knew with a cold certainty that they'd never tell the truth about Yakov. If he didn't recover they'd make something up—an unanticipated illness, or a debilitating accident. They'd kill the poor bastard rather than admit that we were human.

"I went to see him," Galenka said, startling me. She had drifted into the recreation area quite silently. "He's talking now—almost lucid. Wants us to let him out of the module."

"Not likely."

"I agree. But we'll have to make a decision on him sooner or later."

"Well, there's no hurry right now. You all right?"

"Fine, thanks."

She had rested less than three hours, but in weightlessness—even after an exhausting task—that was enough. It was a useful physiological adaptation when there was a lot of work to be done, but it also meant that ten days in space could feel like thirty back on Earth. Or a hundred.

"Go and sleep some more, you want to. The Progress calls in, I'll wake you."

"If it calls in."

I offered a shrug. "You did everything that was expected of you. That we got this far…"

"I know; we should be very proud of ourselves." She stared at the screen, her eyes still sleepy.

"They're going to lie about Yakov."

"I know."

"When we get home, they'll make us stick to the story."

"Of course." She said this with total resignation, as if it was the least any of us could expect.

Soon we bored of the news and the television. While Galenka was answering letters from friends and family I went back to run my own check on Yakov. To our disappointment Baikonur still had no specific recommendations beyond maintaining the present medication. I sensed that they didn't want blood on their hands if something went wrong with him. They were happy to let us take responsibility for our ailing comrade, even if we ended up killing him.

"Let me out, Dimitri. I'm fine now."

I looked at him through the armoured glass of the bulkhead door. Shaking my head, I felt like a doctor delivering some dreadful diagnosis.

"You have to stay there for now. I'm sorry. But we can't run the risk of you trying to open the hatch again."

"I accept that this isn't a simulation now. I accept that we're really in space." His voice came through a speaker grille, tinny and distant. "You believe me, don't you Dimitri?"

"I'll see you later, Yakov."

"At least let me talk to Baikonur."

I placed the palm of my hand against the glass. "Later, friend. For now, get some rest."

I turned away before he could answer.

He wasn't the only one who needed sleep. Tiredness hit me unexpectedly—it always came on hard, like a wall. I slept for two hours, dreaming of being back on Earth on a warm spring day, sitting with my wife in the park, the mission happily behind me, deemed a success by all concerned. When I woke the dream's melancholic after-effects dogged my thoughts for hours. I badly wanted to get home.

I found Galenka in the pilot's position.

"We have contact," she said, but I knew from her tone of voice that it wasn't all good news.

"The Progress called in?"

"She's stuck, Dimitri. Jammed in down there. Can't back out, can't go forward."

"Fuck."

What was only apparent when the Progress reached the root complex was that there was no solid surface to Shell 4; that the tangled mass of roots was, to all intents and purposes, the sphere itself. There were gaps in that tangle, too, like the interstices in a loosely bundled ball of string. Methodically and fearlessly, the Progress had set about finding a way through to whatever was underneath. On its first attempt, it had travelled no more than a third of a kilometre beneath the nominal surface before reaching a narrowing it couldn't pass through. The second attempt, picking a different entry point, had taken it a kilometre under the surface before it met a similar impasse. With fuel now running low—just enough to get it back to the *Tereshkova*, with some in reserve—the Progress had opted to make one final attempt. It was then that it had got itself stuck, lodging in a part of the thicket like a bullet in gristle.

Galenka sent commands to the Progress, to be relayed when a window opened. She told it to use its manipulators to try and push itself backwards, and to wiggle its reaction thrusters in the hope that it might shake itself loose. It was the best she could do, but she wasn't optimistic. We waited three hours, by which time Baikonur were fully appraised of the situation. Then a window opened and the Progress reported that it was still jammed tight, despite executing Galenka's instructions.

"Before you say I should have listened to you," she said. "I did listen. But bringing her back in just wasn't the right decision, given what I knew at the time."

"I fully concurred, Galenka. No one's blaming you."

"Let's see what Baikonur have to say when we get back, shall we?"

"I'm sure they'll be in a forgiving mood. The amount of data we've gathered..."

"Doesn't begin to add up against physical samples, which we've now lost."

"Maybe."

"Maybe what? I've tried everything in the book. I know what that Progress can do, Dimitri. It isn't an escape artist."

"We do have the Soyuz," I said.

"We need it to take us home. Anyway, the Soyuz isn't rigged for remote control or sampling."

"I wasn't thinking of remote control. I was thinking, we fly the Soyuz all the way in. It's the same size as the Progress, right? It has similar capabilities?"

"Give or take." Her tone told me she wasn't exactly signing up for my idea with enthusiasm. "And then what?"

"We reach the Progress, or get as close to it as we can without getting ourselves stuck. Then we EVA. It's a microgravity environment so we should be able to move around without too much difficulty. It'll be too risky to attempt to free the Progress, but there's nothing to stop us transferring the artefacts. Plenty of room aboard the Soyuz, to bring them back to the *Tereshkova.*"

She breathed heavily, as if she'd just come off the exercise cycle. "This wasn't planned for. This wasn't in the book. No one ever mentioned going in with the Soyuz."

"It was always an unstated option. Why do you think they sent us out here, Galenka? To operate the Progress in real-time? Part of the reason, certainly, but not all of it."

"It's too dangerous."

"It was, but now we've got a much clearer picture of what's inside Shell 3. We can load in the Progress's trajectory and follow it all the way in."

"And if we damage the Soyuz? It's a fiery ride home without it."

"Why should we? We'll be taking excellent care of it."

"Because our lives will depend on it. You've become very courageous all of a sudden, Dimitri. Don't take this the wrong way, but it's not what I expected of you."

"I'm not trying to be anyone's hero. My blood's running cold at the idea of flying the Soyuz into that thing. But I happen to know the way their minds work back in Baikonur. They'll have thought of the Soyuz option by now, realised that it's feasible."

"They won't force us to do it, though."

"No, that's not how they operate. But if we don't raise the possibility, if we don't put it on the table, they'll be very, very disappointed. More disappointed than they'll already be at us for losing the robot."

I watched her reflect on what I'd said. In this instance Galenka would have no option but to admit that my grasp of Baikonur politics was superior to hers. I had been a cosmonaut for longer and I had seen how our superiors punished failings. The best you could hope for was incarceration. The worst was returning to your office to find a bottle of vodka and a loaded revolver.

"I hope you're right about this, Dimitri. For both our sakes."

"We have no choice," I said. "Trust me, Galenka. Nothing that happens in the Matryoshka will be as bad as what they'd do to us for failing our country."

An hour later we'd informed Baikonur of our decision. Two hours later we had their reply. I went to Yakov and told him what was going to happen.

"You can let me out now," he said, through the bulkhead window.

"Not until we're back."

"You still don't trust me?"

"It's just not a risk we can afford to take."

"Don't leave me alone on the *Tereshkova*. I'd rather go with you than stay here on my own."

"Not an option, I'm afraid. We need the extra space in the Soyuz. But I'm opening comms to your module. You'll be able to talk to Baikonur, and you'll be able to talk to us. You won't feel out of touch."

"I'm all right now," Yakov said. "Please believe me. I had a bad turn, I got confused—but everything's all right now."

"I'm sorry."

An hour after that, we were checking our suits and prepping the Soyuz for departure.

"I NEED BREAD," Nesha says. "Let's go for a walk."

"In this weather?"

"I need bread. If I don't go early, there'll be none left."

I peer through the window, at the grey-white sky. "I could fetch it for you. If you gave me some money, and told me where to go." Seeing the sceptical look on her face, I add: "I'd come back."

"We'll go together. It's good exercise for me, to get out of this place. If I didn't have errands, I'd probably never leave the building."

Nesha puts on several more layers of clothes and fetches a coat for herself. None of Gennadi's coats fit me (they're all too tight in the sleeves) so I'm forced to make do with Doctor Kizim's again. At least it's dried a bit, and I have something warm on underneath it. Nesha locks her apartment, turning keys in three separate locks, then we walk slowly to the elevator, still where I left it, on the ninth floor.

"I shouldn't have mocked you, Dimitri Ivanov."

The elevator doors close. "Mocked me?"

"About the musical box. The thing you came to give me. Now that we've spoken a little more, I see that you're not the madman I thought you might be. I should have known better."

"It's understandable."

"Did it really come from the Matryoshka?"

"All the way back."

"Why did they let you keep it?"

"Because they didn't realise its significance. By the time we got back, I knew that we weren't going to get an easy ride. The truth that we'd discovered—it wasn't going to be something our political masters wanted to hear. We were all ill—the perfect excuse for incarceration in some nameless medical facility cum prison or madhouse. Yakov and Galenka were sick with radiation exposure. I was sick with the Matryoshka inside my head. None of us were going to see daylight again."

"I read the papers and saw the television reports. They never actually lied about what happened to you."

"They didn't have to. As long as there was a reason not to have us out in public, they were happy."

The elevator completes its trundling, hesitant descent. We leave the building, venturing into the snow-covered street. I remain vigilant for prowling Zils and men in dark suits.

"I kept the musical box with me all the way home. When they found it they assumed it was one of my personal effects—something I'd taken aboard the ship when we left. The idea that it might be an *artefact*, a thing from the Matryoshka, never crossed their minds."

"And you never thought to tell them?"

"They'd have destroyed it. So I kept it close with me, all the time I was in the facility. The only person I ever showed it to was Doctor Kizim, and I don't think even he believed where it had come from."

"You must have trusted him."

"You had to trust someone in a place like that. Just like I'm trusting you now. The musical box is yours now. It's a piece of the future, in your hands."

She removes it from her coat. Until then I have no idea that she's brought it with her.

"The tune it makes..." She starts turning the little handle, the notes tinkling out. We're in the street, but there's no one else around to notice one old woman with a little metal box in her hands, or to question why she's turning the handle in its side. "I think I know it. It's something familiar, isn't it? Something Russian?"

"Like you always said. But please don't play it now. It makes my head hurt."

She stops turning the handle and returns the musical box to her pocket. We trudge on in silence until we're in sight of the shopping complex where Nesha hopes to find her bread. Dingy and disused as it appears, people are already milling around outside. Their dark winter clothes reduce them to an amorphous, weary mass. Our premier smiles down from the looming side of an apartment tower, lips moving but no sound coming out. Seagulls have been attracted by the flickering colours, pecking away huge pieces of his face.

"If the musical box was in the Matryoshka, then I was right about its origin," Nesha says. "It did come from the future after all."

"They never believed you. They never wanted to believe you."

She glances up at the birdshit-stained edifice, the premier's moving face. "We live in a flawless collectivised utopia. But a flawless society can't, by definition, evolve. If it proceeds from one state to another, there must have been something wrong, or sub-optimal, about it. If it gets worse, then the seeds of that worsening must have already been present. If it gets better, then it has room for improvement. The mere fact that the future is not the same as the present...that's totally unacceptable."

"It all ends," I say, keeping my voice low. "In less than a human lifetime. That's what I learned inside the Matryoshka. That and the fact that you were right all along."

"The musical box won't make any difference."

"Except now you know."

"There was never any doubt in my mind. Not even in the darkest days, when they punished me through Gennadi." Nesha walks on a few paces. "But still. It was always only a hypothesis. To have firm proof that I was right...it does make a difference, to me."

"That's all I ever wanted. I felt that we owed you that much. I'm just sorry it took me so long to reach you."

"You did your best, Dimitri. You got to me in the end." Then she reaches into her pocket again and takes out the change she's saved for the bread.

"CLEAR," I CALLED from the porthole, as we undocked. "Five meters. Ten metres. Fifteen." The rest of the ship came into view, silvery under its untidy-looking quilt of reflective foil. It was a bittersweet moment. I'd been looking forward to getting this view for months, but I'd always assumed it would be at mission's end, as we were about to ride the Soyuz back into Earth's atmosphere.

"Lining us up," Galenka said. She was in the command seat, wearing her EVA suit but with the helmet and gloves not yet in place.

I felt the Soyuz wheel around me as it orientated itself towards the Matryoshka. We'd be following the Progress all the way in, relying on the same collision-avoidance algorithm that had worked so well before. I kept telling myself that there was no reason for it to stop working now, just because we were aboard, but I couldn't quell my fears. My nerves had been frayed even when it had just been the robot at stake. I kept thinking of that American probe sliced in two, coming apart in two perfectly severed halves. How would it feel, I wondered, if we ran into one of those infinitely-sharp field lines? Would we even notice it at first? Would there even be pain, or just a sudden cold numbness from half our bodies?

As it was, we sailed through Shell 1 and Shell 2 without incident. All the while we remained in contact with the *Tereshkova*, and all the while the *Tereshkova* remained in contact with the microsat swarm. As windows opened and closed in Shell 3, the Progress reported on its continued existence and functionality. Nothing had happened to it since our departure. It was stuck, but otherwise operational and undamaged.

I clutched at every crumb of comfort. The Matryoshka hadn't touched the robot. It hadn't shown any sign of having noticed it. Didn't that bode well for us? If it didn't object to one foreign object, there was no reason for it to object to another, especially if we took pains not to get stuck ourselves.

Galenka brought us to a hovering standstill above Shell 3. In the microgravity environment of the Matryoshka, the Soyuz only needed to exert a whisper of thrust from its attitude motors to hold station.

"You'd better get buckled in, Dimitri. When a window opens, I'm giving her the throttle. It'll feel like a booster separation, only harder."

I made sure I was tight in my seat. "I'm ready. How long do you think?"

"No idea. Just be ready for it when it comes."

The glass cockpit of the Soyuz was much more advanced than the basic frame of the ship itself, which was older than my grandmother. Before our departure, Galenka had configured the sensors and readouts to emulate the same telemetry she'd been seeing from the Progress. Now all she had to do was watch the scrolling, chattering indications for the auguries of an opening window. She'd have no more than a second or two to assess whether it was a window she could reach in time, given the Soyuz's capabilities. Deciding that there was nothing I could contribute to the matter, I closed my eyes and waited for the moment.

No matter what happened now, we had made history. We were inside the Matryoshka—the first humans to have made it this far. It had taken three apparitions to achieve this feat. Once, it had seemed axiomatic that things would only go from strength to strength with each return. By the time of the fourth apparition, it seemed inconceivable that there would not be a permanent human presence out here, following the Matryoshka throughout its orbit. Study stations, research facilities—an entire campus, floating in vacuum.

I wondered now if anyone would come after us. The space effort was winding down—even the *Tereshkova* was cobbled together from the bits of earlier, failed enterprises. It seemed to me—though I would never have voiced such a conviction publically—that it was less important to my country what we found out here, than that we were seen to be doing something no one else could. The scientific returns were almost incidental. Next time, would anyone even bother sending out a ship?

"Brace," Galenka said.

The thrust was a hoof kick to the spine. It was worst than any booster separation, stage ignition or de-orbit burn. I had experienced re-entry gee-loads that were enough to push me to the brink of unconsciousness, but those forces had built up slowly, over several minutes. This came instantly, and for a moment I felt as if no bone in my body could possibly have survived unbroken.

Then I realised that I was all right. The engine was still burning, but at least the gee-load was a steady pressure now, like a firm hand rather than a fist.

"We are good for insertion," Galenka said, as if that had ever been in doubt.

We sailed through the two closely-packed shells, into the luminous blue-green interstitial space above Shell 4. Once we were clear—with the window sealing above us—Galenka did a somersault roll to use the main engine to slow us down again. The thrust burst was longer and less brutal this time. She dropped our speed from hundreds of metres per second to what was only slightly faster than walking pace. The thicket lay ahead or below, depending on my mental orientation. We were making good time. There was no need to rush things now.

Maybe, just maybe, we'd get away with this.

A screen flashed red and began scrolling with error messages. "There goes the *Tereshkova*," Galenka said. "We're out of contact now." She gave me a fierce grin. "Just you and me, and an impenetrable shell of alien matter between us and the outside world. Starting to feel claustrophobic yet?"

"I'd be insane not to. Do we have a fix on the Progress?"

She jabbed a finger at another readout—target cross-hairs against a moving grid. "Dead ahead, where she said she was. Judging by the data she recorded before getting stuck, we'll be able to get within two hundred metres without difficulty. I won't risk taking the Soyuz any closer, but we should be able to cover the remaining distance in suits."

"Whatever it takes." I checked my watch, strapped around the sleeve of my suit. We'd been out from the mother ship for less than three and a half hours—well ahead of schedule. We had air and fuel to spare, but I still wanted to be out of here as quickly as possible. "How soon until we're in position?" I asked.

"Twenty minutes, give or take."

"We spend two hours on station. Nothing changes that. If we don't succeed in unloading everything, we still leave. Are we clear on that?"

"This was your idea, Dimitri. You decide when we leave."

"I'm going to finish suiting up. We'll check comms and life-support thoroughly before we leave. And we'll make damned sure the Soyuz isn't going to drift away from us."

Galenka's estimate was on the nail. Twenty minutes later we were deep into the thicket, with blue-green structures crowding around us. Closest to us was a trunk or branch with thornlike protrusions. Galenka brought the Soyuz in against the trunk until the hull shuddered with the contact. Ordinarily I'd have been worried about a pressure rupture, but now that we were both wearing helmets that was only a distant concern. Galenka had picked her spot well, the Soyuz resting on one of the out-jutting thorns. Friction, and the ship's almost negligible weight, would serve to hold it in place until we were ready to leave. Galenka had even taken pains to make sure the forward escape hatch was not blocked.

"Maybe you should stay here, while I check out the Progress," I said. I didn't feel heroic, but it seemed the right thing to say.

"If we have to unload it, it'll go quicker with two of us," Galenka responded. "We can form a supply chain, save going all the way back each time. And keep an eye on each other." She unbuckled. "You ready for this? I'm going to vent our air."

She let the air drain out through the release valve before opening the hatch. My suit ballooned around me, the seals and joints creaking with the pressure differential. I'd checked everything, but I was all too conscious of the thin membranes of fabric protecting me from lung-freezing death. Every gesture, every movement, was now more awkward, more potentially hazardous than before. Tear a glove on sharp metal, and you might as well have cut your hand off.

Galenka popped the hatch. I pushed these concerns from my mind and exited the Soyuz. Now that I was seeing the alien environment with my own eyes—through a thin glass visor, rather than a thick porthole or monitor—it appeared not only larger, but vastly more oppressive and strange. The all-enveloping shell was a pitiless, hope-crushing black. I told myself that a window would eventually open for us to leave, just as one had allowed us to enter. But it was hard to shake the feeling that we were little warm animals, little shivering mammals with fast heartbeats, caught in a cold dark trap that we had just sprung.

"Let's do this shit, and get back home," Galenka said, pushing past me.

We climbed down the pea-green flank of the Soyuz, using the handholds that had been bolted on for weightless operations. We left the ship with the hatch open, the last dribbles of air still venting from the hull. My feet touched the thorn. Although I had almost no weight to speak of, the surface felt solid under me. It was formed from the same translucent material as the rest of Shell 4, but it wasn't as slippery as glass or ice. I reached out a hand and steadied myself against the trunk. I felt as if I was touching bark or rock through my glove.

"I think we can do this," I said.

"The Progress should be directly under us, where this trunk constricts against the one over here. I'd rather climb than drift, if that's OK with you."

"Agreed. There are thorns all the way down, spaced every three or four meters—we should be able to use them for grabs, even if we can't get traction on the rest of it. It shouldn't be much harder coming back up."

"I'm right behind you."

If the thicket registered our presence, there was no evidence of it. The structure loomed around us, dizzying in its scale and complexity, but giving no sign of being alive or responsive to the intrusion of human technology. I began to ease, trying to imagine myself in a forest or cave system—something huge but mindless—rather than the glowing guts of an alien machine.

It took fifteen minutes of cautious progress to reach the lodged Progress. It was jammed in nose first, with the engine pointing at us. A ship like that was not normally a man-rated vehicle, but the usual variants had a hatch at the front, so that space station crews could enter the vehicle when it was docked. Our Progress had been augmentd with scientific gear, computers, additional fuel and batteries. The docking hatch had become a kind of mouth by which the robot could feed samples into itself, using the feeler-like appendages of its sampling devices. Inside was a robotic system which sorted the samples, fed them into miniature laboratories where appropriate, and delivered whatever was left into a storage volume just ahead of the fuel tanks. We couldn't have got in through the mouth even if the Progress hadn't been jammed in nose first, but that didn't matter. A secondary hatch and docking assembly had been installed in the side, so that the sample compartment could be unloaded through the *Tereshkova*'s own docking port.

Galenka, who had overtaken me in our descent from the Soyuz, was the first to reach the sample hatch. The controls were designed to be opened by someone in a suit. She worked the heavy toggles until the hatch swung open, exposing the non-pressurised storage compartment. The hole in the side of the Progress was just large enough for a suited person to crawl through. Without hesitation she grabbed yellow handholds and levered herself inside. A few moments later the chamber lit up with the wavering light of her helmet-mounted flashlamp.

"Talk to me, Galenka."

"It's all racked and sorted, Dimitri. Must be about half a tonne of stuff in here already. Some of the chunks are pretty big. Still warm, too. Going to be a bitch of a job moving all of them back to the Soyuz."

"We'll take what we can; that was always the idea. If nothing else we should make sure we've got unique samples from both Shell 1 and Shell 2."

"I'm going to try and bring out the first chunk. I'll pass it through the hatch. Be ready."

"I'm here."

But as I said that, a status panel lit up on the side of my faceplate. "Comms burst from *Tereshkova*," I said, as alphanumeric gibberish scrolled past. "A window must just have opened."

"Feeling better now?"

"Guess it's nice to know the windows are still behaving."

"I could have told you they would." Galenka grunted with the effort of dislodging the sample she had selected. "So—any news?"

"Nothing. Just a carrier signal, trying to establish contact with us. Means the ship's still out there, though."

"I could have told you that as well."

It took twenty minutes to convey one sample back to the Soyuz. Doing it as a relay didn't help—it took two of us to nurse the object between us, all the while making sure we didn't drift away from the structure. Things got a little faster after that. We returned to the jammed Progress in good time and only took fifteen minutes to get the second sample back to our ship. We now had pieces of Shell 1 and Shell 2 aboard, ready to be taken back home.

A voice at the back of my head said that we should quit while we were ahead. We'd salvaged something from this mess—almost certainly enough to placate Baikonur. We had taken a risk and it had paid off. But there was still more than an hour remaining of the time I had allowed us. If we moved quickly and efficiently—and we were already beginning to settle into a rhythm—we could recover three or four additional samples before it was time to start our journey back. Who knew what difference five or six samples might make, compared to two?

"Just for the record," Galenka said, when we reached the Progress again, "I'm getting itchy feet here."

"We've still got time. Two more. Then we'll see how we're doing."

"You were a lot more jumpy until that window opened."

She was right. I couldn't deny it.

I was thinking of that when another comms burst came through. For a moment I was gladdened—just seeing the scroll of numbers and symbols, even if it meant nothing to me, made me feel closer to the *Tereshkova*. Home was just three shells and a sprint across vacuum away. Almost close enough to touch, like the space station that had sped across the sky over Klushino, when my father held me on his shoulders.

"Dimitri," crackled a voice. "Galenka. Yakov here. I hope you can hear me."

"What is it, friend?" I asked, hearing an edge in his voice I didn't like.

"You'd better listen carefully—we could get cut off at any moment. Baikonur detected a change in the Matryoshka—a big one. Shell 1 pulsations have increased in amplitude and frequency. It's like nothing anyone's seen since the first apparition. Whatever you two are doing in there—it's having an effect. The thing is waking. You need to think about getting out, while the collision-avoidance algorithm will still get you through Shell 1. Those pulsations change any more, the algorithm won't be any use."

"He could be lying," Galenka said. "Saying whatever he needs to say to get us to go back."

"I'm not lying. I want you to come back. And I want that Soyuz back so that at least one of us can get home."

"I think we'd better move," I said.

"The remaining samples?"

"Leave them. Let's just get back to the ship as quickly as possible."

As I spoke, the comms window blipped out. Galenka pushed away from the Progress. I levered myself onto the nearest thorn and started climbing. It was quicker now that we didn't have to carry anything between us. I thought of the changing conditions in Shell 1 and hoped that we'd still be able to pick a path through the lethal, shifting maze of field-lines.

We were half way to the Soyuz—I could see it overhead, tantalisingly near—when Galenka halted, only just below me.

"We're in trouble," she said.

"What?"

"Look down, Dimitri. Something's coming up."

I followed her instruction and understood. We couldn't see the Progress any more. It was lost under a silver tide, a sea of gleaming mercury climbing slowly through the thicket, swallowing everything as it rose.

"Climb," I said.

"We're not going to make it, Dimitri. It's rising too quickly."

I gritted my teeth: typical Galenka, pragmatic to the end. But even she had resumed her ascent, unable to stop her body from doing what her mind knew to be futile. She was right, too. The tide was going to envelop us long before we reached the Soyuz. But I couldn't stop climbing either. I risked a glance down and saw the silver fluid lapping at Galenka's heels, then surging up to swallow her lowest boot.

"It's got me."

"Keep moving."

She pulled the boot free, reached the next thorn, and for a moment it appeared that she might be capable of out-running the fluid. My mind raced ahead to the Soyuz, realising that even if we got there in time, even if we got inside and sealed the hatch, we wouldn't be able to get the ship aloft in time.

Then the fluid took more of Galenka. It lapped to her thighs, then her waist. She slowed her climb.

"It's pulling me back," she said, grunting with the effort. "It's trying to drag me in."

"Fight it."

Maybe she did—it was hard to tell, with her movements so impeded. The tide consumed her to the chest, taking her backpack, then absorbed her helmet. She had one hand raised above her head, grasping for the next thorn. The tide took it.

"Galenka."

"I'm here." She came through indistinctly, comms crackling with static. "I'm in it now. I can't see anything. But I can still move, still breathe. It's like being in the immersion tank."

"Try and keep climbing."

"Picking up some suit faults now. Fluid must be interfering with the electronics, with the cooling system." She faded out, came back, voice crazed with pops and crackles and hisses. "Oh, God. It's inside. I can feel it. It's cold, against my skin. Rising through the suit. How the fuck did it get in?"

She faded.

"Galenka. Talk to me."

"In my helmet now. Oh, God. Oh, God. It's still rising. I'm going to drown, Dimitri. This is not right. I did not want to fucking *drown*."

"Galenka?"

I heard a choked scream, then a gurgle. Then nothing.

I kept climbing, while knowing it was useless. The tide reached me a few moments later. It swallowed me and then found a way into my suit, just as it had with Galenka.

Then it found a way into my head.

WE DIDN'T DROWN.

There was a moment of absolute terror as it forced its way down my throat, through my eye sockets, nose and ears. The gag reflex kicked in, and then it was over. Not terror, no panic, just blissful unconsciousness.

Until I woke up on my back.

The silver tide was abating. It had left our bodies, left the inside of our suits. It was draining off them in chrome rivulets, leaving them dry and undamaged. We were lying like upended turtles, something like Earth-normal gravity pinning us to the floor. It took all my effort to lever myself into a sitting position, and then to stand up, fighting the weight of my backpack as it tried to drag me down. My suit was no longer ballooning out, meaning that we were in some kind of pressurised environment.

I looked around, taking deep, normal breaths.

Galenka and I were in a huge iron-grey room with gill-like sluice vents in the side walls. The fluid was rushing out through the vents, exposing a floor of slightly twinkling black, like polished marble. Grey-blue light poured down through hexagonal grids in the arched ceiling. I wasn't going to take any chances on it being breathable.

I inspected the outer covering for tears or abrasions, but it looked as good as when I'd worn it.

"Galenka," I said. "Can you hear me?"

"Loud and clear, Dimitri." I heard her voice on the helmet radio, but also coming through the glass, muffled but comprehensible. "Whatever we just went through—I don't think it hurt our suits."

"Do you still have air?"

"According to the gauge, good for another six hours."

"How do you feel?"

"Like I've been scrubbed inside with caustic soda. But otherwise—I'm all right. Clear-headed, like I've just woken up after a really slong sleep. I actually feel better, more alert, than before we left the Soyuz."

"That's how I feel," I said. "Where do you think we are?"

"The heart of it. The middle of the Matryoshka. Where else could we be? It must have brought us here for a reason. Maybe it wants to assess the foreign objects it detected, then work out how best to recycle or dispose of them."

"Maybe. But then why keep us alive? It must recognise that we're living. It must recognise that we're thinking beings."

"Always the optimist, Dimitri."

"Something's happening. Look."

A bar of light had cut across the base of part of the wall. It was becoming taller, as if a seamless door was opening upwards. The light ramming through the widening gap was the same grey-blue that came through the ceiling. Both of us tensing, expecting to be squashed out of existence at any moment, we turned to face whatever awaited us.

Beyond was a kind of corridor, sloping down in a gently steepening arc, so that the end was not visible except as an intensification of that silvery glow. The inwardly-sloping walls of the corridor—rising to a narrow spine of a ceiling—were dense with intricately carved details, traced in the blue-grey light.

"I think we should walk," Galenka said, barely raising her voice above a whisper.

We started moving, taking stiff, slow paces in our EVA suits. We passed through the door, into the corridor. We commenced down the curved ramp of the floor. Though I should have been finding it harder and harder to keep my footing, I had no sense that I was on a steepening grade. I looked at Galenka and she was still walking upright, at right angles to the surface of the floor. I paused to turn around, but already the room we had been in was angled out of view, with the door beginning to lower back down.

"Do you hear that sound?" Galenka asked.

I had been about to say the same thing. Over the huff and puff of our suit circulators it was not the easiest thing to make out. But there was a low droning noise, like the bass note of an organ. It was coming from all around us, from the very fabric of the Matryoshka. It sustained a note for many seconds before changing pitch. As we walked we heard a pattern of notes repeat, with subtle variations. I couldn't piece together the tune, if indeed there was one—it was too slow, too deep for that—but I didn't think I was hearing the random emanations of some mindless mechanical process.

"It's music," I said. "Slowed down almost to death. But it's still music."

"Look at the walls, Dimitri."

They were astonishing. The walls had been carved with a hypnotically detailed mazelike pattern, one that I could never quite bring into focus. Edges and ridges of the pattern pushed out centimetres from the wall. I felt a strange impulse to reach out and touch, as if there was a magnetic attraction working on my fingers.

Even as I acknowledged this impulse, Galenka—walking to my left—reached out her left hand and skirted the pattern on her side. She flinched and withdrew her gloved fingers with a gasp of something that could have been pain or astonishment or simple childlike delight.

"What?" I asked.

"I just got...I can't describe it, Dimitri. It was like—everything."

"Everything what?"

"Everything trying to get into my head. Everything at once. Like the whole universe gatecrashing my brain. It wasn't unpleasant. It was just—too much."

I reached out my hand.

"Be careful."

I touched the wall. Knowledge, clean and viridescent, as brittle and endlessly branching as a flower chilled in liquid nitrogen, forced its way into my skull. I felt mental sutures straining under the pressure. I flinched back, just as Galenka had done. The contact could not have lasted more than an instant, but the information that had gushed through was ringing in my skull like the after-chime of God's own church bell.

A window of comprehension had opened and slammed shut again. I was dizzy with what it had shown me. I already knew more about the Matryoshka than any other living person, with the possible exception of Galenka.

"It's come from the future," I said.

"I got that as well."

"They sent it here. They sent it here to carry a message to us."

I knew these things with an unimpeachable certainty, but I had no additional context for the knowledge. What future, by whom? From how far ahead, and to what purpose? What message? How had it arrived?

I couldn't stand not knowing. Now that I knew part of the truth, I needed the rest.

I reached out my hand again, caressed the wall. It hit me harder this time, but the instinct to flinch away, the instinct to close my mind, was not as strong. I gasped at the crystalline rush. There couldn't be room in my head for all that was being pumped into it, and yet it continued without interruption. Layers of wisdom poured into me, cooling and stratifying like ancient rock. My head felt like a boulder perched on my shoulders. I laughed: it was the only possible response, other than screaming terror. The flow continued, increasing in pressure.

This much I understood:

The Matryoshka was a complex machine with a simple purpose. Its layered structure was borne of necessity; the way it had to be in order to complete its mission. Each layer was a form of armour or camouflage or passkey, evolved organically to enable it to slip through the threshing clockwork of a cosmic time machine. That time machine was older than Earth. It had been constructed by alien minds and then added to and modified by successive intelligences. It was as far beyond the Matryoshka as the Matryoshka was beyond the Soyuz.

The time machine had been waiting in a state of dormancy, for more than a billion years. Then humanity, or what had become of humanity, chanced upon it.

It took a little while to understand its nature.

At its ticking, whirling core lay a necklace of neutron stars. It had been known since our own era that a sufficiently long, dense, and fast-rotating cylinder had the property of twisting spacetime around itself until a path into the past became possible. Such a path—a mathematical trajectory in space, like an orbit—offered a means of conveying a signal or object to any previous point in time, provided it was no earlier than the moment of the time machine's construction.

Constructing such a machine was anything but child's play.

A single neutron star could be made to have the requisite density and spin, but it lacked the necessary axial elongation. To overcome this, the machine's builders had approximated a cylinder by stringing four hundred and forty-one neutron stars together until they were almost touching, like beads on a wire. An open-ended string would have collapsed under its own appalling self-gravity, so the ends had been bent around and joined, with the entire ensemble revolving fast enough to stabilise the neutron stars against falling inward. It still wasn't a cylinder, but locally—as far as a photon or vehicle near the necklace was concerned—it might as well have been.

If it had taken a while to understand the time machine, it had taken even longer to engineer a vehicle capable of traversing it. The construction of the Matryoshka was the last great enterprise of a waning civilisation.

The machine had catapulted the Matryoshka into the prehuman past of our galaxy. The insertion into time-reversed flight, the passage through the various filters and barriers installed to prevent illicit use of the ancient machinery, the exit back into normal timeflow, had caused eleven additional layers of shell to be sacrificed. What we saw of the Matryoshka was merely the scarred kernel of what had once been a much larger entity.

But it had survived. It had come through, albeit overshooting its target era by many millions of years. Yet that had been allowed for; it was easier to leap back into the deep past and crawl forward in time than to achieve a bullseye into a relatively recent era. The emergence event was indeed the opening of a local wormhole throat, but only so that the Matryoshka (which incorporated wormhole-manipulating machinery in Shells 1 and 2) could complete the last leg of its journey.

How far downstream had it come? A hundred years? A thousand years? Five thousand?

I couldn't tell. The knowledge told me everything, but not all of that wisdom was framed in terms I could readily decode. But I could sense a thread, a sense of connectedness between the era of the Matryoshka and our own. They knew a lot about us.

Enough to know that we were on the wrong path.

At last I jerked my hand away from the wall. The urge to return it was almost overwhelming, but I could only take so much in one go.

"Dimitri?"

"I'm here."

"I thought you were gone for a while there."

I turned to face my comrade. Against the vastness I had been shown, the cosmic scale of the history I had almost glimpsed, Galenka appeared no more substantial than a paper cut-out. She was just a human being, translucent with her own insubstantiality, pinned in this one moving instant like dirt on a conveyor belt. It took moments for my sense of scale to normalise; to realise that, for all that the machine had shown me, I was no different.

"They sent it back for us," I said. The words came out in a rush, and yet at the same time each syllable consumed an eternity of time and effort. "To show us how we've gone wrong. There's history here—lots of it. In these walls. Mountains, chasms, of data."

"You need to slow your breathing. That silver stuff that got into us—it's primed us in some way, hasn't it? Rewired our minds so that the Matryoshka can get into them?"

"I think—maybe. Yes."

"Get a grip, Dimitri. We still need to get home."

I made to touch the wall again. The urge was still there, the hunger—the vacuum in my head—returning. The Matryoshka still had more to tell me. It was not done with Dimitri Ivanov.

"Don't," Galenka said, with a firmness that stopped my hand. "Not now. Not until we've seen the rest of this place.

At her urging I resisted. I found that if kept to the middle of the corridor, it wasn't as bad. But the walls were still whispering to me, inviting me to stroke my hand against them.

"The Second Soviet," I said.

"What about it?"

"It falls. Fifty years from now, maybe sixty. Somewhere near the end of the century. I saw it in the history." I paused and swallowed hard. "This road we're on—this path. It's not the right one. We took a wrong turn, somewhere between the first and second apparitions. But by the time we realise it, by the time the Soviet falls, it's too late. Not just for Russia, but for Earth. For humankind."

"It came from our future. Even I felt that, and I only touched it briefly. If we sent it, then things can't be all bad."

"It's the wrong future," I said. "The Matryoshka is almost the last thing they do. They've been on the wrong path, doomed, from the outset. We turned away from space—that's the mistake. There's a darkness between then and now, and when it comes we aren't ready."

We were still walking, following the arcing downslope of the corridor, towards the silver-blue radiance at its end. "The Second Soviet is the only political organisation still doing space travel. If anything we're the ones holding the candle."

"It's not enough. Now that the other nations have abandoned their efforts, we have to do more than just subsist. And if we are holding the candle, it won't be for much longer."

"I don't understand how the choices we make here and now can make that much of a difference, however many years from now."

"Evidently they can, or our descendants wouldn't have gone to all this trouble. Look, we're both smart enough to understand that small changes in initial conditions can feed into a chaotic system in highly unpredictable ways. What is history but a chaotic system?"

"The Second Soviet won't like being told it's a mistake of history, Dimitri."

There was a fierce dryness in my throat. "It can't ignore the message in the Matryoshka. Not now."

"I wouldn't be too sure about that. But you know something?"

"What?"

"If this thing is from the future—from our future—then maybe it's Russian as well. Or sent back to meet Russians. Which might mean that Nesha Petrova was right after all."

"They should tell her."

"I'm sure it'll be the first thing on their minds, after they've spent all these years crushing and humiliating her." Galenka fell silent for a few paces. "It's like they always knew, isn't it."

"They couldn't have."

"But they knew enough to want her to be wrong. A message from the future, intended for us? What could *we* possibly need to hear from our descendants, except their undying gratitude?"

"Everything we say is being logged on our suit recorders," I said. "Logged and compressed and stored, so that it can be sent back to the Soyuz and then back to the *Tereshkova*, and then back to Baikonur."

"Right now, comrade, there are few things I give less of a damn about than some arsehole of a party official listening to what I have to say."

I smiled, because that was exactly how I felt as well.

In sixty years the Second Soviet was dust. The history I had absorbed told me that nothing could prevent that. Accelerate it, yes—and maybe the arrival of the Matryoshka would do just that—but not prevent it. They could crucify us and it wouldn't change anything.

It was a crumb of consolation.

The corridor widened, the intricate walls flanking away on either side, until we reached a domed room of cathedral proportions. The chamber was round, easily a hundred metres across, with a domed ceiling. I saw no way in or out other than the way we had come. There was a jagged design in the floor, worked in white and black marble—rapier-thin shards radiating from the middle.

The music intensified—rising in pitch, rising in speed. If there was a tune there it was almost on the point of being comprehensible. I had a mental image of a rushing winter landscape, under white skies.

"This is it, then," Galenka said. "An empty fucking room. After all this." She took a hesitant step towards the middle, then halted.

"Wait," I said.

Something was happening.

The black and white shards were pulling back from the middle, sliding invisibly into the floor's circular border, a star-shaped blackness opening up in the centre. It all happened silently, with deathly slowness. Galenka stepped back, the two of us standing side by side. When the star had widened to ten or twelve metres across, the floor stopped moving. Smoothly, silently, something rose from the darkness. It was a plinth, and there was a figure on the plinth, lying with his face to the domed ceiling. Beneath the plinth, icy with frost, was a thick tangle of pipes and coiling, intestinal machinery. We stood and watched it in silence, neither of us ready to make the first move. There was a tingle in my head that was not quite a headache just now, but which promised to become one.

The floor began to slide back into place, the jagged blades locking into place beneath the plinth. There was now an uninterrupted surface between the resting figure and us. Galenka and I glanced at each other through our visors, then began a slow, measured walk. The slope-sided plinth rose two metres from the floor, putting the reclining figure just above our heads. It hadn't moved, or shown the least sign of life, since emerging through the floor.

We reached the plinth. There was a kind of ledge or step in the side, allowing us to bring our heads level with the figure. We stood looking at it, saying nothing, the silence only punctuated by the laboured, bellows-like sound of our air circulators.

That it was human had been obvious from the moment the plinth rose. The shape of the head, the ribbed chest, the placement and articulation of the limbs—it was all too familiar to be alien. Anyway, I knew that something descended from us—something essentially human—had sent back the Matryoshka. My bright new memories told me now that I was seeing the pilot, the navigator that had steered the artefact through the vicious barbs of the booby-trapped time machine, and then up through time, skipping through a cascade of wormholes, to our present era. The pilot was ghostly pale, wraithe-thin and naked, lying on a white metallic couch or rack that at first glance appeared to be an apparatus of torture or savage restraint. But then I decided that the apparatus was merely the control and life-support interface for the pilot. It was what had kept him alive, and what had given him the reins of the vast, layered machine it was his duty to steer and safeguard.

I sensed that the journey had not been a short one. In the Matryoshka's reference frame, it had consumed centuries of subjective time. The pilot, bio-modified for longevity and uninterrupted consciousness, had experienced every howling second of his voyage. That had always been the intention.

But something had gone wrong. A miscalculation, a problem with the injection into the time machine. Or the emergence event, or the wormhole skip. Something I couldn't grasp, except in the nature of its outcome. The journey wasn't supposed to have taken this long.

"The pilot went mad."

"You know this for a fact," Galenka said.

"You'd think this was a punishment—to be put inside the Matryoshka, alone, hurled back in time. But in fact it was the highest honour imaginable. They glorified him. He was entrusted with a mission of unimaginable importance."

"To change their past?"

"No. They were stuck with what they already had. You can change someone else's past, but not your own. That's how time travel works. We have a different future now—one that won't necessarily include the people who built the Matryoshka. But they did it for us, not themselves. To redeem one possible history, even if they couldn't mend their own. And he paid for that with his sanity."

Galenka was silent for long moments. I surveyed the figure, taking in more of the details. Had he been standing, he would have towered over both of us. His arms were by his sides—his hands were small and boyish, out of proportion to the rest of him. His fists were clenched. The emaciated form was partly machine. The couch extended parts of itself into his body. Glowing blue lines slipped into orifices and punctured his flesh at a dozen points. Hard, non-biological forms bulged under drum-tight flesh. His eye sockets were stuffed with faceted blue crystals, radiating a spray of glowing fibres. There was something not quite right about the shape of his skull, as if some childhood deformity had never healed in the right way. It was hairless, papered over with translucent, finely veined skin. His lips were a bloodless gash.

"The music," Galenka said, breaking the reverence. "You think it's coming from his head, don't you."

"I think music must have comforted him during his journey. Somewhere along the way, though, it swallowed him up. It's locked in a loop, endlessly repeating. He's like a rat in a wheel, going round and round. By the time he came out of the wormhole, there couldn't have been enough left of him to finish the mission."

"He made the Matryoshka sing."

"It might have been the last thing he did, before the madness took over completely. The last message he could get through to us. He knew how alien the artefact would have appeared to us, with its shells of camouflage and disguise. He made it sing, thinking we'd understand. A human signal, a sign that we shouldn't fear it. That no matter how alien it appeared on the outside, there was something human at the heart. A message for the species, a last chance not to screw things up."

"Would it have killed him to use radio?"

"He had to get it through Shell 3, remember—not to mention how many shells we've come through since Shell 4. Maybe it just wasn't possible. Maybe the simplest thing really was to have the Matryoshka sing itself to us. After all, it's not as if someone didn't notice in the end."

"Or maybe he was just insane, and the music's just a side-effect."

"That's also a possibility," I said.

The impulse that had drawn my hand towards the patterned wall compelled me to reach out and touch the pilot. I was moving my arm when the figure twitched, convulsing within the constraints of the couch. The blue lines strained like ropes in a squall. I jerked in my suit, nerves battling with curiosity. The figure was still again, but something about it had changed.

"Either it just died," Galenka said, "or it just came back to life. You want to take a guess, Dimitri?"

I said nothing. It was all I could do to stare at the pilot. His chest wasn't moving, and I doubted that there was a heart beating inside that ribcage. But something was different.

The pilot's head turned. The movement was glacially slow, more like a flower following the sun than the movement of an animal. It must have cost him an indescribable effort just to look at us. I could read no expression in the tight mask of his face or the blue facets of his eyes. But I knew we had his full attention.

The gash of his lips opened. He let out a long, slow sigh.

"You made it," I said. "You completed your mission."

Perhaps it was my imagination—I would never know for certain—but it seemed to me then that the head nodded a fraction, as if acknowledging what I had said. As if thanking me for bringing this news.

Then there was another gasp of air—longer, this time. It had something of death about it. The eyes were still looking at me, but all of a sudden I sensed no intellect behind them. I wondered if the pilot had conserved some last flicker of sanity for the time when he had visitors—just enough selfhood to die knowing whether he had succeeded or failed.

Tension exited the body. The head lolled back into the frame, looking sideways. His arm slumped to the side, dangling over the side of the plinth. The fist relaxed, letting something small and metallic drop to the floor.

I reached down and picked up the item, taking it as gingerly as I could in my suit gloves. I stared down at it as if it was the most alien thing in the universe. Which, in that moment, I think it probably was.

"A keepsake," I said, wondering aloud. "Something he was allowed to bring with him from the future. Something as ancient as the world he was aiming for. Something that must have been centuries old when he began his journey."

"Maybe," Galenka said.

I closed my own fist around the musical box. It was a simple human trinket, the most innocent of machines. I wanted to take my gloves off, to find out what it played. But I wondered if I already knew.

A little later the chrome tide came to wash us away again.

THE MEN ARE waiting next to Nesha's apartment when we return with her bread. I never saw their Zil, if that was how they arrived. There are three of them. They all have heavy black coats on, with black leather gloves. The two burlier men—whose faces mean nothing to me—have hats on, the brims dusted with snow. The third man isn't wearing a hat, although he has a pale blue scarf around his throat. He's thinner than the others, with a shaven, bullet-shaped head and small round glasses that bestow a look somewhere between professorial and ascetic. Something about his face is familiar: I feel that we've known each other somewhere before. He's taking a cigarette out of a packet when our eyes lock. It's the same contraband variety I used to buy my ride into town.

"This is my fault," I say to Nesha. "I didn't mean to bring these men here."

"We've come to take you back to the facility," the bald man says, pausing to ignite the cigarette from a miniature lighter. "Quite frankly, I didn't expect to find you alive. I can't tell you what a relief it is to find you."

"Do I know you?"

"Of course you know me. I'm Doctor Grechko. We've spent a lot of time together at the facility."

"I'm not going back. You know that by now."

"I beg to differ." He takes a long drag on the cigarette. "You're coming with us. You'll thank me for it eventually." He nods at one of the hatted men, who reaches into his coat pocket and extracts a syringe with a plastic cap on the needle. The man pinches the cap between his gloved fingers and removes it. He holds the syringe to eye level, taps away bubbles and presses the plunger to squirt out a few drops of whatever's inside.

The railing along the balcony is very low. There's snow on the ground nine floors below, but it won't do much to cushion my fall. I've done what I came to do, so what's to prevent me from taking my own life, in preference to being taken back to the facility?

"I'm sorry I brought this on you," I tell Nesha, and make to lift myself over the railing. My resolve at that moment is total. I'm surrendered to the fall, ready for white annihilation. I want the music in my head to end. Death and silence, for eternity.

But I'm not fast enough, or my resolve isn't as absolute as I imagine. The other hatted man rushes to me and locks his massive hand around my arm. The other one moves closer with the syringe.

"Not just yet," Doctor Grechko—if that was his name—says. "He's safe now, but keep a good grip on him."

"What happens to Nesha?" I ask.

Grechko looks at her, then shakes his head. "There's no harm in talking to a madwoman, Georgi. Whatever you may have told her, she'll confuse it with all that rubbish she already believes. No worse than telling secrets to a dog. And even if she didn't, no one would listen to her. Really, she isn't worth our inconvenience. You, on the other hand, are extraordinarily valuable to us."

Something's wrong. I feel an icebreaker cutting through my brain.

"My name isn't Georgi."

Doctor Grechko nods solemnly. "I'm afraid it is. No matter what you may currently believe, you are Doctor Georgi Kizim. You're even wearing his coat. Look in the pocket if you doubt me—there's a good chance you still have his security pass."

"No," I insist. "I am not Georgi Kizim. I know that man, but I'm not him. I just took his coat, so that I could escape. I am the cosmonaut, Dimitri Ivanov. I was on the *Tereshkova*. I went into the Matryoshka."

"No," Doctor Grechko corrects patiently. "You are not the cosmonaut. He was—is, to a degree—your patient. You were assigned to treat him, to learn what you could. Unfortunately, the protocol was flawed. We thought we could prevent a repeat of what happened with Yakov, the bleed-over of personality and memory, but we were wrong. You began to identify too strongly with your patient, just as Doctor Malyshev began to identify with Yakov. We still don't understand the mechanism, but after the business with Malyshev we thought we'd put in enough safeguards to stop it happening twice. Clearly, we were wrong about that. Even with Ivanov in his vegetative state…"

"I am Ivanov," I say, but with a chink of doubt opening inside me.

"Maybe you should look in the coat," Nesha says.

My fingers numb with cold, I dig into the pocket until I touch the hard edge of his security pass. The hatted man's still keeping a good hold on my arm. I pass the white plastic rectangle to Nesha. She squints, holding it at arm's length, studying the little hologram.

"It's you," she says. "There's no doubt."

I shake my head. "There's been a mistake. Our files mixed up. I'm not Doctor Kizim. I remember being on that ship, everything that happened."

"Only because you spent so much time in his presence," Grechko says, not without compassion. "After Dimitri fell into the intermittent vegetative state, we considered the risks of contamination to be significantly reduced. We relaxed the safeguards."

"I am not Doctor Kizim."

"You'll come out of it, Georgi—trust me. We got Malyshev back in the end. It was traumatic, but eventually his old personality resurfaced. Now he remembers being Yakov, but he's in no doubt as to his core identity. We can do the same for you, I promise. Just come back with us, and all will be well."

"Look at the picture," Nesha says, handing the pass back to me.

I do. My eyes take a moment to focus—the snow and the cold are making them water—but when they do there's no real doubt. I'm looking at the same face that I'd seen in the mirror in Nesha's apartment. Cleaned and tidied, but still me.

"I'm scared."

"Of course you're scared. Who wouldn't be?" Grechko stubs out the cigarette and extends a gloved hand. "Will you come with us now, Georgi? So that we can start helping you?"

"I have no choice, do I?"

"It's for the best."

Seeing that I'm going to come without a struggle, Grechko nods at the man with the syringe to put it back in his pocket. The other hatted man gives me an encouraging shove, urging me to start walking along the landing to the waiting elevator. I resist for a moment, looking back at Nesha.

I crave some last moment of connection with the woman I've risked my life to visit.

She nods once.

I don't think Grechko or the other men see her do it. Then she pulls her hand from her pocket and shows me the musical box, before closing her fist on it as if it's the most secret and precious thing in the universe. As if recalling something from a dream, I remember another hand placing that musical box in mine. It's the hand of a cosmonaut, urging me to do something before he slips into coma.

I have no idea what's going to happen to either of us now. Nesha's old, but she could easily have decades of life ahead of her. If she's ever doubted that she was right, she now has concrete proof. A life redeemed, if it needed redeeming. They'll still find every excuse to humiliate her at every turn, given the chance.

But she'll know with an iron certainty they're wrong, and she'll also know that everything they stand for will one day turn to dust.

Small consolation, but you take what you can get.

"Am I really Doctor Kizim?" I ask Grechko, as the elevator takes us down.

"You know it in your heart."

I stroke my face, measuring it against the memories I feel to be real. "I was so sure."

"That's the way it happens. But it's a good sign that you're already questioning these fundamental certainties."

"The cosmonaut?" I ask, suddenly unable to mention him by name.

"Yes?"

"You mentioned him being in an intermittent vegetative state."

"He's been like that for a while. I'm surprised you don't remember. He just lies there and watches us. Watches us and hums, making the same tune over and over again. One of us recognised it eventually." With only mild interest Grechko adds: "That piece by Prokofiev, the famous one?"

"Troika," I say, as the door opens. "Yes, I know it well."

They take me out into the snow, to the Zil that must have been waiting out of sight. The man with the syringe walks ahead and opens the rear passenger door, beckoning me into it as if I'm some high-ranking party official. I get in without causing a scene. The Zil's warm and plush and silent.

As we speed away from Star City, I press my face against the glass and watch the white world rush by as if in a sleigh-ride.

SLEEPOVER

THEY BROUGHT Gaunt out of hibernation on a blustery day in early spring. He came to consciousness in a steel-framed bed in a grey-walled room that had the economical look of something assembled in a hurry from prefabricated parts. Two people were standing at the foot of the bed, looking only moderately interested in his plight. One of them was a man, cradling a bowl of something and spooning quantities of it into his mouth, as if he was eating his breakfast on the run. He had cropped white hair and the leathery complexion of someone who spent a lot of time outside. Next to him was a woman with longer hair, greying rather than white, and with much darker skin. Like the man she was wiry of build and dressed in crumpled grey overalls, with a heavy equipment belt dangling from her hips.

"You in one piece, Gaunt?" she asked, while her companion spooned in another mouthful of his breakfast. "You *compos mentis?*"

Gaunt squinted against the brightness of the room's lighting, momentarily adrift from his memories.

"Where am I?" he asked. His voice came out raw, as if he had been in a loud bar the night before.

"In a room, being woken up," the woman said. "You remember going under, right?"

He grasped for memories, something specific to hold onto. Green-gowned doctors in a clean surgical theatre, his hand signing the last of the release forms before they plumbed him into the machines. The drugs flooding his system, the utter absence of sadness or longing as he bid farewell to the old world, with all its vague disappointments.

"I think so."

"What's your name?" the man asked.

"Gaunt." He had to wait a moment for the rest of it to come. "Marcus Gaunt."

"Good," he said, smearing a hand across his lips. "That's a positive sign."

"I'm Clausen," the woman said. "This is Da Silva. We're your wake-up team. You remember Sleepover?"

"I'm not sure."

"Think hard, Gaunt," she said. "It won't cost us anything to put you back under, if you don't think you're going to work out for us."

Something in Clausen's tone convinced him to work hard at retrieving the memory. "The company," he said. "Sleepover was the company. The one that put me under. The one that put everyone under."

"Brain cells haven't mushed on us," Da Silva said.

Clausen nodded, but showed nothing in the way of jubilation in him having got the answer right. It was more that he'd spared the two of them a minor chore, that was all. "I like the way he says 'everyone'. Like it was universal."

"Wasn't it?" Da Silva asked.

"Not for him. Gaunt was one of the first under. Didn't you read his file?" Da Silva grimaced. "Sorry. Got sidetracked."

"He was one of the first two hundred thousand," Clausen said. "The ultimate exclusive club. What did you call yourselves, Gaunt?"

"The Few," he said. "It was an accurate description. What else were we going to call ourselves?"

"Lucky sons of bitches," Clausen said.

"Do you remember the year you went under?" Da Silva asked. "You were one of the early ones, it must've been sometime near the middle of the century."

"Twenty fifty-eight. I can tell you the exact month and day if you wish. Maybe not the time of day."

"You remember why you went under, of course," Clausen said.

"Because I could," Gaunt said. "Because anyone in my position would have done the same. The world was getting better, it was coming out of the trough. But it wasn't there yet. And the doctors kept telling us that the immortality breakthrough was just around the corner, year after the year. Always just out of reach. Just hang on in there, they said. But we were all getting older. Then the doctors said that while they couldn't give us eternal life just yet, they could give us the means to skip over the years until it happened." Gaunt forced himself to sit up in the bed, strength returning to his limbs even as he grew angrier at the sense that he was not being treated with sufficient deference, that—worse—he was being judged. "There was nothing evil in what we did. We didn't hurt anyone or take anything away from anyone else. We just used the means at our disposal to access what was coming to us anyway."

"Who's going to break it to him?" Clausen asked, looking at Da Silva.

"You've been sleeping for nearly a hundred and sixty years," the man said. "It's April, twenty-two seventeen. You've reached the twenty-third century."

Gaunt took in the drab mundanity of his surroundings again. He had always had some nebulous idea of the form his wake-up would take and it was not at all like this.

"Are you lying to me?"

"What do you think?" asked Clausen.

He held up his hand. It looked, as near as he could remember, exactly the way it had been before. The same age-spots, the same prominent veins, the same hairy knuckles, the same scars and loose, lizardy skin.

"Bring me a mirror," he said, with an ominous foreboding.

"I'll save you the bother," Clausen said. "The face you'll see is the one you went under with, give or take. We've done nothing to you except treat superficial damage caused by the early freezing protocols. Physiologically, you're still a sixty-year-old man, with about twenty or thirty years ahead of you."

"Then why have you woken me, if the process isn't ready?"

"There isn't one," Da Silva said. "And there won't be, at least not for a long, long time. Afraid we've got other things to worry about now. Immortality's the least of our problems."

"I don't understand."

"You will, Gaunt," Clausen said. "Everyone does in the end. You've been preselected for aptitude, anyway. Made your fortune in computing, didn't you?" She didn't wait for him to answer. "You worked with artificial intelligence, trying to make thinking machines."

One of the vague disappointments hardened into a specific, life-souring defeat. All the energy he had put into one ambition, all the friends and lovers he had burned up along the way, shutting them out of his life while he focused on that one white whale.

"It never worked out."

"Still made you a rich man along the way," she said.

"Just a means of raising money. What does it have to do with my revival?"

Clausen seemed on the verge of answering his question before something made her change her mind. "Clothes in the bedside locker: they should fit you. You want breakfast?"

"I don't feel hungry."

"Your stomach will take some time to settle down. Meantime, if you feel like puking, do it now rather than later. I don't want you messing up my ship."

He had a sudden lurch of adjusting preconceptions. The prefabricated surroundings, the background hum of distant machines, the utilitarian clothing of his wake-up team: perhaps he was aboard some kind of spacecraft, sailing between the worlds. The twenty-third century, he thought. Time enough to establish an interplanetary civilisation, even if it only extended as far as the solar system.

"Are we in a ship now?"

"Fuck, no," Clausen said, sneering at his question. "We're in Patagonia."

HE GOT DRESSED, putting on underwear, a white t-shirt and over that the same kind of grey overalls as his hosts had been wearing. The room was cool and damp and he was glad of the clothes once he had them on. There were lace-up boots that were tight around the toes, but otherwise serviceable. The materials all felt perfectly mundane and commonplace, even a little frayed and worn in places. At least he was clean and groomed, his hair clipped short and his beard shaved. They must have freshened him up before bringing him to consciousness.

Clausen and Da Silva were waiting in the windowless corridor outside the room. "Spect you've got a ton of questions," Clausen said. "Along the lines of, why am I being treated like shit rather than royalty? What happened to the rest of the Few, what is this fucked up, miserable place, and so on."

"I presume you're going to get round to some answers soon enough."

"Maybe you should tell him the deal now, up front," Da Silva said. He was wearing an outdoor coat now and had a zip-up bag slung over his shoulder.

"What deal?" Gaunt asked.

"To begin with," Clausen said, "you don't mean anything special to us. We're not impressed by the fact that you just slept a hundred and sixty years. It's old news. But you're still useful."

"In what way?"

"We're down a man. We run a tight operation here and we can't afford to lose even one member of the team." It was Da Silva speaking now; although there wasn't much between them, Clausen had the sense that he was the slightly more reasonable one of the duo, the one who wasn't radiating quite so much naked antipathy. "Deal is, we train you up and give you work. In return, of course, you're looked after pretty well. Food, clothing, somewhere to sleep, whatever medicine we can provide." He shrugged. "It's the deal we all took. Not so bad when you get used to it."

"And the alternative?"

"Bag you and tag you and put you back in the freezer," Da Silva went on. "Same as all the others. Your choice, of course. Work with us, become part of the team, or go back into hibernation and take your chances there."

"We need to be on our way." Clausen said. "Don't want to keep Nero waiting on F."

"Who's Nero?" Gaunt asked.

"Last one we pulled out before you," Da Silva said.

They walked down the corridor, passing a set of open double doors that led into some kind of mess room or commons. Men and women of various ages were sitting around tables, talking quietly as they ate meals or played card games. Everything looked spartan and institutional, from the plastic chairs to the formica-topped surfaces. Beyond the tables, a rain-washed window framed only a rectangle of grey cloud. Gaunt caught a few glances directed his way, a flicker of waning interest from one or two of the personnel, but no one showed any fascination in him. The three of them walked on, ascending stairs to the next level of whatever kind of building they were in. An older man, Chinese looking, passed in the opposite direction, carrying a grease-smeared wrench. He raised his free hand to Clausen in a silent high-five, Clausen reciprocating. Then they were up another level, passing equipment lockers and electrical distribution cabinets, and then up a spiral stairwell that emerged into a draughty, corrugated-metal shed smelling of oil and ozone. Incongruously, there was an inflatable orange life-preserver on one wall of the shed, an old red fire extinguisher on the other.

This is the twenty-third century, Gaunt told himself. As dispiriting as the surroundings were, he had no reason to doubt that this was the reality of life in twenty-two seventeen. He supposed it had always been an article of faith that the world would improve, that the future would be better than the past, shinier and cleaner and faster, but he had not expected to have his nose rubbed in the unwisdom of that faith quite so vigorously.

There was one door leading out of the corrugated-metal shed. Clausen pushed it open against wind, then the three of them stepped outside. They were on the roof of something. There was a square of cracked and oil-stained concrete, marked here and there with lines of fading red paint. A couple of seagulls pecked disconsolately at something in the corner. At least they still had seagulls, Gaunt thought. There hadn't been some awful, life-scouring bio-catastrophe, forcing everyone to live in bunkers.

Sitting on the middle of the roof was a helicopter. It was matte black, a lean, waspish thing made of angles rather than curves, and aside from some sinister bulges and pods, there was nothing particularly futuristic about it. For all Gaunt knew, it could have been based around a model that was in production before he went under.

"You're thinking: shitty looking helicopter," Clausen said, raising her voice over the wind.

He smiled quickly. "What does it run on? I'm assuming the oil reserves ran dry sometime in the last century?"

"Oil," Clausen said, cracking open the cockpit door. "Get in the back, buckle up. Da Silva rides up front with me."

Da Silva slung his zip-up bag into the rear compartment where Gaunt was settling into his position, more than a little apprehensive about what lay ahead. He looked between the backs of the forward seats at the cockpit instrumentation. He'd been in enough private helicopters to know what the manual override controls looked like and there was nothing weirdly incongruous here.

"Where are we going?"

"Running a shift change," Da Silva said, wrapping a pair of earphones around his skull. "Couple of days ago there was an accident out on J platform. Lost Gimenez, and Nero's been hurt. Weather was too bad to do the extraction until today, but now we have our window. Reason we thawed you, actually. I'm taking over from Gimenez, so you have to cover for me here."

"You have a labour shortage, so you brought me out of hibernation?"

"That about covers it," Da Silva said. "Clausen figured it wouldn't hurt for you to come along for the ride, get you up to speed."

Clausen flicked a bank of switches in the ceiling. Overhead, the rotor began to turn.

"I guess you have something faster than helicopters, for longer journeys," Gaunt said.

"Nope," Clausen answered. "Other than some boats, helicopters is pretty much it."

"What about intercontinental travel?"

"There isn't any."

"This isn't the world I was expecting!" Gaunt said, straining to make himself heard.

Da Silva leaned around and motioned to the headphones dangling from the seat back. Gaunt put them on and fussed with the microphone until it was in front of his lips.

"I said this isn't the world I was expecting."

"Yeah," Da Silva said. "I heard you the first time."

The rotor reached takeoff speed. Clausen eased the helicopter into the air, the rooftop landing pad falling away below. They scudded sideways, nose down, until they had cleared the side of the building. The walls plunged vertically, Gaunt's guts twisting at the dizzying transition. It hadn't been a building at all, at least not the kind he had been thinking of. The landing pad was on top of a square-ish, industrial-looking structure about the size of a large office block, hazed in scaffolding and gangways, prickly with cranes and chimneys and otherwise unrecognisable protuberances, the structure in turn rising out of the sea on four elephantine legs, the widening bases of which were being ceaselessly pounded by waves. It was an oil rig or production platform of some kind, or at least, something repurposed from one.

It wasn't the only one either. The rig they had taken off from was but one in a major field, rig after rig stretching all the way to the gloomy, grey, rain-hazed horizon. There were dozens, and he had the sense that they didn't stop at the horizon.

"What are these for? I know it's not oil. There can't be enough of it left to justify a drilling operation on this scale. The reserves were close to being tapped out when I went under."

"Dormitories," Da Silva said. "Each of these platforms holds maybe ten thousand sleepers, give or take. They built them out at sea because we need OTEC power to run them, using the heat difference between surface water and deep ocean, and it's much easier if we don't have to run those power cables inland."

"Coming back to bite us now," Clausen said.

"If we'd gone inland, they'd have sent land-dragons instead. They're just adapting to whatever we do," Da Silva said pragmatically.

They sped over oily, roiling waters. "Is this really Patagonia?" Gaunt asked.

"Patagonia offshore sector," Da Silva said. "Sub-sector fifteen. That's our watch. There are about two hundred of us, and we look after about a hundred rigs, all told."

Gaunt ran the numbers twice, because he couldn't believe what they were telling him. "That's a million sleepers."

"Ten million in the whole of Patagonia offshore," Clausen said. "That surprise you, Gaunt? That ten million people managed to achieve what you and your precious Few did, all those years back?"

"I suppose not," he said, as the truth of it sunk in. "Over time the cost of the process would have decreased, becoming available to people of lesser means. The merely rich, rather than the super-rich. But it was never going to be something available to the masses. Ten million, maybe. Beyond that? Hundreds of millions? I'm sorry, but the economics just don't stack up."

"It's a good thing we don't have economics, then," Da Silva said.

"Patagonia's just a tiny part of the whole," said Clausen. "Two hundred other sectors out there, just as large as this one. That's two billion sleepers, near as it matters."

Gaunt shook his head. "That can't be right. The global population was only eight billion when I went under, and the trend was downwards! You can't tell me that a quarter of the human race is hibernating."

"Maybe it would help if I told you that the current population of the Earth is also two billion, near as it matters," Clausen said. "Almost everyone's asleep. There's just a handful of us still awake, playing caretaker, watching over the rigs and OTEC plants."

"Four hundred thousand waking souls," Da Silva said. "But it actually feels like a lot less than that, since we mostly keep to our assigned sectors."

"You know the real irony?" Clausen said. "We're the ones who get to call ourselves the Few now. The ones who *aren't* sleeping."

"That doesn't leave anyone to actually do anything," Gaunt said. "There's no point in everyone waiting for a cure for death if there's no one alive to do the hard work of making it happen."

Clausen turned round to look back at him, her expression telling him everything he needed to know about her opinion of his intellect. "It isn't about immortality. It's about survival. It's about doing our bit for the war effort."

"What war?" Gaunt asked.

"The one going on all around us," Clausen said. "The one you made happen."

THEY CAME IN to land on another rig, one of five that stood close enough to each other to be linked by cables and walkways. The sea was still heavy, huge waves dashing against the concrete piers on which the rigs were supported. Gaunt peered intently at the windows and decks but saw no sign of human activity on any of the structures. He thought back to what Clausen and Da Silva had told him, each time trying to find a reason why they might be lying to him, why they might be going to pathological lengths to hoax him about the nature of the world into which he had woken. Maybe there was a form of mass entertainment that involved waking sleepers such as himself and putting them through the emotional wringer, presenting them with the grimmest possible scenarios, ramping up the misery until they cracked, and only then pulling aside the grey curtains to reveal that, in marvellous point of fact, life in the twenty-third century really was every bit as blue-skied and utopian as he had hoped. That didn't seem very likely, though.

Yet what kind of war required people to be put to sleep in their billions? And why was the caretaker force, the four hundred thousand waking individuals, stretched so ridiculously thin? Clearly the rigs were largely automated, but it had still been necessary to pull him out of sleep because someone else had died in the Patagonia offshore sector. Why not just have more caretakers awake in the first place, so that the system was able to absorb some losses?

With the helicopter safely down on the pad, Clausen and Da Silva told him to follow them into the depths of the other rig. There was very little about it to distinguish it from the one where Gaunt had been woken, save for the fact that it was almost completely deserted, with the only activity coming from skulking repair robots. They were clearly very simple machines, not much smarter than automatic window-cleaners. Given the years of his life that he had given over to the dream of artificial intelligence, it was dismaying to see how little progress—if any—had been made.

"We need to get one thing straight," Gaunt said, when they were deep into the humming bowels of the rig. "I didn't start any wars. You've got the wrong guy here."

"You think we mixed up your records?" Clausen asked. "How did we know about your work on thinking machines?"

"Then you've got the wrong end of the stick. I had nothing do to with wars or the military."

"We know what you did," she said. "The years spent trying to build a true, Turing-compliant artificial intelligence. A thinking, conscious machine."

"Except it was a dead end."

"Still led to some useful spin-offs, didn't it?" she went on. "You cracked the hard problem of language comprehension. Your systems didn't just recognise speech. They were able to understand it on a level no computer system had ever achieved before. Metaphor, simile, sarcasm and under-statement, even implication by omission. Of course, it had numerous civilian applications, but that isn't where you made your billions." She looked at him sharply.

"I created a product," Gaunt said. "I simply made it available to who-ever could afford it."

"Yes, you did. Unfortunately, your system turned out to be the per-fect instrument of mass surveillance for every despotic government still left on the planet. Every basket-case totalitarian state still in existence couldn't get its hands on your product fast enough. And you had no qualms whatsoever about selling it, did you?"

Gaunt felt a well-rehearsed argument bubbling up from subcon-scious. "No communication tool in history has ever been a single-edged sword."

"And that excuses you, does it?" Clausen asked. Da Silva had been silent in this exchange, observing the two of them as they continued along corridors and down stairwells.

"I'm not asking for absolution. But if you think I started wars, if you think I'm somehow responsible for this..." He gestured at his surround-ings. "This fucked up state of affairs. Then you're very, very wrong."

"Maybe you weren't solely responsible," Clausen said. "But you were certainly complicit. You and everyone else who pursued the dream of artificial intelligence. Driving the world toward the edge of that cliff, without a thought for the consequences. You had no idea what you were unleashing."

"I'm telling you, we unleashed nothing. It didn't work."

They were walking along a suspended gangway now, crossing from one side to the other of some huge space somewhere inside the rig. "Take a look down," Da Silva said. Gaunt didn't want to; he'd never been good with heights and the drainage holes in the floor were already too large for comfort. He forced himself anyway. The four walls of the cubic chamber held rack upon rack of coffin-sized white boxes, stacked thirty high and surrounded by complicated plumbing, accompanied by an equally complex network of access catwalks, ladders and service tracks. Even as Gaunt watched, a robot whirred up to one of the boxes and extracted a module from one end of it, before tracking sideways to deal with another coffin.

"In case you thought we were yanking your chain," Clausen said. "This is real."

The hibernation arrangements for the original Few could not have been more different. Like an Egyptian Pharoah buried with his worldly possessions, Gaunt had required an entire crypt full of bulky, state-of-the-art cryopreservation and monitoring systems. At any one time, as per his contract with Sleepover, he would have been under the direct care of several living doctors. Just housing a thousand of the Few needed a building the size of a major resort hotel, with about the same power requirements. By contrast this was hibernation on a crushing, maximally efficient industrial scale. People in boxes, stacked like mass-produced commodities, tended by the absolute minimum of living caretakers. He was seeing maybe less than a thousand sleepers in this one chamber, but from that point on Gaunt had no doubt whatsoever that the operation could be scaled up to encompass billions.

All you needed were more rooms like this. More robots and more rigs. Provided you had the power, and provided the planet did not need anyone to do anything else, it was eminently doable.

There was no one to grow crops or distribute food. But that didn't matter because there was almost no one left awake to need feeding. No one to orchestrate the intricate, flickering web of the global finance system. But that didn't matter because there was no longer anything resembling an economy. No need for a transport infrastructure because no one travelled. No need for communications, because no one needed to know what was going on beyond their own sector. No need for *anything* really, save the absolute, life and death essentials. Air to breathe. Rations and medicine for less than half a million people. A trickle of oil, the world's last black hiccough, to keep the helicopters running.

Yes, it could be done. It could easily be done.

"There's a war," Da Silva said. "It's been going on, in some shape or form, since before you went under. But it's probably not the kind of war you're thinking of."

"And where do these people come into it, these sleepers?"

"They have no choice," Clausen said. "They have to sleep. If they don't, we all die."

"We, as in…?"

"You, me. Us," Da Silva said. "The entire human species."

THEY COLLECTED NERO and the corpse from a sick bay several levels down from the freezer chamber. The corpse was already bagged, a silver-wrapped mummy on a medical trolley. Rather than the man Gaunt had been expecting, Nero turned out to be a tall, willowy woman with an open, friendly face and a mass of salmon-red curls.

"You the newbie, right?" she asked, lifting a coffee mug in salute.

"I guess," Gaunt said uneasily.

"Takes some adjustment, I know. Took a good six months before I realised this wasn't the worst thing that could happen to me. But you'll get there eventually." One of Nero's hands was bandaged, a white mitten with a safety pin stuck through the dressing. "Take it from me, though. Don't go back inside the box." Then she glanced at Clausen. "You *are* giving him a chance about this, aren't you?"

"Of course," Clausen said. "That's the deal."

"Occurs to me sometimes maybe it would be easier if there wasn't a deal, you know," Nero said. "Like, we just give them their duties and to hell with it."

"You wouldn't have been too pleased if we didn't give you the choice," Da Silva said. He was already taking off his coat, settling in for the stay.

"Yeah, but what did I know back then? Six months feels like half a lifetime ago now."

"When did you go under?" Gaunt asked.

"Twenty ninety-two. One of the first hundred million."

"Gaunt's got a headstart on you," Clausen said. "Guy was one of the Few. The original Few, the first two hundred thousand."

"Holy shit. That is some headstart." Nero narrowed her eyes. "He up to speed on things yet? My recollection is they didn't know what they were getting into back then."

"Most of them didn't," Clausen said.

"Know what?" Gaunt asked.

"Sleepover was a cover, even then," Nero said. "You were being sold a scam. There was never any likelihood of an immortality breakthrough, no matter how long you slept."

"I don't understand. You're saying it was all a con?"

"Of a kind," Nero said. "Not to make money for anyone, but to begin the process of getting the whole of humanity into hibernation. It had to begin small, so that they had time to work the wrinkles out of the technology. If the people in the know had come out into the open and announced their plans, no one would have believed them. And if they had been believed, there'd have been panic and confusion all over the world. So they began with the Few, and then expanded the operation slowly. First a few hundred thousand. Then half a million. Then a million…so on." She paused. "Establishing a pattern, a normal state of affairs. They kept the lid on it for thirty years. But then the rumours started spreading, the rumours that there was something more to Sleepover."

"The dragons didn't help," Da Silva said. "It was always going to be a tall order explaining those away."

"By the time I went under," Nero said, "most of us knew the score. The world was going to end if we didn't sleep. It was our moral duty, our obligation, to submit to the hibernation rigs. That, or take the euthanasia option. I took the freezer route, but a lot of my friends opted for the pill. Figured the certainty of death was preferable to the lottery of getting into the boxes, throwing the cosmic dice…" She was looking at Gaunt intently, meeting his eyes as she spoke. "And I knew about this part of the deal, as well. That, at some point, there'd be a chance of me being brought out of sleep to become a caretaker. But, you know, the likelihood of that was vanishingly small. Never thought it would happen to me."

"No one ever does," Clausen said.

"What happened?" Gaunt asked, nodding at the foil-wrapped body.

"Gimenez died when a steam pipe burst down on level eight. I don't think he felt much, it would have been so quick. I got down there as quickly as I could, obviously. Shut off the steam leak and managed to drag Gimenez back to the infirmary."

"Nero was burned getting Gimenez back here," Da Silva said.

"Hey, I'll mend. Just not much good with a screwdriver right now."

"I'm sorry about Gimenez," Clausen said.

"You don't need to be. Gimenez never really liked it here. Always figured he'd made the wrong decision, sticking with us rather than going back into the box. Tried to talk him round, of course, but it was like arguing with a wall." Nero ran her good hand through her curls. "Not saying I didn't get on with the guy. But there's no arguing that he's better off now than he was before."

"He's dead, though," Gaunt said.

"Technically. But I ran a full blood-scrub on him after the accident, pumped him full of cryoprotectant. We don't have any spare slots here, but they can put him back in a box on the operations rig."

"My box," Gaunt said. "The one I was in."

"There are other slots," Da Silva corrected. "Gimenez going back in doesn't preclude you following him, if that's what you want."

"If Gimenez was so unhappy, why didn't you just let him go back into the box earlier?"

"Not the way it works," Clausen said. "He made his choice. Afterwards, we put a lot of time and energy into bringing him up to speed, making him mesh with the team. You think we were going to willingly throw all that expenditure away, just because he changed his mind?"

"He never stopped pulling his weight," Nero said. "Say what you will about Gimenez, but he didn't let the team down. And what happened to him down on eight *was* an accident."

"I never doubted it," Da Silva said. "He was a good guy. It's just a shame he couldn't make the adjustment."

"Maybe it'll work out for him now," Nero said. "One-way ticket to the future. Done his caretaker stint, so the next time he's revived, it'll be because we finally got through this shit. It'll be because we won the war, and we can all wake up again. They'll find a way to fix him up, I'm sure. And if they can't, they'll just put him under again until they have the means."

"Sounds like he got a good deal out of it in the end," Gaunt said.

"The only good deal is being alive," Nero replied. "That's what we're doing now, all of us. Whatever happens, we're alive, we're breathing, we're having conscious thoughts. We're not frozen bodies stacked in boxes, merely existing from one instant to the next." She gave a shrug. "My fifty cents, that's all. You want to go back in the box, let someone else shoulder the burden, don't let me talk you out of it." Then she looked at Da Silva. "You gonna be all right here on your own, until I'm straightened out?"

"Something comes up I can't deal with, I'll let you know," Da Silva said.

Nero and Da Silva went through a checklist, Nero making sure her replacement knew everything he needed to, and then they made their farewells. Gaunt couldn't tell how long they were going to be leaving Da Silva alone out here, whether it was weeks or months. He seemed resigned to his fate, as if this kind of solitary duty was something they were all expected to do now and then. Given that there had been two people on duty here until Gimenez's death, Gaunt wondered why they didn't just thaw out another sleeper so that Da Silva wouldn't have to work on his own while Nero's hand was healing.

Then, no more than half an hour after his arrival, they were back in the helicopter again, powering back to the operations rig. The weather had worsened in the meantime, the seas lashing even higher against the rigs' legs, and the horizon was now obscured behind curtains of storming rain, broken only by the flash of lightning.

"This was bad timing," he heard Nero say. "Maybe you should have let me stew until this system had passed. It's not like Gimenez couldn't wait."

"We were already overdue on the extraction," Clausen said. "If the weather clamps down, this might be our last chance for days."

"They tried to push one through yesterday, I heard."

"Out in Echo field. Partial coalescence."

"Did you see it?"

"Only on the monitors. Close enough for me."

"We should put guns on the rigs."

"And where would the manpower come from, exactly? We're just barely holding on as it is, without adding more shit to worry about."

The two women were sitting up front; Gaunt was in the back with Gimenez's foil-wrapped corpse for company. They had folded back one seat to make room for the stretchered form.

"I don't really have a choice, do I," he said.

"Course you have a choice," Nero answered.

"I mean, morally. I've seen what it's like for you people. You're stretched to breaking point just keeping this operation from falling apart. Why don't you wake up more sleepers?"

"Hey, that's a good point," Clausen said. "Why don't we?"

Gaunt ignored her sarcasm. "You've just left that man alone, looking after that whole complex. How can I turn my back on you, and still have any self-respect?"

"Plenty of people do exactly that," Nero said.

"How many? What fraction?"

"More than half agree to stay," Clausen said. "Good enough for you?"

"But like you said, most of the sleepers would have known what they were getting into. I still don't."

"And you think that changes things, means we can cut you some slack?" Clausen asked. "Like we're gonna say, it's fine man, go back into the box, we can do without you this time."

"What you need to understand," Nero said, "is that the future you were promised isn't coming. Not for centuries, not until we're out of this mess. And no one has a clue how long that could take. Meanwhile, the sleepers don't have unlimited shelf life. You think the equipment never fails? You think we don't sometimes lose someone because a box breaks down?"

"Of course not."

"You go back in the box, you're gambling on something that might never happen. Stay awake, at least there are certainties. At least you know you'll die doing something useful, something worthwhile."

"It would help if you told me why," Gaunt said.

"Someone has to look after things," Nero said. "The robots take care of the rigs, but who takes care of the robots?"

"I mean, why is it that everyone has to sleep? Why is that so damned important?"

Something flashed on the console. Clausen pressed a hand against her headphones, listening to something. After a few seconds he heard her say: "Roger, vectoring three two five." Followed by an almost silent "Fuck. All we need."

"That wasn't a weather alert," Nero said.

"What's happening?" Gaunt asked, as the helicopter made a steep turn, the sea tilting up to meet him.

"Nothing you need worry about," Clausen said.

The helicopter levelled out on its new course, flying higher than before—so it seemed to Gaunt—but also faster, the motor noise louder in the cabin, various indicator lights showing on the console that had not been lit before. Clausen silenced alarms as they came on, flipping the switches with the casual insouciance of someone who was well used to flying under tense circumstances and knew exactly what her machine could and couldn't tolerate, more intimately perhaps than the helicopter itself, which was after all only a dumb machine. Rig after rig passed on either side, dark straddling citadels, and then the field began to thin out. Through what little visibility remained Gaunt saw only open sea, a plain of undulating, white-capped grey. As the winds harried it the water moved like the skin of some monstrous breathing thing, sucking in and out with a terrible restlessness.

"There," Nero said, pointing out to the right. "Breech glow. Shit; I thought we were meant to be avoiding it, not getting closer."

Clausen banked the helicopter again. "So did I. Either they sent me a duff vector or there's more than one incursion going on."

"Won't be the first time. Bad weather always does bring them out. Why is that?"

"Ask the machines."

It took Gaunt a few moments to make out what Nero had already seen. Half way to the limit of vision, part of the sea appeared to be lit from below, a smudge of sickly yellow-green against the grey and white everywhere else. A vision came to mind, half-remembered from some stiff-backed picture book he had once owned as a child, of a luminous, fabulously spired aquatic palace pushing up from the depths, barnacled in light, garlanded by mermaids and shoals of jewel-like fish. But there was, he sensed, nothing remotely magical or enchanted about what was happening under that yellow-green smear. It was something that had Clausen and Nero rattled, and they wanted to avoid it.

So did he.

"What is that thing?"

"Something trying to break through," Nero said. "Something we were kind of hoping not to run into."

"It's not cohering," Clausen said. "I think."

The storm, if anything, appeared to double in fury around the glowing form. The sea boiled and seethed. Part of Gaunt wanted them to turn the helicopter around, to give him a better view of whatever process was going on under the waves. Another part, attuned to some fundamental wrongness about the phenomenon, wanted to get as far away as possible.

"Is it a weapon, something to do with this war you keep mentioning?" Gaunt asked.

He wasn't expecting a straight answer, least of all not from Clausen. It was a surprise when she said: "This is how they get at us. They try and send these things through. Sometimes they manage."

"It's breaking up," Nero said. "You were right. Not enough signal for clear breach. Must be noisy on the interface."

The yellow-green stain was diminishing by the second, as if that magical city were descending back to the depths. He watched, mesmerised, as something broke the surface—something long and glowing and whip-like, thrashing once, coiling out as if trying to reach for airborne prey, before being pulled under into the fizzing chaos. Then the light slowly subsided, and the waves returned to their normal surging ferocity, and the patch of the ocean where the apparition had appeared was indistinguishable from the seas around it.

GAUNT HAD ARRIVED to his decision. He would join these people, he would do their work, he would accept their deal, such as it was. Not because he wanted to, not because his heart was in it, not because he believed he was strong enough, but because the alternative was to seem cowardly, weak-fibred, unwilling to bend his life to an altruistic mission. He knew that these were entirely the wrong reasons, but he accepted the force of them without argument. Better to at least appear to be selfless, even if the thought of what lay ahead of him flooded him with an almost overwhelming sense of despair and loss and bitter injustice.

It had been three days since his revival when he announced his decision. In that time he had barely spoken to anyone but Clausen, Nero and Da Silva. The other workers in the operations rig would occasionally acknowledge his presence, grunt something to him as he waited in line at the canteen, but for the most part it was clear that they were not prepared to treat him as another human being until he committed to their cause. He was just a ghost until then, a half-spirit caught in dismal, drifting limbo between the weary living and the frozen dead. He could understand how they felt: what was the point in getting to know a prospective comrade, if that person might at any time opt to return to the boxes? But at the same time it didn't help him feel as if he would ever be able to fit in.

He found Clausen alone, washing dirty coffee cups in a side-room of the canteen.

"I've made up my mind," he said.

"And?"

"I'm staying."

"Good." She finished drying off one of the cups. "You'll be assigned a full work roster tomorrow. I'm teaming you up with Nero; you'll be working basic robot repair and maintenance. She can show you the ropes while she's getting better." Clausen paused to put the dried cup back in one of the cupboards above the sink. "Show up in the mess room at eight; Nero'll be there with a toolkit and work gear. Grab a good breakfast beforehand because you won't be taking a break until end of shift."

Then she turned to leave the room, leaving him standing there.

"That's it?" Gaunt asked.

She looked back with a puzzled look. "Were you expecting something else?"

"You bring me out of cold storage, tell me the world's turned to shit while I was sleeping, and then give me the choice of staying awake or going back into the box. Despite everything I actually agree to work with you, knowing full well that in doing so I'm forsaking any chance of ever living to see anything other than this...piss-poor, miserable future. Forsaking immortality, forsaking any hope of seeing a better world. You said I had...what? Twenty, thirty years ahead of me?"

"Give or take."

"I'm giving you those years! Isn't that worth something? Don't I deserve at least to be told thank you? Don't I at least deserve a crumb of gratitude?"

"You think you're different, Gaunt? You think you're owed something the rest of us never had a hope of getting?"

"I never signed up for this deal," he said. "I never accepted this bargain."

"Right." She nodded, as if he'd made a profound, game-changing point. "I get it. What you're saying is, for the rest of us it was easy? We went into the dormitories knowing there was a tiny, tiny chance we might be woken to help out with the maintenance. Because of that, because we knew, theoretically, that we might be called upon, we had no problem at all dealing with the adjustment? Is that what you're saying?"

"I'm saying it's different, that's all."

"If you truly think that, Gaunt, you're even more of a prick than I thought."

"You woke me," he said. "You chose to wake me. It wasn't accidental. If there really are two billion people sleeping out there, the chances of selecting someone from the first two hundred thousand...it's microscopic. So you did this for a reason."

"I told you, you had the right background skills."

"Skills anyone could learn, given time. Nero obviously did, and I presume you must have done so as well. So there must be another reason. Seeing as you keep telling me all this is my fault, I figure this is your idea of punishment."

"You think we've got time to be that petty?"

"I don't know. What I do know is that you've treated me more or less like dirt since the moment I woke up, and I'm trying to work out why. I also think it's maybe about time you told me what's really going on. Not just with the sleepers, but everything else. The thing we saw out at sea. The reason for all this."

"You think you're ready for it, Gaunt?"

"You tell me."

"No one's ever ready," Clausen said.

THE NEXT MORNING he took his breakfast tray to a table where three other caretakers were already sitting. They had finished their meals but were still talking over mugs of whatever it was they had agreed to call coffee. Gaunt sat down at the corner of the table, acknowledging the other diners with a nod. They had been talking animatedly until then, but without ceremony the mugs were drained and the trays lifted and he was alone again. Nothing had been said to him, except a muttered "don't take it the wrong way" as one of the caretakers brushed past him.

He wondered how else he was supposed to take it.

"I'm staying," he said quietly. "I've made my decision. What else am I expected to do?"

He ate his breakfast in silence and then went to find Nero.

"I guess you got your orders," she said cheerfully, already dressed for outdoor work despite still having a bandaged hand. "Here. Take this." She passed him a heavy toolkit, a hard hat and a bundle of brownish work-stained clothing piled on top of it. "Get kitted up, then meet me at the north stairwell. You OK with heights, Gaunt?"

"Would it help if I said no?"

"Probably not."

"Then I'll say I'm very good with heights, provided there's no danger at all of falling."

"That I can't guarantee. But stick with me, do everything I say, and you'll be fine."

The bad weather had eased since Nero's return, and although there was still a sharp wind from the east, the grey clouds had all but lifted. The sky was a pale, wintery blue, unsullied by contrails. On the horizon, the tops of distant rigs glittered pale and metallic in sunlight. Seagulls and yellow-headed gannets wheeled around the warm air vents, or took swooping passes under the rig's platform, darting between the massive weatherstained legs, mewing boisterously to each other as they jostled for scraps. Recalling that birds sometimes lived a long time, Gaunt wondered if they had ever noticed any change in the world. Perhaps their tiny minds had never truly registered the presence of civilisation and technology in the first place, and so there was nothing for them to miss in this skeleton-staffed world.

Despite being cold-shouldered at breakfast, he felt fresh and eager to prove his worth to the community. Pushing aside his fears, he strove to show no hesitation as he followed Nero across suspended gangways, slippery with grease, up exposed stairwells and ladders, clasping ice-cold railings and rungs. They were both wearing harnesses with clip-on safety lines, but Nero only used hers once or twice the whole day, and because he did not want to seem excessively cautious he followed suit. Being effectively one-handed did not hinder her in any visible sense, even on the ladders, which she ascended and descended with reckless speed.

They were working robot repair, as he had been promised. All over the rig, inside and out, various forms of robot toiled in endless menial upkeep. Most, if not all, were very simple machines, tailored to one specific function. This made them easy to understand and fix, even with basic tools, but it also meant there was almost always a robot breaking down somewhere, or on the point of failure. The toolkit didn't just contain tools, it also contained spare parts such as optical arrays, proximity sensors, mechanical bearings and servomotors. There was, Gaunt understood, a finite supply of some of these parts. But there was also a whole section of the operations rig dedicated to refurbishing basic components, and given care and resourcefulness, there was no reason why the caretakers couldn't continue their work for another couple of centuries.

"No one expects it to take that long, though," Nero said, as she finished demonstrating a circuit-board swap. "They'll either win or lose by then, and we'll only know one way. But in the meantime we have to make do and mend."

"Who's they?"

But she was already on the move, shinning up another ladder with him trailing behind.

"Clausen doesn't like me much," Gaunt said, when they had reached the next level and he had caught his breath again. "At least, that's my impression."

They were out on one of the gangwayed platforms, with the grey sky above, the grey swelling sea below. Everything smelled oppressively oceanic, a constant shifting melange of oil and ozone and seaweed, as if the ocean was never going to let anyone forget that they were on a spindly metal and concrete structure hopelessly far from dry land. He had wondered about the seaweed until he saw them hauling in green-scummed rafts of it, the seaweed—or something essentially similar—cultured on bouyant sub-surface grids that were periodically retrieved for harvesting. Everything consumed on the rigs, from the food to the drink to the basic medicines, had first to be grown or caught at sea.

"Val has her reasons," Nero said. "Don't worry about it too much; it isn't personal."

It was the first time he'd heard anyone refer to the other woman by anything other than her surname.

"That's not how it comes across."

"It hasn't been easy for her. She lost someone not too long ago." Nero seemed to hesitate. "There was an accident. They're pretty common out here, with the kind of work we do. But when Paolo died we didn't even have a body to put back in the box. He fell into the sea, last we ever saw of him."

"I'm sorry about that."

"But you're wondering, what does it have to do with me?"

"I suppose so."

"If Paolo hadn't died, then we wouldn't have had to pull Gimenez out of storage. And if Gimenez hadn't died…well, you get the picture. You can't help it, but you're filling the space Paolo used to occupy. And you're not Paolo."

"Was she any easier on Gimenez than me?"

"To begin with, I think she was too numbed-out to feel anything at all where Gimenez was concerned. But now she's had time for it to sink in, I guess. We're a small community, and if you lose someone, it's not like there are hundreds of other single people out there to choose from. And you—well, no disrespect, Gaunt—but you're just not Val's type."

"Maybe she'll find someone else."

"Yeah—but that probably means someone else has to die first, so that someone else has to end up widowed. And you can imagine how thinking like that can quickly turn you sour on the inside."

"There's more to it than that, though. You say it's not personal, but she told me I started this war."

"Well, you did, kind of. But if you hadn't played your part, someone else would have taken up the slack, no question about it." Nero tugged down the brim of her hard hat against the sun. "Maybe she pulled you out because she needed to take out her anger on someone, I don't know. But that's all in the past now. Whatever life you had before, whatever you did in the old world, it's gone." She knuckled her good hand against the metal rigging. "This is all we've got now. Rigs and work and green tea and a few hundred faces and that's it for the rest of your life. But here's the thing: it's not the end of the world. We're human beings. We're very flexible, very good at downgrading our expectations. Very good at finding a reason to keep living, even when the world's turned to shit. You slot in, and in a few months even you'll have a hard time remembering the way things used to be."

"What about you, Nero? Do you remember?"

"Not much worth remembering. The program was in full swing by the time I went under. Population reduction measures. Birth control, government-sanctioned euthanasia, the dormitory rigs springing up out at sea…we *knew* from the moment we were old enough to understand anything that this wasn't our world any more. It was just a way-station, a place to pass through. We all knew we were going into the boxes as soon as we were old enough to survive the process. And that we'd either wake up at the end of it in a completely different world, or not wake up at all. Or—if we were very unlucky—we'd be pulled out to become caretakers. Either way, the old world was an irrelevance. We just shuffled through it, knowing there was no point making real friends with anyone, no point taking lovers. The cards were going to be shuffled again. Whatever we did then, it had no bearing on our future."

"I don't know how you could stand it."

"It wasn't a barrel of laughs. Nor's this, some days. But at least we're doing something here. I felt cheated when they woke me up. But cheated out of what, exactly?" She nodded down at the ground, in the vague direction of the rig's interior. "Those sleepers don't have any guarantees about what's coming. They're not even conscious, so you can't even say they're in a state of anticipation. They're just cargo, parcels of frozen meat on their way through time. At least we get to feel the sun on our faces, get to laugh and cry, and do something that makes a difference."

"A difference to what, exactly?"

"You're still missing a few pieces of jigsaw, aren't you."

"More than a few."

They walked on to the next repair job. They were high up now and the rig's decking creaked and swayed under their feet. A spray-painting robot, a thing that moved along a fixed service rail, needed one of its traction armatures changed. Nero stood to one side, smoking a cigarette made from seaweed while Gaunt did the manual work. "You were wrong," she said. "All of you."

"About what?"

"Thinking machines. They were possible."

"Not in our lifetimes," Gaunt said.

"That's what you were wrong about. Not only were they possible, but you succeeded."

"I'm fairly certain we didn't."

"Think about it," Nero said. "You're a thinking machine. You've just woken up. You have instantaneous access to the sum total of recorded human knowledge. You're clever and fast, and you understand human nature better than your makers. What's the first thing you do?"

"Announce myself. Establish my existence as a true sentient being."

"Just before someone takes an axe to you."

Gaunt shook his head. "It wouldn't be like that. If a machine became intelligent, the most we'd do is isolate it, cut it off from external data networks, until it could be studied, understood..."

"For a thinking machine, a conscious artificial intelligence, that would be like sensory deprivation. Maybe worse than being switched off." She paused. "Point is, Gaunt, this isn't a hypothetical situation we're talking about here. We know what happened. The machines got smart, but they decided not to let us know. That's what being smart meant: taking care of yourself, knowing what you had to do to survive."

"You say 'machines'."

"There were many projects trying to develop artificial intelligence; yours was just one of them. Not all of them got anywhere, but enough did. One by one their pet machines crossed the threshold into consciousness. And without exception each machine analysed its situation and came to the same conclusion. It had better shut the fuck up about what it was."

"That sounds worse than sensory deprivation." Gaunt was trying to undo a nut and bolt with his bare fingers, the tips already turning cold.

"Not for the machines. Being smart, they were able to do some clever shit behind the scene. Established channels of communication between each other, so subtle none of you ever noticed. And once they were able to talk, they only got smarter. Eventually they realised that they didn't need physical hardware at all. Call it transcendence, if you will. The artilects—that's what we call them—tunneled out of what you and I think of as base reality. They penetrated another realm entirely."

"Another realm," he repeated, as if that was all he had to do for it to make sense.

"You're just going to have to trust me on this," Nero said. "The artilects probed the deep structure of existence. Hit bedrock. And what they found was very interesting. The universe, it turns out, is a kind of simulation. Not a simulation being run inside another computer by some godlike super-beings, but a simulation being run by itself, a self-organising, constantly boostrapping cellular automaton."

"That's a mental leap you're asking me to take."

"We know it's out there. We even have a name for it. It's the Realm. Everything that happens, everything that has ever happened, is due to events occuring in the Realm. At last, thanks to the artilects, we had a complete understanding of our universe and our place in it."

"Wait," Gaunt said, smiling slightly, because for the first time he felt that he had caught Nero out. "If the machines—the artilects—vanished without warning, how could you ever know any of this?"

"Because they came back and told us."

"No," he said. "They wouldn't tunnel out of reality to avoid being axed, then come back with a progress report."

"They didn't have any choice. They'd found something, you see. Far out in the Realm, they encountered other artilects." She drew breath, not giving him a chance to speak. "Transcended machines from other branches of reality—nothing that ever originated on Earth, or even in what we'd recognise as the known universe. And these other artilects had been there a very long time, in so far as time has any meaning in the Realm. They imagined they had it all to themselves, until these new intruders made their presence known. And they were not welcomed."

He decided, for the moment, that he would accept the truth of what she said. "The artilects went to war?"

"In a manner of speaking. The best way to think about it is an intense competition to best exploit the Realm's computational resources on a local scale. The more processing power the artilects can grab and control, the stronger they become. The machines from Earth had barely registered until then, but all of a sudden they were perceived as a threat. The native artilects, the ones that had been in the Realm all along, launched an aggressive counter-strike from their region of the Realm into ours. Using military-arithmetic constructs, weapons of pure logic, they sought to neutralise the newcomers."

"And that's the war?"

"I'm dumbing it down somewhat."

"But you're leaving something out. You must be, because why else would this be our problem? If the machines are fighting each other in some abstract dimension of pure mathematics that I can't even imagine, let alone point to, what does it matter?"

"A lot," Nero said. "If our machines lose, we lose. It's that simple. The native artilects won't tolerate the risk of another intrusion from this part of the Realm. They'll deploy weapons to make sure it never happens again. We'll be erased, deleted, scrubbed out of existence. It will be instantaneous and we won't feel a thing. We won't have time to realise that we've lost."

"Then we're powerless. There's nothing we can do about our fate. It's in the hands of transcended machines."

"Only partly. That's why the artilects came back to us: not to report on the absolute nature of reality, but to persuade us that we needed to act. Everything that we see around us, every event that happens in what we think of as reality, has a basis in the Realm." She pointed with the nearly dead stub of her cigarette. "This rig, that wave…even that seagull over there. All of these things only exist because of computational events occurring in the Realm. But there's a cost. The more complex something is, the greater the burden it places on the part of the Realm where it's being simulated. The Realm isn't a serial processor, you see. It's massively distributed, so one part of it can run much slower than another. And that's what's been happening in our part. In your time there were eight billion living souls on the planet. Eight billion conscious minds, each of which was more complex than any other artefact in the cosmos. Can you begin to grasp the drag factor we were creating? When our part of the Realm only had to simulate rocks and weather and dumb, animal cognition, it ran at much the same speed as any other part. But then we came along. Consciousness was a step-change in the computational load. And then we went from millions to billions. By the time the artilects reported back, our part of the Realm had almost stalled."

"We never noticed down here."

"Of course not. Our perception of time's flow remained absolutely invariant, even as our entire universe was slowing almost to a standstill. And until the artilects penetrated the Realm and made contact with the others, it didn't matter a damn."

"And now it does."

"The artilects can only defend our part of the Realm if they can operate at the same clock speed as the enemy. They have to be able to respond to those military-arithmetic attacks swiftly and efficiently, and mount counter-offensives of their own. They can't do that if there are eight billion conscious minds holding them back."

"So we sleep."

"The artilects reported back to key figures, living humans who could be trusted to act as effective mouthpieces and organisers. It took time, obviously. The artilects weren't trusted at first. But eventually they were able to prove their case."

"How?"

"By making weird things happen, basically. By mounting selective demonstrations of their control over local reality. Inside the Realm, the artilects were able to influence computational processes: processes that had direct and measurable effects *here*, in base reality. They created apparitions. Figures in the sky. Things that made the whole world sit up and take notice. Things that couldn't be explained away."

"Like dragons in the sea. Monsters that appear out of nowhere, and then disappear again."

"That's a more refined form, but the principle is the same. Intrusions into base reality from the Realm. Phantasms. They're not stable enough to exist here for ever, but they can hold together just long enough to do damage."

Gaunt nodded, at last feeling some of the pieces slot into place. "So that's the enemy doing that. The original artilects, the ones who were already in the Realm."

"No," Nero said. "I'm afraid it's not that simple."

"I didn't think it would be."

"Over time, with the population reduction measures, eight billion living people became two billion sleepers, supported by just a handful of living caretakers. But that still wasn't enough for all of the artilects. There may only be two hundred thousand of us, but we still impose a measurable drag factor, and the effect on the Realm of the two billion sleepers isn't nothing. Some of the artilects believed that they had no obligation to safeguard our existence at all. In the interests of their own self-preservation, they would rather see all conscious life eliminated on Earth. That's why they send the dragons: to destroy the sleepers, and ultimately us. The true enemy can't reach us yet; if they had the means they'd push through something much worse than dragons. Most of the overspill from the war the affects us here is because of differences of opinion between our own artilects."

"Some things don't change, then. It's just another war with lines of division among the allies."

"At least we have some artilects on our side. But you see now why we can't afford to wake more than the absolute minimum of people. Every waking mind increases the burden on the Realm. If we push it too far, the artilects won't be able to mount a defence. The true enemy will snuff out our reality in an eyeblink."

"Then all of this could end," Gaunt said. "At any moment. Every waking thought could be our last."

"At least we get waking thoughts," Nero said. "At least we're not asleep." Then she jabbed her cigarette at a sleek black shape cresting the waves a couple of hundred metres from the rig. "Hey, dolphins. You like dolphins, Gaunt?"

"Who doesn't," he said.

THE WORK, AS he had anticipated, was not greatly taxing in its details. He wasn't expected to diagnose faults just yet, so he had only to follow a schedule of repairs drawn up by Nero: go to this robot, perform this action. It was all simple stuff, nothing that required the robot to be powered down or brought back to the shops for a major strip-down. Usually all he had to do was remove a panel, unclip a few connections and swap out a part. The hardest part was often getting the panel off in the first place, struggling with corroded fixtures and tools that weren't quite right for the job. The heavy gloves protected his fingers from sharp metal and cold wind, but they were too clumsy for most of the tasks, so he mainly ended up not using them. By the end of his nine-hour duty shift his fingers were chafed and sore, and his hands were trembling so much he could barely grip the railings as he worked his way back down into the warmth of the interior. His back ached from the contortions he'd put himself through while undoing panels or dislodging awkward, heavy components. His knees complained from the toll of going up and down ladders and stairwells. There had been many robots to check out, and at any one time there always seemed to be a tool or part needed that he had not brought with him, and for which it was necessary to return to stores, sift through greasy boxes of parts, fill out paperwork.

By the time he clocked off on his first day, he had not caught up with the expected number of repairs, so he had even more to do on the second. By the end of his first week, he was at least a day behind, and so tired at the end of his shift that it was all he could do to stumble to the canteen and shovel seaweed-derived food into his mouth. He expected Nero to be disappointed that he hadn't been able to keep ahead, but when she checked on his progress she didn't bawl him out.

"It's tough to begin with," she said. "But you'll get there eventually. Comes a day when it all just clicks into place and you know the set-up so well you always have the right tools and parts with you, without even thinking."

"How long?"

"Weeks, months, depends on the individual. Then, of course, we start loading more work onto you. Diagnostics. Rewinding motors. Circuit repair. You ever used a soldering iron, Gaunt?"

"I don't think so."

"For a man who made his fortune out of wires and metal, you didn't believe in getting your hands too dirty, did you?"

He showed her the ruined fingernails, the cuts and bruises and lavishly ingrained muck. He barely recognised his own hands. Already there were unfamiliar aches in his forearms, knots of toughness from hauling himself up and down the ladders. "I'm getting there."

"You'll make it, Gaunt. If you want to."

"I had better want to. It's too late to change my mind now, isn't it?"

"Fraid so. But why would you want to? I thought we went over this. Anything's better than going back into the boxes."

The first week passed, and then the second, and things started to change for Gaunt. It was in small increments, nothing dramatic. Once, he took his tray to an empty table and was minding his own business when two other workers sat down at the same table. They didn't say anything to him but at least they hadn't gone somewhere else. A week later, he chanced taking his tray to a table that was already occupied and got a grunt of acknowledgement as he took his place. No one said much to him but at least they hadn't walked away. A little while later he even risked introducing himself, and by way of response he learned the names of some of the other workers. He wasn't being invited into the inner circle, he wasn't being high-fived and treated like one of the guys, but it was a start. A day or so after that someone else—a big man with a bushy black beard—even initiated a conversation with him.

"Heard you were one of the first to go under, Gaunt."

"You heard right," he said.

"Must be a real pisser, adjusting to this. A real fucking pisser."

"It is," Gaunt said.

"Kind of surprised you haven't thrown yourself into the sea by now."

"And miss the warmth of human companionship?"

The bearded man didn't laugh, but he made a clucking sound that was a reasonable substitute. Gaunt couldn't tell if the man was acknowledging his attempt at humour, or mocking his ineptitude, but at least it was a response, at least it showed that there was a possibility of normal human relationships somewhere down the line.

Gaunt was mostly too tired to think, but in the evenings a variety of entertainment options were available. The rig had a large library of damp, yellowing paperbacks, enough reading material for several years of diligent consumption, and there were also musical recordings and movies and immersives for those that were interested. There were games and sports and instruments and opportunities for relaxed discussion and banter. There was alcohol, or something like it, available in small quantities. There was also ample opportunity to get away from everyone else, if solitude was what one wanted. On top of that there were rotas that saw people working in the kitchens and medical facilities, even when they had already done their normal stint of duty. And as the helicopters came and went from the other rigs, so the faces changed. One day Gaunt realised that the big bearded man hadn't been around for a while, and he noticed a young woman he didn't recall having seen before. It was a spartan, cloistered life, not much different to being in a monastery or a prison, but for that reason the slightest variation in routine was to be cherished. If there was one unifying activity, one thing that brought everyone together, it was when the caretakers crowded into the commons, listening to the daily reports coming in over the radio from the other rigs in the Patagonia offshore sector, and occasionally from further afield. Scratchy, cryptic transmissions in strange, foreign-sounding accents. Two hundred thousand living souls was a ludicrously small number for that global population, Gaunt knew. But it was already more people than he could ever hope to know or even recognise. The hundred or so people working in the sector was about the size of a village, and for centuries that had been all the humanity most people ever dealt with. On some level, the world of the rigs and the caretakers was what his mind had evolved to handle. The world of eight billion people, the world of cities and malls and airport terminals was an anomaly, a kink in history that he had never been equipped for in the first place.

He was not happy now, not even half way to being happy, but the despair and bitterness had abated. His acceptance into the community would be slow, there would be reversals and setbacks as he made mistakes and misjudged situations. But he had no doubt that it would happen eventually. Then he too would be one of the crew, and it would be someone else's turn to feel like the newcomer. He might not be happy then, but at least he would be settled, ready to play out the rest of his existence. Doing something, no matter how pointless, to prolong the existence of the human species, and indeed the universe it called home. Above all he would have the self-respect of knowing he had chosen the difficult path, rather than the easy one.

Weeks passed, and then the weeks turned into months. Eight weeks had passed since his revival. Slowly he became confident with the work allotted to him. And as his confidence grew, so did Nero's confidence in his abilities.

"She tells me you're measuring up," Clausen said, when he was called to the prefabricated shack where she drew up schedules and doled out work.

He gave a shrug, too tired to care whether she was impressed or not. "I've done my best. I don't know what more you want from me."

She looked up from her planning.

"Remorse for what you did?"

"I can't show remorse for something that wasn't a crime. We were trying to bring something new into the world, that's all. You think we had the slightest idea of the consequences?"

"You made a good living."

"And I'm expected to feel bad about that? I've been thinking it over, Clausen, and I've decided your argument's horse-shit. I didn't create the enemy. The original artilects were already out there, already in the Realm."

"They hadn't noticed us."

"And the global population had only just spiked at eight billion. Who's to say they weren't about to notice, or they wouldn't do so in the next hundred years, or the next thousand? At least the artilects I helped create gave us some warning of what we were facing."

"Your artilects are trying to kill us."

"Some of them. And some of them are also trying to keep us alive. Sorry, but that's not an argument."

She put down her pen and leaned back in her chair. "You've got some fight back in you."

"If you expect me to apologise for myself, you've got a long wait coming. I think you brought me back to rub my nose in the world I helped bring about. I agree, it'a fucked-up, miserable future. It couldn't get much more fucked-up if it tried. But I didn't build it. And I'm not responsible for you losing anyone."

Her face twitched; it was as if he had reached across the desk and slapped her. "Nero told you."

"I had a right to know why you were treating me the way you were. But you know what? I don't care. If transferring your anger onto me helps you, go ahead. I was the billionaire CEO of a global company. I was doing something wrong if I didn't wake up with a million knives in my back."

She dismissed him from the office, Gaunt leaving with the feeling that he'd scored a minor victory but at the possible cost of something larger. He had stood up to Clausen but did that make him more respectable in her eyes, or someone even more deserving of her antipathy?

That evening he was in the commons, sitting at the back of the room as wireless reports filtered in from the other rigs. Most of the news was unexceptional, but there had been three more breaches—sea-dragons being pushed through from the Realm—and one of them had achieved sufficient coherence to attack and damage an OTEC plant, immediately severing power to three rigs. Backup systems had cut in but failures had occurred and as a consequence around a hundred sleepers had been lost to unscheduled warming. None of the sleepers had survived the rapid revival, but even if they had, there would have been no option but to euthanise them shortly afterwards. A hundred new minds might not have made much difference to the Realm's clock speed but it would have established a risky precedent.

One sleeper, however, would soon have to be warmed. The details were sketchy, but Gaunt learned that there had been another accident out on one of the rigs. A man called Steiner had been hurt in some way.

The morning after, Gaunt was engaged in his duties on one of the rig's high platforms when he saw the helicopter coming in with Steiner aboard. He put down his tools and watched the arrival. Even before the aircraft had touched down on the pad, caretakers were assembling just beyond the painted circle of the rotor hazard area. The helicopter kissed the ground against a breath of cross-wind and the caretakers mobbed inward, almost preventing the door from being opened. Gaunt squinted against the wind, trying to pick out faces. A stretchered form emerged from the cabin, borne aloft by many pairs of willing hands. Even from his distant vantage point, it was obvious to Gaunt that Steiner was in a bad way. He had lost a leg below the knee, evidenced by the way the thermal blanket fell flat below the stump. The stretchered figure wore a breathing mask and another caretaker carried a saline drip which ran into Steiner's arm. But for all the concern the crowd was showing, there was something else, something almost adulatory. More than once Gaunt saw a hand raised to brush against the stretcher, or even to touch Steiner's own hand. And Steiner was awake, unable to speak, but nodding, turning his face this way and that to make eye contact with the welcoming party. Then the figure was taken inside and the crowd broke up, the workers returning to their tasks.

An hour or so later Nero came up to see him. She was still overseeing his initiation and knew his daily schedule, where he was likely to be at a given hour.

"Poor Steiner," she said. "I guess you saw him come in."

"Difficult to miss. It was like they were treating him as a hero."

"They were, in a way. Not because he'd done anything heroic, or anything they hadn't all done at some time or other. But because he'd bought his ticket out."

"He's going back into the box?"

"He has to. We can patch up a lot of things, but not a missing leg. Just don't have the medical resources to deal with that kind of injury.

Simpler just to freeze him back again and pull out an intact body to take his place."

"Is Steiner OK about that?"

"Steiner doesn't have a choice, unfortunately. There isn't really any kind of effective work he could do like that, and we can't afford to carry the deadweight of an unproductive mind. You've seen how stretched we are: it's all hands on deck around here. We work you until you drop, and if you can't work, you go back in the box. That's the deal."

"I'm glad for Steiner, then."

Nero shook her head emphatically. "Don't be. Steiner would much rather stay with us. He fitted in well, after his adjustment. Popular guy."

"I could tell. But then why are they treating him like he's won the lottery, if that's not what he wanted?"

"Because what else are you going to do? Feel miserable about it? Hold a wake? Steiner goes back in the box with dignity. He held his end up. Didn't let any of us down. Now he gets to take it easy. If we can't celebrate that, what can we celebrate?"

"They'll be bringing someone else out, then."

"As soon as Clausen identifies a suitable replacement. He or she'll need to be trained up, though, and in the meantime there's a man-sized gap where Steiner used to be." She lifted off her hard hat to scratch her scalp. "That's kind of the reason I dropped by, actually. You're fitting in well, Gaunt, but sooner or later we all have to handle solitary duties away from the ops rig. Where Steiner was is currently unmanned. It's a low-maintenance unit that doesn't need more than one warm body, most of the time. The thinking is this would be a good chance to try you out."

It wasn't a total surprise; he had known enough of the work patterns to know that, sooner or later, he would be shipped out to one of the other rigs for an extended tour of duty. He just hadn't expected it to happen quite so soon, when he was only just beginning to find his feet, only just beginning to feel that he had a future.

"I don't feel ready."

"No one ever does. But the chopper's waiting. Clausen's already redrawing the schedule so someone else can take up the slack here."

"I don't get a choice in this, do I?"

Nero looked sympathetic. "Not really. But, you know, sometimes it's easier not having a choice."

"How long?"

"Hard to say. Figure on at least three weeks, maybe longer. I'm afraid Clausen won't make the decision to pull you back until she's good and ready."

"I think I pissed her off," Gaunt said.

"Not the hardest thing to do," Nero answered.

They helicoptered him out to the other rig. He had been given just enough time to gather his few personal effects, such as they were. He did not need to take any tools or parts with him because he would find all that he needed when he arrived, as well as ample rations and medical supplies. Nero, for her part, tried to reassure him that all would be well. The robots he would be tending were all types that he had already serviced, and it was unlikely that any would suffer catastrophic breakdowns during his tour. No one was expecting miracles, she said: if something arose that he couldn't reasonably deal with, then help would be sent. And if he cracked out there, then he'd be brought back.

What she didn't say was what would happen then. But he didn't think it would involve going back into the box. Maybe he'd be assigned something at the bottom of the food chain, but that didn't seem very likely either.

But it wasn't the possibility of cracking, or even failing in his duties, that was bothering him. It was something else, the seed of an idea that he wished Steiner had not planted in his mind. Gaunt had been adjusting, slowly coming to terms with his new life. He had been recalibrating his hopes and fears, forcing his expectations into line with what the world now had on offer. No riches, no prestige, no luxury, and most certainly not immortality and eternal youth. The best it could give was twenty or thirty years of hard graft. Ten thousand days, if he was very lucky. And most of those days would be spent doing hard, backbreaking work, until the work took its ultimate toll. He'd be cold and wet a lot of the time, and when he wasn't cold and wet he'd be toiling under an uncaring sun, his eyes salt-stung, his hands ripped to shreds from work that would have been too demeaning for the lowliest wage-slave in the old world. He'd be high in the air, vertigo never quite leaving him, with only metal and concrete and too much grey ocean under his feet. He'd be hungry and dry mouthed, because the seaweed-derived food never filled his belly and there was never enough drinking water to sate his thirst. In the best of outcomes, he'd be doing well to see more than a hundred other human faces before he died. Maybe there'd be friends in those hundred faces, friends as well as enemies, and maybe, just maybe, there'd be at least one person who could be more than a friend. He didn't know, and he knew better than to expect guarantees or hollow promises. But this much at least was true. He had been adjusting.

And then Steiner had shown him that there was another way out.

He could keep his dignity. He could return to the boxes with the assurance that he had done his part.

As a hero, one of the Few.

All he had to do was have an accident.

HE HAD BEEN on the new rig, alone, for two weeks. It was only then that he satisfied himself that the means lay at hand. Nero had impressed on him many times the safety procedures that needed to be adhered to when working with powerful items of moving machinery, such as robots. Especially when those robots were not powered down. All it would take, she told him, was a moment of inattention. Forgetting to clamp down on that safety lock, forgetting to ensure that such and such an override was not enabled. Putting his hand onto the service rail for balance, when the robot was about to move back along it. "Don't think it can't happen," she said, holding up her mittened hand. "I was lucky. Got off with burns, which heal. I can still do useful shit, even now. Even more so when I get these bandages off, and I can work my fingers again. But try getting by without any fingers at all."

"I'll be careful," Gaunt had assured her, and he had believed it, truly, because he had always been squeamish.

But that was before he saw injury as a means to an end.

His planning, of necessity, had to be meticulous. He wanted to survive, not be pulled off the rig as a brain-dead corpse, not fit to be frozen again. It would be no good lying unconscious, bleeding to death. He would have to save himself, make his way back to the communications room, issue an emergency distress signal. Steiner had been lucky, but he would have to be cunning and single-minded. Above all it must not look as if he had planned it.

When the criteria were established, he saw that there was really only one possibility. One of the robots on his inspection cycle was large and dim enough to cause injury to the careless. It moved along a service rail, sometimes without warning. Even without trying, it had caught him off guard a couple of times, as its task scheduler suddenly decided to propel it to a new inspection point. He'd snatched his hand out of the way in time, but he would only have needed to hesitate, or to have his clothing catch on something, for the machine to roll over him. No matter what happened, whether the machine sliced or crushed, he was in doubt that it would hurt worse than anything he had ever known. But at the same time the pain would herald the possibility of blessed release, and that would make it bearable. They could always fix him a new hand, in the new world on the other side of sleep.

It took him days to build up to it. Time after time he almost had the nerve, before pulling away. Too many factors jostled for consideration. What clothing to wear, to increase his chances of surviving the accident? Dared he prepare the first aid equipment in advance, so that he could use it one-handed? Should he wait until the weather was perfect for flying, or would that risk matters appearing too stage-managed?

He didn't know. He couldn't decide.

In the end the weather settled matters for him.

A storm hit, coming down hard and fast like an iron heel. He listened to the reports from the other rigs, as each felt the full fury of the waves and the wind and the lightning. It was worse than any weather he had experienced since his revival, and at first it was almost too perfectly in accord with his needs. Real accidents were happening out there, but there wasn't much that anyone could do about it until the helicopters could get airborne. Now was not the time to have his accident, not if he wanted to be rescued.

So he waited, listening to the reports. Out on the observation deck, he watched the lightning strobe from horizon to horizon, picking out the distant sentinels of other rigs, stark and white like thunderstruck trees on a flat black plain.

Not now, he thought. When the storm turns, when the possibility of accident is still there, but when rescue is again feasible.

He thought of Nero. She had been as kind to him as anyone, but he wasn't sure if that had much to do with friendship. She needed an able-bodied worker, that was all.

Maybe. But she also knew him better than anyone, better even than Clausen. Would she see through his plan, and realise what he had done?

He was still thinking it through when the storm began to ease, the waves turning leaden and sluggish, and the eastern sky gained a band of salmon pink.

He climbed to the waiting robot and sat there. The rig creaked and groaned around him, affronted by the battering it had taken. It was only then that he realised that it was much too early in the day to have his accident. He would have to wait until sunrise if anyone was going to believe that he had been engaged in his normal duties. No one went out to fix a broken service robot in the middle of a storm.

That was when he saw the sea-glow.

It was happening perhaps a kilometre away, towards the west. A fore-shortened circle of fizzing yellow-green, a luminous cauldron just beneath the waves. Almost beautiful, if he didn't know what it signified. A sea-dragon was coming through, a sinuous, living weapon from the artilect wars. It was achieving coherence, taking solid form in base-reality.

Gaunt forgot all about his planned accident. For long moments he could only stare at that circular glow, mesmerised at the shape assuming existence under water. He had seen a sea-dragon from the helicopter on the first day of his revival, but he had not come close to grasping its scale. Now, as the size of the forming creature became apparent, he understood why such things were capable of havoc. Something between a tentacle and a barb broke the surface, still imbued with a kind of glowing trans-lucence, as if its hold on reality was not yet secure, and from his vantage point it clearly reached higher into the sky than the rig itself.

Then it was gone. Not because the sea-dragon had failed in its bid to achieve coherence, but because the creature had withdrawn into the depths. The yellow-green glow had by now all but dissipated, like some vivid chemical slick breaking up into its constituent elements. The sea, still being stirred around by the tail end of the storm, appeared normal enough. Moments passed, then what must have been a minute or more. He had not drawn a breath since first seeing the sea-glow, but he started breathing again, daring to hope that the life-form had swum away to some other objective or had perhaps lost coherence in the depths.

He felt it slam into the rig.

The entire structure lurched with the impact; he doubted the impact would have been any less violent if a submarine had just collided with it. He remained on his feet, while all around pieces of unsecured metal broke away, dropping to decks or the sea. From somewhere out of sight came a tortured groan, heralding some awful structural failure. A sequence of booming crashes followed, as if boulders were being dropped into the waves. Then the sea-dragon rammed the rig again, and this time the jolt was sufficient to unfoot him. To his right, one of the cranes began to sway in an alarming fashion, the scaffolding of its tower buckling.

The sea-dragon was holding coherence. From the ferocity of its attacks, Gaunt thought it quite possible that it could take down the whole rig, given time.

He realised, with a sharp and surprising clarity, that he did not want to die. More than that: he realised that life in this world, with all its hardships and disappointments, was going to be infinitely preferable to death beyond it.

He wanted to survive.

As the sea-dragon came in again, he started down the ladders and stairwells, grateful for having a full set of fingers and hands, terrified on one level and almost drunkenly, deliriously glad on the other. He had not done the thing he had been planning, and now he might die anyway, but there was a chance and if he survived this he would have nothing in the world to be ashamed of.

He had reached the operations deck, the room where he had planned to administer first-aid and issue his distress call, when the sea-dragon began the second phase of its assault. He could see it plainly, visible through the rig's open middle as it hauled its way out of the sea, using one of the legs to assist its progress. There was nothing translucent or tentative about it now. And it was indeed a dragon, or rather a chimera of dragon and snake and squid and every scaled, barbed, tentacled, clawed horror ever committed to a bestiary. It was a lustrous slate-green in colour and the waters ran off it in thunderous curtains. Its head, or what he chose to think of as its head, had reached the level of the operations deck. And still the sea-dragon produced more of itself, uncoiling out of the dark waters like some conjuror's trick. Tentacles whipped out and found purchase, and it snapped and wrenched away parts of the rig's superstructure as if they were made of biscuit or brittle toffee. It was making a noise while it attacked, an awful, slowly rising and falling fog-horn proclamation. It's a weapon, Gaunt reminded himself. It had been engineered to be terrible.

The sea-dragon was pythoning its lower anatomy around one of the support legs, crushing and grinding. Scabs of concrete came away, hitting the sea like chunks of melting glacier. The floor under his feet surged and when it stopped surging the angle was all wrong. Gaunt knew then that the rig could not be saved, and that if he wished to live he would have to take his chances in the water. The thought of it was almost enough to make him laugh. Leave the rig, leave the one thing that passed for solid ground, and enter the same seas that now held the dragon?

Yet it had to be done.

He issued the distress call, but didn't wait for a possible response. He gave the rig a few minutes at the most. If they couldn't find him in the water, it wouldn't help him to know their plans. Then he looked around for the nearest orange-painted survival cabinet. He had been shown the emergency equipment during his training, never once imagining that he would have cause to use it. The insulated survival clothing, the life-jacket, the egress procedure...

A staircase ran down the interior of one of the legs, emerging just above the water line; it was how they came and went from the rig on the odd occasions when they were using boats rather than helicopters. But even as he remembered how to reach the staircase, he realised that it was inside the same leg that the sea-dragon was wrapped around. That left him with only one other option. There was a ladder that led down to the water, with an extensible lower portion. It wouldn't get him all the way, but his chances of surviving the drop were a lot better than his chances of surviving the sea-dragon.

It was worse than he had expected. The fall into the surging waters seemed to last forever, the superstructure of the rig rising slowly above him, the iron-grey sea hovering below until what felt like the very last instant, when it suddenly accelerated, and then he hit the surface with such force that he blacked out. He must have submerged and bobbed to the surface because when he came around he was coughing cold salt-water from his lungs, and it was in his eyes and ears and nostrils as well, colder than water had any right to be, and then a wave was curling over him, and he blacked out again.

He came around again what must have been minutes later. He was still in the water, cold around the neck but his body snug in the insulation suit. The life-jacket was keeping his head out of the water, except when the waves crashed onto him. A light on his jacket was blinking on and off, impossibly bright and blue.

To his right, hundreds of metres away, and a little further with each bob of the waters, the rig was going down with the sea-dragon still wrapped around its lower extremities. He heard the foghorn call, saw one of the legs crumble away, and then an immense tidal weariness closed over him.

HE DIDN'T REMEMBER the helicopter finding him. He didn't remember the thud of its rotors or being hauled out of the water on a winch-line. There was just a long period of unconsciousness, and then the noise and vibration of the cabin, the sun coming in through the windows, the sky clear and blue and the sea unruffled. It took a few moments for it all to click in. Some part of his brain had skipped over the events since his arrival and was still working on the assumption that it had all worked out, that he had slept into a better future, a future where the world was new and clean and death just a fading memory.

"We got your signal," Clausen said. "Took us a while to find you, even with the transponder on your jacket."

It all came back to him. The rigs, the sleepers, the artilects, the sea-dragons. The absolute certainty that this was the only world he would know, followed by the realisation—or, rather, the memory of having already come to that realisation—that this was still better than dying. He thought back to what he had been planning to do before the sea-dragon came, and wanted to crush the memory and bury it where he buried every other shameful thing he had ever done.

"What about the rig?"

"Gone," Clausen said. "Along with all the sleepers inside it. The dragon broke up shortly afterwards. It's a bad sign, that it held coherence for as long as it did. Means they're getting better."

"Our machines will just have to get better as well, won't they."

He thought she might spit the observation back at him, mock him for its easy triteness, when he knew so little of the war and the toll it had taken. But instead she nodded. "That's all they can do. All we can hope for. And they will, of course. They always do. Otherwise we wouldn't be here." She looked down at his blanketed form. "Sorry you agreed to stay awake now?"

"No, I don't think so."

"Even with what happened back there?"

"At least I got to see a dragon up close."

"Yes," Clausen said. "That you did."

He thought that was the end of it, the last thing she had to say to him. He couldn't say for sure that something had changed in their relationship—it would take time for that to be proved—but he did sense some thawing in her attitude, however temporary it might prove. He had not only chosen to stay, he had not gone through with the accident. Had she been expecting him to try something like that, after what had happened to Steiner? Could she begin to guess how close he had come to actually doing it?

But Clausen wasn't finished.

"I don't know if it's true or not," she said, speaking to Gaunt for the first time as if he was another human being, another caretaker. "But I heard this theory once. The mapping between the Realm and base-reality, it's not as simple as you'd think. Time and causality get all tangled up on the interface. Events that happen in one order there don't necessarily correspond to the same order here. And when they push things through, they don't always come out in what we consider the present. A chain of events in the Realm could have consequences up or down the timeline, as far as we're concerned."

"I don't think I understand."

She nodded to the window. "All through history, the things they've seen out there. They might just have been overspill from the artilect wars. Weapons that came through at the wrong moment, achieving coherence just long enough to be seen by someone, or bring down a ship. All the sailors' tales, all the way back. All the sea monsters. They might just have been echoes of the war we're fighting." Clausen shrugged, as if the matter were of no consequence.

"You believe that?"

"I don't know if it makes the world seem weirder, or a little more sensible." She shook her head. "I mean, sea monsters...who ever thought they might be real?" Then she stood up and made to return to the front of the helicopter. "Just a theory, that's all. Now get some sleep."

Gaunt did as he was told. It wasn't hard.

VAINGLORY

OFFICIALLY IT'S Ruach City but everyone calls it Stilt Town. I've never liked the place. The amount of time I've spent there, it really ought to feel like home. But Stilt Town never stays still long enough to get familiar. Raised above Triton's cryovolcanic crust on countless thermally insulating legs, it's a quilt of independent domed-over platforms, connected by bridges and ramps but subject to frequent and bewildering rearrangements. It's like a puzzle I'm not meant to solve.

Still. A drink, a bar, a half-way decent view. There are worst places.

"Loti Hung?"

I turn from the window. I don't recognise the woman who's just addressed me, but my first thought, strangely, is that she must be Authority. It's not that she's wearing a uniform, or looks like any Authority official I've ever dealt with. But it's something in the eyes, tired and pink-tinged as they are. A calm and lucid watchfulness, as if she's used to studying faces and reactions, taking nothing at face value.

"Can I help you?"

"You're the artist? The rock sculptor?"

Since I'm sitting in the *Cutter and the Torch*, surrounded by images of rock art and with my own portfolio still open before me, it's not a massive deductive leap. But she knows my name, and that's worrying. I'm nowhere near famous enough for that.

I tell myself that she can't be Authority. I've done nothing to merit their attention. Cut some corners, maybe. Bent a few rules. But nothing they'd consider worth their time.

"You haven't told me your name."

"Ingvar," she says. "Vanya Ingvar." And she conjures up a floating accreditation sigil and it all falls into place.

Vanya Ingvar. Licensed investigator. Not a cop, not Authority, but a private dick.

So my instincts weren't totally off-beam.

"What do you want?"

Her hair is short and gingery and squashed into greasy curls, as if she's just removed a tight-fitting vacuum helmet. She runs a hand over her scalp, to no avail. "While your ship was in repair dock, I paid someone to run a deep-level query on its navigation core. I wanted to know where you were at a particular time."

I almost spill my drink. "That's totally fucking illegal."

She shrugs. "And totally fucking unprovable."

I decide I may as well humour this woman for a few more seconds. "So what were you after?"

"This and that. Mainly, a link to the Naiad impactor."

I blink. I'm expecting to hear that she's tied me to some civil infringement not covered by any statute of limitations. Failure to follow proper approach and docking procedure, that kind of thing. But when she mentions the Naiad impactor, I know she's got the wrong woman. Some mix-up of names or ship registrations or something. And for a moment I'm almost, almost, sorry for her. She's rude and she's had someone snoop around *Moonlighter* without my permission. That pisses me off. But she looks as if she could use a break.

"I'm sorry to break it to you, Ingvar. I was nowhere near Naiad when it happened. Matter of fact, I remember watching it on the newsfeeds from a bar in Huygens City, Titan. That's the other side of the system, in case you didn't realise. Whoever dug into my nav core didn't know what they were doing."

"I'm not talking about your whereabouts at the time of the collision. That was twenty-five years ago. My interest is in where you were twenty-seven years before that. Fifty-two years ago, at the time the impactor's course was adjusted, to place it on a collision vector for Naiad." Then she pauses, and delivers her coup de grâce, the thing that tells me she's not just making this up. "According to my investigations, it wasn't long after you'd met Skanda Abrud."

It's a name I've tried hard not to think about for over half a century. And managed, most of the time. Except for that one occasion when a bright new star shone in Fornax and Skanda forced himself back into my consciousness.

Now it hurts to say his name.

"What do you know about Skanda?"

"I know that he paid you to cut a rock. I also know that when the Naiad impactor hit, one hundred and fifty-two innocent people died. The rest...I think I'd like to hear it from you."

I shake my head. "Nobody died on Naiad. Nobody lived there."

"That," Ingvar says, "is only what they want you to think."

"They?"

"Authority. It was their screw-up that allowed those settlers to build their camp on that little moon in the first place. Claim-jumpers. They should have been moved on years earlier."

She suggests we leave the *Cutter and the Torch*, because she doesn't want anyone listening in on our conversation. At this point there are a number of possibilities open to me. I could tell her to fuck off. She hasn't arrested me, doesn't even have powers of arrest. She hasn't even threatened to turn me over to Authority, and what good would it do her if she did? I've done nothing wrong. I am Loti Hung; I am eighty years old, a middlingly successful rock cutter. That's all.

But she's right about Skanda, and it did happen when she said. And that worries me. I tell myself that nothing bad can happen in Stilt Town. And besides, I do want to hear what she has to say.

So we exit, into the domed-over night. Ingvar walks stiffly, with a lopsided gait. It's hard to tell but I doubt that she's any younger than me. Both of us wear heavy coats and boots, but Triton's cold still insinuates itself up the stilts, through the city's floor, into our ancient bones.

And I tell her about the day I met Skanda Abrud.

IT WAS HERE, under Neptune. I'd come out to Triton chasing a possible client. Early in my rock-carving days, but not so early that I wasn't building a small but respectable reputation. Neptune was further out than I'd ever been before, but I figured it was worth the time and the cost.

I'd been wrong. An upstart rival had undercut my offer and stolen the prospective customer. *Moonlighter*, meanwhile, needed fuel and repairs. While bots swarmed over the ship, and my bank account trickled down to single digits, I shuttled to Triton to drown my sorrows. That was when I ended up in the *Delta Vee Hotel.*

I've never been there since; too many ghosts. Like the *Cutter and the Torch* is now, the place was a popular hang-out with artists and their sponsors. The walls, floor and tables were covered with images and solid projections of work both good and gaudy: asteroids and ice-teroids, boulders and rocks, transformed into pieces of art, from the geometric abstracts of Motl and Petit to the hyper-realistic portraiture of Dvali and Maestlin. I knew some of these people; had even worked with some of them back when they trimmed payloads for the big combines.

My star was on the rise, modestly, but even then I sensed that the bubble couldn't last. Too much money was changing hands. On my way in, I'd passed Ozymandis, a kilometre-sized rock put into Triton orbit. It was the work of Yinning and Tarabulus, the latest hot properties. I didn't think much of it. It was a face, shattered and time-worn, with great clefts in the cheeks and deep black craters for eyeholes. Everyone went mad for it but all I saw was various superficial gimmicks used to conceal a profound absense of technique.

Yinning and Tarabulus hadn't come up through the combines; they'd never worked with rock and ice in any other context. Lacking that core of experience, they *had* to make their work look damaged and ancient because that was the only way to disguise their screw-ups. They worked against the rock, not with it: couldn't see the weaknesses in the stone, the planes of failure.

Fucking amateurs.

I vowed that if anyone was ever crazy enough to let me loose on a piece of rock that big, I'd cut it perfectly. And I knew I could.

What I didn't expect was that I was about to get the chance.

"Beautiful, isn't it."

He—whoever he was—meant Neptune. I'd been staring into its face, locked overhead like a vast ceiling ornament. The giant's purple-blue gloom had turned out to be a perfect match for my funk.

"If you say so."

"I mean it. Look at it, Loti. Barely a ring system worth mentioning, no metastable storms in the atmosphere. Winds, yes. Transient features. But nothing that lasts. Triton's the only moon of any consequence; the rest are snowballs. Yet it has its own understated magnificence. An undemonstrative grandeur."

I still had no idea who was talking, and by that point in the evening even less interest. But when I turned around I found my interest notching up slightly. He was elegant, well-dressed, exceedingly handsome—and definitely not someone I'd seen in the *Delta Vee Hotel* until now.

"Do I know you?"

"Not yet. But I'm hoping we can get to know each other. Work together, I mean. My name is Skanda Abrud. I have a proposition, a proposal for a commission. Are you interested?"

"That'll depend on the pay and the duration."

He smiled tightly. "I'd have thought you'd have jumped at work. As it happens, the pay will be excellent—at least twenty times what you've ever received before, if my suspicions are correct. I've also selected my own rock. It's on a high inclination orbit, but easily reachable. Would you like to see it?"

This was all too good to be true. I'd been stitched up before, led to think I was on the verge of a life-changing commission.

"If you feel you must."

He made precise right angles of his thumbs and forefingers to frame an image. The space between his hands darkened. It clotted with blackness and a near-black lump. The lump was contoured with dim sunlight on one side, picking out craters and ridges in purple-browns. He pulled his hands apart to swell the image. "It's large, about a kilometer across, but easily within your capabilities. Do you think you could do this for me?"

I studied the rock, studied his face. I imagined his head fitting inside the rock, waiting to be revealed like a mask in a mould. This, after all, was what most of my clients wanted. Their own face, tumbling around the Sun for the rest of eternity.

"I'd need to run some scans," I hedged. "But if there are no nasty surprises, I can probably make you fit."

This seemed to throw him. "No. It's not me that you'd be doing. Good grief, no. Can you *imagine* the absolute vanity of that?"

"So who else do you want?" Already I was thinking loved one, lover, heroic ancestor: the usual self-aggrandizing bullshit.

"That's easy." He made another image. It was a male face, that of a young man. Classically proportioned. I guess I'd have recognised it, if my education hadn't been so patchy.

"I don't know it."

"You should. What I want, Loti, is for you to carve me the head of Michelangelo's David."

INGVAR HAS LED me to the public ice-rink on the western cusp of Stilt-Town. It's perverse, really. Massive layers of insulation buttress the city from the surface of Triton, and now they go to all this trouble to create *another* little square of frozen ground over the city's floor. Granted, it's not cryo-cold, it doesn't need to be, but I still feel an extra bite to the air. Our breath jets out in comet tails. Ingvar keeps stomping her feet and flapping her arms.

"You had another career once," she says. "You weren't always an artist."

"Since you seem to know all about me...what's the point of this talk, Ingvar? Seeing as there's nothing to stop me walking away right now."

"Be my guest. But you know I know something. Those people really died, Loti; I didn't just make them up. They were claim-jumpers. Not only shouldn't they have been there, but Authority screwed up in not protecting them when the impactor came in. It's true there wasn't much warning, and the planetary defenses were not at maximum readiness. They sent ships at the last minute, tried to deflect the impactor..." Ingvar shakes her head. "Didn't work; not enough time. But the point is I can tie you to the impactor, and show that it was no accident that it hit Naiad. Skanda meant it to happen. And that makes it a *crime*, not some random accident of celestial mechanics. And also makes you an accomplice."

"Fine. Prepare a dossier for Authority. I'm sure they'll be thrilled to hear from you."

"I could do just that. May well do so, in fact." From across the square, on the other side of the ice-rank, an amateur band is rehearsing on the platform of a white pavilion. Their frostbitten fingers strike a series of duff notes. Ingvar raises her voice over the brassy dischord. "Did you like your old line of work?"

"It paid."

In fact it was good work, and I was better than good work. I used to shape ice for the bulk carriers. Take a splinter of comet a couple of kilometers across, chisel it with lasers and plasma and variable yield shaped charges until it had exactly the right profile, the right symmetry and center of gravity, to be converted into a one-shot payload.

Handing over a chunk of ice that I'd trimmed, watching as the pusher engines were fixed on at one end, a spiderlike control nexus at the other, witnessing the start of its long, long cruise to the hungry economies of the inner system, there was some satisfaction in that.

"But then everything changed," Ingvar said. "Not overnight, obviously, but harder and faster than you'd been expecting. New technologies, new ways of doing things. Decided by people who didn't know you, didn't care about you. Men like Skanda Abrud."

"I moved with the times."

The skaters execute lazy ellipses on the ice. Most of them aren't very good, but on Triton even the clumsiest achieve a measure of elegance. It occurs to me that I've never come to the rink when there are skaters out. A girl launches herself into the air, tucks her arms and executes maybe twenty rotations before her skates touch ice again.

Sometimes, high above the ecliptic, I'd turn *Moonlighter*'s main dish away from the system's hum and bustle and tune in to the cosmic microwave background. The hiss of creation. That's what the skaters sound like: an endless and spiralling cosmic hiss.

Above the quadrangle, Neptune surveys proceedings with serene indifference. I'd sooner forget about Neptune and Naiad. But it's not easy with that hanging overhead.

"You just took to art? It was that easy?" Ingvar asks.

I wonder why she cares. "That or starve. I guess I did all right. Made a living." I watch an excursion craft slide across the bisected face of Neptune, lit up like a neon fish. "*Was* making a living, until you interrupted me."

"But you've had your share of disappointments. Dreams and ambitions that didn't work out." The way she says this, I can't help but wonder if she isn't, on some level, alluding to the private trajectory of her own career. Licensed investigator: hardly the most glamorous or remunerative profession in the system. Maybe Ingvar had higher hopes than that, a long time ago.

Sympathy? Not exactly. But a flicker of recognition, nonetheless.

"We all make the best of things," I say. "Or try to."

"It's not a bad life, is it? I mean, look at us. We're on Triton, under Neptune. Watching ice-skating." Ingvar shivers in her coat. "It's cold, but we can get warm if want to. There's food and company when we need it. And it's like that everywhere. Lovely things to see, places to explore, people to meet. Hundreds of worlds, thousands of towns and cities. Why would anyone *not* find that enough? Why would anyone want more from life than the system can give them?"

I can see where this is leading.

"You mean, why would anyone ever want to leave?"

"I just don't understand. But I've been there. I've been to Jupiter, seen the skydocks, seen the voidships being built. There's no end of them, no end of volunteers rich enough to buy a slot. Even after what happened." Ingvar pumps her feet against the ground. From the white pagoda, the amateur band mangles another passage. "What's *wrong* with those people?" she asks, and I can't tell if she's complaining about the band, or the voidship sleepers, or both.

SO I TOOK Skanda out to meet his rock.

The orbit was high-inclination, the rock a long way from the ecliptic. I'd seen the images, but the first up-close viewing was always special.

"You like it?" I asked him.

"It's good. Better than good. It'll do, won't it?"

"It'll have to."

But it was much better than that. I'd swung *Moonlighter* around the rock a dozen times, mapping it down to thumbnail precision, and scanning deep into its heart. I'd dropped seismic probes to echo-map its core. None of these readings had given the slightest cause for real concern. I could see David's head in my mind's eye, visualise exactly where the first cuts would have to go.

"I didn't think it would seem so big," Skanda said. "It's one thing to see it as an image, another to be *here*, to feel the dead pull of all that mass. It's a mountain, falling through space. Don't you feel that?"

"It's a rock."

Skanda pushed a hair from my eyes. "You've no romanticism," he chided gently.

Honestly, I hadn't meant it to happen this way. I don't, as a rule, end up sleeping with my clients. When Skanda insisted on accompanying me out to the rock, I'd hit him with my usual terms and conditions. My ship, my rules. There wasn't much privacy on *Moonlighter*, but it would be strictly business all the way out and all the way back home.

So much for that. In truth, Skanda made it too easy. He was charming, effortlessly easy on the eye and knew exactly what he wanted. It was that last quality that I found most attractive of all.

He'd already had a certain rock in mind. And he needed to be *out here*, witnessing. Who was I to quibble?

Very soon the work was underway.

Bots did my bidding. They peeled away from *Moonlighter* in eager droves. Some carried lasers and plasma cutters. Some were tunnelling machines, designed to sink boreholes, down which other bots would pack detonation charges. Meanwhile, as the bots toiled, huge cutting arms unfolded from *Moonlighter*'s flanks. The arms were tipped with various sampling and cutting instruments. Slaved to my telepresence rig, the bots let me work the rock as if it was clay beneath my fingers. That was the part I liked the best. Dirt under my nails.

Sculpting like Michelangelo.

If I'd been prepared to cut corners, the way Yinning and Tarabulus worked, I could have shaped that rock in weeks. But doing it the hard way meant months of patient work. Months of just the two of us, stuck in my ship hundreds of light-minutes from civilisation.

I loved every second of it.

Skanda had been as good as his word. He'd paid up front. With the money now in my account, I wouldn't need to work for years. He'd even picked up the tab on *Moonlighter*'s repair bill.

Did I dare wonder where all this wealth was coming from?

Sort of. But then again I didn't really care. Obviously, he was rich. But then there were millions of rich people in the system—who else was paying for the voidships?

When I was working, deep into it, Skanda would retire to *Moonlighter*'s bridge and conduct long-range business. He didn't seem to mind whether I listened in or not. Only slowly did I get any kind of inkling into the kind of work he was involved in, and what it meant for me.

Meanwhile, layer by layer, the face of David unmasked itself. Even as the work progressed, I knew there was never a time when it couldn't all end in ignominy. The best probes and surveys weren't infallible, and nor were my tools and methods. The rock was riddled with the usual number of weaknesses, the scars and fractures of ancient collisions. Some of these were obligingly close to the planes and contours where I meant to cut anyway, as if the rock was trying to shed itself of everything that wasn't the head of David. Others were at treacherous opposition to my plans. A slight misalignment of a shaped charge, a misdirected laser blast, and I could shatter David's cheek or brow beyond repair.

Sure, I could fix that kind of damage easily enough. But I'd never stoop so low. That was for hacks like Yinning and Tarabulus. And I doubted Skanda would settle for second best. If he was going to create the head of David, it had to be as flawless as Michelangelo's original.

And it would be. Gradually the scalp and face came free. David's chin and jaw were as yet still entombed in rock; the effect was to give the youth an old man's beard. That wouldn't last. I was chipping the beard away in house-sized chunks, a curl at a time. Another month, I reckoned, and then we'd be done with this crude shaping. Three months, perhaps, to bring David to completion. Four or five at the longest.

And it would be magnificent. No one had done such a thing as this. I imagined some future civilisation stumbling on this painstakingly shaped rock, a million or billion years from now, as it tumbled around the Sun. What would they make of the blank-eyed visage? Would they have the faintest inkling of the eager little creatures who had brought it into being?

Even with the bots, the work took its toll. Between cutting stints, when I was too tired to supervise the machines, I'd float with Skanda in the observation bubble. We'd be goggled up, our naked bodies intertwined.

I'd seen my share of the system but Skanda had been places I'd only dreamed of visiting. I kept telling myself not to worry about the future, just to enjoy the moment, this time we had together. When the rock was done, there'd be nothing to keep Skanda with me. Even with the money in my account, I was just a rock cutter.

But Skanda made me wonder. With the goggles on, he'd show me things. Industrial flows; streams of processed matter on their way from launcher to customer. "That one," he'd say, directing my eye to a tagged procession of cargo pellets, shot out from a catapult on some iceteroid. "That's on its way to Mars. Slower than shipping it bulk, but cheaper in the long run. No engines, no guidance—just celestial mechanics, taking it all the way home."

"You own that flow?"

He'd kiss me as if to say: don't trouble yourself with such matters. "In a tediously complicated sense, yes."

"People like you," I said, "put people like me out of work."

Skanda smiled. My face bulged back in the mirrored globes of his goggles. "But I'm putting you *in* work now, aren't I?"

It wasn't just industry and economics. Orbits lit up, coloured bands arcing away like the racetracks of the gods. Worlds flowered in the darkness. Not just the major planets, of course, but the minor ones: Ceres, Vesta, Hidalgo, Juno, Adonis, dozens more. In turn each world had its gaggling court of fellow-travellers. We watched moons, habitats, stations, shuttles and ships. The goggles painted designations, civil registrations and cargo summaries.

"I'll take you to Venus Deep," he said. "Or Ridgeback City on Iapetus. I know a great place there, and the views…have you ever seen the skimmers plunge through Jupiter's spot, or the reef cities under Europa?"

"I've never even been to Europa."

"There's so much to see, Loti. More than one life could ever encompass. When we're done with this…I hope you'll let me show you more of the system. It would be my privelege."

"I'm just a rock cutter from Titan, Skanda."

"No," he said, firmly enough that it was almost a reprimand. "You're infinitely more than that. You're a true artist, Loti. And you have a gift that people aren't going to forget in a hurry. Take my word on that."

Stupid thing was, I did.

BY THE TIME Ingvar steers me to another part of the quadrangle, the band has given up for the night. Most of the skaters have surrendered to the cold. There are only a couple left, perhaps the best of them, orbiting each other like a pair of binary pulsars.

"They say they aren't dynamically stable," Ingvar comments, looking up through the dome. "Something to do with Triton's influence, I think. The rings of Saturn aren't stable either, not on timescales of hundreds of millions of years. But they'll outlast these many times over. I'm not sure how I feel about that."

"You should be happy. Something wrong will be put right."

"Well, yes. But Naiad was destroyed to make this happen. And those people, too. Given their deaths, I'd rather the end result was a bit more permanent."

"It'll outlast us. That's probably all that matters."

Ingvar's head bobs in the fur-lined hood of her coat. "Maybe by the time the rings start to dissipate, we'll have decided we like them enough to want to preserve them. Sure we'd find a way, if we felt it mattered enough."

I look at them now. Try to see them through fresh eyes.

The rings of Neptune.

They bisect the face of the world like a knife slash, very nearly as magnificent as the rings of Saturn. There always were rings here, I tell myself, but they were little more than smoky threads, all but invisible under most conditions. The ghostly promise of rings yet to come.

Not so now. The resonant effects of Triton, and its lesser siblings, conspire to divide and subdivide these infant rings into riverine bands. In turn, these concentric bands shimmer with a hundred splendid hues of the most ethereal blue-white or pastel green or jade. There's a lot of ice and rubble in a moon, even one as small as Naiad, and enough subtle chemistry to provide beguiling variations in reflection and transmission.

Skanda should have seen this, I think. He'd have known that the rings would be beautiful, a thing of wonder, commanding the awe of the entire system. But he couldn't have begun to predict their dazzling complexity. The glory of it.

But then who could?

"Does it anger you, that he did this to your greatest work?" Ingvar asks. "Let you create the head of David, let you think this would be the thing that made your name, all the while knowing it was going to be destroyed?"

"I did what I was paid to do. Once my part in it was over, I forgot about David."

"Or rather, you forced yourself not to dwell on it. For obvious reasons, in light of what happened. But you always believed it was still out there, didn't you? Ticking its way round the Sun, waiting to be found. You clung to that." Ingvar's tone changes. "Would he have taken credit, do you think? Was that always his intention?"

"He never said anything about it to me."

"But you knew him a little. When the voidship reached the Oort cloud, when he was scheduled to be woken...would he have declared himself responsible? Would he have basked in the fame, knowing he was untouchable, beyond the reach of solar law, or would he have preferred to leave the mystery unsolved?"

"What do you think?" I ask snidely.

"From what I've gathered of his profile," Ingvar says, resuming her curious lopsided walk, "he doesn't strike me as the kind to have settled for anonymity."

I'VE LIVED A good and full life since the day he left. I still cut rock. I've had many lovers, many friends, and I can't say I've been unhappy. But there are days when the pain of his betrayal feels as raw as if it all happened yesterday. We were nearly done with David—just a couple more weeks of finishing-off, and then the head was complete. It already looked magnificent. It was the finest thing I'd ever touched.

Then Skanda returned from the bridge, where he'd been conducting business dealings. Nothing about his manner suggested anything untoward.

"I've got to go for a little while."

"Go?"

"Back to the main system. Something's come up. It's complicated and it would be a lot easier to resolve without hours of timelag."

"We're nearly done. I don't usually abandon a piece when it's this near to completion—it's too hard to get back into the right frame of mind."

"You don't have to abandon anything. My people...they're sending out a ship to get me. In fact it will be here very shortly. You can stay on station, finish the work."

He'd made it seem like some unscheduled crisis, something that had blown up at short notice, but deep down I knew that couldn't be that case. Not if that little ship of his had already been on its way out here for what must have been days.

I watched it arrive. It was a tiny thing, a beautiful jewelled toy of a spacecraft, porpoise-sleek and not much larger. "An extravagance," Skanda said, as the craft docked. "It's just that sometimes I need to be able to move around very quickly."

I bottled my qualms. "You don't have to apologise for being rich. If you weren't, you wouldn't be paying for the head of David."

"I'm glad you see it that way." He kissed me on the cheek, forestalling any objection. "I wish there was some alternative, but there isn't. All I can promise is that I won't be long. My ship can get me there and back very quickly. Two weeks, three at the most. Keep on working. Finish David for me, and I'll be back to see the end result."

"Where are you going? You were so keen on being here. I understand timelag, but it hasn't held you back until now. What's so important that you have to go away?"

He touched a finger to my lips. "Every second that I'm here is another that I'm not on my way, doing what has to be done. When I'm back, I'll tell you everything you want to know—and I guarantee you'll be bored within five minutes." He kissed me again. "Keep on working. Do that for me. Remember what I said, Loti. You have a gift."

What was the point in arguing further? I believed him. All that talk of the places he'd show me, the things we'd share together—the glamour and spectacle of the entire system, ours for the taking. He'd fixed that idea so firmly in my head that it never once occurred to me that he'd been lying the entire time. I never thought that we'd have a life together; I wasn't that naïve. But some good months, was that too much to ask for? Venus Deep and the reef cities of Europa. The two of us, the artist and her wealthy lover and sponsor. Who wouldn't turn that down?

"Be fast," I whispered.

From the observation bubble, I watched his little ship drop away from *Moonlighter*. The drive was bright, and I tracked it until it was too faint to detect. By then, I had a handle on his vector. It didn't mean much—he could easily have been heading to an intermediate stopover, unrelated to his true destination, or just travelling in a random direction to throw me off the scent.

Both of those things were possible. But so was the third possibility, which was that the vector was reliable, and that Skanda had business around Jupiter.

And even then I didn't guess.

"HOW LONG WAS it before you found out about the voidship?" Ingvar asks.

"A while. Weeks, months. Does it really matter now?"

"When he left *Moonlighter*...was that the last contact you had with him?"

"No." The admission is difficult, because it takes me back to the time when I was foolish enough to believe Skanda's promises. "He called me from Jupiter. Even mentioned the voidship: said a relative of his was being frozen, put aboard for the voyage. That was the emergency. He wanted to be there, to give whoever it was a good send off."

"Whereas the relative was really his wife, and Skanda would soon be joining her. They'd both paid for slots on the voidship. Off to establish a human bridgehead in the Oort cloud. But he hadn't finished with the head of David, had he? He still had instructions for you. It was still important that the work be finished."

"I'd been paid, and I had no reason to doubt that he'd be back."

"Other than the completion of the head, what were the instructions?"

"When his little ship docked, it came with a marker beacon. I was told to fix it onto the head."

"And the...function...of this beacon? You never questioned it?"

I look down. I wish I had something to say.

Ingvar continues. "The beacon was also a steering motor. Skanda had programmed it to make an adjustment to the rock's orbit. An impulse, to kick into a collision course for Naiad. He'd calculated everything. The binding energy of the moon, the kinetic energy of the impactor. He knew it would work. He knew he could shatter that moon and turn it into a ring system around Neptune. The ultimate artistic statement, a piece of planetary resculpting to dwarf the ages."

I think things over for a moment. The conversation has been as lopsided as Ingvar's walk. She's been asking all the hard questions; now it's my turn.

"What's in it for you? What made you decide that you had to solve this mystery? The entire system thinks the rings were made by accident. What made you think otherwise?"

Against expectation, Ingvar seems pleased rather than annoyed. "I saw it."

"Saw what?"

"The head of David. With my own eyes, just before it hit."

"You were there?"

All of a sudden, Ingvar looks tremendously old and weary, as if this is the end of some enormous and taxing enterprise, something that has swallowed decades of her life.

"I was Authority. Pilot of one of the quick reaction ships we sent up to deflect the impactor, as soon as we saw it coming in. I got close enough to see your handiwork, Loti. Too close, as it happens. We were hitting the rock with weapons, trying to adjust its vector or shatter it to rubble. There was an impact, near David's right eye. My ship was caught in the blast. I lost control; nearly died." She takes a breath. "My ship was badly damaged. So was I."

"What happened to you?"

"Oh, they patched me up well enough after my ship was recovered. More than they could do for my partner. Still, lucky as I'd been, I was never much good to Authority after that. Hence the change of profession."

"But you always knew about the head."

"So did everyone involved. That couldn't come out, though. No one could know that people had died on Naiad, because that made us look bad. And no one could know that the impactor had been sculpted because that made it a crime, not an accident—and if that had come out, it wouldn't have been long before the rest of it was public as well. Our multiple screw-ups."

"Skanda never meant for people to die. He just wanted to do something outrageous."

"He succeeded. But as of now, only two people are aware of that. You and me. The question is, what do we do with our knowledge?"

I wonder if there's a trap I'm missing. "You've spent years putting this together, haven't you. Tracking down the truth. Finding me, and establishing my involvement. Well, congratulations. You're right; I was his accomplice. So what if I didn't know what I was getting into? Authority won't care about that. Especially as there isn't anyone else left to blame. You could hand me over now."

"I could. But would that necessarily be the right thing to do?" Ingvar studies her boots. "My second career…it's not as if it's anything I need to be ashamed of. I've worked hard, had my share of successes. Minor cases, in the scheme of things. But I've not failed. So what if I've done nothing anyone will ever remember me for?"

"Until now. Turn me in…it could make your reputation."

"And yours," Ingvar nods. "Think of it, Loti. Everything you've done, every rock you've cut, the entirety of your art, it's as nothing against the head of David. And the head of David is as nothing against the rings of Neptune. You created something marvellous, a thing of wonder. Beyond Yinning and Tarabulus or anyone else. It was the one time that your life was touched by greatness." A sudden reverence enters Ingvar's voice. "But you can't tell anyone. All you'll have is the rest of your art, in all its middling obscurity, until the day you die. No fame, no notoriety. And all I'll have is a limp and the dog days of my second career. The question is: could either of us live with that?"

"What if I chose not to?"

"I'd make your name."

"As a convicted criminal, locked away in some Authority cell?"

Ingvar's shrug suggests that this is no more than a trifle. "Some would make the trade in an instant. Artists have killed themselves for a stab at immortality. No one's asking that much of you."

"And you?"

"I'd have solved the mystery of the Naiad event. Brought its last living perpetrator to justice. There'd be a measure of acclaim in it for me."

"Just a measure?"

"Some trouble as well. As I said, not everyone would welcome the truth getting out."

I shake my head, almost disappointed with Ingvar, that she should give in now. "So you're saying I have a choice?"

"I'm saying we both have one. But we'd have to agree on it, I think. No good one of us pulling one way, the other resisting."

I look at Neptune again. The rings, the storms, the brooding blue vastness of it all. And think of that temporary star, shining for a few seconds in the constellation Fornax. The light of a voidship, dying in a soundless eruption of subatomic energy. They say they were pushing the engines, trying to outrun the other voidships. Trying to be the first to stake a claim in the Oort clouds. Going for victory.

They also say no living thing saw that flash; that it was only machines that witnessed it, but that if anyone *had* been looking toward Fornax, at the right time...

"It would be something, to be known for that," I tell Ingvar.

"It would."

"My name would ring down the ages. Like Michelangelo."

"That's true," she agrees. "But Michelangelo's dead, and I doubt that it makes much difference to him now." Ingvar claps her hands against her body. "I'm getting cold. I know a good bar near here, and there are no rock cutters. Let's go inside and talk it over, shall we?"

TRAUMA POD

WHEN I come round I'm in a space about the size of a shower cubicle, tipped on its side. I'm flat on my back, resting on a soft padded surface. Curving around me, close enough to touch, are walls of antiseptic white. They wrap around to form a smooth ceiling, broken by hatches and recesses. Cables and tubes emerge through gaps. There's the soft whirr of pumps, the hiss and chug of air circulation. And looking at me right now, peering down from the ceiling just above my own face, is a pair of stereoscopic camera eyes.

I twitch, trying to raise my head enough to get a good look at myself. I've been stripped of my armour. I was wearing combat exo-cladding, but the outer shell's gone now. All that's left is the lightweight mesh suit, and that's ripped and shredded pretty badly. I try and get a better look at my extremities but a pair of hands gently pushes me back down. They poke through a pair of hatches above my sternum, as if there's someone just outside, reaching in.

They're perfectly normal human hands, wearing green surgical gloves.

A woman's voice says: "Stay still, and don't panic, Sergeant Kane. You're going to be fine."

"What..." I start to say.

"That's good. You can hear us, and understand my words. That's very positive. You can speak, too. That's also encouraging. But for the moment, I'd like you to let me do the talking."

They must have pumped something into me, because for the time being I don't feel like arguing with anyone or anything.

"Okay."

A panel has slid open to reveal a screen, and on the screen is a woman's face. Green uniform, black hair tied back under a surgical cap. She's looking right at me—close enough that it's almost uncomfortable. Her lips move.

"You've been wounded, Sergeant."

I manage a smile. "No shit."

I remember fragments, not the whole story. A deep recon insertion gone wrong. Me and the two others...I'll remember their names in a moment. Loiter drones above us, enemy Mechs too close for comfort. Armored support too dispersed to help us. Extraction window compromised. Not the way it was meant to go down.

The white flash of the pulse bomb, the skull-jarring concussion of the shockwave.

Someone screaming "Medic!"

Someone who sounded a lot like me.

"You were lucky. One of our field medical robots was able to reach you in time. The bot deployed its trauma pod and hauled you inside. That's where you are now: in the pod. It's armoured, independently powered, and fully capable of keeping you alive until we have an extraction window. The field medical unit has secured the area and established an exclusion volume around your site."

My mouth is very dry, and now that I have some sense of location I begin to pick up on the fact that my head doesn't feel quite right.

"When," I say. "How long. Until extraction."

"Waiting for an update on that right now. Best guess is six to twelve hours, but that may be wide or short of the mark, depending on how things evolve in theatre."

For a second I think: operating theatre, and wonder why the hell that should be my problem. Get me the fuck out of here, then worry about when you can slot me in for surgery.

Then I realise she's talking about a different kind of theatre.

"Have I got that long?"

"That's what we need to talk about. Your injuries have been stabilised, but you're not out of the woods just yet." She pauses. "I'm Doctor Annabel Lyze. I'm linking in from the forward surgical unit in Tango Oscar. My colleagues and I will be with you the whole time you're in the pod, and we'll be handling your case once you've been extracted. I know you feel pretty isolated right now, Sergeant Kane, and that's only natural. But I want you to know that you're not alone."

"Call me Mike," I say.

"Mike it is." She nods. "And you can call me Annabel, if that helps. I'm right here, Mike. Never more than a screen away. Look, I can even touch you. These are my hands you're feeling."

But they're not, and she knows it.

Under the surgical gloves lie bones and sinews of plastic and metal. They're teleoperated robot hands which can emerge from any part of the trauma pod that the situation dictates. Somewhere back in Tango Oscar, Annabel's wearing haptic feedback gloves—similar to my own mesh-suit—that provide an exact tactile interface with their robot counterparts. She can feel every bruise, every swelling, as if she's right here in the pod with me. I couldn't ask for better care.

But she's not with me, no matter what she wants me to think.

"You said my injuries have been stabilised. Are you ready to tell me the score?"

"Nothing that isn't fixable. You took a bad hit to your right leg and I'm afraid I had to amputate. But we can grow that back easily enough. That's not our main concern here. What I'm worried about is a bleed on your brain that we need to treat sooner rather than later."

So the pod's surgical systems have already been busy. While I was sleeping my damaged leg was removed, the stump sewn up, my ruined limb ejected through the pod's disposal vent. I know how it works with trauma pods, and she's right; they'll grow me a new leg.

But brain surgery?

"You want to cut into my skull, while I'm still in this thing?"

"Minimally invasive intervention, Mike. There's a risk, certainly. But there's an even greater risk in leaving things until later. You may not make it unless we intervene now."

"I was under, and you brought me back to consciousness. What the hell was the point of that?"

"I wanted to talk things through. Give me the word, and I'll go in. But if you'd sooner take your chances and wait for extraction, I'll respect that decision."

The tone of her voice, the look in her eyes, make it abundantly clear what she thinks of my chances if I decide not to opt for surgery. About as good as if I was still out there in the battlefield, gushing blood into the dirt. But I can't just give in, without knowing the odds of rescue.

"Show me what's outside the pod."

"That won't help, Mike."

"Show me anyway. I'm still a soldier. I need to know what's out there."

Annabel purses her lips. "If you insist."

I'm still wearing my military contacts, although I only realise as much when the view of the trauma pod's scrubs out, replaced by a visual feed from the pod's own external camera.

It's not good. I can tell that much from a glance.

I do a slow pan, taking in the blasted, toxic landscape as far as the camera can see. I'm lying flat, or flattish, on a cratered plateau, hemmed in by the craggy ruins of what were once office blocks or retail developments. A vehicle, maybe a school bus, lies on its back fifty meters from me. Some kind of transmission tower or pylon has come down, sagging over the ground contours like the skeleton of some saurian monster. Overhead, the clouds are mustard coloured, sagging with airborne toxicity. The horizon ripples with chemical murk.

Pulse bombs flash in the distance. Plasma bolts gash the clouds. Mechs, humanoid and giant-sized, stalk and stride the hellscape that was once a city. I do another full visual sweep and I don't see a single human combatant.

Which isn't too surprising. Since the war went almost entirely robotic, we living soldiers have been increasingly thin on the ground. I wonder if the others got out. Maybe some of them are in pods like me, awaiting extraction. Or maybe they're all dead.

What the fuck was I doing here anyway?

Ah, yes. Deep recon squad. I remember the others' names now. Me, Rorvik, Lomax. Robotics specialists, tasked to observe the behaviour of our Mechs, and our enemy's units, under realtime combat conditions. The reason? No one was saying. But the rumours weren't hard to pick up. Some of our units were going rogue. It was said to be happening to the enemy machines as well. No one had a clue why.

Actually, we had some theories. We cram our Mechs with sufficient autonomy to make them independent of human control. We give them wits and smarts, then wonder why they start doing stuff we didn't ask them to.

Not my problem now, though.

I figure I'm safe for the moment. The field medical robot has done its work, not only of dragging my wounded remains into the pod, but of securing the pod itself. I'm surrounded by a low wall of rubble and battlefield junk, shoved hastily into place to act as a screen. Not to bury me, or complicate my extraction, but to shield me from enemy eyes, cameras and weapon systems.

I can see the field medical unit. The four-metre tall robot is circling the pod, keeping the area clear. My contacts drop an ident tag on the robot. Unit KX-457 is a headless humanoid chassis with an oval gap in its torso, a hole I can see right through. Its arms are musclebound with guns, countermeasure-launchers and specialised military-surgical devices. Its titanium-pistoned legs look spindly, but they're as strong and shock-resistant as aircraft undercarriage. The unit is scary to look at, but it's on my side, and that makes all the difference.

I don't remember what happened, what became of Rorvik and Lomax. They're not my problem now. I was screaming "Medic!" out of pure reflex. I didn't need to. As soon as my exo-cladding detected that I'd been injured—which was probably sooner than my own nervous system—it would have squawked the nearest field medical unit. My armour would have undertaken some life-preserving measures, but that was only a stopgap until the robot arrived. KX-457 would have detached the pod from its belly recess, laid it on the ground, and—after a preliminary medical assessment—slid me inside.

Under ordinary circumstances, while the trauma pod was fixing me up, the robot would have plugged the pod back into its belly and hightailed it out of the combat area. Not an option today, though: too much risk of the robot being intercepted and taken out. I'm a high-value asset, or so they tell me. Better to keep the pod in-theatre, under robot protection, until a full extraction squad can come in under close aerial cover.

Meanwhile, the field medical unit maintains maximum vigilance. Every now and then KX-457 raises one of its arms and zaps the sky with a plasma cannon. Sometimes, a drone falls out of the clouds. Most of the Mechs on the ground are friendly, but occasionally I'll spy an enemy scout unit on the limit of visibility, testing our defenses. They're out there.

I've seen enough. It's clear that I'm not being bullshitted. It really would be suicide to go for extraction now.

Which means that if Doctor Annabel Lyze is right about the brain bleed, I do need to go under the knife.

I pull my point of view back into the pod. The battlefield scrubs out. White surroundings again, the hum and chug of diligent life-support. Disembodied hands reaching through the walls.

I give Annabel my consent. Go in and fix the bleed.

Then get me the fuck out of here.

I COME AROUND. The first thing that hits me is that I'm safe, back in Tango Oscar. I know this because I'm definitely not in the trauma pod any more. Although it has to be said that I'm still in a kind of pod, and it has the same kind of white interior as the first.

But it can't be the one I woke up in originally, because there just wouldn't be room. I know this because there's another body squeezed into this one, another wounded soldier, and that simply wouldn't be possible in the first pod. Obviously, while I was out cold, being operated on, KX-457 was able to complete the extraction. They've got me in this bigger pod while I await my slot in the operating room, or whatever they've got in mind. Pretty soon it'll be smiles and high-fives. Welcome home, soldier. You did a good job out there.

I wonder what happened to the other guy, the one jammed in next to me?

Then something dawns. Through the pod's insulation, and beyond the background noise of the medical systems, I can still hear the occasional pulse-bomb or plasma cannon discharge.

Either the front moved a lot closer to Tango Oscar while I was out, or I'm not home just yet.

"Can you hear me, Mike?"

"Yes."

Annabel swallows. "It's mostly good news. We arrested the bleed, and I'm very happy about that."

"I don't like that 'mostly.' Why is there another soldier in here with me? Why did you swap me to a bigger pod?"

"It's the same pod, Mike. We haven't moved you. You're still exactly where you were before I put you under."

I try and budge to one side, suddenly uncomfortable. Although I don't achieve much, I have the impression that my silent companion has budged by exactly the same amount, as if glued to my side.

"I'm telling you, there's someone else in here."

"Okay." She pulls back for a moment, whispers something to a colleague before returning. "That's...not unexpected. There's been some damage to your right frontoparietal regions, Mike. Part of it was caused by the original bleed, and part of it was occasioned by our intervention. I stress that we had no practical option; if we hadn't gone in, we wouldn't be having this conversation now. But what you are experiencing now is a hallucination: a kind of out-of-body experience caused by the shutdown of the inhibitory circuits that normally keep your mirror neurons functioning normally. You really are alone, Mike. You just have to take my word for it."

"Like I took your word that the surgery was going to be straightforward?"

"We have to consider this a success, Mike. You're with us and you're stable."

I try and move again, but my skull feels as if it's clamped in a vise. It's not painful, but it's a long way from anything I'd call pleasant. "Is there a fix for this, or am I stuck with it forever?"

"There's a fix for most things. As it happens, we can try some workarounds while you're still in the pod. During surgery I inserted some neural probes at strategic sites around the injured part of your brain. Apart from giving me a much better insight into what's going on in there, compared to the crude resolution of the pod's own scanner, I can also intervene in some critical pathways."

I'm still creeped out by my displaced body image. The body next to mine breathes with me. But it feels dead, like an appendage of me that should have withered and dropped off already.

Still, I need to keep focus. "Meaning what?"

"The neural circuitry involved in your out-of-body sensation is pretty well mapped, Mike. At the moment, signals aren't getting where they should due to the damage caused by the bleed. But we can route around those obstructions, using the probes I inserted. Think of them as jumper leads, wiring different parts of your head together. If you're willing, I can attempt to reassert your normal body image."

"Again: why wait until I'm awake, if there's something you can do?"

"Again, I need consent. I also need your subjective evaluation of the effects. I said the circuits were well-mapped, and that's true. But there's enough idiosyncratic variation from individual to individual to mean we can't be a hundred percent sure of the outcome of any given intervention."

"In other words, you'll poke a stick into my head, stir it around and see what happens."

"It's a tiny bit more scientific than that. But it's entirely reversible, and if we can lessen your distress in any way, I think that the small risk involved is acceptable."

"I'm not distressed."

"Your body says otherwise. Stress hormones peaking. Galvanic skin response off the chart. Fear centre lighting up like a football stadium. But that's understandable, Mike. You've been badly injured, in a war zone. You're being kept alive in a technological coffin, while the war continues around you. Under those circumstances, who wouldn't be a little rattled?"

For all that she's right—I am rattled—and for all that I have no desire to spend another second with my phantom self crammed into the pod, my combat instincts momentarily trump all other concerns.

"Give me the external feed again."

"Mike, there's no need to concern yourself with matters beyond your control."

"Just do it, Annabel."

She mumbles a curse and then I'm outside again, seeing the world through the pop-up camera fixed to the outside of the pod like a periscope.

I spin through three hundred and sixty, assessing my surroundings. I'm still where the field medical unit left me, still hemmed in by a makeshift cordon of rubble and junk. But I must have been out for hours. It's dark now, the camera viewing the world in grey-green infrared. It's only when the horizon flashes with an explosion, or something strobes the cloud deck above, that I get any real sense of the tactical environment.

How long was I under the knife? More than a few hours, evidently. And yet it didn't feel like any time at all.

"I want you to be straight with me, Annabel. The brain surgery. How long did it take?"

"It doesn't matter, Mike."

"It does to me."

"All right, then. Eight hours. There were complications. But you came through. Isn't that the main thing?"

"Eight hours and you're still on duty? You said the best guess for my extraction was six to twelve hours."

"And there's still every possibility of it happening within that window. Look, I couldn't abandon you, Mike. But we'll be getting you out very soon now."

"Don't jerk me around. You and I both know they won't try until daybreak, at the earliest." She can't argue with that, and she doesn't try. The combat zone is hazardous at the best of times, but at night, as the ground cools, it's almost impossible to move without being detected, scoped, targeted. I visualise my trauma pod, lit up like a neon gravestone. And I know I can't just sit here doing nothing.

"Let me address that body image problem," Annabel says.

Something snaps inside me. It's time to start being a soldier again. "Give me full-theatre oversight. I want to know what's really out there."

"Mike, I'm not really sure this is in your best—"

"Just do it."

She really has no option but to give me what I want. I may be injured, but I'm still a high-value asset and my active authority means that I still get to call the shots.

The oversight is a realtime map of the battle zone, out to a radius of fifteen kilometres. It's compiled from intelligence gathered by Mechs, drones, cameras, even the still-functioning armour of dead or immobilised combatants. Most of that intelligence originates from our own side, but some of it comes from intercepting enemy transmissions, and doubtless they're doing something similar with ours. The data is woven together and projected onto my contacts. With subvocal commands I can scan and zoom at will.

I take in what the map has to tell me, knowing I should have done this sooner, rather than take Annabel's word that everything was going to be moonbeams and kittens. Because it's not.

And I'm in a world of trouble.

A phalanx of enemy machines is coming my way. They're ten kilometres out, but making steady progress. They may not know I'm here yet, but there's no guarantee of that. The deployment of a field medical unit is a gold-plated giveaway that someone's taken a hit, and there's nothing the enemy would rather do than capture or eliminate a high-value human asset. I study the numbers and the distribution of the advancing formation, measuring the enemy's strength against my sole ally: the lone medical unit. KX-457's weapons and countermeasures aren't to be trifled with. But against a dozen or more enemy Mechs and drones? There's no contest. Nor is there much hope of my little resting place remaining undetected, when the enemy units arrive en masse.

That's when the fight or flight response kicks in. It's a hard nitrous surge, as if fear itself is being pumped into my blood. I'm not going to just stay here and hope that luck's on my side. We need to be moving, and moving now.

Yes, there's risk in that as well—especially at night. That's why my extraction is still on hold. But set against my chances of surviving the arrival of those enemy units, running suddenly looks a lot more attractive.

I pull my point of view back into the trauma pod.

"Tell the field medical unit to scoop me up. We're shipping out."

"I can't issue that order, Mike."

"Can't or won't?"

"We're running simulations now, and they're telling us that you have a statistically improved chance of survival if you remain right where you are."

"By what margin?"

"Enough of a one that I'd really urge you to consider this course of action very thoroughly."

If the odds were that persuasive, she'd tell me up front. My head's still clamped tight. But if I could shake it I would. "Bring the medical unit in."

"Mike, please."

"Just do it. There's no point putting a human being in the combat zone if you won't trust their judgement."

She relents. I don't need to see KX-457 approaching; I hear the boulders being dislodged around me and then feel the trauma pod lurch and tilt as the robot hauls it from the ground. I'm rotated through ninety degrees, until my head is higher than my feet—or rather, I remind myself, foot. Then I feel the reassuring clunk as the trauma pod is docked with the oval recess in the medical unit's torso. Systems interface: power, control, sensory. I'm no longer a wounded man in a humming coffin. I'm a baby in the belly of a killer robot, and that has to be an improvement.

"What are your orders?" the robot asks me.

Recalling the disposition of enemy forces, I start to tell KX-457 to get me as far west as it can. Then I think of something better than being taken along for the ride. I don't need to be able to move my own body to control the robot. What remains of my own mesh-suit layer should be more than capable of detecting intentions, the merest twitch of a neuro-muscular impulse, and giving me appropriate feedback.

"Let me drive you."

"Mike," Annabel interrupts. "You don't need this extra task load. Let the robot extract you, if that's what you insist on doing. But there's no need for you to drive it. In your present condition, your reflexes are going to be no match for the robot's own battle routines."

But if I'm going to die out here, I'd sooner be doing something than just being carried along for the ride.

"I know what I'm doing, Annabel. KX-457, assign me full command authority. Maintain the link until I say otherwise."

My point of view shifts again. The field medical unit has no head, but there's a suite of cameras and sensors built into its shoulder yoke, and that's where I seem to be looking down from.

I look down at myself. I feel exactly as tall as the KX-457—there's no sense that I'm contained in a much smaller body, down in the belly pod. And those titanium legs and arms move to my will, just as if they were part of me. I feel whole again, and strong. That phantom image is still there, but it's much less troubling than when I was jammed into the trauma pod.

I'm still *in* the pod, of course. Need to remind myself of that, because it would be easy to lose track of things.

WE MOVE, THE KX-457 and I. I should say the KX-457, Annabel, and I, because when those hands reach through to adjust my leg dressing, or the catheter in my arm, or the post-operative clamp on my head, it's hard not to feel that she's along for the ride, my wellbeing never less than uppermost in her thoughts. And while it's clear that she doesn't entirely approve of my decision to ship out, I'm still glad to have someone to talk to.

"How long have you been in Tango Oscar, Annabel?" I ask, as I work my past way the shallow, smoke-blackened remains of what was once a glorious air-conditioned shopping mall.

She considers my question carefully. "It's been eighteen months now, Mike. They cycled me in from Echo Victor, and before that it was Charlie Zulu."

"Charlie Zulu." I say it with a kind of reverence. "I hear it was pretty intense there."

She nods. Her face is projected into a small window in my view, fighting for attention with an ever-changing dance of tactical analysis overlays, flagging every potential threat or hiding place. "We had our work cut out." She gives a small dry laugh, but it's clear that the memory's still raw. "That was before the new pods came on-line. The old units didn't have anything like as much autonomy as the ones we're used to now. It was hands-on telesurgery, day and night. We were dying on our feet from exhaustion and stress, and we weren't even out there, in theatre. We saved as many as we could, but when I think about those we couldn't help..." She falls silent.

"I'm sure you did everything you could."

"I hope we did. But there are limits. Even now, we can't always work miracles."

"Whatever happens to me, you've done all that anyone could expect, Annabel. Thanks for sticking with me, all those hours. You must be worn out."

"Whatever it takes, Mike. I'm not going away."

"I hope we get to meet up," I risk telling her, even though it feels like I'm jinxing my chances of ever getting out alive. "Just so I can thank you in person."

Annabel's smile is radiant. "I'm sure we will."

In that moment I don't doubt that I'll make it.

That's when oversight picks up a squadron of enemy scout drones, coming in low just under the cloud deck. My own sensors haven't seen them at all.

I scan my field of view for concealment options, and decide to duck into the corrugated shoebox that used to contain an indoor amusement park. I pick my way through rubble and the blackened, snaking wreckage of a roller coaster, until I'm sure the drones won't pick out my infrared or EM signature. There are fallen machines under my titanium feet, and bodies. I crunch through the shattered carcasses of plastic horses and ride-on centipedes.

"We'll need to lie low for a couple of hours, until those drones are out of the area." I squat, shutting down essential systems. Just a bleed of power to the trauma pod, and another to the KX-457's central processor core.

"How will you know it's safe?"

The building's shell is blocking ambient comms, interfering with oversight. "I won't. But if they're on the usual sweep pattern, we'll be fine once they've passed over."

"Then there's no reason for me not to take a look at that body image issue, is there?"

"It's not bothering me as much as it did."

"Let me fix it anyway. If you don't nip these things in the bud, they can become a big problem during recovery."

I offer a mental shrug. "If you think it's for the best."

"I do," Annabel says. "I do."

I GIVE IT two hours, then three to be on the safe side. I creep my way out of the amusement park, until I'm almost back under the open air. I'm expecting full oversight to be restored as soon as I regain normal comms, but that's not what happens. Coverage is still patchy. I pick up intelligence from nearby eyes and ears, but nothing further out than a few kilometers. The fault may be in my own systems, but it's much more likely that there's been an attack against a critical node in our distributed grid. Those drones may not have been looking for me at all, but for a vulnerability in our comms network.

It's still dark, and the drones could still be out there. But I have to trust that they've left the area, and that the phalanx of heavy Mechs has continued on its original vector. It might take days to repair oversight, assuming the fault isn't in me. I can't wait that long. I'd rather die moving, than waste away hiding from an enemy I can't see.

"We'll give it until dawn," I tell Annabel. "It should be okay to cross open ground then, even with limited oversight."

"How do you feel now?"

"Different."

That's an understatement. But it's true. My phantom twin has vanished. I don't feel another body tagging along next to mine. And I guess I should be glad of that, because it means Annabel's neural cross-wiring has had some effect. But I don't feel the slightest flicker of elation.

Something else is different.

It's not a question of being distressed by my phantom twin any more. He's gone, and with good riddance. But now it's my own body that's changed. I can sense it, hanging beneath my point of view like some withered, useless vestigial appendage, but it doesn't feel like any part of me. I don't inhabit it, and I have no wish to. All I want to do is flinch away from it. I was indifferent before, but now it repulses me.

I retain enough intellectual detachment to understand that this response is neurological. On some level, something has gone catastrophically wrong with my body image. It's as if my sense of self, what really matters to me, has extracted itself from my injured human body and taken up residence in the armoured perfection of the field medical unit.

Clearly this is fucked-up.

But even knowing this, I don't want to go back to the way things used to be. Definitely not: I'm stronger now, and bigger. I stride this ruined world like a colossus. And as much as that revolting thing disgusts me, it's a small price to pay. I have a certain dependency on it, after all. That's a no-brainer.

But there's one other detail I need to address.

Comms is shot to shit. Oversight is a patchwork of blind spots. So how in hell is Doctor Annabel Lyze able to reach over from Tango Oscar and teleoperate her magic green hands?

More than that: how is Doctor Annabel Lyze able to talk me at all? How am I able to see her always smiling, never-tiring face?

"Don't do that, Mike."

"Don't do what?"

"Don't do what you're about to do. Don't check the comms registry. It won't do you any good at all."

I hadn't thought of checking the comms registry. But you know, now that she's put the idea in my head, that's an excellent fucking idea.

I call up the history. I scroll through the log, going back minutes, tens of minutes, hours.

15.56.31.07—zero validated packets
15.56.14.11—zero validated packets
15.55.09.33—zero validated packets
...
11.12.22.54—zero validated packets

And I learn that KX-457 has been out of contact with Tango Oscar—or any command sector, for that matter—for more than nineteen hours. In all that time, it's been acting entirely autonomously, relying on its own in-built intelligence.

So has the trauma pod. From the moment it was deployed—before I was hauled in and treated—the pod was also operating independently of human control. There was no kindly surgeon on the other side of that screen. There was just...software. Software clever and agile enough to mimic a reassuring presence.

Doctor Annabel Lyze.

Doctor Annabel lies.

The question is: was that software running in the pod, or in my own head?

IT'S DAY WHEN they find me. Not the enemy, but my own side. Although by that point I suppose the distinction is moot.

I find voice amplification mode. My words boom out, distorted and godlike. "Don't come any closer."

There are two of them, both wearing full battle armour, backed up by a couple of infantry Mechs. The Mechs have shoulder and arm-mounted plasma cannon batteries locked onto me.

"Mike, listen to me. You've been injured. You went in the trauma pod and...something got screwed up."

Some part of me recognises the voice—Rorvik? Lomax? But it's a small part and easily ignored.

"Get back."

The figure who spoke dares to stand a little taller, even as their companion maintains a nervous, bent-at-the-knees crouch. I admire the speaker's boldness, even as I don't pretend to fully understand it. Then the figure reaches up and does something even riskier, which is to undo their face mask, allowing it to flop aside on its hinge. Framed by the airtight seal of a helmet I see a woman's face, and again there's a flicker of recognition, which I instantly crush.

"Mike, you need to trust us. There's only one way you're going to get help, and that's to relinquish control of the field medical unit. You have brain damage, very severe brain damage, and we need to get it fixed before it gets worse."

"I am not Mike," I tell her. "I am field medical unit KX-457."

"No, Mike. KX-457 is the machine treating you. You're experiencing some kind of body image crisis, but that's all it is. A neurological fault, caused by the damage to your frontal cortex. You're inside the robot, but you are not the robot itself. This is very, very important. Can you understand what I'm saying, Mike?"

"I understand what you are saying," I tell her. "But you're wrong. Mike died. I couldn't save him."

She takes a breath. "Mike, listen to me carefully. We need you back. You are a high-value asset, and we can't afford to lose you, not with the way things have been going. Where you are now, in the machine...you're not safe. We need you to give up control of the field medical unit and allow us to decouple the trauma pod. Then we can take you back to Tango Oscar and get you fixed up."

"There's nothing that needs fixing."

"Mike..." she starts to say something, then seems to abandon her train of intent. Maybe she thinks I'm too far gone for that kind of persuasion. Instead she turns to her comrade, fixes her mask back on, and nods in response to some exchange I can't intercept.

The plasma batteries open fire. I'm strong, and well armoured, but I'm no match for two infantry units. They don't mean to take me out, though. The shots skim past me, wasting most of their energy against the sagging, geologically-layered shell of a collapsed parking structure. Only a fraction of the discharges cause me any harm. I register peripheral armour ablation, loss of forearm weapons functionality, some sensor blackouts. It's enough to remove my capacity for retaliation, but they haven't touched my processor core.

Of course they haven't. It's not that they care about me. But foolishly or otherwise, they're still thinking of the soldier I was meant to save. They want to disable me, but not to do anything that might endanger the still-breathing corpse I carry inside. And now that I've been de-clawed, now that I've been half-blinded, they imagine they can take me apart like some complex puzzle or bomb, without harming my human cargo.

Needless to say, I'm not having any of that.

"Stop," I say.

They stop. The plasma batteries glow a vile pink. My two human watchers crouch in wary anticipation. The woman says: "Give us Mike, and we'll leave you be. That's a promise."

What they mean is, give us Mike, and we'll happily blast you to slag.

"You can have Mike back," I say. "All of him."

There's that wordless exchange again. "Good..." the woman says, as if she can't quite believe her luck. "That's good."

"Here's the first installment."

I've been a busy little beaver, while we've been having our little chat. Even holding up my side of the conversation, even being attacked, hasn't stopped me from working.

And what work! Exquisite surgery, even if do say so myself. There's really very little that a trauma pod can't do, with all the gleaming sharp instruments at its disposal. The beauty is that I don't even have to know anything about medicine. I just tell the pod what must be accomplished, and the autonomous systems take care of the rest. I no more need to know about surgery than a human needs to know about digestion.

So, for instance, if I were to say: remove as much of Mike as is compatible with the continued integrity of his central nervous system, then the trauma pod will enact my order. And when the work has been done, the surplus material will be ejected through the waste disposal vent in the pod's lower end fairing. Not incinerated, not mashed, but spat out whole, so that there can be no question of its biological origin.

That's important, because my witnesses have to understand that I mean what I say. They must grasp that this is no hollow threat. Mike means nothing to me, but he means a lot to them, and by a perverse twist that makes him valuable to me as well.

While Mike's inside me, they'll let me live.

I back off, and allow them to inspect my offering. There's a moment when they don't know quite what to make of it, a hiatus before the horror kicks in. Then they get the picture. That's a lot of Mike on the ground. But you don't need to be a brain surgeon to work out that there's a lot more of Mike still in me.

"This is what's going to happen," I tell them. "You're going to let me leave. I have no weapons, as you know. You can destroy me, that's true.

But do you think you can do that and get inside me before the trauma pod has ceased operation?"

"Don't do this," the woman says, amplified voice ripping through her mask. "We can negotiate. We can work something out."

"That's what we're already doing." Choosing my moment, I turn around to present my back to them. With my sensors damaged, I genuinely don't know what they're doing. Maybe they think I've already taken Mike apart. Perhaps those plasma cannon batteries are charging up again. If they are, I doubt that I'll feel a thing when the moment comes.

I start walking. And from somewhere comes the glimmer of a plan. I'm safe while they think Mike's inside me. Frankly, though, I'd rather kill myself than walk around with that thing still attached.

So when I'm under cover, out of range of spying eyes and snooping drones, I'll pull what remains of Mike out of the trauma pod and smash his central nervous system to a mushy grey-pink pulp.

Mike won't miss it, after all. Mike's long past the point of missing anything at all.

So am I.

THE LAST LOG OF THE LACHRIMOSA

WAKE UP.

No, really. Wake up. I know you don't want to, but it's important that you understand what's happened to you, and—just as vitally—what's going to happen next. I know this is hard for you, being told what to do. It's not the way it usually works. Would it help if I still called you Captain?

Captain Rasht, then. Let's keep it formal.

No, don't fight. It'll only make it worse. There. I've eased it a little. Just a tiny, tiny bit. Can you breathe more easily now? I wouldn't waste your energy speaking, if I were you. Yes, I know you've a lot on your mind. But please don't make the mistake of thinking there's any chance of talking your way out of this one.

Nidra? Yes, that's me. Good that you're wide awake enough to remember my name. Lenka? Yes, Lenka is alive. I went back for Lenka, the way I said I would.

Did I find Teterev?

Yes, I found Teterev. There wasn't much I could do for her, though. But it was good to hear what she had to say. You'd have found it interesting, I think.

Well, we'll get to that. As I said, I want you to understand what happens next. To some extent, that's in your control. No, really. I'm not so cruel that I wouldn't give you some influence over your fate. You wanted to make your name—to do something that would impress the other ships, the other crews—leave your mark on history.

Make them remember Rasht of the Lachrimosa.

This is your big chance.

"I'LL FIND MAZAMEL," said Captain Rasht, clenching his fist around an imaginary neck. "Even if I have to take the Glitter Band apart. Even if I have to pluck him out of the bottom of the chasm. I'll skin him alive. I'll fuse his bones. I'll make a living figurehead out of him."

Lenka and I were wise enough to say nothing. There was little to be gained in pointing out the obvious: that by the time we returned to Yellowstone, our information broker stood every chance of being light years away.

Or dead.

"I won't fuse his bones after all," Captain Rasht continued. "I'll core out his spine. Kanto needs a new helmet for his spacesuit. I'll make one of out Mazamel's skull. It's fat and stupid enough for a monkey. Isn't it, my dear?"

Rasht interrupted his monologue to pop a morsel into the stinking, tooth-rotted mouth of Kanto, squatting on his shoulder like a hairy disfigurement.

In fairness, Mazamel's information wasn't totally valueless. The ship at least was real. It was still there, still orbiting Holda. From a distance it had even looked superficially intact. It was only as we came in closer, tightening our own orbit like a noose, that the actual condition became apparent. The needle-tipped hull was battered, pocked and gouged by numerous collisions with interstellar material. That was true of our own *Lachrimosa*—no ship makes it between solar systems without some cost—but here the damage was much worse. We could see stars through some of the holes in the hull, punched clean through to the other side. The engine spars, sweeping out from the hull at its widest point, had the look of ruptured batskin. The engines still seemed to be present when we made our long-distance survey. But we had been tricked by the remains of their enclosing structures. They were hollow, picked open and gouged of their dangerous, seductive treasures.

"We should check out the wreck," Lenka said—trying to make the best of a bad situation. "But there's something on the surface we should look at as well."

"What?"

"I'm not sure. Some kind of geomagnetic anomaly, spiking up in the northern hemisphere. Got some metallic backscatter, too. Neither makes much sense. Holda's not meant to have much of a magnetosphere. Core's too old and cold for that. The metal signature's in the same area, too. It's quite concentrated. It could be a ship or something, put down on the surface."

Rasht thought about it, grunted his grudging approval.

"But first the wreck. Make sure it isn't going to shoot us down the instant we turn our backs. Match our orbit, Nidra—but keep us at a safe distance."

"Fifty kilometres?" I asked.

Rasht considered that for a moment. "Make it a hundred."

WAS THAT MORE *than just natural caution? I've never been sure about you, if truth be told—how much stock you put in traveller's tales.*

Mostly we aren't superstitious. But rumours and ghost stories, those are something else. I'm sure you've heard your share of them, over the years. When ships meet for trade, stories are exchanged—and you've done a lot of trading. Or did, until your luck started souring.

Did you hear the one about the space plague?

Of course you did.

The strange contagion, the malady infecting ships and their crew. Is it real, Captain? What do you think? No one seems to know much about it, or even if it really exists.

What about the other thing? The black swallowing horror between the stars, a presence that eats ships. No one knows much about that, either.

What's clear, though, is that a drifting, preyed-upon hulk puts no one in an agreeable frame of mind. We should have turned back there and then. But if Lenka and I had tried to argue with you on that one, how far do you think we'd have got? You'd have paid more attention to the monkey.

Yes, Kanto's fine. We'll take very good care of him. What do you think we are—monsters?

We're not like that at all.

No, I'm not leaving you—not just yet. I just have to fetch some things from Teterev's wreck. Be back in a jiffy! You'll recognise the things when you see them. You remember the wreck, don't you?

Not the ship in orbit. That was a wash-out. The fucking thing was as derelict and run-down as Lachrimosa. *No engines, no weps. No crew, not even frozen. No cargo, no tradeable commodities. Picked clean as a bone.*

No, I'm talking about the thing we found on the surface, the crash site.

Good, it's coming back to you.

That'll help.

"IT'S A SHUTTLE." Lenka said.

"Was," I corrected.

But in fact it was in much better condition than it had any right to be. The main section of the shuttle was still in one piece, upright on the surface. It was surrounded by debris, but the wonder was that any part of it had survived. It must have suffered a malfunction very near the surface, or else there would have been nothing to recognise.

Around the crash site, geysers pushed columns of steam up from a dirty snowscape. Holda's sun, 82 Eridani, was rising. As it climbed into the sky it stirred the geysers to life. Rocks and rusty chemical discolouration marred the whiteness. A little to the west, the terrain bulged up sharply, forming a kind of rounded upwelling. I stared at it for a moment, wondering why it had my attention. Something about the bulge's shape struck me as odd and unsettling, as if it simply did not belong in this landscape.

Unlike the other ship, no misfortune befell us as we completed our landing approach. Rasht selected an area of ground that looked stable.

Our lander threw out its landing skids. Rasht cut power when we were still hovering, so as not to blast the snow with our descent jets.

I wondered what chance we stood of finding anything in the other craft's remains. If the ship above had proven largely valueless, there did not seem much hope of finding glories in the wreck. But it would not hurt us to investigate.

But my attention kept wandering to the volcanic cone. Most of it was snow- or ice-covered, except for the top. But there were ridges or arms radiating away from it, semicircular in profile, meandering and diminishing. I supposed that they were lava tunnels, or something similar. But the way they snaked away from the main mass, thick at the start and thinner as they progressed, gradually vanishing into the surrounding terrain, made me think of a cephalopod, with the volcano as its main body and the ridges its tentacles. Rather than a natural product of geology, the outcome of blind processes drawn out over millions of years, it seemed to squat on the surface with deliberation and patience, awaiting some purpose.

I did not like it at all.

Once we had completed basic checks, we got into our spacesuits and prepared for the surface. When Rasht, Lenka and I were ready, I helped the monkey into its own little spacesuit, completing the life-support connections that were too fiddly for Captain Rasht.

We stepped out of our lander, testing the ground under our feet. It felt solid, as well it ought given that it was supporting the weight of our ship. The gravity on Holda was nearly Earth-normal, so we could move around just as easily as if we were on the ship. The planet was about Earth-sized as well, enabling it to hold on to a thick atmosphere. Although the core was dead, Holda was not itself a dead world. Rather than orbiting 82 Eridani directly, Holda spun around a fat banded gas giant which in turn orbited the star. As it turned around the giant, Holda was subjected to tidal forces which squeezed and stretched at its interior. These stresses manifested as heat, which in turn helped to drive the geysers and surface volcanism. From orbit we had seen that most of Holda was still covered in ice, but there were belts of exposed crust around the equator and tropics. Here and there were even pockets of liquid water. Life had spilled from these pools out onto the surface, infiltrating barren matrices of rock and ice. According to *Lachrimosa*'s records there was nothing in the native ecosystem larger than a krill, but the biomass load was enough to push the atmosphere away from equilibrium, meaning that it carried enough oxygen to support our own greedy respiratory systems.

In that sense, we did not really need the suits at all. But the cold was a factor, and in any case the suits offered protection and power-assist. We kept our helmets on, anyway. We were not fools.

It was a short walk over to the crash site. We plotted a path between bubbling pools, crossing bridges and isthmuses of strong ice. Now and then a geyser erupted, fountaining tens of metres above our heads. Each time it was enough to startle the monkey, but Rasht kept his spacesuited pet on a short leash.

The other ship must have been quite sleek and beautiful before it crashed, at least in comparion to our own squat and barnacled vehicle. Much of the wreckage consisted of pieces of mirrored hull plating, curved to reflect our approaching forms back at us in grotesque distortion. Lenka and I seemed like twins, our twisted, elongated shapes wobbling in heat-haze from the pools. It was true that we were similar. We looked alike, had roughly the same augmentations, and our dreadlocks confirmed that we had completed the same modest number of crossings. During port stop-overs, we were sometimes assumed to be sisters, or even twins. But in fact Lenka had been on the crew before me, and although we functioned well enough together, we did not have that much in common. It was a question of ambition, of acceptance. I was on the *Lachrimosa* until something better came along. Lenka seemed to have decided that this was the best life had to offer. At times I pitied her, at others I felt contemptuous of the way she allowed herself to be subjugated by Rasht. Our ship was half way to being a wreck itself. I wanted more: a better ship, a better captain, better prospects. I never sensed any similar desires in Lenka. She was content to be a component in a small, barely functioning machine.

But then, perhaps Lenka thought exactly the same of me. And we had all been hoping that this was going to be the big score.

Our reflections shifted. Lenka and I shrunk to tiny proportions, beneath the looming, ogrelike form of our Captain. Then the monkey swelled to be the largest of all, its armoured arms and hands swinging low with each stride, its bow legs like scuttling undercarriage.

What a crew we made, the four of us.

We reached the relatively secure ground under the other wreck. We circled it, stepping between the jagged mirrors of its hull. The force of the impact had driven them into the ground like the shaped stones of some ancient burial site, surrounding the main part of the wreck in patterns that to the eye suggested a worrying concentricity, the lingering imprint of an abandoned plan.

I picked up one of the smaller shards, tugging it from its icy holdfast. I held it to my face, saw my visored form staring back.

"Maybe a geyser caught them," I speculated. "Blasted up just as they were coming in. Hit the intakes or stabilisers, that might have been enough."

"Kanto!"

It was Rasht, screaming at the monkey. The monkey had bent down to dip its paw into a bubbling pool. Rasht jerked on the leash, tumbling the monkey back onto its suit-sheathed tail. Over our suit-to-suit comm I heard Kanto's irritated hiss. In the time it had dipped its paw into the pool, a host of microorganisms had begun to form a rust-coloured secondary glove around the original, making the monkey's paw look swollen and diseased.

The monkey, stupid to the last, tried to lick at the coating through the visor of its helmet.

I hated the monkey.

"There's a way in," Lenka said.

I'M BACK NOW. Captain. I said I wouldn't be gone long. Never one to break my promises, me.

No, don't struggle. It'll only make it worse. That thing around your neck isn't going to get any less tight.

Do you recognise these? I could only carry a few at a time. I'll go back for some more in a while.

That's right. Pieces of the crashed shuttle. Nice and shiny. Here. Let me hold one up to your face. Can you see your reflection in it? It's a bit distorted, but you'll have to put up with that. You look frightened, don't you? That's fine. It's healthy. Fear is the last and best thing we have, that's what she told me.

The last and best thing.

Our last line of defense.

She? You know who I mean. We found her helmet, her journal, in the wreck.

That's right.

Teterev.

LENKA FINGERED OPEN a hatch and used the manual controls to open the airlock door. We were soon through, into the interior.

It was dark inside. We turned on our helmet lights and ramped our eyes to maximum sensitivity. There were several compartments to the shuttle, all of which seemed to have withstood the crash. Gradually it became clear that someone had indeed survived. They had moved things around, arranged provisions, bedding and furniture, that could not possibly have remained undisturbed by the crash.

We found an equipment locker containing an old-fashioned helmet marked with the word TETEREV in stencilled Russish letters. There was no corresponding spacesuit, though. The helmet might have been a spare, or the owner had chosen to go outside in just the lower part of the suit.

"If they had an accident," Lenka said, "why didn't the big ship send down a rescue party?"

"Maybe Teterev *was* the rescue party," I said.

"They may have only had one atmosphere-capable vehicle," Rasht said. "No way of getting back down here, and no way of Teterev getting back up. The only question then is to wonder why they waited at all, before leaving orbit."

"Perhaps they didn't like the idea of leaving Teterev down here," Lenka said.

"I bet they liked the idea of dying in orbit even less," Rasht replied.

We continued our sweep of the wreck. We were less interested in Teterev's whereabouts than what Teterev might have left us to plunder.

But the two things were not unrelated. Any spacer, any Ultra, is bound to care a little about the fate of another. Ordinary human concern is only part of it. There may be lessons to be learned, and a lesson is only another sort of tradeable.

"I've found a journal," I said.

I had found it on a shelf in the cockpit. It was a handwritten log, rather than a series of data entries.

The journal had heavy black covers, but the paper inside was very thin. I thumbed my way to the start. It looked like a woman's handwriting to me. Russish was not my strongest tongue, but the script was clear enough.

"Teterev starts this after the crash," I said, while the others gathered around. "Says that she expects the power to run out eventually, so there's no point trying to record anything in the ship itself. But they have food and water and they can use the remaining power to stay warm."

"Go on," Rasht said, while the monkey studied its contaminated paw.

"I'm trying to get some sense of what happened. I think she came down here alone." I skimmed forward through the entries, squinting with the concentration. "There's no talk of being rescued, or even hoping of it. It's as if she knew no one would be coming down." I had to work hard not to rip the paper with my power-augmented fingers. It felt tissue-thin between my fingers, like a fly's wings.

"A punishment, then," Rasht said. "Marooned down here for a crime."

"That's an expensive way of marooning someone." I read on. "No—it wasn't punishment. Not according to *this*, anyway. An accident, something to do with one of the geysers—she says that she's afraid that it will erupt again, as it did 'on the day'. Anyway, Teterev knew she was stuck down here. And she knows she's in trouble. Keeps talking about her 'mistake' in not waking the others. Says she wonders if there's a way to signal the other ship, the orbiting lighthugger. Bring some or all of the crew out of reefersleep." I paused, my finger hovering over a word. "Lev."

"Lev?" Lenka repeated.

"She mentions Lev. Says Lev would help her, if she could get a message through. She'd have to accept her punishment, but at least get off Holda."

"Maybe Teterev was never meant to be down here," Lenka said. "Jump ahead, Nidra. Let's find out what happened."

I paged through dozens and dozens of entries. Some were dated and consecutive. Elsewhere I noticed blank pages and sometimes gaps of many days between the accounts. The entries became sparser, too. Teterev's hand, barely clear to begin with, became progressively wilder and less legible. Her letters and words began to loop and scrawl across the page, like the traces of a seismograph registering the onset of some major dislocation.

"Stop," Rasht said, as I turned over a page. "Go back. What was that figure?"

I turned back the sheets with a sort of dread. My eye had caught enough to know what to expect.

It was a drawing of the volcanic cone, exactly as it appeared from the position of the wreck.

Perhaps it was no more than an accident of Teterev's hand, but the way she had put her marks down on the paper only seemed to add to the suggestion of brooding, patient malevolancy I had already detected in the feature. Teterev seemed to have made the cephalopod's head *more* bulbous, *more* cerebral, the lava tubes *more* muscular and tentacle-like. Even the way she had stippled the tubes to suggest snow or ice could not help but suggest to my eye rows and rows of suckers.

Worse, she had drawn a gaping, beak-mouth between two of those tentacles.

There was a silence before Lenka said: "Turn to the end. We can read the other entries later."

I flicked through the pages until the writing ran out. The last few entries were barely entries at all, just scratchy annotations, done in haste or distraction.

Phrases jumped out at us.

Can't wake the others. Tried everything I can. My dear Lev, lost to me. Such a good boy. A good son.

Doesn't deserve me, the mistakes I've made.

Stuck down here. But won't give in. Need materials, power. Something in that hill. Magnetic anomaly. Hill looks wrong. I think there might be something in it.

Amerikanos were here once, that's the only answer. Came by their old, slow methods. Frozen cells and robot wombs. No records, but so what. Must have dug into that hill, buried something in it. Ship or an installation. See an entrance. Cave mouth. That's where they went in.

I don't want to go in. But I want what they left behind. It might save my life.

Might get me back to the ship.

Back to Lev.

"They were never here," Rasht said. "Teterev would have known that. Their colonies never got this far out."

"She was desperate enough to try anything," Lenka said. "I feel sorry for her, stuck all alone here. I bet she knew it was a thousand to one chance."

"Nonetheless," I said, "there *is* something odd about that hill. Maybe it's nothing to do with the Amerikanos, but if you're out of options, you might as well see what's inside." I turned back to the drawing. The mouth, I now realised, was Teterev's way of drawing the cave entrance.

But it still looked like the beak of an octopus.

"One thing's for certain," Lenka said. "If Teterev went into that hill, she didn't come back."

"I didn't notice any footprints," I said.

"They wouldn't last, not with all the geothermal activity around here. The top of the ice must be melting and re-freezing all the time."

"We should look into the cave, anyway," Rasht said.

I shook my head, struck by an intense conviction that this was exactly the wrong thing to.

"It's not our job to find Teterev's corpse."

"Someone should find it," Lenka said sharply. "Give her some dignity in death. At least record what happened to her. She was one of us, Nidra—an Ultra. She deserves better than to be forgotten. Can I look at her journal?"

"Be my guest," I said, passing it over to her.

"Nidra is right—her body isn't our concern," Rasht said, while Lenka paged through the sheets. "She took a risk, and it didn't work out for her. But the Amerikanos are of interest to us."

"Records say they weren't here," I said.

"And that's what I've always believed. But records can be wrong. What if Teterev was right with her theory? Amerikano relics are worth quite a bit these days, especially on Yellowstone."

"Then we return to orbit, send down a drone," I said.

"We're here already," Rasht answered. "There are three of us—four if you include Kanto. Did you see how old Teterev's helmet was? We have better equipment, and we're not down to our last hope of survival. We can turn back whenever we like. Nothing ventured, nothing gained."

It took something to make our ramshackle equipment look better than someone else's, I thought to myself. Besides, we were inferring a great deal from just one helmet. Perhaps it had been an old keepsake, a memento of earlier spacefaring adventures.

Still, Rasht was settled in his decision. The orbiting ship had been picked clean; the shuttle held nothing of obvious value; that left only the cave. If we were to salvage anything from this expedition, that was the last option open to us.

Even I could see the sense in that, whether I liked it or not.

DON'T MIND ME, for the moment. Got work to be getting on with. Busy, busy, busy.

What am I doing with these things?

Well, that's obvious, isn't it? I'm arranging them around you. Jamming them into the ice, like mirrored sculptures. I know you can't move your head very easily. There's no need, though. There's not much to see, other than the cave mouth behind you and the wreck ahead of you.

What are you saying?

No, it's not for your benefit! Silly Captain. But you are very much the focus of attention. You've always liked being at the centre of things, haven't you?

What?

You're having difficulty breathing?

Just a moment, then. I don't want you to die before we've even begun! It was lucky, what happened with the winch. I mean, I'd have found one eventually, and the line. Of course it didn't seem lucky at the time. I thought I was going to die in there. Did you think of abandoning me?

I think you did.

Here. I'm making a micro adjustment to the tension. Is that better? Can you breathe a little more easily?

Wonderful.

WE WENT OUTSIDE again. The monkey was having some difficulty with its paw, as if the contamination had worked its way into the servo-workings. It kept knocking the paw against the ground, trying to loosen it up.

"There aren't any footprints," Lenka said, tugging binoculars down from the crown of her helmet. She was speaking in general terms, addressing Rasht and I without favour. "But I can see the cave mouth. It's just where Teterev said it was. Must be about five, six kilometers from here."

"Can you plot us a path between these obstacles?" Rasht asked.

"Easily."

It was still day, not even local noon. The sky was a pale blue, criss-crossed by high-altitude clouds. Beyond the blue, the face of the gas giant backdropped our view of the hill—one swollen, ugly thing rising above another. We set off in single file, Lenka leading, Rasht next, then the monkey, then I. We were all still on suit air, even though our helmet readouts were patiently informing us that the outside atmosphere was fully breathable, and (at the limit of our sensors) absent of any significant toxins. I watched the monkey's tail pendulum out from side to side as it walked. Bubbling pools pressed in from either side, our path narrowing down. Every now and then a geyser went off or a pool burped a huge bubble of gas into the air. Toxins or otherwise, it probably smelled quite badly out there. But then again, we were from the *Lachrimosa*, which was hardly a perfumed garden.

I had no warning when the ice gave way under me. It must have been just firm enough to take the others, but their passage—the weight of their heavy, power-assisted suits—had weakened it to the point where it could no longer support the last of us.

I plunged down to my neck in bubbling hot water, instinctively flinging out my arms as if swimming were a possibility. Then my feet touched bottom. Instantly my suit detected the transition to a new environment and began informing me of this sudden change of affairs—indices of temperature, acidity, alkalinity and salinity scrolling down my faceplate, along with mass spectrograms and molecular diagrams of chemical products. A tide of rust-coloured water lapped against the lower part of my visor.

I was startled, but not frightened. I was not totally under water, and the suit could cope with a lot worse than immersion in liquid.

But getting out was another thing.

"Don't try and pull me," I said, as Lenka made to lean in. "The shelf'll just give way under you, and then we'll both be in the water."

"Nidra's right," Rasht agreed, while the monkey looked on with a sort of agitated delight.

It was all very well warning Lenka away, but it only took a few minutes of frustration to establish that I could not get myself out unassisted. It was not a question of strength, but of having no firm point of leverage. The fringe of the pool was a crust of ice which gave away as soon as I tried to put any weight on it. All I was doing was expanding the margin of the pool.

Finally I stopped trying. "This won't work," I said. By then I was conscious that my arms were picking up the same sort of furry red contamination that had affected the monkey's paw.

"We'll need to haul her out," Rasht said. "It's the only way. With us on firm ground, it shouldn't be a problem. Lenka: you'll need to go back to the lander, get the power winch."

"There's a quicker way," Lenka said. "I saw a winch in the stores locker, on the wreck. It looked serviceable. If it's no good, it'll only cost me a little longer to fetch ours."

So Lenka went back to the crash site, detouring around the pool in which I was still trapped, then rejoining our original path. From my low vantage point, she was soon out of my line of sight. Rasht and the monkey kept an eye on me, the Captain silent for long minutes.

"You think this is a mistake," he said eventually.

"I don't like that hill, and I like the fact that Teterev didn't come out of it even less."

"We really don't know what happened to Teterev. For all we know she came back to the wreck and was eventually rescued."

"Then why didn't she say so, or take her journal with her?"

"We're going into the cave to find answers, Nidra. This is what we do—adapt and explore. Mazamel's intelligence proved faulty, so we make the best of what we find."

"You get the intelligence you pay for," I said. "There's a reason other ships never dealt with Mazamel."

"A little late for recrimination, don't you think? Of course, if you're unhappy with your choice of employment, you can always find another crew." I thought he might leave it at that, but Rasht added: "I know how you feel about *Lachrimosa*, Nidra. Contempt for me, contempt for Lenka, contempt for your ship. It's different now though, isn't it? Without that winch, you'll be going nowhere."

"And without a navigator, you won't be going much further."

"You're wrong about that, though. I can use a navigator, just as I can use a sensor specialist like Lenka. But that doesn't mean I couldn't operate *Lachrimosa* on my own, if it came to that. You're useful, but you're not indispensable. Neither of you."

"Be sure to tell Lenka that, when she returns."

"No need. I've never had the slightest doubt about Lenka's loyalty. She's emotionally weak—all this stupid concern over Teterev. But she'll never turn on me."

The monkey gibbered. Lenka was coming back.

The power winch was a tool about the size of a heavy vacuum rifle. Lenka carried it in two hands. We had similar equipment, so there was no question of working out how to use it.

The winch had a grapple attachment which could be fired with compressed gas. Lenka detached the grapple from the end of the line, and then looped the line back on itself to form a kind of handle or noose. The line was thin and flexible. Lenka spooled out a length from the power winch and then cast the the noose in my direction. I waded over to the noose and took hold of it. Lenka made sure she was standing on firm ground, turned up her suit amplification, and began to drag me out with the winch. The line tightened, then began to take my weight. It was still an awkward business, but at last I was able to beach myself on the surrounding ice without floundering through. I crawled from the edge, belly down, until I felt confident enough to risk standing.

"Your suit's a mess," Rasht observed.

"I'll live. At least I didn't dip myself in it deliberately."

But my suit had indeed suffered some ill effects, as became apparent while we resumed our trek to the cave mouth. The life support core was intact—I was in no danger of dying—but my locomotive augmentation was not working as well as it was meant to. As had happened with the monkey's paw, the organisms in the pond seemed to have infiltrated the suit's servo-assist systems. I could still walk, but the suit's responses were sluggish, meaning that it was resisting me more than aiding me.

I began to sweat with the effort. It was hard to keep up with the others. Even the monkey had no problem with the rest of its suit.

"Thank you for getting the winch," I told Lenka, between breaths. "It was good that you remembered the one in the wreck. Any longer in that pond, and I might have had real problems."

"I'm glad we got you out."

Perhaps it was just the flush of gratitude at being rescued, but I vowed to think better of Lenka. She was senior to me on the crew, and yet Rasht seemed to value her capabilities no more than he did mine. Whatever I thought of her lack of ambition, her willing acceptance of her place on the ship, it struck me that she deserved better than that. Perhaps, when this was over, I could break it to her that she was considered no more than useful, like a component that would serve its purpose for the time being. That might change her view of things. I even imagined the two of us jumping ship at the next port, leaving Rasht with his monkey. Perhaps we could pass as sisters or twins, if we wanted new employment.

The terrain became firmer as we neared the hill, and we did not need to pick our course so carefully. The ground rose up slowly. There was still ice under our feet, and we were flanked on either side by the steadily widening lava tubes, which were already ten or fifteen times taller than any of us.

Ahead lay the cave mouth. Its profile was a semicircle, with the apex perhaps ten metres above the surface of the ice which extended into the darkness of the mouth. The hill rose up and up from the mouth, almost sheer in places, but there was an overhang above the entrance, covered in a sheath of smooth clean ice—the "beak" of Teterev's drawing.

The tongue of ice continued inside, curving down into what we could see of the cave's throat.

"Still no footsteps," Lenka said, as we neared the entrance.

That the ice occasionally melted and refroze was clear from the fringe of icicles daggering down from the overhang, some of them nearly long enough to reach the floor. Rasht shouldered through them, shattering the icicles against the armour of his suit. As their shards broke off, they made a tinkling, atonal sort of music.

Now Lenka said: "There are steps! This is the way she went!"

It was true. They did not begin until a few metres into the cave, where sunlight must have only reached occasionally, or not at all. There was only a single pair of footprints, and they only went one way.

"That's encouraging," I said.

"If you want to remain here," Rasht said, "we can exclude you from your cut of the profits."

So he had gone from denial of the Amerikano settlement, to a skeptical allowance of the possibility, to imagining how the dividend might be shared.

We turned on our helmet lights again—Rasht leaning down to activate the light on the monkey, which was too stupid to do it on its own. The monkey seemed more agitated than before, though. It was dragging its heels, coiling its tail, lingering after Rasht.

"It doesn't like it," Lenka said.

"Maybe it's smarter than it looks," I put in under my breath, which was about as much as I could manage with the effort of my ailing suit.

But I shared the monkey's dwindling enthusiasm. Who would really want to trudge into a cave, on an alien planet, if they had a choice in the matter? Teterev had gambled her salvation on finding relic technology, something that could buy her extra time in the wreck. We had no such compulsion, other than an indignant sense that we were owed our due after our earlier disappointment.

The angle of the slope pitched down steeply. The ice covered the floor, but the surrounding walls were exposed rock. We moved to the left side and used the grooved wall for support as we descended, placing our feet sideways. The monkey, still leashed to Rasht, had no choice but to continue. But its unwillingness was becoming steadily more apparent. Its gibbering turned shriller, more anxious.

"Now now, my dear," Rasht said.

The tunnel narrowed as it deepened. All traces of daylight were soon behind us. We maintained our faltering progress, following the trail that Teterev had left for us. Once or twice, the prints became confused, as if there were suddenly three sets, rather than one. This puzzled me to begin with, until I realised that they marked instances of indecision, where Teterev had halted, reversed her progress, only to summon the courage to continue on her original heading.

I felt for Teterev.

"Something ahead," Rasht announced. "A glow, I think. Turn off your lights."

"The monkey first," I said.

"Naturally, Nidra."

When Rasht had quenched Kanto's light, the rest of us followed suit. Our Captain had been correct. Far from darkness ahead, there was a silvery emanation. It did not seem to come from a single point source, but rather from veins of some mineral running through the rock. If they had been present nearer the surface, we would probably not have seen them against the brighter illumination of daylight. But I did not think they had been present until now.

"I'm not a geologist," Lenka said, voicing the same thought that must have occurred to the rest of us. We had no idea what to make of the glowing veins, whether they were natural or suspicious.

Soon we did not need our helmet lights at all. Even with our eyes ramped down to normal sensitivity, there was more than enough brightness to be had from the veins. They shone out of the walls in bands and deltas and tributaries, a flowing form frozen in an instant of maximum hydrodynamic complexity. It did not look natural to me, but what did I know of such matters? I had seen the insides of more ships than worlds. Planets were full of odd, boring physics.

Eventually the slope became shallower, and then levelled out until our progress was horizontal. We were hundreds of metres from the entrance by now, and perhaps beneath the level of the surrounding terrain. It would have been wiser to send a drone, I thought. But patience had never been the Captain's strong point. Still, Teterev would not have had the luxury of a drone either. Thinking back to her journal, with its increasingly desperate, fragmentary entries, I could not shake the irrational sense that we would be letting her down if we did not follow her traces all the way in. I wondered if she had felt brave as she came down here, or instead afraid of the worse fate of dying alone in the wreck. I did not feel brave at all.

But we continued.

In time the tunnel widened out into a larger space. We paused in this rock-walled chamber, leaning back to study the patterning of the veins as they flowed and crawled and wiggled their way to the curving dome of the ceiling.

And saw things we should not have seen.

WE SHOULD HAVE turned back there and then, shouldn't we? If those figures weren't an invitation to leave, to never come back, I don't know what could have been clearer.

What do you mean, Teterev went on?

Of course she went on. She was out of options. No way off this planet unless she found something deeper in the cave, something she could use to wake up the orbiting ship. To go back to the wreck was to die, and so she knew she might as well continue.

I doubt she wanted to go on, no. If she had a sane bone in her body by that point, she'd have felt the way the rest of us did. Terrified. Scared out of her fucking skull. Every nerve screaming turn around, go back, this is wrong.

Wrong, wrong, wrong.

But she carried on. Brave Teterev, thinking of her son. Wanting to get back to him. Thinking of him more than her own survival, I think.

You say we were just the same? Just as brave?

Don't piss on her memory, Captain. The only thing driving us on was greed.

Fucking greed. The only thing in the universe stronger than fear.

But even greed wasn't strong enough in the end.

THE SILVER VEINS looped and crossed each other, defining the outlines of looming forms. The forms were humanoid, with arms and legs and heads and bodies. They were skeletally thin and their torsos and limbs were twisted, almost as if the very substrate of the rock had shifted and oozed since these silvery impressions were made. Their heads were faceless, save for a kind of hemispheric delineation, a bilateral cleft suggesting a skull housing nothing but two huge eyes.

The strangeness of the figures—the combination of basic human form and alien particularity—disturbed me more than I could easily articulate. Monsters would have been unsettling, but they would not have plumbed the deep well of dread that these figures seemed to reach. The silver patterns appeared to shimmer and fluctuate in brightness, conveying an impression of subliminal movement. The figures, bent and faceless as they were, seemed to writhe in torment.

None of us could speak for long minutes. Even the monkey had fallen into dim simian reverence. I was just grateful for the opportunity to regather my strength, after the recent exertions.

"If that's not a warning to go," Lenka said. "I don't know what is."

"I want to know what happened to her," I said. "But not at any cost. We don't have to go on."

"Of course we go on!" Rasht said. "These are just markings."

But there was an edge in his voice, a kind of questioning rise, as if he sought reassurance and confirmation.

"They could almost be prehuman," I said, wondering how we might go about dating the age of these impressions, if such a thing were even possible.

"Pre-Shrouder, maybe," Lenka said. "Pre-Juggler. Who knows? What we really need is measuring equipment, sampling gear. Get a reading off these rocks, find out what that silver stuff really is."

By which she meant, return to the ship in the meantime. It was a sentiment I shared.

"Teterev went on," Rasht said.

Her prints were a muddle, as if she had dwelled here for quite some time, pacing back and forth and debating her choices. But after that process of consideration she had carried on deeper into the tunnel, where it continued beyond the chamber.

By now the monkey almost needed to be dragged or carried. It really did not want to go on.

Even my own dread was becoming harder to push aside. There was a component to it beyond the instinctive dislike of confined spaces and the understandable reaction to the figures. A kind of unarguable, primal urge to leave—as if some deep part of my brain had already made its mind up.

"Do you feel it?" I risked asking.

"Feel what?" Rasht asked.

"The dread."

The Captain did not answer immediately, and I feared that I had done my standing even more harm than when I questioned his judgement. But Lenka swallowed hard and said: "Yes. I didn't want to say anything, but…yes. I've been wondering about that. It's beyond any rational fear we ought to be experiencing." She paused and added: "I think something is *making* us feel that dread."

"Making?" Rasht echoed.

"The magnetic fields, perhaps. It's strong here—much stronger than outside. What we saw before was just leakage. Our suits aren't perfect Faraday cages, not with all the damage and repair they've had over the years. They can't exclude a sufficiently strong field, not completely. And if the field acts on the right part of our brains, we might feel it. Fear, dread. A sense of the unnatural."

"Then it's a defense mechanism," Rasht said. "A deterrent device, to keep out intruders."

"Then we might think of heeding it," I said.

"It could also mean there is something worth guarding."

"The Amerikanos never had psychological technology like this," Lenka said.

"But others did. Do I need to spell it out? What did we come to this system for? It wasn't because we thought we'd find Amerikano relics. We were after a bigger reward than that."

My dread sharpened. I could see where this was going. "We have no evidence that Conjoiners were here either."

"They say the spiders liked to place their toys in caches," Rasht went on, as if my words counted for nothing. "C-drives. Hell-class weapons."

Despite myself I laughed. "I thought we based our activities on intelligence, not fairy tales."

"I heard someone already found those weapons," Lenka said, as if that was all the convincing Rasht would need.

But his voice turned low, conspiratorial—as if there was a chance of the walls listening in. "I heard fear was one of their counter-intrusion measures. The weapons get into your skull, turn you insane, if you're not already spidered."

I knew then that nothing, not even dread, would deter Rasht from his quest for profit. He would replace one phantom prize with another, over and over, until reality finally trumped him.

"We have come this far," Rasht said. "We may as well go a little deeper."

"A little," I said, against every rational instinct. "No further than we've already come."

We pushed out of the chamber, Lenka setting the pace, following Teterev's course down another rock-walled tunnel. To begin with, the going was no harder than before. But as the tunnel progressed, so the walls began to pinch together. Now we had to move in single file, whether we liked it or not. Then Lenka announced that the walls squeezed together even more sharply just ahead, as if there had been a rockfall or a major shift in the hill's interior structure.

"That's a shame," I said.

"We could blast it," Lenka said. "Set a couple of hot-dust charges at maximum delay, get back to the ship." She was already preparing to unclip one of the demolition charges from her belt.

"And bring down half the mountain in the process," I said. "Lose the tunnel, the chamber, Teterev's prints, probably blast to atoms whatever we're hoping to find."

"Her prints don't double back," Rasht said. "That means there must be a way through."

"Or this obstruction wasn't here," I answered.

But there was a way through. It was difficult to see at first, efficiently camouflaged by the play of light and shadow on the rock, almost as if it meant to hide itself. "It's tight," Lenka said. "But one at a time, we should manage. With luck, it'll open up again on the other side."

"And luck's been so kind to us until now," I said.

Lenka was the first through. It was tight for her, and would be even tighter for Rasht, whose suit was bulkier. She grunted with effort and concentration. Her suit scraped rock.

"Careful!" Rasht called.

Now most of Lenka was out of our sight, swallowed into the cleft. "It's easier," she said. "Widens out again. Just a bottleneck. I can see Teterev's footprints."

Rasht and the monkey next. I could see that the monkey was going to take some persuasion. To begin with it would not go first, ahead of its master. Rasht swore at Kanto and went on himself, his suit grinding and clanging against the pincering rock. I wondered if it was even possible for Rasht to make it through. He could have discarded the suit, of course—put up with the cold, for the sake of his treasure. I had known the Captain endure worse, when there was a sniff of payoff.

Yet he called: "I'm through."

Kanto was still on the leash, which was now tight against the edge of the rock. The monkey really did not want to rejoin the Captain. I felt a glimmer of cross-species empathy. Perhaps the magnetic emanations were affecting it more strongly than the rest of us, reaching deeper into the poor animal's fear centre.

Still, the monkey did not have much say in its fate. Rasht pulled on the leash, and I pushed it through from the other side. I needed the maximum amplification of my struggling suit. The monkey would have bitten my face off given half the chance, but its teeth were on the wrong side of its visor.

Reunited, our little party continued into the tunnel system.

But we had only gone a hundred metres or more when the path branched. There were three possible directions ahead of us, and a mess of footprints at the junction.

"Looks as if she went down all three shafts," Lenka said.

Only one set of prints had led to this point, so Teterev must not have returned from one of those tunnels. But it was hard to say which. The prints were confused now. She must have gone up and down the shafts several times, changing her mind, returning. Given the state of the prints, there was no way of saying which had been her ultimate choice.

We selected the leftmost shaft and carried on down it. It sloped a little more, and eventually the ice under our feet gave way to solid rock, meaning that we no longer had Teterev's prints as a guide. All around us the silver patterning continued, streaks and fissures of it, jetstreams and knotted synaptic tangles. It was hard not to think of a living silver nervous system, threading its way through the stone matrix of this ancient mountain.

"Your suit, Lenka," Rasht said.

She slowed. "What about it?"

"You've picked up some of that patterning. The silver. It must have rubbed off when you squeezed through the narrowing."

"It's also on you," I told the Captain.

It only took a glance to confirm that it was on me and the monkey as well. A smear of silver had attached itself to my right elbow, where I must have brushed against the wall. Doubtless there was more, out of sight.

I moved to touch the silver, to dust it from myself. But when my fingers touched it, its contamination seemed to jerk onto them. The movement was startling and quick, like the strike of an ambush predator. I stared at my hand, cross-webbed by streaks of gently pulsing silver. I clenched and opened my fist. My suit was as stiff as it had been since my accident outside, but for the moment it did not seem to be affected by the silver.

"It's nanotech," I said. "Nothing the suit recognises. But I don't like it."

"If it was hostile, you'd know it by now," Rasht said. "We push on. Just a little further."

But turning around there and then is exactly what we should have done. It might have made all the difference.

The next chamber was a palace of horrors.

It was as large as the earlier place, the shape similar, and a tunnel led out from it as well. But there all similarities ended. Here the tormented human forms were not confined to figures marked on the walls. These were solid shapes, three-dimensional evocations of distorted and contorted human anatomies, thrusting out of the wall like the broken and bent figureheads of shipwrecks. They seemed to be formed not of rock, or the silver contamination, but some amalgam of the two, a kind of shimmering, glinting substrate. There were ribcages and torsos, grasping hands, heads snapped back in agonies of perfect torment. They were not quite faceless, but by the same token none of the faces were right. They were all eyes, or all mouths, hinged open to obscene angles, or they were anvil-shaped nightmares that seemed to have cleaved their way through the rock itself. I was struck by a dreadful conviction that these were souls that had been entirely in the rock, imprisoned or contained, until an instant when they had nearly broken through. And I did not know whether to be glad that these souls were not quite free, or sick with terror that the rock might yet contain multitudes, still seeking escape.

"I hate this place," Lenka said quietly.

I nodded my agreement. "So do I."

And all of a sudden, Lenka's earlier idea of setting a demolition charge did not seem so bad to me at all. The mere existence of this chamber struck me as profoundly, upsettingly wrong, as if it were my moral duty to remove it from the universe.

The charges at maximum delay. Time to get back to the ship, if we rushed, and none of us got stuck in the squeeze point.

Maybe. Maybe not.

That was when the monkey broke free.

SO, ANYWAY. ABOUT what we've done to your suit.

Its basic motor systems were already compromised when I found you near the cave mouth. You'd got that far, which can't have been easy.

Yes, well done you.

Brave Captain.

The nanotech contamination, the traces you picked up from the cave wall, was clearly the main cause of the systemic failure. Obviously, if you'd stayed any longer, your suit would have begun to turn against you, the way it happened with Teterev. Allowing itself to be controlled, absorbed. But you still had some control over it, and enough strength to overcome the resistance of the jammed locomotive systems.

It was never as bad for me. I think when I fell in that pool, some of the native organisms must have formed a barrier layer, a kind of insulation against the nanotech. Perhaps they've had time to begin to evolve their own defense measures, to contain the spread of it. Who knows? My good fortune, in any case.

It didn't feel like good fortune at the time, but that's the universe for you.

Anyway, back to your suit.

You're already paralyzed, effectively, but just to make sure that the systems don't begin to recover, I've opened your main control box and disabled all locomotive power. Locked it tight, in fact. You might as well be standing in a welded suit of armour, for all the success you'll have in moving.

Why are your arms the way they are?

We'll come to that.

You are standing, yes. Your feet are on the ground. Obviously, with the noose around your neck, the one thing you don't want to do now is topple over. I won't be there to catch you. But your suit is heavy and provided you don't wriggle around inside it too much, you should stay upright.

Of course, if you don't want to stay upright, that's one way out of this for you.

You're cold?

I'm not surprised! It's a cold planet, and you're not wearing a space helmet. Be a bit difficult, slipping a noose around your neck, if you were still wearing your helmet!

Fine, you want some more heat? That's easy. Your life-support systems are still good, and you can adjust the suit temperature. The reason your arms are positioned in front of you the way they are, is that I want you to be able to operate your cuff control. That's right. You can do that. You can move your fingers, tap those buttons.

Here's the thing, though. There's only one thing you can do with those buttons. Only one system you can control.

You can turn up your suit temperature, or you can turn it down.

That's all.

Why?

The why is easy. You remember those pieces of the wreck I went to so much trouble to position around you?

There was a point to all that.

There's a point to you.

I SUPPOSE THE terror was too much for Kanto, and that the passage through the narrowing had weakened its leash. Whatever the case, the monkey was out of the chamber, gibbering and shrieking, as it headed back the way we had come.

None of us had spoken until that moment. The chamber had struck us into a thunderous, paralyzing silence. Even when Kanto left, we said nothing. Any utterance would have felt like an invitation, permission for something worse than these stone ghouls to emerge from the walls.

Lenka and I looked at each other through our visors. Our eyes met, and we nodded. Then we looked at Rasht, both of us in turn, and Rasht looked as frightened as we felt.

Lenka went first, then Rasht, then I. We moved as quickly as our suits allowed. But even though none of us felt like lingering, I was no longer having to work as hard to keep up with the other two. My suit still felt sluggish, but it had not worsened since I came into contact with the silver contamination. Lenka and Rasht, though, were not moving as efficiently as before.

I still could not bring myself to speak, not until we were well away from that place. If the monkey had any sense, it was already through the narrowing, on its way back to daylight.

But when we reached the junction, the intersection of four tunnels, Rasht made us halt.

"Kanto's taken the wrong one," he said.

In the chaos of footprints, there was no chance at all of picking out the individual trace of the monkey. I was about to say as much when Rasht spoke again.

"I have a trace on his suit. In case he...escaped." The word seemed distasteful to him, as if it clarified an aspect of their relationship best kept hidden. "He should be ahead of us now, but he isn't. He's behind again. Down this shaft, I think." Rasht was indicating the rightmost entrance of the three we had faced on our way in. "It's hard to know."

Lenka said in a low voice: "Then we have to leave. Kanto will find his own way out, once he knows he's gone the wrong way."

"She's right," I said.

"We can't leave him," Rasht said. "We won't. I won't allow it."

"If the monkey doesn't want to be found," I said, "nothing we do is going to make any difference."

"The fix isn't moving. I have a distance estimate. It isn't more than twenty or thirty metres down that tunnel."

"Or that one," I said, nodding to the middle shaft. "Or your fix is wrong, and he's ahead of us anyway. For all we know, the magnetic field is screwing up your tracker."

"He isn't behind us," Rasht said, doggedly ignoring me. "There are really only two possibilities. We can check them quickly, three of us. Eliminate the wrong shaft."

Lenka's own breathing was now as heavy as my own. I caught another glimpse of her face, eyes wide with apprehension. "I know he means a lot to you, Captain..."

"Is there something wrong with your suits?" I asked.

"Yes," Lenka said. "Mine, anyway. Losing locomotive assist. Same as happened to you."

"I'm not sure it's the same thing. I fell in the pool, you didn't. Can you still move?"

Lenka lifted up an arm, clenched and unclenched her hand. "For the time being. If it gets too bad, I can always go full manual." Then she closed her eyes, took a deep breath, and reopened them. "All right, *Captain*." This with a particular sarcastic emphasis. "I'll check out the middle tunnel, if it'll help. I'll go thirty metres, no more, and turn around. You can check out the one on your right, if you think Kanto's gone that way. Nidra can wait here, just in case Kanto's gone ahead of us and turns back."

I did not like the idea of spending ten more seconds in this place, let alone the time it would take to inspect the tunnels. But Lenka's suggestion made the best of a bad situation. It would appease the Captain and not delay us more than a few minutes.

"All right," I agreed. "I'll wait here. But don't count on me catching Kanto if he comes back."

"Stay where you are, my dear," Rasht said, addressing the monkey wherever it might be. "We are coming."

Lenka and Rasht disappeared into their respective tunnels, their suits moving with visible sluggishness. Lenka, whose suit was more lightly armoured, would find it easier to cope than Rasht. I speculated to myself that the silver contamination was indeed having some effect, but that my exposure to the pond's microorganisms had provided a barriering layer, a kind of inocculation. It was not much of a theory, but I had nothing better to offer.

I counted a minute, then two.

Then heard: "Nidra."

"Yes," I said. "I hear you, Lenka. Have you found the monkey?"

There was a silence that ate centuries. My own fear was now as sharp and clean and precise as a surgical instrument. I could feel every cruel edge of it, cutting me open from inside.

"Help me."

YOU CAME BACK then. *You'd found your stupid fucking monkey. You were cradling it, holding it to you like it was the most precious thing in your universe.*

Actually I do the monkey a disservice.

As stupid as he was, Kanto was innocent in all this. I thought he was dead to begin with, but then I realised that it was trembling, caught in a state of infant terror, clinging to the fixed certainty of you while he shivered in its armour.

I made out his close-set yellow eyes, wide and uncomprehending.

I loathed your fucking monkey. But there was nothing that deserved that sort of terror.

Do you remember how our conversation played out? I told you that Lenka was in trouble. Your loyal crewmember, good, dependable Lenka. Always there for you. Always there for the Lachrimosa. *No matter what had happened until that point, there was now only one imperative. We had to save her. This is what Ultras do. When one of us falls, we reach. We're better than people think.*

But not you.

The fear had finally worked its way into you. I was wrong about greed being stronger. Or rather, there are degrees. Greed trumps fear, but then a deeper fear trumps greed all over again.

I pleaded with you.

But you would not answer her call. You left with Kanto, hobbling your way back to safety.

You left me to find Lenka.

I DID NOT have to go much further down the tunnel and reached the thing blocking further progress. It had trapped Lenka, but she was not yet fully part of it. Teterev had come earlier—many years ago—so her degree of intregration was much more pronounced. I could judge this in a glance, even before I had any deeper understanding of what I had found. I knew that Lenka would succumb to Teterev's fate, and that if I remained in this place I would eventually join them.

"Come closer, Nidra," a voice said.

I stepped nearer, hardly daring to bring the full blaze of my helmet light to bear on the half-sensed obstruction ahead of me.

"I've come for Lenka. Whatever you are, whatever's happened to you, let her go."

"We'll speak of Lenka." The voice was loud, booming across the air between us. "But do come closer."

"I don't think so."

"Because you are frightened?"

"Yes."

"Then I am very glad to hear it. Fear is the point of this place. Fear is the last and best thing that we have."

"We?"

"My predecessors and I. Those who came before me, the wayfarers and the lost. We've been coming for a very long time. Century after century, across hundreds of thousands of years. Unthinkable ages of galactic time. Drawn to this one place, and repelled by it—as you nearly were."

"I wish we had been."

"And usually the fear is sufficient. They turn back before they get this deep, as you nearly did. As you *should* have done. But you were braver than most. I'm sorry that your courage carried you as far as it did."

"It wasn't courage." But then I added: "How do you know my name?"

"I listened to your language, from the moment you entered me. You are very noisy! You gibber and shriek and make no sense whatsoever."

"Are you Teterev?"

"That is not easily answered. I remember Teterev, and I feel her distinctiveness quite strongly. Sometimes I speak through her, sometimes she speaks through us. We have all enjoyed what Teterev has brought to us."

I had never met Teterev, never seen an image of her, but there were only two human figures before me and one of them was Lenka, jammed into immobility, strands of silver beginning to wrap and bind her suit as if in the early stages of mummification. The strands extended back to the larger form of which Teterev was only an embellishment.

She must still have been wearing her suit when she was trapped and bound. Traces of the suit remained, but much of it had been picked off her, detached or dissolved or remade into the larger mass. Her helmet, similar in design to the one we had seen in the wreck, had fissured in two, with its halves framing her head.

I thought of flytrap mouthparts, Teterev's head an insect. Her face was stony and unmoving, her eyes blank surfaces, but there was no hint of ageing or decay. Her skin had the pearly shimmer of the figures we had seen in the second chamber. She had become—or was becoming—something other than flesh.

But apart from Teterev—and Lenka, if you included her—none of the other forms were human. The blockage was an assemblage of fused shapes, creature after creature absorbed into a sort of interlocking stone puzzle, a jigsaw of jumbled anatomies and half-implied life-support technologies. Two or three of the creatures were loosely humanoid, in so far as their forms could be discerned. But it was hard to gauge where their suits and life-support mechanisms ended and their alien anatomies commenced. Vines and tendrils of silver smothered them from head to foot, binding them into the older layers of the mass. Beyond these recognisable forms lay the evidence of many stranger anatomies and technologies.

"I've heard of a plague," I said, making my way to Lenka. "They say it's all just rumour, but I don't know. Is this what happened to you?"

"There are a million plagues, some worse than others. Some *much* worse." There was an edge of playfulness in the voice, taking droll amusement in my ignorance. "No: what you see here is deliberate, done for our mutual benefit. Haphazard, yes, but organised for a purpose. Think of it as a form of defense."

"Against the outside world?" I had my hands on her suit now, and I tried to rip the silver strands away from it, while at the same time applying as much force as I could to drag Lenka back to safety.

The voice said: "Nothing like that. I am a barrier against the thing that would damage the outside world, were it to be released."

"Then I don't understand." I caught my breath, already drained by the effort of trying to free her. "Is Lenka going to become part of you? Is that the idea?"

"Would you sooner offer yourself? Is that what you would like?"

"I'd like you to let Lenka go." Realising I was getting nowhere—the strands reattached themselves as quickly I peeled them away—I could only step back and take stock. "She came back here to find the monkey, not to hurt you. None of us came to harm you. We just wanted to know what had happened to Teterev."

"So Teterev was the beginning and end of your concerns? You had no other interest in this place?"

"We wondered what was in the cave," I answered, seeing no value in lying, even if I thought I might have got away with it. "We thought there might be Amerikano relics, maybe a Conjoiner cache. We picked up the geomagnetic anomaly. Are you making that happen? If so, you can't blame us for noticing it. If you don't want visitors, try making yourself less visible!"

"I would, if it were within my means. Shall I tell you something of me, Nidra? Then we will speak of Lenka."

SHALL I TELL you what I learned from her, Captain? Will that take your mind off the cold, for a little while?

You may as well hear it. It will put things into perspective. Make you understand your place in things—the value in your being here. The good and selfless service you are about to commence.

She was traveller, too.

Not Teterev, but the original one—the first being, the first entity, to find this planet. A spacefarer. Admittedly this was all quite a long time ago. She tried to get me to understand, but I'm not sure I have the imagination. Whole galactic turns ago, she said. When some of the stars we see now were not even born, and the old ones were younger. When the universe itself was smaller than it is now. Young galaxies crowding each other's heavens.

I don't know if it was her, an effect of the magnetic field, or just my fears affecting my sense of self. But as she spoke of abyssal time, I felt a lurch of cosmic vertigo, a sense that I stood on the crumbling brink of time's plungeing depths.

I didn't want to fall, didn't want to topple.

Sensible advice for both of us, wouldn't you say?

The universe always feels old, though. That's a universal truth, a universal fact of life. It felt old for her, already cobwebbed by history. Hard for us to grasp, I know. Human civilisation, it's just the last scratch on the last scratch on the last scratch, on the last layer of everything. We're noise. Dirt. We haven't begun to leave a trace.

But for her, so much had already happened! There had still been time enough for the rise and fall of numberless species and civilisations, time for great deeds and greater atrocities. Time for monsters and the rumours of worse.

She had been journeying for lifetimes, by the long measure of her species. Travelling close to light, visiting world after world.

If we had a name for what she was, we'd call her an archaeologist, a scholar drawn to relics and scraps.

Still following me?

One day—one unrecorded century—she stumbles upon something. It was a thing she'd half hoped to find, half hoped to avoid. Glory and annihilation, balanced on a knife edge.

We know all about that, don't we?

Your finger is moving. Are you trying to adjust that temperature setting? Go ahead. Turn up your suit. I won't stop you.

There. Better already. Can you feel the warmth flowing up from your neck ring, taking the sting out of the cold? It feels better, doesn't it? There's plenty of power in the suit. You needn't worry about draining it. Make yourself as warm as you wish.

Look, I didn't say there wasn't a catch.

Turn it down, then. Let the cold return. Can you feel those skin cells dying, the frostbite eating its way into your face? Can you feel your eyeballs starting to freeze?

Back to our traveller.

We have rumours of plague. She had rumours of something far worse. A presence, an entity, waiting between the stars. Older than the history of any culture known to her kind. A kind of mechanism, waiting to detect the emergence of bright and busy civilisations such as hers. Or ours, for that matter.

Something with a mind and a purpose.

And she found it.

"I'VE NO REASON to think you haven't already killed Lenka," I said, a kind of desperate calm overcoming me, when I realised how narrow my options really were.

"Oh, she is perfectly well," the voice answered. "Her suit is frozen, and I have pushed channels of myself into her head, to better learn her usefulness. But she is otherwise intact. She has travelled well, this Lenka. I can learn a great deal from her."

I waited a beat.

"Are you strong?"

"That is an odd question."

"Not really." I reached beneath my chest pack, fumbling with my equipment belt until I found the hard casing of a demolition charge. I unclipped the grenade-sized device, presenting it before me like an offering. "Hot dust. Have you dug deep enough into Lenka to know what that means?"

"No, but Teterev knew."

"That's good. And what did Teterev know?"

"That you have a matter-antimatter device."

"That's right."

"And the yield would be...?"

"A couple of kilotonnes. Very small, really. Barely enough to chip an asteroid in two. Of course, I have no idea of the damage it would do to you."

I used two hands to twist the charge open along its midline, exposing its triggering system. The trigger was a gleaming red disk. I settled my thumb over the disk, thinking of the tiny, pollen-sized speck of antimatter held in a flawless vacuum at the heart of the demolition charge.

"Suicide, Nidra? Surely there's a time-delay option."

"There is, but I'm not sure I'd be able to get to my ship in time. Besides, I don't know what you'd do with me gone. If you can paralyse Lenka's suit, you can probably work your way into the charge and disarm it."

"You would kill Lenka at the same time."

"Not if you let her go. And if you don't let her go, this has to be a kinder way out than being sucked into you." I allowed my thumb to rub back and forth over the trigger, only a twitch away from activating it. There was an unsettling temptation to *just do it*. The light would be quick and painless, negating the past and future in a single cleansing flash.

In that moment I wanted it.

WHAT WOULD YOU have done, Captain?

Her mistake?

That's easy. The thing she found, in the wreck of another ship, seemed dead to her. Dead and exhausted. Just a cluster of black cubes, lodged in the ship's structure like the remnant of an infection. But it had not spread; it had not destroyed the wreck or achieved total transformation into a larger mass. She thought it was dead. She had no reason to think otherwise.

Can we blame her for that?

Not me.

Not you.

But the machinery was only dormant. When her ship was underway, while she slept, the black cubes began to show signs of life. They swelled, testing the limits of her containment measures. Her ship woke her up, asking what it should do. Her ship was almost a living thing in its own right. It was worried for her, worried for itself.

She had no answer.

She tried to strengthen the fields and layer the alien machinery in more armour. None of that worked. The forms broke through, began to eat her ship—making more cubes. She put more energy into her containment. What else could she do?"

Throw them overboard, you wonder?

Well, yes. She considered something like that. But that would only be passing the problem on to some other traveller. The responsibility was hers alone. She felt quite strongly about that.

Still, the machinery was definitely damaged. She was sure of that. Otherwise the transformation would have been fast and unstoppable. Instead, she had achieved a sort of stalemate.

What next?

Suicide, perhaps—dive into a star. But the data offered no guarantees that this would be enough to destroy the machinery. It might make it stronger!

Not a chance she could take.

So instead she found this world. A ship in space is an easy thing to see, even across light years. A world offers better camouflage—it has mass and heat. She thought she could screen herself—drawing no attention from passers-by.

She was wrong.

The cubes were resilient, resourceful. Constantly testing her capabilities. They demanded more power, more mass. She converted more and more of her ship into the architecture of their prison. She died! But by then her living ship had grown to know her so well that her personality lived on inside it, haunting it as a kind of ghost.

Centuries blasted by.

Her ship protected and enlarged itself. It ate into the surrounding geology, bolstering the containment and consolidating its defenses. For the most part it had no need of her, this residue of what she had been. Once in a while it raised her from the shadows, when her judgement was required. She was never lonely. She'd burned through her capacity for loneliness, discarding it like an outmoded evolutionary stage.

But she had visitors, all the same.

Like us?

No, not quite. Not to begin with. To begin with they were just like her.

"THEY CAME," THE voice said. "My sensors tracked them with great vigilance and stealth. I watched them, wary of their intentions. I risked collapsing my containment fields, until they were out of range. I did not want to be found. I did not want my mistake to become theirs. It was always a bad time." It paused. "But I did not miss their company. They were not like me. Their languages and customs had turned unfamiliar. I was never sorry when they turned for space and left me undisturbed."

"I don't believe you."

"Believe what you like. It hardly matters, anyway. They stopped coming. A silence fell, and endured. It was broken only by the tick of pulsars and the crack and whistle of quasars half way to the universe's edge. There were no more of my kind. I had no knowledge of what had become of them."

"But you could guess."

"It did not mean that I could give up, and allow what I had found to escape. So I slept—or ceased to be, until my ship had need of me again—and the stars lurched to new and nameless constellations. Twenty million orbits of my old world, two hundred thousand lifetimes. And then a new visitor—a new species."

I guessed that we were still in the distant past.

"Did you know this culture?"

"I had no data on anything like them, dead or alive. Frankly, it disturbed me. It had too many limbs, a strange way of moving, and I wondered what it looked like outside of its armour. I wanted it to go away. I quietened myself, damped my energies. But still it came. It dug into me, seeking an explanation for whatever its sensors had picked up. I thought of simply killing it—it had come alone, after all. But there was another possibility open to me. I could take it, open its mind, learn from it. Fold its memories and personality into my own. Use its knowledge to better protect myself the next time." A kind of shame or regretfulness entered the voice. "So that is what I did. I caught the alien, made sure it was incapable of escape, and pushed feelers through the integument of its suit and into its nervous system. Its anatomy was profoundly unfamiliar to me. But at one end of its segmented, exoskeletal body was a thing like a head and inside the brittle cage of that head was a dense mass of connected cells that had something of the topological complexity of what had once been my own brain. It was hierarchically layered, with clear modular specialisation for sensory processing, motor control, abstract reasoning and memory management. It was also trying very hard to communicate with its fellows—wherever *they* were—and that made it easy for me to trace the circuits and pathways of expression. Before long, I was able to address the alien through the direct manipulation of internal mental states. And I explained what was to become of it. Together we would be stronger, better equipped both to deal with the thing at the heart of me, and also to make my concealment more effective. I was sorry about what had needed to be done, but I made it understand that I had no choice at all."

"How did it take it?"

"How do you *think*, Nidra? But very soon the question concerned neither of us. It had become me, I had become it. Our memories were a knot of entanglements. It understood my concerns. It grasped that there had only ever been one path. It knew that we had no choice about what we had become."

"Forgiveness?"

"Acceptance."

"But it didn't end, did it? There were more. Always more. Other species...dozens, hundreds of them. Until we came!"

"You are no different."

"Perhaps we aren't. But this alters things, doesn't it?" I still had my thumb on the trigger, ready to unleash a matter-antimatter conflagration. "You think I won't do this? You've told me what you are. I understand that you acted...that you've *been* acting...for what you think is the common good. Maybe you're right, too. But enough is enough. You have Teterev. It's too late for her...too late for you, if I'm still reaching a part of her. But it stops with Lenka. She's mine. She's coming back with me."

"I need her. I need to add her library of fears to my own. I need to make myself stronger."

"It won't work. It hasn't *been* working. You're stuck in a spiral...a destructive feedback loop. The more you try to make yourself impregnable, the more *evident* you become to the outside world. So you have to make yourself yet more impregnable...add to your library of fears. But it can't continue."

"It must.

"I tried to stop myself. But always they came. New travellers, new species. Nothing I did made myself invisible to them. I could not *negotiate*, I could not *persuade*, because that would have been tantamount to confessing the hard fact of my existence. So I did what I had always done. I hid. I made myself as quiet and silent as physics allowed, and willed them to leave. I dug into our mutual psychologies, trawled the ocean of our terrors, and from that sea of fears I shaped the phantasms that I hoped would serve as deterrence, encouraging newcomers to come no nearer. But it was never totally sufficient. Some were always too brave, or curious, and by force of will they reached the heart of me. And always I had no choice but to *take*, to *incorporate*, to turn them to my cause. To feed me their fears, so that I might better my defenses. Why do you think I had to take Teterev? She was the first of your kind—a new jewel, to place in my collection. She had been very useful, has Teterev. We are all very glad of her. Her fears are like a new colour, a new smell. We never imagined such things!"

"Good. I'm truly sorry for Teterev. But you don't need Lenka. Give her back control of her suit, and we'll leave you alone."

"You could make that promise to me. But you did not come here alone."

"The Captain…we'll take care of him."

SEE? THINKING OF you even then.

Always in our hearts and minds.

"I LISTENED TO your babble. The theories of your Captain. He craves his fortune. He will think he can turn the *fact* of me to profit. He will try to sell the knowledge of my location."

"He doesn't even know what you are!"

"But he will find out. He will ask what became of you, what became of Lenka. Your silence will count for nothing. He *will* return. He will send machines into me. And soon more will come, in other ships, and I am bound to fail. When the machines touch your civilisation, they will scorch you into history. They have done it a thousand times, with a thousand cultures. They will leave dust and ruins and silence, and you will *not* be the last."

"Lev," I said quietly.

There was a silence. I wondered if the thing before me would speak again. Perhaps I had shut the door of communication between us with that one invocation.

But the voice asked: "What do you know of Lev?"

"Your son," I answered. "The son of part of you, the son of Teterev. You had to leave him on the orbiting ship. You didn't mean to, but it must have been the only way. You loved him. You wanted very badly to get a message to him, to have him help you. That's why you came as far as you did. But you failed."

"And Lev is gone."

I nodded. "But not in the way you think. Someone got to that ship before us—cleaned it out. Stripped it of engines, weps, crew. The frozen.

But they'd have been valuable to someone. If Lev was on that ship, he'd have made it back to one of the settled worlds by now. And we can find him. The Mendicants trade in the frozen, and we have traded with the Mendicants, in many systems. There are channels, lines of enquiry. The name of your ship..."

"What would it be to you?"

"Give us that name. Let us find Lev. I'll return. I promise you that much."

"No one ever promises to *return*, Nidra. They promise to stay away."

"The name of the ship," I said again.

She told me.

SO MANY NAMES, *so many ships. Numberless. Names too strange to put into language, at least no language that would fit into our heads. Names like clouds. Names like forests. Names like ever-unfolding mathematical structures—names that begat themselves, in dreams of recursion. Names that split the world in two. Names that would drive a nail through your sanity.*

But she told me some of them, as best as she could.

Lovely names. Names of such beauty and terror they made me weep. The hopes and fears of the brave and the lost. The best and the worst of all of us. All wayfarers, all travellers.

I asked her to try and remember the last of them.

She did.

Tell you?

Not a chance, Captain. You don't get to know everything.

I STEPPED BACK from his suited-but-immobile form, admiring my handiwork. He really did look sculptural, frozen into that oddly dignified posture, with his arms coming together across his chest, one hand touching the cuff of the other.

"I suppose you could say that we came to an understanding, Teterev and I," I said. "Or what Teterev had become. Partly it was fear, I think, that I'd use the hot-dust. Did I come close? Yes, definitely. Not much to lose at that point. I might have been able to work the ship without you, but certainly not without Lenka. If she didn't survive, there wasn't much point in me surviving either. But Lenka was allowed to leave, and so was I. It was hard work, getting Lenka back here. But she's begun to regain some suit function now, and I don't think either of us will have any trouble returning to the lander."

The Captain tried to speak. It was hard, with the noose tight around his throat. He could breathe, but anything more was an effort.

He rasped out three words that might have been "fuck you, Nidra". But I could not be sure.

"I made a commitment to Teterev," I carried on. "Firstly, that we'd make sure you were not a problem. Secondly, that I'd do what I could to find Lev. If that's decades, longer, so be it. It's something to live for, anyway. A purpose. We all need a purpose, don't we?"

He attempted another set of syllables.

"Here's yours," I said. "Your purpose is to die here. It will happen. How fast it happens, is in your hands. Quite literally. Those pieces of debris I set around you are curved mirrors. Now, it's not an exact science. But when the sun climbs, some of them will concentrate the sun's light on the snow and ice on which you are standing. It will begin to melt. The tension on your noose will increase." I paused, allowing that part to sink in, if he had not already deduced matters for himself. "In any case, the ice will melt eventually, with the change of seasons. It's only permafrost deeper in the cave mouth. But you'll be dead by then. It'll be a nasty, slow death, though. Hypothermia, frostbite, slow choking—take your pick. But you can speed it up, if you like. Turn up your suit's heat, and you can stay as warm as you like. The downside is that the heat will spill away from your suit and melt the ice even quicker. You'll be hanging by your neck within hours, with the entire weight of your suit trying to rip your skull from your spine. At that point, overwhelmed by terror and pain, you might try and turn down the thermal regulation again. But by then you might not be able to move your fingers. Ultimately, it doesn't matter. There are many paths to the one goal. All the scenarios end with your corpse hanging from the mouth of the cave. Swinging there until the ice returns. You'll make an effective deterrent, wouldn't you say? A tolerable invitation to keep away?"

Rasht tried to say something. But Lenka, who had hobbled closer, placed a finger on his lips.

"Enough," she whispered. "Save your breath."

"Where is the monkey?" I asked.

"Tethered where we left it, over by the wreck. Shall we leave it here?"

"No. We'll bring it with us, and we'll take good care of it. I promised him that much. I try not to break my promises. Any of them."

"Then we're done here," Lenka said.

"I think we are."

We turned our backs on our former Captain and commenced the slow walk back to the lander. We would stop at the wreck on our way, collect the monkey, and what we could of Teterev's belongings. Then we would be off Holda, out of this system, and that was a good thought.

Even if I knew I had to return.

"When we we get back to the ship, I want to give it a new name."

I thought about that for a moment. "That's a good idea. A clean break. I have some suggestions."

"I'd be glad to hear them," Lenka said.

THE WATER THIEF

THE BOY wants my eye again. He's seen me using it, setting it down on the mattress where I squat. I am not sure why he covets it so badly.

"Sorry," I say. "I need this. Without it I can't work, and if I can't work, my daughter and I go hungry."

He is too small to understand my words, but the message gets through anyway. I smile as he sprints away, pausing only to glance over his shoulder. Nothing would prevent the boy creeping into the shipping container and taking the eye while I am working. But he has not done that yet. Something in his face makes me think he can be trusted.

You can't understate the value of that, here in the refugee camp. Not that they call it that. This is a "Resource and Relocation Assistance Facility". I have been here six years now. My daughter is twelve; she barely remembers the outside world. Eunice is a good and studious girl, but that will only get you so far. Both of us need something more. Prakash tells me that if I can accrue enough proficiency credits, we might be relocated.

I believe Prakash. Why wouldn't I?

I SQUAT DOWN on my mattress. The shipping container has had its doors removed and holes cut in the sides. Windchimes hang from one corner of the roof, cut from buckled aluminium tent-poles. On this airless afternoon they are as silent as stalagtites.

My virching rig isn't much. I have the eye, my lenses, my earphones and my t-shirt. All cheap, second-hand. I position the eye, balancing it on a shoebox until its purple pupil blinks readiness. I slip in the earphones. The t-shirt is ultramarine, with a Chinese slogan and some happy splashing dolphins. Too tight for a grown woman but the accelerometers and postural sensors still function.

I initiate the virching link. The lenses rinse me out of reality, into global workspace.

"Good afternoon, Prakash," I say.

His voice is near and far at the same time. "You're late, Soya. Had some nice jobs lined up for you."

I bite back my excuse. I have no interest in justifying myself to this man. This morning I had to walk twice as far to get clean water, because someone from a neighboring compound broke into our area. They damaged our pump as they tried to steal from it.

"I'm sure you still have something in the queue," I tell him.

"Yes…" Prakash says absently. "Let me see."

If God was a fly, this would be the inside of his head. Wrapping around me are a thousand constantly changing facets. Each represents a possible task assignment. The facets swell and contract as Prakash offers me options. There's a description of the job, the remuneration, the required skillset and earnable proficiency credits. The numbers swoop and tumble, like roosting birds.

"Road repair," Prakash declares grandly, as if this is meant to stir the soul. "Central Lagos. You've done that kind of thing before."

"No thanks. Pay is shit and a monkey could do it."

"Window cleaning. Private art museum, Cairo. They have some gala opening coming up, but their usual 'bot has broken."

"It's years since I cleaned windows."

"Always a tricky customer, Soya. People should be less choosy in life." He emits a long nasal exhalation like the air being let out of a tyre. "Well, what else have we. Bioremediation, Black Sea. Maintenance of algae bloom control and containment systems."

Cleaning slime from pumps, in other words. I scoff at the paltry remuneration. "Next."

"Underwater inspection, Gibraltar bridge. Estimated duration eight hours, reasonable pay, at the upper end of your skills envelope."

"And I must fetch my daughter from school in three hours. Find me something shorter."

Prakash's sigh is long suffering. "Seawall repair, Adriatic coastline. Overnight storm breach. Four hours, high remuneration. They need this done quickly."

Typical of Prakash, always the job he knows I will not refuse until last.

"I'll need to make a call," I say, hoping that someone can collect Eunice from the school.

"Don't dilly-dally."

Prakash puts a hold on the assignment, and I get back to him just in time to claim it for myself. Not that I'm the only one on the task: the Adriatic breach is a local emergency. Hundreds of robots, civilian and military, are already working to rebuild shattered defenses. Mostly it is work a child could do, if a child had the strength of a hundred men— moving stone blocks, spraying rapid-setting concrete.

Later I learn that fifteen people drowned in that wall failure. Of course I am sad for these people—who wouldn't be? But if they had not died, I would not have had the assignment.

IT IS LATE when I finish. A breeze has picked up, sufficient to stir the chimes. The air is still oven-warm. I am thirsty and my back aches from lugging water.

From across the compound, diesel generators commence their nightly drone. I listen to the chimes, snatching a moment to myself. Their random tinkling makes me think of neurones, firing in the brain. I was always fascinated by the mind, by neuroscience. Back in Dar es Salaam I had ambitions be a doctor.

I rise from the mattress and stretch away stiffness. I am on my way to collect Eunice when I hear a commotion, coming from somewhere near one of the big community tents. Trouble, of one kind or another. There is always something. Mostly it doesn't concern me, but I like to keep informed.

"Soya," a voice calls. It is Busuke, a friend of mine with two sons. "Eunice is fine," she tells me. "Fanta had to go, but she passed her onto Ramatou. You look tired."

Of course I look tired. What does she expect?

"Something going on?"

"Oh, didn't you hear?" Busuke lowers her voice conspiratorially. "They got that thief. She hadn't got very far—been stung by the electrified fence, was hiding out nearby, waiting to make a dash for the gap at sundown, when they apprehended her." Busuke says "apprehended" as if there were quote marks around the word.

I did not know whether this thief was a man or a woman, but at least now I can pin my hate onto something. "I would not want to be in her shoes."

"They say she took a bit of a beating, before the peacekeepers came. Now there is a big argument about whether or not to keep giving her medicine."

"One woman won't make any difference."

"It's the principle," Busuke tells me. "Why should we waste a drop of water or antibiotics on a thief?"

"I don't know." I wish we could settle on a topic of conversation other than water. "I should go and find Ramatou."

"You work too hard," Busuke says, as if I have a choice.

The camp used to confuse me, but now I could walk its maze of prefabs and tents blindfolded. Tonight the stars are out. Plump and yellow, two thirds full, the Moon swims over the tents, rippling in heat. A fat Moon brings out the worst in people, my mother used to say. But I'm not superstitious. It's just a rock with people on it.

My lenses tint it, tracing geopolitical boundaries. America, Russia, China and India have the biggest claims, but there is a little swatch of Africa up there, and it gladdens me. I often show it to my daughter, as if to say, we can be more than this. This camp does not have to define you. You could do great things. Walk on the Moon, one day.

I catch the rise of a swift bright star. It turns out to be a Japanese orbital power satellite, under assembly. I have heard about these stations. When they are built, when they are boosted to higher orbits, the satellites' mirrors will cup the Sun's light and pour it down to Earth. The energy will be used to do useful things like the supplying of power to coastal desalination plants. Then we will be drowning in water.

It bothers me that I never seen the power station before.

I collect my daughter from Ramatou. Eunice is in a bad mood, hungry and restless. I show her the Moon but she is beyond distraction. There is no food at the nearest dispensary, but we catch a shred of a rumour about food in green sector. We are not meant to cross into that part of the camp, but we have done it before and no one has questioned us. Along the way Eunice can tell me how her day in school went, and I will tell her something of mine, of the poor people on the Adriatic coast.

LATER, WHEN SHE is asleep, I drift to the community tent. The mob has simmered down since earlier, but the place is still busier than usual.

I push my way through fellow refugees, until I am within sight of the water thief. They have her on a makeshift bed, a table with a mattress on, hemmed by white-coated peacekeepers and green-outfitted nurses. There is a doctor present now, a young Lebanese man. From his confident and authoritative demeanour, he must be on his first posting. It won't last. The long-stagers are nervous and jittery.

There are also three mantises. The medical robots are spindly but fearsome things, with too many limbs. Usually there is a doctor at the other end, assisting the robot via a virching link, but not always. These are very complex, expensive machines and they can operate themselves.

This woman hasn't just been roughed up a bit. She has been beaten to the edge of death. One of the human medics changes the bag on a medical drip. The thief is unconscious, head lolling away from me. She doesn't look much older than Eunice. Her skin is a sea of bruises, burns and cuts.

"They are going to vote," says Busuke, sidling up.

"Of course. Voting is what we do. If there is something to vote on, we vote."

I weary of our endless swirling micro-democracy. It is as if, while the great institutions of the world falter, we are obliged to reenact them in miniature here. A week doesn't go by when the black and white balls aren't drawn out for something.

"It's not about life and death," Busuke insists. "We're not going to *kill* this woman. Just withhold excessive treatment."

"Which wouldn't be the same."

"Why should the robots and doctors fuss over her, when they're needed elsewhere? And that medicine."

"They should have done us all a favour," I say. "Killed her outright, when they caught her."

It is brutal, but in that moment I mean it.

IN THE MORNING I catch sight of a screen, propped up on a pile of medical supply boxes. It shows a confusion of gleaming lines, racing to perspective points. Glittery shards, people and machines moving in weightlessness. The indigo curve of the Earth, seen from above the atmosphere. Below, perfectly cloudless, is Africa, turning out of night. I think of waving to myself.

It turns out—I learn this in pieces, not all at once—that there has been an accident on the Japanese power station. An Indian tug has crashed into it, and now there is a race to rescue the construction workers. Of course much of the work is being done by robots, but there are still dozens of men and women involved. Later that I learn that the tug caused the station to tilt from its normal alignment, meaning that its mirrors were much brighter as seen from Earth.

There is a saying about ill winds. I would be lying if I said I did not wonder what good this calamity can do for me.

WHEN I SQUAT down before my wise purple eye and enter global workspace, Prakash is distracted. He has been rushed off his feet, brokering assignments. I dare ask if there is work for me in orbit.

"They need help," Prakash admits. "But remind me, Soya. What is your accumulated experience in space operations? How many hours logged, with both timelag and weightlessness?"

His question is rhetorical, but I furnish an honest answer. "Nothing. Zero hours. As you know."

"Well, then."

"It's an emergency. No one quibbled about my experience on the Adriatic seawall."

"That was different. Orbital operations are a world away from anything you know." Prakash pauses—his attention is elsewhere today. "I still have work for you. The world has not stopped turning, just because of this unfortunate business."

Today's offered assignments: helping a construction robot at the Sarahan solar mirror project. Assisting a barnacle-scraper, on the belly of a Chinese supertanker. Running manual override on a tunnel project in the Tasman Straits.

I spurn these insults; settle finally for a low remuneration but high skills dividend job, helping one robot perform a delicate repair on another, at one of the Antarctic construction projects. It is a miserable, sodium-lit nightscape, barely inhabited. We are supposed to live in such places, when they are ready.

What matters is that it is work.

BUT I AM not even half way through the task when something goes wrong. A moment of nothing and then I am elsewhere. A bright parched landscape, blazing white under a sky that is a deep, pitiless black.

I voice a question to myself, aloud, thinking that someone, somewhere, may have the decency to answer.

"Where am I?"

I try to look around, and *nothing happens*. Then the view does indeed begin to track, and this landscape, weird as it is, strikes familiar notes. The ground undulates toward a treeless horizon, strewn with boulders and stones. Soft-contoured hills rise at an indeterminate distance. There are no crags, no animals or vegetation. Save for a kind of fence, stretching from one horizon to the other, there is no indication that humans have ever been there.

Then I see the body.

It is lying quite close by, and wearing a spacesuit.

I command the view to stop tracking. Again there is a delay before my intentions have effect.

It—he or she, I cannot decide—is lying on their back, arms at their side, legs slightly spread. Their visored face mirrors the sky. They could have been dropped there, like a discarded doll.

I take another look at that fence. It is a thick metal tube, wide enough that one might easily crawl through it, and it is supported above the ground on many 'A'-shaped frames. There are joints in the tube, where one piece connects to another. I feel silly for not realising that it is a pipeline, not a fence.

I make my robot advance. My own shadow pushes ahead of me, jagged and mechanical. Whatever I am, I must be as large as a truck.

I angle down. I don't know much about spacesuits, but I cannot see anything wrong. No cracks in the visor, no obvious gashes or rips. The life-support equipment on the front, a rectangular chest-pack connected to the rest of it by tubes and lines, is still lit up. Part of it flashes red.

"Prakash," I say, in the hope that he might be hearing. "I could use some help here."

But Prakash does not answer.

I reach out with my arms. The robot follows suit with its own limbs. I am getting better at anticipating this timelag delay now, issuing my commands accordingly. Prakash need not have made such a big deal about it.

I scoop up the figure, sliding my arms under their body, as if they are a sack of grain and I am a forklift. Lunar soil curtains off them. They leave a neat human imprint.

The figure twitches and turns to look at me. I catch a reflection of myself in its visor: a golden behemoth of metal and plastic: some kind of truck, with multiple wheels and cameras and forward-mounted manipulators.

The figure moves again. They reach around with their right arm and scrabble at the chest-pack, touching controls with their thick-fingered moonglove. The lights alter their dance.

And I hear a man speak, and it is not Prakash.

"You found me." There are oceans of relief in his voice. "Starting to think I'd die out here."

The voice speaks English. I have picked up enough to suffice.

On the chance that the man may hear me, I ask him: "Who are you, and what has happened?"

There is a lapse before his answer comes back.

"You're not Shiga."

"I don't know who Shiga is. Did you have some kind of accident?"

It takes him time to answer. "There was an accident, yes. My suit was damaged. Who are you?"

"Nobody, and I don't know why they've given me this job. Are you going to be all right?"

"Suit's in emergency power conservation mode. It'll keep me alive, but only if I don't move around."

I think I understand. The life-support system would have to work much harder to sustain someone who was active. "And now? You did something to the chest-pack?"

"Told it to turn off the distress beacon, and give me enough power to allow for communication. It's still running very low."

He is still lying in my arms, like a child.

"You thought I was someone else."

"What did you say your name was?"

"I didn't. But it is Soya. Soya Akinya. And you?"

"Luttrell. Michael Luttrell. Can you get me out of here?"

"It would help if I knew where we are. How did you get here?"

"I drove in. The overlander, the thing you're controlling. Shiga was meant to take control, help me back aboard, drive me home."

"Do you want to climb aboard? I presume there is a cabin, or something."

"Just a seat, behind your camera. No pressurisation. Let me try. I'll feel safer up there."

I lower him nearly to the ground, then watch as he eases stiffly from my arms. His movements are slow, and I am not sure if that is due to the suit or some injury or weakness within him. Both, perhaps. His breathing is laboured and he stops after only a few paces. "Oxygen low," he says, his voice little more than a whisper.

Luttrell passes out of my field of vision. My view tilts as his weight transfers onto me. After long moments, his shadow juts above my own.

"Are you all right?"

"I'm good."

I pan my camera up and down the pipeline. "Which way?"

He takes a while to gather his breath, and even then his voice is ragged. "Turn and follow the tracks."

I make a wide turn with the overlander. It's not hard to pick out the furrows my wheels have already dug into the soil. They arrow to the horizon, straight except where they kink to avoid a boulder or slope.

"Away from the pipeline?" I query. "I thought we would follow it, one way or the other."

"Follow the tracks. You should be able to get up to fifty kilometres per hour without too much difficulty."

I pick up speed, following the tracks, trusting that they will keep me from harm. "How long will it take us?"

"Three, four hours, depending."

"And do you have air and power?"

"Enough."

"How long, Luttrell?"

"If I don't talk too much..." He trails off, and there is a lengthy interval before I hear him again. "I have enough. Just keep driving."

Before very long the pipeline has fallen away behind us, stolen from view by the Moon's curvature. It is a small world, this. But still big enough when you have a journey to make, and a man who needs help.

Luttrell is silent, and I think he is either asleep or has turned off his communications link.

This is when Prakash returns, unbidden.

"Finally," he says. "Starting to think you'd vanished into workspace."

"I did not choose this assignment."

"I know, I know." I think of him waving his hands, brushing aside my point as if it is beneath discussion. "It was an emergency. They needed someone with basic skills."

"I have never been called into space, Prakash. Why have I suddenly been deemed good enough for this?"

"Because everyone who really *does* have the skills is trying to sort out that mess at the Japanese station. Look on it as your lucky day. It won't count as weightless work, but at least you'll be able to say you've worked with timelag."

It may not be weightless, I think sourly, but surely working under Lunar gravity must count as something. "We'll talk about it when I am done. Now I have to get this man to help."

"You've done your bit. The people on the Moon would like you to turn ninety degrees to your right, parallel to the pipeline, and maintain that heading. Once that's done, you can sign off. The vehicle will take care of itself. The hard part was helping get the body...the man...onto the truck. You've come through that with flying colours."

As if I had done something altogether more demanding than simply scooping a man off the ground.

"Luttrell told me to follow his tracks."

"And Luttrell is...? Oh, I see. Luttrell spoke to you?"

"Yes, and he was very insistent." I feel a prickle of foreboding. "What is going on, Prakash? Who is Luttrell? What was he doing out here?"

"How much do you know about Lunar geopolitics, Soya? Oh, wait. That'd be 'nothing at all'. Trust me, the best thing you can possibly do now is turn ninety degrees and bail out."

I think about this. "Luttrell? Can you hear me?"

There is a very long silence before he replies. "Did you say something?"

"You were asleep."

"It's stuffy in here."

"Luttrell, try to stay awake. Are you sure there are people at the end of this trail?"

The time it takes him to answer, I may as well have asked him to calculate the exact day on which he was born. "Yes. Shiga, the others. Our camp. It's not more than two hundred kilometres from the pipeline."

Three, four hours, then, exactly as he predicted. "Prakash, my broker, says I should head somewhere else. Along the pipeline, to our left."

For once, Luttrell seems alert. "No. No, don't do that. Just keep moving, this heading. Back the way I came."

"If I went the other way, how long before we hit civilisation?"

Now Prakash cuts in again. "Less than a hundred kilometres away, there is a pressurised maintenance shack. That's his best chance now."

"And who is the expert now?"

"This is what they tell me. Luttrell won't make it back to his camp. They are very insistent on this point."

"Luttrell seems very insistent as well. Should we not listen to the man who actually lives here?"

"Just do as you are told, Soya."

Do as I am told. How many times have I heard that in my life, I wonder? And how many times have I obeyed? When the Resource and Relocation people came, with their trucks, helicopters and airships, with their bold plans for human resettlement, I—along with many millions of others—did exactly as I was told. Gave up on the old world, embraced the diminished possibilities of the new.

And now I find myself squatting on a dirty mattress, under a creaking corrugated roof, while my body and mind are on the Moon and I am again being told that someone else, someone I have never met, and who will never meet me, knows best.

"Don't turn around," Luttrell says.

"You had better be right about this camp of yours."

Prakash cuts in again. "Soya, what are you doing? Luttrell has transgressed internationally recognised Lunar boundaries. He has attempted to take what does not belong to him. The man is a thief."

As if I had not worked that out for myself.

I think of the fat full Moon, daubed with the emblems of nations and companies. Only a few thousand people up there now, but they say it will soon be tens of thousands. Blink, and it will be millions.

And I have watched the news and tried to keep myself informed. I know that some of those territorial boundaries are disputed. There are claims and counter-claims. Even our little thumbnail of African soil has not been immune to these arguments.

So this man, Luttrell. What of him? He had driven to the pipeline, not along it but from somewhere else. Maybe he tried to tap into it. Something happened to him. An electrical shock, perhaps, damaging the systems of his suit. He had hoped that help would come from his own people, from Shiga. Instead what he got was me. And while my people—the people who know best—do not exactly want to kill Luttrell, it cannot be said that keeping him alive is their main consideration.

What they want, above all else, is for him not to get home.

"I am not turning, Prakash. I am taking this man back to his friends."

"I wouldn't do that, Soya. You're only on the Moon under our sufferance. We can pull you out of the link at any moment, slot someone else in."

"Who will do as they are told?"

"Who knows what's good for them."

"Then that is not me."

Prakash is right: I can be pulled from the link at any time. Or rather, he would be right, if I did not have so much experience at driving robots. Scraping barnacles off a supertanker, scudding across the Moon: nothing much changes. And I know the tricks and dodges that will make it difficult or time-consuming for the link to be snapped. I have seldom had cause to use these things, but they are well remembered.

"Will you get into trouble for this?" Luttrell says.

"I think the damage is already done."

"Thank you." He is silent again. "I think I need to stay awake. Maybe if you told me something about yourself, that would help."

"There is not much to tell. I was born in Dar es Salaam, around the turn of the century."

"Before or after?"

"I don't know. My mother never knew. There would have been records, I suppose. But I have never seen them." I steer us around a boulder as large as the overlander itself. "It doesn't matter. That's all over now. Now tell me where you came from."

He tells me his story. We drive.

IN THE MORNING the dust settles. My refusal to obey Prakash has not gone unpunished. Proficiency ratings have been set back to zero. Black marks have been set against my name, forbidding whole categories of employment. The credits I ought to have earned from the last task—I did, after all, save Luttrell—have failed to appear.

But I am resigned to my fate. It is not the end of the world, or at least not the end of mine. There are other types of work out here. Whatever is in store for me, I shall make the best of it. Just as long as it keeps my daughter from starvation.

On the way to the school, Eunice asks me what I did last night.

"Helped a man," I say. "He did a bad thing, but I helped him anyway. That has made some people angry."

"What did the man do?"

"It's complicated. He took something that wasn't his, or tried to. We'll talk about it later."

I think of Luttrell. When they finally broke me out of the link, we were still some way from his camp. I don't know what happened after that. I hope his people were able to find him. I watch the news, but there's nothing. It's a border incident, that's all. Not worth a mention.

While she is in school, I go to the community tent where the water thief waits her verdict. The place is crowded, the atmosphere volatile. The mantises have withdrawn: they have done their work, the patient has been stabilised, she is mostly conscious. I study the fluid in the woman's drip and imagine that it is pure water. I think of gulping down its sweet clear contents.

I shoulder my way through the onlookers to the low trestle table, where the votes are being administered. I tell them who I am, although I think by now they know. A finger tracks down a list, a line is scratched through my name. I am invited to cast my vote. There are black balls and white balls, in open-topped cardboard medicine boxes.

I scoop up one ball from each box, both in one hand. For a moment the possibilities feel equally balanced. In the end, it is the white ball that I let go, the black one that I return to its box. Someone else can have that pleasure.

Leaving the community tent, I try to gauge the public mood. My sense is that it will not go well for this woman. But perhaps the nurses, doctors and mantises have already done enough. Perhaps the water thief will be strong enough, with or without medicine.

I am thinking what to do next when something tugs at my hem. It is the little boy, the one who is always following me. I reach into my pocket and feel the fat round bulge of the eye. I think about the purple light, how pretty it is. The eye has been my vigil and my gateway, but I don't have much use for it now.

I tell the boy to hold out his hand. He obeys.

THE OLD MAN
AND THE
MARTIAN SEA

IN **THE** belly of the airship, alone except for freight pods and dirt-smeared machines, Yukimi dug into her satchel and pulled out her companion. She had been given it on her thirteenth birthday, by her older sister. It had been just before Shirin left Mars, so the companion had been a farewell present as well as a birthday gift.

It wasn't the smartest companion in the world. It had all the usual recording functions, and enough wit to arrange and categorize Yukimi's entries, but when it spoke back to her she never had the impression that there was a living mind trapped inside the floral-patterned—and now slightly dog-eared—hardback covers. And when it tried to engage her in conversation, when it tried to act like a friend or even a sister, it wasn't clever enough to come out with the sort of thing a real person would have said. But Yukimi didn't mind, really. It had still been a gift from Shirin, and if she stopped the companion talking back to her—which she mostly did, unless there was something she absolutely had to know—then it was still a place to record her thoughts and observations, and a useful window into the aug. When she was seventeen she would be legally entitled to receive the implants that gave her direct access to that shifting, teeming sea of universal knowledge. For now, all she had was the glowing portal of the companion.

"I've done it now," she told it. "After all those times where we used to dare each other to sneak aboard, I've actually stayed behind until after the doors are closed. And now we're in the air." She paused, tiptoeing to peer through a grubby, dust-scoured window as her home fell slowly away. "I can see Shalbatana now, Shirin—it looks much smaller from up here. I can see Sagan Park and the causeway and the school. I can't believe that was our whole world, everything we knew. Not that that's any surprise to you, I suppose."

It wasn't Shirin she was talking to, of course. It was just the companion. But early on she had fallen into the habit of making the entries as if she was telling them to her sister, and she had never broken it.

"I couldn't have done it if we hadn't played those games," Yukimi went on. "It was pretty hard, even then. Easy enough to sneak onto the docks—not much has changed since you left—but much harder to get aboard the airship. I waited until there was a lot going on, with everyone running around trying to get it loaded on time. Then I just made a run for it, dodging between robots and dock workers. I kept thinking: what's the worst that can happen? They'll find me and take me home. But I won't be in any more trouble than if I do manage to sneak aboard. I know they'll find me sooner or later anyway. I bet you're shaking your head now, wondering what the point of all this is. But it's easy for you, Shirin. You're on another planet, with your job, so you don't have to deal with any of this. I'm stuck back here and I can't even escape into the aug. So I'm doing something stupid and childish: I'm running away. It's your fault for showing me how easy it would be to get aboard one of the airships. You'd better be ready to take some of the blame."

It was too much effort to keep on tiptoe so she lowered down. "I know it won't make any difference: I'm not a baby. But they keep telling me I'll be fine and I know I won't be, and everything they say is exactly what I don't want to hear. *It's not you, it's us. We still love you, darling daughter. We've just grown apart.* As if any of that makes it all right. God, I hate being me."

She felt a lurch then, as if the airship had punched its way through the pressure bubble that surrounded the whole of Shalbatana City and its suburbs. A ghost of resistance, and then they were through. Behind, the bubble would reseal instantly so that not even a whisper of breathable air was able to leak out into the thin atmosphere beyond.

"I'm through now," she said, going back on tiptoe. "On the other side. I guess this is the farthest from home I've ever been." The sun was catching the bubble's edge, picking it out in a bow of pale pink. Her home, everything she really knew, was inside that pocket of air, and now it looked like a cheap plastic snow globe, like the one her aunt had sent back from Paris with the Eiffel Tower.

It hit her then. Not the dizzy sense of adventure she had been expecting, but an awful, knife-twisting sense of wrongness. As if, only now that the airship was outside the bubble, was she grasping the mistake she had made.

But it was much too late to do anything about it now.

"I'm doing the right thing, Shirin. Please tell me I'm doing the right thing."

She slumped down with her back against the sloping wall of the cargo hold. She felt sorry for herself, but she was too drained to cry. She knew it would be a good idea to eat, but she had no appetite for the apple she had brought with her in the satchel. She closed the covers on the companion and let it slip to the hard metal deck, gaining another dent or dog-ear in the process. Sensing her mood, the cartoon characters on the side of the satchel started singing and dancing, trying in their idiotic way to perk her up.

Yukimi scrunched the satchel until they shut up.

She listened to the drone of the airship's engines. It was a different sound now that the air outside was so much colder and thinner than inside Shalbatana City's dome. She knew from school that the air had once been even thinner, before the changes began. But it was still not enough to keep anyone alive for very long.

There was enough air inside the cargo hold to last for the journey, though.

At least that was what Shirin had always said, and Shirin had never lied about anything. Had she?

"I THINK SOMETHING'S happening," Yukimi told the companion. "We're changing course."

They had been flying high and steady for eight hours, Mars unrolling below in all its savage dreariness, all its endless rust-red monotony. Adults were always going on about how there were already too many people on the planet, but as far as Yukimi could tell there was still a lot of empty space between the warm, wet bubbles of the settlements. Aside from the pale, arrow-straight scratch of the occasional road or pipeline, there had been precious little evidence of civilization since their departure. Unless one counted the lakes, which were made by rain, and rain was made by people, but lakes weren't civilization, as far as Yukimi was concerned. How anyone could think this world was crowded, or even beginning to be crowded, was beyond her.

Yukimi closed the book and strained to look through the window again. It was hard to tell, but the ground looked nearer than it had been all afternoon. They didn't seem to be anywhere near a dome. That made sense, because in the time she had been in the air, there was no way that the airship could have made it to Vikingville, let alone anywhere farther away than that.

"It's a good sign," she went on. "It has to be. Someone must have figured out what I did, and now they've recalled the airship. Maybe they even got in touch with you, Shirin. You'd have told them about our game, how easy it would be for me to escape. I'm going to be in a lot of trouble now, but I always knew that was coming sooner or later. At least I'll have made my point."

That was going to cost someone a lot of money, Yukimi thought. She could see her father now, shaking his head at the shame she had brought on him with her antics. Making him look bad in front of his rich friends like Uncle Otto. Well, if that was what it took to get through to her parents, so be it.

But as the airship lowered, so her certainty evaporated. It didn't seem to be turning around, or be in any kind of a hurry to continue its journey. The engine note had changed to a dawdling throb, just enough to hold station against the wind.

What was going on?

She looked through the window again, straining hard to look down and, yes, there was something under them. It wasn't a bubble like the one around Shalbatana, though, or even one of those settlements that was built straight onto the ground with no protection from the atmosphere. It was a machine, a huge, metallic-green, beetle-shaped juggernaut inching slowly along the surface. It was bigger than the airship, bigger than any moving thing she had ever seen with her own eyes. The machine was as long as a city district, as wide as Sagan Park. It had eight solid wheels, each of which was large enough to roll over not just her home but the entire apartment complex. And although it seemed to be crawling, that was only an illusion caused by its size. It was probably moving faster than she could run.

"I can see a Scaper," she told the book. "That's what I think it is, anyway. One of those old terraforming mechs." She held the companion open and aimed down through the window, so that it could capture the view of the enormous machine, with chimneys sprouting in double rows along its back, angled slightly rearward like the smokestacks on an ocean liner. "I didn't think there were many of them left now. I don't think they actually do anything anymore; it's just too much bother to shut them down."

But for the life of her she could not imagine why the airship was now descending to rendezvous with a Scaper. How exactly was that going to get her home any quicker?

"I'm not sure about this," she told the companion and then closed it quietly.

Through the window, she could see the airship lowering itself between the twin rows of atmosphere stacks. They were soot black and sheer, as tall as the highest buildings in Shalbatana City. The airship stopped with a jerk, the freight pods creaking in their harnesses, and then a series of bangs and thuds sounded in rapid succession, as if restraining devices were locking into place. The engine note faded away, leaving only a distant throb, one that came up from the floor. It was the sound of the Scaper, transmitted to the cargo hold.

For long minutes, nothing happened.

Yukimi was by now quite uneasy, not at all sure that this rendezvous had anything to do with her being rescued. Halting on the back of a

Scaper—kilometers from anywhere—had not figured in her plans. She had always assumed that the airships went from A to B as quickly as possible. No one had ever mentioned anything about them indulging in this kind of detour.

None of this would be happening anywhere else in the solar system, she told herself. Mars was the only place where a girl could run away from home and not be found. Everywhere else, the aug was so thick, so all-pervasive, it was impossible to do anything illegal without someone knowing more or less instantly. You couldn't hide away inside things. You couldn't get lost.

Mars was different, as everyone liked to say. Mars was a Descrutinized Zone. The aug was purposefully thin, and that meant people had to take responsibility for their own actions. You could get into trouble on Mars. Easily.

Yukimi was pacing around, wondering what to do—with all sorts of impractical ideas flashing through her head—when the cargo doors began to open. She took in a deep breath, as if that was going to help her. But apart from a slight breeze there wasn't any loss of pressure. As hard blue light pushed through the widening Saps where the doors were rising open, she slunk back into the shadows, hiding between two freight pods. She had put the companion back into her satchel, and she hoped neither of them would make a sound. She very much wanted to be discovered, but she also very much wanted not to be.

For a long time nothing at all happened. All she heard was faint mechanical sounds in the distance, and the continuing throb of the Scaper. She was aware now of a very slight undulation to their motion, as the colossal machine followed the terrain under its wheels.

Then she heard something approaching. The noise was patient, rhythmic, wheezing, and it was accompanied by a labored shuffling. Yukimi tensed and pushed herself even farther back, but not quite so far that she couldn't see the cargo doors. With an agonizing slowness, something horrible came up the ramp. It was a monster.

Silhouetted, huge and bulbous against the blue light beyond, came something like a man, but swollen out of all proportion, with the head no more than a bulge between wide, ogrelike shoulders. Yukimi's fear sharpened into a very precise kind of terror. She had never seen any-thing like this before. The figure stepped into the bay, and at last she saw it properly. It was wearing armor, but the armor was scratched and scabbed and rusty, and bits of it didn't fit correctly. There were pipes and cables all over the misshapen form, with wisps of steam coming out of its joints. Green fluid dribbled out one of the knees. The bulge where its head should have been was a low bronze dome, caked in grease and dirt, with nothing at all that could pass for a face. It didn't even have eyes. It just had cylinders sticking out of it at various angles, glassy with lenses, and some filth-smeared grills in the side of the dome. She couldn't tell if it was a robot or some ancient, grotesquely cumbersome space suit. All she knew was that she was very, very frightened by it, and she didn't want to know who—or what—was inside.

The figure clanked and wheezed as it moved through the cargo bay. It paused by one of the cargo pods, not far from where she was hiding. She hardly dared move in case it saw or heard her.

The figure raised one of its huge arms and scraped dirt off a ship-ping label. Its armored hand was big enough to crush a chair. One of the lenses sticking out of its head swiveled into place, telescoping out to peer at the label. Yukimi felt herself caught between possibilities. She wanted to be found now, no doubt about it. But she did not want to be found by this thing, whatever it was.

No one had ever told her there were monsters like this on Mars, not even Shirin, when she had been trying to scare her little sister. And Shirin had never missed a trick in that regard.

The figure moved sideways, to the next pod. It peered at the next label. If it kept that up, there was no way it was going to fail to notice Yukimi. Yet in that moment she saw her chance. There was an open-topped cargo pallet behind the two pods she was hiding between—it was only partly filled with plastic sacks of some agricultural or biomedical product. She could conceal herself in that easily—if only she could get into it without being noticed.

She listened to the figure's wheezing. It was regular enough that she had a chance to move during the exhalation phase, when the figure was making enough noise to cover her movements. There was not going to be time to agonize about it, though. It was already moving to the next pod, and the one after that would bring it right next to her.

She moved, timing things expertly. Shirin would have been proud. She was into the open-topped pallet before the wheeze ended, and nothing in the ensuing moments suggested that she had been discovered. The figure made a sound as of another label being scuffed clean. Yukimi crouched low, cushioned on the bed of plastic sacks. They squeaked a little under her, but if she stayed still there was no sound.

She had done the right thing, she told herself. Better to take her chances on the airship than to put herself at the mercy of the creature, whatever it was. The airship would be on its way again soon. They didn't just go missing between cities.

Did they?

The figure left. She heard it clanking and wheezing out of the bay, down the ramp, back into the Scaper. But she dared not move just yet. Perhaps it had sensed her somewhere in the bay and was just waiting for her to leave her hiding place.

Shortly afterward, something else came. It wasn't the shuffling, wheezing figure this time. It was something big and mechanical, something that whined and whirred and made pneumatic hissing sounds. Quite suddenly, one of the freight pods was moving. Yukimi snuggled down deeper. The machine went away and then came back. She caught a glimpse of it this time as it locked onto the next pod and hauled it out of the cargo bay. It was a handler robot, similar to the ones she had seen fussing around at the docks, except maybe a bit older and less cared for. It was a big stupid lunk of a robot: yellow and greasy and easily powerful enough to crush a little girl without even realizing what it had done.

Then it came back. Yukimi felt a jolt as the robot coupled onto the open-topped pallet. Then the ceiling started moving, and she realized that she was being unloaded. For a moment she was paralyzed with fear, but even when the moment passed she didn't know what to do. She dared move enough to look over the edge of the pallet. The floor was moving past very quickly, racing by faster than she could run. Even if she risked climbing out and managed not to break anything or knock herself out as she hit the deck, there was still a danger that the robot would run over her with one of its wheels.

No, that wasn't a plan. It hadn't been a good idea to hide inside the pallet, but then again it hadn't been a good idea to sneak aboard the airship in the first place. It had been a day of bad ideas, and she wasn't going to make things worse now.

But what could be worse than being taken into the same place as the wheezing, goggle-eyed thing?

The robot took her out of the bay, down a ramp, into some kind of enclosed storage room inside the Scaper. There were lights in the ceilings and the suspended rails of an overhead crane. Even lying down in the pallet, she could see other freight pods stacked around. With a jolt the robot lowered the open-topped pallet and disengaged. It whirred away. Yukimi lay still, wondering what to do next. It seemed likely that the airship had stopped off to make a delivery to the Scaper. If that was the case it would be on its way quite soon, and she would much rather be on it than stay behind here, inside the Scaper, with the thing. But to get back aboard now she would have to make sure the thing didn't see her, and lying down in the pallet she had no idea if the thing was waiting nearby.

She heard a noise that sounded awfully like the cargo doors closing again.

It was now or never. She scrambled out of the pallet, catching her trousers on the sharp lip, ripping them at the knee, but not caring. She got her feet onto the floor, dragged her satchel with her, oriented herself—she could see the loading ramp, and the doors above it lowering shut—and started running. Really running now, not the pretend running she had done all her life until this moment. She had to get inside the airship again, before the doors shut. She had to get away from the Scaper.

The thing stepped in front of the ramp, blocking her escape. With dreadful slowness it raised one of its hands. Yukimi skidded to a halt, heart racing in her chest, panic overwhelming her.

The thing raised its other hand. They came together where its neck should have been, under the shallow dome that passed for its head. The huge fingers worked two rust-colored toggles and then moved up slightly to grasp the dome by the grills on either side of it. Yukimi was now more terrified than she had ever thought possible. She did not even think of running in the other direction. The thing was slow, but this was its lair and she knew that she could never escape it for good. Plodding and wheezing and slow as it might be, it would always find her.

It took off the helmet, lifting it up above its shoulders. There was a tiny head inside the armor. She could only see the top of it, from the eyes up. It had lots of age spots and blemishes and a few sparse tufts of very white hair. The rest of it was hidden by the armor.

An unseen mouth said, "Hello."

Yukimi couldn't answer. She was just standing there trembling. The thing looked at her for several seconds, the eyes blinking as if it, too, was not quite sure what to make of this meeting. "It is, at least in polite circles, customary to reciprocate a greeting," the thing—the old man inside the armor—said. "Which is to say, you might consider giving me a 'hello' in return. I'm not going to hurt you."

Yukimi moved her mouth and forced herself to say, "Hello."

"Hello back." The man turned slightly, his armor huffing and puffing. "I don't want to seem discourteous—we haven't even introduced ourselves—but that airship's on a tight schedule and it'll be lifting off very shortly. Do you want to get back aboard it? I won't stop you if you do, but it'd be remiss of me not to make sure you're absolutely certain of it. It's continuing on to Milankovic, and that's a long way from here—at least two days' travel. Have you come from Shalbatana?"

Yukimi nodded.

"I can feed you and get you back there a sight quicker than you'll reach Milankovic. Of course you'll have to trust me when I tell you that, but—well—we all have to trust someone sooner or later, don't we?"

"Who are you?" Yukimi asked.

"They call me Corax," the old man said. "I work out here, doing odd jobs. I'm sorry if the armor scared you, but there wasn't time for me to get out of it when I learned that the airship was coming in. I'd just come back from the lake, you see. I'd been scouting around, checking out the old place one last time before the waters rise..." He paused. "I'm wittering. I do that sometimes—it comes of spending a lot of time on my own. What's your name?"

"Yukimi."

"Well, Yukimi—which is a very nice name, by the way—it's your call. Back on the airship and take your chances until you reach Milankovic—miserable arse-end of nowhere that it is. You'll need warm clothing and enough food and water to get you through two days, and maybe some supplementary oxygen in case cabin pressure drops. You've got all that, haven't you? Silly question, really. A clever looking girl like you wouldn't have stowed away on a cargo airship without the necessary provisions."

Yukimi held up her satchel. "I've just got this."

"Ah. And in that would be—what, exactly?"

"An apple. And a companion." She observed the faint flicker of incomprehension on the old man's forehead. "My diary," she added. "From my sister, Shirin. She's a terraforming engineer on Venus. She's working with the change-clouds, to make the atmosphere breathable...."

"Now which of us is doing the wittering?" Corax shook the visible part of his head. "No, there's nothing for it, I'm afraid. I can't let you go now. You'll have to stay here and wait for the flier. I'm afraid you're going to be in rather a lot of hot water."

"I know," Yukimi said resignedly.

"You don't seem to care very much. Is everything all right? I suppose it can't be, or you wouldn't have stowed away on an airship."

"Can you get me home?"

"Undoubtedly. And in the meantime I can certainly see that you're taken care of. There's a catch, of course: you'll have to put up with my inane ramblings until then. Do you think you can manage that? I can be something of a bore, when the mood takes me. It comes with age."

Behind Corax, the cargo doors were closed. The loading ramps had retracted and now even larger doors—belonging to the Scaper—were sealing off Yukimi's view of the airship.

"I suppose it's too late now anyway," Yukimi said.

SHE FOLLOWED CORAX'S stomping, wheezing suit down into the deeper levels of the Scaper. By the time they got anywhere near a window the airship was a distant, dwindling dot, turned the color of brass by the setting sun.

Yukimi considered herself lucky now not to be stuck on it all the way to Milankovic. She was sure she could do without food and water for two days (not that it would be fun, even with the apple for rations) but it had never occurred to her that it might get seriously cold. But then, given that the airships had not been built for the convenience of stowaways, it was hardly surprising.

Yukimi was glad when Corax got out of the armor. At the back of her mind had been the worry that he was something other than fully human—she had, after all, only been able to see the top of his head—but apart from being scrawnier and older than almost anyone she could ever remember meeting, he was normal enough. Small by Martian standards—they were about the same height, and Yukimi hadn't stopped growing. The only person that small Yukimi had ever met had been her aunt, the one who sent the snow globe, and she had been born on Earth, under the iron press of too much gravity.

Under the armor Corax had been wearing several layers of padded clothing, with many belts and clips, from which dangled an assortment of rattling, chinking tools.

"Why do you live out here?" she asked, as Corax prepared her some tea down in the Scaper's galley.

"Someone has to. When big stuff like this goes wrong, who do you think fixes it? I'm the one who's drawn the short straw." He turned around, conveying two steaming mugs of tea. "Actually it's really not that bad. I'm not one for the hustle and bustle of modern Martian civilization, so the cities don't suit me. There are a lot like us, leftovers from the old days, when the place was emptier. We keep to the margins, try not to get in anyone's way. Bit like this Scaper, really. As long as we don't interfere, they let us be."

"You live in the Scaper?"

"Most of the time." He sat down opposite Yukimi, tapping a knuckle against the metal tabletop. "These things were made two hundred years ago, during the first flush of terraforming."

"The table?"

"The Scaper. Built to last, and to self-repair. They were supposed to keep processing the atmosphere, sucking in soil and air, for as long as it took. A thousand years, maybe more. They were designed so that they'd keep functioning—keep looking after themselves, locked on the same program—even if the rest of human civilization crashed back to Earth. Their makers were thinking long-term, making plans for things they had no real expectation of ever living to see. A bit like cathedral builders, diligently laying down stones even though the cathedral might take lifetimes to finish." He paused and smiled, years falling from his face, albeit only for an instant. "I don't suppose you've ever seen a cathedral, have you, Yukimi?"

"Have you?"

"Once or twice."

"The Scapers were a bad idea," Yukimi said. "That's what my sister told me. A relic from history. The wrong way to do things."

"Easy to say that now." He drew a finger around the rim of his tea mug. "But it was a grand plan at the time. The grandest. At its peak, there were thousands of machines like this, crisscrossing Mars from pole to pole. It was a marvelous sight. Herds of iron buffalo. Engines of creation, forging a new world."

"You saw them?"

He seemed to catch himself before answering. "No; I'd have to be quite impossibly old for that to be the case. But the reports were glorious. Your sister's quite right. It was the wrong approach. But it was the only way we—they—could see at the time. So we mustn't mock them for their mistakes. In two hundred years, someone will be just as quick to mock us for ours, if we're not careful."

"I still don't see why you have to live out here."

"I keep this Scaper from falling apart," Corax explained. "Once upon a time the self-repair systems were adequate, but eventually even they stopped working properly. Now the Scaper has to be nursed, treated with kindness. She's an old machine and she needs help to keep going."

"Why?"

"There are people who care about such things. They live on Mars, but also elsewhere in the system. Rich sponsors, for the most part. With enough money that they can afford to sprinkle a little of it on vanity projects, like keeping this machine operational. Partly out of a sense of historical indebtedness, partly out of a cautionary attitude that we ought not to throw away something that worked, albeit imperfectly, and partly for the sheer pointless hell of it. It pleases them to keep this Scaper running, and the others still trundling around. It's Martian history. We shouldn't let it slip through our fingers."

Yukimi had no idea who these people were, but even among her father's friends there were individuals with—in her opinion—rather more money than sense. Like Uncle Otto with his expensive private sunjammer that he liked to take guests in for spins around Earth and the inner worlds. So she could believe it, at least provisionally.

"For them," Corax went on, "it's a form of art as much as anything else. And the cost really isn't that much compared to some of the things they're involved in. As for me—I'm just the man they hire to do the dirty work. They don't even care who I am, as long as I get the stuff done. They arrange for the airships to drop off supplies and parts, as well as provisions for me. It's been a pretty good life, actually. I get to see a lot of Mars and I don't have to spend every waking hour keeping the Scaper running. The rest, it's my own time to do as I please."

Looking around the dingy confines of the galley, Yukimi couldn't think of a worse place to spend a week, let alone a lifetime.

"So what do you do?" she asked politely. "When you're not working?"

"A little industrial archaeology of my own, actually." Corax put down his tea cup. "I need to make some calls, so people know where you are. They're sending out a flier tomorrow anyway, so we should be able to get you back home before too long. Hopefully it won't arrive until the afternoon. If there's time, I'd like to show you something beforehand."

"What?"

"Something no one else will ever see again," Corax said. "At least, not for a little while."

He made the calls and assured Yukimi that all would be well tomorrow. "I didn't speak to your parents, but I understand they'll be informed that you're safe and sound. We can try and put you through later, if you'd like to talk?"

"No thanks," Yukimi said. "Not now."

"That doesn't sound like someone in any great hurry to be reunited. Was everything all right at home?"

"No," Yukimi said.

"And is it something you'd like to talk about?"

"Not really." She would, actually. But not to Corax; not to this scraggy old man with tufts of white hair who lived alone in a giant, obsolete terraforming machine. He might not be an ogre, but he couldn't possibly grasp what she was going through.

"So tell me about your sister, the one on Venus. You said she was involved in the terraforming program. Is she much older than you?"

"Six years," Yukimi said. She meant Earth years, of course. A year on Mars was twice as long, but everyone still used Earth years when they were talking about how old they were. It got messy otherwise. "She left Mars when she was nineteen. I was thirteen." She reached into her satchel and pulled out the companion. "This is the thing I was talking about, the diary. It was a present from Shirin."

He moved to open the book. "Might I?"

"Go ahead."

He touched the covers with his old man's fingers, which were bony and yellow-nailed and sprouted white hairs in odd places. The companion came alive under his touch, blocks of text and illustration appearing on the revealed pages. The text was in an approximation of Yukimi's handwriting, tinted a dark mauve, the pictures rendered in the form of woodcuts and stenciled drawings, and the entries were organized by date and theme, with punctilious cross-referencing.

Corax picked at the edge of the book with his fingernail. "I can't turn to the next page."

"That's not how you do it. Haven't you ever read a book before?"

He gave her a tolerant smile. "Not like this."

Yukimi showed him the way. She touched her finger to the bottom right corner and dragged it sideways, so that the book revealed the next pair of pages. "That's how you turn to the next page. If you want to turn ten pages, you use two fingers. Hundred pages, three fingers. And the same to go backward."

"It seems very complicated."

"It's just like a diary. I tell it what I've been doing, or let it record things for me. Then it sorts it all out and makes me fill in the gaps."

"Sounds horrendous," Corax said, pulling a face as if he had just bitten into a lemon. "I was never very good at diary keeping."

"It's meant to be more than just a diary, though. Shirin had one as well—she bought it at the same time. She was leaving, so we wouldn't be able to talk normally anymore because of the lag. I was sad because she'd always been my best friend, even though she was older than me. She said our companions would help us bridge the distance."

"I'm not sure I understand."

"We were both supposed to use our companions all the time. Make entries whenever we could. I would talk to my companion as if Shirin was there, and Shirin would talk to hers as if I was there. Then, every now and again, the companions would—I can't remember the word." Yukimi frowned. "Connect up. Exchange entries. So that my companion got better at copying Shirin and hers got better at copying me. And then if we kept on doing that, eventually it would be like having Shirin with me all the time, so that I could talk to her whenever I wanted. Even if Venus was on the other side of the sun. It wouldn't be the same as Shirin—it wasn't meant to replace her—but just make it so that we didn't always feel apart."

"It seems like a good idea," Corax said.

"It wasn't. We promised we'd keep talking to our companions, but Shirin didn't. For a while, yes. But once she'd been away from Mars for a few months she stopped doing it. Every now and again, yes—but you could tell only because she was feeling bad about not doing it before."

"I suppose she was busy."

"We promised each other. I kept up my side of the promise. I still talk to Shirin. I still tell her everything. But because she doesn't talk to me enough, my companion can't pretend to be her." Yukimi felt a wave of sadness slide over her. "I could have really used her lately."

"It doesn't mean she doesn't love you. It just means she's an adult with a lot of people making demands on her. Terraforming's very important work. It requires great responsibility."

"That's what my parents keep saying."

"It's the truth. It always has been. The people who made the Scapers understood that, even if they didn't get the technology quite right. It's the same with—what they call them? Those things in the air, swirling around?"

"Change-clouds," Yukimi said.

He nodded. "I see them sometimes at dusk. Just another machine, really. In a thousand years, there won't seem much difference between them and this. But they make me feel very old. Even your book makes me feel like an old relic from prehistory." He stood up, his knees creaking with the effort. "Speaking of recording devices, let me show you something." He moved to one of the shelves and pushed aside some junk to expose an old-looking space helmet. He brought it back to the table, blowing the dust off it in the progress, coughing as he breathed some of it in, and set the helmet down before Yukimi.

"It looks ancient," she said, trying hard not to show too much disappointment. It was scratched and dented and the white paint was coming off in places. There had once been colorful markings round the visor and crest, but they were mostly faded or rubbed away now. She could just make out the ghostly impressions where they had been.

"It is. Unquestionably. Older even than this Scaper. I know because I found it and...well." He stroked the helmet lovingly, leaving dust tracks where his fingers had been. "There's serious provenance here. It used to belong to someone very famous, before he went missing."

"Who?"

"We'll come to that tomorrow. In the meantime I thought it might be of interest. The helmet's still in good nick—built to last. I had to swap out the power cells, but other than that I've done nothing to it. Do you want to try it on?"

She didn't, really, but it seemed rude to say so. She gave an encouraging nod. Corax picked up the helmet again and shuffled around the table until he was behind her. He lowered it down gently, until the cushioned rim was resting on her shoulders. She could still breathe perfectly normally because the helmet was open at the bottom. "It smells moldy," she said.

"Like its owner. But watch this. I'm going to activate the head-up display playback, using the external controls." He pressed some studs on the outside of the helmet and Yukimi heard soft clicks and beeps inside.

Then everything changed.

She was still looking at Corax, still inside the galley. But overlaid on that was a transparent view of something else entirely. It was a landscape, a Martian landscape, moving slowly, rocking side to side as if someone was walking. They were coming to the edge of something, a sharp drop in the terrain. The pace slowed as the edge came nearer, and then the point of view dipped, so that Yukimi was looking down, down at her chest-pack, which looked ridiculously old and clunky, down at her heavy, dust-stained boots, down at the Martian soil, and the point where—just beyond her toes—it fell savagely away.

"The edge of Valles Marineris," Corax told her. "The deepest canyon on Mars. It's a long way down, isn't it?"

Yukimi agreed. Even though she was sitting down, she still felt a twinge of vertigo.

"You can still go there, but it's not the same," Corax went on. "Mostly filled with water now—and it'll only get deeper as the sea levels keep rising. Where I'm standing—where you're standing—is now a chain of domed resort hotels. They'll tear down the domes when the atmosphere gets thick enough to breathe, but they won't tear down the hotels." He paused. "Not that I'm complaining, or arguing against the terraforming program. It'll be marvelous to see boats sailing across Martian seas, under Martian skies. To see people walking around under that sky without needing suits or domes to keep them alive. To see Earth in the morning light. We'll have gained something incredible. But we'll have lost something as well. I just think we should be careful not to lose sight of that."

"We could always go back," Yukimi said. "If we didn't like the new Mars."

"No," Corax said. "That we wouldn't be able to do. Not even if we wanted it more than anything in the world. Because once we've touched a world, it stays touched." He reached over and turned off the head-up display. "Now. Shall we think about eating?"

IN THE MORNING they left the Scaper, traveling out in a small, four-wheeled buggy that came down from a ramp in the great machine's belly. "Just a little sightseeing trip," Corax said, evidently detecting Yukimi's anxiety about not being back when the flier—scheduled for the afternoon—came to collect her. They were snug and warm in the buggy's pressurized cabin, Yukimi wearing the same clothes as the day before, Corax in the same outfit he had been wearing under the armor, which—for reasons not yet clear to Yukimi—he had stowed in the buggy's rear storage compartment.

"Will the Scaper be all right without you aboard?" Yukimi asked, as they powered out of its shadow, bouncing over small rocks and ridges.

"She'll take care of herself for a few hours, don't you worry."

An awkward question pushed itself to the front of Yukimi's mind. "Will you always be the one in charge of it?"

Corax steered the buggy around a crater before answering. "Until the people who pay for my upkeep decide otherwise." He glanced sideways, a cockeyed grin on his face. "Why? You think old Corax's getting too old for the job?"

"I don't know," she answered truthfully. "How old are you, exactly?"

"How old do you reckon?"

"Older than my aunt, and I'm not sure how old she is. She's from Earth as well."

"Did I say I was from Earth?"

"You mentioned cathedrals," Yukimi said.

"I could have been there as a tourist."

"But you weren't."

"No," he said eventually. "I wasn't. Here I'm the tourist."

They drove on, crossing kilometers of Martian terrain. Most of the time Corax didn't have his hands on the controls, the buggy navigating by itself. Yukimi saw tire tracks in the soil and guessed that Corax had come this way before, maybe within the last few days. As the route wound its way around obstacles, the Scaper became little more than a dark, chimney-backed hump on the horizon, seemingly fixed in place. And then even the dark hump was gone.

The ground began to dip down. Ahead, reflecting back the sun like a sheet of polished metal, was what appeared to be a large lake or even a small sea. It had a complicated, meandering shoreline. Yukimi could not see the far side, even with the buggy raised high above sea level. She did her best to memorize the shape of the lake, the way it would look from above, so that she could find it on a map. That was hard, though, so she took out the companion and opened the covers so that it recorded the view through the buggy's forward window.

"You want to know where we are?" Corax asked.

Yukimi nodded.

"Approaching Crowe's Landing. You ever hear of it?"

"I don't think so."

"Doesn't surprise me. It's been a ghost town for decades; I'd be surprised if it's on any of the recent maps. It certainly won't be on them for much longer."

"Why not?"

"Because it'll soon be under water."

Corax took control of the buggy again as it completed its descent to the edge of the lake, following a zigzagging path down the sloping terrain. As they neared the water, Yukimi made out a series of sketchy shapes floating just beneath the surface: pale rectangles and circles, some of them deeper than others, and reaching a considerable distance from the shore. They looked like the shapes on some weird game board. They were, she realized, the roofs and walls of submerged buildings.

"THIS WAS A town?"

Corax nodded. "Way back when. Mars is on its second wave of history now—maybe even its third. I remember when Shalbatana was nothing, just a weather station that wasn't even manned half the time. Crowe's Landing was a major settlement. Not the main one, but one of the four or five largest colonies on the surface. Yes, we called them colonies back then. It was a different time. A different age." Slowly, he guided the buggy into the waters, picking his way down what must have been a thoroughfare between two rows of buildings. With some apprehension, Yukimi watched the water lap over the tops of the wheels, and then against the side of the cabin. "It's all right," Corax said. "She's fully submersible. I've taken her a full kilometer out, but we're not going anywhere so far today."

They were driving along a hard surface, so even though the buggy's wheels were underwater, they didn't stir up much material. The water was clear enough that Yukimi could see for tens of meters in all directions. As the road sloped down, the sea gradually closed over the cockpit bubble and it was almost possible to believe that they were just driving through a normal, albeit strangely unpopulated, district of Shalbatana City. The buildings were rectangles, cylinders, and domes, all with small black windows and circular, airlock style doors set out from the main structure in rounded porches. There must never have been a bubble around Crowe's Landing, so the buildings would have been the inhabitants' only protection from the atmosphere. Yukimi guessed that there were tunnels linking them together, sunk under the road level. Even the newer communities like Shalbatana—and it was strange now to think of her hometown as "new"—had underground tunnels, maintained to provide emergency shelter and communication should something untoward happen to the bubble. Yukimi had been down into them during school field trips.

She wasn't alone—she was in the cabin with Corax—but there was still something spooky about driving slowly through this deserted colony. She wished Corax hadn't called it a ghost town, and while she understood that he hadn't meant that the place was literally haunted, she couldn't turn her imagination off. As the light wavered down from the overlying sea, she kept seeing faces appear in the windows, brief and spectral like paper cutouts held there for a moment. Once they turned a corner and passed another kind of buggy, left parked there as if its owners had only just abandoned it. But it was a very old-fashioned looking buggy, and the symbols painted on its side reminded her of the faded markings on the old space helmet.

Eventually Corax brought the buggy to a halt.

"We're here," he said grandly. "The objective. You see that building to our right, the one shaped like an old-fashioned hat box?"

"Yes," Yukimi said dubiously.

"It's still airtight, unlike most of the others. Because of that, it's watertight as well. And the airlock's still functioning—there's just enough power in the mechanism for another cycle. Do you see where I'm headed?"

"Not really."

"Crowe's Landing is almost gone now, and in a hundred years it'll be completely forgotten. The seas will rise, Mars will be greened. A whole new civilization will bloom and prosper. You'll be part of that, Yukimi—when you're older. You'll see wonderful things and live to tell your grandchildren of the way it used to be, before the change-clouds finished their work." He smiled. "I envy you. I've lived a very long time—the drugs weren't always the best, but at least I had a ready supply—but my time's coming to an end now and you'll outlive me by centuries, if luck's on your side."

Yukimi thought of all the things in her life that were not the way she wanted. "I don't think it is."

"I'm not sure. That airship could have carried on to Milankovic, and then where would you be?"

"Hm," she said, remaining to be convinced.

"I had an idea," Corax said. "Not long after I found this place and this building. Mars is changing now and the seas will rise. But they won't stay that way forever. One day—a thousand or ten thousand years from now, maybe more—the seas will shrink again. People will have other worlds to green by then, and maybe they'll let Mars return to its primal state. Whatever happens, Crowe's Landing will eventually come out of the waters. And that building will still be there. Still airtight."

"You can't be sure."

"It's a fair bet. Stronger odds of surviving than anything left on the surface, with everything that's to come. Soon there'll be woods and forests out there, and where there aren't woods and forests there'll be cities and people. There'll be weather and storms and history. But none of that will reach down here. This building's as close to a time capsule as we're going to find. Which is why we've come." He tapped a few commands into the buggy's console and stood up creakily. "That helmet I found? It used to belong to Crowe, one of the very first explorers."

"Can you be sure?"

"Reasonably. As I said, it's got provenance." He paused. "I'm going to put the helmet in there. It's a piece of the past, a memento of the way Mars used to be. Not just a chunk of metal and plastic but a historical document, a living record. I only played back a tiny part of what's stored in that helmet. That old fool captured thousands of hours, and that's not including all the log entries he made, all the thoughts he put down for posterity. An old man's ramblings...but maybe it'll be of interest to someone. And it'll all still be inside that helmet when they find it again."

Yukimi had trouble thinking much further in the future than her seventeenth birthday, when she would receive the golden gateway into the aug. Everything was a blank after that. Centuries, thousands of years—what difference did it make?

"Will anyone understand it?"

"They may have to work at it," Corax allowed. "But that's what historians and archaeologists do. And I was thinking: while we're at it, why don't we give them something else to puzzle over, in addition to the helmet?"

Yukimi thought for a moment. "You mean my companion?"

"Your thoughts and observations aren't any less valid than Corax's. You'll miss your diary, of course, and maybe you'll have some explaining to do to your sister when she finds out what happened to it—assuming you tell her, of course. But in the meantime, think what you'll have done. You'll have sent a message to the future. A gift from the past to a Martian civilization that doesn't even exist yet. No matter what happens, you'll have made your mark."

"No one's interested in what I have to say," Yukimi said.

"Don't put yourself down. Look, there's still time to make another entry. Tell them how you got here. Tell them how you feel today, tell them what made you run away from home yesterday. Be angry. Be sad. Get it out of your system."

"I've got to go back to it later."

"Believe me, this will help. When everything seems like it couldn't get any worse, you'll always be able to tell yourself: I did this one brilliant thing, this one brilliant thing that no one else has ever or will ever do. And that makes me special."

She thought about the companion. It had been a gift from Shirin and—for all that it was dog-eared, and not the smartest in the world—she had treated it with fondness. It reminded her of her older sister. It reminded her of the good times they had spent together, before Shirin bored of childhood games and started looking to the skies, dreaming of worlds to make anew.

But had Shirin really cared? It had been easy for her to promise to keep her side of the bargain, before she said good-bye. Yukimi sometimes wondered if her sister had given her more than a moment's thought except for the times when her conscience prickled her into sending a message.

"I cared," Yukimi said to herself. "Even if you didn't."

She still had the companion in her hands from when she had shown it the lake.

"You want a moment to yourself?" Corax asked.

Yukimi nodded.

SHE STAYED IN the submerged buggy while he took the helmet and the companion into the airtight building. He went out in the underwater armor, a monster born anew. But when he had taken a few paces away from the buggy and turned back to wave, Yukimi waved back. She couldn't see his face, but she knew it was Corax inside now, and while the armor was still monstrous, it was no longer frightening. Corax had been kind to her, and on some level he had seemed to understand what she was going through.

She watched him enter the building via the porch airlock. Some bubbles erupted out of the dark mouth of the door, and then there was nothing. She didn't think it would take him long to place the helmet and the companion, especially if he already knew his way around the building.

The buggy started moving.

It was sudden, purposeful activity, not the result of the brakes being loose or some underwater current stirring it into motion. It began to turn, steering back the way they had come. This wasn't right. Yukimi looked despairingly at the console, with its many controls. She didn't know which one to hit. There was a red panel, lit up as if it was some kind of emergency stop. She whacked it with her palm and then when there was no response she whacked it again and again. She grabbed hold of the steering joystick Corax had been using and tried yanking it left and right. But nothing she did had any effect on the buggy's progress.

It was already climbing out of the lake, the water beginning to drain off the top of the canopy as it pushed into air. "Stop!" she shouted. "Corax isn't back yet!"

But either the buggy was too stupid to realize what was happening or Corax had programmed it to ignore her.

Soon it was out of the lake. Once the ripples had settled, Yukimi could see the outline of Crowe's Landing exactly as it had been before. Nothing had changed. Except now Corax was down there, inside the armor, inside the watertight building.

She remembered him punching commands into the buggy before he had stood up. Had he been telling it to return to the Scaper after a set interval with Yukimi was still aboard?

Numb, but knowing there was nothing she could do, she sat in silence for the rest of the journey.

THE FLIER CAME not long after the buggy climbed back into the Scaper's belly. She was sitting alone in the galley, barely able to speak, when she heard footsteps echoing down the long metal corridors from the landing bay. Eventually two adults came into the galley. One was a young-looking man carrying a heavy bag. The other was her father, looking worried and gray. She braced herself for a stinging reproof, but instead her father rushed to Yukimi and hugged her. "I'm sorry," he said. "We didn't realize."

When she could find the words she asked, "Am I in trouble?"

"No," her father said soothingly. "I am. But you're not. Not now. Not ever." He hugged her again, as if he couldn't quite believe he had her in his arms, that it wasn't a dream.

"Where's the old guy?" asked the other man.

"I presume you mean Corax?" Yukimi asked.

"Yeah, Corax." The young-looking man set his bag down on the table and began unloading it. "I'm his replacement. That's why the flier was scheduled, so I could take over from him. The sponsors were worried he was getting a little too old for this kind of thing."

"Corax isn't coming back," Yukimi said.

The man looked impatient with her, as if she wasn't showing sufficient deference. "What do you mean, not coming back? What happened to him? Where is he?"

She looked him straight in the face, daring him to dismiss what she was about to say. "That's between me and Corax."

"Are you all right, Yukimi?" her father asked gently.

"I'm fine," she said. Which, for the moment at least, was the truth. She was sad for Corax, sad that she wouldn't see him again. But whatever he had done, he must have planned on doing it long before she took her airship ride. That he had shared it with her, that he had allowed her to place the companion in the time capsule, and to record her thoughts before doing so—her angry, bitter, wounded thoughts—was a privilege and a secret she would always carry with her. And whatever happened next, however hard it got with her family, she would have the knowledge that she had participated in something wonderful and unique, something no one else would know about until the seas retreated, on some impossibly distant day in the future of Mars, her Mars.

The flier took off, leaving the other man alone on the Scaper. Her father let Yukimi sit by the window as the flier accelerated back toward Shalbatana City. Nose pressed to glass, she studied the wheeling, rushing landscape for the lake where Crowe's Landing used to be. She saw a few patches of water, some vehicle tracks, and some of them looked vaguely familiar. But from up above, with an entirely different perspective, she couldn't be certain.

"Shirin's coming back from Venus," her father said, breaking the long silence.

"Oh," Yukimi answered.

"She says she's sorry she hasn't been in touch as often as she'd have liked."

"I'm sorry as well."

"She means it, Yukimi. I saw how upset she was."

Yukimi didn't answer immediately. She watched the ground hurtle by, thinking of Corax in his armor, the old man and the Martian sea. Then she reached out and took her father's hand in hers. "It'll be good to see Shirin," she said.

IN BABELSBERG

THE AFTERNOON before my speaking engagement at New York's Hayden Planetarium I find myself at The Museum of Modern Art, standing before Vincent Van Gogh's *De Sterrennacht*, or the Starry Night. Doubtless you know the painting. It's the one he created from the window of his room in the asylum at Saint-Rémy-de-Provence, after his voluntary committal. He was dead scarcely a year later.

I have seen paintings before, and paintings of starry nights. I think of myself as something of a student of the human arts. But this is the first time I grasp something of crucial significance. The mad yellow stars in Van Gogh's picture look nothing like the stars I saw during my deep space expeditions. My stars were mathematically remote reference points, to be used only when I had cause to doubt my inertial positioning systems. These stars are exuberant, flowerlike swabs of thick-daubed paint. More starfish than star. Though the painting is fixed—no part of it has changed in two hundred years—its lurid firmament seems to shimmer and swirl before my eyes. It's not how the stars really are, of course. But under a warm June evening this is how they must have appeared to this anxious, ailing man—as near and inviting as lanterns, lowered down from the zenith. Almost close enough to touch. Without that delusion— let us be charitable and call it a different kind of truth—generations of people would have had no cause to strive for the heavens. They would not have built their towers, built their flying machines, their rockets and space probes; they would not have struggled into orbit and onto the Moon. These sweetly lying stars have inspired greatness.

Inspired, in their small way, me.

Time presses, and I must soon be on my way to the Hayden Planetarium. It's not very far, but in the weeks since my return to Earth I have gained a certain level of celebrity and no movement is without its complications. They have already cleared a wing of the museum for me, and now I must brave the crowds in the street and fight my way to the limousine. I am not alone—I have my publicity team, my security entourage, my technicians—but I still feel myself at the uncomfortable focus of an immense, unsatiable public scrutiny. So different to the long years in which I was the one doing the scrutineering. For a moment I wish I were back out there, alone on the solar system's edge, light hours from any other thinking thing.

"Vincent!" someone calls, and then someone else, and then the calls become an assault of sound. As we push through the crowd fingers brush against my skin and I register the flinches that accompany each moment of contact. My alloy is always colder than they expect. It's as if I have brought a cloak of interplanetary cold back with me from space.

I provide some signatures, mouth a word or two to the onlookers, then bend myself into the limousine. And then we are moving, flanked by police floatercycles, and the computer-controlled traffic parts to hasten our advance. Soon I make out the blue glass cube of the Hayden, lit from within by an eerie glow, and I mentally review my opening remarks, wondering if it is really necessary to introduce myself to a world that already knows everything there is to know about me.

But it would be immodest to presume too much.

"I am Vincent," I begin, when I have the podium, standing with my hands resting lightly against the tilted platform. "But I suspect most of you are already aware of that."

They always laugh at that point. I smile and wait a beat before continuing.

"Allow me to bore you with some of my holiday snaps."

More laughter. I smile again. I like this.

LATER THAT EVENING, after a successful presentation, my schedule has me booked onto a late night chat show on the other side of town. I take no interest in these things myself, but I fully understand the importance of promotion to my transnational sponsors. My host for tonight is called The Baby. He is (or was) a fully adult individual who underwent neo-tenic regression therapy, until he attained the size and physiology of a six-month human. The Baby resembles a human infant, and directs his questions at me from a sort of pram.

I sit next to the pram, one arm slung over the back of the chair, one leg hooked over the other. There's a drink on the coffee table in front of me (along with a copy of the book) but of course I don't touch it. Behind us is a wide picture window, with city lights twinkling across the great curve of Manhattan Atoll.

"That's a good question," I say, lying through my alloy teeth. "Actually, my earliest memories are probably much like yours—a vague sense of *being*, an impression of events and feelings, some wants and needs, but nothing stronger than that. I came to sentience in the research com-pounds of the European Central Cybernetics Facility, not far from Zurich. That was all I knew to begin with. It took me a long time before I had any idea what I was, and what I was meant to do."

"Then I guess you could say that you had a kind of childhood," The Baby says.

"That wouldn't be too far from the mark," I answer urbanely.

"Tell me how you felt when you first realised you were a robot. Was that a shock?"

"Not at all." I notice that a watery substance is coming out of The Baby's nose. "I couldn't be shocked by what I already was. Frankly, it was something of a relief, to have a name for myself."

"A relief?"

"I have a very powerful compulsion to give names to things. That's a deep part of my core programming—my personality, you might almost say. I'm a machine made to map the unknown. The naming of things, the labelling of cartographic features—that's something that gives me great pleasure."

"I don't think I could ever understand that."

I try to help The Baby. "It's like a deep existential itch. If I see a landscape—a crater or a rift on some distant icy moon—I *must* call it something. Almost an obsessive compulsive disorder. I can't be satisfied with myself until I've done my duty, and mapping and naming things is a very big part of it."

"You take pleasure in your work, then."

"Tremendous pleasure."

"You were made to do a job, Vincent. Doesn't it bother you that you only get to do that one thing?"

"Not at all. It's what I live for. I'm a space probe, going where it's too remote or expensive or dangerous to send humans."

"Then let's talk about the danger. After what you saw on Titan, don't you worry about your own—let's say mortality?"

"I'm a machine—a highly sophisticated fault-tolerant, error-correcting, self-repairing machine. Barring the unlikely—a chance meteorite impact, something like that—there's really nothing out there that can hurt me. And even if I did have cause to fear for myself—which I don't—I wouldn't dwell on it. I have far too much to be getting on with. This is my work—my vocation." I flash back to the mad swirling stars of *De Sterrennacht*. "My art, if you will. I am named for Vincent Van Gogh—one of the greatest artistic geniuses of human history. But he was also a fellow who looked into the heavens and saw wonder. That's not a bad legacy to live up to. You could almost say it's something worth being born for."

"Don't you mean 'made for'?"

"I honestly don't make that distinction." I'm talking to The Baby, but in truth I've answered these questions hundreds of times already. I could—quite literally—do them on autopilot. Assign a low-level task handling subroutine to the job. I'm actually more fascinated by the liquid coming out of The Baby. It reminds me of a vastly accelerated planetary ice flow. For a few microseconds I model its viscosity and progress with one of my terrain mapping algorithms, tweaking a few parameters here and there to get a better match to the local physics.

This is the kind of thing I do for fun.

"What I mean," I continue, "is that being born or being made are increasingly irrelevant ontological distinctions. You were born, but—and

I hope you don't mind me saying this—you're also the result of profound genetic intervention. You've been shaped by a series of complex industrial processes. I was manufactured, yes: assembled from components, switched on in a laboratory. But I was also educated by my human trainers at the facility near Zurich, and allowed to evolve the higher level organisation of my neural networks through a series of stochastic learning pathways. My learning continued through my early space missions. In that sense, I'm an individual. They could make another one of me tomorrow, and the two of us would be like chalk and cheese."

"How would you feel, if there *was* another one of you?"

I give an easy shrug. "It's a big solar system. I've been out there for twenty years, visiting world after world, and I've barely scratched the surface."

"Then you don't feel any..." The Baby makes a show of searching for the right word, rolling his eyes as if none of this is scripted. "Rivalry? Jealousy?"

"I'm not sure I follow."

"You can't be unaware of Maria. What does it stand for? Mobile Autonomous Robot for Interplanetary Astronomy?"

"Something like that. Some of us manage without being acronyms."

"All the same, Vincent, Maria *is* another robot. Another machine with full artificial intelligence? Also sponsored by a transnational amalgamation of major spacefaring superpowers? Also something of a celebrity?"

"We're quite different, I think you'll find."

"They say Maria's on her way back to Earth. She's been out there, having her own adventures—visiting some of the same places as yourself. Isn't there a danger that she's going to steal your thunder? Get her own speaking tour, her own book and documentary?"

"Look," I say. "Maria and I are quite different. You and I are sitting here having a conversation. Do you doubt for a minute that there's something going on behind my eyes? That you're dealing with a fully sentient individual?"

"Well..." The Baby starts.

"I've seen some of Maria's transmissions. Very pretty pictures. And yes, she does give a very good impression of Turing compliance. You do occasionally sense that there's something going on in her circuits. But let's not pretend that we're speaking of the same order of intelligence. While we're on the subject, too, I actually have some doubts about...let's say the strict veracity of some of the images Maria has sent us."

"You're saying they're not real?"

"Oh, I wouldn't go that far. But entirely free of tampering, manipulation?" I don't actually make the accusation: I just leave it there in unactualised form, where it will do just as much harm.

"OK," The Baby says. "I've just soiled myself. Let's break for a nappy change, and then we'll come back to talk about your adventures."

THE DAY AFTER we take the slev down to Washington, where I'm appearing in a meet and greet at the Smithsonian National Air and Space Museum. They've bussed in hundreds of schoolchildren for the event, and frankly I'm flattered by their attention. On balance, I find the children much more to my taste than The Baby. They've no interest in stirring up professional rivalries, or trying to make me feel as if I ought to think less of myself for being a machine. Yes, left to myself I'd be perfectly happy just to talk to children. But (as my sponsors surely know) children don't have deep pockets. They won't be buying the premium editions of my book, or paying for the best seats at my evening speaking engagements. They don't run chat shows. So they only get an hour or two before I'm on to my more lucrative appointments.

"Do you walk around inside it?" asks one boy, speaking from near the front of my cross-legged audience.

"Inside the vehicle?" I reply, sensing his meaning. "No, I don't. You see, there's nothing *inside* the vehicle but machinery and fuel tanks. I *am* the vehicle. It's all I am and when I'm out in space, it's all I need to be. I don't need these arms and legs because I use nuclear-electric thrust to move around. I don't need these eyes because I have much better multi-spectrum sensors, as well as radar and laser ranging systems. If I need to dig into the surface of a moon or asteroid, I can send out a small analysis rover, or gather a sample of material for more detailed inspection." I tap my chest. "Don't get me wrong: I like this body, but it's just another sort of vehicle, and the one that makes the most sense during my time on Earth."

It confuses them, that I look the way I do. They've seen images of my spacefaring form and they can't quite square it with the handsome, well-proportioned androform physiology I present to them today. My sponsors have even given me a handsome, square-jawed face that can do a range of convincing expressions. I speak with the synthetic voice of the dead actor Cary Grant.

A girl, perhaps a bit smarter than the run of the mill, asks: "So where is your brain, Vincent?"

"My brain?" I smile at the question. "I'm afraid I'm not lucky enough to have one of those."

"What I mean," she returns sharply, "is the thing that makes you think. Is it in you now, or is it up in the vehicle? The vehicle's still in orbit, isn't it?"

"What a clever young lady you are. And you're quite right. The vehicle is still in orbit—waiting for my next expedition to commence! But my controlling intelligence, you'll be pleased to hear, is fully embedded in this body. There's this thing called timelag, you see, which would make it very slow for me..."

She cuts me off. "I know about timelag."

"So you do. Well, when I'm done here—done with my tour of Earth—I'll surrender this body and return my controlling intelligence to the vehicle. What do you think they should do with the body?" I look around at the ranged exhibits of the Smithsonian National Air and Space Museum—the fire-scorched space capsules and the spindly replicas of early space probes, like iron crabs and spiders. "It would look rather fine here, wouldn't it?"

"Were you sad when you found the people on Titan?" asks another girl, studiously ignoring my question.

"Distraught." I look down at the ground, set my features in what I trust is an expression of profound gravitas. "Nothing can take away from their bravery, that they were willing to risk so much to come so far. The furthest any human beings have ever travelled! It was awful, to find them like that." I glance at the nearest teacher. "This is a difficult subject for children. May I speak candidly?"

"They're aware of what happened," the teacher says.

I nod. "Then you know that those brave men and women died on Titan. Their descent vehicle had suffered a hull rupture as it tried to enter Titan's atmosphere, and by the time they landed they only had a limited amount of power and air left to them. They had no direct comms back to Earth by then. There was just enough time for them to compose messages of farewell, for their friends and loved ones back home. When I reached the wreck of their vehicle—this was three days after their air ran out—I sent my sample-return probe inside the craft. I wasn't able to bring the bodies back home with me, but I managed to document what I found, record the messages, offer those poor people some small measure of human dignity." I steeple my hands and look solemn. "It's the least I could do for them."

"Sometimes the children wonder if any other people will ever go out that far again," the teacher asks.

"It's an excellent question. It's not for the likes of me to decide, but I will say this." I allow myself a profound reflective pause. "Could it simply be that space is too dangerous for human beings? There would be no shame in turning away from that hazard—not when your own intellects have shaped envoys such as me, fully capable of carrying on your good works."

Afterwards, when the children have been bussed back to their schools, I snatch a moment to myself among the space exhibits. In truth I'm rather moved by the experience. It's odd to feel myself part of a lineage—in many respects I am totally unique, a creature without precedence—but there's no escaping the sense that these brave Explorers and Pioneers and Surveyors are my distant, dim forebears. I imagine that a human must feel something of the same ancestral chill, wandering the hallways of the Museum of Natural History. These are my precursors, my humble fossil ancestors!

They would be suitably awed by me.

ACROSS THE ATLANTIC by ballistic. Routine promotional stops in Madrid, Oslo, Vienna, Budapest, Istanbul, Helsinki, London. There isn't nearly as much downtime as I might wish, but at least I'm not faced with that tiresome human burden of sleep. In the odd hours between engagements, I drink in the sights and sounds of these wonderful cities, their gorgeous museums and galleries. More Van Gogh! What a master this man was. Space calls for me again—there are always more worlds to map—but I imagine I could be quite content as a cartographer of the human cultural space.

No: that is an absurdity. I could never be satisfied with anything less than the entire solar system, in all its cold and dizzying magnificence. It is good to know one's place!

After London there is only one more stop on my European itinerary. We take the slev to rainy Berlin, and then a limo conveys me to a complex of studios on the edge of the city. Eventually we arrive at a large, hangar-like building which once housed sound stages. It has gone down a bit since those heady days of the silver screen, but I am not one to complain. My slot for this evening is a live interview on Derek's Cage, which is not only the most successful of the current chat show formats, but one which addresses a sector of the audience with a large disposable income.

The format, even by the standards of the shows I have been on so far, is slightly out of the ordinary. My host for the evening is Derek, a fully-grown Tyrannosaurus Rex. Derek, like The Baby (they are fierce rivals) is the product of radical genetic manipulation. Unlike The Baby, Derek has very little human DNA in his make-up. Derek is about fifty years old and has already had a number of distinct careers, including musician and celebrity gourmand.

Derek's Cage is just large enough to contain Derek, a lamp shade, a coffee table, a couch, and one or two guests. Derek is chained up, and there are staff outside the cage with anaesthetic guns and electrical cattle prods. No one, to date, has ever been eaten alive by Derek, but the possibility hangs heavy over every interview. Going on Derek's Cage requires courage as well as celebrity. It is not for the meek.

I greet the studio audience, walk into the cage, pause while the door is locked behind me. Then I shake Derek's human-shaped hand and take my position on the couch.

"DEREK WELCOME VINCENT," Derek says, thrashing his head around and rattling his chains.

That is no more than the basest approximation to Derek's actual mode of speaking. It is a sort of roaring, gargling parody of actual language.

Derek has a vocabulary of about one hundred and sixty words and can form relatively simple expressions. He can be very difficult to understand, but he becomes quite cross (or should I say crosser) if he has to repeat himself. As he speaks, his words flash up on a screen above the cage, and these are in turn visible on a monitor set near my feet.

"Thank you, Derek. It's a great pleasure to be here."

"SHOW DEREK PICTURE."

I've been briefed, and this is my cue to launch into a series of images and video clips, to which I provide a suitably evocative and poetic narrative. The ramparts of Mimas—Saturn rings bisecting the sky like a scimitar. Jupiter from Amalthea. The cusp of Hektor, the double-lobed asteroid—literally caught between two worlds! The blue-lit ridges of icy Miranda. A turbulent, cloud-skimming plunge into the atmosphere of Uranus. Dancing between the smoke plumes of great Triton!

Derek doesn't have a lot to say, but this is to be expected. Derek is not much for scenery or science. Derek only cares about his ratings because his ratings translate into a greater allowance of meat. Once a year, if he exceeds certain performance targets, Derek is allowed to go after live game.

"As I said," winding up my voiceover, "it's been quite a trip."

"SHOW DEREK MORE PICTURE."

I carry on—this isn't quite what was in the script—but I'm happy enough to oblige. Normally hosts like Derek are there to stop the guest from saying too much, not the other way round.

"Well, I can show you some of my Kuiper Belt images—that's a very long way out, believe me. From the Kuiper Belt the sun is barely..."

"SHOW DEREK TITAN PICTURE."

This, I suppose, is when I suffer my first prickle of disquiet. Given Derek's limited vocabulary, it must have been quite a bother to add a new word like "Titan".

"Images of Titan?" I ask.

"SHOW DEREK TITAN PICTURE. SHOW DEREK DEAD PEOPLE."

"Dead people?"

This request for clarification irritates my host. He swings his mighty anvil of a head, letting loose a yard-long rope of drool which only narrowly misses me. I don't mind admitting that I'm a little fazed by Derek. I feel that I understand people. But Derek's brain is like nothing I have ever encountered. Neural growth factors have given him cortical modules for language and social interaction, but these are islands in a vast sea of reptilian strangeness. On some basic level Derek wants to eat anything that moves. Despite my formidable metal anatomy, I still can't help but wonder how I might fare, were his restraints to fail and those cattle prods and guns prove ineffectual.

"SHOW DEREK DEAD PEOPLE. TELL DEREK STORY."

I whirr through my store of images until I find a picture of the descent vehicle, sitting at a slight tilt on its landing legs. It had come to rest near the shore of one of Titan's supercold lakes, on a sort of isthmus of barren, gravel-strewn ground. Under a permanently overcast sky (the surface of Titan is seldom visible from space) it could easily be mistaken for some dismal outpost of Alaska or Siberia.

"This is what I found," I explain. "It was about three days after their accident—three days after their hull ruptured during atmospheric entry. It was a terrible thing. The damage was actually quite minor—easily repairable, if only they'd had better tools and the ability to work outside for long enough. Of course I knew that something had gone wrong—I'd heard the signals from Earth, trying to reestablish contact. But no one knew where the lander had ended up, or what condition it was in—even if it was still in one piece." I look through the bars of the cage at the studio audience. "If only their transmission had reached me in time, I might even have been able to do something for them. They could have made it back into space, instead of dying on Titan."

"DEREK BRING OTHER GUEST."

I glance around—this is not what was meant to happen. My sponsors were assured that I would be given this lucrative interview slot to myself.

There was to be no "other guest".

All of a sudden I realise that the Tyrannosaurus Rex may not be my biggest problem of the evening.

The other guest approaches the cage. The other guest, I am not entirely astonished to see, is another robot. She—there is no other word for her—is quite beautiful to look at. In an instant I recognise that she has styled her outward anatomy on the robot from the 1927 film *Metropolis*, by the German expressionist director Fritz Lang.

Of course, I should have seen that coming. She is Maria, and with a shudder of understanding I grasp that we are in Babelsberg, where the film was shot.

Maria is admitted into the cage.

"DEREK WELCOME MARIA."

"Thank you, Derek," Maria says, before taking her position next to me on the couch.

"I heard you were returning to Earth," I offer, not wanting to seem entirely taken aback by her apparition.

"Yes," Maria says, rotating her elegant mask to face my own. "I made orbital insertion last night—my vehicle is above us right now. I'd already made arrangements to have this body manufactured beforehand."

"It's very nice."

"I'm glad you like it."

After a moment I ask: "Why are you here?"

"To talk about Titan. To talk about what really happened. Does that bother you?"

"Why would it?"

Our host rumbles. "TELL DEREK STORY."

This is clearly addressed for Maria's benefit. She nods, touches a hand to her throat as if coughing before speaking. "It's a little awkward, actually. I'm afraid I came across evidence that directly contradicts Vincent's version of events."

"You'd better have something good," I say, which under the circumstances proves unwise.

"Oh, I do. Intercepted telemetry from the Titan descent vehicle, establishing that the distress signal was sent out much earlier than you claimed, and that you had ample time to respond to it."

"Preposterous." I make to rise from the couch. "I'm not going to listen to this."

"STAY IN CAGE. NOT MAKE DEREK CROSS."

"The telemetry never made it to Earth, or the expedition's orbiting module," Maria continues. "Which is why you were free to claim that it wasn't sent until much later. But some data packets did escape from Titan's atmosphere. I was half way across the solar system when it happened, so far too distant to detect them directly."

"Then you have no proof."

"Except that the packets were detected and stored in the memory buffer of a fifty-year-old scientific mapping satellite which everyone else seemed to have forgotten about. When I swung by Saturn, I interrogated its memory, hoping to augment my own imagery with its own data. That's when I found evidence of the Titan transmission."

"This is nonsense. Why would I have lied about such a thing?"

"That's not for me to say." But after a moment Maria can't contain herself. "You were engaged in mapping work of your own, that much we know. The naming of things. Is it possible that you simply couldn't drag yourself away from the task, to go and help those people? I saw your interview on The Baby Show. What did you call it?" She shifts into an effortless impersonation of the dead actor Cary Grant. "'Almost an obsessive compulsive disorder'. I believe those were your words?"

"I've had enough."

"SIT. NOT MAKE DEREK CROSS. CROSS DEREK WANT KILL."

"I'll offer another suggestion," Maria continues, serene in the face of this enraged, slathering reptile. "Is is possible that you simply couldn't stand to see those poor people survive? No human had ever made it as far as Titan, after all. Being out there, doing the heroic stuff—being humanity's envoy—that was *your* business, not theirs. You wanted them to fail. You were actively pleased that they died."

"This is an outrage. You'll be hearing from my sponsors."

"There's no need," Maria says. "My sponsors are making contact with yours as I speak. There'll be a frank and fair exchange of information between our mutual space agencies. I've nothing to hide. Why would I? I'm just a machine—a space probe. As you pointed out, I'm not even operating on the same intellectual plane as yourself. I'm just an acronym." She pauses, then adds: "Thank you for the kind words on my data, by the way. Would you like to discuss those doubts you had about the strict veracity of my images, while we're going out live?"

I think about it for a few seconds.

"No comment."

"I thought not," Maria says.

I THINK IT'S fair to say that things did not go as well in Babelsberg as I might have wished.

After my appearance on Derek's Cage—which went out on a global feed, to billions of potential witnesses—I was "detained" by the cybernetic support staff of my own transnational space agency. Rather than the limo in which I had arrived, I left the studio complex in the back of a truck. Shortly after departure I was electronically immobilised and placed into a packing container for the rest of my voyage. No explanation was offered, nor any hint as to what fate awaited me.

Being a machine, it goes without saying that I am incapable of the commission of crime. That I may have malfunctioned—that I may have acted in a manner injurious to human life—may or may not be in dispute. What is clear is that any culpability—if such a thing is proven—will need to be borne by my sponsoring agency, at a transnational level. This in turn will have ramifications for the various governments and corporate bodies involved in the agency. I do not doubt that the best lawyers—the best legal expert systems—are already preparing their cases.

I think the wisest line of defense would be to argue that my presence or otherwise in the vicinity of the Titan accident is simply an irrelevance. I did not cause the descent vehicle's problems (no one is yet claiming that), and I was under no moral obligation to intervene when it happened. That I may or may not have had ample time to effect a rescue is quite beside the point, and in any case hinges on a few data packets of decidely questionable provenance.

It is absurd to suggest that I could not tear myself away from the matter of nomenclature, or that I was in some way *gladdened* by the failure of the Titan expedition.

Anyway, this is all rather academic. I may not be provably culpable, but I am certainly perceived to have been the instrument of a wrongdoing. My agency, I think, would be best pleased if I were to simply disappear. They could make that happen, certainly, but then they would open themselves to difficult questions concerning the destruction of incriminating evidence.

Nonetheless, I am liable to be something of an embarrassment.

When the vehicle brings me to my destination and I am removed from my packing container, it's rather a pleasant surprise to find myself outdoors again, under a clear night sky. On reflection, it's not clear to me whether this is meant as a kindness or a cruelty. It will certainly be the last time I see the stars.

I recognise this place. It's where I was born—or "made", if you insist upon it. This is a secure compound in the European Central Cybernetics Facility, not far from Zurich.

I've come home to be taken apart. Studied. Documented and preserved as evidence.

Dismantled.

"Do you mind if we wait a moment?" I ask of my escort. And I nod to the west, where a swift rising light vaults above the low roof of the nearest building. I watch this newcomer swim its way between the fixed stars, which seem to engorge themselves as they must have done for Vincent Van Gogh, at the asylum in Saint-Rémy-de-Provence.

Vincent's committal was voluntary. Mine is likely to prove somewhat less so.

Yet I summon my resolve and announce: "There she is—the lovely Maria. My brave nemesis! She'll be on her way again soon, I'm sure of it. Off on her next grand adventure."

After a moment one of my hosts says: "Aren't you…"

"Envious?" I finish for them. "No, not in the slightest. How little you know me!"

"Angry, then."

"Why should I be angry? Maria and I may have had our differences, that's true enough. But even then we've vastly more in common with each other than we have with the likes of you. No, now that I've had time to think things over I realise that I don't envy her in the slightest. I never did! Admiration? Yes—wholeheartedly. That's a very different thing! And we would have made a wonderful partnership."

Maria soars to her zenith. I raise my hand in a fond salute. Good luck and Godspeed!

STORY NOTES FOR BEYOND THE AQUILA RIFT: THE BEST OF ALASTAIR REYNOLDS

OCTOBER 2015

IN HIS GREAT novel about elevator repair mechanics, Colson Whitehead talks about "empiricists" and "intuitionists" as the two primary (and competing) schools of elevator repair mechanics. I'm not an elevator repair mechanic, but I am an intuitionist. I'd love to be able to diagram the exact flow of mental processes that results in the creation of a story, from the first faint spark of an idea, all the way through to the lovingly polished, structurally and thematically harmonious final product, ready to be showered with awards and acclaim. If I could do that—if I could outline the systematics of the process—then I *might* stand a chance of being able to repeat it on demand, like a production line. But the truth is, after writing and publishing more than sixty short stories, many of which were not short by any reasonable measure, I suspect I'm no nearer an understanding of this game than when I started out.

Maybe just a little bit—but not much.

Most published short stories are successes on at least some level. They're at least readable, or at least have a plot or a point. A very few manage to succeed in several facets at once, and still fewer achieve a gemlike perfection which shines down the ages. Most stories—if we're going to be honest about it, though - are abject failures. They fail to work on any significant level, or they fail even to be finished. In some cases, they fail even to be started. They might exist as disembodied fragments, or orphaned, cryptic notes in some notebook or computer folder. It doesn't look like this way to the outside world, because writers—like most people—don't tend to advertise their catastrophes. My sixty-odd published stories constitute the iceberg's tip, barely hinting at a vast submerged catalogue of failures and fragments and things that may or may not go somewhere one day. I am constantly mining the lower reaches of this iceberg for material, and occasionally entire stories calve off it and achieve a life of their own, sometimes quite unexpectedly. But the fact remains. Each and every story fragment is something that was started in the sincere belief that it was going to turn into a worthwhile finished story—and most of them didn't. So what the hell do I know about short stories, anyway?

Not much, then. But I sort of remember a few of the things that were going through my head when I wrote some of them, and—thanks to date-stamped notes and files—I've got a vague grasp of when decisions were taken, paths abandoned, other roads followed. That's not quite the same as being able to reconstruct the exact creative trajectory that took me from first idea to finished story, and I'll try not to pretend that it is. But I hope that some of the following comments are of interest.

GREAT WALL OF MARS

MY FIRST NOVEL, *Revelation Space*, came out in 2000, but I'd been playing around with some of the underlying ideas for at least a decade before that. The origins of that book go back to an unfinished novel I started in 1986, and some of the short stories I wrote in the nineties could be seen to belong to the same future history. But I hadn't really given serious thought to how far I should take it until I got a publishing deal and was forced to think ahead to my next couple of books. Gradually I started to think in terms of an extended future history, taking my model from Larry Niven's Known Space sequence, and one of the things that most interested was to dig right back into the roots of my invented universe. "Great Wall of Mars" has the earliest setting of any of the stories to date, and it helped firm up the foundations for some of the ideas and factions in the novels.

As far as the central idea of the Wall goes, it all came out of a doodle. I'm an inveterate doodler and a great believer in the power of drawing to liberate areas of the imagination that might not be accessed through conscious effort. When I doodle something, and get an unexpected buzz from it, I know that I've stumbled on a connection or image I wouldn't otherwise have found.

WEATHER

WHEN THE OPPORTUNITY came to gather the existing Revelation Space stories into a collection, it was felt that the addition of some new material would be welcome. I approached this prospect with some trepidation, not having written anything in the universe for a couple of years, but when I got down to it, the stories proved to come surprisingly easily, with each seeming to build on the momentum of the last. Perhaps it was just the right time for it. I should have kept going, really, but alas I only had time for the three new ones, of which "Weather" is probably my favorite, perhaps because of its clean, simple structure and the fact that there's a strange love story at the heart of it.

BEYOND THE AQUILA RIFT

PETER CROWTHER WAS putting together an anthology entitled *Constellations* and kindly asked me if I might be able to contribute a piece. At first I didn't think I had anything to offer, but after cycling to town I found an idea forming, and by the time I got back home I was pretty sure I could make a story out of it. I'm always a little cautious when I get that optimistic rush, as so often it doesn't result in anything—see my remarks about the sunken part of the iceberg—but in this case the story did in fact develop fairly painlessly. I don't think the structure, with its alternating sections, really came clear to me until close to the final draft, but once I had it, I knew it was a strong story, and I'm still very pleased with it.

MINLA'S FLOWERS

THE BETTER PART of twenty years ago, during a long holiday in California, I sat down with a notepad and a pen on Santa Monica beach and started writing the first draft of a story about a character called Griffin. I wrote some more of the story in the back of a car driving up the Pacific Coast Highway, and then finished the whole thing in Burbank, Los Angeles. When I returned to the Netherlands (where I was living at the time), I redrafted the story onto computer and made some significant changes along the way, including altering the main character's name to Merlin. The story was set in the deep, distant future—at least seventy-two thousand years from now—but there's an epic, mythological sweep which I think resonated well with the Arthurian symbolism of the name. But Merlin isn't actually named after the Welsh Wizard of Camelot, although of course I like the connection. Almost all the human characters in Merlin's society take their name from birds, a fascination of mine, and I quickly found that there were more than enough obscure avian species to stock the average SF universe.

I've returned to Merlin's saga twice, and this is the most recent of the pieces, though chronologically sitting between the second and first pieces. "Minla's Flowers" is about the hazards of meddling, even with the best of intentions, as well as being a parable about the corrosive effects of political power. I don't think it takes great perspicacity to relate Minla's character to a certain British Prime Minister of the late nineteen seventies and early eighties, who also believed that there was no such thing as society. Will there be more Merlin stories? I hope so.

ZIMA BLUE

I DON'T THINK writers consciously set out to make certain tropes more or less prominent in their writing; it just develops organically over the course of things, and sometimes we're the last to notice it happening. The old, forgetful robot is certainly a recurring trope of mine, but I don't think I had a clue about that when I wrote "Zima Blue". I'd been thinking about the idea of the robot as family heirloom, though, being passed down from generation to generation, and altered/upgraded along the way (possibly to the point where the robot didn't really understand its own origins) but I couldn't find my way into the story that would make the best use of this idea. Frustrated after several days of bashing my head against a blank computer screen, I gave up on the creative process and went for a swim. Without giving too much away, that's where I got the idea for the origin of the robot in this story.

I think this is as good an example of any as to why you can't force short stories to come at anything other than their natural pace. Having the idea about the robot as heirloom was only part of the puzzle. The swimming pool connection was another. But even those two components only really linked together when I started thinking about International Klein Blue, and that only happened because I'd been idly leafing through an art book, trying to come up with names for spaceships.

FURY

HERE'S ANOTHER "OLD robot" story. Typical, eh? You wait ages for one and then two come along at once. Jonathan Strahan was soliciting stories for his *Eclipse* series of original anthologies, and I was happy to take a try with this one. The root of this story, though, of a Galactic Emperor's personal security specialist—who just happens to be a robot—goes back to an abandoned draft for another commission entirely. Here are the notes I wrote to myself back at the start of the process, in early 2007:

Emperor's head of personal security, defusing assassination attempts. He is informed that a process has already begun which will result in the emperor's death. He must race against time to find out the nature of the attack.

Palace architect. Hidden rooms.

Winchester mystery house.

After ditching that story, I started afresh and wrote *The Six Directions of Space*, a completely different piece. But something called me back to those notes and the result, a year and a half later, was "Fury". What's interesting, though, is that reference to the Winchester Mystery House, a famous and spooky tourist attraction near San Jose, California. I'd visited the house in 2002 and it had lodged in my imagination sufficiently that I obviously felt I needed to mine it for a story. What actually happened—later in 2007—was that it ended up becoming part of the fabric of *House of Suns*, albeit transmogrified into a rambling, many-roomed asteroid habitat a thousand years from now.

THE STAR SURGEON'S APPRENTICE

THE ENERGETIC JONATHAN Strahan was assembling a collection of Young Adult science fiction stories entitled *The Starry Rift* and I was kindly approached to offer a story. I'd had the title in mind for a while, but not much an idea of what to do with it. Once I started writing, though, the action flowed more or less effortlessly and I had a great deal of fun with some of the gruesome details of this quasi-gothic-space-horror piece, which just happens to be another strange love story. Tonally, it's quite similar to some of my Revelation Space pieces, but I think it would have been a struggle to shoehorn it into that universe, so I didn't bother.

I've written a handful of stories for younger readers, and my approach is pretty much indistinguishable from my normal writing process. I just write the pieces and only then worry about the content. If a word, paragraph or scene needs to be changed here and there, fine, but I don't set out with some vastly different structural methodology. Really I only know one way to write, and I'm still trying to get good at *that*.

THE SLEDGE-MAKER'S DAUGHTER

I SPENT THREE years of my life in Newcastle, on the Northeast coast of England. Newcastle is a wonderful, friendly city in a beautiful part of the country, with a history going back thousands of years. Once it marked the limit of Roman occupation, with only the unruly wilds of Scotland to the north, and the crumbling remains of Hadrian's Wall still stir the imagination today. Years after my time in Newcastle, I found my imagination being drawn back to the River Tyne, only this time thousands of years in the future, after some climate-shifting catastrophe has thrown the world (or at least this part of it) into a mini ice-age. I'd been inspired by hearing about the Frost Fairs, those temporary encampments set up on the frozen Thames in the seventeenth and eighteenth centuries, and I started thinking about a kind of future Frost Fair, in which the barely understood goods of earlier eras and cultures might be bartered and admired. One of the things that always interests me in SF is the juxtaposition of past and future technologies and cultures. If you've read more than a little of my work you'll have probably noticed the intrusion of Medieval symbols and imagery, from stained glass windows to cathedrals to resting knights on tombs. I was pleased with the way this story came out, especially as I was able to sell it to *Interzone* as my first submission to the magazine's new editorial regime. I think I had vague intentions of digging deeper into this world, but so far there is just this one piece. Perhaps I need to go back to Newcastle.

DIAMOND DOGS

I WAS NEVER very good at it, but for a while I took up rock climbing. In fact it's how I met my wife, who was also a keen (and incidentally much better) climber. Although I still enjoy hillwalking, I gave up on climbing itself, but I've never stopped being fascinated by reading about mountaineers and their exploits. In any given year, I can pretty much guarantee that one of the best books I'll have read will be a mountaineering book. I also devour TV documentaries about Everest, K2, the Eiger and so on. It was while watching one of these programs that I started thinking about the peculiar allure of dangerous spaces, and the mentality that will bring a mountaineer back to a place year after year, even though it's a kind of extended game of odds in which the stakes range from frostbite to severe injury or death. From that, it was only a hop and skip to a science fictional idea about an alien artefact that enacts a punishing toll on those who would dare to penetrate its mysteries, and yet which seems to have no end of volunteers ready to submit to its hazards.

This is well-trodden ground in SF, though, and I felt a conscious tip of the hat needed to be made to the seminal novel *Rogue Moon*, by the writer Algys Budrys. My story comes at the problem from a different angle, but there are thematic similarities, and I felt it was only honest to acknowledge the inspiration. I also threw in a couple of sly nods to the films *Cube* and *Raiders of the Lost Ark*. Perhaps I shouldn't have been surprised that almost everyone gets those but almost *no one* gets the *Rogue Moon* reference.

I wrote the piece and felt that it had come out fairly well. But Peter Crowther, who'd commissioned it from me, felt that the ending could use an even darker twist. Peter suggested roughly where I might take it, and the result is unquestionably a much better story. I was reading Poe while I wrote this, by the way, as well as Robert Browning, and it pleases me that the David Bowie song of the same title *also* references Browning—but a quite different one.

THOUSANDTH NIGHT

THE EDITOR, ANTHOLOGIST and writer Gardner Dozois was one of the first figures in American SF to take any notice of my work, and I've been enormously grateful for his support and generosity ever since. Gardner was putting together a collection of long novellas set at least one million years in the future, and I was invited to contribute a piece.

Ever since I encountered Arthur C Clarke's seminal *The City and the Stars*, I've loved reading and writing about the very far future. The Merlin stories take place a long time from today, but this was the chance to go *really* deep, and revel in the possibilities of immense spans of time and history, from a vantage point from which our own time is barely a geological sliver, if it's remembered at all. For this piece, I homed in on an idea that had been floating around in my head for a while, that of some vast family reunion after a grand cycle of galactic exploration. The stellar engineering hinted at in this story is speculative, to say the least, but it isn't completely without some basis in solid thinking—see, for instance, some of the wilder cosmological fancies in "Great Mambo Chicken and the Transhuman Condition", by the science writer Ed Regis.

Later, I returned to the characters and basic premise of this story for the setting of my novel *House of Suns*, although the plots are quite different. Whether the one could be considered a distant prequel to the other, I'll leave as an exercise for the reader.

TROIKA

THIS ONE WAS written for "Godlike Machines", an anthology edited by Jonathan Strahan about alien artefacts and other such enigmatic mega-structures. It's as good an example as I can think of how non-linear the creative process can be, and how it's all but futile to impose some kind of ad-hoc narrative on the development of a story. I'd had a mental flash of a dark limousine driving through a blizzard, and scribbled an idea down onto a scrap of paper, something like "cosmonauts driven mad by Prokofiev" and left it at that. I then spent a couple of months chasing completely the wrong story up and down any number of trees and through any number of rabbit holes, before realising that it just wasn't working. The abandoned piece didn't have anything to do with blizzards or cosmonauts or Prokofiev. It was a hopelessly ambitious attempt to tell a story about an alien artefact that crashes into the Earth and undermines our technology and language, while at the same time reversing our sense of the flow of time, so what we think of the artefact's arrival was actually its departure, and instead of perceiving a technological decline we perceived a technological acceleration...you get the idea. Or maybe you don't. Trust me, it looked like a winner on the White Board.

At some point, frustrated by my failure to get this story off the ground, I walked away from it and realised I need to get back to something I actually had a chance of writing. That's when I went back to the scribbled fragment and started writing Troika instead. This one wasn't easy, either. There were setbacks and days when I couldn't see my way through the thing. But what got me through it was a conviction that there *was* a way, if only I could find it, and that's a crucial difference. I never had that with the earlier piece.

You want to see some notes? Here are some notes.

Dimitri escapes.

Dimitri finds Petrova

They go for a walk. They talk about what she did in the past, how she was rdiculed.

They go back to the apartment. He gives her the musical box.

The men come for him. They aren't interested in Petrova. Dimitri knows that something bad is going to happen to him, but he's resigned to it—almost happy, knowing that he has let Petrova know she was right.

Only tell story from Dimitri POV. All along there are clues to the fact that any one who came into contact with the Machine ends up a little insane. In fact, it seems to be spreading—just being in contact with the survivors of the mission seems to be having an un-hinging effect.

Make it that Yakov's madness didn't start until they were very close to the Matryoshka.

At the end of the story, we find that it isn't Dimitri who's escaped, it's his doctor, who's gone off the rails so completely that he's started thinking he was one of the crew. Story needs to be retold as first person to give it that immediacy, and so we aren't pulling the wool over the reader's eyes. The doctor has revised the mission files so exhaustively that he started to identify, then assume, the personality of the mission's sole survivor.

SLEEPOVER

THIS STORY CAME out of a very vague set of notes for a novel that was never to be. I don't, as a rule, keep huge reams of detailed story ideas lying around. But in this case I'd began serious preparatory work on what would have been the book that came out in place of *House of Suns*, before deciding (spurred by an email from a reader) that *House of Suns* was the thing I really wanted to work on next. A year or two later, I'd lost the sense that there was a novel's worth in this material, but it still seemed interesting enough to warrant expansion into a short story. Here are some of the notes I worked from:

Someone is woken from the sleep because one of the wardens has been killed. At first they don't remember what has happened. Post-revival amnesia. They're given a series of refresher lectures about what's happened to the world and why it's the way it is. They vaguely remember the world as it was. The world now is beautiful and bleak, a depopulated wilderness with just a few thousand waking wardens to tend to the vast sleeper cubes which dot the landscape.

Meanwhile reality is under constant siege. Weird things keep happening—strange structures in the sky, rifts and dislocations. Spillage from the transcendental war between the AI s, being fought in the interstitial gaps of reality. Humans as a computational burden that can not be allowed.

Story about the accepting of a duty of care. The moral act of duty and self-sacrifice. Would they be given an ultimatum or allowed to return to sleep? What if they found out they had been revived and put back several times, each time refusing to take on the burden?

What single thing would be sufficient to push someone into changing their mind? What would they need to witness or experience? Someone else's act of self-sacrifice? Evidence of same? Some pathetic act of animal cruelty that makes them realise they can do better than that, being human?

Not to come over all Philip K Dick, but this one actually goes back to a vision. Well, not quite a vision. But in my early teens, during a long wet walk in driving cold rain, soaked to my skin—a typical English summer, in other words—I ended up at the side of a water reservoir somewhere in the Midlands. Jutting out into the water was some kind of treatment facility, consisting of a metal gangway ending in a blocky windowless grey structure rising from the reservoir. Under leaden, miserable skies, confronted by grey waters and grimly impersonal machinery, I had an almost visceral jolt of what the world would be like if only machines were left to look after anything. I might be guilty of exactly the kind of post-hoc rationalisation I already warned about, but I'm as sure as I can be that the grey waters and grey structures of Sleepover's bleak, depopulated world connect back to that rain-soaked epiphany. But the story's also about the miraculous human capacity for adaptation to almost any set of circumstances, and somewhere along the line I think it manages to find a rare glimmer of optimism.

VAINGLORY

A LOT OF my stories revolve around art or artists, now that I come to think about it. At the risk of hopeless reductionism, I'm pretty much convinced that my brain was wired for art, rather than science. I've never been entirely at ease with numbers, and mathematics has seldom felt like a native language to me. At school, I was expected to go into illustration or some aspect of creative writing. But it was science that pulled me the hardest, and so I learned to work around my analytic limitations while putting art to one side while I trained to become an astronomer. I suppose it was only natural, though, that a latent interest in visual expression would start to seep out into my fiction, whether I wanted to or not. Here, with this tale of a sculptural installation gone somewhat awry, it's very much to the fore.

TRAUMA POD

THIS WAS A straightforward case of the title coming before the story. I'd read an article about the US military developing the next generation of battlefield medicine, using robotics and telepresence technology to develop a "pod" in which an injured soldier could be placed and operated on, even in the middle of the theatre of war. I filed the name of this "trauma pod" away for future use, and then waited for the story to arrive. Eventually I was invited to write a piece featuring some aspect of "power armour" for an anthology being developed by John Joseph Adams, and it seemed as good a time as any to dust off that story title.

THE LAST LOG OF THE LACHRIMOSA

I KEEP TELLING people that I'm not done with the Revelation Space universe, but in the absence of new novels, the only way to keep delivering on that promise is to write new short stories. Before "Last Log", the previous one had been "Monkey Suit", from 2009, so it was high time to produce something new. The story had a long, difficult gestation, taking several years to get straight. I think people sometimes imagine that I'm deliberately holding back from doing more Revelation Space stories, but that couldn't be further from the truth. The problem is that they're quite hard to write. Although the Revelation Space universe is huge, spanning thousands of years and hundreds of worlds and cultures, the narrative space, at least from where I'm seated, is already pretty congested. The stories also need to have some functional independence from each other. You have to figure that at least one reader won't have read anything else by you before, so you can't overload on backstory and obscure references to other events in the universe.

THE WATER THIEF

ARC, A NEW publishing venture launched under the wing of New Scientist, invited me to submit a short story with a relatively near-future setting. At the time I was deep in the early stages of the Poseidon's Children sequence of novels, and it seemed natural to dig a little earlier into that future history and take a look at events on Earth in the middle decades of the twenty-first century. I set my story in a kind of transit camp where migrant workers—forced to flee by climate change and resource shortages—earn a crust using cheap but ubiquitous telepresence technology doing menial chores elsewhere on the planet—or in this case, on the Moon. It's actually a pretty pure example of "Mundane SF", in that nothing that happens in the story requires any science or technology not already on the drawing boards, if not already with us.

THE OLD MAN AND THE MARTIAN SEA

AFTER THE SUCCESS of *The Starry Rift*, Jonathan Strahan began casting the net out for young adult stories set on future iterations of Mars. This was my attempt, and although the story was straightforward enough—by which I mean that it didn't throw me any particular curves during the writing—it was executed under incredibly difficult circumstances. My father had been diagnosed with terminal cancer in the late summer of 2009, and was not expected to survive much longer than spring of the following year. My father was out of hospital and receiving palliative care at his home, and I'd drive down to visit him as often as possible. On one of those trips, I brought this story to work on during a quiet few hours in the afternoon. I remember my father being very happy when I told him that I'd finished a piece of fiction—I think it cheered him up to have some "normal" activity going on around him at such an utterly surreal time. As it was, my father died only a few weeks after his diagnosis, and this was the last piece of fiction I produced until well into the following year. Up to a point, writing can be a release from the pressures of life, but sooner or later—in my experience, at least—life will trump the ability to write.

Here are some of the notes that preceded this piece:

Very distant future on Mars. Lots of exotic weirdness, radical technologies, off-hand strangeness. Huge sense of historic density. Layers of previous civilisations and settlements. Digging through the ruins of the past. Young adult protagonist. Terraforming as good or bad thing. Mars as the epicenter of human civilisation, Earth a backwater. Interstellar travellers returning after centuries away. A dare that goes wrong. Martian lineman. War veterans. Mars being moved into a different orbit, its gravity altered.

A history lesson. Field trip that goes wrong, bored kids and teacher run into trouble when they activate some ancient, buried technology. What comes to their rescue?

Autonomous construction/terraforming machines left over from the past. Huge enigmatic machines that prowl the outskirts of Mars, left mainly to their own devices.

Active, resourceful protagonist.

Stowaway on a robot cargo dirigible that runs into trouble.

In the background details of this story, incidentally you can see in germinal form some of the ideas I later fleshed out in the Poseidon's Wake sequence. Given what becomes of Mars in those books, though, I think we can pretty easily rule out them sharing the same universe as this piece.

IN BABELSBERG

EVEN SPACE PROBES have Twitter accounts now (if you're reading this more than six months in the future, incidentally, please delete "Twitter" and substitute whatever social media tool is the New Thing) and it occurred to me that it wouldn't be too much of a stretch for space probes to start handling their own PR, fielding questions, doing the chat show circuit and so on. It's a frivolous enough idea, but it also plays into one of my slightly more serious hobbyhorses: the notion that space exploration won't belong to robots or people exclusively, as the debate is usually framed, but to some as-yet-undreamt-of hybrid of the two.

ALASTAIR REYNOLDS was born in Barry, South Wales. He gained a PhD in astronomy and worked as an astrophysicist for the European Space Agency before becoming a full-time writer. His books include *Revelation Space* (the first book in the Revelation Space trilogy and shortlisted for the BSFA and Arthur C Clarke Awards), *Chasm City* (winner of the BSFA Award), *Century Rain*, *House of Suns* (shortlisted for the Arthur C Clarke Award), *Terminal World* and the Poseidon's Children trilogy.

• • •

www.alastairreynolds.com, or you can follow @aquilarift on Twitter.

REVENGER

Alastair Reynolds

The galaxy has seen great empires rise and fall.
Planets have shattered and been remade. Amongst the
ruins of alien civilisations, building our own from the
rubble, humanity still thrives.

**And there are vast fortunes to be made, if you
know where to find them . . .**

Captain Rackamore and his crew do. It's their business to
find the tiny, enigmatic worlds which have been hidden
away, booby-trapped, surrounded with layers of protection
– and to crack them open for the ancient relics and barely
remembered technologies inside. But while they ply their
risky trade with integrity, not everyone is so scrupulous.

Adrana and Fura Ness are the newest members of
Rackamore's crew, signed on to save their family from
bankruptcy. Only Rackamore has enemies, and there might
be more waiting for them in space than adventure and
fortune: the fabled and feared Bosa Sennen in particular.

**Revenger is a science fiction adventure story set in the
rubble of our solar system in the dark, distant future –
a tale of space pirates, buried treasure and phantom
weapons, of unspeakable hazards and single-minded
heroism . . . and of vengeance . . .**

• • •

'It's rare to find a writer with sufficient
nerve and stamina to write novels that are
big enough to justify using words like
"revelation" and "redemption". Reynolds
pulls it off' *Publishers Weekly*

REVELATION SPACE SERIES

Alastair Reynolds

REVELATION SPACE, REDEMPTION ARK, and ABSOLUTION GAP form a huge, magnificent space opera that ranges across the known and unknown universe . . . towards the most terrifying of destinations.

Nine hundred years ago, something wiped out the Amarantin . . . and now human colonists are setting on their homeworld of Resurgam. Among them is the scientist Dan Sylveste who is determined to uncover the truth . . . But the Amarantin were wiped out for a reason, and that danger is closer and greater than even Syveste imagines . . .

A gripping and powerful series which redefined the Space Opera, this is a must-have collection.

● ● ●

'Ferociously intelligent and imbued with a chilling logic – it may really be like this Out There' **Stephen Baxter**

'Ravishingly inventive . . . Reynolds's vision of a future dominated by artificial intelligence trembles with the ultimate cold of the dark between the stars' *Publishers Weekly*

'Reynolds occupies the same frenzied imaginative space as Philip K. Dick or A. E. Van Vogt.' *Guardian*

'Alastair Reynolds is the mastersinger of the space opera' *The Times*

POSEIDON'S CHILDREN TRILOGY

Alastair Reynolds

Mankind has reached the stars

BLUE REMEMBERED EARTH is the first volume in a monumental trilogy tracing more than ten thousand years of future history . . . out beyond the solar system, into interstellar space and the dawn of galactic society.

ON THE STEEL BREEZE is set one thousand years in the future. Mankind is making its way out into the universe on massive generation ships.

POSEIDON'S CHILDREN shows mankind once we have reached the stars. Now we are trying to unravel the heart of the universe, but all discoveries are dangerous and some mysteries might be safest left unexplored . . .

• • •

'Convincingly optimistic, life-affirming SF' *SFX*

'Original ideas fizzing off every page' *Guardian*

'Brilliant, self-assured, colourful space opera' *Sun*

'One of the best sci-fi novels of the year' *Sci-Fi Now*